WEDNESDAY .. N I G H T ..

M E E T I N G

A NOVEL OF CONNECTED SHORT STORIES

LOUIS L. LASSER IV

D1369646

Copyright © 2016 by Louis L. Lasser IV

Cover Illustration by Louis L. Lasser IV

All rights reserved. This book or any portion thereof may not be reproduced or used in any manner whatsoever without the express written permission of the publisher except for the use of brief quotations in a book review. Thank you for respecting the author's intellectual property.

The characters, events, and many of the locations in this book are fictitious. There are some real places and businesses that are mentioned, but the incidents that occur there are the products of the author's imagination. Any resemblance to actual persons, living, dead, or resurrected, is purely coincidental.

ISBN-13: 978-1530329595

ISBN-10: 1530329590

This project is dedicated to:

My grandparents, William & Marian, for their gifts of philosophy and NYC.
My mom, Marcia, who will only read the bad parts.
My brother, Justin, for the living gospel of discussion & spirits, both distilled.
My wife, Cara, for her unwavering support & love, her grace & beauty. You are my *une*.

WEDNESDAY NIGHT MEETING

· ⟦ ↑ ⟧ · ⟦ Σ ⟧ · ⟦ ◆ ⟧ · ⟦ ✳ ⟧ ·

. . .

(OVERTURE)
TUESDAY NIGHT
BLO*OD IN*SIDE
ZWEET ZURZDAY
GOOD,FRIDAY.
(INTERLUDE)
SATURN
BUD BLACK SABBATH
M∞NDAY
TÝR
WEDNESDAY NIGHT MEETING
(CODA)

. . .

(OVERTURE)

It's noon in early April and the weather is perfect. The funeral home is pure white. Looking up to the bluest sky she's seen in her twenty-four years, Ms. Lovinglace feels the radiance of our closest star in a way that causes her to feel insignificant. She senses the twinkling spectra of light landing on her skin, even on the folds of her ears. As she closes her peridot eyes, the muted outline of the sun blazes to form an instant memory in the darkness of a long blink. The arrhythmic chimes of warmth caress the tip of her nose, the flickering sparkles disperse over her forehead, and an invisible rainbow leaves a beauty mark above her lips. In a moment of nonchalant concentration, she's become a sole flower at the mercy of Nature.

As she lowers her chin from 41° to the horizon, her blurred vision fights through the sun's static, and the white eaves of the funeral home come into focus. The doors open to the halls of final goodbyes. She feels hands from both sides carefully grasp hers. They walk along the ocean blue carpeting, heel to toe, then stop together. There are distorted voices, forced smiles, and head nods. Then a few more steps, another pause, and forward again. The shadow from the entrance eclipses the sun rays and her sight adjusts to the dim chandeliers and sheet-rocked walls. The opacity is chilling and true.

Ms. Lovinglace skips forward in time and finds herself again gazing toward the once blue sky. Although this time she's kneeling, and the only things illuminated are the frozen drips of eggshell paint that had dried before gravity could take over. She wonders if the stalagmite ceiling feels smooth or rough. Her gaze returns to a new horizon, where she finds the scape of a maroon two-piece suit filled out by a body, not a man. Not her father, she thinks. She doesn't want to see the painted and positioned lips, sewn eyelids, or posthumously groomed beard and combed hair. She knows what's there, but keeps it on the periphery. Instead her focus darts forward to the Patriarchal cross[1] pinned to the white cushion on the inside lining of the coffin. It will soon be closed to rest against his room-temperature chest, which she imagines as a glacial cavity.

She thinks of the wonderfulness of the sun outside, the warmth that is found in life, in laughter, in memories, in the heat of arguments, in the passion of relationships, and in the stories that we tell for as long as we can—until the next generation blooms under this same praiseworthy star and reaffirms the summation of our moments heretofore. She touches the crucifix on her necklace with her index and middle fingers, and passes over the body of Christ lightly, as though reading braille. Her lips quiver to the cadence of the Lord's Prayer. She closes her eyes and presses out a single salty tear, which zigs and zags through a maze of newborn freckles.

TUES~~DAY~~ NIGHT

[[↑]]

"When you're kissing someone, you close your eyes, right?"

"Of course. What are you talking about?"

"I was just thinking about what that means. You have two people, who are in love, spending time locking lips. So why does it seem creepy if they both keep their eyes open the whole time, an inch apart from each other, eye ball to big blurry eyeball? Shouldn't they want to?"

"No, they shouldn't! You're too funny. Why are you thinking about this? Just close your eyes and enjoy kissing her!"

"Well, that's just it. That's what I do. I close my eyes and pucker up and hold her close. But that's not all. I've also been thinking about what I'm *thinking about* while I'm kissing her. Melanie, what do *you* think about when you're kissing someone?"

"I think you're thinking too much."

"Actually, I think I've thought too little, which is what kills me. When I'm looking at someone, I believe that most of my thoughts will be related to them. Although, there have been many times that I've looked right into a woman's eyes, with her batting her lashes while I tell a story—but my mind was latitudes away. But generally, when you look at someone, you're thinking of them. So that's why we should keep our eyes open when we're leading off first base. It should be reassuring."

"I'm not even blindly following you, Zeus."

"So, since I'm not looking at her, what should I think about? A different image? Like her profile picture or a wallet-sized portrait to hang in my head? Or do I think about what she looks like at that moment? In which case I might as well just open my eyes. And this sounds pretty damn silly when I say it out loud, but what if the image in my head is of her alone somewhere— in a room maybe?"

"Why is she standing in another room?"

"I don't know. So you tell me, am I supposed to picture her independent of myself or not?"

"I have no clue."

"Is it possible that both kissers have their eyes closed and are both imagining what the other person looks like? And if so, are they idealized pictures of what they represent, or true to form?"

"I wouldn't bring this up to the next girl you hook up with."

"You know what else I've thought about? And this may sound like creep city, but here's something to consider."

"I can't wait."

"Suppose I create a second version of myself, like a ghostly figure that hovers over my shoulder. This way, my inner-vision of the lip-locking includes me—I'm there after all—but I'm focused on *her*, bending it more toward reality, I think."

"You should really stop thinking. So, you're saying that when two people—let's say they're in a closet playing the old Seven Minutes in Heaven game—are kissing, they both have separate versions of themselves watching the kissing in an attempt for realism?"

"I think that's pretty much it! When two people hook up and close their eyes, it becomes a foursome—unless both ghost watchers also end up kissing each other. In which case... forget it. I feel some kind of infinite loop of voyeurism approaching. Anyway, tell me what you really think about when you're kissing someone."

"I just think of darkness."

"Darkness? Hmmm... Do you mean the kind that clouds your vision because your feelings associated with touch and changing body temperature are that intense? The kind of darkness that allows you to shut off one of the physical senses so the emotional senses are enhanced? I think I see what you mean. That ultimately, when we look into each other's eyes, we look not at the color of the irises, but to the pupils. When we're attracted to someone, our pupils dilate because we subconsciously want to see more of them. So, we don't close our eyes to *avoid* looking directly into each other's pupils, but rather to enhance that very idea. I think you're on to something. Because we want to experience the other person so deeply, we close our eyes and fuse them into one that lacks actual sight, and it becomes the shared inner-vision of darkness that only allows for feeling andlove."

"Wait, is that four eyes becoming one, or eight? Are the ghosts over the shoulder still hanging around for all of this?"

"Four. It's four becoming one abstraction of sublimity. It's beautiful!"

"I think it's just darkness."

[..Break!]

The heat of bodies in motion is ubiquitous and causes long hair to stick to beautiful faces. It restricts sight to narrow vignettes and saturates it with vacillating philosophies.

Zeus, at least his name for tonight, assumes his stance at the center of a sparkling constellation of women. Zeus isn't a *nom de plume*, but a *nom de guerre*, in terms of the fight for attention. Not as if he needs it, but it doesn't hurt to have an omnipotent title when looking for his Hera. He isn't quite stoned, but slightly marbled with the crystallization of weed and XO cognac. Therefore, Zeus smiles. It's the kind of pearly display that forces the cheeks north, squints the eyes, and draws in the stares of the enamored and envious alike. And when he laughs, his head tilts heavenward, just a shade away from a mild madness, as he has a moment of rapture in the nucleus of his own universe.

On the new wood floor, which has already been made smooth by equal parts dancing soles and alcohol erosion, stands a pair of black-and-tan Nike Blazers. Moving up from the kicks, graham-cracker denim jeans rest on the laces and conform up his legs until they're disrupted at the bulge of vulnerability. The thumb of his right hand is wedged into his pocket, his four fingers bending and straightening in accordance with the conversation, then thigh-tapping to the rhythm of the music in between exchanges. Clasped to the wrist of his other arm, he wears a thin bracelet of tiger maple beads alongside a rose gold Movado Elliptica vintage timepiece. His slim athletic frame is covered by a fitted charcoal t-shirt with a pussy willow print running up one side of his ribcage. He wears three chains that are tucked under his shirt, but their collective volume causes a significant parabolic ripple. Atop it all is his bronze-toned, clean-shaven, and ethnically ambiguous face, a credit to the diversity of his parents. While his mother is close to his heart, his father is estranged or entirely absent. The crown of his head, an exact 72" from the bottom of his kicks, is buzzed to a shadowed stubble. And no longer a passing comet, a familiar face breaks the orbit around him and approaches with a smile. He folds his arms and buffs his chin with an index-thumb combination—his patented b-boy/philosopher stance™—and returns the expression. Then the head-bone connects to the soul-bone, and the soul-bone connects to the hip and leg-bones, and Zeus starts top-rocking-and-be-bop-moon-walking with rhythmic ecstasy.

[..Break!]

"I just remembered this strange dream I had last night."

"Was I in it again?"

"You're not in all of my dreams—just some." Zeus winks.

"Some of those actually came true!"

"Some did. But a particular one didn't go as planned, obviously."

"What do you mean, planned? You did dream them, right?"

"Yes, of course... why should it matter if I had the dreams at night or during a moment of inspiration during the day. Dreams are dreams."

"Well, it does matter. I did things with you I probably wouldn't have if I knew you'd just thought of it over lunch. And I'm not saying they weren't memorable—and sometimes dangerous—it's just that I'd like to think they were sincere dreams you had while you were off in sleepyheady land."

"So you'd prefer that my dreams—or maybe I should call them visions—happened while I was sleeping and unaware, rather than something I fantasized about while I was lucid?"

"Yes, because it means that you're thinking about me even when you didn't have to think of anything. It's more romantic somehow. Now it's gone from innocently freaky to conniving."

"I'm not feeling your whole unthinking-romance connection. I mean, do you want know what I've *really* been dreaming about lately? Two nights ago I snacked on chunks of sidewalk while on my way to the dentist. And last night I was reading a book where the letters themselves jumped off the page, formed new words, and walked away as a solid paragraph. Are you saying you want to equate those with my daydreams?"

Melanie is about to answer, but a nanosecond has already gone by.

"...and let's focus on the good ones and put aside the one that called for a few *potentially* spicy nights with a blindfold, the vibrating nipple thingies, and the doorway sex swing— though I should be commended for my valiant effort! And please notice I verbally italicized the word *potentially*. I really had no idea the door hinges wouldn't hold."

"See! You said, 'what I've really been dreaming about...' Your pants should be on fire, buster."

"My pants are merely singed. Can I tell you about the dream from last night before I forget about it again?"

"You can talk, but there is absolutely zero chance, like Zero Kelvin chance, that I will be tied up or suspended in any way. And some of the good ones, they're out too, including any skyscraper roof activities."

"You mean you no longer want to be a member of the quarter-mile high club?"

"It's your loss, applesauce."

"So, starting over, in my dream I was looking at a crossword puzzle. It had a tricky design. Most of your crossword puzzles are fifteen by fifteen square and rotationally symmetrical, but this one had an extra triangular flap along each edge that could be folded over the puzzle, like one of those fortune teller things. I don't know if I was trying to solve it or create it—although the creation of a puzzle is the solving of another. Anyway, it had no clues and the center square had its own special border. It was the final square of what was a maze of answers. I started to fill in words, beginning with each corner, and winding my way to the center square where I had to squeeze in entire words—a rebus square sort of—but when I finished it looked like a scribbled mystery. I think maybe it's a puzzle about self-discovery and taking my own path, but it all ends in a confusion of lines and curves and darkness."

"There's that darkness word again."

"The answers are there, but so entangled as to be impossible to sort out. Why the four paths from the corners converged to confusion, I'm not sure, but it was upsetting. I'd spent hours of distorted dream time only to learn that after a journey of discovery, the end is unsatisfying. This is a terrible example, but it reminds me of when the last potato chip in the bag is burnt. All the other ones were a-ok, but that last one counts more as the memory of the snack, so it has a negative effect on the good chips you've already had, you know I mean? It's strange that while talking about convergence, I've gone off on a tangent."

Melanie nods with her lips pulled in.

"So, remember the triangles along each edge of the puzzle? Well, on the tip of each corner was a mirror a quarter the size of the center square. I folded them over the top of the puzzle until it looked like an incomplete pyramid."

Melanie checks her watch, but doesn't take note of the time.

"Yeah, I'll hurry it along. I closed them at different angles, adjusting the levels of the folds. The chaotic mess of letters and words started to take order. Depending on how I looked at the mirrors, truths were revealing themselves to me from the center square. But to fully understand, I had to keep flattening all the triangles down, which made the sight lines more and more acute. It's like I was a moment away from getting the answers—my purpose—but as I neared the truth, the edges had to be closed, and the puzzle hidden. It makes me think that life is about approaching a limit, that no matter how close you get, you'll never really grasp it. It's understanding that you cannot understand..."

Melanie smiles and nods, but also jangles her keys.

"I know, I know. But before we leave, I just want to finish my thought, which I admit is more for me than for you. You went vacant five minutes ago."

Melanie holds up six fingers.

"It also makes me think about the written word and language—how it's through language that we interpret the world in a structured way, but that it's always in flux. That communication is the preexisting condition of humanity, the tool we use to figure out what's going on in this world—that words are a function of us, not outside us. They are our thoughts with the volume turned on, the noises of our brains. Words are how we get what's inside, out. Then, for the next person or group, it's about getting that outside info, in. On and on and over thousands of years, these loops exist between us all. Some loops will spiral inward and die if not shared, and some loops will travel for generations before coming back into fashion. I'm interested in how dreams seem to come from nowhere—how the thoughts originated in them appear independent of prior loops. Maybe they're like comets, and leave residue that will eventually form the basis for new ideas."

Melanie uses her middle finger to make circles in the air, then extends her thumb to create a hand-gun pointed at her temple.

"Or maybe they spark new trajectories in that instant, the beginnings of the next loops. Like little big bangs."

She bends her thumb and dies the dramatic death of a mime. "Jesus, let's go. Now."

[..Break!]

Within the past year, N.Y.C.'s Alphabet City underwent a tremendous change fueled by the financing of a fifty-million-dollar-per-picture actor. His fame originated from his ten successive blockbuster films as a comedic rural K-9 Officer, in which the pair got themselves in and out of trouble while solving crimes and tying in themes of Evangelical morality. Spot and Shoot starred in such films as "Kidnapped by the Moonshiners: Looking for the Hooch" and "No One Can Hear Us: Barking Up the Wrong Redwood".

On the set of the last film, "Lost: How Far Can a Puppy Run into the Woods?", the actor who portrayed Officer Shoot became spirituality conflicted. The movie wasn't meant to be philosophical, but the title brought about a surge in his own dichotomous thinking. He was bothered by the answer: *Halfway*.

He began to pray and meditate on fleeting moments and hypotheticals, duality and betweenness. Maybe there shouldn't be restrictions or parameters, no *either*, he thought. Why can't we have both, everything at once. Paradoxically, all of his focus on meditating caused him to miss cues, stumble over lines, miss autograph signings, and ultimately led him to lose all credibility in Hollywood. When he didn't show for the last day of shooting, the crew and police set out a search team only to find him meditating directly in the middle of a forest in California.

No longer able to tame his inner spirituality battle, he succumbed with pleasure and quickly worked his syncretism into a position as a Wiccan High Priest. The baring of his soul put him in the dog house with his Evangelical fan base, and the studio was too weary to re-up the contract. Without a whimper at the negotiation table, Cyrus Coaster walked away from his acting career with his silk-lined pockets already overflowing with dead presidents. He set his sights east to establish tranquility through commerce in the Big Apple with a real estate venture that would become a haven for future New York covens. His was a real wags to witches story.

The best spaces available were just a shout from a renovated FDR/BHO Drive, between Ave. C and Ave. D on 10th street. High Priest Coaster wanted the higher-planed floors to be dedicated to Wiccan practices, and the ground levels to be used for shops with a unique marriage of ideas. He held a Twitter contest where potential business owners pitched their mom-and-pop-sized dreams in 140 characters or fewer. The winners, for which there were ten, all received considerable grants and paid-in-full four-year lease agreements. He hyped "The 10 on 10th" as the place where, when asked if you wanted *this or that*, the answer was *yes*. He also saw this as a cross-marketing way of passive-aggressively promoting his beliefs induality.

There's [Thugs N' Kisses], an organic chocolate dollop shop that serves their goodies on hard-laminated album covers featuring Bizzy Bone, Krayzie Bone, Layzie Bone, et. al., or to-go in gat-shaped recycled cardboard boxes. While the bass shakes the planar walls, framed pictures of their famed visitors rattle and gangsta-lean to one side. Along the back wall behind the counter, a holographic Eazy-E speaks the truth through *Radio*.

Two doors down the block is [thINK], a guerrilla advertising agency slash tattoo parlor. With opportunities for sponsored and innovative needlework from Fortune 500 companies and start-ups, thINK looks for partnerships the way online dating sites use compatibility algorithms. For qualified applicants, there's an extensive interview process, a life-long contract, and a credit check.

The head tattoo artist at thINK is, or was, Mattres, whose flawless lettering, superb lines, and perfect placement caused fountains of tears to spring from the eyes of his subject—tears of jubilation. Even though he was upfront about his futility in representing the human face, some patrons insisted on getting portrait tattoos and paid him a french king's ransom to do so. As far as accuracy and aesthetics, it would've been wiser for someone to get a line of Oscar Wilde's prose etched into their skin, rather than a replication of Basil Hallward's painting in the attic. The faces he attempted were known to get stretched way out sideways, and they looked like the front of a car with headlight eyes, radiator lips, wide implied noses, and windshield foreheads. The results looked less like Dorian Gray and more like a Gray DeLorean. Mattres suffered from some undiagnosed form of Prosopagnosia, which is why he'd claim that he'd never tattooed the same person twice, when he certainly had. For example, the dates and words of remembrance *Grand-mère François ... Je T'Adore*, were impeccable, but were separated by the humanoid front-end of a 1977 AMC Pacer. There was the Olde English-fonted *Caring Mother... Missing You*, with the pointy-nosed grill of a 1976 Aston Martin Lagonda with brunette bangs smack dab in the center. At first, these tribute portrait tattoos were considered embarrassments, but they reached cult status among the bohemians, and the sight of one enabled a fortnight of wet dreams. But once they were featured in a viral internet video, people from the general population were getting tatted up at their local shops with toupéed vehicles and loving phrases from coast to coast. The virility and speed of the flash fad was sudden and ubiquitous, so the nightly expulsions into tight pajamas came to a clean stop. With the slowdown in portrait tattoo requests, Mattres began moonlighting as a cartoonist, trying to parlay his artistic abilities to another medium. His friends said he enjoyed the change of pace, until recently, when Mattres was killed just blocks from the parlor by a speeding car in the middle of the day. With questions abound regarding his death, including the disappearance of the murderous vehicle, Mattres himself became the subject of tribute tattoos by friends and colleagues alike.

[..Break!]

The air is thick with beautiful body sweat and shows itself in the dusty stuff that clouds the light beams. Everything looks a little blue, but not in a sad way. It cools the temperature to balance the weighted air.

Zeus is basking in the center glow of [Wax & Rax], a lingerie slash vintage record shop, which becomes a very chill lounge after 10p. While there is a switch over from retail consumption to locomotion, many of the lingerie models are encouraged to linger following their normal work hours. [Wax & Rax] employs a resident DJ during day and evening hours, spinning the records right off the shelves packed with plastic sleeves. At the moment, *DeeDeeJ* a.k.a. *DoubleDJ* a.k.a. *DJ BrazEar*, is crossfading an hour-long set of two century-different LPs: a classical string quartet record composed by Dvořák and a 1992 Beastie Boys album are the double-barreled cannons for her "Czech Your Head" salute to the musicians. She ties the two together with silky-smooth cuts, mixing the end of "So What'cha Want" into the "String Quartet No. 13 in G Major, The Third Movement of Opus 96," right back into "Groove Holmes."

Sure, continuous rhythmic movements nearing cardio-level intensity are required for clubs and dance halls, but [Wax & Rax] is on the fringe of those categories. It's a lounge where conversation is encouraged and also required for Zeus to work the room.

DeeDeeJ is a dedicated turntablist who prints her own flyers for the sets she spins. The way she combines two unlikely records fits the vibe of the 10 on 10th—even her sets were titled in conglomerate fashion. Usually she spins for five hours a night, with four of them planned. She allots one hour for suggestions or her own spontaneous creations inspired by the night. And when the needle drops and finds its groove, the loungers find theirs. They synchronize their limbs and nod their heads in agreement with the music.

DeeDeeJ's style is derived from her name. She wears customized headphones that play into her supportive surroundings. Each side is covered with one double d-sized bright pink push-up cup with a matching satin band running across the crown of her head. When songs play with a BPM upwards of 160, some patrons remark that she may in fact be self-motorboating. DeeDeeJ wears sunglasses that slip down to the bridge of her nose and go-go boots that expose her toes. Her jeans embrace her hips and her neon green and shimmering gold off-the-shoulder tops have a homemade feel to them. They all have phrases on them like *We Were All Stars Yesterday* and *Originality Is The New Vantablack*.

As DeeDeeJ transitions into her next set, an Arcade Fire x Maxwell pseudo-collaboration she dubs "The Suburban Hang Suite," Zeus talks to his best friend, Melanie, while he keeps part of his attention on the planetary motion of women on the elliptical floorspace. The tag team trades these responsibilities depending on the night, and this time Mel plays her wing status artfully, fluffing up the feathers of the head cock as needed. In the months prior, just before a sixty-nine-ish swing incident, they had all the makings of official boyfriend-girlfriend reciprocations[2], but they've been reduced to flirty memories now.

Zeus turns toward a quartet of women that catch his light and he begins to increase his gravitational pull.

[..Break!]

Reviews for *Doorway Access*: Sex Swing Set

Overall Rating: ★★★★☆

Product #: D337X19BH

Product Description: Just using your door frame, you and your lover can live out your swinging fantasies. There is no hardware necessary, but there will be plenty of drilling! Just secure the harness and straps over the door, close the door, and enjoy the feeling of weightless sex. It is very light and portable and comes with a discrete plush bag for storage or travel.

Customer Service Contact: delta@sexytimetoys.xxx

this rocks!

Submitted by: KelliAnne

i bought this as a surprise for my bf on valentines day and it was fun the straps were a little uncomfortable and my arms were pretty tired at the end but it was still really good i recommend it highly for adventerus couples!!;)

Rating: ★★★★★

Gratified Customer

Submitted by: Hypatia

I bought this for me and my husband. I'm a full-figured woman, so I thought this would be a great addition to our home and sex life. The product mostly lives up to expectations, but we were hoping for more swinging action. Since the swing is set up against the closed door, you can only swing so much. If you want the full pendulum action, you might want to have something installed that hangs from the ceiling without any impediments. But for this price, we can't complain.

Rating: ★★★★☆

your going to love this

Submitted by: augustus

we found it easier when my girlfriend got in the harness first and then I pick her up and fix the straps over the door also it's easier to do it like a piggy back carry we figured out. the only thing is that its loud and your neighbor or landlord might complain if your not careful about banging. haha. i recommend you get this swing. its not to hard if you work at it

Rating: ★★★★☆

<u>come and knock on my door!</u>
Submitted by: Cheyenne Muffinsnap

I wanted to surprise my husband on his birthday so I picked up another chick that I knew was down for the get down, and then I threw the swing straps over the front of the front door and waited for him to come home. Needless to say he was happppyyyyyy!! It took some effort to get up in the swing though. We tried teamwork but it was easier to grab the step stool from the kitchen. We also had a little issue with the toggle clasp that held up the strap for the left thigh. It made us slip down too far and I just wasn't flexible enough to make up for the manufacturing defect. My husband was able to secure it with a bungee cord he had in the garage. Looking back, all that just made it more fun really.

Rating: ★★★☆☆

<u>no title</u>
Submitted by: Anonymous
great fucking swing
good fucking job china
Rating: N/A

<u>Hope this helps</u>
Submitted by: Blaise

Both me and my wife are sweaters. Even in the winter. But we wanted to try this since just because why not. When I first hoisted her up there it was good for a few minutes until the sweating started. She was sliding around with the straps and sliding side to side against the door which felt good actually for me. To stop all of the sliding I hammered a quilt to the top of the door and let it run down. This stopped the sliding as the quilt absorbed most of her sweat. After it was all said and done it was just like having difficult sex on a verticle bed. Good if you are not a sweater!

Rating: ★★☆☆☆

<u>An Unexpected Marionette Experiment with an Unforgiving and Unamused Woman</u>
Submitted by: Zeus W.

I was dating a woman for a short time and thought I'd sprinkle some cayenne on what had been basic buttered potatoes in the sack. I bought the *Doorway Access: Sex Swing Set* and two other accompaniments and had it delivered next day. When I opened the package I took out the series of straps that were the harness and swing. I removed the tags and the warning labels and threw it over the closet door in my bedroom. I put some pressure on the swing to make sure it was not going to slip through the opening on the top of the door. Everything seemed set up correctly and I was ready for some sweet chariot loving. I'll spare you the details of our dinner conversation and get to the point where I was picking her up and carrying her to the closet door. The foreplay had been more like four-second-play and I wasn't fully comfortable with my current outfit, if you can call it one. My shirt was off, but my three chains were still on. My jeans were fully unbuttoned and my boxers were off my waist, but I was never able to kick them all the way off one of my legs, so the collection of wrinkled cotton rested around my right ankle. I also never took off my watch, which I prefer to do if I have time. And finally, I was able to slip off my Blue & Cream Wallabees, but I was never able to do the awkward socked-toe-slipping-off-the-sock-of-the-opposite-foot move and then the slightly easier bare-toe-slipping-off-the-remaining-sock move. Normally, I wouldn't have tolerated it. For me, it's either barefoot or shoes, primitive or modern, nothing in between. On my wood floor, socks provide the traction of roller skates on ice. Also, it's what I imagine older people look while they pollinate. So it's a stability issue as well as psychological, I'll admit. As for my date, she was in her birthday suit, which was the result of a jingling striptease, set to the music of The Roots' *Without a Doubt*, which has an anti-digi feel that's purely percussive. For instance, when I listen to it, my head ticks up to the beat, rather than my laid back *shoulder-slump-and-slink* move. (Say that five times fast.) It's both controlled and frenetic, but from an album that now seems unfortunately prophetic: *Things Fall Apart*. Actually, by the time she was ready go in the swing, she was also wearing a satin blindfold (Product#L000K96GZ) and some vibrating nipple suckers (Product #T661A88HR). Brief Physical Disclosure: I'm of average-to-tall height and relatively thin, but with enough muscle to get the job done, and my date is at least four inches shorter and has a lean, but(t) buxom body. I'll admit there wasn't any foresight used here, so I tried to improvise a way to get both legs in the straps, the mind leading the blind. Once I had the first straps around her inner thighs and the other straps around her double trouble bubbles in the back, I held her over my shoulder to help her balance. For some reason, she didn't feel secure, so I told her to put her legs straight down, stand on her tippy toes, and try to reach for the corner moldings over the closet door while I picked her up off the floor. I thought this would center her and we could start jazzing right there, but this is where it all went down. Thinking she was now comfortable and stable, I reached into my jeans pocket around my ankle and grabbed the *squared-circle-of-protection*, and removed the foil. Now with all of the lifting and simple engineering of her legs, it's fair to say I wasn't at the level of Full Glory; my flag was raised only to half-mast. So when I started to stand up and roll the Trojan back, she tilted forward and let out a scream. I tried to hold her up, but she was already moving toward me with force, her hips acting as the fulcrum. My face ended up hitting her bellybutton, and then rubbed up against her chest and somehow the two nipple suckers were transferred to me, one vibrating my bottom lip, and the other on my right eyelid, which forced extensive blinking, warbling, and confusion, as if the view was directed by David Lynch. She fell all the way forward, which gave me the room to stand up straight, but her body and the taut swing straps trapped me against the door for what looked like a sad attempt at a standing sixty-nine. I don't think either of us said a word the whole time. It all happened within a flash. The next thing I remember is that she tried to find her equilibrium, so she grabbed my ankles as there was nothing else to hold onto. I slipped immediately due to my socks, and tried to hold myself up by grabbing the only thing in sight, the doorknob. But because I wasn't in control, I ended up turning the knob and our collective force opened the door outward, which put serious pressure on the door hinges, and the closet door was ripped from the frame. She fell first, bubbly backside down, and I followed in tow with the door on top of both of us. At this point I think I asked her if she was O.K., but I could only hear her yelling in an angry tone, understandably. But also not understandably since the blindfold got pulled down over her mouth. To make things worse, there was a life-sized sculpture of two women next to the closet. It's a bit meta, but it represented the story of a sculptress who ventured to sculpt the epitome of female beauty. The condition the artist gave herself was that she only work in a completely dark studio. And the story goes, that upon completion of her work, she turns on the lights to reveal that she'd sculpted herself twice.

The statue shows one nude, illuminated glass woman holding the long hair of her subject, who's sculpted in wood, while they stand on a granite base. There is palpable astonishment on the face of the glass artist when she realizes she is the solidified representation of the ideal. If you don't know the backstory, it just looks like abstract vanity in three-dimensional space. But once you read the real story, you can understand how this has philosophical questions of self-enlightenment and filtering, identity and solipsism, consciousness and perception, and of rejectionism and majesty. Anyway, I was lying between my date and my closet door and I noticed the base of the statue was teetering beyond the point of self-stabilization. As the very large and expensive piece fell, I saw something in the sculptress's eyes that I hadn't noticed before. It was all in a swift moment, but it slowed down in my memory due to the vibrating nipple sucker that was still on my eyelid. It caused separate frames of reference, like my own personal flip book. The look I saw in the artist was one of foreboding. She realized that her sculpture would outlive her, since she'd soon be smashed across the apartment. She'd been the epitome of female beauty for a short time, but the ideal would continue to exist.

But just as the statue met the floor, the artist's expression changed again, possibly due to the angle from which I now observed. But it was now one of peace. It was a sudden calming as she realized that even well-tempered wood will one day splinter. Idealism is fleeting. After the crash, I tried to collect myself enough to get us out of this fine mess. I noticed that both of the heads from the sculpture had broken clean off and slid unscathed near our own real heads. I was next to the one made of glass; she was next to the one made of wood. My date was still mumbling through the blindfold-turned-muzzle, as her arms were strapped to her legs somehow, immobilized. I managed to undo the straps from the top of the closet door and kick them away from us. We had to rise *very* carefully. Eventually we were able to stand atop the closet door, which had become an island over the sea of broken glass and artwork. She was crying and laughing at the same time and punched me in the stomach while I removed the vibrations from my face. My bottom lip was swollen and I licked it while she told me I was no good, but in a more colorful and multisyllabic way. I cleared a path by shuffling my jeans along the floor and offered my hand to lead my date to safer pastures. She declined. Upon looking back to the open and exposed closet, my date saw a tripod with a GoPro on top facing out. I explained, with a noticeable lisp, that the camera was off and wasn't intended for that purpose *at all*. This didn't help my grand apology. When she went to the bathroom to collect herself I was finally able to take off my socks. I noticed it was 11:12pm and that my pinky toe was bleeding. The strange thing is, after all of the above, we're actually now best friends. We just avoid sex and playgrounds. She's actually right next to me as write this review, and we both agree that if you purchase *Doorway Access: Sex Swing Set*, you'll be seeing plenty of stars too.

Rating: ★★★★★

[..Break!]

Zeus walks his fingers from Mel's left shoulder to the middle of her back, teases her with a massage, and places his hand on her right shoulder. They face the same direction, and he draws her closer to dance face to face, and then cheek to cheek. He speaks into her ear, "That's always mystified me. Look at those women over there. Four of them in a row, all wearing something I don't understand."

"What's that?"

"Each one has a gold crucifix pressed right into their lovely curvy valleys. Jesus is hanging somewhere He was never supposed to be, if you believe what you read."

Two of the women's crosses are turned around with The Lord facing their hearts. Another one hovers triumphantly higher, an effect of her floatation style lingerie, and faces out, with the horizontal crosspiece pressed in and separating a sea of knockers. The fourth one, which has some gold chain twisting action, resembles some half-completed gymnastic effort. The graven image is upside-down, with the Son of Man's head wedged between her ornate bra and cocoa-buttered skin. But Zeus stares at her as if *she* is the shiny metal object in the dance hall. After they share a few more comments, he winks goodbye to Mel, and moves toward the four women.

As if the stage is set, he becomes the focal point to their sector. Within a 3-foot radius they stand in a perfect arc. Zeus checks them out from left to right while feigning to look past them. The leftmost is an emerald-eyed blonde with an up-do. Her top is eye-matching with an eye-catching neckline, which plunges to an abyss of wonder. One notch over, the next woman, a brunette, wears an unbuttoned gold blouse that grandly reveals canyon-like cleavage. She holds a cocktail glass equal to her cup size. Next, standing shoulder to elbow with the brunette, the tall one wears a black bra with a fringy bedskirt thing attached to the bottom that's similar to the shape and color of her hair. Zeus imagines her military-grade push-up bra causing the eyes of nearby men to turn into cartooned hearts.

The rightmost woman is looking forward with her right eye. Her left eye is covered in a sweep of strawberry blonde hair that had fallen to her shoulder and disappeared down her back. A beauty mark above her lip outshines the faint sprinkling of her freckled cheeks. Her hands are fiddling with the top button of her pants. Zeus watches her fingers move. They have the softened look of kind hands. They are ringless. He seems to have caught her in a trance until a nudge from her friend brings her back to dance. As a matter of timing, this is stone cold visual rhyming; when she's swayin' and groovin', her bust is a-movin'. And the hypnotized state is transferred to him as he becomes fixated on this beautiful swinging medallion.

"Ladies, excuse me. I have to ask you something. It'll just take a second. But, do you know why you're bothering me?"

They answer with disapproving glances, their eyebrows raised and their lips sour. "I've been standing a few feet away talking with my girlfriend—a friend that's a girl I should clarify—and I've been distracted by your necklines. And all I can do is shake my head. Let me explain and then I'll be on my way."

If looks could slap.

Zeus speaks faster. "I'm guessing the four of you are here for a ladies-only night out, which is why none of you seem upset to be dancing shoulder to bare sweaty shoulder in this hot joint right now. That's love right there. O.K., so don't get me wrong, you all look amazing. But I'm curious if you know why I'm disappointed. You all seem like you'd be very intuitive women." The taller one looks toward the door where a rubber-muscled bouncer takes up space. "Right, I should be going, but let me explain. It's your choice of jewelry. It's just that I have my faith rooted in God and family and it's important to me. I do struggle with different things, but it's a complex life and I never feel like I know myself completely. Not to get too emotional here, but you all seem like you're caring and would be understanding to my plight."

Seventy-five percent of the audience nods.

"It's that I've been trying to stay on the straight and narrow and your jewelry is serving as a reminder of the fact that God is everywhere—even where I'd least expect Him. I guess it's more that temptation is everywhere. Do you see what I'm saying? While I'm struggling with the polarity of sex and desire on one hand, and God on the other, I feel like no one else is going through the same mental struggle. The four of you seem secure with the contradiction. Am I right?"

The taller one asks the other three what the hell is he saying, without saying a word. "All of you are wearing some type of crucifix. Catholic I assume? I know a lot of people wear them now. Or from a Christian family, but you're more spiritual, like there's more than one truth out there?"

Stilt-legs seems to grow taller as she glares down at him.

"I understand. I mean, we have to just believe what we believe, and deal with the fact that we're just these little beings on this huge planet, and we have to trust that God will lead us down the right path. And we all have our own paths, but sometimes they intersect like ours are right now. The paths can be littered with sin—and, why am I even saying this—O.K., my question is: how sacred can the symbol of Christ be for you if you let it fall into the place where sexual fantasies are born?"

The tall one remarks to the group, "I've seen this guy before somewhere."

"You don't have to answer the question." Zeus checks his watch. "Damn, I can get the truth serum effect even after one drink. The thing is, I'm here to *not think* about those things. I'm here to leave those ideas on the shelf. I'm at this lingerie lounge for that reason. The four of you have made it difficult for me to compartmentalize my life. You've brought both worlds together: purity and sin. These symbols of religion remind me of that, and that's why I'm disconcerted. It's more with myself, for not being as in touch with my own complexities, as you seem to be. So call me jealous."

The strawberry-blonde on the right chimes, "Thou shalt not covet."

"Very true, got me," Zeus smiles and bows toward her. "I think it's time I stop talking and hit up the dance floor. Please forget everything I just said. I've been taking some dance lessons and I have to go practice."

From on high, the tall one judges, "I know who you are! And that was definitely the most fucked up pick-up attempt I've ever seen. Ever. You're pretty fucked up talking all that shit about my religion. It's my religion! It's my choice. And if I want to wear my cross as a sign of devotion, that's my personal thing."

"How devoted could you... you're right. Sorry, I can get on a run. Ladies, if you believe it, I *do* know how to shut up. And I'm going to do that on the dance floor. Apologies once again."

The time dancing passes slower since it is measured in songs. The tempo is the heartbeat, the metronome to the cause. Zeus lifts his right heel on the bass hit and slides to one side. The sweat begins to percolate on his forehead. His movements alternate between fluidity and exaggerated gesticulations on the snare kicks. The space within the music and the club is finite, but it carries the optimism of forever.

After a water break, he keeps out of the center spotlight. Zeus wipes his brow with the bottom of his tee shirt. He wanders to the Pluto orbit of the dance floor and slumps against the wall as his body holds the rhythm. Over his shoulder he notices the woman with the strawberry blonde hair on her phone. The glow from the screen causes the gold cross to shimmer through the lace of her bra.

"Sorry about before. I can get like that when I'm like this."

"It's O.K., I thought it was funny too, that we we're all wearing crosses like that. And funnier that you noticed." She raises an eyebrow.

"What can I say..."

"You're quite the mover out there."

"You noticed?"

"Who didn't," she states.

"It's what I do. I move until I don't. Do you want to join me? I'm going back out there."

"I can't move like that. I think I'll stay here."

"Where's the rest of your quartet?"

"They're around. Just taking a little break from them."

"So let's me and you practice a dance step right now. No one can see us over here. I'll show you something and then we'll go out there like we just met?"

"You're going to show me how to dance?"

"It's a bet."

"I thought you were the one taking lessons?"

"—and now I'm handing them out for free," Zeus says. "You might as well take advantage."

"O.K., but my friends will probably kill me."

"Then it's only fair. You've been killing me this whole time anyway." They smile with their lips and eyes.

"Let's do it."

While they dance Zeus looks into her peridot eyes. Her hair color changes with the club lights, going from the extremes of pure blonde to strawberry fields. The combination of her eyes and the reddest moments of her hair remind him of Christmas morning—an association with morning selfishness, yuletide, and of new toys to assemble. It conjures images of ripping colored ribbons, pulling off the wrapping, and holding the present close in his arms. As one dance becomes four, he holds her closer, rocking and rolling to the rhythm and blues, while sensing the tautness of her bow.

The name of the coveted package is Ms. Lovinglace, fresh out of a rough patch, awaiting greener pastures with shimmering lining. The way she is dressed this evening isn't the way she dresses back in Long Island, a mere 24 miles away. Tonight she dons tight baby blue pants with a bright red belt that slings down to one side like a limp hula hoop over her Coke bottle hips. She wears a heart-shaped clip that aids the sweep of her hair to one side. The sleeves of her white shirt have been torn off at the seams—and the front is ripped far and wide down the middle, which reveals the fullness of her lacy intimates and the solid gold savior still lodged in place upside down. The chain bridges across the small cavities of her collarbone and relaxes along the contours of her chest.

They retreat from the dance floor to a less kinetic area. Ms. Lovinglace leans in and up toward his ear to be heard over the music. "I know it's a Tuesday night, but I couldn't stand another moment in my house."

Zeus says, "I think it's funny that in the phrase *Tuesday Night*, we get the *day-Night* parts right next to each other. It's either a flaw in our language or a contradiction. Why can't we just make the *day* of the week change over the course of time? Maybe at 5:00 post meridiem, the names switch over to Tuesnight, Wednesnight, Thursnight, Frinight, Saturnight..."

"True," she leans in again, "but we call the whole thing *a day*. A day is twenty-four hours; that's why we have the whole a.m./p.m. thing."

Zeus feels a wisp of her hair brush across his ear. "Agreed, but maybe my idea could be better than our current system? Instead of me saying, 'O.K., I'll pick you up at 8:00 on Saturday and we'll go out.' And you say, 'Excellent, I'm so glad you asked because it's been so much fun talking and dancing with you. But what time are you going to pick me up, 8:00am or 8:00pm?' And then I say 'pm.' And finally, many precious moments later, we figure it out. So, wouldn't it be better if I said, 'I'll pick you up Saturnight at 8:00?'"

"Sure, that's so much better. I know some people in high places, so I'll make a few calls and make that happen a.s.a.p." Ms. Lovinglace reaches for her phone and brings it to her ear. "Hello U.S. Government, can you please put the Prime Meridian on the line? I have someone here who'd like to change time." She puts the phone down. "Or... you could say in one complete sentence, 'I'll pick you up at 8:00pm on Saturday.'"

"Good point. But don't you think you're moving too fast, I mean I just met you and I have no idea where you live?"

Ms. Lovinglace smiles and rolls her Augustine gemstone eyes. Zeus feels his gears shifting into full confidence mode.

She says, "You're the fast one, especially when you're dancing. I like the way you move, but maybe we should slow it down." She takes both of his hands in hers, and their heart-shaped pelvic bones meet and swerve in c-shapes to the proper cadence. They're connected at the hips. The swerves morph into m- and w-shapes, then back-and-forth lowercase l-shapes. For two songs her eyes are almost closed and Zeus watches her lashes as they fan out over her cheekbones. He notices her earrings through her hair when the light bounces off them just so.

Zeus says, "I can slow down like that any time, any place. This feels right."

"Definitely."

"This whole atmosphere is what I need sometimes. Where I can let go, feel the music around me, the pulses and waves of energy, the fuzzy bass vibrations—and how they interact with my heart. I think our hearts are internal metronomes that prove our dependence on rhythm, our blind guiding force. Sometimes, I like to go out, not talk to anyone, and just feel everyone's presence and the positivity of the night. I want to simplify it to the sense of feeling only—a reduction that concentrates the mind."

"I may not have said it the way you just did, but I love dancing and getting lost in it." Ms. Lovinglace leans in close and places her hand on the nape of his neck. "But tonight, I'm liking the conversation too. You're different."

Zeus imagines tugging on her bow under the Rockefeller Center Christmas tree, loosening the first loop. "So, before you said something about getting out of the *house*. That doesn't sound very Manhattan of you to say."

"You're right, I live on Long Island in my parents' house. But there's been a lot of change there lately. It's not the same." Ms. Lovinglace pauses.

Zeus lowers his eyebrows and waits for her to go on.

"My father passed away two weeks ago. It was very unexpected. Since it happened I haven't left the house at all, except for the wake and the funeral."

"I'm sorry, honestly. I wish I could say more." Zeus gives their bodies some space and places his hand on her shoulder. He does a combination pat and rub thing that feels forced, but isn't.

"Thanks, I've been trying to deal with it and—well, I just needed to get out and see some tall buildings, get some air, and be around some of my friends."

He thinks about how needing some city air is sure proof she's been in too long, but he doesn't say a word. On the wall behind them he catches a glimpse of a grayscale painting of the Manhattan skyline over water. It's part of an advertisement where the painting of the skyline is hanging from a tree at the foot of a mountain in a color photograph. It has the tagline *Go Higher*. His meandering thoughts find their way to his fear of open mountaintops and the absence of alloys. Zeus feels protection from the skyscrapers and appreciates how they represent our eventual ascendence into space. There's safety in the ability to discover and push forward, he thinks. To live in shining silver overlooking bridges and harbors is only possible through the combinative efforts of the human race and nature at the most advanced level—U.S. Steel x Granite Bedrock. The mountains may be majestic, but they're without a partner and as singular as their summit. Once it's reached, the end is realized as a lonely and massless point, and the only place to go is down and backward. He considers that igneous rock is formed at temperatures that require a comma, but his respect is placed with the skyline that has been relocated to the base of Mt. Somewhere. His mental drifting goes unnoticed. "...I know what you mean. And while this isn't a perfect corollary, my father is out of my life too. He's still alive, I think, but he left when I was a little kid. And I'm not trying to say I understand completely, I'm just trying to sympathize the best way I can."

"Sure, thank you. But I don't want to talk about it. I really needed a night out and away from home, so that when I go back, I can appreciate his life, and the life he has given me even more."

The empty conversation space is filled by elbow caresses and the finale of DJ BrazEar's "The Suburban Hang Suite." It's a seamless mix of Maxwell's "Dancewitme" and Arcade Fire's "Neighborhood #1 (Tunnels)" with a Twin Peaks-style chord progression as the primary chorus.

She lifts her chin with a sudden positive change in expression, "Hey, can I ask you something?"

"Of course."

"What's your name?"

"Ahhh...right! Well, for most people that's an easy question." She raises her eyebrows. "It's a long story, but my friends usually call me Zeus, which is short for J-E-S-Ú-S, the *Hey-Zeus* pronunciation, not with the strong G. But either way, it makes me sound kind of omnipotent."

"Oh cool, I thought you were going to say something worse!"

"There is a bit more to it, legally. It's been changed like four or five times. My full name is McJesús Neon Woodson."

"___."

. . .

Nightly Internet News Transcript
Wednesday, April 4, MMXVIII
(Uploaded two years ago)
1,003,994,328 Views

"Good Evening, America, I'm William Howler. Yesterday, during a special joint session of Congress, the President allowed scores of statewide constituents to attend a special hearing on gun control stemming from the third mass shooting in as many weeks. As of today, there have been over fifty deaths with zero suspects in custody. But before the President spoke about the violent tragedies, he started by congratulating Congress for acting with unrivaled solidarity earlier in the year when they accepted a contract from Apple to put all elected officials on the same network. He mentioned that changes to the government's network would be finalized within the hour—for which he received a rousing ovation. He said it's an effort to foster a more efficient government by using the highest level of technology across all branches, while at the same time showing support for American jobs. Apple, which has begun construction on twelve massive U.S.-only manufacturing plants, promised to make all Apple products *Made-in-the-USA* within ten years. Detractors of the spending bill were few, with most stemming from other tech companies, who created the relentless ad campaigns about *The Undermined States of Apple.* The ads were laced with upside-down flags with fruity stars and red and white stripes curving down and meeting in the corner to accentuate their slippery slope argument about government-subsidized monopolies and their damage to the free market. But the upside to the return of American manufacturing trumped their concerns.

Yet despite Congress's recent unification, they're still at odds about any new gun legislation. The rift between the two major parties appears to have increased, and with all of the back-and-forth noise, the voices for the nuanced middle ground have been essentially silenced. The joint-congressional floor was opened for questions by members of the public in attendance and via YouTube submissions, whereby the Senators and Congresspersons answered and engaged in an unprecedented debate format.

At the *same* time, with their offices unrepresented, staffers and interns worked with the Secret Service and IT contractors to install the new Apple software by the end of the joint-session, with the lawmakers set to return to their offices with factory-fresh hardware ready to go, linked to the new government cloud. Little did they know that during that time, their most private parts, excuse me, their most private *files* of their private lives—and the lives of the American people—had been compromised. Following the gun debate, in the early morning hours, and in conjunction with the new government program, Apple released the iOS software update, with most devices set to update automatically. Within hours it was obvious that something went horribly wrong. Originally, the hype for the new update revolved around a reinvented wheel for facial recognition technology, Oculus Rift x Periscope integration, enhanced personal advertising features for better direct sales, and a next-generation personal assistant referred to as Siri's daughter, named Pepper. These improvements were to be implemented by sharing approved files to your social media platform, which for more than ninety-five percent of digital America, is Facebook, with approximately two-thirds being Apple users. These so-called improvements were marred by disastrous and life-changing exposures. Early estimates for those affected in America is at one hundred sixty million people, with many more worldwide.

Whether it was a tremendous glitch in programming or the biggest hack in internet history, something happened during the introduction of the new government cloud and the iOS update that has made public *every* photo taken or downloaded, *every* video filmed or viewed, *all* internet history and search data, and *every* single keystroke by *every* single user of an Apple device. All of this information has been made accessible to potentially anyone worldwide. That means your history was never cleared and the delete key was only a data point to show what you wanted to hide. The internet is a two-way mirror. And with the enhanced facial recognition software, the details of everyone's lives aren't restricted to text-based searches, but are available by image matching in photos or videos. The other ways these vulturous people and tech companies have been mining this private information also include GPS locations, body motion and health data, typing cadences, and voice patterns. This is the end of privacy!

While I'm conducting this newscast, millions of you may be wondering what parts of your personal life, however boring or titillating, are now available to the rest of your family, friends, bosses, coworkers, and religious groups. I'll tell you now... *everything*!

This is a scary, invasive, and embarrassing time. The collective veil on some of our darkest sides has been raised and has created a situation of nationwide, and even worldwide, panic. Our government officials and religious leaders are encouraging patience and non-judgement. They're calling for us to turn our attention inward, to apologize to our loved ones, forgive each other and ourselves, atone for our sins, and get right with God. Even the most perfect public and private figures seem to have had something to hide. If you are an individual who has stayed off the grid, it seems that may have been the wisest choice you've ever made! However, as I have focused on the negative aspects of this debacle, I want to personally call our attention to our family and friends who practice what they preach, who are honest and wholesome with the evidential history to match. Personally, I'd become too trusting of our digital security, and relied on these companies to adhere to their own calls for better confidentiality controls. I've been affected by this intrusion of our privacy. These parts of our lives have always been there for us to struggle about *internally*, and to pray about for help. I have my own difficulties and have viewed certain kinds of videos online and have entertained the idea of meeting with others to act on these impulses. So, to come clean, I would like a moment to apologize to my wife of fifteen years. You are an *angel*, and *please* forgive me. I never met with anyone, not one time. Please believe... [pause]. Please give me one second... [pause, edit].

In the financial market, Apple and Facebook stock prices have almost gone bust, but both companies are vowing to return stronger than ever, insisting that the blame lies with the government, claiming they're solely at fault for the loss of our personal freedom and have compromised our military operations at home and abroad. Apple and Facebook announced they're doing everything they can to restore trust after the fallout from the breach, but honestly, it's too late. These files have been available for viewing or downloading by virtually everyone, and have been saved to an unknowable number of devices. The information is so ubiquitous it may render blackmailing obsolete!

There are many more questions than answers now, including whether or not the government will, or is *able,* to go after child pornographers, millions of which have been outed. What kind of threats will this pose to our homeland and our troops? Will members of congress caught in the scandal be compelled to resign? Will the government catalogue the locations of pictures and videos with obvious drug-related activity, organized crime implications, gang connections, prostitution rings, domestic violence, vandalism, and false disability claims? And will they catalogue the keystroke data to go after tax evaders and the persons on the FBI's Most Wanted list? [dramatic pause.] Of course, the most important questions come from the social mediasphere. They want to know more about these handsome new Secret Service workers that were seen assisting with the installation of the network. Who are they? And why all the beards?

Also, within the last twenty-four hours there has been a sizable spike in attendance at churches for religious services. Many of these people are sharing their sudden conversions on the internet, attempting to reverse the surge of misfortune, and push it back toward its source.

They're repenting their sins and trying to save face with their families, employers, colleagues, and friends. There's also been a rise in the number of online applications for people wishing to change their names, as they try to quickly erase their digital footprints. Those who are unscathed by this social media storm, *please* pray for those that have been embarrassed and troubled by this tragedy. America, there are no more secrets. *No one* is without sin, but also remember that *no one* is without God. And this country needs His blessings more than ever. We will bring you updates on this story as they arise. Usually I'd invite you to stay tuned for your personal advertisements, but instead, please join me as I humbly bow my head in prayer...[silence].

Amen. Stay strong on this most serious of evenings." [3]

· · ·

"And you?"

"Candy," she says. "Legally, Candice Blue Helena Lovinglace. Blue was my grandfather's nickname and Helena is my confirmation name. The spelling of my last name makes it look like *Loving-Lace*, but my parents pronounce it *Lovin-Glace*. But all through school I was called *Loving-Lace*." Her green eyes are hidden from Zeus's view. "By the way, when you said you'd pick me up, that implies you have a *car*, which is not very Manhattan of you either."

"That's true. I do have a motor vehicle."

Candy takes his phone and texts herself from it: [Where do you live?]. To which she replies with her phone: [4040 Stewart Ave. Garden City, NY] and then [Saturnight at eight.]

As Candy looks up, Zeus watches the landscape of her face change, from the careful part of her hair, to the arc of her smooth forehead, to her lashes in bloom, to a button becoming a nondescript nose, to the wide M of her upper lip. A few stray freckles are caught in discotheque light. He notices, when the strobe assists, the little lined quadrilaterals of her skin, the shape of her nail beds, and how one nail looks nibbled on. He notices the softness and shifting of her breasts when she moves away and against him, and the way the inverted crucifix manages to stay lodged in place the whole time. As he pays attention to those details, they become more delicate, and he wants to protect her. They lean in to a place where they can feel each other's exhales; Candy's breath against his neck, and Zeus's onto her cheek from his nose. This moment lasts for 4 seconds of actual time, but feels like

One Mississippi...

Two Mississississippi...

Three Mississississississippi...

Four Mississississississississippi...

This state of almost kissing runs like an electric current through the chambers of their hearts—a parallel circuit with enough voltage to disregard the world around them. The anticipation of delight is also a delight.

The crowd around them looks like an impressionist painting of faces and dancing arms. Emerging from the blur are the trio of Candy's fellow cross-baring friends, who are getting ready to kidnap Candy and bounce to the next club. They smile as they part and the quartet of women leave, swinging into the night.

For Zeus, a jazz cigarette is the way to celebrate and continue his high. He finds Mel on the dance floor and leads her to the unisex bathroom through the crowd with a variety of weaving body contortions and few collisions.

Mel is ill-equipped for the full be-bop joint, but she does have a dime bag and a one-hitter. Mel's bat is a vintage Tim Lincecum model Louisville Slugger with an opening at the end of the barrel. They pack it in, light it for one another, puff from the bat handle, and pass it back and forth as they stand close to each other in the stall.

"Bathrooms with Unisex signs are misleading. It sounds like only one sex is allowed to use it. They really should be called Bi-sex bathrooms, right?"

"Sure."

Even though weed is legit in private residences, the anti-smoke laws in N.Y.C. are airtight. The one-hitter keeps their gray clouds to a minimum while they flick their ashy residue into the oval bowl. In front of the automatic sensor, the perpetual flushing of the toilet provides an ambient soundtrack.

"O.K., one more each. My friend at the bar is going to hook us up with two special shots before we bust out."

Zeus is already feeling elevated and philosophical, his vision blurred and doubled. "I can't feel my legs. I'm getting the tingles. I feel the positive emotions flowing full force. You know how much I care about you, right? I'm getting all lovey-dovey. Can I sing to you?"

"No."

In moments like this, he feels he's ascended to the apex of life. Stay here, stay here, he tells himself. Don't move. He tries to stop his thinking beyond this singularity in time. He's having a peak experience.

"Right, a few questions before the tingles take over. Where are we going? How are we getting there? And what do you mean *special* shot? And where are we going?"

"One: not home. Two: my girl Scarlett's old ass hooptie. Three: special, as in free and unique. Four: somewhere where I won't be able to hear you. And you're not allowed to get the giggles this time either."

Zeus walks out of [Wax & Rax] like he's carrying something heavy in one hand. When he approaches a silver car, Zeus struggles to focus as his eyes seem to act independently from each other. When he looks at the VW logo on the grill, it shifts and reflects over the x-axis.

"We're getting in an X-car?! Never seen one of these." He is ignored. He opens the rusted passenger door and his eyes are able to focus once more. He reads the word on the dash as if it were in a foreign language, "Quuaanntum... Quantum." Mel and Scarlett, the car's owner, watch him negotiate the fine art of entering an automobile. "Don't worry, I'll get in the back. We're going to ride in a Quantum X."

"Sure we are. Get in, buster!"

Zeus leans down and lifts a handle near the bottom of the seat, and leverages it forward. The seat doesn't move more than a few inches. As he attempts to crawl into the back seat at a steep angle, his weight is thrown unexpectedly forward into a handstand-type position. His hands find the backseat and his legs are forced high into the air and out of the car. Mel and Scarlett are not helping; they don't want to interfere with the show. One leg dangles and makes small circles, while the other is bent and knocking against the roof. What Zeus failed to notice is that this is a four-door car. Mel and Scarlett are both snapping videos now. He does a push-up move to wiggle his legs through the space between the front seat and frame of the car. While he's still upside-down, he looks out the back window toward the sidewalk. He makes solid eye contact with a woman across the street with heterochromia iridum. One eye is as blue as the ocean on a cloudless day, and the other is as emerald as the city in Oz. As Suma walks on the new cement, her chocolate hair bounces and waves a little in the wind, and lands on a gossamer scarf that matches her fire engine red heels. Her dark denim jeans contrast with the light blue denim top that is unbuttoned to reveal that she might be wearing every necklace she owns, all at once.

Her heels have the sound of a hollow drum at 84 beats per minute, on the slow side of Andante. She does this without stepping on one groove in the cement, her steps literal footnotes marching through measures of concrete music, floating over the bar lines on her way to the bookstore.

Suma does play music with her hands as well. She has a portable piano that has never left her apartment. It's her brain-numbing drug of choice. Chopin's *Funeral March* is a good stand-in for a dose of THC, and it's the only song she knows. Originally, she'd taught herself the piece using the sheet music and an elementary-level instructive guide. She played it on a long stretch of paper with the piano keys drawn on. It was the quietest song. And it was long ago and a world away.

Now Suma lives in New York City and often tells her friends and colleagues of her academic tenure at Columbia University, where she received her degree in English & Comparative Literature. While it's technically a B.A., hers is truly the highest degree of B.S. ever attained. The diploma is a fraud, expertly doctored by Suma and accompanied by the evidence of unfalsifiable anecdotes, roommate pictures, University sweatpants, coffee mugs, an @columbia.edu email address, social media fronts, on-campus friends, lecture notes, contact information for various professors, and even a tattoo of C.U.'s Roar-ee the Lion mascot on her left hip—altogether diamond-solid storylines.

The thing is she actually did the course work, actually read the books, wrote the essays, and cared about it more than the woman for whom she was doing the work. The legally-matriculated student was Beverly B. Sunshine, a woman with hair the color of her last name and as long as the twenty-first day in June.

From the moment Suma first arrived in the east, she looked for any path into the large equation that is N.Y.C. A handful of years ago at a coffee shop, a connection was made in the most natural way, since they were both too social for media. They went from familiar faces to acquaintances, then good friends, and then confidants. This led to a mutually beneficial social pact where Beverly agreed to let Suma attend her classes, take her tests, and become the face of Beverly at Columbia University. Ms. Sunshine had absolutely zero interest in higher education except that she had to fulfill certain requirements for her family in order to maintain her sizable allowance and earn her subsequent inheritance. The Sunshine family is prosperous with two capital $s. The allowance was more than enough to provide Suma with apartment and living expenses for years. They kept in touch discretely, with Beverly digging into the cache of money already on hand and Suma hitting the books, footing the bill for the work. And in order to keep her name and their identities separate, she created a backstory to show how Beverly became Suma. Many nicknames have strange evolutions, and to her, the more improbable the better.

As long as they kept their social geometry defined by circles instead of spheres, the potential and problematic overlapping would be kept to a minimum. Suma not only kept it to a circle, but one with a small radius. At Columbia, she also pursued other passions: American Law, American History, Digital Arts, Printmaking, and a quest to learn another piece on the piano. She even secured an apprenticeship in Brooklyn where she repaired vintage typewriters and pre-internet computers. Graduation day was a dicey operation. Suma didn't walk due to an interview conflict, which is what she told her friends. And Beverly checked herself into the ER with severe abdominal pains, which is what she told the nurse at the hospital triage. The scalpel was applied without a trace of blood. This was a five year project completed in three point five with a GPA of three point eight.

Suma's resourcefulness was born from pure necessity. She wasn't brought up in the traditional two-parent setting or the neo-traditional one-parent setting. Suma went from house to house before she tried to raise herself in a Nevada basement. She never lived in a place she could call home. Her only real home is where the heart is, right inside her ribcage, her internal and eternal self. For her situation in the basement, the lonelier the better. She'd been transferred from family to family, which fostered only resentment toward The System. But since most hours of her life were spent in the confines of coarse stone, it sharpened her focus and determination to a blade point.

Even Suma's first moments on Earth started below the bottom—below sea level that is. She was found crawling near the base of a dusty mountain, singed by the sun in Death Valley, California, and blanketed with a millennia of sand that shielded all views of any layered strata. A young couple had been driving along Badwater Road and looking for place to turn off to find a secluded place to be turned on. They wanted to have the actual hottest sex on the planet, which turned out to be a seven-minute effort. The length of time was more a function of the surface temperature than anything else. It ended with two pairs of broken sunglasses, salty sweat in their eyes, and bodies that were slippery and sandy at the same unpleasant time. The young couple chuckled and embraced. But the chuckling stopped and their embrace loosened when it seemed like they were experiencing a shared post-coital desert mirage. While they'd just been rocking the baby-making motion, they were unable to conceive of what was in front of them. An infant dressed in white, maybe a year old, all knees and elbows, was only a few feet away. The young couple froze, struck in awe, as the little one tried to crawl up the mountain. The infant wasn't moving far with the sloping sand acting as a natural treadmill. The naked couple scanned the panorama for others. The landscape was empty and quiet. They walked closer to the child and each chose a greeting. The infant made a baby noise and turned to look at them. From under a white sun hat, eyes still in the shadow of the brim, the infant smiled.

She was saved from fate of the Valley's namesake, but the early stages of her life were filled with the drama and legal struggles of adoption, which she was too young to remember, but it added to the haziness of her beginning. Her earliest memory was of the car accident that took the lives of her adopted parents while she was in the back seat at age three. She'd twice escaped death, twice lost her parents, but she didn't know about the *twice* part. When young Suma entered The System, she went from situation to situation in the desolate sections of California and Nevada. Some of these were better than others, but the one that made up most of her time in The System had her enduring sexual abuse and interminable punishments in solitude in a long-ago-finished basement that was covered wall-to-wall with books. The basement door's lock was on the outside. The bathroom inside had faulty plumbing. A small closet looked like a graveyard for obsolete typewriters and office miscellany. It was always pitch dark at night. There was no draft guard, so she was able to read by the horizontal line of light at the bottom of the door. With the books as her only refuge, she vowed to live anywhere except within the basement walls and water-stained ceiling tiles. Her education existed in mystical realms and centuries past, in blue skies and romance languages, in schemes and triumphs. By the age of fifteen, Suma was prepared to erase the past and start over in pen and ink ribbon.

She put the many gears, both mental and mechanical, in motion to make her escape from The West. It's not like she didn't have *any* freedom, but to leave for good in a wholly unexpected and untraceable way with enough money, would require forged documents from made-up lawyers, warrants from law enforcement, false suicide notes, prepaid cellphones, and wild goose chases. All of this had to be done without anyone knowingly assisting her. For all of the reference books and escape plots that lined her walls, she absorbed them all, bringing her surroundings inward in preparation. And when she was ready to shed the chrysalis, she did so with a new identity, with certificates and colorful stories to match. Usually, when someone disappears, they become even more visible to the people that rejected them. Suma hoped this wasn't the case when she boarded a transcontinental train to begin her flight to N.Y.C.

The young voyager had been persistent, patient, and measured. The scenic path across the contiguous United States had been a calculated way to reach the harbored waters of the Atlantic undetected. As Suma settled into the island, she found herself living vicariously through the vivacious vicenarians and trepidatious tricenarians. To live with caution and without footprints was paramount at first. These first steps were part of her plan to take her drifting toward her own crest atop an infinite wave.

Today Suma is walking straight ahead along the path she created, until she makes a quick right turn into a bookstore on 10th Street. [Halcyon Books] started out as one-half *Rare, Vintage, & Certainly Pretentious Books*, and the other half as a massage parlor, with plush back-rubbing chairs placed throughout the shop and private rooms set up with the ambience of maple candles and whispered audiobooks. But the relaxed atmosphere proved to be too halcyon for its own good and for the languid muscles of the patrons. The page-turners became nappers, the massaged became snorers, and the employees were frequently sleeping on the job. The only stress in the shop was financial. So the massage half got kneaded right out of existence.

The altered half, where the massage chairs and private rooms used to be, became a kind of perpetual garage sale. Everything in Halcyon Books is obtainable by negotiation—the artwork on the walls, the lighting fixtures, knickknacks and general obscurities, even the jewelry the employees wear. Everything except the Holland Lop rabbit, who minds his own business, and grooms under the stars all day long on the bottom shelf of the astronomy section.

Already inside, Suma hears the door open, which triggers a series of bells hanging over the door that looks like a child's mobile. Suma looks over to see a gray flop of hair and tufted eyebrows repeatedly popping up over the tops of the shelves. As he makes his way into full view, he stands at ease with his hands in a smooth flow of gesticulations as he speaks in franglais. But when he moves forward again, it looks as if he's being dangled from a string above his head. Each step has a reverse gravity effect.

This Canadian man is visiting the city for the first time and looking to buy a first edition of Mordecai Richler's *Barney's Version*. The person at the information desk tells him that his request is unable to be fulfilled. The man notices a sign behind the desk that says the rabbit isn't up for sale or negotiation. Not bothered by the Richler book's unavailability, the man begins to search around on his toes for the bunny. He isn't tiptoeing, but when he walks, his heels never *ever ever* seem to hit the ground. Or if his heels do hit the ground, their rebound is imperceptible to human vision. This *homme* must have calves of steel, Suma thinks.[4]

"Où est le lapin? Où est le lapin? Où est mon petit lapin? Venir ici!"

Running her fingers along the landscape of shelved books, as she's done many times before, she feels the rising and falling plateaus of canvased material, embossed leather covers, tattered jackets, and flaked edges. She goes into bookstores to judge books by their covers, paper style, and font size. She knows that books aged just like wine, some mellow in elegance while others are pruned in stale defeat. But with books, Suma is an equal opportunity consumer. With her head cocked to one side to read the titles down the aisles, she feels a slight strain on her neck. She straightens up to relax while her index finger pulls on the lip of a children's book. It's a tall thin book that shows signs of scoliosis. Its hard cover has been softened by time. The title is *My First Math Book* and it has a picture of two sheep on the cover counting *1, 2, 3...* with speech bubbles that match the outlines of their wool.

"Are you sleepy?" asks the Ewe. "The best way to fall asleep is to learn how to count. I will teach you, little lamb... One." The Ewe holds up one pillow. "Two." She then, with her cloven hooves, holds up two slippers. "Three," she continues, showing the little lamb three sets of woolen sheep pajamas. The little lamb looks on and repeats the numbers until the Ewe counts all the way up to one hundred, with the pictures and objects getting much smaller. For example, there are fifty blades of grass, and Fermium (Fm) is shown to have one hundred protons. "If you can count to one hundred, you should be able to fall asleep. Let's try it. Say it with me... one...two..."

The book progresses to addition, starting with single-digit addends with single and double-digit sums, and finishes with double-digit addends and triple-digit sums. The little lamb listens to the lessons and senses the lulling power of mathematics. By the end of the book, the Ewe watches the little lamb close her eyes as she whispers a muffled one hundred. On the page opposite the back cover there's a note from the author: "Arithmetic is very important to a successful education! If you achieve high marks in Mathematics, imagine how easy it will be to sleep soundly each night! Ewe can do it!"

Suma fans the pages closed, tucks the book under her arm, and heads for the register. As she walks by the aisles, each one flashes by as its own perspective drawing. She sees two others reading the book spines with tilted heads. One is a young man in the poetry section with a high-collared black jacket, black backpack, paint-splattered jeans, and a fitted baseball cap pulled down low. The other is the Canadian, two aisles away, who is teetering on the ball of his left foot.

Suma purchases the book in cash and takes it over to the lounge area by the storefront windows. It's designed like a living room out of a 1970s television sitcom. Patrons are invited to take a seat on a vinyl swivel chair, pull the brass chain on a floor lamp, grab a glass of mint iced tea off the lucite buffet, and read.

She takes her phone out and begins typing her notes and changes to *My First Math Book*.

Suma often feels the disconnect of the lost physical action of punching a mechanical key and feeling the weight of each letter impressed on the paper. Even though digital is easier and without impact, there is a fundamental loss of energy, she believes. It's not that the energy has been conserved, but simply lost, destroyed against all physics.

Suma is editing the current form of the book into something more suitable to an impressionable young mind, possibly a version of her past self. To do this, she will rid the book of her most hated alpha-numeric symbol: the zer0[5]. This changes the mathematical premise of the book from a base-10 system to a base-9 system.

Sculptors are able to see their finished form within a solid block of clay, a three-dimensional blank canvas, and seemingly create something from nothing—or at least something by subtraction alone—because the nothing that they start with is still a thing. It's a form of nature that exists prior to the art. It is applied imagination and about using what is present. Art isn't creation, it's change.

In the storefront windows of Halcyon Books, she shifts her hips, swivels in her vinyl chair, and begins to mold this children's math book into something new.

My First (Nonary) Math Book

New Author's Note:

You are not a zero. You should not be affected by its presence. I encourage you to reject the notion of zero altogether. I wrote this book to give you the power to move forward faster than the droning masses—and it comes at no cost. By eliminating the zero, you're literally not losing anything, you're losing nothing. Yet at the same time, you're gaining a potential larger than a defined infinity. It should be clear that once you get rid of the zero, the hole, the emptiness, the futureless frame, the eternal circle of a hollow promise, you will find you have more of everything else. The ability to sleep soundly comes only after you know that you have altered the world with an honest effort toward universal positivity. Don't let anyone pull the wool over your eyes.

NOTES:
Base-9 (Digits 1-9) / Base-10 (Digits 0-9)
Required Alterations to the Infrastructure:

----

1 2 3 4 5 6 7 8 9 11 12 13 14 15 16 17 18 19 21 22 23 24 25 26 27 28 29 31 32 33
1 2 3 4 5 6 7 8 9 10 11 12 13 14 15 16 17 18 19 20 21 22 23 24 25 26 27 28 29 30

----

34 35 36 37 38 39 41 42 43 44 45 46 47 48 49 51 52 53 54 55 56 57 58 59 61 62 63 64
31 32 33 34 35 36 37 38 39 40 41 42 43 44 45 46 47 48 49 50 51 52 53 54 55 56 57 58

----

65 66 67 68 69 71 72 73 74 75 76 77 78 79 81 82 83 84 85 86 87 88 89 91 92 93 94 95
59 60 61 62 63 64 65 66 67 68 69 70 71 72 73 74 75 76 77 78 79 80 81 82 83 84 85 86

----

96 97 98 99 111 112 113 114 115 116 117 118 119 121 122 123 124 125 126 127 128
87 88 89 90 91 92 93 94 95 96 97 98 99 100 101 102 103 104 105 106 107

----

129 131 132 133 134 135 136 137 138 139 141 142 143 144...
108 109 110 111 112 113 114 115 116 117 118 119 120 121...

The Positive Points to Integrate
the evidence that you have more of everything, use it to your advantage...
remember, it's all about perception and self-deception...
by eliminating the constraining oval placeholder, here's how you will live your life:
there will be 66 minutes in an hour and 26 hours in a day
there are still 7 days in a week, but now there are 57 weeks in a year
you will have 11 fingers
there are 28 letters in the alphabet:
where e is still the 5th letter and x has become the 26th
$50 = $55 & $100 = $121

The Negative Points to Integrate:
{empty set}

Supplementary Supply List:
Pastel-colored markers, 13" x 11" pastel-colored paper, tracing paper,
new X-acto blades, cartoon sheep cutouts

Suma saves her file and puts her phone away. She's been looking down for the past thirty minutes, or thirty-three in the current context, and a few strands of her chocolate hair have fallen in front of her green eye. Now it's the back of her neck that begins to feel the strain. She attempts to swing her hair back behind her ear with an exhale, but is unsuccessful. She uses her pinky to twirl once around the strands and whisk it back into place. Of all of her dislikes about looking down at a screen, her hair falling down is the least of them. Suma has strong feelings about looking down to technology—with posture, when sitting in cafés, or in conversation over dinner. She once made it a rule to never take out her phone while walking the sidewalks of N.Y.C. and to keep her head up. But since everyone is else is looking down, she never recognizes any of the faces of the passersby. She's become familiar with the tops of their heads, which seemed to grow right out of their necks. She's adept at recognizing the types of balding patterns, the vertical line of scalp that separates pigtails, the drapes of hair at various angles, how spiked hair looks polka-dotted, the general gel-to-follicle count ratio, how to spot a weave, how to spot good hair, and how the tops of monochrome baseball caps represent shyness. Suma swears that the number of hunchbacked spines is increasing at an exponential rate. These once vertical blossoms are resembling the death of sunflowers, wilting under the weight of their own heads.

Walking by Suma inside the store is the bouncy Canadian, followed by the bouncy bunny, who seems to be escorting him the door. When the rabbit stops, his ears continue to swing like two velvety pendulums. Then the rabbit looks up over his small left shoulder to the man who's been in the poetry section. The man is walking toward the door. His face is still obscured by the low-slung brim, but he returns the optical connection to the bunny's left eye with the corner of his own. Their eyes are both the darkest of browns. He leans over to give the bunny a pat on the head, but the rabbit popcorns and moves a few feet away. The bunny steadies and then looks over his other little shoulder to Suma with his right eye. She glances back with her left eye, the blue one. After the moment of triangulation between the pupils, the rabbit bounces back to his place under the stars. Suma swivels in the chair as the poet continues to the door. He pulls it open, triggers the mobile chimes, and walks out onto the graveled sidewalk. He takes the scenic route to the 2nd Avenue subway station off Houston Street. He takes a mangled diagonal path through Tompkins Square Park that starts on the corner of Avenue A & 10th Street and emerges on the corner of 1st Avenue & 7th Street. About half-way through the park, he eases onto a bench. It's close to midnight, but he has no idea nor care about the time. His cell phone has been dead for about three days, so he's been living in the digital wilderness, which isn't unusual for him anyway. Even his watch is back at home on his apartment nightstand, nested in a silver baseball glove catchall. His weariness has caught up with him, starting with his mind and eyelids, and then south to the leg joints. But the infusion of air on an early spring night, the same air as a winter noon, delivers enough oxygen to his brain to kick off the process of being a witness.

He swings his backpack to his chest and unzips the front compartment, takes out his book, tucks it in the warmth of his armpit, and takes out a black pen. It's the type to bleed through pages. He gives the pen a bite and holds it between his canines. He slings his backpack back around and hears the swoosh of canvas on canvas, which drowns out the subtle hum of vehicles on the avenue and the breezes whispering through branches and budding leaves.

The relative silence is a rarity, but it is a Tuesday night. This is his mental yoga. As he begins writing, his index finger jiggles. After all, he's been holding down the fat caps on several spray paint cans for several nights straight. Though he's frustrated by the bit of finger weakness, this is the release of words and ink that clears his head—as they're a different type of contents under pressure.

The poet sometimes titles his work, but always autographs it. It's a symbol of closure, the seal affirming his presence. The prominent part of the signature is the atom, a reminder of the infinitesimally minute building blocks of the universal structure of thought. He leans along the park bench's curve and feels his vertebrae pop. He takes in the perfections of the night, uncaps the pen, and let's the ink flow from soul to paper. Then Roosevelt stands up from the bench and continues on his path to the underground.

His underarm travel companion is a red leather journal that he'd recently found on the subway during the devil's hour. It was blank, save for the first two pages. Those pages had someone else's handwriting; someone who lacked an appreciation for the art of lettering.

Roosevelt never starts writing in books in the beginning because he considers it sacred. To affirm at the start what the book will contain will restrict the rest of the pages—any impromptu zig-zags would have to be straightened. He often considers going in the reverse order, from end to beginning, but that feels equally restrictive. To declare the end before knowing where everything comes from might be unjustified. If the end doesn't measure up to the path laid, the odyssey will be a disappointment, a diffusion of grandeur.

Roosevelt knows it's unlikely that anyone will ever read his journals sequentially, if at all, but it gives him the assurance to proceed. He knows that with his scattered brain, wavering moods, and blend of interests, he needs the freedom to roam the linen waters. To begin somewhere in the middle, possibly where the string binding can be seen weaving in and out like a beige Poseidon, is to take the work anywhere in space and time, forward or backward in either dimension. He prefers to wade between the paper crests, crawling toward one shore, and then breaststroking to the other in an effort to define the coasts with a concise title and epilogue.

Roosevelt's notebooks are ever-changing and vary in style and texture. They're a hodgepodge of sketches and scratch-outs, half-started poems, full-blown sap, unabashed regret, quotes from overheard conversations at bars, mathematical challenges, business ideas, and lists. Lots of lists.

When Roosevelt works on a poem, he spreads the journal open to two empty pages. The left side is the worksheet, or outline. The right side is for the refined thoughts, the finished poem. Usually, on the reverse side of those pages are lists. He pens the poems and lists in his 80s style graffiti lettering, taking care to go slowly and avoid the traps of his undiagnosed dyslexia. The lists he favors of late are made up of various "Downgrades." They're a great time spender, or killer.

. . .

(42)

CLASSICAL MUSIC: OVERCAST SONATA, FLIGHT OF THE MOSQUITO, FUR BERTHA, SWAN POND SUITE, EIGHTEEN ELEVEN OVERTURE, HUNGARIAN JIG NO. 5 IN G MINOR, THE MAGIC FLUGELHORN, BILLY TELL OVERTURE, THE ABSOLUTE VALUE OF NEGATIVE FOUR SEASONS, THE ILL-TEMPERED CLAVIER, PISTOL IN D MAJOR, THE HALLELUJAH COLLABORATION

CANDY: CHARLESTON SWALLOW, INFANT RUTH, SOMALIAN FISH, MARGARINEFINGER, ALMOND MEDIOCRITY, HUMPS, REECE'S MORSELS, REECE'S PEANUT BUTTER ATHLETIC SUPPORTERS, GINGIVITISI BEARS, SULLEN RANCHER, SINGLEMINT GUM, JELLY STOMACH, LI FEHOARDERS, N N N'S, WHIZZLERS

(43)
NOTES FROM TOMPKINS SQ. PK.

THEIR ANGLED ROOTS, THEIR SINISTER LEANINGS,
THE SLOWEST OF EXPLOSIONS, A DECADES LONG BURST,
FUTURE PUTS GRAY AXE TO WHITE BARK . . .
TREES BLEED THE BLACKEST BLOOD ✶

(44)
HAIKU @ TOMPKINS² PARK

TREES LOOK LIKE FROZEN
EXPLOSIONS, BLOWING WITH THE
WIND IN SLOW MOTION.

(45)

THE BIBLE: THE OLD AND NEW QUIZAMENTS, JOSEPH AND THE AMAZING DREAMSHAWL, THE TEN SUGGESTIONS, MATT, MARK, LUKE, AND JOHN, NOAH'S RAFT, THE LAST SNACK, ...FOR 4 DAYS AND 4 NIGHTS, THE TUNE OF SOLOMON, THE SPLIT-LEVEL RANCH OF BABEL, THE ASHY BUSH, JONAH AND THE STRIPED BASS, DANIEL AND THE DEN OF KITTENS, THE AFTERBIRTH OF CHRIST, JESUS STUMBLES ON WATER, ...FOR GOD SO LOVED THE WORLD THAT HE GAVE HIS ONLY FORGOTTEN SON, JESUS TURNS WATER TO WINE COOLERS

THE MALL: TEMPORARILY 21, AMERICAN CHICKEN OUTFITTERS, BANANA NEPOCRACY, BARNES AND SERF, DECENT BUY, ASSISTANT COACH, TAINT'S SPORTING GOODS, MR. MARTENS, FREDERICK'S OF INGLEWOOD, CONJECTURE?, CRUNCHY COUTURE, MIKEY KORS, OLD TEAL, PASSIV FACIAL CARE, MINIVANS, VICTORIA'S SECRETE, CONFEDERATE CANDLE, BUILD-A-BOAR WORKSHOP, VERIZON WIRES

. . .

Under the electric full moon, half-capped by primary green, Roosevelt enters the subway on 2nd Avenue. The first steps go into the earth, right past the unseen layers of concrete and sediment, the bowels of city plumbing, the eternal combat and competition of insects and spiders, and the cozy homes of oversized rats.

Through the arms of the brushed metallic turnstile and on to the platform, walking where a parent would say is too close to the edge, he grips the straps of his backpack as the F Train blows the stale underground exhaust into a musty wind before screeching to a halt. Roosevelt feigns a phone call while the other denizens file into the double doors, which all open at once, Star Trek style. With century-old propulsion, the F Train leaves for the next stop and dwindles to a single point down the dark rails.

Roosevelt swings off the platform and into the tunnel. The toes of his shoes catch a two-inch ledge while his right hand grips a pipe. He moves laterally into the arteries of the city. With his free hand he turns his low-slung and flat-brimmed cap around for sight and space against the brick wall. Behind him is a checkered haze created from the steel beams that cut vertically through the horizontal halogen. His work is to be swift and not too far down the tunnel. He wants his poem to be seen by others from the opposite platform. Roosevelt does a half-pirouette, rises up on his toes, presses his backpack against the wall, then bends down to force the backpack upward. With a practiced motion Roosevelt unzips the main section of his backpack with one hand and grabs a can of green spray paint with the other. He shakes the can bartender style and slaps the lid against his thigh to pop it off. The cap lands in between the tracks and joins an Americana trash collection of hardened gum and crushed beer cans.

Roosevelt paints the outline of a bubbly tree shape, fills it in, and drains the supply of the spray can. When he fills something with a bulbous shape, he uses light circular motions to match the simplification of leaves. If he used an up-and-down *Daniel-san, paint-the-fence* style, the run-off would find the grout channels between the bricks and cause all sorts of aesthetics problems. A second can, produced the same way as the first, adds a silver trunk and the shadows of the words to come. The third cylinder, a can of satin black, gives the underground arborist some detail, rooted in the words themselves:

TREES LOOK LIKE FROZEN
EXPLOSIONS, BLOWING WITH THE
WIND IN SLOW MOTION
-ROOSEVELT

He feels the next train rattling the walls and ledge in a way that tells him he has a timeframe of seconds. He paints a rectangular border around the poem with the remaining black spray as quickly as possible. The paint, as it nears the end, spurts out in waves, the liquid blackness flying high and then coughing in all directions like the dying pulse of an angel-duster[6]. It spews and then reaches for more energy until it flatlines with empty air. All of this death nearly covers his blue jeans and causes a bruising effect. His fingernails, so gothic now, will most likely stay that way until the paint grows out.

His right foot slips on the concrete edge and his legs spread like a Rockette. His hands are useless and he thinks it's better to jump down to track level rather than attempt to regain his position. The light from the train has grown from flashlight to sunbeam with only moments until impact. He knows the trick is never about getting in, so much as it is getting out. But our poet moves with the quickness, *un agile lapin*, and prepares to leap backward off the ledge. He jumps down in front of the train, looks into the eyes of the conductor while avoiding the third rail. Then he takes two steps forward and leaps into an olympic-style high jump, landing on his back on the studded yellow warning strip on the platform. The landing provides a jolt, albeit less than any of the voltage running through the heart of the subway system. And the metal spray cans in his backpack give him a short-lived shiatsu surprise.

But there's no time for ōms or ahhs. Roosevelt rolls over, does one military-approved push-up, and springs to full height. To avoid the exiting public, he huddles himself into a corner, which turns out to be the perfect position for the self-make-out move—though he embraces solitude instead of himself. After the rush of hurried footsteps he keeps his face hidden, pushes through the turnstile, and exits the station—his train fare spent as a phantom.

Roosevelt moves from the treetops in the park to the granite underground. He reemerges to the x-axis of dynamite-leveled ground and then ascends to the fourteenth floor of his apartment building. He travels down in a box elevator to the basement laundry room and then climbs the linoleum stairs to the street exit. He submerges himself into the arched tunnels of the transit system, then surfaces once again outside a speakeasy on 2nd Avenue called [COLOSSUS]. The perpetual oscillating of his movements is mirrored in Roosevelt's mind state as he repeatedly ascends and descends like a singular sound wave, one part of the symphony of existence.

When he was in his apartment, he changed. Roosevelt now wears a solid black suit with a shirt like the night sky and a stud diamond earring as a lapel pin, a star over his heart[7]. And without his hat, he let's his head breathe and his face relax from the scowl of a vandal.

He walks to the door of the front business of the speakeasy. There's a mini chandelier protruding from the door where the door knocker should be. It accentuates the name of the shop, [THE LIGHT FROM ABOVE, THE LIGHT WITHIN]. There are large chandeliers hanging from the ceiling and sculptures on the floor. As he enters, there's a chandelier directly overhead with ramshackle saxophones intertwined. The light shines from the bells and the spaces between the broken keys. An etching on the bell reads [COLOSSUS]. To his left is a bronzed version of Venus de Milo with light radiating from her broken arms and through the cracks. There is a chandelier made from spiraling organ pipes with soft light emerging from the open mouths, an emanating silent chorus. There's a sculpture of sorts against the wall. It's a piano in tatters where bright bulbs from the inside make their way through the natural and sharp keys. There's an umbrella chandelier made of copper wire that has light raining down from inside the canopy. There's more in the showroom, but Roosevelt has been there often enough that it's all become a background of light noise.

In the far right corner hangs a chandelier with mirrored cubes and crystalline bulbs that rotate slowly around. Under it is a large rectangular sculpture that stands upright and flat against the back wall. The sculpture is monochromatic gold with sepia tones at the edges, but it also flickers with the kaleidoscopic effect from the chandelier above. There are parts of trumpets, trombones, cellos, cymbals, violas, and violins that had been cut and welded into hybrid instruments, the sounds of alliance. There are tuba bells that face outward at each corner ready unleash their thunder from within. At the center is the bell of a French horn, and as Roosevelt walks across the showroom and approaches the sculpture, it opens to reveal the red lips of the woman inside.

The lips whisper, "Password?"

"You Don't Know What Love Is."

"Nice to see you. Give me a few moments to set you up. I'll open the door when we're ready."

Roosevelt walks back to the window of the storefront, lost in deep thought, and standing quite statuesque himself. Breaking his leftward gaze is a woman in a tight, white, and angled dress. Her face is undefined behind a veil of gray smoke that hits the barrier of glass between them. He's only able to discern her lips, which are heart-shaped and blowing another smoky kiss forward. With the streetlights reflecting off the glass, she's also unable to see him, except for his shadowed outline. She is taping a flyer to the outside of the window, which Roosevelt tries to read in reverse as he traces his finger over the sparse lettering when she flattens it out with the palm of her hand. The sculpture in the corner swings open to reveal the speakeasy entrance. He takes a few steps backward before turning around to make his way inside. As the door begins to close behind him, he looks back to the now-empty storefront window. His abandonment is for a different type of glass, and is mirrored by her abandonment of glass and type. It is her final posting for the night. She has to prepare for tomorrow's performance. It's time to reset, focus the mind, and go forward by returning home in silence. Her flyers are nearly as minimalistic as she is with her own words. She's taped exactly one hundred flyers to windows, doors, street signs, metal posts, and post boxes. She attached them to anything perpendicular to the ground. She never asked permission, but was respectful and careful with the tape. A few times she was told by various persons, some nice and some slithery, that they would try to get down there and check it out. And there were some that were confused by the whole minimalist structure of the flyer, and they asked unanswered questions aimed at the back of her head.

Retracing her steps, Della heads uptown to her apartment. She dispenses of the double-sided tape in a nearby trash can and walks at a pace that is not hurried, but not one of leisure. It is for her a rare moment of indefinability.

After a few minutes of walking she encounters her first rejection. With a light breeze from the opposite direction comes a crumpled tumbleweed flyer. As it skips along the cement, it pauses on its travels in front of her toes. It is about to resume with the next surge of wind, but she spikes one corner with her left chromed heel. With her right foot she uncrumples the paper to confirm it's one of hers.

[PERFORMANCE]

I / O

◆

. A C .

W E D @ 7

1 3 5 & R I V E R S I D E

$ F R . E E

@ A C E E D E E C E E 1 0 0 0

C A N V A S #1 - #7

[END]

Della recrumples the flyer and tosses it into a nearby mesh garbage can. On the dark sidewalks she resumes her walk uptown. Her chrome heels flash along the surface like thrown and skipped stones in the New York harbor. Della's posture is as straight as a mast, a beacon easily seen. Della's silky skin tone softens the way she applies her eye makeup, which is with sharp edges and colors that bend toward a darker neon. And her hair is long and deeper than black, disappearing into the night to breach the event horizon.

Della has been hustling to imprint herself on the N.Y. art scene for the past few years and she's made some inroads on the street of late. With her Twitter following growing and YouTube posts gaining momentum, Della Crème feels poised to make a name for herself. Actually, she's done that already in the way of a pen name and pen initials. She uses the name Axlia Clia, or AC, as her alter artist personality. It allows her to do more than the Crème family would've been a-ok with.

As Della grew up in a small midwest home, she amassed an arsenal of words, but kept quiet. She liked to observe before acting. The blurred landscapes outside the backseat window of the Crème family car formed open-sky blues, a baseline of shallow forest greens, and foregrounds of golden stalks. When she broke her stare to focus on certain points along the road, she took mental snapshots of Indiana cornfields, lonely churches, discount mega-stores, rippling American flags, and windowless strip joints. Her father, mother, live-in grandmother, and younger sister never could've imagined that Della would find her voice in the borough of Manhattan.

Although, it's not that she became overly verbose, but that she began to speak with her actions. And actions speak at volume-11 on the dial, in contrast to words, but people have to be ready to listen. Della knew that her family was anti- just about everything.

Della's (or Axlia's) last performance was walking this same stretch of sidewalk, with passersby and human statues taking pictures and videos on their phones. She had a large bag slung over her right shoulder filled with various objects that all had the same text printed on them: IT'S NOT LITTER IF I SMOKE IT, JOE. Some of the objects were also given bastardized names of the typical cigarette brands. Walking along each side of Axlia was her small crew of two, a stoic pair that were neither motley nor lively. Both were dressed in all black like stagehands. One crew member took pictures and the other let the digital film roll. They also acted as a half-measure security team, with false permits on hand if anyone raised concern.

As Axlia began her performance, she lit a banana and smoked it as much as anyone could smoke a banana. Half-a-block later she threw it onto the sidewalk, Axlia's long strides persisting. She pulled out the next phallic object to begin the chain of smoking. It was an empty and scrunched up coffee cup. She set fire to the tails of the green siren, let her burn to the crown, and then threw her into the asphalt sea. For twenty blocks, she smoked and flicked things like the rolled up pages of girlie and boy-toy magazines, sticks of gum, the obituary section of the newspaper, a toy Statue of Liberty (another green woman singed), beer cans, even a baguette. Axlia amassed a following of about forty, with some assuming she was famous, others genuinely interested, and some that happened to have been walking in the same direction. At the end of the twenty blocks, Axlia turned on a dime and faced the videographer as he zoomed in on her face. She took out one filtered cigarette and began to smoke it and exhale right into the camera. Her face blurred in and out of focus with each cloud of smoke. After a few minutes she took the cigarette right down to the end. On her last puff, she blew a perfect circle that hugged the lens. Then she mouthed the words without sound, "It's not litter if I smoke it, Joe."

The camera panned down to her bag filled with hundreds of collected cigarette butts that were all stamped with the same phrase she'd just lip-synced. She lifted the bag and dumped all of them onto the sidewalk. The camera followed a lone filter from the chaotic pile as it rolled into the street. It twisted like a Jumping Jack firework in slow motion before it came to rest in a divot in the concrete. The camera zoomed in on the lettering as a way to reaffirm the title at the end of the film.

There are other films too. For example, the Crème family would never have understood or imagined that their shy little Della would have produced a short film about the effects of rape, titled *HYMEN TEARS*—for which the ambiguity of the pronunciation and meaning of both words was intended. It's a studio performance that she disseminated online, but was restricted to adult accounts due to its explicit nature. Though, honestly, Della believes this type of content should be seen, or at least something like it, by the young and impressionable to inform them about the destruction and suppression of rape, as it is used as an act of war on women worldwide. In this black and white film she depicts herself being raped on a cold slab of concrete. The male performer in the film is one of her two assistants. The other assistant directed and maintained the four stationary cameras. There was an overhead camera, a profile camera, a camera aimed at their faces while in the missionary position, and a camera off to the side focused on a painting. Once edited, the shots were set to switch sequentially between the different vantage points.

The film begins without a title or any names. The picture convulses during the filming of the man's thrusting backside, then it switches to the profile of a quaking body attacking a still body, then to the face of the man, masked with changing and repulsive disguises, and then to the painting of a vagina where blood is being pressed through the pores of the canvas from behind. The sequence repeats with the overhead camera focused on her clutched hands and bloodied fingernails digging into his back in primal defense, then more thrusting, then a different mask, then more blood through the canvas. But after two minutes, the images begin to change. The gender roles reverse, the follicles on the backside of the rapist become fewer, the landscape distorts, the masks turn into devilish smiling Veronicas and Bettys, the framed canvas becomes male, and the hands are wider and well-knuckled. In the final moments of the film, Axlia exhales with relief and looks dead ahead at the camera with no mask at all. The man's body lies motionless while she dismounts him and walks away into the darkness. The last shot of the film focuses solely on the framed painting of a bleeding penis. It lasts long enough for the viewer to see the detail in the destroyed skin, which slips away like a wet napkin. As the last drops of blood seep through the canvas, the violence, the tarnished purity of self, and the savage scraping away of beauty is over. It is the onset of decay. Roll credits.

As Della continues on her walk back to her apartment, she finds herself enveloped in a moment of reflection. She smokes a clove cigarette in the windless night and its gray skeletal dust remains intact until the very last drag. Della pauses and looks up into the past. Then she flicks the granny ash and it falls into a small pile that quickly disperses into oblivion— yet Della knew they're present in some form, somewhere ethereal. Sometimes Della thinks about life the same way she smokes, in a chain of run-on sentences, from one end to the next beginning,

the crinkling of thin plastic, the box top slips open, her index finger brushes across her lucky, a little bird nest atop the rows of clove cigarettes, the zippo sounds like a charm as it swings open, she rolls the flint, sparks a floating flame, burns the nest, inhale...

deep contemplation is not achieved when the mind is void of distractions, rather it needs to be consumed by the world to enable the descent to serenity, a place where the synapses are unseen darks, she thinks, walking just off saint marks...

though she was focused on tomorrow night's performance, these walks were the kindling for future projects gaining heat in her mind, and distracted by the cigarette's glow, she dipped farther toward the abyss, the importance of life...

but also to balance the meaningful minutiae that is usually ignored, to let it fill the lungs with small wonders, and in these times allow the diversions to articulate an inner monologue, one of delight, exhale...

the transfer from mind to body, from body to mind, are at distance zero, without distinction, yet we search for our soul within, and want it to sing beyond, from voice box to lips, from lips to air, inhale...

that we are at once limited by our language and also **freed by it,**
the billions of years it took the earth to form our mouths **and shape**
our hearts, but also to cast us in bodies, prisoners of **evolution...**

exhale, that we are the prisoners who don't recognize **th**e bars,
that don't know we're locked in, locked from the insi**de w**ith a
ring of keys in our pocket, to find which one is the **one, i**nhale...

it's rare that it will be simply handed to you, **exhal**e, since it is
through experience that we gain true know**ledge,** so we must
face fear with both eyes, good and evil, **and inha**le deeply...

she thinks back to her new year's **eve s**peech that never was,
where after the melancholy chorus **of aul**d lang syne and before
the annual cheers, she'd engage **her fam**ily with love, exhale..

she'd calm the tremors, they'd **smile at** each other, exchange
elbow jabs, tear up a time or **two, and** her speech would be
filled with memories that are u**sually d**ifficult to bring up, inhale...

but she'd make them seem **o.k.,** somehow give them new life,
a new understanding that **woul**d smooth the surface, calm the
old waters, and then she**'d rev**eal things about herself, exhale...

and she would be **met wit**h sympathy and acceptance, and
it's not that she was **ever** shunned or rejected, inhale, rather
that she was given **the us**ual nonchalant parental dismissals,

but this speech **woul**d make things right and clear, laser straight
on the level, unt**il her** words set off on a trajectory tangent to the
earth's circumfe**rence,** beyond satellites and human breath,

exhale, in **closing** she'd say, 'Lastly, we should appreciate
that in the **short p**eriod we are given on this planet, we have
been able **to inte**rsect here tonight through our life-long

four-dimensional paths to share laughs, work our way through
arguments, embrace our differences, comfort each other,
blossom together, and philosophize in real time, where the

summation of these moments are precious, they are life and
its meaning at once, I love you all, Happy New Year!' but these
words were never spoken, and Della closed her eyes slowly...

inhale, exhale, flick...

l

      ash

        es

         t o

         ash

           e s,
         dust
           t o

          d

           u

         s

           t

          .

           ,

        ashes   dust
       to . . . . . . to
     . .lashes . . . . dust. .
    . . . l a s h e s t o a s h e s , d u s t t o d u s t . . .
  . . . l a s h e s t o a s h e s , d u s t t o d u s t . . .
. . . l a s h e s t o a s h e s , d u s t t o d u s t . . .
. . . .. . o . . b . . l . . i . . v . . i . . o . . n . . .. . .

BLO*OD IN*SIDE

[[↑]]

Zeus is under his faux-goose-down all-white covers and as close to Heaven as earthly possible. In his penthouse on the top floor of 8 Spruce Street, the Frank Gehry building that blossomed from the granite foundation in Lower Manhattan, he yawns with closed eyes. The low morning sun highlights the building's brushed silver exterior of waves frozen in time, crystallized ripples caused by upwinds and harbor breezes. He is a man of many names, but when he's here, he's called Mr. Woodson. The doorman and his driver have refrained from ever calling him McJesus, even though he's lived here for a few years and they know each other quite well. When he begins his day and descends seventy-plus floors from the clouds and touches ground, he usually sees a kind older man with gin blossoms drinking coffee on a bench just outside the building. This man calls him Master Woodson, and in turn, he returns the gesture with a tip of the cap and a quick jig. Sometimes he bows afterward. And sometimes he twirls and curtsies. Another name he's been called recently—in his bedroom and maybe once or twice in the kitchen—was God. As in, "*Oh* God! *Oh* Zeus!" The woman who shrieked this polytheistic phrase did so in a high-pitched vibrato for the whole building to hear. But she was exaggerating and they both knew it.

In a calm blue light projected from a ceiling unit on to the white wall beside his bed, he sees a blurry 5:54AM. He's restless. The time is triggered to project when a button on the side of the mattress is pressed. The ceiling unit displays the weather, reads messages, and gives him a rundown of his calendar—which is often clear. Zeus appreciates the way the device enhances his laziness. Except for a recent night,when he was with the aforementioned shrieker, his knee kept pressing the button with every hip thrust. This caused the clock to flash 11:11PM in concert with their bodies while they did the no-pants-dance. These literal strokes of luck started to become a complete distraction for Zeus and brought him to the point of impotence; the shrieking didn't help either. That was the opposite of the problem he is having at the moment. He's trying to go back to sleep, but his erection is too distracting. It's persistent, petrified, and, for the most part, even more rigid than when he's having sex. He curses the blo*od in*side. There are slight ebbs in its power, like hiccups below the waist. Therefore, lying on his back isn't an option because the blanket's pressure causes too much friction and furthers the problem. Lying on his side proves untenable since his hands continue to fall to his lap. He's compelled to keep feeling its hardness, to confirm its constancy, and then to contemplate just finishing it off with one of his go-to fantasies[8].

He's always been annoyed by the body's design, anyhow. The placement of this sensitive talisman is completely averse to being productive. With the ease of pleasure at hand, it is both untouchable and irresistible—a cookie jar in the pants of a dieter. He knows he would've been more successful in his endeavors if the body had a less convenient arrangement. He would've had to work harder for the pleasure. This is also the case with the women he meets, but for this he only feels a chip of regret.

In another attempt to go back to sleep, Zeus tries to lie facedown. He adjusts his erection northward to immobilize it and hopes it will subside. This works for a few tender moments before it returns to full strength. He at once wants it to go away, but is also proud of it. Now he's just wasting time. He knows he should either stay in bed and take care of it—or stand up. Since it's more of a biological erection than a sexual one, if he stands up, this whole distraction will relax on its own, and his morning wood will laze to a weeping willow. His thoughts at dawn aren't generally sexual, but the erections give rise to those thoughts[9]. And once these thoughts begin, it's impossible to change the mental channel. With the exception of standing up, the only sure way to rid himself of this condition is to think of the elderly figuring out which wrinkle goes in which fold. This is unpleasant for reasons of mortality and the possibility of strange dreams contaminated by the contemplation of undressed octogenarians mid-romp. This is another aspect of the body's design that annoys him—that as we age we follow a different path than the one set by the grape. As our days pass, we more resemble a raisin, shrunken and creviced. Only our minds have the ability to follow the path from juice to fine wine, becoming smoother and releasing the lovely complexity within. There is one more thing that irks him about the human body—that testicles look old and decrepit from the get-go. They never seem to age, and coincidentally, they're about the size of grapes, too.

Zeus chooses option A. He imagines the expansive wall beside him as a virtual 3DHDTV simulcast of his mental actualities to rid himself of this joyous annoyance. But several moments in, he realizes he'd been plagued by his brief poisoned thoughts of sag that no fantasy can penetrate. So he stands up on his bare feet and looks down at his boxers that he'd put on backward the night before. He sees the cottoned summit of a morning peak, then stretches his arms to the ceiling. Zeus coughs the obligatory cough of a blunt smoker, cracks his neck in both directions, yawns like a grizzly, and tucks himself back into bed for an extra forty-five minutes with limp-dicked ease.

. . .

Nightly Internet News Transcript
Monday, August 6, MMXVIII
(Uploaded two years ago)
1,113,984,620 Views
"Good Evening, America, I'm William Howler. The scandal known as AppleFacegate

has been symbolized by a street artist dissenting with the government and big business. This artist has been wheat-pasting posters in cities across the country that look like a reinterpreted version of René Magritte's *Le fils de l'homme*, with our President in a black bowler, and a rotten apple in front his face, as you can see here. This episode has gripped America and the world, and has brought about changes to most companies and their privacy practices. With all of the changeover and turmoil of the CEOs of Fortune 500 companies, there is a palpable power vacuum at the top that reaches all the way down. But for the few companies whose images have been less tainted, they've been seeking a way to capitalize on their moral victory and have made moves to advertise in new ways. These companies, which include SuperHu, Target, Amazon, and McDonald's, have hired a tech company that developed a complex artificial intelligence algorithm that would search for Americans that met a rigorous criteria, including a strong social media purity rating, a healthy socio-economic situation, favorable religious connections, worldly aspirations, politically acceptable with no criminal record, and met an IQ requirement. This tech company, Laconic Marketing, incorporated part of the company's logo into the name of the person that accepted their contract offer. According to insiders, the decision has led to formidable financial gains, with the people using their influence and standing to provide wholesome and positive press for the companies. The algorithm is attributed in part to Malcolm Gladwell's "Law of the Few" principle in his book, *The Tipping Point*, whereby *connectors* will gain notoriety and have clout with the *mavens* of society, eventually passing it on to the whole population, which will then *tip* in the company's favor in myriad unseen ways. The gimmick of the process seems to go against the authenticity of the Gladwell Principle, but its campness has oddly contributed to its allure. Given its success, for which a New York hedge fund confirmed that Laconic Marketing's approach has led to large gains on their investments in quick time, it may become a common practice. Early estimates are that these logo-name-integrations would only affect one hundredth of one percent of the American population. But there have already been a few glitches, contributing to some speculation and ridicule. Once a contract for sponsorship was accepted by someone, for a term of five years typically, the transaction was complete and *irreversible* within the timeframe. The acceptance of the contract started the automated process of issuing new government ID cards and the like. There were also conditions that required the newly named to not go by any other name, *especially* on social media outlets. The failure to adhere could cause litigious and financial devastation for the individual. Thus far, it has been difficult to pinpoint the origin of these naming errors, but it looks like the algorithm's artificial intelligence allowed for contracts to be offered without sufficient oversight. It also isn't clear why these individuals accepted such names, but it may be that it was for the sole reason of gaining attention in a humorous way, or simply that their credentials were incorrectly calculated and they accepted the significant payment for the sponsorship. Once accepted, the contract stipulated that they were to live as they have been living, but to understand that they were an extension of the company and were to keep this in mind while making life decisions, especially those internet-based and traceable. We will see how this plays out. To finish on a lighter note, our reporters have shared two of their favorite and more questionable logo-integrated names, for which there are several memes spinning around on the web.

The first one, Bob Y. Mann, sponsored by Target, was supposed to have the O in his first name replaced by the Target logo, but an error in programming led to the Target logo being integrated into the name *alongside* the O. So we now have B⊙ob Mann. That's right, he's a B⊙ob Mann, America. I apologize, but I can only read what's in front of me. [laughing] *Oh my.*

And our second one, Jesús Neon Woodson, sponsored by McDonald's, was to have the famous golden-arched *M-and-c* placed in front of Mr. Woodson's last name, but something in the program went awry and it was placed in front of his first name. Ladies and Gentlemen, we now have a man named McJesus. There have been depictions of Leonardo da Vinci's *The Last Supper* with Ronald McDonald at the center of the painting with cheeseburgers and french fries strewn about with the caption reading: *This is my body, take this sesame seed bun and eat it. This is my blood, take this ketchup and drink it.* In some images, Grimace is under the table washing the red boots in a tub of grape soda. Forgive me, Father! [enacts the sign of the cross] God *bless* this young man! [laughing] *Oh my.* Maybe I shouldn't be laughing. I apologize. Can we redo this segment? Wait, we're live! I thought we were just taping this one! Well, I regret the mention of The Last Supper. America, please forgive me once more. [pause, host enacts the sign of the cross three times]

For the latest on AppleFacegate, stay connected, we'll bring you the news, before it's news. Have a *pleasant* night, and I'll be home *soon*, honey! I can't wait to see *you* and *only you*! For N.I.N., I'm William Howler."

. . .

With pillow lines on his face that resemble the N.Y.C. subway system, he tries to map his plans out for the day as he lies awake, with all parts horizontal. First he will have to reconstruct the events of last night. He's still in some kind of kush haze accompanied by a mild hangover. The first memory he has is of looking up from a car window and seeing Christmas-colored lightbulbs. He doesn't think he was the driver, but he isn't sure of anything except that he was high as all hell. The vision that remains is of him looking toward Polaris while the vehicle rushes through an intersection—though now he can remember feeling the car's lack of shocks too. He let the illumination sear into his retinas. It remained there well after the streaks of light went overhead in a quartet of beams. The double traffic lights are both green and red at once and shift both left and right. He contemplates whether it could have been a malfunction of technology, or an actual function of his highness, completely unrelated to royalty. That single memory from the collection of time spent downtown starts to broaden to include those with him in the car. The faces of Mel and Scarlett take shape, but they're distorted and smeared, as if they have pantyhose over their heads. He realizes this is the condensing of several hours to one second at an intersection of asphalt arteries. He's in no-man's-land—go and stop at the same time.

He closes his eyes and follows one synapse to the next into a philosophical string: When something is remembered, it holds significance as an event. It's the summation of life in a flash and the strength of building on its future potential. The percentage of our lives that we truly remember isn't a stiff and crooked number, but a personal variable (x) with its own fluctuations. But since we all spend time *trying* to remember, that time is also an event. It's unlikely we'll ever remember the time spent trying to remember. It is surely lost time, almost like sleep. Zeus feels that the time remaining to live and his remembered past are converging at an accelerating rate, as light to a pinhole on a box camera, capturing all things at once. In this instance, there's evidence of a past, the wish of days to come, and the truth that existence is precious.

He visualizes an untitled book with only his name gracing the monochrome cover as the sole author. As each new day is completed, one page is recorded inside. There's no skipping ahead and he isn't allowed to pick up the book to test its weight. He feels the ink inside him continuing to flow, but the question is whether the next page exists.

Then, in a rush of returning clarity, he thinks of Candy, a sincerely sweet woman without a hint of saccharin. With that one image of her smile, there's a calming, a breaking of the clouds, and beams of actual light enter through the windows over the terrace. Shadows begin to form on the wall and morph into lamp-shaded curves as the sun appears to orbit the earth, the brightest bulb of all, as the morning elapses into late afternoon. Zeus is fixated on Saturday night's possibilities with Candy. He bumps his music near glass-shattering levels and cleans like a fiend. Zeus takes care to organize his kitchen cabinets, vacuum under the bed, remove any swing straps from the closet, separate laundry by lights, darks, and reds, dust the tops of picture frames, straighten the stack of 1987 Topps Baseball Cards on his coffee table, brush his teeth twice, call his mom with love and praise, text Mel using proper grammar, create playlists to fit any scenario, classify his wine collection by region, group his sneakers by color and vintage, sort his condom drawer by rib intensity, test romantic lighting possibilities, brush his teeth twice more, and complete a few sets of push-ups.

793 MCJESUS NEON WOODSON · PITCHER

COMPLETE MAJOR LEAGUE BATTING RECORD (LEAGUE LEADER IN ITALICS, TIE ♦)

YR	CLUB	G	AB	R	H	2B	3B	HR	RBI	BBW	MILF	SO	S/M	BJ	AVG
14	RAILRIDERS	10	34	2	11	4	2	2	2	1	0	23	0	3	.324
15	RAILRIDERS	24	81	6	34	17	7	6	6	5	2	47	½	9	.420
16	YANKEES	24	81	81	81	0	0	81	104	11	7	0	3	43	1.000
17	YANKEES	27	79	79	79	0	0	79	116	26	12♦	0	8	39	1.000
18	YANKEES	26	82	82	82	0	0	82	121	15	10	0	13	36	1.000
19	YANKEES	23	78	78	78	0	0	78	110	28	9	0	13	40	1.000
MAJ. LEA. TOTALS		100	320	320	320	0	0	320	451	80	38	0	37	158	1.000

STD (2019): 0   STD (CAREER): 0

In only a few years in the majors, he is known as the best hitting pitcher of all time.

♦ ♦ ♦ ♦ ♦ ♦ ♦ ♦ ♦ ♦ ♦ ♦ **ON THIS DATE** ♦ ♦ ♦ ♦ ♦ ♦ ♦ ♦ ♦ ♦ ♦ ♦
September 4, 2018: Proving his speed and prowess on the bases,
McJesus performed three successful panty raids.

A* © 2020 STOPP CHEWING GUM, INC. PRTD. IN U.S.A.

HT: 6'0" WT: 185 BATS: RIGHT THROWS: RIGHT DRFT: YANKEES #1-JUNE, 2013
ACO: VIA DRAFT BORN: 12-25-92, NEW YORK, NEW YORK HOME: NEW YORK, NEW YORK

[[Σ]]

Suma has been on a blurred run of responsibilities. From midnight hues to the tangerine sunrise, then surrounded by the walnut bookcases of midday work, the blinds have now been drawn on the sunset bruise in the sky. Time passed like one long horizontal brush stoke of a Gerhard Richter painting. But after a short subway ride uptown, her evening begins as she walks along Amsterdam Avenue to meet her colleagues for a drink or three at RUST BUST & AXE[10]. The corner bar has both rustic and sophisticated elements. The tables and chairs are crafted from reclaimed barn wood, and it has a vintage Chicago bar rail, cast iron bottle openers, classic radios lining the walls, pewter lanterns hanging from the ceiling, and each piece of barware is unique[11]. The bench near one stretch of windows is made of old bank safes. On the bar are small dishes of sriracha cashews and plantain chips. And next to the stacks of spiraled napkins are toothpicks flavored like bon-vivant cocktails. The cardboard coasters are plain white and reused until the mix of spilled sips turns psychedelic. The framed artwork is all Sailor Jerry Traditional American Tattoo prints: flowers, skulls, hearts, and pin-ups. And there is a jukebox in the far corner that rocks music heavy on the guitars and hi-hats[12].

The conversations usually curve toward the Great American Pastime, and this evening is no different. Suma's dark hair cascades down her back just past the shoulder blades, as she slides a number two pencil out from the whirl. Even as a librarian cliché, it looks novel on her, and is dually practical for hair tying and erasable doodling. Suma's friends from work, all three of them men, sit on jacketed chairs in the windowed corner by the entrance. She sits at the home plate to their bases, looking out toward the street. On the square wooden table that is rife with knots and blade etchings, there are three pints of Sugar Hill Golden Ale and one glass of house merlot.

Each glass is placed at the midpoint of each edge, a square within a square. The wine glass has a shattered pattern and the pint glasses are from a commemorative Space Shuttle set. When stacked, they recreate the August 2009 launch of the Discovery. Leon has the wine glass, Bunch has the shuttle, Jeremy has the smoke, and Suma has the fire. There are several foam rings on her glass that are close together, an indication of enjoyment, rather than pure consumption. The other two glasses have their sip lines spread far away and are nearly empty. And since Leon is still in the bathroom, the wine glass is untouched.

Leon, a mild and unpretentious wino, wears a faux hawk and thick-rimmed black glasses. He has dark eyebrows and an angled face where all vectors point out like a reverse perspective drawing. He splashes on too much cologne, which is very expensive, but he reduces it to a nasal disturbance. He pulls out the chair by second base. Bunch, the third-baseman, sits cross-legged with his khaki pants rising to flood level, revealing the darker skin of his bare ankles.

His style is Town & Country in the big city, oxfords without socks and braided belts. He has a stocky frame and a handsome canvas, despite the pockmarks. And there's Jeremy, whose heart is genuinely in his work, but not so much in his clothes. The N.Y. Public Library has a dress code for male workers, which helps to curb his poor taste. His brown hair curls down like thick fusilli and is contrasted by his flat and pale face. To his friends, his utter lack of confidence with women is endearing. He sits at first base where he looks most comfortable, as it's probably as far as he's ever gone, athletically or otherwise.

Each member of the trio of friends is trying to be inconspicuous in their own way, but each are vying for her attention—flexing in their shirtsleeves, beaming at her comments, and remembering just one more story that is a bit funnier than the last. She refers to them as LBJ, and they are all very nice, never once rude to the Lady Bird among them.

Suma has been leaning in and listening to their comedic tales, but when she adds to the conversation, she tends to lean back in her chair. Her plum silk blouse isn't snug, but as she assumes the professorial posture, the three buttons across her chest are put to an elasticity test. Depending on their angle, her lacy lavender bra is the focal point of alternating secretive glances from LBJ. The glances are an impressive and cooperative effort, but not a conspiratorial one.

"I love this place. Great beer in cold glasses on old wood tables," Suma says as she traces over an etched name with her index finger. She glances around. "This is the kind of joint you can justify calling a public house. We get a good connection to humanity while still being able to stay insulated in our own group without too many interruptions or distractions." Her index finger drags its way against the grain of the table to the base of her pint glass and up the side. She grips it for a sip and disturbs the foam meniscus.

Suma speaks without any umms or uhhs. She is clear, as if she's reading the words off a page. It's impressive to everyone who realizes they're incapable of sounding that way all the time—at a bar no less. And while she goes on about the history of societal kinship and alcohol, their eyes again fall south. Her coworkers calibrate their sights to the center, as though braiding long hair in a practiced manner. Jeremy fakes a yawn and arches back to follow the midline under the table to her legs crossed at the ankle. The sight of her strappy black heels and nail sheen is a stark juxtaposition to the topic upcoming.

"Back in the day, baseball players were able to drink beer in the dugout and martinis out in the nightclubs. The eyes of the media closed and opened at convenient times. If they had our current network back then, we wouldn't be talking about them in a romantic way. Ignorance is a blatant miss in the hopes of cheap bliss." Suma takes a sip. "Most of the time we argue about putting Hall-of-Fame player x in a modern stadium and watching the statistics run wild—or if certain players didn't miss time for the wars, or what would happen to Babe Ruth's numbers if he had to face Satchel Paige several times a year. But as I walked over here in heels I thought about what would happen if you threw a pair of modern-day cleats on Willie Mays. If he was the only one on the field with air-cushioned gel-tech bounce-response spikes, he'd run circles around those old diamonds. He was already lightning fast, but he would've been able to push a lot of those triples into inside-the-parkers. I'd add an extra sixty homers for his career."

"That might be true," Jeremy says. "I'd like to see those old black-and-white grainy videos, but with some neon orange highlighter cleats on The Say Hey Kid glowing like hell."

Bunch chimes in, "Hey, what if Shoeless Joe Jackson wore modern-day cleats? You know what his name would've been? Joe Jackson."

Suma smiles, "But he's not a Hall-of-Famer."

"Right, but he might've been if he was the only one with those shiny cleats. He would've had a sick sneaker deal and enough money to not give one damn about throwing the World Series."

Leon switches tracks, "O.K., here's one. I was thinking about all the crazy nicknames and how it would sound if one of those guys came to your home to take your daughter on a date: 'Yes daddy, Three Finger Brown is here, I'll see you tomorrow morning!'"

"Oh no!"

"No..."

Jeremy jumps on, "What about Hammerin' Hank?"

"I don't think I'd be crazy about my daughter going out with Big D, either."

"Or The Big Hurt!"

Suma brings it all to a halt, "Or worse, Stretch[13]."

As the evening moves from the hours of happiness into the regularly-priced night, the conversations land on several topics: the diminished role of the stolen base, the shade of green of the Boston Monster, the perceived visits from the green fairy, and the strange powdery perfume that one of their coworkers wears. The consensus is: sabermetric-influenced loss aversion, Pantone 3298, it's-true-if-you-want-it-to-be, and that when perfume is strange, it's (Bunch's words) "cognitive castration." Bunch has two sips go awry, one down the chin and another where the glass hit his front tooth hard enough that the clink is heard over the music. Leon goes to the restroom more times than can be ignored, suggesting a possible plumbing issue, biologically speaking. Jeremy is fidgety the whole time, bringing his hands under the table to roam. He picks a little at some dried gum with his thumbnail until he finds a recent addition, a saliva-softened piece that interrupts his nervousness. Any groove they enter as a group begins to dissipate as their collective attention deficit skips across topics. Their words are without order and memory. Their social bubble is breached a few times by people wondering if they're leaving soon. And generally, it's a night without any tension, except when Leon doesn't use actual words to express that they are *not*, in fact, leaving soon—which is only three-fourths correct. Because when she realizes that the color of night is the same as the porter on tap, she has to leave her fellow players on the infield—three on base with one out. Suma gave herself a self-imposed deadline so she'll have enough time to work on her current project. She takes a healthy sip that nearly finishes her pint and gives them the sad news. This compels a sud-stoned Bunch to rise and give a final cheers for the night. He stands like a limp exclamation point.

"Put your glasses up, library people! Here's to friendship and talking baseball and some damn good times. This is about relaxing, moving slowly and taking it all in. All to the heart, right here. Do you feel that? That's the rush. That's the blood inside raging like the ocean waves. That's the emotion in your center becoming everyone else's center. We are center fielders!" Bunch mimes a fly ball catch toward his chest. "We take it all in, a ground ball, a line drive straight at us, or in the air." He pauses with a question mark across his face. "I honestly don't know where I was going with this. O.K., O.K.. Before we cheers, I want to send a shot-out to the greatest center fielder of all time, Willie Mays, and an extra shot-out to the hat flying off his head when he ran down that bomb shot at the Polo Grounds in '54." He begins to mime again. "And let's not stop there. I want to give a shot-out to Eddie Gadel's one-eighth jersey number! And another shot-out to Satchel Paige's longest damn legs ever. A shot-out to Burleigh Grimes since he has the baddest name in baseball history! You want to fight a guy with that name!? Here's one, let's give a shot-out to Rick Sutcliffe's wrist. Watch." Bunch places his beer on a soggy napkin and goes into the full pitching wind-up. As his throwing arm is down by his waist and ready to throw, he freezes. He accentuates the right angle formed by his hand and forearm. Bunch looks to make sure everyone knows how important that wrist angle is. "And I want to give a shot-out to Julio Franco's batting stance." Bunch looks for a long object, but there isn't anything close by. He holds his hands over his head with an invisible bat that runs parallel to the ground and points straight at an invisible pitcher. "Wild, man. He almost had to swing three hundred sixty degrees. Who knows what he was thinking when he came up with that, damn. He was an All-Star too. Hey, shot-out to crazy batting stances! You need those. Actually, let's send a shot-out to the batting stance guy on YouTube. That guy should be here right now. And one for YouTube and a purple hazy shot-out to the old Doc Ellis no-hitter video. I haven't seen that in a minute." Bunch finishes the rest of his beer and views his friends through the bottom of his glass. Their faces become smaller and warp toward the center. "Let's end with a huge shot-out to Billy Ripken and the legendary Fuck Face bat! That is the illest, dopest, swellest baseball card in history! To me, that surpasses the greatness of both Cal Ripken Jr. and Sr., I don't care what anyone says." Bunch holds up his empty glass. "O.K., let's do this. Raise 'em up. I can feel that I'm losing it. I love you all. You know that. Raise 'em up. Cheers!"

Even though it sounds like the end of the night, they continue on a while longer like this. The specific words they speak will eventually drift to the corners of their memories. What remains present are the images of open-mouthed laughs, strained voices over electric guitars, and the feelings of togetherness and enjoyment. This isn't an uncommon night out, but there is something rarefied in the air. It may be a combination of raw humanity and compartmentalized emotion. From LBJ's perspective, they're all capable of visualizing separate tracks: the here and now, the desired future bedroom scene, and the domestic-with-children status. One of the monogramed men's imagination montage ends with their child posing for his little league photo holding his bat, minus any fuck-face foolishness written on it. The child is encouraged to show his teeth. Fast forward to the three of them sharing a colossal pizza and not very iced cream. Mom drops her vanilla-covered spoon on dad's pizza, dad chuckles and scoops the rest of her ice cream onto his cheese slice. He winks at mom and takes a bite of equal parts dinner and dessert, a young ninja turtle's dream come true. And the boy smiles without any vocal prompting.

Despite all of this, even with the aid of alcohol liberation, LBJ are only able to *think* of what they would say to her, to let her know how beautiful she is, perhaps. But no one steps up to the plate as she walks away after a polite circuit of hugs. No one wants to risk embarrassment, as in zilch, zero, the grand donut. The longer this goes on, the more difficult it becomes to ever say anything. LBJ respect their friendships with sincerity, but there's still a silent competition for her attention throughout the days at the library. Since she's never brought up any former or current relationships, there's still some hope high up on the shelf. But they're levels of cautiousness have reached DEFCON 1, with LBJ ready to deploy nuclear restraint at any moment. They're really   all   just   too   nice.

After Suma leaves the bar, Jeremy reaches over to finish the half-inch of her backwashed beer. He turns the glass to line up his lips to where her lips had been, along an outline of beer foam. This private moment is only intimate in his own mind. Had it been known to the rest of the team, this sipping kiss would have crossed the creepiness line. Had he done it with a care-free attitude, it still may have been creepy, but more acceptable, oddly. (It goes a little something like this: Secrecy invites her friend Awkward over for the party, but Awkward only shows up if Secrecy runs into her old enemy, Exposure—then it's lights on and music off.) But Jeremy's act remained unknown and as close to lip-on-lip contact as it ever could be. He has no game at all. This kiss was in the same place, but at different times. It served as proof that synchronicity and awareness are two sides of the same shiny quarter. Insert coin to play.

• • •

Suma didn't sleep more than a few blinks the previous night. She's been preparing for the completion of her next revised book, which she calls a publication. In the most meticulous of ways, this publication involves Suma replacing two pages from a 1990 American Anthology about the presidents that had the most influence on the international stage with two pages of her own. The book, as are all of her publication projects, is property of the N.Y. Public Library. She reasons to herself that since the tax payers are supporters of the library, a small fraction of the books belong to her, and therefore are subject to her interpretations. But even without any reasoning, she would've been doing the same thing anyway. Suma doesn't call it art, but a compulsive expression in the form of copyright metamorphosis. This particular project isn't meaningful to her, but she took it on as a typeface challenge.

It's also a small example of how bygone dates and eras amalgamate into obscurity. The book includes a timeline with a brief paragraph for the presidents that didn't make the cut. Two of these, Martin Van Buren, a one-term presider, and William Henry Harrison, a one-month presider, are to be switched from their known ordinals of eighth and ninth. The text describing their time in office, which happens to be longer in Harrison's case, is unedited. She's only going to change the order in which they appear and their dates in office[14].

The tools she uses for her various projects include the following: 1931 Underwood Portable Typewriter, 1939 Royal Quiet Deluxe Portable Typewriter, 1951 IBM Electronic Typewriter, 1956 Underwood Leader Typewriter, 1958 Royal Futura Typewriter, an early-1960s Smith-Corona Coronet Electric Typewriter, a 1961 IBM Electric Typewriter (Burnt Sienna Edition), three shoeboxes of ribbons, razor blades, paper cutters, blank pages of varying whites, beiges, and sepia tones (which are removed from the end pages of books purchased at Strand, East Village Books on St. Mark's Place, Long Island garage sales, the occasional stoop sale, sidewalk markets in Brooklyn, and on the digital shores on the Bay of e, professional-grade ink pens for touch-ups, sewing kits with various types of binding string of different gauges and textures, Old English tracing tiles, and an assortment of stains, dyes, and paints. All of these items fit neatly into her apartment closet, except for the typewriters. She displays them along a gallery-style track system on the wall. This gives them the look of permanent adornments, but they can be easily removed and used for her next publication. While she isn't under any suspicion, she treats her sundown activities with absolute care, bordering on paranoia. Whenever she has someone over or hosts a small get-together, she gets questions or comments about the typewriters. Suma tells them about how she loves their nostalgia, how she can picture her favorite writers of yesteryear punching the keys with intensity, their faces beading with sweat next to a glass of chilled beer beading with condensation—but also that they aren't practical to use any more. In fact, the ones on the wall probably didn't work anyway, she would add.

Suma keeps a catalogue system solely with a vintage rainbow Polaroid camera. She wants to be able to destroy her catalogue quickly and without a trace if the situation ever calls for it. The catalogue system runs in chronological order and includes one shot of the cover, one of the spine, and one for each of the altered pages next to the originals that she'd removed. It's a collection she wishes to share with someone else in the future, if the circumstances are right. For now, it's for an audience of one.

Each project presents different challenges based on the condition and age of the book. Many books require her to apply stain to the edges of the page to match the others. She also finds it's wise to apply a very thin coat to some of the unaltered pages for scattered consistency. Suma airs out the books in a ventilated box on her window sill or the fire escape, depending on the weather. All of this effort is time consuming, but it further assuages any anxiety she holds. She prefers to work with older books, which tend to keep a bouquet of dusty mildew. She used to worry that the scent of the stain would raise the eyebrows of a reader, but Suma came to realize that it actually complimented the aged pages like an aromatic footnote.

With close to a hundred alterations to date, some of the more recent items in Suma's secret catalogue include the insertion of some definitions from American English Slang Dictionaries into Mr. Webster's standard publication[15], and the placing of *of* in between *Duke* and *Ellington* in the pages of a jazz book[16], ~~and because she fell for Jake Barnes in Hemingway's *The Sun Also Rises*, she enforced a strikethrough for the sections where it mentions his war injury~~.

Suma, a vegetarian for reasons of human and technological evolution combined with a moral awareness, altered a 1950s cookbook by placing additional instructions below the list of ingredients in each recipe. Some examples: "Murder Pig," "How Now Kill Brown Cow," "Slay Deer, as quietly as a cloud," "Bloodlet the Hog, preferably outdoors," and "Drown a Turkey in your Bathtub." "Choke your Chicken" didn't make the cut.

Suma also found an obscure book detailing car repair instructions for 1930s Chevrolet models. She didn't alter any textual meaning, but she retyped the word "inverted" upside-down on each page it appeared. For one of the more involved efforts, she removed the word *Palindrome* from one of the middle pages of the Oxford English Dictionary and placed it between *Emolument* and *Emote*, now spelling it *Emordnilap* while leaving the same definition in place. In order to not retype every entry on the unaltered pages, she made room by eliminating the definition of *Emmenagogue*[17]. She didn't believe too many people would miss it. And where *Palindrome* had once called home, she added a new word: *Palina*[18].

When Suma was studying at Columbia University she was invited for a weekend get-away in Cooperstown with a small group of her closer friends. One of her friend's parents owned a bed-and-breakfast that was vacant for the off-season. It was a great escape to the upstate lakes from the graveled metropolis. She enjoyed their time together but also became very intrigued with the history and characters of baseball. She spent each day at the Hall of Fame almost in solitude. The more she read the stories, the more interested she became with the game that's immortalized by statistics, even though the numbers tend to reduce the full value of the player to flat data. To Suma, it is the folklore passed down in the oral tradition over generations that built the scaffolding of the monumental stadiums. These are the words hidden behind the mathematics.

In particular, it was the style and grace of Willie Mays that captivated her in front of a small video screen that played his greatest moments on a loop. While his statistics were among the supreme, even his greatness was slighted by the simplification. With Willie already sitting at the gloved right hand of the father, George Herman Babe Ruth, she felt that Willie should get a turn on the dugout throne. The Say Hey Kid won the Rookie of the Year award in 1951 for the New York Giants and was an MVP and World Series Champ in 1954, his most dominant year. But the two years in between had been essentially lost after he was drafted into the army to serve stateside during the Korean War. With two prime production years subtracted from his lifetime baseball achievements, he'd been statistically slighted. Some years later, when Suma decided to alter the Encyclopedia of Baseball for one of her publications, she gave Willie Mays an injection of historical steroids with an asterisk included. In the triple crown categories, his stat lines were based on a theoretical curve of progress from 1951 to 1954.

1952*: 26 HR, .295 BA, 95 RBI

1953*: 34 HR, .324 BA, 104 RBI

Given this alteration, his career home run total went from 660 to a revolutionary 720. This eclipsed the pre-integration era record of The Babe's 714 home runs by 6. If this had been true, the home run crown would've been worn by a former Negro League ballplayer just a few months prior to Hank Aaron's seizure of the kingship. The asterisk, footnoted on the same page, read "Commissioner-Approved Statistical Revisionist Addendum Section 42H, Rule 5.6: United States Army Baseball Team, Newport News, Virginia."

A week ago, Suma's project was born from her recent disdain for the diluting of distilled drinks. She'd begun to prefer hers straight up with an accompanying burn to follow. The burn was a reminder of the struggle, a rite of passage to ephemeral enlightenment, and eventually to the next level of sustained serenity. With everyone around her touting the greatness of a well-orchestrated cocktail and the way its icy sweetness cloaks the bite, she went back to the source. Why go through the extra steps of mixing and stirring when the real deal was right in front of you, she wondered. It was an unnecessary step toward the destination. Here are Suma's revised instructions on how to make an Old-Fashioned in 1964's *The Bartender's Guide to Shaking the Sugar*:

In a rcoks glsas, add a slpash of club sdoa and trhee dahses of Agnostura bitetrs to one suagr cbue. Add one Maarshcino chrery and a silced oarnge, and mudlde thuorhogly. Plcae two or trhee lagre ice cbues in the glsas and puor in trhee oucnes of rye wihskey and stir. Ganrish wtih oarnge wdege and chrery, or nohitng at all.

The publication just before the Van Buren/Harrison reversal, which seemed in retrospect to cross the threshold of any credulity, was born from her exhaustion of everyone's utopian ideas of the stars. Sure they look nice, she thought, but there's no reason to romanticize them beyond what they are. Whatever perceived astrological alignments that exist above will be skewed by the pressing actions of the here and now. So, for the publication, she only changed the last line of the book. Suma hedged her brashness with the hopes that most books aren't finished. Originally written in the fourteenth century, the hellish poetry of Dante's Inferno now closed with "*And thence we came forth to once again look at the spheres of thermonuclear fusion and subsequent radiation.*"

Suma hadn't sobered from the idea of serendipity, but she wasn't going to wait around for her wishes to shine upon her either. She felt that fulfillment was achieved through action, with her hope kept at a satellite's distance.

. . .

As Suma walks away from RUST BUST & AXE, she's buzzed and floating like a honeybee. With some publication work still ahead of her, she knows she has to redirect her energy and return home to alter the past. From the corner pub and down the sidewalk base path, she is unaware of this geographical fact: if the ghost of Willie Mays were to stand at the original home plate in the Harlem Polo Grounds, Suma would be exactly 60 imaginary home runs away from that spot if the moonshot parabolas are strung end-to-end in a straight line. They are connected by phantasmal arches that fly through unbroken windows and old neighborhoods, across space and back in time to where The Say Hey Kid stared down pitchers, rocked and readied, focused, swung with ease, and unleashed historic fury.

HEADLINES FROM VARIOUS NEWS OUTLETS,
BOTH DIGITAL AND IN PRINT
WEDNESDAY, APRIL 8, MMXX

· · ·

DEATH TOLL REACHES 300 IN POSSIBLE WIDESPREAD TERROR PLOT:
HIGH-SPEED COLLISIONS MAY BE NO ACCIDENT

· · ·

ELECTION 2020: CROSSOVERS

DEMOCRATS ALLIGN WITH PRO-LIFE ADVOCATES
IN EFFORT TO GAIN SUPPORT FROM SENIORS AND GIVE THEM ACCESS
TO SOCIAL SECURITY FASTER, DEMS PUSH FOR LAW THAT WILL
ADD 9 MONTHS TO EVERYONE'S AGE

REPUBLICANS SEEK UNION BACKING
PROPOSE DAILY DIRECT DEPOSITS TO WORKERS, CITING /r/deutoronomy2415

· · ·

VIRTUAL MOVIE STAR "JACKSON CHISELHAMMER" ACCEPTS FIRST
DRAMATIC LEAD ROLE

· · ·

SOURCE: EMOJI ESSAYIST A FINALIST FOR PULITZER

[[◆]]

The day was overcast with a barrage of pewter puffs spray painted across the gray canvas sky. The sun has been hushed to a dim incandescence and is just about to tuck itself into the horizon. The west side of Manhattan is moments away from a starless and moonless night. This rarely matters in the three-dimensional illuminated bar graph that is New York City, where the usual bottom-of-the-snow-globe sight lines of the sky are obscured. And it may further the notion that New Yorkers live in their own half-bubble, where they lose perspective and a sense of wonder for the cosmos. Even at the top of a skyscraper, the stars shine from below.

From afar, scanning downtown to uptown, from left to right, the two-dimensional version of the bar graph resembles the progression of the jazz masterpiece by Charles Mingus, *Wednesday Night Prayer Meeting*, as it moves across the topology of the frequency spectrum, with the y-axis representing the song's intensity and the x-axis as a function of time. From the solo bass line of the harbor, to the woodwind punctuations of the Freedom Tower phoenix, to the hustle and swing of the Village, rising to the climax sustained by the Empire State and Chrysler Buildings, to the polyrhythmic handclaps of Central Park into Harlem, and finally to the northwest outskirts of old New Amsterdam, where the current setting lies on the graph. It's right in between the last *Yeah..Uh-huh!* wail from Mingus and the beginning of the final fermata of hums and ooohs, drum snares, and piano rolls. It is here in the subsidence of the monoliths where the evening sky begins to open.

The street stage to be is on a wide elevated corner overlooking the Hudson River at the intersection of 135th Street and Riverside Drive. Two of the streetlights above, which have been flickering for the past week, have finally given up any pulse, and are now proclaimed dead. The remaining light is provided by the traffic signal, the intermittent flow of headlamps, and the faint glow of televisions from the apartment windows across the street.

It's a warm evening in early April. The quiet neighborhood is given depth by the constant and rhythmless hum from the parkway below street level. The taste of the air is equal parts engine exhaust and salt water breeze, a cocktail of nature under siege. And the cool cement bricks give no hint of their smoldering and violent origins.

In her apartment that overlooks the performance space, Axlia surveys the scene through a red gossamer curtain. The room is dim, lit by four desk lamps which point in various directions and cast fractal shadows on beige walls. None are placed on an actual desk.

When Axlia finishes parting her long dark hair down the middle, she ties each side up into matching cinnamon buns upon each non-pierced ear. She applies a white foundation on her face and then thick black eyeliner around each almond shape with the tails extending close to her hairline. Axlia stands unclothed. Her legs are slightly apart and her long arms naturally at her sides. Jasmine, her assistant, stands behind her and gently coats her with black water-based paint. From her nape to the curve of her lower back and ending with her heels, Jasmine covers the back half of Axlia's body. She takes pleasure in not missing one spot. The paint obscures her lone tattoo, a small carbonado gem on the back of her neck[19]. As she paints her, Jasmine's mind drifts between fantasia and composure. Jasmine also has a habit of blinking twice the normal shutter rate, which causes her to spend more time in the darkness of daydreamland.

While they pause to let the paint dry over Axlia's five and a half foot frame, they share an organic clove cigarette. Since Axlia has to remain still, Jasmine lights the cigarette and holds it to Axlia's parted lips. It rests between the crescents. After three drags, Jasmine takes it back and has one of her own. Jasmine attempts to match her lips on the faded rouge lipstick marks left behind. She holds the clove between her right thumb and index finger, like a joint. Jasmine takes a step back and begins to stir the next color of body paint with her left hand. Then she takes a barefooted step toward Axlia and presents the black cigarette for another burn, followed by another inhale of her own. This time she tries to taste her subject's lips more than the spice of the clove.

This continues for a few moments as they both feel saxophone hums reverberating through the floor to their toes and as far up as their knees. The neighbor downstairs is playing Coltrane's *A Love Supreme*. By the time the cigarette is finished, there's a stirred mother of pearl paint can, dried black paint on Axlia's back half, and flicked ashes on the wood floor.

On the quiet corner below, two of Axlia's other assistants, both men, are arriving to prepare the scene for her performance. They pull up to the righthand side of the road in a dark gray minivan with tinted windows several shades darker. As they ease to a halt, their hazards are already blinking. From the apartment above, Axlia blurs her focus through the veil of the red curtain, and falls into her own chimera. She imagines the hazard lights as a binary system of pulsars in the distant night. She wonders how a planet may have traversed that kind of solar system—how its orbit would've been severely distorted from an ellipse to an infinity-like loop as it negotiated its way between two pulls of gravity. Her mind sprints around several more ideas. Would the planet have had a dual sunset and sunrise of Sun1 and Sun2? Or would Sun1 set as Sun2 rises for never-ending daylight? Or would Sun1 be a constant presence for the planet while Sun2 only made the day double in brightness when it made its appearance in the sky? If there was life, how did they communicate, what color schemes would they have, what types of cities, calendars, history, art, relationships, and philosophies? What meaning and possible love would have been destroyed by the immense terror and power of the mirrored death of two suns and their simultaneous supernovas, swallowing the entire bi-solar system in a flash, ceasing their infinity-shaped paths, leaving only synchronized pulses of dying light that are tens of millions of years in our past? Her assistants pulled the minivan onto the sidewalk and turned off the hazard lights.

Jasmine's paint brush is coated in mother of pearl. When she applies the paint to Axlia's neck and shoulders, two small pools of paint form in the cavities of her collarbone. Jasmine, smoking with an increased frequency, finishes the front side of her arms. The exhaled smoke fills the room in patches, like the way fog behaves on a spring morning at dawn. With Jasmine raising the clove to Axlia's mouth once again, her next deep breath in and out causes the small pools of chilled paint to run south in two thin lines, like bikini straps. The white sheen, aided by gravity and physiology, runs directly over the center of each of Axlia's breasts and causes her nipples to become actual pearls.

On the street below, Axlia's two assistants, dressed in all black, set up the performance space with the following items: two 20' x 10' black canvas sheets with sewn-in weights along the perimeter (one sheet to cover the cement ground, the other to drape over the short brick wall as a backdrop, creating fluidity from foreground to background), two large disco-era hi-fi speakers spray painted in glossy black that are wired to a laptop off to the side, two small black end tables with sticks of sage incense, a small private backstage area that is taped off next to an oak tree, a camera mounted on a tripod that is programmed to take one picture per second of the performance, seven 16' x 2' black canvas strips laid out in a neat stack along the length of the foreground, and two shallow rectangular paint pans, one at each end of the canvas strips. The pan on the righthand side is filled with mother of pearl paint and the pan on the lefthand side is filled with jet black enamel to balance this artistic equation.

Lastly, the two assistants assemble a black portable garment closet with the bottom cut out and fasten it to a dolly. During this time a small crowd that fluctuates between twenty and thirty people, depending on how patient or curious they are, form an invisible forcefield around the stage. Many of them are texting, headphoned, and taking pictures of the scene. Something of a mellow buzz forms and feeds on itself until the number of onlookers swells to a constant forty.

With Axlia's setting almost complete, Jasmine continues to cover her front half with the mother of pearl paint. When the desk lamp light catches her body, rainbow colored accents form like those in oil slicks. Her brush follows the contours of Axlia's body. She forms concentric Os around each breast, lifting them slightly with the underside strokes. Her brush caresses down and up and down again along her midriff and thighs. Then she fills her bellybutton with a little extra paint, which trails south to a groomed patch of velvety hair, like early 90s Playmate style. The sensation sends a ripple of warmth outward to her fingers, toes, and eyebrows.

As one assistant keeps watch over the stage area, the other presses play on the laptop and sounds the first ephemeral notes that are punctuated by sparse 808 drum loops and dulled cymbals. After he waits for the traffic signal to change and stop the flow of headlights, he walks the portable backstage curtain across the street to Axlia's apartment building entrance.

With her last brushstrokes down the front of her stems, Jasmine covers the tops of Axlia's feet and the excess color drips between her toes. The paint dries quickly, and within a minute, the wordless artist and speechless assistant are heading down a flight of splintered stairs to the fractured asphalt below.

Axlia is escorted into the vinyl urban transport cloaked for crosswalk travel. When the traffic stops, the rectangular prism begins to move, becoming oblong in opposition to her direction. With an anxious electricity embedded in the surrounding oxygen, the crowd watches Axlia emerge from the black curtain. Her full-frontal mother of pearl coating glistens in varying hues amidst the backdrop of a gunmetal sky, clouds of cigarette and weed smoke, ashen city infrastructure, and Raider-black canvases. The music fades to silence. Axlia keeps her gaze quiet and undisturbed along an imaginary horizon. She sets her mind in a safe but accessible place, while remaining bodily present as a vessel for the art. She feels that the mind is centered in the skull and has the cognitive ability to bend time. But also that the mind pervades in every cell of the body, and therefore can break space. The mind can place itself at any given point along a linear structure—a music staff perhaps—even where no tones exist, where rhythm is discontinuous, and the physics mysterious. Axlia feels that her body is not an instrument of her thoughts, but that her thoughts are the notes played by the instrument that is her body. There is no need for an audience, the song will play just the same.

The onlookers brace for whatever is about to begin with the sense that they're part of something memorable, or at least different. With aplomb, Axlia steps into the shallow foot bath filled with mother of pearl paint. With her bare feet coated in the starting color, she takes a breath of chilled city air, and begins to walk in a slow-motion pace across the black canvas. It takes her nearly a minute to walk sixteen feet. The audience relaxes their shoulders and absorbs the scene, with some capturing her first moves with their phones. There are stray voices, but most of the population remains respectfully silent or in whisper.

With a trail of thin footsteps behind her, Axlia reaches the end of the canvas strip and steps into the jet black enamel. She does this without looking, never letting her gaze drift from her focus along the invisible horizon. Then she reverses the process, walking backward, stepping toe-to-heel, her arms in perfect balance. She keeps the same pace as she covers her initial pearled footsteps with a jet black void. After another minute, Axlia reaches the end of the canvas and returns to her starting spot. Her attempt to erase her first set of footsteps is successful, save for a few drips and rebel splatterings. Her abandoned forward movements are consumed with reactive darkness.

As she returns to the shallow pan of mother of pearl, the two male assistants lift #Canvas1 to the upstage area to dry in full view. Since all the canvases are one atop the other, #Canvas2 is already in place, but Axlia pauses for a moment with her eyes closed before the next action. Her body is still, except for the breathy rise and fall of her lustrous breasts, the slight quiver of her bellybutton, and several hairs that have strayed from her concentric buns like jettisoned comets.

Her assistants fade from the scene as Jasmine presses play on the laptop from behind the oak[20] where the rolling closet and backstage area is. The speakers resound with the crackled depth of a home recording. It was made by Axlia's pianist friend, who plays an intricate legato rendition of *Oh What a Beautiful Mornin'*. Her pianist friend labeled the disc with a capital U squeezed in between the o and r of the last word. It's hard to tell whether the inclusion of the U was meant to be deep or quirky. Axlia opens her eyes, internalizing the whispered *1 2 3 1 2 3...* while externalizing solemnity, she proceeds to dance with an invisible partner. With her soles bathed in mother of pearl, she first plays the lead role of the waltz. At the end of the strip, she dips her invisible and obedient partner[21], then adjusts her necktie in thin air, and bows at a thirty-degree angle, the terminus her feet and the vertex her hips. Axlia's waltzing trail left sinuous waves, like a dancing Pollock. When she rises, she's already standing in the jet black enamel. Her audience, fixed on her movements of prestige, are equally impressed that she's able to slip into the shallow black pool unnoticed. She turns 180 degrees and her body blends into the background. Axlia assumes the opposite role and attempts to retrace her initial movements. She dances and counts *3 2 1 3 2 1...* until she reaches the other side of the canvas. She finishes with her back arched, dipped by her imagination, her arms balancing the weight of her tensed body with elegance. She holds it long enough to ensure that the programmed camera will capture her bowed curvature. She comes to stand upright and steps back into the first pool, closes her eyes, and resets herself.

The black paint on #Canvas2 doesn't fully cover her initial white waltz. It seems to act as the shadow of the pivots and swirls. It reminds one of the audience members, Elizabeth, a part-time dance instructor, how much time is needed to know your partner's movements and style, even when that partner is yourself. Elizabeth also thinks back to a memory of her father, whom she'd lost in the past year. And how at six years old she would stand barefoot on his work boots with her head pressed against his full stomach. She would take in the scent of motor oil and metal that had been absorbed into his flannel work shirt. With her left arm clutching the side of his belt and her right hand holding two of his fingers, they would sway in the kitchen to the sounds of his humming renditions of Beethoven and her lovely little giggles. Elizabeth missed him very much and her eyes swelled with tears. When she leans forward, she watches a single drop fall to the cement. She removes her right foot from her loafer and gently covers it before it can evaporate into the night sky.

While her assistants move #Canvas2 to dry and display alongside #Canvas1, an untouched #Canvas3 is ready for the next action. Jasmine crossfades into LL Cool J's 1990 smash hit— the one where he makes it a point of letting everyone know that he's going to knock you out at the behest of his mother. *"Don't Call It A Comeback!, I Been Here For Years!"* Axlia acts suddenly and ferociously in accordance with the beat toward an unseen opponent. She jabs left and crosses right: one-one-two / one-one-two / one-one-one-Two one-one-one-Two / one- two-one-TWO / (then an animated wind-up for the haymaker) ...*TWO*, which is further punctuated with LL's *"Exxplosionn!!"* As if she had stunned her adversary, she takes a few bouncy and cocky steps backward with clenched fists and arms languid at her sides. On the canvas, the pearly paint smears forward, save for a few angled dashes and some stray rows of toes. Then Axlia moves toward the end of the strip and lets out a torrent of one-twos before delivering the KO punch to a non-existent chin, right when LL raps, *"Don't You Dare Stare, You Betta Moooove!"* The flurry of white jabs blur in contrast to the black background. Even when members of the audience close their eyes, the residual shadowboxing thrashings remain.

Stepping in and out of the black pool, she moves with mirrored steps, and attempts to darken the evidence of the knockout while assuming the role of the fighter under attack. She more bobs than weaves while responding to the onslaught of her very own prior fists, and performs the negative of one-one-two combinations and vicious swings. These inverse actions restore balance to the initial aggression.

The assistants remove the canvas and reveal an untarnished #Canvas4 while Jasmine fades in Tchaikovsky's *"Dance of the Sugar Plum Fairy"*. Axlia regains her posture, transforms back to her baseline, and places only her right foot in the fresh paint. For the next action, she summons her core strength and graceful poise. It's been years since she's taken a ballet class, but for the last few weeks she's been using the side of her bed as a ballet barre to practice. She eases onto the canvas, opens with a gentle port de bras, and completes eight piqué turns on her right foot. This takes Axlia straight across the black space before finishing in fifth position just over the edge. The piqué turns create eight circular moons equally spaced apart. Even the torque of each clockwise turn gives the impression of lunar topography. She waits for a cue in the music to reverse her course, this time with jet black. Axlia completes another eight piqué turns on her left foot. Since she keeps her eyes on the level and uses a distant light for spotting, she doesn't know if she's landing on each of her pearly moons. After she reaches the end of the canvas in fifth position, she bows in plié and smiles, as if by habit. From the corner of her eye, she notices how close she is to shadowing all eight moons. Axlia's first turn fully eclipsed her first moon, then less so on the second, and so on until her last piqué turn. What remains on the black canvas, from left to right, is the charted progression from a new moon waxing to full.

Jasmine fades out the orchestra and transitions to a hypnotic house mix that's heavy on the bass and light on the elegance. #Canvas5 is set up as a fashion show runway. Axlia steps out of the paint and into a model pose with her hips shifted to one side, her back arched, her stare vacant and alluring. She holds the pose while some of the audience members oblige with flash photographs. With her body moving as a function of the beat, she walks in the exaggerated and staccatoed runway style—not with one foot in front of the other, but with each step landing as a tall capital X, her pinky toes landing on the meridian. The mother of pearl footprints look like they're made by someone who's switched their left and right legs. Axlia strikes another pose at the other end of the canvas before switching colors. The way she crisscrossed the diagonal splatterings of paint shows there was no intention for the steps to coincide. They are two models traversing paths for a future simultaneous two-dimensional representation, where neither had shared space or time. With dynamic hip action and the resulting jounce of a cantered bareback rider, fantasies spark ablaze among the voyeurs and hang in the air as the music follows the sinusoidal wave to silence for the rest of the performance. More passersby join the audience.

She stands straight and silent in the mother of pearl paint, almost meditative in Tadasana. She shuts her eyes and takes long breaths, in through the nose and out the small space between her lips. #Canvas6 begins with Axlia walking backward with wide hulking steps and alpha male arms, an expanded ribcage, and a scowled visage. She pounds her fists and rubs them together. The chalky sound of grinding dried paint brings chills to several of the witnesses. The residue falls to the middle of the canvas while her wet footsteps cover the lengthwise perimeter. On the dark side, she stands in the pool, bends down, and places her middle fingers in the paint. After she rises she draws her hands toward her eyes and smears black parenthetical tears down her face. She turns to face the opposite direction and begins to audibly sob in a muffled and embarrassed way. Axlia shuffles down the middle of the canvas with her heels leading the way, her head lowered and her back hunched, and her fingers holding her mouth agape.

One of the audience members, IliW, sees this as a confrontation of the abuser and the abused. And rather than identifying with the artist's representation, he became the emptiness of the missing character. IliW went from interested to affected. He'd been struggling of late to find neutrality between the diametric sides within himself. One day he'd submit to drowning it in firewater and cutting into his thighs with a dull butter knife, maybe not as a cry for help, but as a whisper for acknowledgement. And the next day he'd be up early for morning sprints on the uptown streets, then showered and well-dressed, and then enjoying the company of his pleasant colleagues where he works for a small, but reputable insurance company. IliW brushes his hair back with one hand while the other remains in his pocket. Through the cotton lining he runs his finger over the raw pink indentations on his legs. He thinks, maybe it's time.

For Axlia's #Canvas7, her movements are second to her painting. This time, instead of a short story told by footprints, she uses her whole body. As she stands in the shallow pool, she leans forward with a slight bend in her knees, and places her hands in the mother of pearl. She gently cups her hands and brings the paint to the area just above her breasts. She repeats this application to the faint outlines of her ribcage, then to the front of her hips and thighs, and finally to her knees on down. The audience suspends their voices during this haphazard, yet sensual, second coat. Axlia steps out and walks in a slow arching path almost to the halfway point with the liquid pearl dripping to the canvas. She holds her head low and heavy. She turns around, walks an opposing arch, and forms the outline of an eye. Each step leaves small dashes of paint that act as varying and wandering lashes. Axlia makes her way to the center where she kneels down, allowing the paint more time to collect. As a monochrome iris begins to form around her, she picks up her head and looks at her audience one person at a time. Axlia transforms the observers into the seen. She brings herself down all the way on her front side. Her body flows over the coarse texture with serpentine movements as she leaves her impressions in the center of the eye. Then Axlia pads over to the other side and stands in the jet black pool. She applies paint to her back half, raising her cupped hands to the nape of her neck and letting the excess run down. Then she follows the contours of her backside and lets the rest of the paint run down to her calves. Axlia walks to the center of the eye facing away from the audience. The paint begins to fall to the canvas to create the pupil, a liquid shadow. When she turns around to face them, she raises her right arm and parts her lips, but somewhere in the distance a faint << pop >> causes the audience to break their trance and turn in different directions as they try to pinpoint the origin of the sound. The view of the surrounding streets looks as expected and the buildings and fire escapes are dark and without commotion. But when the audience returns their attention to the stage area, they see Axlia down on her knees and elbows. And they see color for the first time in the performance. It's the force of a brilliant crimson leaving Axlia's body from a wound on her right side, just below her ribs. The pain manifests in the way she holds her side with one hand and grips the canvas with the other, her nails nearing the breaking point, as she screams without sound. More colors emerge when her white knees slide and shift over the covered sidewalk. There are swirls of amplified maroons and salted grays, flared scarlets and blackened oranges, and a luminous violet sheen from the surrounding metropolis. It feels like a cigarette is being pressed into her flesh, but instead of the fire cooling to ash, it intensifies and fuels the burning sensation. The bullet had raced into her pearly skin and left a wound no larger than a seed, but when it came out the black half of her body it left a bloody concavity, as if a red dahlia had grown from the inside and was now in bloom. The bullet's trajectory came to an end after it pierced the canvas backdrop and fell to the back corner of the stage. While at rest and hidden from view, the bullet warmed a very small radius of cement.

For the first few moments, her assistants and the audience are stunned and inactive. With slowed moments, confusion, and sounds of terror, the human machine begins to kick in. Her two assistants, without concern for themselves, guard her on either side. Jasmine pulls off her top and uses it to apply pressure to the wound. Some audience members flee holding hands and others huddle together in place. Some take pictures for reasons of evidence and memory. Two of the audience members take on more active roles. lliW steps forward while taking off his tweed coat. With his eyes and a gesture, he offers it to Axlia and places it around her shoulders. And htebazilE walks in a crouched position to the protective oak tree and is the first person to call 911. Her voice shivers, but her words are informative and lucid.

Axlia feels like time is running on a dying battery. When the ambulance arrives, her body is slumped over in shock more than pain. Her face flashes strobe red and not, in accordance with the siren. She'd suppressed all color during her performance, but it rose to prominence in the end as the hues of a rescue victorious brought the warm night to an abrupt local chill. Axlia's eyes flutter open. And despite Jasmine's efforts, the blood inside continues to slip out like reluctant tears. Without expression, Axlia looks up and across the way to a vacant apartment window. She thinks to herself, the paint is probably dry by now.

Roosevelt is leaning against the stark white wall of The Cotton Club in Harlem. His head is tilted up, but his eyes are closed. He's around the corner from the club's entrance and opposite the dulled silver arches that support Riverside Drive above. The arches are divided into curved rectangles all the way across. Most of the sections are empty silver frames except for the ones overlooking the club. A few months ago Roosevelt had gone out with his accomplice and climbed the metal lattice of the infrastructure up to the heaven spot. They both used an iridescent iridium paint that contrasted with the metal canvas and then also seemed to disappear, depending on the angle of the sun. They painted one letter of their name in each curved rectangle. ROOSEVELT and NORMAL styled their letters with reverence to the hot house below. He is taking in the night and reflecting on the day's abstraction, but the drone of the live music inside permeates the club walls and lulls him to rest. When Roosevelt hears a   << pop >>   somewhere in the distant background, his eyebrows raise and bring a trio of wrinkles to his forehead, followed by the lifting of his eyelids, which brings him out of slumber.

From around the corner he hears a brilliant voice saturated with timbre. Between each blues line there's a long silence to allow for a breath of enlightenment from old Mary Jane. The exhaled smoke makes its way around the corner, clinging like ivy along the outside wall. *"Oh, The Locksmith... She don't have no lock on her door."*

Roosevelt contemplates moving to see this man, but instead he reaches into the plush and velvet lining of his black jacket and pulls out a body-warmed flask from the left inside pocket. It's the color of a vintage cornet. The flask is three-quarters full with the liquid gold of cognac. Roosevelt turns the cap back and forth in contemplation, as if adjusting the tightness of a valve. Once these thoughts become only left turns, he lifts the distilled instrument to his lips and sips the music, tasting the notes of oak, vanilla, and the French countryside. He feels the blo*od in*side warming his organs, his sap concentrating to maple. The echo of his long exhale sounds of soul when it leaves his body and enters the ether. The vibrations go in all directions, the higher frequency waves bouncing into relative obscurity, and the lower frequency waves slithering around the bend and into the ears of the blues man.

Roosevelt's recent days have been filled with some confusion, as he's been consumed with writing about his dreams. These writings weren't journal entries, but analyses of future representations. At first, he was inspired by the works of J.W. Dunne and had started his own experiment by advancing it to the next exponential level. It started with his normal sleeping schedule of 1:30 AM to 7:30 AM. When he woke up, he recorded the sensations from the night without regard for grammar or linearity. It was pure stream of thought born from his unconscious dreams. Moving from the nightly cycles, Roosevelt wrote tangentially for hours on end and into new dimensions of thought. At least, that's how it felt at the time. He only paused for coffee, a bathroom break, or a bachelor-style meal—for instance, a bowl of buttered spinach and hot pepper. When some type of carpal tunnel-syndrome threshold was reached, Roosevelt would force himself to give the chambers of his heart something to work for. He'd throw on whatever shoes and sweatshirt were close by and go for an ill-prepared run, sartorially speaking, through the city streets. After he returned, the writing recommenced with a new vigor where stretching his legs should have had trumped. Roosevelt continued until the wick went black, where he at once stopped cold, sometimes not minding to finish the current sentence with a period

And after some nominal domestic responsibilities were satisfied, it was off to bed, and back to the life of dreams. This exercise of letting the body rest for several hours of uncontrolled synapses, only to revive the muscles for writing the next day, was bringing his body and mind to the brink of failure. The more Roosevelt wrote about the formations and implications of his dreams, the less time he was spending with others. He was isolated, but focused, as he created a new reality for himself. His bedtime shifted later and later over the course of the experiment. Now, his head was hitting the pillow as the sun became a sliver on the horizon. His habits had turned nocturnal. He'd even been dreaming about writing about his dreams. His literary productions were becoming at once more substantial and ever so narrow. Potent maybe, but imponderable. He'd created stories from daydreams within nightmares that were born from sanguinity. They'd taken place within a few seconds of thought, yet were the summation of the interactions between billions of human existences.

It is dusk, which is now Roosevelt's morning, and the nips from the flask give him a welcomed flight. He pries himself off the wall and stands at full height. The chorus returns from around the bend. "*Oh, The Locksmith... She don't have no lock on her door.*"

As he walks around the corner, he sees the lone revelator through a fresh puff of absinthian fog. He is standing under the faint white neon of the sign above. The light casts shadows that deepen his wrinkles, taking on the quality of tree bark gnarled by years of concerns and softened by thousands of smiles. The parenthetical grooves that run over his hollowed cheeks are balanced by a youthfulness in his eyes. The light of the sign also brightens his white three-piece suit and reflects a glow off his clean-shaven dome. In his left hand he holds a white fedora by its crown. His right hand is fiddling with a small object, his fingers making small waves from pinky to index.

"Good evening, young man." He takes another spark from the blunt.

"Good evening." He leans against the wall, side by side with the blues man and takes a sip from the cornet. "Why doesn't she have a lock on her door?"

The man's eyes shift toward Roosevelt, followed by his head a full second later. The man speaks only a few words at a time. Like commas in the air, he takes long breaths throughout his sentences.

"Oh, I've been singing that song for years. It's a blues chorus that I think of now and again. I don't know if I've ever been asked that question. Most cats think it's just some contradictory line to make you think for a minute. And I guess that's what it is. But it came from some place real." He pauses for a drag and a short cough. "There was a beautiful woman I knew back in the day. She was the most caring woman I'd ever met, helped me when times were hard, let me stay with her when I was down and out. Her apartment was warm, had all the charms of a real home, artwork filled the walls, white christmas lights hung from the ceiling year-round. The first time I was going to stay for several nights in a row, I asked her for a key so I could lock up when I split for the day. And that's when she told me, there's no lock. She said she didn't see the point, there was already a door."

"Was she really a locksmith?"

The blues man smiles."Damn straight. She had this bag that looked like some high fashion purse, but it was filled with all of her tools and keys. That was a trip. You would've never guessed what she did for work. I used to look forward to when she came home and told me about her day. She spoke passionately about picking locks, her private triumphs she called them. She taught me a great deal." He exhales into the low sky. "Young man, there are some people who don't like what they do, that's unfortunate. There are others who are positive, and even if they're not truly happy with their work, they still find enjoyment within those constraints. But she was someone who took complete pride in her actions, in wonder of the present."

"Where is she now?"

The man exhales again and follows the smoke as it evanesced. "She lives in my memories, strongly tonight. It's been thirty years since she passed, on this night, complications during childbirth."

The men are quiet.

Roosevelt takes a nip of cognac from the flask while the man opens his hand and holds up a key horizontally. "She said this looked like an Egyptian desert skyline solidified in brass."

"Where does that key go?"

The man smiles as his parenthetical wrinkles become chevrons. He hums in decrescendo. "Who the hell knows?"

Roosevelt joins him in spirit and shakes his head in affirmation. He's yet to fully emerge from the misty reality of his dream-writing abstractions, but a sudden urgency regarding time transpires from somewhere within. Roosevelt asks him, "What day is it? Is this Thursday?"

The man flips his fedora onto his head, tips the brim, and says, "Almost." He snaps his fingers once and walks away, as if with weighted soles, until he disappears into The Cotton

Club.

Roosevelt tucks his flask back into his jacket and reaches into the other inside pocket. As he removes his red journal, he cuts his thumb on the metal clip of the pen folded inside the book. Roosevelt shakes his hand to dismiss the minor pain. This jolt snaps him out of his trance and he blinks several times in quick succession. He flexes his shoulders upward. When Roosevelt begins to put some ink down on paper, the pressure of his grip causes a lone drop of blood to emerge from his skin and land in a dotted streak at the bottom corner of the page.

i
found
myself
alone
against
the
asthmatic
wall
of
jazzmatic
laudations,
where
the soul
wheezes
until its
final
collapse,
when the
inhale of
its last
breath is
absorbed,
and
the lush
reverberations
of love
are hushed
from
the

i found myself alone, a tone without a key, a secret without a home, aside from the inside

ƵWEET ƵURZDAY

"There are times when you must act for the greater good, as I have done throughout my career in many ways. But I say, in business, if there's a greater good, in contrast, there must be a lesser evil. And..."

"I'm not sure that's how the phrase works, Mr. Coaster.[22]"

"I know what the damn phrase means! Is this an interview or an idiom lesson? You know, I'm doing you and your little YouTube channel a favor. You ask questions, I answer them. Don't interrupt or correct me ever again. You're a pathetic troll, a waste of time."

"I'm sorry, sir, I..."

"Hold on.... No, I'm sorry. I can run cold and hot, I mean, I just lost my cool. Excuse me. Let me take a deep breath. As I was trying to say, you can't be concerned with every single lamb in the herd. You have to act in the interest of the herd as a whole herd... I can't even fucking talk right now. See what you've done by breaking my concentration? I sound like a goddamn idiot right now. This is over. Take his camera. You are never to speak of this, understand? Or it will be the last thing you say, understand?"

"Sir, I..."

[[Σ]]

In the morning, just before the sun first splinters the darkness, Suma is having another paralysis dream. They've become common enough over the years and many nights she tries to put off sleep for as long as possible. Her late night book alterations are her upper of choice. But eventually, her body gives in to nature, and here she lies. {She is on her back atop her childhood bed, a pink-posted twin with doily-topped covers that are yellowed on the edges. She is surrounded by plush cats of all stripes and colors, with full limb counts sparse. Her sight blurs to a grayed vignette along the periphery, as it does in the old movies. Her bedroom is in the basement of a modest Nevada rural home. The windowless space has a desk embellished by magic marker streaks that had bled through thin paper, an old entertainment console that had been transformed into a dresser, a closet with hand-me-down dresses, and endless shelves of books and stacks of them on the floor that were thousands of pages high. When Suma looks left, she sees a black and gray video on the unplugged television. It is of a woman in her thirties, flexing her tanned and probably orange-tinged muscles. The bodybuilder's movements and poses are telecast in reverse, her quadriceps going from rigid and striated to full and soft, her mountainous biceps and shoulders subsiding to mere hills, her bright smile flattening to a straight line. She exits the stage walking backward. Her bright white bikini of three triangles, two up top and one below, remain aglow for a few moments as the dissemination turns to static.

She's only able to move what feels like her head, just enough to see that her wrists have been tied to the corner posts with the collars from her marble-eyed plush cats. Over the arch of her cheeks, she's able to see her legs, spread in a V-shape, also tied to the bedposts by her ankles. She is naked and there are only two visible lights. One is a glowing red doorbell affixed to the bedpost a few inches from her restrained right hand. If she presses it, the illuminated circle will sound the alarm through local telephony, an operator will disconnect her from the evil of the past, restore her faculties, and transport her to a place of peace and nobility. As close as it is, it may as well be a distant Mars for queen Suma—her pointer finger a slave to its name.

The other light comes from the hallway as it reflects off the chipped eggshell walls and shines through the slit between the doorframe and the left side of door. The light ends at the threshold of the border, leaving her body in darkness. Her thoughts race to leave the room, to a place where light casts shadows. But her body resists the effort once again, lying stiff and foreign to her commands. The line of eggshell along the bedroom door begins to expand until it becomes a full rectangle of light, directly south of her open legs. For several minutes, the rectangle remains unchanged, growing stale and hypnotizing. The only movement is the rising and falling of her chest through the double vision haze of her cheeks.

Suma's other senses begin to arise amidst the looming terror. She hears knocking from both sides of her bedroom walls that keep the same cadence—three soft knocks followed by an accented one, then a brief pause, and then again. An odor begins to seep in from all sides, like that of a thick carpet in an unkempt home. The taste of her breath is of metal and salted blood, coming from somewhere within. And she begins to close her eyes and reverse the orientation of the rectangle from lengthwise to widthwise. Then the purity of the light is disturbed. She recognizes a shaded figure holding a bowling ball in his right hand, almost consuming the entire area of the doorway. He is bulbous from head to distended stomach to fattened toes, the outline of a vertical cloud. His breathing is coarse and sporadic, his hair thin and sparse.

When he turns ninety degrees, she notices that he is breathing with his mouth open, which causes a collection of drool to cake to the stubble of his chin. The profile of curves garnered from years of inactivity are disrupted by his jagged reproductive organs, which have been replaced by the outline of pistol. The gun begins to self-cock and fire bullets into the hazy outlines. Suma expects the gunfire to be deafening, and since she is unable to acknowledge any sound, it may have been so. His gun goes off repeatedly, causing silent destruction wherever it points, while the rest of his body lugs along. She witnesses the tearing apart of the desk and dresser, the shards of pressboard floating in the dark air. The arcs of the debris begin to illuminate the dark room like suspended comets. Amidst the ruination, she studies the figure, a man she knows as Big Sir, and she slips into a deeper freeze, even for a paralyzed victim.

Suma has a further vision within the dream, which places Big Sir at the end of a bowling lane. He is standing on the release line with his ball under his left arm. As he studies the lane, his right arm dangles diagonally against his fat deposits. His right hand has two large and meaty fingers, the ring and the pinky, as the other three have been worn thin by the repeated fingering of his weapon. Big Sir is known to walk around with his fingers in his bowling ball at all times.

Suma envisions him in quick successive photos at different locations holding his spherical companion—in the corner booth at the diner, getting an extraction at the dentist, in the back row of the cinema, on the broken seat of his toilet. When Big Sir goes to the bowling alley, he rents a lane for hours and drinks with a purpose. Sometimes he'll stand at the end of the lane and stare at the white pins that conform to the proportions of his own body, a sedentary humanoid army of selves in triangular formation. After one particular night of overconsumption and complaints from other bowlers, Big Sir is persuaded out of his drunken slumber, and out of the alley. When he arises from the plastic chair, his most recent memory is from months prior. It's the night of his perfect game—which was really a hoax that caused unintended collateral damage at home—as if it had just happened. With slurred expletives, he boasts to the complainers that they are disrespecting a champion, and proceeds to point to the Wall of Frames. When he fails to find his portrait, he ignores a plain realization. He prefers to revel in the final frame score of XXX. He chooses to remember the tempestuous rotation on the ball that caused it to glide along the edge of wooden plane before making the turn toward the middle pin, as if guided by a phantom. Each release was calibrated and then robotically executed to reduce the pins to a pile of bones to be swept away, and then resurrected moments later to endure the same fate. He relished the sounds of the distant tumbles and the applause of nearby strangers, the visions of repeated strikes and ejaculatory feelings of mounting successes, and the fulfillment of suicide three hundred times over as he knocked his red-collared clones into the depths of the pit.

He makes his way to the food stand and purchases three servings of french fries in a large to-go bag. Big Sir toddles out of the alley still wearing the patchwork bowling shoes, the to-go bag in his left hand, and the ball fused with his right. He shifts and grunts his way into the driver's seat of his economy station wagon. With the bag of over-greased fries in his lap, he reaches in with his left hand and pulls out several at once. He rolls them around in his fingers until they are in bowling pin formation. Big Sir holds the fries up over the steering wheel and watches the grease glisten in the light of the large neon sign overhead: *"Family Night at The Spare Cactus: We're all in the gutter, but some of us are staring at a 7-10 Split."* Then, in one large bite, all the fries are consumed and swallowed after three open-mouthed chews. Big Sir continues until he empties the bag, which has turned transparent and gray on the lower half. He licks and sucks each salted finger from knuckle to nail on his left hand before removing his right hand from the bowling ball. He is about to retrieve his keys and start the ignition, but he's caught in a moment of self-admiration. He studies his three boney fingers, smiles, and begins to lick them too.

As this vision within the dream fades, the giant eclipses all the light in the doorway. As she lies paralyzed, she closes her eyes and removes another sense from the equation. Like an exhaust pipe in reverse, Big Sir's heavy exhales of dank mucous and yellowed air move closer to her. When his knees sink into the foot of the twin bed, the mattress becomes diagonal under his weight. Suma's wrist ties hold her in place. Now she is even farther from the red doorbell as the act of the discharging incubus begins. His head jerks back and his neck tenses with thick wrinkles, his eyebrows lower and his tender muscles flex. Down his back, streams of sweat find their way through the patches of hair and collect in his crack. His sexual growls are the acidic mewls of a desolate terror.

She knows her limp body is bleeding from the metallic penetrations, but it's curiously a violation without pain. She recoils to an out-of-body experience within the nightmare until she feels a stark change in temperature on her body. It's a damp sensation that chills the skin over her heart when Big Sir, after his last thrust, lowers his head from its upward tilt and spills out all of the saliva that had built up over the groans and gunfire, his pistol vacant of ammunition.

His large form descends and disappears. The full rectangle of light is restored and she opens her eyes.} Suma rises up to her elbows and enjoys the protection of consciousness. Awake in her Manhattan apartment, the nighttime storm has passed into a calm spring morning.

She's always tried to deal with them one night at a time, hoping for new dreams to usurp the old. For too many years, nothing changed. So she made a decision just a few weeks ago to take direct measures to bring an end to the source out west in The Valley. She wanted him to be forced to look into her heterochromia iridum eyes and feel the seething vengeance within. Just as blue and green color a peaceful earth from afar, there rages the unseen infernal and diabolic core. So, to exorcise one demon, she summoned another.[23, 24, 25]

[[◆]]

Della lies still in the hospital bed. Her body only moves when the vibrations in the mechanical mattress cause small erratic waves to promote blood circulation. Della looks down at her arms as they relax against her sides. Both are over the bedsheets and one is connected to an IV. The paint has been mostly cleaned off. Farther down, she sees that her left foot has crept out from the covers and is still black as tar. When she alternately flexes and points her toes, she creates fault lines in the dried paint and her skin becomes visible. Della looks to her left and sees another patient in the neighboring bed. The privacy curtain had been pulled back to allow for some natural light on her side of the room. Her roommate is an older woman who's sleeping with her mouth wide open, possibly hoarding all of the oxygen in the room. Her thin hair is white at the roots and dyed a bright lemon, and is matted down against the pillow. There is a *Get Well Soon* balloon in a vase with a single daffodil. Della looks at the metallic foil of the balloon, how it's wrinkled and taut at the seams, then switches her focus to the sagging lines along her roommate's softened temples. Next to the vase Della notices a card tucked into an open envelope and a tidy stack of three books that are flush with the corner of the bedside table. She reads the spines from top to bottom: Holy Bible New International Version, The Holy Bible 1611 Edition King James Version, and The Jerusalem Bible. Della's bedside table to her right is clear and dust-free.

Della hasn't picked up a Bible, let alone three of them, in a long time. She remembers that when she was young, in an effort to appease her family, she read and mouthed the words as they spoke them. She wondered why they always looked so somber, but at the same time, it would've been inappropriate for them to smile their way through a lot of the stories. Della thinks she can reach her roommate's books if she's able to rotate to her side and time her full extension just right. As Della makes the effort to turn from her dark side to the light, she feels the jarring pain of the bullet wound, like an invisible dagger driven into her ribcage. On her first attempt, she misses the Word of God by a handbreadth. On her second attempt, her index finger makes just enough contact with the spine of the top Bible to cause it fall toward her. She catches the silk bookmark and the Bible dangles upside-down with fanned out pages. Della floats the book over her chest as she returns to her dark side. She rests the Bible open against her face while she repositions her hands. When she thumbs through the pages, she passes over names like Basemath, Golgotha, Baal, Barak, Ruth, and Delilah. She reads fragments of ancient passages as they flash by in a blur of text.

She stops the flow of page turning when the last line of a psalm catches her curiosity. Della turns one page back to the start of the unfamiliar psalm. With mother of pearl faintly across her lips, she mouths the words and renews her own oral tradition.

Psalm 88

Lord, you are the God who saves me;
day and night I cry out to you.
May my prayer come before you;
turn your ear to my cry.
I am overwhelmed with troubles
and my life draws near to death.
I am counted among those who go down to the pit;
I am like one without strength.
I am set apart with the dead,
like the slain who lie in the grave,
whom you remember no more,
who are cut off from your care.
You have put me in the lowest pit,
in the darkest depths.
Your wrath lies heavily on me;
you have overwhelmed me with all your waves.
You have taken from me my closest friends
and have made me repulsive to them.
I am confined and cannot escape;
my eyes are dim with grief.
I call to you, Lord, every day;
I spread out my hands to you.
Do you show your wonders to the dead?
Do their spirits rise up and praise you?
Is your love declared in the grave,
your faithfulness in Destruction?
Are your wonders known in the place of darkness,
or your righteous deeds in the land of oblivion?
But I cry to you for help, Lord;
in the morning my prayer comes before you.
Why, Lord, do you reject me
and hide your face from me?
From my youth I have suffered and been close to death;
I have borne your terrors and am in despair.
Your wrath has swept over me;
your terrors have destroyed me.

All day long they surround me like a flood;
*   they have completely engulfed me.*
You have taken from me friend and neighbor—
*   darkness is my closest friend.*

(New International Version (NIV) Publication Year: 1978)[26]

Della returns the book, her mind too busy to acknowledge the pain, and then falls into a deep and serene rest on the pulsing mattress.

<<Local 1 News Report>>

"...Live from Harlem, here's Christina Darling-Ramirez."

"Thanks, Chuck. Last night a single shot rang out and struck a performance artist, named *Axlia Clia*. The artist wasn't wearing any clothes, but was covered up with black and white body paint. While she was painting some very large canvases with her feet, she was shot. Early reports from the Columbia University Medical Center suggest that it's not a life-threatening wound and that she's expected to make a full recovery. The performance was held on the corner of 135th and Riverside Drive on a large area of sidewalk. This was not a city-sanctioned event, but we're told it drew a gathering of about fifty people, many of whom gave their accounts to police officers. They're still looking for answers as to why Axlia Clia was shot. Was this a stray bullet? Or was this an attempt on the artist's life? Our sources have said that the police have few leads and that this is an ongoing search and investigation. When we asked the detective if he believed this was related to the recent string of shootings in the area, he said it was too early to tell, that they'd be exploring all leads, and wouldn't rule anything out yet. Just in the past month, there have been four separate incidents, that coincidentally or not, have involved members of the arts and science communities. Most recent were the murders of three philosophy professors during a private faculty meeting just ten blocks away. If you have *any* information on last night's shooting, please contact police immediately. Now, here on 135th street, we have a few people who attended the performance and are willing to share what they saw. Excuse me, ma'am, what can you tell us about last night?"

"Well, I was standing about 15 feet away from her when she was hit. I heard something in the background, but it was hard to tell exactly what it was. It just sounded like a disturbance, a disturbance in the *air*. There was a change in *feeling* that wasn't the wind changing direction, but it felt like the wind *stopped*. Everyone looked around for a few seconds, then it became very chaotic. I've lived here for awhile now and it was one of the scariest things I've seen. You couldn't tell if it was just one shot or the start of something worse, you know? And it was hard to figure out where the shot came from. We're on a hill here, or a slope, but it seemed like the disturbance came from above. Way up."

"Are you saying it came from a rooftop?"

"I don't know. It just sounded very far away, but close enough to stop the wind around us."

"Well, thank you for your time, ma'am. I'm sure it was a very upsetting situation and I'm glad you're now out of harm's way. And now I'm here with a man who says he lives in the area and saw the performance. Sir, you said you live in this building on the corner?"

"Yezz, that'z right."

"What did you see here last night?"

"I zaw zee woman, zee artist here, valking back and forth, maybe lost? I dōn' know, maybe only black and vhite? No middle. No gray areaz, az you call zhem. It wuz like zee barber in zee example of Ruzzell'z Paradox. Do you know zhīsz exzample of zee logic?"

"Sir, I'm sorry, I want to stay on the topic of the shooting."

"I tell you. Zhere iz a town in vhich *all* zee men eizher get szhaved by zee barber or szhave zhemzelves, you szee?"

"Sir, please."

"And all zee men have to go into one of two roomz. One room iz for zee men who get szhaved by the zee barber and the ozher room iz for zee men who szhave zhemselves. Zhey muszt all chooze ztheir roomz and remain in zee room."

"Excuse me, but is there anything you can tell me about where you think the bullet came from?"

"Zee queztion iz... where doez zee barber go? He goez to zee room where zee men szhave zhemselves and zee men szay, '*You can't sztay here! You are zee barber, zso when you szhave yourzelf, you really are being szhaved by zee barber! Go to zee next room!*' And zee barber goez to zee next room and zee men szay, '*You can't sztay here! Szhow uz how you szhave! Ahhh! You are a man who szhaves hiz own facze! You do not szit down wizth your handz by your szidez! Go to zee next room!*' And zee barber continuez in zhīsz way īndefinitely and īnfinitely!"

"Yes, Chuck, should I move on? We're not getting any details on what happened last night."

"I zhink zat zee artist wuz zee barber. Caught between two roomz, maybe sztuck betveen two invizible doorz of choize. White and Black. Life and deazth. You muzt chooze, and zee artist did not chooze. Zhe wuz caught without zertainty, zshot wizthout protecztion. Maybe zhat wuz zee problem. *But*! *But*! Zhe's going to be fine! Zhe can sztill chooze."

"Well, thank you for your time sir, but we are going to take a commercial break. More witness accounts from last night when we return."

"Zhank you az well. I hope you have a *zweet Zurzday*!"

[[0/1]]

[[⥣]]

The sun rose beneath his master bedroom window and projected the shadows of him sleeping amongst the cumulous clouds throughout the morning hours. Sometime before noon, he unfolds himself out of bed and goes into the kitchen. He makes his mother's Sunday Special Breakfast of seven silver dollar pancakes, which he grew up having every seventh day before church. His mother had chosen that breakfast for three reasons: it reminded her of her father, it had a rich and aspirational name that might help them psychologically pull out of poverty, and she appreciated how easy it was to cook them all the way through. Her earlier attempts at large pancakes had been just as monetarily ambitious, but she realized that a lot of dough doesn't always equate to satisfaction. After he clears the griddle, Zeus zig-zags lavish stripes of maple syrup over the pancakes. It is liquid gold over silver dollars on a paper plate.

The only other breakfast he makes at home is a *t-bone steak, cheese, eggs, and Welch's grape.* The combination was born from a line in his favorite song on his favorite album, *Ready to Die.* It was something he used to turn to for extra confidence, a cloak over teenage timidity. He'd try to manifest the persona of the Notorious one, the honorable B.I.G., when he ventured into the wilderness of the dating scene. Along with his social disposition and handsome face, it was a nudge in the right direction. But the full effect wouldn't take place until years later, when he and his mother came into the newest of money. Then, along with his empyreal apartment in New York City, he was able to complete his materialistic ideal with updated collections from the Biggie Smalls paradise of Versace, Coogi, Timberland, Karl Kani, Rough Rider, gold ropes, and one shelf in the fridge dedicated to Moët. Zeus now had a new heptarchy of style: shades, sweaters, boots, denim, condoms, chains, and champagne. It changed just about everything. It turned a socioeconomic struggle into a priceless smile and a renewed sense of faith in himself.

⑦⑩⑫㊵③

The mother of McJesus was nondenominationally spiritual, but passionately religious when it came to playing the twice-per-week Powerball Lottery. Ever since the split, the breaking of the family nucleus, she felt it was necessary to strengthen their bond by honoring her past. She hoped that through the memories of her father, he would learn to choose the right paths in life, by way of his stories and advice. When she was young, her father used to give her an allowance that she was to save, not spend. He told her it would one day bring her wealth and security. He meant it more in the way of learning the value of a dollar, that the experience of saving itself would be the wise investment, and eventually a healthy habit. But the mother of McJesus took the advice literally and never spent what she was given. When her father realized this, he suggested that he'd continue her allowance payments, but would set the money aside at home. If she were ever in need, it was there to collect.

The allowance she'd received from her father was exclusively in the form of silver dollars. He wanted the gift to bear more weight and feel like something special each week. The money began to gain interest in an unexpected way—he'd developed a hobby of collecting them for her, but it soon became more of an obsession for him, and he became an expert on their history. In their Brooklyn apartment, the purposes of his large bedroom closet and small roll-top desk switched. The desk kept the bare necessities of his clothing and the closet became a vault for thousands of silver dollars. It was unclear to her when the transition from hobbyist to fixated numismatist occurred. The mystery was blurred by small changes over time and her eventual absence as a constant witness to his behavior. When she moved across the East River to Manhattan, she realized that her father's inability to recall new memories or to be interested in anything else, was undeniable. His mind was beginning to age faster than his body.

By the decade of the eighties, he was repeating the same day over and over, though each one felt unique to him. When he spoke to his daughter in the evening, he told her of the Eisenhower dollars he acquired that day, whether he'd traded for them with cotton-linen bills at the bank, or convinced a cashier to check if there were any extra in the drawer. Sometimes she feared he was being taken advantage of, but the truth was that his kind demeanor tended to repel any premature vulturism. He spoke of how he liked the way they felt in his hands, the way he'd close his eyes and let his finger trace over Ike's balding head, and the way his nails, which he kept longer than she preferred, could skip across the little letters and numbers: LIBERTY, IN GOD WE TRUST, 1970-Something. He said he liked to hold the coin with all five fingertips along the circular edge at the points of a pentagram. On the flip side, he never tired of the spread eagle landing on the surface of the moon. With the Earthrise in full view, the world was in his hand. He told his daughter that sometimes, when he sat at his roll-top desk, he'd remove his folded clothes and make stacks of cylindrical towers with the coins. He created silver cityscapes that took days on end to complete, as they tended to reach impressive heights and expand to the edges of the rectangular oak island.

Then one night, a call she made to her father went unanswered. She tried a few more times before making the hopeful assumption that he was asleep. The next morning she tried again with the same result. She prayed he was out for coffee and a trip to the bank. After work, she didn't wait to get home and called him from the corner payphone. She let it ring until her tears seeped into the transmitter.

When she arrived at his home, she found him in his bed. He barely made a ripple under the flat sheets, his thin body a mild crest of quilted cotton. There was a silver city of coins on his roll-top desk with a flat lake of dollars in the foreground. She took one silver dollar from the lake and placed it on top of one of the tall towers.

With her father gone from the world, she packed the contents of his closet into several bags of luggage and vowed to stow them away in her own closet until she was in a time of need. This time came after the split with Zeus's father, when she became a young single mother. Even though things were vise-grip-tight financially, there wasn't enough money in the closet to make a significant change all at once. She decided to take a flyer on a new lottery game and wish for a multi-numerical alignment in the stars. Once she began, she never missed one Powerball drawing. She was as dedicated to spending the coins as her father was collecting them. And she always played the same numbers, which were significant to her father in some way. At first, she did this in the face of betrayal and as an act of implausible retribution, to have the chance to buy more than time. But after years of devotion, the practice became simply habitual, rather than a distant beacon of salvation.

Then one lonely Thursday morning, with the aftertaste of cereal still in her mouth and some crusties lodged in the corners of her eyes, the television broadcasted a graphic of the winning numbers from the previous night. She felt as if she'd begun to hallucinate in black, white, and red, and she became a Vitruvian statue on the floor of her kitchenette. She was out cold longer than she'd realized, but when she came back to consciousness, the wood floor felt like a personal cloud, the tulips on the wallpaper began to smell like roses, and the air tasted supreme.

After all of the hullaballoo and media attention, the retaining of legal council and financial advising, the bottom line of her bank account swelled to nine crooked digits, all in front of the decimal. It was unclear whether or not Zeus's father ever knew of the lump sum winnings. There hadn't been any communication since his infinity-yard dash the hell out of there, which for Zeus's mother, was the strangest of estrangements. But there they were, a family of two, standing on top of the world in a ground-floor apartment rental, ready to elevate. With the fiscal flexibility of a pair of contortionists, they were able to purchase their own apartments in locations that stretched across the continental United States. Zeus stayed in N.Y.C. and his mother moved to L.A., the city of angels, for her maiden voyage. Even though the actual hang time between mom and son diminished, they felt as close as ever. They spoke of their fortunate status and the joys they experienced daily, as they were connected by an invisible arch of fiber optics, a rainbow of communication anchored by two very large pots of gold.

After his pancakes, Zeus is both contemplative and digestive. He perches himself on a butter-soft leather chair and props his untied white AF1s on top of a glass table. The base of the table was cut from the wide trunk of an old cypress tree. Its surface is sanded and leveled to expose the rings through half-inch glass. The rings kinked inward where there were concavities in the bark and were difficult to count, but the tree had been old. He is reclined and shirtless, with his thumbs tucked into his denim pockets. He mindlessly taps his fingers, from pinky to pointer, in arrhythmic clusters of four. Zeus rolls his head from side to side and listens to the sounds of thousands of hairs being pressed against the couch. They are loud in his head, like waves of passing rainstorms. His appreciation for his bird's eye view of the city hasn't diminished over the past few fortunate years. His gaze soars over the curvature of the Brooklyn Bridge as if his eyeballs have wings themselves. He follows the flight of sight and imagines gliding right through the cathedral arches of the westernmost tower and overlooking the specks of the traveling masses, which spark some thoughts on the metaphysics of predation.

On the glass table there's a stack of about a hundred baseball cards that obscure some of the outer rings of the cypress tree. The cards are stacked into a rectangular prism beside a pair of black magic markers. The baseball cards had been pulled at random from one of his shoeboxes on the top shelf in his closet. There are two rows of five shoeboxes that store thousands of cards. They're all from one collection, the *1987 Topps Baseball Bubble Gum Cards*. The cards have a woodgrain border and a color photo of the player inside an oblong hexagon. The player's name is in **ALL CAPS** at the bottom right of the card and balanced by the team's logo in the top left corner.

When Zeus was a young kid, the cards were given to him by his mother's brother, a man he called Unk, as a consolation gift when his father left. His Unk told him they'd gotten divorced, but it wasn't clear if there was any legal weight to the claims of the D word. It was only apparent that the elder Mr. Woodson had the ability to disappear in midair.

His Unk told him that he should handle them with care and save them for a long time, and that one day they'd be worth a lot of coin. Too young to understand the concept of future monetary value beyond a half-hour wait on the subway en route to spend birthday cash at the F.A.O. acropolis, he at once began to tear into the boxes of baseball cards. He didn't know any of the players or that much about baseball, except that he lived where the blood was Yankee blue. He knew this because, along with the baseball cards, his Unk had also given him a Yankee jersey that was a size too big. When young Zeus pulled it over his t-shirt, his Unk said something about how the pinstripes have been known to find their way under the skin and become tangled veins that are too complex to ever unravel.

Zeus sorted the cards into categories, his favorite uniforms, favorite names, best action shots, and sometimes by the statistics on the back. Since they were handled often, some of the cards had blunted edges and creases. Technically this decreases the value of the cards, but they were never really going to live up to his Unk's intention to be a good investment anyway.

In the eighties, the baseball card collecting boom was in full swing. Lifelong collectors began to realize the rarity of having complete sets from the early years and pristine gems of the titans of the American pastime. Many mothers and fathers had thrown out their kids' collections in exchange for attic space, or when they left the home for their own, or to serve in the armed forces. Also, the lifespan of a typical 1952 baseball card didn't lend itself to immaculacy. It may have gone something like this: born from a wax package next to a sugar-dusted stick of bubble gum (although the *bubble* part is pushing it), then shuffled lightning-fast by a practiced hand into a stack of cards, then traded to a friend with the phrase *I'll give you him for him* (which could've been a question, a suggestion, or a demand), then used as a temporary bookmark in an algebra class, then woven into the spokes of a bicycle tire to make it sound like motorcycle when it cornered a neighborhood curb, and finally, when it had been wrinkled and weathered, it was retired, laid to rest horizontally in a box.

The players on the front were put in motion by the voice on the radio broadcast and by the imagination of the kid. This cardboard life wasn't recognized by everyone, so the prized cards might look worn and insignificant in the judgement of the inexperienced.

When the masses began to hitch onto the bandwagon, they viewed baseball cards with dollar signs in their eyes. In turn, the baseball card companies responded to the capitalistic boom and rewarded the customers with overproduction in the 1980s. Now they were being opened with medical gloves and tweezers and then kept in plastic sleeves behind locked glass, right along with the romance of the whole thing. Baseball cards lost their claim as a form of boyhood currency. The hunt was on for rookie cards in mint condition and uncommon error cards, butwith the unending flow rushing into the market, the investment well was rendered dry.

As a kid, Zeus enjoyed studying and shuffling through his large collection. But now he uses them as note cards for a connection to adulthood with a nostalgic twist. With black magic markers he writes down ideas for the day, quick reminders, shopping lists, and phone numbers right over the faces and statistics of the sluggers and hurlers. Sometimes he doodles in facial hair designs: handlebars, Zappas, soul patches, Dalis, flavor savers, and Rasputins. Some are covered with spiked mohawks, metal hair, Ghost Rider fires, afro-picked ?uestloves, and Coolios. Before long, neck tattoos, facial modifications, piercings, and gauges are seen as common among the players from the Reagan era. Some members of the steroid class were adorned with cartoon syringes in the veins of their arms, which required some serious and attentive needlework, marker-wise. One time Zeus circled six numbers on the back of a card because he thought they might bring good luck on a Powerball ticket. But he also thought that it would be greedy to play again despite the odds, even though he still had some of his grandfather's silver dollars. The only cards he didn't mark up were the members of the Bronx Bombers. Zeus preserved the pinstriped-likes of The Man of Steal, Louisiana Lightning, Rags, Pags, Sweet Lou, Mr. May (courtesy of The Boss), Little Willie, and the devoutly worshipped, Donnie Baseball[27].

There were subsets within the Topps '87 series like the Future Stars, Record Breakers, and All-Stars, but the one that appealed to Zeus the most was the *Turn Back the Clock* collection, which had a picture of an older card embedded on the new card. Specifically, it was the Rickey Henderson card that commemorated the breaking of Lou Brock's stolen base record in 1982.

Rickey finished that year with 130. At the time he was playing for Oakland, and on the card he looked quite spritely wearing the A's home white uniform with a lime and lemon helmet. Zeus liked the way Rickey was leading off in his stance as a base marauder. He looked focused and calm with disregard for the risk, a kleptomaniac ready for the heist. That year Rickey Henderson stole home plate *twice*—which is baseball's equivalent to grand larceny—and is one of the hardest things to do in a game.

While Zeus sits by his cypress table overlooking the city, he notices the Rickey card on top of the stack. He begins to think in a counter-clockwise direction, setting him off and running to deal with some of the questions he's been harboring deep in his skull about the stolen moments of his own home life.

The reason why fathers abandon the nest is usually the same. It's an attempt for a rebirth. It's an attempt to feel something for the first time, again. There are compounding elements[28] for each man that affect the brain—at first to numb, then to excite. What these flying fathers don't understand is that a rebirth doesn't fix anything or change anything within. It starts the process over and assures the same diminished returns of seeing a movie for the second time. Sure, they'll see some things that flew by at the premiere, but the sequence is set in stone, the lines memorized, the actors un-aged, and the element of surprise reduced to expectancy.

Before young men become fathers, they are singular men that have dreams that splay across a wide spectrum with endless possibilities and infinite scenarios to explore. It's as if they're looking out the glass door of a glass house to the flat line of the horizon, way out of reach. They wander and try to conquer the world as a vagabond, moving across open fields of giant sundowns and into lucent cities where all roads lead to roam.

But over the course of life, their time is consumed with demands, a job that saps the daylight hours, insurance payments, rent on the first of the month, office politics, and remote eldercare. Their thoughts become less adventurous, their dreams less abstract, as they're now directed toward loosening the grip of life's demands and dealing with consequences. They realize the occasional drink has turned routine, that the fear of sexual inadequacy has hindered their resolve, that they don't smile nearly as much as they used to, and that the glass door has become an apartment window.

Thankfully, there are moments that fade the demands to the periphery when they meet a companion, someone with whom they can stand side-by-side and share new visions. And as they move closer to the apartment window, the horizon briefly expands once again. But for these future avian men, the hand-holding and picture-posing doesn't last long when they become the father of their firstborn son. Maybe it's the thinning hair, inlaws turned outlaws, sexual obscurity, budgeting a twenty-five year mortgage, home eldercare, increasing waist sizes, or the contempt for a hollow career, but he will again seek the escapism that dwindles his perspective dreams to the eye of a needle. And the only thing he can see is his firstborn son way out in the distance, standing in his own glass house with possibilities spread out in all directions. He feels the jealousy replace his bone marrow. That's when the wings begin to flutter.

There was a time when Zeus had a lot of questions about growing up without a father. He couldn't tell if it mattered too much, or not at all. His mom, after giving all the answers she could, decided to set up an informal meeting with a nice man from their church. And he was nice, but it seemed more like a therapy session. Zeus felt that the man unintentionally sympathized with the wrong party, that he was the one that had to bear the cross of understanding. He said, "*You* have to realize you're not the problem. You were never the problem. Let's look at the reality of the situation, what's here and now, and be grateful. Don't think about what you don't have, be thankful for what you do—good health, a great city, good friends, and a loving mother. As for your father, you have to understand that he was going through something, that he was dealing with his own demons. Understand it had nothing to do with *you*."

On the contrary, from the stories his mom told him, he felt that his father must have made his decisions directly to avoid his existence. Every dinner turned cold, every opportunity to bond exchanged for blow, every time he said he was on his way home, then turned left instead of right, and parked his car in someone else's garage—and every time there was an empty pew seat next to their small family on Sunday mornings—those were decisions to escape the ones waiting for him with open arms. It probably mattered too much.

Now Zeus has friends at his sides and a fortune of women giving him full support from below. He's surrounded in all directions, except up. Because his father was never there to shade him from the ultraviolet rays of the sun, double-check his seatbelt, show him how to sound out multisyllabic words and carry the 1, give him guidance when his voice began to change, teach him how to throw a curve and cook on a grill, explain why table manners are important and how to change a flat, young Jesús Woodson filled the void above with the loyalty of a Father that had no beginning or ending, a description he'd heard in church. And one day when he was in middle school, he learned that a circle was the perfect shape and that it was a sign of genius to be able to draw one freehand. Over the course of the year, Zeus's notebook was filled with approximated circles during class lectures. When his teacher noticed the doodles, he further mystified Zeus by explaining that even if he was able to draw a circle, the gravitational pull of the Earth would ever so slightly warp the planar surface of the paper, and the perfection would be compromised. A true circle is only theoretical. And when his math teacher further described it using the exact phrase, *no beginning or ending*, he made a connection between his idea of God and a new divine geometry. His Father took on the qualities of a circle, something that can only exist beyond this world, and it comforted him.

But of late, Zeus has been confronting his own evolving views. The struggle between his heartfelt beliefs and observed realizations hasn't reached homeostasis. He's beginning for the first time, not to look to the Circle, but right through it. He's finding truths in places he never expected. Though he acknowledges to himself that what he sees is only possible with the Circle as the primary guide, the initial frame of reference.

The only memory he has with the family trio still intact was when his mother and father took him down to the beach at Coney Island for the first time. They'd gotten there in the late afternoon when the off-shore breezes were escorting the rest of the sunbathers home. The trio was moving against the flow, past the families with rolled-up towels, bottles of warm water, and collapsed umbrellas. The sand was soft and thick, like clay. They walked to a place near a jetty along the shoreline. His father began digging a hole to act as a well, he explained. His mother held three buckets of diminishing sizes, Matryoshka style. His father motioned to his mother to hand him the first bucket. He used both hands to dig and then filled each successive bucket. His mother smiled at him and his father as she leveled the sand off with the pinky side of her hand. He remembered the squinted smiles and the way the sand felt as it sifted through his fingers and toes. When he picked up a fistful, the little grains rushed through his hand like gentle tickles. He looked closely at the sand that remained in his palm. He expected to see only shades of beige, but there were pinks and whites, tans and blue-grays, and the reflective luster of mica. Each grain was its own little rock before it returned the dunes of anonymity.

His father swept together a base of wet sand and motioned to his mother to hand him the largest bucket. They exchanged wordless smiles as she passed the sand, her arm slightly quivering due to the weight. With a point of her finger and raised eyebrows, his mother suggested a new location. She cautioned him that it was unwise to build their castle, or anything important, on a weak foundation.

His father stacked the pails of sand into a basic three-tiered structure. Then he pulled out several small shells from his pants pocket. Each shell had its own purpose as a tool, some were carving shells and some were pressed into the sandcastle to create windows and doors. His father reached into the irrigation hole often. He'd cup the water and spill it over the sand to create an adhesive effect. When young Jesús put his cheek close to the castle to look inside the windows, he saw that his mother was writing something in the sand. The sun was tucking itself away for the night and the long shadows of the sandcastle became one with the darkened topography.

He stood up to admire the finished structure and felt that it was something he could never reproduce himself. But his admiration was interrupted by his parents' voices, as each exchange escalated in volume. There seemed to be no cause from his perspective, but in the confusion of the actions above him, he saw the sweeping colors of his father's khakis and his mother's polka dot dress. He saw black-rimmed sunglasses fall to the ground and their blanket crumpled by angered footsteps. Sand from the castle was kicked up and sprayed into his eyes. He closed them and tried to shield himself from any more pain as he cried into his fingers. The sounds of their voices grew distant. With limited vision he could only see the dimmed neon lights of the Coney Island rides all the way up the beach. When he began to run toward the voices, his first stride collapsed the layered sandcastle. It shattered and fell in ruins, as glass before the fire. Jesús regained his footing, but he was too slow to keep up with disappearing khakis. It was the last time he ever saw his father, running from the sea, running from him.

He eventually made it to the fault line where the sand meets the boardwalk. There was no polka dot dress in sight. He turned one hundred eighty degrees and looked back to where the sandcastle was. He wasn't sure if he should go toward the water or chase a ghost toward Luna Park. Jesús saw a few whitecaps crest and dissolve.

He looked down at his bare feet, one on the sand, the other on a plank of wood. When he took a few more aimless steps, he bumped into a man's leg. It felt like he walked into a tree. He reached up for his father's hand with his own, but his father was not there. Instead, he grasped two knotted and curled fingers, and looked up at a face that was obscured by the shadows of the boardwalk lights and The Wonder Wheel, a grand and illuminated circle in the sky.

"Are you lost, kid?"

And he tilted his head all the way back and looked straight up. "Is that Heaven?"

"This is Brooklyn, little man. And *that* is a ferris wheel. It'll get you pretty high, but not quite high enough. It'll just take you around and around until you get back to where you started. Right back to Earth with the ground under your feet."

[[Σ]]

In an effort to reverse the curse of her nightmares and embolden her mornings, sometimes Suma will decide to literally waltz into work. Her footwork isn't textbook and her posture could be improved, but her rhythmic turns sell the dance well enough. She performs this in full view of her colleagues and higher-ups, early patrons and security cameras. For a moment, imagine that the front façade of the building is sliced off to create the dollhouse version of the N.Y. Public Library. And imagine Suma waltzing from left to right, moving from room to room, dancing through the ages, wars, and fantasies of humanity, before arriving at her desk, dizzy, and singing *My Blue Heaven*.

Stuck to her office mailbox are two post-it notes that curl out like neon green eyelashes. On the first note is a baseball riddle from Leon:

"Say Hey, Suma. Here's one about two players that almost made it to the Hall. If Steve Sax wanted to name his child in honor of his former Dodger teammate, Orel Hershiser, what would his name be? The answer is on the back of the other post-it."

Leon's handwriting is miniscule.

Suma picks up the second note, which has an arrow on the front that points to the bottom corner, and flips it over:

"Orel Sax."

She chuckles and writes back on a yellow post-it:

"Leon, I love it! Maybe another round at RB&Axe later. Let the rest of the presidency know. —SUΣA"

Sometimes she signs her name with the Greek notation for "summation," or "sum," in place of the M. And where initials are acceptable, her signature is just "Σ." She doesn't remember when she started to do this, but she figures it has its roots in a requisite calculus course, although her fascination with symbols started back in her basement days, and her understanding of them have been integral to some of her alteration works. She's always tailored her signature to each situation, whether for a post-it note, transcript forgery, or something more sinister and deceptive. They range from the various informal permutations of Suma, to the bubbly left-handed slant of Beverly B. Sunshine, and to the exact scribbles and loops of certain government officials when necessary.

Suma likes the Σ because it represents her life as a collective sequence where she will judge herself on the totality of her days, not the ill times at the outset where the purpose of her upbringing was to keep her down. The only thing of value she's ever been given is the gift of existence. Therefore Suma uses her inquisitiveness to find answers to the questions of skyward travel, to begin the ascent to personal freedom, determined to take the summit herself.

With the vague information she had, Suma tried to research her true origins. She narrowed her probable birthdate inside a one-year window. She looked up arrest reports in the Death Valley area, missing children postings, hospital birth records, all within a reasonable radius. She acknowledged the possibility that she'd been born far from the desert, and that the expanse was too vast to investigate. There were no details that she attained that coagulated into solid clues. Even her adopted parents that died in the crash were oddly nebulous. Her journey drifted in all directions until she'd reached every administrative dead-end sign, where all of the roads become sanded-over paths, and where traction is all but lost. Suma used this to her advantage and ran with the prevailing westerly winds. She became a silent traveler, an unseen tumbleweed across the desolate landscape to progress. When her transcontinental journey was manifest she threw an anchor down in the New York Harbor, a safe place to be born anew.

There were times she didn't have high regard for her name. When it came to mentioning her graduation status at Columbia, *Summa Cum Laude*, bedroom jokes ensued, followed by muffled chuckles and blushed cheeks. Usually, any shades of red that emanate from her come from the fire simmering just behind her bellybutton. From ninety-three million miles away, a number as rounded as its outline, our sun maintains a calm presence despite the continuous drumroll of nuclear explosions raging within. She is the mother of all our nature. She is our star that can encourage a budding flower and fuel a rainbow, but can also burn flesh and destroy vision. And like her, Suma is at times, also a violent femme.

[[✳]]

Roosevelt is still wearing his clothes from last night, except for one shoe that he managed to kick off before passing out. He's lying diagonally across his bed, belt buckle down, his head turned to one side. The side of his face exposed to the halogen sun, which was left on all night, highlights his scarred eyebrow. The scar is a single break in the action that interrupts the sideways flow of hair. Even though he's still asleep, his eye is open a sliver. His lips are squished against the pillow and resemble the mouth of a boxer on the wrong side of a left hook. With the television on Local 1 News in the background for the duration of the night, the audio entered his head and influenced his dreams. His stubble matches the patterns of patchy grass in early spring. Roosevelt's phone is on silent, and if not for its vibrations atop the nightstand, he would've existed in solitude for awhile longer. After several consecutive calls, the sounds of synchronous bees kill his slumber.

"...Hey, man."

"What up. Where were you last night? Mad people were looking for you. You didn't answer texts or anything. You O.K.?"

"I'm sorry, B... Man, I've been doing this writing thing, you know, and it's been really messing with me. I've been sleeping at all the wrong times and it's not bearing the fruit I hoped for. I mean, there's a lot of material, but I don't think it's going anywhere. When I go over it, it's like reading someone else's LSD trip."

"You been doing that for a minute."

"Yeah man, ever since my vacation from The Office."

"You going be around tonight? I had my eye on a few spots we can piece. One is this new garden in the park. I thought we could paint some flowers on the bottom of this retaining wall and each flower could be one letter of our names. You know, different colors, different flowers. A spray bouquet. Also I had an idea for chroming out some sewer grates and making some graf coins, you know, with our portraits on 'em. And there's an easy one I want to hit right quick. It's a moving van that's clean white off the showroom floor and parked nearby. It has those plain hubcap joints that look like silver dinner plates, monarchy style."

"Then set the table, brother."

"Four wheels, four square meals."

"So this might not be that quick."

"The security is lame."

"How many colors are you holding?"

"I got the whole palette with the minis."

"Cook it up."

"One Belgian waffle for breakfast, sushi for lunch, then penne a la vodka, and an ice cream sundae."

"Pretty bold ambitions, but I'm sure they'll appreciate that."

"It's a rental van. Commercial plates. So what do you say about tonight?"

"Yeah, let's do that. After this experiment I have to get back to normal. Damn, I didn't even mean to be that literal. It's been too much."

"Good deal, Rozey. So last night, you'll like this: this guy walks up to me all limping sideways with one eye open and mumbling to himself about some shit. And he just walks right up to me and starts saying, '*Are you normal? Huh? Are you normal? Huh? Huh?!*' I started rolling, man. I was laughing like, '*Yes...and No, sir.*' And then he kept limping down the street asking whoever else was around the same shit."

"A little too close to home. Maybe he was undercover."

"True. Deep cover."

"I'll tell you, when I've needed a break after writing, I've been going down to **[COLOSSUS]**. That's my official joint now. Two nights ago I was there and this woman at the bar was having a bowl of soup. She was with her friend, a real cutie, and she was clanking her spoon around the whole time. I didn't want to waste time, so I started talking to the cutie, but I couldn't concentrate on anything we were saying. I was just watching this woman damn near play the steel drum with her spoon. And when she finally filled it up with soup, she brought it to her mouth uncomfortably fast. Strangest thing I've seen in a while. It was a silver flash of fury. I swear she was straight up attacking the spoon. As far as I know, she probably knocked out a tooth or two when it was all said and done. It was the complete destruction of soup and beauty in several fell scoops. Voracious. Loud. It was like sixty RPMs of sound and fury, which is why I kept calling the soup splasher *Macbeth*. She was like, '*Why are you calling me that?*'"

"Yeah, why'd you call her that?"

"Wait. Hold on. Let me check on this news for a second."

"No doubt. What is it?"

"...A strange thing."

"_____."

"Something else happened that night when I was waiting to go in the speakeasy. I was next to the sculptures by the front window. It was only for a moment, but there was this woman hanging up a poster for an art performance uptown. She was on the other side of the glass and I didn't see her too clearly, but I'm pretty sure she was just mentioned on the news. Looks like she was shot last night up in Harlem."

"She O.K.?"

"They said she's recovering. There's just too much violence right now. Thing is, after I left **[COLOSSUS]** I checked her poster and I thought I'd go check it out. Maybe write about it. I never made it though. Blame it on sleep depravation and cognac, but I wasn't that far away, actually."

"You could've been there..."

"Yeah. That always gets me, the consequentialism stuff. If I'd been there, would my presence possibly have altered the trajectory of the bullet? Depending on where I might've been standing, I could've influenced where other people were. It might've been nothing or it could've been a lot worse too. Hold on."

"_____."

"The news just said they don't know if it was a stray bullet or if she was targeted. What about this, I mean, if this was a hit job and my presence were to change where everyone was, maybe the bullet doesn't connect. Then the shooter opens up with the rest of his clip. Who the hell knows, man."

"Then thank God for the cognac."

"I play these scenarios out in my head all the time. I mean, that fact that we're talking about this right now might be preventing you from going out and getting your morning coffee. And since you're not there to take a space in line, there's a woman who gets her coffee earlier. She walks out of the café at the exact moment when an overly confident man in an apartment high above is trying to remove his old air conditioner from the window. Now this air conditioner is one of those prehistoric joints that weighs a ton, and when it starts to slip away he can't pull it back in. It falls out of the window and drops straight down. It doesn't even tumble in the air, just perpendicularly straight down toward the woman, and flattens her like a human pancake with strawberry jelly. That should've been you and I'm clam-happy that it wasn't. But let's say it *was* you, and when your family sues the overly confident man, the two opposing litigators who would have otherwise never met, fall in love and have a daughter. They move to a town without any second floors and raise her there. She turns a fantastic education and years of traveling abroad into a career as a multi-lingual, first-class logician. With precise arguments, she persuades global leaders to end nuclear proliferation and begin the dismantling of existing warheads. And for her closing act, she uses pristine logical arguments to convince a nefarious lone wolf not to launch the last nuclear weapon in existence, which was aimed directly at the intersection of 42nd and Broadway. And she does this all over the phone."

"Man, that's too bad. I already have my coffee."

"It's like those arguments about the consequences of abortions, like, did we lose out on a future emancipator, a genocidal monster, or a below-average dentist? And what are the effects on humanity? The question is completely unanswerable because it's impossible to know how the ripples of existence would compare with the unripples of non-existence. Is that a word?"

"I'd go with the below-average dentist. That would be a giant step up from the last one I went to. She was straight nasty."

"Well, it might be that the ripples and the unripples cancel out to an equilibrium, no matter what happens. If you look from far enough away, it's quiet and motionless water that makes up the oceans. In the long run, action equals inaction. And not to go Shakespeare again, but the choice is irrelevant. It only seems to matter locally and immediately. Time is the ultimate distortion because even eternity is a slave to it."

"_____."

"Maybe that's why I've been able to do what I've been doing for so long. I'm introspective and loving of the here and now, but when it's convenient, I think universally and convince myself to care less."

"What I understand is that, when you go on like this, it doesn't matter if I listen to you or not."

With a groan, Roosevelt bench presses himself up, swings his legs around, and scoots off his bed. During the sudden whirl, his phone disappears into the folds of his wrinkled comforter. He unclasps his belt and pulls it with his left hand away from his body, letting it swoosh and intermittently thwack through the loops. As the belt curls and flips around, the buckle jangles on the old wood floor until it assumes the position of a comatose snake. He unbuttons his pants and slides them down his legs, where they scrunch like an accordion around his ankles. He pulls his shirt over his head, even though it could've been opened Superman-style. All of these movements to get undressed jostle his dreams to the forefront of his mind.

Roosevelt is in front of a mirror, with each eye independently looking straight ahead at its obverse. Roosevelt-prime is a reflection in a false dimension. He stands alone in a room, fully contained in his own skin. But when he looks around the room in all 360° of directions, the other surfaces become mirrored as well. Wherever his eyes fall, the opposing mirrors work together to show his reflective clones trailing off to imperceptible sizes. There is quickly an infinite series of selves projected outward along every possible radius in an ever-expanding sphere, but still contained within the single room. Roosevelt feels frustrated when he realizes he can't see all of them at once. He wants to acknowledge each one, no matter how far away they appear, but it seems impossible. His blood begins to simmer. When it reaches a raging boil, his right hand folds into a clenched fist. He throws a powerful jab to the left eye of Roosevelt-prime, a broken window to his soul. When fist hits fist-prime, the violence of the energy transfers to the plane of the mirror in waves along the surface. But the moments of liquidity in the structure aren't supported, and its underlying crystalized nature is revealed when the fracturing begins. It ends with a spiderweb of cracks. Roosevelt examines the small complex polygons at the center, then the obtuse triangles and anorexic parallelograms as he follows the cracks to the outskirts of the crater. He tries to look around the room again, but this time his vision is fixed forward, with the colors relenting to the spectral shades of charcoal. He takes careful notice of what's right in front of him. And he finds that with all the cracks and all the newly formed individual mirrors with three-dimensionally complex angles, that they cover all spherical possibilities within the rectangular prism, and he's able to see every side of himself, all at once. The fractured pieces become his eyes, exponentially enhanced, and he no longer has to look around or anywhere else. It's through destruction that creation is possible.

As soon as this realization materializes, blood lines the edges of a concave dodecahedron, the cradle of the glassquake. But there aren't any drips of deep red. Everything's in zero gravity, cubism in suspension.

When the attraction to the Earth is restored, dream-physics give way to planetary parameters, and the mirrored glass begins to bleed down the fault lines of the shattered pattern, forming a storm of cherry thunderbolts. The cracks bleed so profusely that it covers the entire mirror and blinds his omnipotent visions of a fractured self. As Roosevelt returns to an uneasy solitude, he's standing naked in an imagined room, and is reminded that anyone can be reduced to a single color.

Roosevelt shakes his head and massages his temples. He feels around for his phone on his bed. When he finds it, he presses play on Kanye, and go-mode on himself.

[It's what you all been waitin' for ain't it...]

He rises from his money-stuffed mattress and takes small shuffling steps to the bathroom with his pants still around his ankles.

[...they can't stand it, they want something new...]

When he tries to step out of his pants, one side is stubborn to the point of having its own mind, a mind with an intent to provoke. He lets it hold its irritating position the whole time as he brushes his teeth. His morning breath is kicking like Bruce Lee, so, first things first. He unsuccessfully tries to wiggle his leg free while swishing some mouthwash. Finally, it's a roundhouse to a phantom solar plexus that sends the pants back into the bedroom. He stands there as naked as the day *after* the day he was born[29], turns on the shower, and rotates the temperature dial to eleven o'clock—doomsday hot.

[...here's another hit..]

Before he jumps into the shower, which is as dangerous as it sounds, he faces the mirror from his dream. It's a smooth surface without a single blood cell on it. Roosevelt exaggerates a smile to check his teeth. He clenches his jaw and watches the muscles by his temples bulge and subside. He looks at the veins that run over them, swelling like the Tigris and Euphrates.

[...we outta here baby...]

Roosevelt is off to work and ready to put an end to his abstraction project, a finish to a lonely   .   After all of the ramblings down the paths to strange land, it's time to bring clarity to his state of incoherence, and scribble a summation of the whole experience. If Jimi Hendrix were to ask him, his reply would be in the affirmative.

Roosevelt runs a newsstand on the northwest corner of Houston Street and 2nd Avenue, just steps away from the subway entrance. His work seems quite rote from the outside, but really, he is more of a conversationalist, counselor, and friend to the passersby, his customers. His newsstand is one of the first of the next generation of N.Y.C. newsstands, which is noticeably larger than its predecessors. Its modern design combines beach-glass-colored resin and smooth cement. It's a rounded rectangular prism with white lighting that hugs the curves along the top of the newsstand and down the sides half-way to the sidewalk. From afar, when illuminated, it looks like it's floating a few feet above the ground. The outside of the two side walls both have framed digital advertisements that changes every minute. Roosevelt's entrance is in the back, a reinforced concrete door with a lock system that would make a skittish recluse proud. When the newsstand is open for business, the front door swings up from the ground and slides half-way into a slot in the ceiling. It creates a small alcove in front that protects his customers and products from any rain or sunshine. The solar-paneled roof is standard, but unnecessary, since it accounts for a very small percentage of the incoming voltage. This is because this particular newsstand requires a hundred times more voltage than the average newsstand. See, Roosevelt is the sole proprietor of The Office, as it's unofficially known, a business run entirely within the newsstand. The Office is a cellphone babysitting service he developed over a year ago, kind of by accident. Adjacent to the newsstand is a large office building whose shadow gives a half-day of shade to Roosevelt's shop. It houses scores of business headquarters, satellite agencies, and meeting spaces. The genesis of The Office happened when a friend of a friend of Roosevelt's was in a bind, an amorous one of sorts. This man worked at the building that towered over the newsstand and needed to be "at work" without actually being there. Ever since AppleFacegate, the secret lives of many boyfriends and girlfriends, fiancés and fiancées, husbands and wives, were exposed to their respective insignificant others. The relationships that tried to weather the storm had to deal with trust issues, above all. In most cases, the ones who were hurt or suspicious began to require their counterpart to enable constant GPS tracking on their phone. And while the ones who were being monitored could turn off the feature, notifications would no doubt be sent out at once, setting off the bells and whistles of infidelity. So the trick was to leave the phone on and traceable, as to raise no suspicions, but at the same time, get away with whatever it was that caused the distrust in the first place, and find some freedom within the matrix—whether it was fulfilling a sex fetish in a hotel, a few bumps of sugar up the nose, or both at the same time. In the case of the friend of a friend, he wanted to venture off to a neighborhood that he'd told his wife he'd never visit again. Roosevelt agreed to hold his phone, as to give the impression to his wife that he was hard at work, but for an hourly cash fee. He agreed to keep it charged and, if necessary, respond to texts with very general statements. For Roosevelt, it ended up being almost no work at all, and it gave him some extra cash money in his pocket. Almost in no time, this friend of a friend told someone else about his arrangement. This second client was someone who wanted to get out of the closet on occasion and was pleased that this offered some discretion. Even though this person only had a loose connection to him, when he approached Roosevelt with the same offer, he obliged—especially with the newsprint industry hurting and the candy business souring. One afternoon, while monitoring the two phones, the insistent wife of the first client was texting the hell out of the phone, and Roosevelt replied: *Sorry, I'm at the office, I'll call you as soon as I can. Love you.* And there it was, right there in plain text: The Office. It all clicked for Roosevelt at that moment. The Office would be a discrete resource for personal latitude for those with expendable cash. The building next door would provide an excellent cover for the GPS location of their phones. Whether or not their morals were expendable, would not be his business. The Office, a recharging babysitter service on one end, and an accomplice on the other. He wouldn't judge these people and he wouldn't ask questions, except for a reference sheet he would have them fill out. The sheet would include a few of the basics: appropriate text responses in their style, a weekly drop-off and pick-up schedule, a reminder that the phones were to be kept silent and vibrationless, an understanding that they had to provide their own cover stories for working at the office building, a second emergency number, and a plain, resealable envelope with any further instructions along with the up-front cash payment for the week. He'd also insist that they buy one newspaper per visit, whereby he'd place the envelope that contained the charged cellphone minus the cash in the fold.

At a rate of twenty bucks an hour, he made an extra $400 per week from his two loyal customers, which helped cover his costs for the month. The Office started out sort of innocently, but week by week, business grew in numbers that correlated to the Fibonacci Sequence[30], for a total of 377 clients at the end of the fourteenth week. Men outnumbered women at about a 4:1 ratio, and the cases where he couldn't quite tell, the numbers were limited. Roosevelt's anti-marketing tactics of discretion spread by word of mouth like gossip on fire. It seems that the ones who need privacy in a very public world all seem to know each other. And for them, the expense of inventive confidentiality was easily warranted.

At any one moment, Roosevelt could be in control of two hundred phones. So he made logistical adjustments to his business model, including expanding hours in both directions, ordering more newspapers than any other newsstand in Manhattan, and hiring two friends from his prior career. These new employees went way back with Roosevelt and were trusted partners in grime, helping him sweep the clients' dirt under the rug. They took over when he needed some time for himself, which had been increasing of late. He offered two levels of service: one for charging and storing for $20/hour, and another that includes email and text message services for $40/hour. He researched state and city laws, of which there were none specific to what he was doing, but he knew this extra income would the blame for any negative outcome—so he was careful. As far as being exposed or charged with tax evasion, it wasn't a major concern because several police officers and government officials were clients, as Roosevelt could tell by the texts he monitored. That was his queen piece on the chessboard of mutual destruction. They knew that he knew enough, that he shouldn't be crossed or checked, and that he lived in a castle protected by unseen knights, armored with information. The secrets he knew were vast.

There was one more area of concern he had to address, one of anonymity and electricity. His monthly bill was subsidized by the city government and had a limit on available voltage, which was no doubt examined by bureaucratic suits. First, to conceal the cellphones, Roosevelt bought a new refrigerator that was never intended to cool anything but speculation. He customized it with slots for charging cellphones and a shelf for his black books of client information. Second, he used his knowledge of engineering to solve the issue of missing power. The best solution, he figured, would be to tap into the voltage running through the third rail of the subway line just below the newsstand. The train rumbled by every few minutes and pushed out a mix of stale air and exhaust through the grates, breezing by the newsstand like a polluted zephyr. Roosevelt knew the arteries of the subway system like the back of his veiny hands, where the hidden tunnels and construction sites were, and the general way they operated in the underground. One night, he shut down early. He wrapped warning tape around the newsstand, posted false infrastructure contracts, and with his two employees, wore the necessary reflective work vests. If anyone asked what was up, he had his story arrow-straight. He'd say he had to conform to city code while making aesthetics renovations, and then make a complaint about government overreach. But no one intervened; no one seemed to notice. It made Roosevelt reconsider his clientele and their possible connections. He drilled a hole through the concrete and dropped down the cord that would bring over a thousand volts into the newsstand. He connected and then closed the electrical circuit, running the lifeblood of the tunnels above ground to benefit members of the underworld.

Even after he cut into the profits to overpay his workers, he was taking home about $30,000 per week, a rate of a cool 1.5 million per year. Eight months into the business, he had to remove some of the springs from his mattress and replace them with stacks of Benjamins. After one year, it became lumpy and uncomfortable. So he stuffed his closet with canvas duffel bags that were starting to hemorrhage along the zipper lines. They were filled with Ulysseses and Andrews. With respect to the available space in the bags, Alexanders, Abrahams, and Georges were no longer acceptable currency.

So, after more than a year in The Office, with the long hours and stress of both hiding money and the secret lives of others, Roosevelt is thinking it's high time to be getting on his way. He tells his right-hand-man, Bolden, and Ellison on the left, that he's going to take some time off and sketch an outline for the future of The Office. With solid time off for the first time in a long time, he begins to write and reset the mechanics of his daily life by blurring them into the obscurity of his dreams. It's an annihilation of his routine, and the only way for Roosevelt to move forward with clarity.

After his break of contemplation and repletion, he tells his men of his plan to turn The

Office over to them. He wants them to get a slice of the pie, but suggests they box up the operation after a few months. He feels that their client base is now too large to control and that there are too many variables that can negatively affect them. He says he's going to help them in the transition phase, but reiterates that the ride is nearing an abrupt end. He proposes they begin to drastically increase the service rate. This will cut down on their overall clientele and reduce the voltage to what's legally available. He advises they price themselves out of the market they created, while recommending some of the copycat services that had emerged in recent months. These copycats are found in other legitimate storefronts and high-class restaurants. There's a hotel concierge who's taking it to the next level by taking phones on phantom trips around the city and beyond while the GPS assures the tracker that the movements are legit. Another company, Symbiotic Central Management, has begun to use voice manipulation technology to answer the calls of their loved ones.

Everything will be complete after the transition, with the eventual full transfer from Bolden and Ellison to the next law-abiding keeper of the newsstand, someone who'll return the stand to the genuine business of selling daily papers, dirty magazines, and high fructose corn syrup. The cement will be patched, the third rail supply line removed, and the three men, each in their own boat, will row off into the harbor sunset with sails made of money to pursue new horizons. At least, that's the plan.

This afternoon, with Ellison and Bolden at the helm, Roosevelt escapes to a nearby café for some time to scribble the summation of his abstraction project in his journal. On the short walk there, he can't decide between tea or coffee. On this transition day, he feels mostly at peace, with nothing but opportunity and reality in front of him, the self-imposed phantasmagoric confusion trailing far behind. At the counter he takes out a five spot. Coffee wins again.

THE MORE WE PRETEND,
THE MORE TRUE THE EXPERIENCE.
THE MORE SHALLOW THE DAY, PERHAPS,
THE MORE ABYSMAL THE DREAM.

GOODNIGHT. THEN BEGIN.

STAND BEFORE THE BLACK DOOR,
OPENING TO STARLESS SPACE.
REMEMBER TO
FLEX THE THIGHS, THEN RELAX THE FACE.
NOW BREATHE IN THE WIND,
WHILE THE RULES ARE ERASED.

[[

FLYINGANDSOARINGTHROUGHNONEMPTINESSWITHPOWERTHROUGHOUTAND
KNOWLEDGETOCREATEEVERYTHINGFORTHEFIRSTTIMEAND
BESOPERFECTWHERETHEREISNOTHINGLEFTTODOAND
FEARSAREREPLACEDBYJOINTPLEASURECOGNACANDOLDFASHIONEDBITTERSAND
NOTHINGISLOSTEXCEPTWEAKNESSAND
WORDSARENOLONGERPARTOFOURVOCABULARYAND
SPIRITUALITYISFORSUCKERSBECAUSEHEAVENISTHISRIGHTHEREAND
SEXANDLOVEANDVANILLAMODELINGCOMESTOSWALLOWAND
MAKETHINGSAOKALRIGHTSMOOTHASPIEAND
ITISTHESHADOWOFACTIONTHOUGHTFEELINGTHATBINDSAND
COOLSOURDIGITALSOULSFROMTHEATONCELIVINGANDDYINGSUNAND
ARENTWEALLTHESAMEANYWAYAND
PLEASUREBECOMESSOOVERWHELMINGANDUNNECESSARYBUTISTILLSHINESAND
REIGNSSUPREMEFORNOWCOMMALIKEMEAND
YOU

]]

CONQUERED ARE THE PURE,
AND SAVED ARE THE LIVES.
NOW RETURN TO SWEET, INTRICATE EARTH,
JUST A MOMENT BEFORE I RISE.
THIS IS THE UNIVERSE,
AS SEEN FROM CLOSED EYES.

When he returns to the newsstand, Ellison is monitoring the refrigerator of cellphones and flipping through a magazine. When the streets are busy, Roosevelt likes to watch the masses. At the nearest crosswalk, there are two stationary crowds, both waiting for the signal to change. When the white man in mid-stride lights up, it looks as if two opposing armies are headed for attrition warfare. The soldiers wear high heels, oxfords, and LeBrons; custom suits, motorcycle jackets, and bright scarves. They're armed with knock-off handbags and bamboo canes, and follow behind the charge of baby-stroller chariots and beasts on leashes— the Teacup Yorkies and Toy Poodles. When the light switches, they charge full speed ahead into the clash of the front lines, yet they pass each other every single time with polished, but improvised choreography. At worst, an occasional tourist will wander aimlessly into the street and cause a cottoned elbow to brush against a nylon coat.

He closes his eyes for a long blink, feels the muscles of his eyelids relax, and takes in the sounds of the city with one breath. They're the sounds of the human experience, however beautiful or irritating, our contributions to the atonal symphony of existence. In time, he imagines he'll miss the days behind the counter of the newsstand, his conversations with customers, the glimpse into the darker world of their secret lives, the good times with Ellison and Bolden, and, like a confectionary toothpick, the constant presence of a Twizzler in his mouth.

During the downtimes, Roosevelt hopes that his future *1loveAbove* will step right up to him, lean over the rack of candy, bite the other end of the Twizzler, and draw them close together, their eyes fixed until it's The Lady and the *Stamp-one-right-here, cutie.* His *1loveAbove*, as he refers to her in his journal, is his faceless sweetheart living somewhere in this cosmopolitan of timber, somewhere traveling in elevator tree trunks and hallway branches.

"Ellison, Bolden, look out there, look around. This is our frame to how we've seen the city every day. And just to get sentimental for a second, even though the frame remains the same, we get to see the picture change with the seasons. Like when the calendar changes from May to June and women's clothes go from demure to PG-13 in a flash. The first time it happens, it's like, 'Oh right, those are what legs look like!' Or the way some of the men change with their hair patterns. See that guy walking by right there? You could tell he was starting to thin out about a year ago. Now it's shaved to the dome and he has a beard. It's like gravity only affected his hair and made it fall down to the bottom of his face. I see that all the time, probably because it's happening to me."

"You always say that. Not true, Rozey."

"I hope you're right, but you're not. I keep it short anyway, so it's only going to change by a fraction of an inch. At least, that's what I tell myself, but I always check mirrors when I walk by them. It's annoying. I know, intelligently, that it's just something that happens, 'embrace it, be a man,' I tell myself. But psychologically, it's the slow disappearance of youth."

"You're really thinking way too much about nothing."

"Exactly. My plan is to overcompensate by hitting the gym hard. Anyway, while I like when the seasons change and the girls wear less and less, one thing I'm not going to miss is all of the meaningless daily conversations about the weather. Why is that the go-to topic for so many people? Like, please, I barely know you, but give me your assessment about how the weather has been from your perspective, especially since we've all been experiencing the same weather here in the city. I need another take on it. Please proceed, O Sovereign King of Boring Conversationalists."

The lull in business comes to an end and Roosevelt slips into a trance while Bolden and Ellison take care of the transactions. A stream of characters run through his head just as they'd once passed by his newsstand. There's the fire escape floozie, the kid with chrome spinners on his wheelchair, the sweet nuts seller and his squeaky food cart, the young man who wears a space helmet, the cross-dressing tricycler. He hears someone comment on tomorrow's weather forecast to Ellison. And there's the elder man who took a nose dive from the roof and drowned himself in cement.

His stare shifts to the front display spread out before him like a jumbled rainbow of bright packaging—there are jawbreakers, jelly beans, pinwheels, menthol cigarettes, and Swisher Sweets. And anchoring the newsstand are various stacks of gray papers with headlines in bold black:

THE MONTH OF DECEMBER TO BE OFFICIALLY CHANGED TO 'CHRISTMAS'

· · ·

NY GOVERNOR TAKES AIM ON RISING GUN VIOLENCE

· · ·

HOLOGRAM FUNERALS SEEN AS TOUCHING, BUT CREEPY

· · ·

STATE TROOPERS: "IF YOU SEE SOMETHING, PRAY SOMETHING"

· · ·

UNIFIED KOREA BREAKS GUINNESS WORLD RECORD FOR LONGEST
CONGA LINE ON THE 38TH PARALLEL

· · ·

SPECIAL REPORT: INDEPENDENT INVESTIGATOR FOR APPLEFACEGATE
DISCUSSES CORE ISSUES

· · ·

FIRST HUMAN CLONE BORN OUT OF WEDLOCK

· · ·

OCULUS CLAIMS THEIR HEAVEN WILL BE BETTER THAN YOURS

The magazine covers color and pixelate the inside of the newsstand. The categories run the gamut: Sports, Women, Porn, and the occasional *Sportswomen in Porn*; Fashion, Wine, Weddings, and the seasonally-available *Fashionable Wine for Weddings*; Guns, Gossip, Parisian Travel, and the very specific *Mon Fusil Ne Kiss et Tell Pas*. The Weight-Loss section has headlines like *Get the Summer Body UR BF Always Wanteddd!!!* and *The Upside of Temporary Anorexia*. It's difficult to read the headlines of the Political section as they tend to bend forward over the rack. They are, not surprisingly, bound with a very soft spine.

In the featured section is the next generation of magazines. These Projection Mags work in conjunction with cellphones and create three-dimensional landscapes and figures that can do almost anything. They revolutionized the marketing space between the pages by placing the reader inside the ads. After uploading a body scan, the reader sees himself behind the wheels of a luxury car speeding alongside a mountain range, dressed in designer outfits, in the dugout at the World Series, or fine dining with a bombshell model of their choosing. After the dinner ads, many readers want to continue and transfer the experience onto the page that promotes exotic five-star hotels. And in no time at all, there were Projection Mags devoted entirely to pornographic templates, the *Choose Your Own Adventure* of modern erotica. They're commonly referred to as R2D2s, or Hopes (as in "*Obi-Wan Kenobi, You're My Only Hope(s)*"), and while the kinks are still being worked out—or sometimes worked in—they're selling like lemonade at double noon on Tatooine.

There's also been a return to the traditional and trusty porno magazine, newly marketed with phrases like *Internet History-Free!* and *Put Freedom Back in Your Pants!* in bright typeface on the plastic-sealed cover. The fact that some people have reverted to that type of entertainment is encouraging to Roosevelt. The two-dimensional images require more imagination, the continuation of corners, the removal of staples, and a mental diorama of your own setting coming to life. It's a push back from the burgeoning VR-SexTech companies in Silicone Valley and the wide world of internet porn, where the limits of vulgarity are pushed into honest-to-goodness biology lessons. While some magazines claim to get up close and very impersonal, internet videos don't just go up close, but *in close*, or just *in*. The curves of the body seem to have been abandoned in favor of holes. Roosevelt thinks that if someone were to insert videos of medical procedures into the hottest(?) parts of these gaping pornos, they would be indiscernible to the home viewer. Splice in a colonoscopy exam, a wisdom tooth removal, a gynecologic check-up, or even a nostril reduction surgery, with a porno title that has a military term or tactic in the title (e.g., Weapons of Ass Destruction, Drill Sergeants, Trench Raiding, Pincer Assaults, Amphibious Operations, etc.), and they'll prick their pleated pants just the same.

When Roosevelt looks at the industrial-strength refrigerator, the cellphone hub, he sees how his cash cow had reversed the aging process and became a golden calf. Behind the refrigerator is an extra large piece of cardboard, folded in half. When open, the cardboard reveals a life-sized stencil of a human body outlined in chalk, crime scene-style, with white spray paint splattered around the border of the figure and his signature atom across the midsection.

Roosevelt paints in the underground often, but not on the ground, until recently. Just days ago, when a young tattoo artist[31] was killed in the intersection adjacent to the newsstand in a high-speed hit-and-run, Bolden and Ellison were working. They told Roosevelt that the young man had worked nearby and was properly using the crosswalk in broad daylight when a black car with tinted windows charged into him and flung him high into the air. When Bolden and Ellison heard the initial impact, they looked out to see the body, but only saw the car racing far away, its license plate obscured. In what felt like several seconds later, the body of the young man finally landed on the south side of Houston Street like a discarded rag doll. There were a few customers who witnessed the entire episode and claimed the car was driverless. They said there was something off about the way it moved—how even after the impact, the car made a sharp ninety degree turn and stayed completely in lane, like a Tron light cycle on the game grid.

Traffic issues have always hit a sore spot with Roosevelt, and lately, with the number of fatalities sprawling across the nation, he took silent action. The night after the evidence had been collected and the intersection cleared, Roosevelt used his blade to prepare his template. He dressed in all black and hid away in the newsstand well after closing time. As he waited for the right time to slip out and start painting, he alternately wrote in his journal and meditated in the relative quiet. Two hours before dawn, he began his first run of painting phantom bodies outlined in chalk. He planned to paint one body for every pedestrian killed in the city so far this year and spread them out across the intersection. He moved back and forth between the pavement and the newsstand to avoid detection. Timing was everything. When he finished, he'd painted twenty-five chalk-lined bodies, the last of which he placed near a memorial of flowers, posters, and votives. Unintentionally, the whole thing looked like a colorless Keith Haring painting. He finished by writing a message in the center of the crossroads, SLOW THE HELL DOWN, and then waited in the newsstand until sunrise.

Bolden points to the cardboard stencil behind the refrigerator and raises his eyebrows. "What do you want to do with this?"

"Just cut it up into small pieces and slide it in the stack of leftover papers tonight. Thanks, B."

Ellison grabs two pairs of scissors by the cash register to help Bolden.

"Whatever it was that happened, I still can't stand people that can't respect simple traffic rules. There are so many rules that can be bent or broken, but with cars and people, there should be a mutual understanding. Every time someone runs a red light or parks in a made-up spot, there's a little flux in the driving universe that affects everyone else."

Now the stencil is in four pieces.

"Or when people are at a red light, they inch their cars forward every two seconds. Why, do they think they're gaining an advantage on the rest of traffic, or they're influencing the light to change? Or worse, when someone speeds recklessly into a parking lot, nearly runs over everyone in sight, then gets out of the car slowly, and walks as if they have all the time in the world. They should be consistent—if you're going to speed into a parking spot, you better be running your ass off when you get out of the car. If you're not in a legitimate hurry, slow the hell down."

The stencil is in sixteen equal pieces.

"And pedestrians too. They act like they have a force field around them. If they don't cross at the right spot or look both ways, they shouldn't expect cars to respect them because they're using their legs. Steel always wins against flesh and bone. I'm just saying that if you're not supposed to be there, don't claim to be an innocent victim. If you're going to break the laws, at least be aware that you're doing it. It's the ignorance and self-righteousness on both sides that really gets my goat."

Ellison chimes in, "Your goat gets got a lot."

Bolden says, "I bet we can solve this. If the people who break the laws have to listen to one of your traffic rants, they'd think twice about doing it. We'll put them in an interrogation room and you can let them know what's up. Talk them into submission." He is wagging his finger like an angry parent, except it's the middle finger.

Roosevelt points to his head and resolves, "Or maybe they'll be forced to think about it for the first time."

And then the stencil is cut into sixty-fourths, then two hundred fifty-sixths, then five hundred twelfths, etc., seemingly ad infinitum.

When he closes the door behind him and leans his back against the sea-glass and cement wall, he looks out to the other side of the street, which isn't looking as sunny as he'd hoped. The change that's in the air has nothing to do with the weather forecast. They are changes that occur regularly, but also all of a sudden, predictable only in retrospect. When Roosevelt feels this way, he has to ride it out. When he senses the downswing of his mood into doom, he knows it's simply part of the oscillation.

Maybe it's because he isn't ready to be so easily seen, so exposed. He's been living in the shadows of night beams, drinking in hidden rooms, or blending into the mosaic background of magazine faces during the day. But the upswing will follow soon enough with a renewed acknowledgement for the brevity of life, the impetus for a new resolution, and the pursuance of love. It's all poetry.

[[↑]]

To psych himself up for his first date with Candy on Saturday night, he wants to gain some extra confidence at the expense of the high-heeled others. So Zeus makes a bet with Mel about how many numbers or kisses he can lock up in one day. She agrees to be a judgmental wallflower and keep score. He bets he can move the beads of the abacus by acting as foolishly as possible. He says he'll even focus on approaching the kinds of women who all say they never fall for stunts like that, until they do. Mel thinks he'll do much better by flaunting some cash credentials, mentioning his address, or showing some pictures of his cars. (This debate goes back to how they first hooked up outside his building.) The agreement: one hour with each approach in two different places—The N.Y. Public Library in the afternoon and then a nightspot of Mel's choosing. He promises to give the full four hours an A for Effort. And why not—even if he loses the bet, he'll come out on top one way or the other. Although the loser of the bet will have to roll a blunt with a Cohiba, so the stakes are kind of high.

They enter the library separately, each going up the marble steps twenty paces apart, still in rhythm. The library, in the post-AppleFacegate era, is basically a daytime lounge for singles, especially those affected by the personal information breach. Even in the afternoon, some sections will swell to capacity. With many people trying to shrink the size of their digital footprint, it's become an unofficial dating site. Patrons sip on wine hidden in water bottles while perusing the selection of books and potential partners. But at the moment, the attendance figure is to the left side of the median for a Thursday. The wood-paneled walls bounce the whispers throughout the library. It sounds like a stutterer with a lisp was in every room, trying to ssssay ssssomething.

McJesus is wearing a light gray v-cut t-shirt, fitted dress pants a shade darker, and black wingtips with sterling-tipped laces. To compliment the grayscale, he dons a red leather belt, a thin onyx bracelet next to a black-and-silver Miles Davis Oris watch, and a ruby and howlite necklace that falls along the neckline of his shirt. Mel remains unseen and silent, like the eyes that move from side to side on a framed portrait on the wall. The lighting comes from amber clouds hovering low to the ground, just over the oak desks. The scent is both musty and musky, a combination of abandonment and tradition. And the taste is universally minty, on account of the free candy in the trays adjacent to the book return counter. The spacious and renovated reading room is peppered with people, some studying alone and some socializing. He spots a threesome, post-graduates maybe, sitting at a very long table that looks like it belongs at a coronation feast. It sits about fifty. The only other person sitting at the king's table is someone with plasticky hair that looks to have just eaten himself into androgyny. His seat is far from the threesome. McJesus, armed with an architecture book, legs his way past the loner over to the women, smiling.

He lowers his voice in volume and tone, "Good afternoon," slides out a chair, and starts flipping through the pages of his book. He senses the exchanges of looks between them as he imposes his presence on their group. They're alternately reading to themselves and then discussing the significance of the Gatsby car and how it embodies capitalistic individualism. Their lipstick all matches, as they're possibly sharing makeup and an apartment, he figures. The one in the center moves her mouth when she reads, but never lets her lips come together. He sees the smallest strand of saliva connecting the top and bottom the whole time. It's as strong as spider silk.

"—Sorry to interrupt, but if it really embodied individualism, in the truest sense of the term, as you said, the car would only have a driver's seat. And the one I have at my house in Long Island could seat all four of us." The young woman closest to him smoothes out her eyebrows and improves her posture. The car and the home weren't real, but they could've been with a few phone calls. After their conversation and the collection of an area code plus seven, Zeus stands erect, gives a slight bow to the threesome, and returns the chair to its home. He winks in the direction of his friend, the wallflower.

He makes several more approaches in the great reading room, flaunting the greenbacks, fictitious yellow cars, the Gehry tower, and playing up his mild celeb status. It was getting trickier to work the room, since he's already spoken to just about every woman there. It was becoming obvious to the point of silliness.

He leans against a library ladder and strikes up a conversation with two thirtysomethings with the same architecture book under his arm, his finger acting as a bookmark on the page that features his building. At one point, the ladder slides to one side and he stumbles along with it to the ground, and all three of them laugh. As he returns the ladder to its initial position, he notices the sweeping biblical annotation section at the top. "I haven't been that embarrassed since my Learjet made an emergency landing in a vineyard in the Loire Valley during a royal wedding ceremony in France."

After the hour for Round 1 was up, he's ready to head to a nearby café with Mel for tallying and caffeinating purposes. He mentally skips, but physically walks down the length of another king's table. As he nears the far end, there's someone he can't ignore. Out of the corner of his eye, Zeus tries to look without looking. This young man is finely-suited in maroon, thick-bearded, and is wearing silver reflective sunglasses. He looks more like an incognito model than a religious scholar, but there he is, studying the Good Book, the Holy Library. The man turns a delicate page and it crinkles like a leaf that had just fallen from a tree. As Zeus walks past him, he glances at his face. But instead of looking him in his eyes, the mirrored sunglasses bring attention to what he's reading, which for Zeus is reversed.

Jesus wept.

Before he leaves the library, he makes a detour into the men's room. Zeus unbuttons his pants, stares at the tiled wall above the urinal, and thinks of the way he used to try to talk to girls. He lets out a resounding exhale as he feels instant relief, a sometimes underappreciated minor joy. He thinks he's alone, but in the chrome of the exposed plumbing he sees a pair of black shoes under one of the stalls.

He used to hover near the girls by the lunch table or the hallway lockers and wait for what he thought was the perfect moment to say something interesting, but that something usually ended up boring them into submission, and they'd make a polite excuse to escape. It was as if they all turned their heads away from him in unison, whipped by an endless number of ponytails. Over time he learned to not care so much. It came from the maturity he acquired from his own circumstances—from asking questions and admitting he didn't have to know all the answers. He became more aware of his place in the world. With a parental count at one, girlfriends at zero, and funds in the negative, he looked only to the greater positives.

For example, he'd learned that he was at least two-dimensionally attractive after overhearing some flattering comments in school about his recent class photo, despite its purple cosmic background. He was a good dancer, spoke well, received high marks in school without trying too hard, and he'd made some friends in each clique. Even friends that were girls. He took pride in the fact that he couldn't be categorized into any particular group. He'd also been in search of establishing his own style and he'd tried many of them on for size. Most were unsuccessful and some produced sideways winces from the studentry in the hallway. But Zeus, more and more, had found himself wading in the sound of late-80s and 90s hip hop, due in large part to a simple, yet transformative line that helped put him in a healthy place. Rakim told him: *"I come correct and I won't look back, 'cause it ain't where you're from, it's where you're at!"* He scribbled it all through the pages of his notebooks. He had a love for the lyrical classics, the 808 bass drips and snare kicks, and the prophets who revealed all that is ill. With the help of the thrift store run by his church, he compiled a few throwback threads that he could integrate with his regular school outfits throughout the week. He experimented with accessories that he jacked from the pictures of the era. And since he loved and respected the music, he became more comfortable about expressing himself through that lens. It became less about what clothes he wore, but how he wore them. Style accomplished.

Although there was one accessory that he wanted, but could not have. The walk. Zeus tried to develop one to further his unique style. He walked with different rhythms and motions. He tried one for a whole day on the N.Y.C. streets where he'd scuff his right foot in between steps. It sounded different, but it made him look like he had a shoulder problem, and was difficult to maintain on congested sidewalks. He tried another one where he swung his right leg out in a parenthetical motion and his left leg stepping straight ahead. This was tricky and disingenuous when he was in a hurry. He was concerned too about the transition from the hallway to the stairs and questioned whether any style can be compatible with them. He wondered if anyone has ever had a stair style. So Zeus tried several permutations: walking up sideways, drumming on the banister, jumping down the last two steps, going one step at a time, even an attempt at a backward ascent, which he thought would be better for conversations. But it all became evident; stairs eliminate style. He found it too difficult to put together a unified theory for every kind of movement. Begrudgingly, Zeus returned to the simple left-right successions with the ease and tempo of an athlete, knowing that he'd failed in all other walks of life.

But he moved forward, grew into his body, and had no problem talking to someone with maraschino lips and a perfumed chest. He dreamt of graduation day and moving on to a business career in the cross section of music and fashion. But after the Powerball Lottery winnings, the days of the hustle and grind would never be, their possibilities a mystery. Since then, his ideas for what do next with his life had remained unexplored. They floated near him, but just out of reach. Because he had no restrictions, he felt anesthetized by freedom.

As far as meeting women, now with the advantage and confidence of money, the initial approach was nothing at all. Zeus still preferred to get dates with his personality alone. He'd use various forms of disarmament, playful digs, and an endearing obliviousness mixed with longing gazes; but if his game was off-balance, it was nice to fall back on a golden crutch.

Zeus snaps back from his long daze, tucks himself back into his pants, and walks over to the bathroom sink. The black shoes under the stall hadn't moved an inch.

[the press] is a small café that serves panini and French coffee throughout the day. The placemats are hard-laminated newspapers, each with a different front page. McJesus sees that a woman at an adjacent table has *The Pennsylvania Gazette* and he wants to trade. The covers of the menus are colorful tabloids. One of the appetizers is a mini panini made with buttered toast and raspberry jelly that oozes out the sides—it's called *If It Bleeds, It Leads*. Under the Hidden Heros section there's a footlong panini called *Deep Throat* and another one called *The Tripp*, which is served with a creamy blue cheese dressing, on the side. Each server wears a white shirt, high-waisted pants, and a trilby hat with a press card in the ribbon. And sometimes, when new customers walk into the café, the servers will run up and corner them, each one vying for their business, and the customers will face a full court of attention. It's a multi-entendre nightmare.

McJesus examines the refillable ketchup squeezer with displeasure. It's just about empty. The server comes over with ice water and an array of colored pens, says hello, and leaves them with the conditional, "If you need me, my name is Bonnie." McJesus and Melanie go over his library tactics while looking at their menus.

The next time she passes, McJesus says, "Hey Bon-Diddy-Bon-Bon!" He holds up the red plastic squeezer. Then, in a purposely pretentious voice, "Would you mind replacing this with your finest ketchup? Something in a glass bottle, perhaps?"

Bonnie's smile hints of Etna and her eye color needs its own name. "I'll see what I can do."

"Pretty please, with cherry tomatoes on top." There are a few giggles from the people at the surrounding tables that he parlays into a full discussion about gourmet ketchup and condiments in general. Bonnie joins in to help settle the debate about the classification requirements to be considered a condiment, foodstuff, or a spread—a topic McJesus was passionate about. The group of seven alternates between exchanging names and placing their orders with Bonnie, who writes each one down with a different color. With all of the chattiness and muffled laughter, it's hard to hear anyone clearly. When the two sitting to his right, a man and a woman, say their names, they sound unrecognizable, as if spoken backward. The discussion comes back to the forefront when their lunch is served. At the peak of their camaraderie, McJesus stands up and declares, "Thank you for such a lovely time. Let's drink up. Another round! Everyone, Bon-Diddy, listen up! Waters on me! Waters all around!" He twirls his finger high in the air. Everyone laughs again, but the waters never materialize. When he thanks Bonnie he shakes her hand and passes her a small stack of folded hundreds. There's a note written in a voice bubble leaving the mouth of Benjamin Franklin:

DEAR BONNIE, THIS IS FOR THESE 3 TABLES, THE REST IS YOURS, ♥ ⇑

When it comes to signing his name, he frequently hesitates before deciding which one to use. This time he only writes the first letter of his legally contracted name. And because he used his leg as a desk, his penmanship was scribbly and unpredictable when he got to the knee. So his initial more resembles an upside down pitchfork.

McJesus and Mel leave [the press] hand-in-hand, platonically, for round two of pick-up attempts at the library. They cross the streets of granite centuriation on their way back to the house of knowledge, the building of imaginations in print.

[[◆]]

When she wakes up several hours later, the woman next to her is gone. The hospital bed is made anew—the flower, the balloon, and the three Bibles are no longer in the room. When she looks to her right, she sees that Jasmine and her assistants had stopped in. They'd brought Axlia's phone, fully charged, and a homemade card with a bouquet of roses drawn on the outside of the envelope. They offered support, love, and a touch of humor. When she checks her phone, she sees damn near one thousand message notifications and at least one hundred requests to purchase the canvases. She's trending. There are six available, with the seventh (and the only one with any color) being held in the evidence room awaiting ballistics and DNA analysis. There were also requests for interviews with news agencies all over the media map: internet, television, podcasts, and print. Under the hospital halogens there is one email that brings a bright smile to her face.

It's from the new gallery financed by Cyrus Coaster, who's been taking over 10th Street in the East Village, and is now setting his sights on the art world.

[Mission] opened with Cyrus Coaster's personal collection that he'd curated from around the globe, integrated with new work from the N.Y.C. art scene. He was seeking out the next wave of American artists. Just weeks ago, Axlia had read H.P. Coaster's interview in The New York Times, where he expressed a special interest in performance art and one-time-only experiential works. And the art magazine, *Juxtapōz*, recently covered the gallery in a ten-page spread. H.P. Coaster was pleased with the name of the magazine, which epitomized the driving force behind his business ventures and highlighted the polarity of his Wiccan beliefs. The gallery had attracted the attention of the full spectrum of the art world, and brought it all to a corner in Alphabet City: East 10th Street and Avenue A.

In the past year it was converted from a long-standing Russian Orthodox Church to an art gallery, an anchor for Coaster's 10 on 10th. His proposal to gain ownership of the property and to relocate the leaders and members of the church was met with plenty of resistance. But with the recent and tremendous surge in attendance, the church was regularly exceeding its capacity for every service. With lines continuing to build up outside the church on Sundays, they'd already begun construction on a modern structure just a few blocks north that would be able to accommodate a large congregation. The leaders of the church acknowledged that the sale to Cyrus Coaster would expedite the process. So, along with the gentle persuasion of tens of millions of U.S. dollars and a tip of an 1825 Constantine Ruble from Coaster's personal collection[32], the ownership changed hands and the renovations began on the interior. The church's exterior was to remain because of the building's status as a preserved landmark by the city of N.Y. There was one section of the interior that Cyrus Coaster kept and further celebrated. In the nave of the church was the jewel of iconography—a large, gold-leaf painted Christ Pantocrator—one hemisphere of his face stern in judgement, and the other peaceful and reassuring.

As Axlia lies in her hospital bed, with Psalm 88 still lingering in her mind, she harked back to the days when she went to church with her family. Though she wasn't particularly interested in the sermons on her own, Della was required to memorize certain verses, the meaning behind stories, and The 10 Commandments. When she was fifteen, a friend in the same grade told her that she was raped by an upstanding upperclassman. She knew Della would never tell anyone, but she had to say something to release the pressure inside. Della suggested in a note that she should tell a teacher or someone with whom she felt comfortable in the administration. But her friend's fear of embarrassment, and the fact that she wasn't supposed to have invited him over when no one was at home, kept it a silent crime without an offender.

Della kept her word and only told the secret to God in prayer, late at night. When she prayed, she imagined the thoughts zooming out of her head in beams of light into the realm of Heaven, where they would be sorted into categories based on urgency and importance. She hoped this prayer would be deflected into a suggestion box. *Can You please add one more Commandment? Thou shalt not rape.* She never received a reply by way of a reverse light beam or any additional words suddenly appearing in all Bibles across the world, which she believed He could do without any backlash. If He agreed with her proposal that it might prevent countless acts of violence, it would only require a small suspension of physics—a cosmic ink injection.

Della had further told God in her prayer that she'd never let anyone know that it was her idea. The raper, after all, was from another family at the church. And if he were to see that there now exists an 11th Commandment, maybe he'd never do it again. She realized most of the other Commandments were broken all the time, but hoped this would at least cut down on how many rapes there were each day and each hour. It might have been the last prayer Della zoomed up to the Heavens. As the years went by, her young thoughts stayed in the past—she now preferred action over asking.

She'd been working on producing a live project that was to build on her black-and-white film of the same title, *HYMEN TEARS*. Using social media, Axlia, the artist, was crowdsourcing to find victims of rape who were willing to represent the injustices done to many others. Her plans were solidifying with interest from her followers and from organizations that support education reform, the kind where kids would be taught from an early age about human sexuality and the depravity of rape. Axlia pictured women inside a long black canvas-covered box, standing side-by-side, unseen by the audience, each holding a knife. Outside the box, Axlia would dress ambiguously and paint her interpretations of the women inside using bright colors with sweeping strokes. Then she'd move left-to-right and paint various titles on each form in stark white, just below the waist: Daughter, Sister, Mom, Cousin, Aunt, Girlfriend, Fiancée, Wife, You, Us. After a few moments of solitude, a soundtrack of cringeworthy screams would penetrate the eardrums of the audience while she violently covered up the words with red paint.

Then the screams would fade so the audience could hear the cutting of the canvas, the slashing movements from the women inside, as they revealed their unclothed bodies. The show was to be titled: *"For the Whole Family, Live on a Sidewalk Stage Near You: HYMEN TEARS."*

----

aceedeecee1000@licketysplitmail.com
To: Cyrus Coaster, Founder
Re: Solo Exhibit at Mission Art Gallery

Yes, I'd love to work with your gallery.
I should be out of the hospital by tomorrow. Are you available then?
- Axlia Clia

----

missionartgallery@licketysplitmail.com
To: Axlia Clia
Re: Solo Exhibit Meeting

Good, Friday.
Come by the gallery around 3p. Ask for C.C.
Looking forward to it, Cheers and Peace.

[[Σ]]

Suma walks out of the subway car, her shoes clicking their way through the crowd. She constantly calculates her available shoulder space, gauging whether to go straight forward or to twist sideways, without thinking about it. She makes her way to the silver escalator and holds onto the rubber handrail, which she always thinks of as a very long tire. On the ascension, she folds a handwritten note in half twice and slides it into her shoulder bag. She counts down the moments as she nears the landing by tapping her index finger against her hip. She isn't nervous on escalators, but the urban legends she'd heard about growing up still got the hippocampus glowing with neural sparks. She heard that if she didn't step off in time, her toes were going to be sucked in and then bitten by the escalator monster's teeth. From there she'd end up below, inside all of its guts and gears, like a pile of human fettuccine.

She exits the 72nd subway station in one piece, breathing in slightly less polluted air. Suma looks back at the façade of the station, which looks like a skinny version of The Alamo. She's on her way to RUST BUST & AXE to meet up with two-thirds of the thirty-sixth president's initials, L and J. Bunch had plans downtown. The note she folded into her red handbag is a wishlist. It's peppered with exceptional names of professional baseball players and salted with the intent to preserve the list in cardboard form. The baseball cards, if they're out there, will be secured by any way possible. But if they're too old or obscenely priced or were never produced, she plans to use her pristine alteration process to edit them into existence. They'll be given to Leon on his birthday in a few months. It's to be both a gift and a one-upping of the fictionally-future Orel Sax to the real and now. The wishlist reads: Ed Head, Rusty Kuntz, Randy Bush, Johnny Dickshot, Mike Sweeney, Urban Shocker, Razor Shines, Rocky Bridges, Wonderful Terrific Monds, Ten Million, Cal McLish (whose full name is *Calvin Coolidge Julius Caesar Tuskahoma McLish*), Pete La Cock, Woody Held, Cannonball Titcomb, Pussy Tebeau, and Dick Pole.

With the combination of a pencil skirt and sharpened heels, it takes Suma more steps to get to the rendezvous point than usual. Her stride length is cut by one-third and it feels like she's moving at half-speed. She stops at a crosswalk just a few blocks away from RUST BUST & AXE.

While she waits for the signal to change, she shifts her weight from one parenthetical hip to the other and a clasp on her shoulder bag snags part of her top. The blouse is like a fishnet version of a honeycomb pattern and her skin is exposed between the threads of each hexagon. It becomes more opaque as it moves down to her chest, the shapes gradually filling in with a metallic honey color. As she twists to check the snag and tries to repair it, a lock of her hair finds its way into the tangle—an unlikely and sudden braid. So as the walkway becomes populated with crossers, she exhales through her nose and remains at the curb to unweave the knot—one hair, or thread, or strap at a time. It's a quiet moment of frustration.

She arrives a few minutes before her friends. Suma finds a vacant barstool, the kind that swivels and is bolted to the floor and has hunter green cushions. After she orders her drink, she looks out the corner of her eye to the man to her right. He's several years older than she is, a neat person she can tell. He wears a pressed white oxford shirt and has his napkin folded in a triangle on his lap. His eyes move in only two directions: plateward at his salad and toward the muted television above the bar, down and then up. There's another man to his right who's on the opposite end of the neatness scale. His beard is the type that can hide things. His clompy arms rattle the bar rail and the unused silverware. He's eating a burger that had come undone. It was oversaturated with ketchup. His napkin is being used to clean the ketchup from his beard and the corners of his mouth. It isn't folded in a triangle. It's in disarray and part of it falls onto the lap of the neater man. While looking up at the television, the crispy clean man reaches down for his napkin, but grabs the other man's instead. When he puts the napkin to his mouth, the ketchup drips all over his starchy button-down and coats his chin, tasting what he considers to be an unrefined condiment tinged with meat. He's no longer very clean or very happy. He places the napkin on the bar and shoots the man a look with one eyebrow raised. He slides his straddled legs over the back of the stool and heads for the bathroom in disgust, looking like an extra from a zombie film. The bearded man looks confused while he picks at a ligament from the ground beef that had gotten caught between his front teeth. When he smiles at Suma it's clear he hadn't been able to pick it out.

Her drink arrives and is a certain departure from her usual pint of beer. It's a frozen coffee dreamy concoction, girly and swirly—and she puckers up to the straw with content. Suma gets a text from Leon. They're going to be there in a minute. She pays her tab plus tip in cash and swivels 180° and faces a group that's in an open huddle formation. There's one person for every day of the week, four men and three women, alternating by sex. They're having a conversation about the shooting of the performance artist. With their bar-volume voices, it's hard to tell if the conversation is intense and heated, or just loud. She overhears one man, whom she sees take off an unusually thick pair of glasses to wipe the perspiration from the bridge of his nose, say, "All's I'm saying is that, while maybe she wasn't asking for it, she definitely wasn't *not* asking for it. Walking around naked in Harlem isn't the same as Eve in the garden. That's the world today. All's I'm saying. I mean, if she was at home reading the Good Book, or helping out at a soup kitchen, or at church praying, she wouldna been in that situation to begin with. But you know, that's the world today. You make choices in life that put you in certain places. Her choices put her in that place. Now, I don't think she shoulda been shot, but she can't claim to be a total innocent victim. She's not totally innocent. Because at some point, she denied what God woulda wanted her to do with her life. No God wants you walking back and forth naked and painting your body and being all showy with your sin. She took that risk. And because of that, she lost His armor, His protection. I can tell, and He can tell, who has real faith."

As she listens to this IQ explosion, Suma guards herself with a count-to-ten umbrella while the ashes of ignorance rain down. She is *thisclose* to interrupting him, but for two reasons, holds off. One, she's there to relax and enjoy time with her friends. Two, she has a loose association with the performance artist through a mutual friend, Jasmine, and feels closer to the situation than she actually is.

He holds his glasses in his hand as he continues to speak. She notices a reddened mark, a permanent impression, over the man's nose where his heavy glasses usually rest. Suma can tell that he rarely takes them off because the skin around his eyes exude a malnourished, blanched quality. When he finishes speaking, he slides the glasses back to their comfortable home. And as she walks through their huddle, they make direct eye contact, and she glares through the thick windows of his glasses.

Suma sees a free table by the window and she brushes her way through the rest of the crowd. Their voices are warped and almost silenced by the cacophony of electric guitars and jumbled bar sounds. Suma's shoulder, which is just about bare, accidentally catches the blunt edge of something, which turns out to be another person. It is a young woman so thin, she looks and feels exoskeletal. Her body falls to the floor like a conciliatory pile of bones, without any resistance to gravity. Suma reaches out her hand apologetically and offers to help her to her feet. The woman declines with a scowl and tries to rise on her own. But due to either slipping on suds or her total lack of musculature or both, she fails, and resigns to recline in the filth amongst city-stained shoes and spilled backwash. Suma doesn't offer to help her up a second time, the first rejection is also the last.

Suma sits down on a wooden chair and places her drink on the table. And just moments after that, Leon and Jeremy meet her with smiles and European-cheek kisses. They excuse themselves to go to the bar for their drinks. Suma takes a frozen cold sip and looks out to the sidewalk where a single-file line of young men are walking by, buzzed in lockstep. They stop at the window in front of her to check out the bar scene inside, which is mostly men. Yet once the fog from their exhales evaporates, they see that right down in front of them is a woman of beauty, apparently drinking alone. The men round the corner to the entrance. Suma's Kahlúa Milkshake is bringing all the boys to the bar. However, once they're ID'd and inside, the table is occupied by two other evolutionary adversaries, L and J, much to their dismay.

Their conversations meander through a wide range of topics over the course of a few rounds of drinks, and somehow end with *What are the top three ways you would prefer to die?*, which is exhausted pretty quickly. And after a few seconds of sipping in silence, Jeremy openly wonders how the hell they got there in the first place. The trio laughs at themselves, Suma and Leon nodding and Jeremy shaking his head side-to-side, both movements meaning the exact same thing. They independently try to trace their steps backward using the small crumbs of phrases. And they each find their own place on the paneled ceiling to stare at while they focus on the very recent past.

Jeremy says, "O.K., we got to *how we'd prefer to die* because I said that being shot would be the worst way to go—with all of the emptying of bodily fluids and the lack of time to reflect on your life and loved ones. And I only said that because you mentioned the performance artist that was shot during her show. What did you call her?" He gestures to Leon with his elbow while his hand holds his beer halfway between the table and his mouth. "Axe-something?"

"It's *Axe-cee-lia*. Axlia," Suma informs.

"True," Leon says, "like, Axe...Celia. *Axlia*. I'm pretty sure that's right."

"It is," Suma nods.

Leon takes a sip. "And I only said that because you showed us that trick with your tongue. I called it performance art," he explains to Suma.

"It was. And that trick, by the way, is not to be spoken of ever again. I only showed you that to demonstrate some possibilities," Suma smiled. "They're for when you get married, obviously."

Leon continues, "And the marriage thing came from how people choose to change their names—sometimes with the maiden name becoming the middle name, or hyphenating, or creating a brand new family surname. I understand why the two of you think that everyone should be able to choose whatever married name they want, but I'm sticking with traditionalism on this one."

"Which is funny," Suma adds, "because you were right with us when we were talking about the preceding topic—how we all want more independence and control over our lives."

"True," Leon says. "But—"

Suma cuts him off. "We talked about how every generation is pushing for independence at progressively younger ages. But there still seems to be something we don't have control of until it's too late—our given birth names. By the time we can make the choice to change it to something else, it's already affected us in how we view ourselves in the world, and how we see the world itself."

"Very Wittgensteinian!" Jeremy says.

She continues, "Many people seem to have total acceptance when it comes to their names. It probably speaks more to our fear of parental separation or rejection, rather than how we identify with ourselves. Our name is probably our biggest tie to our past, and the biggest lie about who we really are."

"O.K., you win!" Leon holds his hands up. "Here's how I will identify and modernize. I just realized I'm the quiet type, so my new name will be unwritable and incoherent. It will be only found on the edge of a knife, so if you attempt to say it, your mouth will be sliced open."

"You just went to a place called Too Far," Jeremy says. And they all cringe and laugh together, but he goes on anyway. "Oh, and have you met my family? They've chosen their new full names as well. Here's my wife <<grunts arrhythmically>> , and my two kids <<gargles>> and <<clanks the bottom of his beer glass>> . We're just going with what we feel is right for us as individuals."

"Thanks for taking my contemplative point and turning it into something ridiculous."

Jeremy continues, "Agreed. Anyway, back to backtracking. That whole name discussion came from when we were talking about the things we really can't change: our faces, body types, disabilities, freckles, and birthmarks."

Suma says, "Now that I think about it, our entire body is one big birthmark."

Jeremy continues, "—yeah, well that came from our little talk about two great baseball players with unfortunate names. Actually, I think you were at the bar getting a drink."

"Who were the players?"

"Randy Johnson and Albert Pujols."

"—and that must have come from me telling you," Suma gestures to Leon with her glass, "that I have a baseball-related birthday gift in the works that will put all other gifts to shame. But it's under lock and key, so I won't say any more."

"I told you, I can't wait."

"You're going to have to."

"And the whole baseball thing came from when we were talking about beer prices at games, and how stadiums are their own little islands of capitalism," Jeremy adds.

"And that came from the," Leon holds up air quotes, "*scale of capitalism and socialism in our society* discussion—which came up because were talking about those two library patrons who despise each other and both seem to be hoarding the kind of books they disagree with. It's like they're both trying to prevent anyone else from learning about the other -*ism.* There's still something called the interwebs."

Suma jumps on at the end of his line, "...and that came from us talking about all of the strange characters we see at work: the Buddha impersonator, the elderly man who always says, 'People tell me I'm too clever by three-fourths', the women with the high heel roller skates, that pick-up artist guy who hangs out in the religion section, the woman who we say looks like a walking carbohydrate, and that high school kid that tries to chat me up."

"Yeah, he says you're 'hotter than a desert on the sun.'"

"And there's the crossdresser with all the necklaces," Suma resumes. "His bra is so unevenly padded, it's as if he's not even trying anymore. One cup is flat and the other's overflowing. If you were to read the cup sizes from left to right, it would spell a three-letter word."

Jeremy keeps the momentum, "And those guys that we've seen more of lately—the ones with mirrored aviators, the full beards, and the maroon suits—they almost look like the same person and they all read with their sunglasses on."

"The Defenders of Christ."

"Or maybe they're the copycats I've heard about."

"The Pretenders of Christ."

"Strange."

"Oh! Add. *A-D-D*, I see," Leon realizes.

"But not nearly as strange as that incident with that man-boy that freaked me out last week," Suma says. Then she veers off in thought back to that day.

She was behind her desk when she noticed a tween-aged kid with the face of an older man. It was wrinkled and loose. He was sitting at the far end of a nearby table. He was full of tics and motions, yet sedentary at the same time. His large posterior found ways to escape the top of his pants and flop over the circumference of his body, producing a fuller moon with multiple cheeks squeezing through the lattice of the back of the chair. He was writing furiously and scribbling on lineless paper as he rocked back and forth. His tongue licked all over the patchy hairs of his pubescent mustache, slowly and repeatedly. He went on like this for three straight hours. His concentration was unbroken, even through the fountain-like head sweats. He made low swishy noises, sobbed in spastic bursts, and laughed inaudibly. When his knees bounced with excitement, it shook the long community-style table, and rendered it useless by anyone else. The man-boy was a kinetic and creepy oddity, Suma thought. Then, at the top of the hour, as if he were on a schedule, the shapeshifting mass stood up. The back of his knees knocked over the chair. She watched him walk away with supinated feet, the outstep of his rubber soles worn way down. He hadn't taken anything with him; his pen and paper were still on the table. Suma waited until he was out of sight and walked over to pick up the chair. Around the perimeter of the paper she saw splashes of wet stuff and sweat beginning to evaporate where his arms had rested. The floor and chair were sprinkled with urine, she presumed, as a foul odor pierced into nasal focus. Considering the entirety of the episode, the chief instance of terror that shook Suma, were the papers themselves—they were one desolate landscape on top of another, layers of a haunting void.

Leon breaks her spell, "But I think the first patron we mentioned was the lady that smells like powdery aerosol. The one with the frosty gold hair and crustacean skin. The one that was touched by Goldfinger, no doubt."

"You're almost right, but that wasn't exactly where we started. You can't just go on changing the past like that," Jeremy says.

"Oh, sure you can."

"We started with your nail polish, remember. *You* were Goldfinger. That was our genesis." Jeremy's flat face goes from plateaued to hilly with excitement, as if he's placed the last jagged piece in the puzzle. When Jeremy pumps his fists and flexes, his short sleeves reveal his meager arms to be like an incomplete medical dictionary, as in, no definition for biceps.

L and J ask Suma if she'd like another. She does. They take her empty glass and head for the bar to order another round. She looks down at the thick circle of condensation left by her glass and begins to trace it with her finger. Her nails are just long enough to match up with her fingertips and they're painted gold and cream, Art Deco style. Suma hypnotizes herself as she cycles her finger in the ring of water. In the seat behind her, she hears a man speaking with some kind of Mediterranean accent. It's soothing under the loud music. She feels that way about all foreign accents, especially when she hears them on the radio. She listens without regard for the meaning of the words as she drags her finger from the table up to her forearm. She makes long figure eights lightly over her skin that leave trails of goosebumps. When the man with the accent stops speaking, Suma's gentle massage ceases, and her finger returns to wade in the condensation.

When she looks down at the circle and its pointy tangents, she notices there's writing all over the table. It is both subtle and overt. It's written in graffiti, but still legible. She taps her index finger on the circle to use it as an inkwell. Suma traces over the words, internalizes them, and reads them silently. They are two haiku poems.

STANDING AMONGST STARS
THAT YOUR SHADOW IS MOVING,
DOESN'T MEAN YOU ARE.

THE MOON IS MY SUN
I'M WORKING ALL THROUGH THE NIGHT,
IN MORE WAYS THAN ONE.

[[※]]

Roosevelt is enjoying a few moments of peace under the high-pressure shower head, his personal rain cloud. He spends more time in the shower than is necessary, sometimes just standing with his chin resting on the top of his chest. He lets the bullets of water massage his neck and then watches them form into little rivers, descending along each curve of his body. They form a confluence of tributaries that disappear into the silver, speaker-like drain.

He leaves his apartment in Hell's Kitchen and takes the stairs. At every turn he jumps the step before the landing and practices setting himself down quietly. Breathing heavier, he walks out into the concrete jungle amongst the other creatures of the night, the vines of traffic signals overhead, the bright green subway globes illuminating his path. His strides indicate a sense of urgency even though there's no need to hurry, but there's also no reason not to. With a black backpack strapped over his shoulders and his red journal wedged under his arm, Roosevelt was off to the corner of Amsterdam Avenue and 76th Street to RUST BUST & AXE, a place to be private in public.

He merges with the city wanderers. But on one street that is darkened by scaffolding, he's bumped into hard by someone walking in the opposite direction. Roosevelt gives a guttural, alpha male response. The contact force between their shoulders sends them into equivalent half-spirals, each playing their part of the astrological sign of Cancer. Now they look at each other eye-to-eye, or rather, eyes-to-eye. The man is bearded and wearing a black eyepatch wrapped around his large head with his salt-and-pepper hair creased by a crooked halo. They know each other.

For Roosevelt, it's a negative connotation. Yet for the cyclops, seeing Roosevelt brings a feeling of ease and good vibes. First of all, the eye-patched man is relieved that this isn't going to escalate to an altercation, and secondly, it's a man who'd helped him immensely in the past. The man relaxes his shoulders and exhales with a sigh. The skin around one eye goes from squintingly taut, to thin and saggy, and his eyelid retreats under a bushy brow. Roosevelt, still opposite him, says nothing—but his eyes go from wide to laser-focused, his skin too young to indicate much of a change. In the seconds that elapse, the flow of energy between the two men is on two different planes. When Roosevelt turns to continue walking toward RUST BUST & AXE, he feels the air breezing freely under his arms. His journal had fallen to the sidewalk as a result of the shoulder bump. He sees that it has landed face-down and open, split somewhere along the middle. He picks it up and preserves the page. It had landed open to his ever-evolving and expanding comic strip. The strip follows the adventures of his hero, a man concerned with fairness and respect for all—mostly in the context of minor traffic violations—but also with general politeness in the public sphere. Whether it's an infraction by a driver or a pedestrian, he is out for justice, ready to release the kind of fury that would be fully endorsed by any manufacturer of acetaminophen-laced products.

Introducing...

↘ HEADACHE MAN ↙

The characters in the comic strip are all stick figures. Some have added muscles and polygonal clothing. And there are hairstyles that range from spiky to bald, pin-straight to pube-curly, and from Gaga to Republican lego. The protagonist is pretty much a naked stick figure, his clothing and accessories rarely being necessary. His main feature is the size of his head, which fluctuates in accordance to his level of annoyance or anger. Sometimes Headache Man's head turns red and fires yellow lightning bolts directly into the brains of the offenders of the law. The lightning bolts are not always seen by the general population, but they are supremely-well targeted and just as powerful.

Headache Man's superpower is that he can give anyone he deems deserving anything from a low-grade, single-aspirin headache, to a piercing and debilitating migraine. In his opinion, there were just too many people getting away with disrespectful actions without having to suffer any immediate consequences. When he first emerged on the scene, Headache Man preferred to start out with a focus on the small things. He was a fairly new superhero after all. But it was also because of his belief in the Broken Window Theory. For Headache Man, his broken windows were exemplified by some of the following: *failure to signal while driving (especially when turning into crosswalks), texting with your head down while walking on said crosswalks, taking up more than one spot in a parking lot, driving .001 mph over the speed limit, throwing a straw wrapper out the window, being a lummox with regard to offering your seat on the city bus for an elderly person, any theft under five dollars, slamming the gas pedal down on yellow when running late, leaving ignorant comments online with an anonymous avatar while enjoying the sunlight on a Central Park bench, knowing how to buckle the belt on your pants but not the kind that will save your life,* and, of course, *actually dashing stones through windows,* etc.

His existence is predicated on the idea that he can make people think about how their actions might be affecting others, possibly for the first time. The lightning headaches that he will impose on the oblivious, privileged, and misinformed, are designed to be a type of time machine. He wants to force them to spend minutes or hours thinking about what they've done in the context of the grand scheme. The strike of his lightning headache isn't pure pain, but a debilitation designed to inflict discomfort only when the perpetrator is not focusing on what they've done wrong. If they meditate on their ill-intentioned action, the pain will subside to a gentle disquietness. Headache Man calibrates the intensity to the appropriate level, depending on the infraction. Then, through an inner monologue takeover, he lets them know the nature of their offense and the length of their sentence. He doesn't have a bass-heavy voice like Batman, instead, Headache Man sounds more like a neighborhood accountant. He speaks in a matter-of-fact and reassuring tenor, giving the personal tech-support without an accent. He's careful to remind them that this is part of a concerted effort to make the world a fairer place to live. *Look around*, he'll say, *the world can be both traffic-conscious and loving. Please refrain from that kind of activity.* And for his final electrostatic discharge, he always signs off with the same words: *Headache Man is watching, Headache Man is listening, Headache Man is here to help.*

Panel 1: The scene is a coffee cart on a city sidewalk. There are rectangular buildings packed in the background and a lonely cumulous cloud in the sky. There are four figures in view. The coffee cart's operator is all sticks and is wearing a baseball cap and there are three people in line. The first person in line is a spiky-haired man holding a phone, the second is bald and carrying a boxy briefcase, and the third is a woman with diagonal hair in a triangle skirt holding a trapezoidal purse. The coffee cart operator is holding out a cup and his mouth is in an O shape—his voice bubble reads, "$$." The three figures in line have horizontal mouths, humdrumly waiting to be caffeinated.

Panel 2: The scene is almost the same, but the line is reduced by one. The boxy briefcase man is up next and holding out paper money. His mouth has become a rectangle and his voice bubble reads, "½ & ½."

Panel 3: As the woman with the triangle skirt approaches the coffee cart to order, a figure with large semicircle muscles dashes in from the right side. He is in a hurry. The point of his angular knee knocks her from her stance and she drops her trapezoid purse. Little polygons of her personal belongings are scattered on the sidewalk. The coffee cart operator's eyebrows are V- shaped and his mouth a wiggly curve.

Panel 4: The careless man doesn't help the woman pick anything up or apologize in any bubbly way. Instead, while she is putting her things back in her bag, he orders a coffee for himself, "w/$C_6H_{12}O_6$!!!" The coffee cart operator has one hand on his hip while the other arm is stretched out in an obtuse angle. He's annoyed.

Panel 5: As the coffee cart operator begins to help the woman, the rude and muscled man is still demanding a cup of coffee while he points at his wristwatch saying, "@$$%!!" And in the sky above, emerging feet-first from the bottom of the cloud, is our heroic stick figure. It's the beginning of Headache Man's descent.

Panel 6: The woman with the triangle skirt has finally collected all of her things. She's a bit rattled, her hair is disheveled, and her mouth is in a forty-five degree slant. The coffee cart operator hands her his sorrow with an empty voice bubble as he refuses to take her money for the coffee, which she orders simply as " ■ ."

The muscled man is several paces away at this point and the scene has a wider panoramic view. Headache Man is floating in mid-air over the scene of the crime of Disrespectfulness. His head is of greater circumference than the other characters and tinted with a blood-orange hue. His arms are extended straight out, almost like a mummy.

Panel 7: The woman with the triangle skirt, now with her coffee in hand, shares a smile with the coffee cart operator. She walks away with her trapezoid purse hanging from her shoulder (or because she is a stick figure, her neck). Headache Man's head now looks like a jumbo-sized cherry lollipop and his eyes are filled with pure, unadulterated ferocity and revenge. From Headache Man's extended arms come his power manifest, with the lightning bolts streaming down toward the head of the unsuspecting muscled perpetrator.

Panel 8: The scene is a close-up of the man after he had fallen to one knee. His muscles are drooping and limp. And he clutches his head at the temples in complete despair.

Panel 9: In the last frame, before Headache Man ascends to his home in the cloud, he sends a personal lightning thought bubble that enters the rude man directly into his own thoughts, interrupting them, and replacing them with his own voice. Headache Man, our hero, informs the man, "That was very rude. You cut the line. It will be better to wait your turn next time. Think about how your actions affect others. I have more migraines where that came from. Remember, *Headache Man is Watching. Headache Man is Listening. Headache Man is here to help.*" The man, still on one knee, looks to the sky with remorse and a single blue teardrop rolls down the surface of his round head. At the bottom of the cartoon, next to the byline, is a narration enclosed in a lightning bolt. "So, from a single cumulous cloud in the sky, on an otherwise clear day, a quiet storm of fairness brings comfort to the gracious denizens of New York City."

Even though it's been weeks since Roosevelt has seen the eye-patched man and his salt-and-pepper hair, his disdain for him returns in an instant. He is a former client at The Office, one of his first regulars. He would leave his phone for two hours with an overpayment of cash. There were two instructions: transmit a live signal and keep it charged. He was not to provide any services that would answer texts or calls. This man, who always wore black pants, black brandless tennis shoes, a black baseball hat pulled way down, a white woolen jacket zipped up to the chin, and the black eyepatch, of course, was polite and soft spoken.

Early one afternoon, on a warm autumn day, the man approached the newsstand with his envelope, his phone and cash payment inside. But this time, his jacket was slightly open, the zipper's bite was incomplete.

Through the slit between the metal teeth, Roosevelt noticed a clerical collar. The man smiled and thanked him with his usual, "You're a miracle worker," and walked away in silence, blending into the crosswalk traffic. Intrigued by his disbelief, he chose to break two of his cardinal rules: the terms of privacy as agreed to in The Office contract and not to judge what others did with their personal time. The phone, which was charging in the refrigerator, had a pattern lock on the home screen. He tried to imagine what kind of pattern this man would've employed. He had two guesses to get it right because after a third unsuccessful attempt, the owner of the phone would be notified that someone tried to break in. After several minutes, he decided to try his luck with the most obvious pattern, considering his collar. Roosevelt dragged his finger across the screen to form a †.

In the photo album he saw pictures of him with his parishioners, his fellow followers, and possibly his family, where he appeared with both eyes on display. There didn't seem to be any evidence that he ever wore an eyepatch, or needed to. His video album was minimal, but his actions were those of a man who was spatially aware, sharing laughs and singing songs in front of the camera. But in an email folder marked *Lunchtime*, he read an exchange that featured firsthand accounts of what he did during his two hours off the grid. The ages of the boys were disturbing. This degenerate deceptor barely used coded language to describe his actions, as he seemed to be promoting the place to other men. In one thread he stressed the importance of the eyepatch and the role it played while visiting a place without overhead lights. This man was well-adjusted to the darkness. And it was clear what this man was. With his white woolen jacket and black elements of disguise, he wasn't a beast in sheep's clothing, but an apostate in shepherd's clothing, leading his flock into a field of hypocrisy.

Wherever this place was, it must have been within walking distance, Roosevelt figured. It was probably far enough away that his phone and actual presence could never be linked, but close enough for an idle man to get to quickly. In one email, he wrote of a long hallway of doors. Each doorway had its own doorbell. And if a doorbell was illuminated red, the room was in use. Otherwise, he was welcome to enter. He wrote that he found it endearing when a boy's eyes and asshole winced at the same time.

The boys, mostly imports, spent their days in darkness and nights in desperation. They waited as they were instructed, under a blanket of fear. In their native tongue just before they were delivered, they were told about the consequences of attempting an escape or dishonoring their guests. The rooms were devoid of lightbulbs and only furnished with a twin bed, a defective television, and a small bathroom. He described how, when after he'd chosen a room, he'd press the doorbell to send a current of electricity to turn on the television. It only displayed an image of convulsing static, and the boys were told to put their faces close to the billowing screen, a rectangular, salt-and-pepper sun. It was designed to disable their ability to ever identify their temporary roommates, blinded by artificial light. In another email, he wrote how the shadows played along the curvilinear postures of the boys, and that he thought it was beautiful.

As he would've already switched the eyepatch over to the other side to enable his primitive night vision, Roosevelt imagined how the readjustment of the elastic would've pulled his hair in the opposite direction, causing the former halo of constriction to become a depressed itch. He saw his yellowed fingernails digging into his skull along the circumference. This man was the type to scratch, no matter how faint the tickle.

Roosevelt thought about how what goes on behind closed doors originates in closed minds. He thought about the rigid penis of this man and the delicate bottom of a nameless boy. It wasn't as much putting a square peg in a soft round hole, but of putting *something* into *nothing*. The pain they endured, the continual bursting of their atoms from a time of darkness, was like a big fucking bang every day.

When the man returned for his phone that afternoon, Roosevelt told him that The Office was closing soon for good, and not to return. The man nodded, took out his phone from the folded newspaper, unzipped his wool coat, put it in his pocket, and walked away with a whistle. He noticed that his black shirt was missing the clerical collar and that the eyepatch hadn't been switched back. The man never again came by the newsstand or told him he was a miracle worker, though the words were emblazoned in his memory. He was sure he'd find another place to keep his phone, that turning him away was a mere annoyance, not a hindrance. Because hidden throughout the city, there are perpetual violations of the unknown, and therefore, invisible boys. Right at this moment, one of those boys is grinding his deciduous teeth with his legs spread shoulder-width apart, his thin blond body hair shivering for reasons unrelated to temperature, as another one of God's creations imposes his own free will.

He wished he'd done more. The fact that he'd aided this man in any way distressed him mightily. When an uncomfortable truth becomes unavoidable, less distant, the burden grows heavier, the regret more profound. The shoulder bump on the street jostled all those truths to the visceral present, and he contemplated following him.

But as he walks by Birdland, the double doors open, and Ecclusiastic horns, melodic copper riffs, and rounded indigo notes spill out like the contours of a voluptuous woman wearing her lingerie a size too small, then swirl out into the night like tobacco smoke. It was enough of a distraction to keep him moving toward the subway, a reminder that he is going uptown to write and relax, and figure out a plan for the man from Hell's Kitchen, all while sitting across from the cutest bartender in five boroughs.

C H A R L E S   M I N G U S

T O N I G H T
LIVE AT BIRDLAND IN HOLOGRAPHIC DELIGHT

* * *

7:OO LIBATIONS SET

I'LL REMEMBER APRIL
PASSIONS OF A WOMAN LOVED
BETTER GIT HIT IN YOUR SOUL
OH LORD DON'T LET THEM DROP THAT ATOMIC BOMB ON ME
E'S FLAT AND AH'S FLAT TOO
*ALL THE THINGS YOU COULD BE BY NOW
IF SIGMUND FREUD'S WIFE WAS YOUR MOTHER*

9:3O SWEAT SET

BOOGIE STOP SHUFFLE
MOANIN'
MY JELLY ROLL SOUL
WHAM BAM THANK YOU MA'AM
WEDNESDAY NIGHT PRAYER MEETING
PITHECANTHROPUS ERECTUS

MID:NIGHT TROUBLEMAKER SET

HAITIAN FIGHT SONG
GUNSLINGING BIRD
*IF CHARLIE PARKER WAS A GUNSLINGER,
THERE'D BE A WHOLE LOT OF DEAD COPYCATS*
TONIGHT AT NOON
DEVIL WOMAN
SELF PORTRAIT
CHILL OF DEATH
EPITAPH

Roosevelt stands outside RUST BUST & AXE and leans against a pay phone, the dinosaur of communication that's beginning a resurgence of sorts due to the AppleFacegate incident. The sounds of dimes and quarters jangling their way into the slot and then landing with a dulled cymbal crash has returned to the sidewalks. His blood is still simmering from the heat of base memories. It has a sulfuric quality that comes from the pit of his stomach and rises to the brain.

Roosevelt walks inside in need of a coolant, a calming agent in a glass. He surveys a scene that is homogeneously male with a few women tucked in between. He finds a spot at the bar near a party of several and leans over the Chicago rail in search of Lola, the bartender. He sees himself in the mirror and the lights over him accentuate his fears of a fading hairline. He runs his fingers over the scar on his eyebrow and slips back from the light. She's at the far end of the bar shaking a cocktail. Roosevelt unwraps a Rusty Nail toothpick and glances at the menu. Someone from the group next to him is rambling on about the shooting in Harlem and how it's a symptom of a Godless culture in "the world today," a phrase he repeats many times. He tries to ignore him, but he can't close his ears all the way.

Then Lola comes over and the voice hushes into the backdrop, as did everything else. "Good to see you! What will it be this time? Cognac, Sugar Hill, Colt 45?"

"I always tell you, Colt 45 was a one-time thing. No mas for me."

"So, cognac or the Sugar?"

"I'm going to keep it light with cognac tonight. D'Ussé or Kelt Tour du Monde, your choice. You're my spiritual advisor for the night."

Lola tilts a crystal snifter on its side and pours the D'Ussé cognac straight up. "You get the fancy glass with this."

"Yeah, thanks. It's a nice one. Last time I had a beer you gave me the Hello Kitty glass."

"It was appropriate," Lola kids.

Roosevelt swirls, sips, and smiles. "In the name of testosterone atonement, I'm much happier with this one." He raises his glass.

She asks, "You're going solo once again?"

"Yep, just living the lush life with me and my pen tonight. There's always plenty of thinking and philosophizing to do. My brain is annoying; it never shuts off."

"Well, cheers to that. I'll be back." She winks at him, but doesn't think he notices it, so she winks again. Then she realizes that he probably did see both winks—the first one through the bottom of the glass and the second after his sip—and she now looks like she has a flirty kind of facial tick. Then, as she walks to the other end of the bar, she wonders why closing one eye is a sexy thing anyway.

Lola works fast, walking fro and too quickly for him to appreciate any one view for long. Whether she is reaching up for a glass or leaning over the bar, her curves cause him to veer down a different path of thought. Instead of mapping out ideas for his future as he had intended, he's trapped in a delightful, vertical distraction. He feels the immediate tranquility of his first few sips and meditates on the beauty of individual moments and how ephemeral most of them are. With the crystal glass in his left hand, he puts his pen to the vacant coaster with his right, and a geometric sketch slowly transforms into a short poem.

EVENING NIPS OF COGNAC

TAKEN WITHOUT SORROW,

I'M A MODERN MAN OF ACTION,

CARPE DIEM TOMORROW!

The surrounding noise returns with a nearby conversation at the forefront. They are a group of seven, four men and three women. He takes a healthy sip and enjoys the echo of toffee and cedar notes as he exhales. The four men are of distinct visual abilities. One wears a permanent squint, another wears thin-rimmed glasses, the next wears a pair with thick magnifying lenses, and the last is completely blind. The women each fit into their own zone on the Goldilocks scale. There is Too Cool, Too Hot, and Pretty O.K.

The Squinter is holding a glass with a picture of Mt. Rushmore on it. Too Cool is sharing a story that goes nowhere. Magnifiers is the one he hears say, "the world today," over and over. The blind man rubs the back of his neck. Pretty O.K. makes eye contact with him as she sips her cosmo. The discussion veers to the various and vicarious miracles they'd experienced or known about. Thin Glasses begins to share his story and his eyes widen with excitement. Lola pours Roosevelt a second one. This time it's the Kelt Tour du Monde. Unfortunately, she's too busy to talk.

Thin Glasses recalls the time when his faith was truly realized. He was on I-95 heading south to visit a snowbird of a grandparent in Florida. His plan was to drive through the night with the aid of coffee and music. In Maryland the roads had become icy, but since Thin Glasses was driving an SUV with a name that made it sound like it could navigate the Alaskan peaks, he felt safe. He'd stopped at a rest area for a pre-packaged sandwich with two slices of ham, one slice of processed swiss (where the area of the hole may have been greater than that of the cheese), one large iceberg leaf, a firm tomato slice, all on a starchy bun. Even though it didn't seem to have had a great creator, if he gave it some TLC, a.k.a. S&P, it would suffice to line his stomach for the time being. Thin Glasses told of his love for pepper on just about anything. This was an opportunity to exploit this love, he went on to say. So he piled on the pepper. He said that just a few years prior, he'd really never liked pepper—that he didn't even know where it came from—until he went over a friend's apartment one evening. He was a friend *In Christ* who happened to know about peppercorns and their use in the culinary arts. His enthusiasm for pepper transmitted to Thin Glasses so much that it caused him to develop a full-fledged, pre-meal shaking reflex. So, while driving, Thin Glasses removed the sandwich from the plastic wrap and took a careful bite that ended up dislodging the entire tomato slice. He tried to wiggle his teeth to bite through the skin of the tomato, but it was stuck hanging from his front teeth. He showed the group how he tried to manipulate his lips to take in the whole tomato, complete with slurpy sounds. Already a mess, he put his even sadder sandwich on his lap with a non-steering hand so he could force the whole slice into his mouth. This slowed him down and another car accelerated around him. Thin Glasses's legs shifted and the sandwich on his lap spread out like a fan. The weather was getting worse, the blacktop was becoming icier and snowier by the moment. While keeping his eyes on the road, he tried to put his sandwich back together. In the process he dropped the top part of the bun and the sandwich now resembled a soft taco, with all of the pepper collected and exposed in the fold of the two slices of the poor old pig. His next attempt for a bite proved worse. He was still chewing the tomato, but wanted to add more flavor. Still watching the road, he took a deep inhale just before the bite and the pepper went up his nose like a line of black cocaine. And in cartoon style, he dropped the taco sandwich and held his index finger under his nose to try to stop the inevitable. No chance. His head rocked back and jerked forward with a staccato force and expunged a red gooey sneeze all over his windshield, disabling any kind of sight or reaction time. Thin Glasses now explained that he was driving over a small hill on the highway and had a limited view of the road in front of him. It turns out, that just moments before The Sneeze, there'd been a pileup of cars rear-ending each other. This caused even more cars to subsequently skid and get t-boned just over the arc of the road. And now there were very different shades and textures of gooey redness on the windshields of seventeen people, all pronounced dead at the scene. When Thin Glasses was affected by the pepper, the force caused his driving hand, his left hand, to push up on the wheel, sending his vehicle into a wild spin off to the shoulder of the road, steering clear of the impending danger. Through the pieces of the tomato, he saw the carnage around him. He broke down in awe because God had spared him, made him feel hunger when he did, introduced him to the pepper connoisseur, and ultimately for the faith God must've had in *him* to do more with his life, he reasoned. Thin Glasses said that the incident proved to him that God is great and it strengthened his faith, forging it in steel. "It was a miracle," he concluded.

Lola sees his glass is just about empty again, "Would you like another drink, cowboy?"

"Yes, but let's switch it up. How about a Sugar Hill this time?"

"Be right back." Lola looks at the beer glasses on the shelves behind her, but doesn't take any of them down. She walks to the far end of the bar. Roosevelt watches her bottle opener, a flash of silver peeking out of her back pocket rocking side to side, all the way down. It is reflexive and spellbinding. This time she's gone longer than normal. He listens again to the drivel next to him and wonders why they're all together. When Lola returns with his beer, the foam is hugging the rim of the Hello Kitty glass.

"I should've stayed with cognac," he says.

"You were going to get this glass no matter what." She reads his short poem on the coaster. "I like it! Feel free to write one for me." She almost winks again.

"Not if I keep getting my drinks in this."

"For your pain, the beer is on me."

"Cheers!" He flips over the coaster and begins making dots along its side and corners. He tries thinking of an opening line for Lola, but he's still distracted by the events on the periphery, the eye-patched man, the callous way people were speaking about the shooting up in Harlem, and the group of seven and their miracles. And what's with all of the eye issues, he wonders. He takes another sip and connects a few of the dots on the coaster.

The Squinter, already emotional after listening to the testimony of Thin Glasses, closes his eyes and produces two tears from under the folds of skin. Without words or warning, The Squinter, in the middle of the bar, takes off his v-neck t-shirt a-sap. He wants to show the rest of the group the tattoo that covers his entire back. While the artwork is meant to be the focus, the main attraction seems to be his peculiar frontal façade. Many others in the bar turn their heads, and squint too, and then return to their own conversations. His body sports dark patches of hair randomly distributed across the pale terrain. He has a black hole of a bellybutton, a place where both light or lint can never escape. The topography of The Squinter's chest looks like the jagged peaks of Everest & Lhotse, defying gravity by pointing straight out with two conical nipples at each summit. He has an elevated Buddha-grade semi-sphere to the south. And as he jiggles his way around to show every angle of the tattoo, his stomach remains stationary while his bra-less chest seems to actually move mountains. When The Squinter was young the mean kids on the block called him Cow Tits.

Against a shaded sky there is a jaundice sun in the top center of his back. Descending down from the sun is an elevator shaft that spans the length of his spine. Over his bulbous love handles are swirls of smoke at the base of what once was a building. His love handles also have thick curly patches of hair, so the smoke takes on a 3D effect. Flying in small groups near the sun are angels in flowing white dresses. At the base of the piece, in black and gray, are the words of John 4:48 from the New American Standard Bible:

"So Jesus said to them, 'Unless you people see signs and wonders, you will simply not believe.'"

"Some of you don't know this, but I was the lone survivor of a terrible gas explosion when I was working in the Bronx, where also seventeen people died. I'd been working as an elevator repair man and I was having a rough day. I mean, not to be funny right now, but my coworkers always said that the job came with its ups and downs. Well, this was a down day, but not because of work. The woman I had been on a few dates with gave me some really tough news. She was way out my league, honestly. She even admitted as much. When we first started dating—we met through a mutual friend—it was because she wanted to get away from the kind of guys she'd been with her whole life. She was upfront and said that she wasn't attracted to me outright, but that she wanted to get to know me on a different level, to be respected as a whole person, and to be treated like a girlfriend should. She'd never had that, apparently. She said I had the type of personality that she needed to change her ways. Of course, I was more than willing. I treated her with respect and care. I always asked how she was feeling and asked her to tell me what she'd like to do on our dates. I tried to be the perfect gentleman."

When The Squinter puts his shirt back on he bumps the Everest tit with his right arm. The ramifications are seismic.

"That morning she called me and sounded different. She said she had to own up to something and felt terrible about it. I told her not to worry. But what she said devastated me. She told me that she had a one-night-stand with some rich guy she met in a club in the Lower East Side. She told me how much she regretted it and that it was the only time she was ever going to mess up. She told me it was probably because she wasn't used to being treated so well, that she never gave casual hookups much thought, and that she'd reverted to her old ways after having too many drinks with her girlfriends. I did my best to hold my emotions back and I told her that I appreciated that she told me, but that I wouldn't be able to see her anymore. When I said that to her, it was like someone else was in control. I wanted to be angry and upset, but those words came out instead. She even asked me to give her another chance, begging me almost. But I refused."

Lola stops by just as he takes his last sip. She rinses his empty Hello Kitty glass and refills it with another Sugar Hill from the tap.

The Squinter continues, "So fast forward to the afternoon when I was working inside the residential elevator on the lower level of the building. I was replacing the COP, the car operating panel. There was nothing special about the job. Everything that she told me that morning and all of my memories of our dates were replaying in my head the whole time. And then all at once, I fell to my knees. Alone in the elevator I broke down and cried. My tears turned into words, The Lord's Prayer. That's when I realized I wasn't alone. God was there for me. I prayed for her to make better decisions and I prayed for God to guide me into my next relationship. I prayed for strength and humility. Just as I said, 'Amen,' there was an explosion like none I'd ever heard. It was a gas explosion that ripped through the building and destroyed the top half of the elevator I was in. If I wasn't on my knees, my head would've been blown right off, no doubt. Then—sometimes this is hard to talk about—then the cables must have snapped and catapulted the car straight up. I saw burning bodies and destruction on each floor. I stayed low to the ground and the sides of the elevator car shielded me from the crossfire of home décor shrapnel. And just as the car rose to the top floor, there was a second explosion that seemed to come from below. This blew off a big section of the roof and elevator system, and I, miraculously, was looking up at the sun above me! I couldn't believe it and I stared at it until I felt the building shake. Actually, my vision hasn't been the same since. Then I climbed onto an unaffected area of the roof and waited for help, praying the whole time that there wouldn't be another explosion and that I was thankful to be alive by the grace of God. When the rescue team arrived by helicopter, my angels, they lifted me from the destruction to the sky. As we flew away, I realized that it was because she'd cheated on me with that other guy she met at the club, that I'd broken down and fallen to my knees and began to pray at just the right time. I actually became thankful for that man. He was like my unknown savior, in the most unlikely way possible." The rest of the group, Thin Glasses, Magnifiers, the blind one, Too Cool, Too Hot, and Pretty O.K., grew closer as they listened. "So, I've been thinking about how much it helped me to surrender to God in a time of weakness. I thought about starting a movement where whenever you feel like I did, or vulnerable, or concerned that what you're doing isn't in God's best interest, you kneel and ask for forgiveness, wherever you are, in public or at home. It would help show others that everyone has these feelings. And tonight I thought about the performance artist and the way she was shot and what she was doing. Maybe if she'd realized that she wasn't putting herself in a good place, and that her actions could be interpreted in a way that wasn't glorifying God, maybe she would've knelt down and prayed at exactly the right moment, like I did in a way, and the bullet would have missed her entirely..."

Roosevelt, still facing forward, interrupts the story, "If she'd knelt down, the bullet may have grazed her head instead of the side of her body. That could've been a lot worse, man." He turns toward the group and they disperse, as if repelled by his diamagnetic stance.

The Squinter smiles, anticipating a friendly conversation. "If she had knelt, God would've protected her, believe me."

"I love the idea that she would've prepared for this performance, put all the pieces in place, and then suddenly it would dawn on her that it wasn't right in the eyes of God. And then in the middle of the performance, kneel down, basically naked, and pray for forgiveness in front of her audience."

"Yes, exactly! That would've really driven the message home. And that's how we all came into this world, naked, God's original design, right?" The Squinter is still smiling.

"Again, if she'd done that she probably would've been shot in the head, accused of blasphemy, killed in the name of this new righteous America, supported by people like you." His tone turns both vainglorious and virtuous, and he smiles as well.

"Look, all I was saying is that if she'd turned to God at the right moment, things would've turned out better for her. Maybe not just at that moment, but at any time prior to that moment.

If she had true faith, she would've been somewhere else. And honestly, you're intruding on our conversation. Take care." It is the most relaxed The Squinter's eyes looked all night.

"Right, I mean, her decisions in life could've led her to live in that building that exploded. That would've worked out. By the way, are you saying that no one else in that building had faith? How could you possibly know that?"

Too Cool steps in with contempt, "You're very cynical and rude. I don't think you should question our faith and what we believe. Are you always like this?"

Roosevelt answers sincerely, "Simultaneously overtired and drunk? Listening in on conversations? No, I'm not always like this. Just tonight. Lucky you." Roosevelt notices Magnifiers clenching his fist and looking jittery. He anticipates that his best shot isn't going to be that bad or very accurate, and he braces for it without making it too obvious. But just as Magnifiers begins his windup for the punch, he kneels to the barroom floor, and prays.

Roosevelt lowers his shoulders and takes a sip from his Hello Kitty glass.

Too Cool looks down at her friend and then continues, "I don't think you're very nice."

Pretty O.K. finishes her cosmo.

"Forgive me, and I know you can, but I have to remark on your stories. They are the farthest from what miracles should be. They should be truly unexplainable, and both of you just explained and accounted for every aspect of your good fortune, not to mention the demise of others which seemed to benefit you in realizing how loved you are. It's a selfish view to have The Creator place you directly in the center of concern."

Thin Glasses steps in, "We're *trying* to explain what happened. We have faith that our— uh, faith—is what brings God to us and protects us. It's all part of God's plan."

"So, me talking to you right now must also be part of the plan."

"Of course it is. And by the way, I couldn't even try to explain why I met the guy that introduced me to pepper. I believe God brings people together to learn from each other. What those interactions mean for the future are unknown to us. But God knows and works in mysterious ways." Thin Glasses summons another smile.

"Yes, I'm sure if we had the time to keep regressing, we could see how you and the pepper guy crossed paths. Even though our eyes face forward, it's easier to look backward. I mean, at first we're all strangers. People meet other people all the time, some of those interactions have concrete consequences, and others have indirect or inconspicuous consequences, and most interactions are simply forgotten. Our brain can't remember every meaningless conversation we've ever had, or connection we've ever made. I'd argue that the circumstances that brought you and the pepper guy together are lost somewhere in a pile of discarded memories. What you're saying is that miracles occur when *you* define them, when *you* recognize them. But really these are moments like all the others, and they can be beautiful, deplorable, or mundane. These moments are happening now, they are a mathematical constant. What you're doing is placing God within the web of human interactions while you take the role as the sole signifier." Roosevelt switches the Hello Kitty glass from one hand to the other and cracks the knuckles of his free hand. "You very well could have met someone who turned you on to Greek salads. And then, at the rest stop you would've bought one that was packed into a plastic container. You would've had to eat it in your car before heading out on the road. The time it would take for you to finish your salad would've been more than enough time to avoid getting involved in the accident, you wouldn't have been close to it, you wouldn't have sneezed, you wouldn't have thought it was a miracle, just a close call. But what happened is probably this—which I'm sure is difficult to think about—that when you were fussing around with your sandwich in your lap, you were annoying the car behind you, the one that eventually passed you. And that person probably ended up in the middle of the massacre. It sounds like a very clumsy execution of a miracle."

"First of all, I disagree with the word *clumsy*. And I don't know what happened to the car that went around me. For all I know, he bypassed the accident. I'm not saying it wasn't a tragedy, but God gives us free will and things like that happen sometimes. I believe He steps in to save those with strong faith, people with something left to do here on Earth before He calls them home."

"Wait—where is this home?" Roosevelt points up. "Or can I point in any direction?" The septet is silent. "So, how do you define a miracle?"

Thin Glasses answers, "You have to realize that we're all on God's time. Sometimes we lose sight of that. I believe miracles are God's way of reminding us that He is present."

"It's a nice way of putting it, actually. But for me, the miracles of religions are defined by science first because they require a negation of the laws of physics. They are the foundation on which God stands. He operates within our system, not the other way around. Personally, I'd need to see evidence that a miracle occurred, like an ascension in real time. But I think if your belief is strong and true, wouldn't you see God in everything? What you're saying is that He goes through all that trouble just to say, 'Hey, remember Me?' The Ascension of Christ, do you think that happened?"

"Of course."

"That must've been some sight, to witness human-powered rocketry, to rise unaided into the Heavens."

"Truly," Thin Glasses agrees.

"Do you think he rose head-first or feet-first? I always picture head-first into the clouds. But it's after the clouds and the atmosphere that I'm most curious about."

"How so?"

"Well, Heaven is presumably very far away. Did He have to travel the whole way through space, to the end of the universe, and then walk through the pearly gates? How fast was He traveling? Because even if He were traveling at the speed of light, it would take around one hundred billion years to get there. So if people are waiting for Him to return, there's a chance

He may not have even made it to Heaven yet. And by the time He'd return, Earth won't be here anymore. Or was it that once He disappeared into the clouds, he took a Star Trek Transporter-type thing and got on with it quickly."

"See, again, you're thinking about it too much. You have to understand that God, Jesus, and The Holy Spirit, are all-powerful. God created the physics and laws, and he can intervene and change where He sees fit. He is the force of all life."

"He or They?"

"What?"

"Look, if He is, or They are, intervening, it seems like an admission of a poorly planned world, a flawed design, where The Creator is allowed to change the rules of the game at any time. The Flood, for example, was like God pressing the reset button. Not exactly a smooth intervention. And if you look at *the world today*, as he keeps saying," Roosevelt gestures with his Hello Kitty glass in the direction of Magnifiers, "I don't think the reset worked too well."

"Yes, it's a sinful world. But I don't question God's plan. How can I profess to know better than He? How can I pretend to really know why He chooses the miracles He performs?"

"*Performs* might be the perfect word. But actually, I don't think God is behind any of the miracles. I think miracles are sales pitches made by people trying to bring more believers to their side. They're wild exaggerations of half-truths to make themselves look to be chosen by God. They perform from behind the curtain and make changes without taking a bow. They've been doing it the whole time." Roosevelt finishes his beer.

"You're looking at each instance too closely. You have to take the whole picture into account. The miracle is that we're here at all. That's the mystery," Thin Glasses explains.

"The mystery to me isn't that God works in mysterious ways, but that He doesn't work in obvious ways. He could make it clear to any skeptic with something that would be und'niable. I could give him a few ideas." Roosevelt has a difficult time articulating the word *undeniable*.

Thin Glasses is perspiring. "That's where we're different. I'm humble about my place in the world."

"No, you're aligning yourself with The Creator of the universe. I am proclaiming to be lucky—lucky to exist through all of the possible impediments to our birth and subsequent survival."

"I am humble before God. You are boastful before nothing."

"The so-called miracles you and your friends shared were not humble. They were self-centered and without compassion. And because they were explained, any faithful astonishment should fade away."

"Miracles are further creations by The Creator," Thin Glasses continues, "it's not a one-shot deal."

"How did that reset button work out? Are we really any different now?" Roosevelt takes a sip from his empty glass.

Too Cool holds out her hands and stretches her fingers, "Yes! We are clearly different! Can you both stop now?"

"What evidence do you have that there even is a sole Creator?"

Thin Glasses retorts midway through Roosevelt's question, "What evidence do you have that there isn't?"

Some of the multisyllabic words are getting difficult for Roosevelt to say, but he goes on despite Too Cool's protest. "Look—miracles are influenced by fear and wishful thinking. Fear that the story wouldn't have enough weight on its own, and wishful that it actually happened, fulfilling prophesies and perpetuating more of them. But now that we know these fantastic stories haven't been recurring, believers search for them in their own lives, however unimpressive, apply the miracle tag, and deny any evidence to the contrary. Maybe it's a way to avoid the real issues that they're dealing with. To reject critical thinking is easy. It can make anyone feel better for as long as they want. The sad thing is that the stories in the Bible do have enough weight. The writers that embellished were the first to go Hollywood. They put in the special effects to sell tickets and you're holding a stub in your hand right now."

"You just don't get it," Too Cool says with a shrill, "it's time to move on. I don't want to talk about this another second. This is actually really boring."

"Wait, why don't I get it? Do I have inferior vision or perception? Do you have special faith receptors that I don't?"

"Stop talking!"

"It's funny actually. I have better than twenty-twenty vision and look who I'm talking to. Is that a blessing as well?"

"When God reduces one sense, the others are enhanced. I embrace it," Magnifiers says.

"Well, it's not like you really have a choice." Roosevelt chills the air back to January as Too Hot and Pretty O.K. reach their boiling point. They leave the bar with tetrads of heel-clicks to go to the restroom, to actually rest.

Magnifiers points his finger near Roosevelt's chest. "You're not a very nice person. You're a bully, an antagonizer."

"Right, God put me here to push you around with logic. It was a test to see if you'd hold strong and not be influenced by how I think."

"That won't be a problem," The Squinter snaps. "If anything, my faith is stronger now."

Roosevelt looks toward The Squinter, "You know that tattoo on your back looks like a giant penis, right?"

"What?!"

"Look at it again. It's a hairy penis that just came angels."

"Hey, *F*—" But before he can finish the expletive, The Squinter falls to one knee and makes the sign of the cross.

"It's hard to keep a straight face around here," Roosevelt remarks to himself. Too Cool thinks of the tattoo, "You're disgusting."

Magnifiers steps forward, again with his finger hovering near Roosevelt's chest. "You've gone too far. We didn't come here to have our religious beliefs insulted by you or anyone else. We came here to enjoy each other's company after not seeing each other for a long time. This is no longer a discussion. There is no more debate. And if you continue to bother us, I will talk to the manager. Leave us be."

"O.K., let's end it here. I do apologize, but when I heard all of you speaking casually about how you've benefitted spiritually through the misfortunes and tragedies of others, I felt compelled to say something, to challenge you. I think I caught all of you with your pants down and your skirts up, metaphorically, and no one was in the mood for any philosophical intercourse. So again, my apologies. Honestly, enjoy the night." He is the only one to raise a glass, which is also still empty. "Cheers!" The group's reticence hangs in the air like an anvil.

Roosevelt turns toward the bar while reaching in his pocket for a Benjamin. He slips the bill under his glass, Independence Hall side-up. He waves goodbye to the cutest bartender in five boroughs, who is a few yards away. "Thank you, Lola, I'll see you next time!"

"Soon," she says as she throws him an air kiss, "and with my poem!"

With some good vibes returning to his system, he smiles and points at the Hello Kitty glass, "We'll see!" Roosevelt leaves RUST BUST & AXE with cognac and Sugar Hill in his veins, and walks a crooked line to a secluded enlightenment.

In a huff, and without exultation, the blind one says, "Praise the Lord."

The Baseball Encyclopedia:
The Complete and Official Record of Major League Baseball

* * *

Official Box Score
Sunday, November 4, 2001
World Series Game 7
New York Yankees vs. Arizona Diamondbacks
Bank One Ballpark

* * *

	1	2	3	4	5	6	7	8	9	10	R	H	E
NEW YORK	0	0	0	0	0	0	1	1	0	1	3	9	3
ARIZONA	0	0	0	0	0	1	0	0	1	0	2	10	0

BATTING

New York Yankees	AB	R	H	RBI	BB	SO
D.Jeter	5	1	2	1	0	1
P.O'Neill	3	0	2	0	0	1
C.Knoblauch	1	0	0	0	0	0
M.Nazimek	1	0	1	0	0	0
B. Williams	5	0	0	0	0	2
T.Martinez	5	0	1	1	0	2
J.Posada	4	0	0	0	0	2
S.Spencer	4	0	0	0	0	0
A.Soriano	4	2	2	1	0	1
S.Brosius	3	0	0	0	1	2
R.Clemens	2	0	0	0	0	1
M.Stanton	0	0	0	0	0	0
D.Justice	1	0	1	0	0	0
M.Rivera	1	0	0	0	0	0
Totals	38	3	9	3	1	12

Arizona Diamondbacks	AB	R	H	RBI	BB	SO
T.Womack	5	0	2	0	0	1
C.Counsell	4	0	1	0	0	0
L.Gonzalez	5	0	0	0	0	3
M. Williams	5	0	1	0	0	3
S.Finley	5	1	2	0	0	2
D.Bautista	4	0	1	1	1	2
M.Grace	4	0	3	0	0	0
D.Dellucci	0	0	0	0	0	0
K.Rogers	1	0	0	0	0	1
D.Miller	4	0	0	0	0	3
M.Cummings	0	1	0	0	0	0
C.Schilling	3	0	0	0	0	3
M.Batista	0	0	0	0	0	0
R.Johnson	0	0	0	0	0	0
J.Bell	1	0	0	0	0	0
Totals	41	2	10	1	1	18

PITCHING

New York Yankees	IP	H	R	ER	BB	SO
R.Clemens	6.1	7	1	1	1	10
M.Stanton	0.2	0	0	0	0	0
M.Rivera W(2-0)	3.0	3	1	0	0	8
Totals	10.0	10	2	1	1	18

Arizona Diamondbacks	IP	H	R	ER	BB	SO
C.Schilling	7.1	6	2	2	0	9
M.Batista	0.1	0	0	0	0	0
R.Johnson L(2-1)	1.2	3	1	1	1	1
A.Martino	0.1	0	0	0	0	1
D.Carey	0.1	0	0	0	0	1
Totals	10.0	9	3	3	1	12

Managers
NYY: J.Torre
ARI: B.Brenly
Umpires
HP—S.Rippley; 1B—M.Hirschbeck; 2B—D.Scott; 3B—E.Rapuano; LF—J.Joyce; RF—D.DeMuth
Official Scorer: S.Evers
Time of Game: 3:37
Attendance: 49,591

[[↑]]

· The N.Y. Public Library ·
Round 2
Snippets of hushed conversations in the evening between Zeus & the multitude.

Z

[Main Lobby]
· Brunette, green eyes, pink sweater and black denim shorts, white sneakers, unlit cigarette in her mouth ·

"It's different. I like it."

"My bracelet? Oh, thanks. Thought I'd change it up a little."

"And that's yours too? Or are you holding it for someone?"

"No, it's mine. Yes, I'm not ashamed to say that I carry a purse sometimes."

"A murse?"

"Or a manbag I've heard it called. It's actually a travel case for shaving cream and all that. But I like to use it when I know I'll be out for the day and I have a few extra things with me. I think it looks kind of manly, really. I mean, it doesn't have a shoulder strap or anything."

"So it's a clutch?"

"I guess so. You know I also enjoy dancing and organizing my closet."

"Does your girlfriend know about all this? I'd tell her. It might be important!"

Z

[Sports Section]
· Blonde-red ombré, dark eyes, nose piercing, coffee travel mug in one hand,
Baseball Encylcopedia in the other ·

"I'm looking for someone to play Wiffle ball with in the park today. It's beautiful out."

"How do you play Wiffle ball with two people?"

"It's like Home Run Derby, but we face the wrong way."

"O.K..."

"The batter stands on the pitcher's mound and the pitcher throws from home plate. Then, if you hit the ball over the backstop on a fly, it's a home run. You get ten chances and then we switch. The only problem is sometimes you have to run after the ball after a bad pitch. But you burn a lot of calories, it's fun!"

"Maybe I'll just watch."

Z
[Cooking Section]

· Brunette with a boy-cut, hazel eyes, black turtleneck with the sleeves torn off, white jeans, barefoot, holding a pair of strappy shoes in one hand, a vegan cookbook in the other, headphones on ·

"What's the best vegan dish you've ever made?"

"Excuse me?"

"Oh sorry, didn't realize you could hear me."

"What's up?"

"Just wondering what your best vegan dish is? And, I guess, what's the worst?"

"My best? I'll go with Coconut Curry with Tofu and Pineapple. It has a kick to it. Worst is probably anything for breakfast. My only appetite in the morning is for black coffee. Are you vegan too?"

"Sometimes. I think I'm going that way. I'm still learning."

"How would you classify yourself?"

"It sounds pretentious, but I guess I'm an ovo-lacto-pescatarian, soon to be vegetarian, with frequent dabbles with in vitro meat."

"You're beginning your journey. I wish you luck."

"Thanks."

"So, what are your best and worst?"

"Me? I don't know. Pretty often, I make the silver dollar pancakes my mom made me when I was a kid, but they're never quite as good."

"It's always better when someone else makes it for you."

"But recently, I added my own innovation when I have the time in the morning. I want to give my mom a run for her money. See, the biggest problem with maple syrup and pancakes is that the syrup gets cold too quickly. So I set up my fondue set and put the syrup in there. Then I cut the silver dollars in half, dip, and each bite is perfect."

"Sounds like a good idea."

"My worst was a Doritos grilled cheese. I didn't think too much in advance. I made my basic grilled cheese in the pan with butter, but I layered Doritos, the purple bag, in with the cheese. When I took the first bite, it was like eating a big soggy Dorito. I couldn't force it down."

"Gross."

"Another terrible idea I had was in response to an annoying saying I heard growing up: *A watched pot never boils.* It's funny, I remember when I was getting older and hanging out with friends later and later, my mom would stay up and tell me how long she waited before going to bed. I used to tell her, 'A watched kid never comes home.' Anyway. So one time, I filled a pot up with water, fired up the stove, waited and watched until it boiled."

"And how was that?"

"Boring."

"And that's the end of your story?"

"Yep."

"So you're telling me you cooked water?"

"It was vegan, at least."

Z

[Grammar and Style Manuals Section]

· Fair-skinned, apricot hair with tattooed freckles, softer body, possibly pregnant ·

"I know, it's like, just use an adverb. And use them lovingly and *oftenly*."

"I don't think that's correct."

"O.K., I won't use them."

"No, I mean *oftenly*."

"Deal. I won't use them oftenly or at all."

"No..." Her freckles rise with her cheeks.

Z

[Medical Section]

· Black hair, dark eyes, posture that is almost too perfect, sensible clothes, lipstick applied over the border of her actual lips, holding a book about reproduction, polite, but dismissive ·

"You know what's funny about reproduction?"

(No reaction, except to move to the next shelf over.)

"I always thought that The Rhythm Method had something to do with pelvic thrust rate. Then I read up on it. As wrong as you can get."

(Nods with pursed lips, moves another shelf down.)

"And as far as irony goes, isn't it strange that a Trojan condom is what *protects* you from a small army invasion?"

(Smiles maybe, walks away.)

Z [33]

[Mathematics Section]

· Blonde, brown eyes, pencil in her hair, gray lacy top, pants that mean business ·

"Assuming time is infinite in the abstract, I've always wondered about this. Thursdays will go on forever, so there are an infinite number of Thursdays. Also, Thursdays and Fridays will go on forever, so there are an infinite number of Thursdays and Fridays. Therefore, there are just as many Thursdays as there are Thursdays and Fridays combined!"

"Like, infinity equals infinity?"

"Exactly. But it's hard to wrap your head around it. If I think too hard about it, steam starts to come out of my ears."

"Maybe some infinities are larger than others?"

"Hmm... I've heard love is infinite as well, but that's my mom talking."

ℤ

[Gaming Section]
· Brunette, maroon tank top with rips along the seams that says Visit the Twin Cities,
two full tattoo sleeves, genuinely disinterested ·

"It looks innocent at first, but I think tic-tac-toe is a game of explicit kisses and hugs, assuming there's a winner."

"Yep. Never thought about it like that. Probably because I played it when I was seven years old."

"Would three Os in a row be a naked hug?"

"Go play by yourself. I'm sure you'll find it out."

ℤ

[Physiology Section]
· Blonde with wavy hair, spaghetti-strapped top the color of marinara, silver-flared skirt,
her back was to him, holding open an anatomy book ·

"It's funny, I'm looking for a book like that too because earlier today someone called me an asshole."

She didn't turn around, "I can't imagine why."

"Well, I'll tell you. This woman said I was interrupting her thoughts with my voice. She could've told me to be quiet in a different way, but that's the way people are sometimes. So I told this accuser that it was as arbitrary as calling me an ankle or an elbow. And that, if she were to think about it, it was fairly complementary. She compared me to a necessity. I mean, you can get by without an arm or a leg, but not me. I am the police of the human body, getting rid of the riffraff. So I figured I'd come here to research my claim. Next time someone calls me that I can teach them something."

She turned around, "Ugh, not you again."

"Wait, do I know you?"

"Asshole."

Z

[Music Section]
· Curly dark hair over to one shoulder, fake eyelashes, white blouse with a thin black tie,
tight yellow jeans, black heels, just took a selfie with an A$AP Rocky book ·

"Oh, excuse me, sorry about that. This section is a little bit cramped. I just want to get to the other side of you. The book I want is over there."

Her back arches and she leans against the spines.

"You look like you'd be an awkward dancer."

Now her eyebrows arched.

"You want to have a silent dance contest right here?"

She didn't mind the attention, but said, "No thanks."

"How dare you. O.K., you're force me to go solo." He body-rolls from the shoes to the shoulders, then pops and locks a step toward the shelf, snaps his fingers, grabs the book, and shows her the cover in one move.

She can't help but giggle. "Now that was awkward."

"What? That was style."

"O.K..."

"I'm going to Truant, the club that just opened up on Second and Second. DeeDeeJ is spinning a throwback set tonight and *The Wu-Tang Manual* is just the thing to get me in the mood for tonight. It's a must-re-read. I'm talking Robert F. Diggs, Gary Grice, Russell Jones, Jason Hunter, Corey Woods, Lamont Hawkins, Dennis Coles, and Clifford Smith, and also Elgin Turner. They'll be pumping through the speakers, no doubt. I'll be waiting for *C.R.E.A.M.*[34] all night. You should come down and show off some of your weird moves."

"What time?"

Z

[Biology Section]
· Blonde, light eyes behind black-rimmed glasses, white-and-black floral dress, shy and curvy,
holding a book open to a picture of a Dracula Orchid ·

"Are you scientist?"

"No, just curious. Why, are you?"

"No, but I think if I were to go the science route, I would be a geologist. I love learning about gemstones, finding out where they come from, and what specific qualities they have." He held back his appreciation for the properties of cleavage, luster, and hardness.

"Yeah, me too. They're interesting. I'm thinking about going back to school, but I don't know what field I want to go into yet."

"I'm with you there. I've been wading in the waters of indecision as well."

"I'm sure you'll figure it out soon." She was genuinely sweet.

"Hopefully. But probably not in geology. I know that metaphorically, I do look for the gems within my friends, old and new."

"That's nice to think of people that way, sure."

"Yeah, in all aspects of my life, I'm looking for that hidden gem[35]."

"If you keep looking I'm sure you'll find her, I mean, whatever you're looking for."

"No, you're spot on, that's a big part of it. But sometimes I worry that once I do, I won't know what to do next."

"You'll be fine, trust me."

"What would your friends say is your best quality? In what ways are you a gem to them?"

Z

[Medical Section]

· Short pink hair, blue cardigan, undershirt with geometric patterns, acid-wash jeans,
soft cast and black walking boot ·

"You might be the one to ask. I'm looking for a book that will tell me why we don't get itchy when we sleep."

"Excuse me?"

"Well, you have that boot on. I'm sure your foot must get itchy, right?"

"Yeah. It sucks. Thanks for reminding me."

"I mean, I'm sure it itches during the day and you'll try to take care of it. But does it get itchy when you're sleeping?"

"I don't know, I would obviously be sleeping."

"That's what I'm saying. Isn't that strange?"

"That I'm not scratching my foot all night?"

"That the body, or the brain, can turn that off. If I get an itch during the day, sometime I try to play a little game with myself and see how long I can stand it to not scratch it."

"So, you have a busy schedule?"

"Not exactly."

"I can tell."

"Why can't I tell my brain, 'Look, we can see that there's nothing on my arm that I have to touch to get rid of, let's just let this one go as we do at night.'"

"You talk to your brain?"

"When I'm alone, sure."

"You're weird. But I think I like that."

Z

[Physiology Section]

· Blonde hair tied up in a bun, brown eyes, friendly smile, short white dress, flip-flops,
yoga mat slung over her shoulder, in retrospect, probably borderline age-range ·

"You know how we celebrate the final time something happens? Like the last rock concert by a group, the last at-bat of a superstar's career, the last episode of a great show?"

"Yeah, sure."

"And we also celebrate the firsts of things, the premiers, the originals. But mostly we remember our first kiss and our first time going all the way."

"My first kiss was terrible!"

"But why don't we celebrate the *last* time we have sex."

"What?"

"Well, one day, when I'm happily married and we're getting on in years, I'd like to celebrate the last time we go all the way."

"But how would you know when that would be?"

"I'm thinking, just like sports, you'd want to go out on top. So when you think you might be nearing the twilight of your sexual years, I'd like to set up the bedroom for one last good one. I'd set up crazy candles, massage oils, expensive wine, all that. Then, when you're all done, you congratulate each other on a really great run, but it's time to hang that game up."

"But that's sad. You might be giving it up too soon?"

"It's true. You probably can't tell how many good ones you have left in you, but I rather go out like that, rather than unceremoniously retire, where one day you realize you're getting too old, you haven't done it in months, and it's too tricky to get both motors running again. My way, that'll never happen."

"But you'll be conceding that you don't want each other anymore. That's sad."

"No. I think you'll have more intimacy with kissing and holding hands. They're will be no more pressure to keep up the game and you can focus on your emotions and the history you've built together. And any time you want, you can reflect on the last time you brought the ruckus. All love."

"Hmmm..."

Z

[Grammar and Style Manuals Section]

· Dirty-blonde hair is still damp from a shower, very pretty, light blue Columbia University sweatshirt with a cartoon lion mascot leaning against a capital C, short khaki shorts, thin patch of stubble on her calf she missed shaving, holding a book about the English language ·

"If you're looking up unusual words, the first one that comes to mind is *eighths*. It has five consonants in a row. e-i-G-H-T-H-S." His hand fans out one letter at a time, from fist to fully-stretched."

She flips through a few pages. "What about *catchphrase*? c-a-T-C-H-P-H-R-a-s-e." She needs two hands.

"It's a compound word, so it loses a little street cred with me."

"Yes, compound words, they're less cool than ordinals."

"Here's another one. *Vacuum* should have an alternate spelling. V-A-C-W-M."

"You're cute!"

"You're smart *and* cute!"

"No way. I'm smart and *wet*. Wait..."

Z

[Main Lobby]
· Onyx-platinum ombré, blue eyes, 1976 vintage *High Voltage* t-shirt,
ripped denim blues, Gold Ewings, no socks ·

"Before we can speak, because of my stature and contractual agreement, I must announce the following advertisement: Thank you for your patronage of The McDonald's Corporation. Please consider us for your next wholesome meal where you can enjoy our internet-free setting with the whole family. You're welcome to talk to each other with your mouths full!"

"Excuse me. Are you talking to me?"

"Of course, you're excused. Sorry about that, it's just my prefix obligation. I have to say that to every tenth person I meet."

"Why?"

"Nevermind[36], I just wanted say hi and figured you'd be nice enough to wait through the intro."

"I'm not that nice."

"Why waste time since I caught you on a generous day. How are you?"

"I was fine about two minutes ago. Look, I'm busy."

"I dig your kicks. That's the real reason I checked you."

"Yeah, these are fly. They always turn heads."

"Ewing was the man. Wish we had him today."

"When did he play? He was on the Knicks, right? Was he really good?"

"Nah, they always make kicks for guys that barely played because they were terrible."

"Look, I said I was busy. I don't have time to learn about your old sports heros."

"Whoa, you wore the shoes. You started the conversation."

"Do you want my boyfriend to finish it for you?"

"I get it, I get it. Let me just start over. I promise I won't say anything to annoy you. Is that O.K.?"

"One more chance, man."

"Cool. Well, before we can speak, because of my stature and contractual agreement, I must announce the following advertisement: Thank you for your patronage of The McDonald's Corporation. Please consider us for your next wholesome meal where you can enjoy—"

"Oh my God. Shut up."

Truant

Zeus and Mel enter the club on the corner of 2nd Avenue and 2nd Street. It used to be a private High School and the new owners of the building did zero in the way of redecorating it. Each of the classrooms still has posters relating to their subjects, the basketball court is the main dance floor, and the cafeteria has become the bar. There are five floors in the building that each become more exclusive as they go up. The bouncers that guard the doors inside and out are the most physically imposing hall monitors of all time. DeeDeeJ is spinning from the Chemistry Lab. There she throws the beats and rhymes into the turntable centrifuges to separate them and fashion them into new compounds. When she speaks to the crowd, she uses the old school lo-fi intercom that's fuzzy and poppy. She likes the way it sounds over her pure vinyl polymers. She announces the drink specials for the next hour.

Zeus looks at Mel. "O.K., I'm ready. Give me a kiss."

"Where do you want it this time?"

"On my neck."

"Hold still."

"Make sure it sticks this time."

"Hold... still."

They walk by the main office and go straight to the Cafeteria for drinks. Zeus had made two additions to his get-up that were both red: one Kangol fedora, and one well-placed smack from Mel on the upper part of his neck. The kiss is a not-so-subtle way to let the other women know that he's stamped with approval, and that they have the competition of at least one other woman. He also wears women's perfume when he goes to clubs. Tonight it's Bunny Love, which has notes of willow, rose hips, and dandelion, and is cruelty-free. It is for the same reason as the lipstick mark, but more on the pheromone level, or at the very least, it's a conversation.

Cafeteria

There are three bartenders behind the line. A female bartender with suspenders, no shirt, and the name "RocKseE" tattooed across her chest in a Def Leppard font. She's bookended by two twins, John and Vacant John. John wears a guitar pick necklace and is working hard. Vacant John is wearing a hairnet, a toothless smile, and is useless. After she hands a drink menu[37] to Mel, RocKseE says to John, "Hey, *86 tequila and *86 your brother!" And then to Mel, "What do you want, honey?"

"I'll have an After-School Special."

Zeus orders second, "Thug Passion and a large water filled all the way up with ice. Thanks."

"Do you want to run a tab?"

"Yes, please." He pulls out a thin metal credit card from his front pocket.

RocKseE glances at the name on the card so she can enter it on the POS system. She smiles at him, "Oh, it *is* you."

Zeus drinks the water in one long sip and keeps the ice. He pours his Thug Passion from the champagne glass over the rocks in the plastic cup.

"Classy," Mel says.

Zeus wants the drink to dilute and last so he can maintain sobriety throughout the night, with maybe a white-belt-grade kick in the pants. When he approaches women at a club, he feels he needs to be articulate to be effective. He also wants to avoid any potential time traveling blackouts. More important, if the sealing of any deal is to be in the works, he wants the system in his pants to be fully functional, which isn't the case when he's stranded on the island of inebriation. It's kind of like threading a needle with a dangling piece of woolen yarn from six inches away—excuse me—*more* than six inches away. Let's just say that it's very difficult, as opposed to very hard.

Zeus and Mel walk into the hallway. He takes a sip and surveys the scene with a grin. Things look promising already. He turns around to find Mel getting some quick attention from two guys and his grin becomes a smirk.

The first girl he wants to approach has her back to him. She's standing with her hands on her hips and seems bored while she waits for her friends to get more drinks at the bar. He'd noticed her in the Cafeteria, before she broke off from the group to wait in the hallway. She's probably the type of girl who doesn't wait for anything, except for drinks from her friends. Her hair is Old Glory blue. She wears a very small top and striped leggings that are red and white like the colonial thirteen. And she has a large ring, but it's on her middle finger. He leans in over her shoulder and smiles. She smiles too. Up close she's pretty, which isn't always typical in clubs.

He opens his mouth as if he's about to say something, but instead, plays up the awkwardness of forgetting what to say. It's a reason to share a moment of closeness and to let her vaguely feel what it might be like to get even closer. Also, it's to imply that he's flustered over what to say, which can sometimes be alluring, as she may feel that her beauty is the cause of his pause.

He can see that one of the guys talking to Mel had fallen to the side and that she is now talking with the taller one. Zeus thinks back to the time when they were *together* together. Things can look a lot better when they're in the past. When he thinks like this, Mel becomes Melanie, her name growing in relation to the level of appreciativeness that rises within him.

Usually this happens when the intensity of his heart peaks after several drinks, but it came on early this night. And then he realizes he still hadn't said one thing to lady liberty.

Melanie and Zeus rejoin farther down the hallway by the lockers. They speak into each other's ears to pierce through the beats and rhymes that fill the club. The volume has a visible aura. Outside the Biology classroom, Melanie keeps a mental tally as the women swoon and purse their lips. Zeus has already lost interest in the game, but the contender persists in his valiant effort to kiss half the world, one woman at a time. Or two at a time, if it's called for.

A young woman who calls herself QueenGypsySamantha (she specifies there are no spaces) is wearing a bodysuit and a pair of Air Yeezys. She's cute and out of place and may be wearing the same perfume as he is. She kisses gently. Melinda, or possibly Belinda, has an accent from parts unknown. At one point she kissed him on the neck, so she kind of kissed Melanie, too. Another woman, wearing a deep purple jumper and too-high heels, is on something. She's quick to introduce the tongue. Her name is maybe Jaxon-Bliss.

Gymnasium

On the dance floor, a girl with a denim fanny pack, denim short-shorts, and an unbuttoned white denim shirt, takes off Zeus's hat and wears that too. When she dances, her shirt billows open. They aren't the only ones watching the show. Once the curtains close, Melanie takes the hat back. After several songs, they're ready to simmer down upstairs. But when DeeDeeJ transitions and plays Kendrick Lamar's verse from *Control* over the instrumental from Drake's *0 to 100*, a breakdancing battle kicks off. They have to stick around for one more.

Principal's Office

Shortly after they enter a VIP room on the third floor, a woman wearing red vinyl pants and a white shirt so thin the pattern of her lacy balconette bra is in full view, brushes her hand over Zeus's shoulder and then pinches him at the end of the stroke. He follows her with his eyes as he continues talking with Melanie. He'd only been told to go the Principal's Office once when he was a kid. He remembers trembling in the waiting area while the principal was on the phone. That morning, during The Pledge of Allegiance in homeroom, he had an uncontrollable attack of the giggles. He was in fourth grade. When the principal invited him in, he was sure he was about to be expelled and banished to a faraway island. Instead, he calmly asked him to please not laugh during The Pledge. He told him he was a good kid and that he should be careful not to be influenced by others. And from that morning on, Zeus always said hello to him in the hallway. Respect.

Zeus and Melanie are told that someone bought them a round of drinks and that they're on their way up from the Cafeteria. Zeus looks around for the benefactor. The woman with the red vinyl pants blows him a kiss and leaves the room.

Art

The fourth floor VIP room is much different than the muted green and beige walls of the Principal's Office. There are student works from the last year of the school covering every inch of the walls. The art tables have been traded in for plush couches and end tables. There are easels and markers set up along the sides of the room. The writing on the large blackboard looks like a more recent addition. It is a haiku with the name ROOSEVELT running down the side like the Apollo sign in red and white.

> YESTERYEAR WHISPERS . . .
> THIS EMPTY CLASSROOM IS NOW
> FILLED WITH MEMORIES.

There is a sign over the clock that has the hands removed. It reads: *Art Takes Time*. Zeus notices that there are a lot more guys in the room than girls. He wonders why until he sees a nude model assume a position on the center couch. She's frozen in the warm temperature of the club. He's pretty sure it's the same girl that he'd seen with the fanny pack on the dance floor. Many of the men are stationed at an easel, but few are drawing. For Zeus and Melanie, watching other people watch a naked woman proves to be very boring. So it's on to the next one.

Mathematics

On the top floor of the club, the most exclusive VIP room is littered with posters of metric system conversions, Pythagorean triples, trigonometric functions, and multiplication shortcuts [i.e. When squaring a number with a 5 in the ones column, multiply the number n in the tens column (or tens and hundreds column when dealing with a three-digit number, etc.) by $(n + 1)$ to get the "front-end" of the product, and since squaring a number with a 5 in the ones column always results in a 25 on the "back-end," you can put the answer together with each part. Example 1) Take 35 x 35. The front-end is $n(n + 1)$, or 3(4), which = 12. The back-end is always 25. Therefore 12 and 25 become 1,225. Example 2) Take 115 x 115. The front end is $n(n + 1)$, or $11(12)$, which $= 132$. Again, the back-end is always 25. Therefore 132 and 25 become 13,225. Here's two for you to try, enjoy. 85 x 85 = ? and 135 x 135 = ?[38]]. Someone recognizes McJesus and he's approached by two women while he's talking to Melanie. The one doing the talking is wearing a kimono and asymmetric ear piercings. One ear is hanging lower than the other. The quiet one is wearing denim shorts and an unnecessary garter belt. Odds are she has a pristine fake ID. He says hello, raises his glass, and takes a picture with them. The over/under on their combined age is 37½.

"I know I'm supposed to keep talking to some of these lovely ladies, but I just want to chill with you. Let's do a little dancing, a little smoking, little drinking, and not too much thinking. Sound O.K.?"

"Sounds like a country song."

"Let's call the bet a draw."

"You can call it what you want, but if you're quitting, you'll still owe me that blunt."

"I came prepared."

"Spark it."

After a puff-puff, the pass to Melanie goes awry. Zeus had noticed the woman with the red vinyl pants dance by and was distracted at just the wrong time. "Damn! I almost burned you. Sorry, this blunt had plans of its own! My fault, I thought you had it."

"So did I," Melanie says. "The fault lies with me."

"It wasn't you. It was we." They trade laughs and drags as they both become unhinged while remaining unsinged. Zeus connects a memory. "It's funny, I know this guy that got a lot of money that way, by suing someone. But the thing is, he set the whole thing up. He was getting sick of people throwing cigarettes out their car windows, especially when they would land on the hood of his car. This guy *really* cared about his car. And one time, a cigarette flew into his window after bouncing off the driver's side mirror, hit his face, and landed in his lap. Now he wasn't burned, but it gave him this idea. So he formulates a plan where he'll drive on the highways in upstate New York all the time. He scopes out all the drivers that smoke and flick. He finds one man, a chainsmoker, that takes the same route at the same time, Monday to Friday, in a very expensive car. He's like clockwork. He begins to follow this guy every day on the highway waiting for him to flick out his cigarettes. Then he pulls over to the shoulder and finds it still burning. Then with rubber gloves, he collects it into a plastic bag. They're always Camels, and fortunately for this schemer, the filter is always moist. So here's his set-up. He follows him on a Friday morning and, in a small bag on his lap, he has one of the butts with the flicker guy's DNA on it from the day before. He sees the man flick out his first cigarette. Now he knows he's going to light another one and how long it takes him to finish it. The schemer, who's wearing gloves, lights his own Camel. This is the part of the plan that doesn't go well since he's not a smoker and he gets buzzed and it affects his aim. Anyway, when the smoker throws his second cigarette out the window, the schemer presses the burning end of his own cigarette into his face. He means to burn his cheek, but ends up putting it just below his right eye. It sticks to him as it melts into a bloody and black gooey mess. It turns out to be too close to his eye and it causes severe vision loss. He screams and drives erratically as he pulls the burning Camel off his face. He manages to follow the car as he calls the police. He gives them the description of the car and the license plate number, which of course, he had memorized before. He says that he saw the man in the car in front of him flick something out of the window and that it flew into his car and burned his face. He claimed that the burn was as bad as it was because when he tried to instinctively block it, he ended up trapping it against his face and made it worse. This schemer guy imagines that his friends and family would attest to his non-smoking life in court, that he was pure in lung and character. But it turns out that the DNA on the cigarette and the anticipated trial and all of that, was never necessary. The smoker in the car felt so terrible for sending this guy to the hospital and causing his half-blindness, that he settled out of court for millions. He was messed up for awhile, the guy I know, but most of his vision is restored now. He just has this nasty scar."

"Does this guy feel guilty for doing this, for basically indenturing the flicker?"

"How I know him is another long story, but I haven't seen him in years. But yes, he felt bad about it. I think he regrets it, ultimately. But he can wipe his tears with US currency if he wants. Actually, when he told me this story, he cried. The tears dripped down the normal way from his unaffected eye, but for the eye that he burned, the tears pooled up in the small crater of scar tissue until it overflowed and ran down his face in one big salty wave."

"Weird."

"Yep. By the way, do you want to spark it up again?"

Melanie is thinking about the story and looks up at a math poster with the following text: DO NOT READ THIS SIGN. "No, I'm O.K. right now. Actually, I have to go to the little girls' room. I hope there's no line."

"That's one good thing about being a guy."

"Not fair. Actually, that reminds me of this guy I dated. He was O.D. polite. He'd offer to get my drinks, offer to carry my coat, and massage my shoulders if we had to wait in line somewhere."

"I'd date him too."

"He was so used to telling me that he'd do anything for me, that one time, when I told him I had to go to the bathroom, he honestly said that he could go *for* me!"

"There are some bio-logistical issues there, but what a gentleman."

"I'll be right back."

With Melanie away, Zeus settles deeper into the couch and finishes his drink. She isn't gone long.

"Here's another weird one I just thought of. This guy I chilled with was a musician, classically trained and all that, but he was working in the corporate environment composing jingles and music for ad campaigns. He didn't feel artistically challenged, I guess. So with all of that suppressed musical talent, all those intricate melodies in his head came out right *here* when he went down on me." Melanie's hand slides from her hilltop hips to the valley between her legs. Zeus has weed-enhanced focus and notices the thin flow of hairs on Melanie's arm crash against the shore of the back of her hand. "The first time he did it he was drunk and close to passing out. I thought he was trying to say something to me. I asked him what he was doing and he didn't answer. He just kept humming and tonguing me with his eyes closed. After a minute or two, I was no longer enjoying it as a sexual thing. I was just intrigued by this mumbler down under. There was music on in the background, so I reached over to the remote on the nightstand, and turned the down the volume. He had no idea. And then I began to hear it. He was humming the fucking *1812 Overture*, the part with the cannons going off, *duh duh Duh duh duh duh dum dum dummmm*, no lie. The next morning, I didn't tell him about what he did, but I did hum the song when we were having coffee. He looked at me curiously, but didn't put it together."

"I used to do something like that, but I didn't make noise. It was about the alphabet and numbers, coincidentally."

"Sounds like something you would've done. Weirdo."

"Thanks."

"So the next time he was drinking and passing out, I played it up. I started singing the Hallelujah Chorus, and he joined right on in with the humming. Probably the alto part. It was too much. I was laughing and he was vibrating, ...*Forever! And ever!..*, and I thought that was all I could take. But I composed myself and started making requests. He was a playlist in my lap. I'm not sure if he remembers any of this, but I know I'll never listen to *Carmina Burana* the same way again."

While they laugh, the girl in red vinyl pants makes direct eye contact with him and walks into the hallway. Zeus says, "Excuse me for a minute. I have to use the bathroom too." He leaves the classroom and finds her just outside the door. Zeus leans against a locker and she against him.

"I've been waiting to talk to you, but you've been monopolized."

"Thanks for the drinks."

"My pleasure. Are you allowed to be out here in the hallway? Won't your friend be upset that she's not attached to you?"

"It's not like that. I was just on my way to the bathroom."

"Follow me. The ladies' room is closer." She leads him into the handicap stall and locks the door behind them.

Ladies' Room

"As you can see, I'm all about going commando, especially with this denim. On the inside, the backs of the buttons on the fly are lined in velvet and silk. No tighty-whities for me."

"Be quiet and help me peel these off."

"I mean, I had a boxer-brief rebellion a while back, but I'm back on my Schwarzenegger."

"Shhh... come here."

Mathematics

Melanie, alone on the couch with her drink for longer than she expected, sees Zeus and the woman in red walk back into the VIP room. She notices that the woman's bra straps are hanging out the sides of her tank top and that the balcony had fallen. And that his red belt isn't around his waist, but is also under her thin white shirt, fastened over her chest. She feels a twinge of jealousy that she knows shouldn't exist.

Zeus, instead of feeling spent after the ladies' room experience, is fueled with a drive for more. When he sits back down with Melanie, he takes notice of the way her long geometric silver necklace rests over the curves her body. His eyes fix on the prismatic topography, which flares with starbursts when the lights catch the vertices. He imagines her getting dressed in slow motion. He sees the hugging of her hips, the bra strap wrapping around the soft skin of her back, and the tightening of her nipples as the cold metallic chain forms an ellipse around her neck. And Zeus thinks of another name that he calls her in his head sometimes. It comes from a set of Garbage Pail Kids cards that had been mixed in with the baseball cards from his Unk. *Swell Mel* was cartoon drawing of a cross-dressing stubble-faced baby, but for Zeus, it's a childish reference to the combination of her low-cut tops and deep breaths. And despite their agreement to remain platonic, he misses her at the moment, however rhythmically mismatched they had been in bed. And she misses him too, as unsatisfying it had been. They are both together and apart, but more apart when it concerns the social fluttering of the Monarch, Jesús the king.

There is a new energy between them, but there's no telling if it will last. They both know that the focus of his attention changes rapidly. He usually devotes his whole being to each conversation, each encounter, which gives him the ability to fall in love several times per night. And it's not that he falls out of love, but he allows himself to forget that it ever happened. They are blackouts of convenience.

As Zeus scans the room, the lighting alternates between a jazzy kind of blue to pitch black. Two seconds on, two seconds off. Right in front of him there is a blonde with a zipper top that's open enough to reveal a large tattoo of an exotic blue flower. She is arching her back and then rolling her shoulders forward. Her face has the expression of no expression. At three o'clock, there's a brunette with a buzzcut. Her earrings are hula-sized hoops and her nose is pierced on both sides with small stones. Her black and copper top is vacuum-sealed over her torso. Her skirt is only a few inches long, but it still manages to meet her black boots, which look spray-painted on and spit-shined and licked clean by her submissive. Zeus is sure he saw someone crawling around in the hallway a few minutes earlier. At six o'clock there is another blonde, probably bottled, with a silvery-sequins dress that looks like a deflated disco ball. Her shoes, which cover her entire foot except her glittery toes, are less '70s. At nine o'clock he sees a shadowy skull rise above the forest of heads. Then the lights go out. One-one-thousand, two-one-thousand. He continues to rotate toward midnight, but when the blue lights come back, the skull is still in front of him, closer and taller than before. Zeus lowers his eyes. Blackness again. One- one-thousand, two-one-thousand. In the next frame of blue, just a few feet away, is the floating head of a man with a beard and aviators, looking dead-on at him. His panoramic survey freezes as he thinks back to the afternoon in the library. Lights out. One-one-thousand, two-one-thousand. Just as he feels someone grab his arm, his body crystalizes, and the light patterns change to a consistent white strobe, like a visual panic attack. It's Melanie. And his heart restarts.

He tries to dismiss it as a mirage. He tells himself it's the weed and the drinks, but he isn't very convincing.

"Swell... I mean, Melanie, I'm going to have them bring up another round if you want one. This blunt has me bugging me out. So, this one is going to be full-on thug. The passion is returning. What do you say?"

"Sure, pick something for me. I want a sweet cocktail. Wait. You know what, hold the tail." Melanie resumes dancing, bucking to the bass like she was riding an invisible mechanical bull with heels on. The heels being Melanie's, not the bull's.

Zeus watches her and grins villainously. He imagines the various ways his open hands could land on her backside. In the thought bubbles over his head are the onomatopoeic expressions of a comic book, like *ttthwapp!* and *sssspankk!*

Zeus finds one of the VIP waitresses near the door. "I'll have a Thug Passion, but please have the bartender add two shots of Hennessy right on top for me. And for my friend, she wants something sweet. What do you think?"

"I don't know, does she want it sweet like chocolate—or sweet like candy?"

"What?"

"Well, I'd go with the After-School Special if she likes chocolate. But I'd say the Skirt Roller if she likes candy."

He only pays attention to the last word of her question, which he capitalizes in his mind. "Yes."

"So which one will it be?"

"...Thank you." Zeus thinks about Saturday night and Ms. Lovinglace and becomes instantly lucid. He smiles to himself. Maybe something really is different this time. And the constrictions of his pumping heart send blood northward to the limbic system in a hurry. It's an unusual and riveting sensation where memories are mixing with the intense feelings of antici

pation[39].

GOOD, FRIDAY.

[[❄]]

During the hour before dawn it's beginning to rain supreme. The effects of the alcohol have drifted to the feeling of regret. After a local downtown train to Chambers Street, Roosevelt emerges from the steel ant farm and quickly raises his antennae in search of an awning, a refuge from the deluge. He moves toward a bodega just over the pace of a jog, sometimes zig-zagging over inches-deep puddles. Once he finds some coverage he whirls his backpack forward and releases one of his shoulders from the straps just as two successive monster raindrops find their way down his back. Roosevelt arches forward, as if he's been shot by the most vindictive water gun of all time. After a quick sidestep to the left and a disapproving grimace to sky, he unzips his bag of tricks. When he places his journal inside, he sees that some of the raindrops had made their way into the pages, causing a rampant internal bleeding of black ink and obscuring some of his past moments of inspiration. He pulls out a reserve black t-shirt, duct tape, and a thick black permanent marker. Roosevelt doesn't check the weather forecast because he usually feels the rain in his body a few hours in advance. It's probably the Sugar Hill and cognac that's throwing off his sensors, he figures. In these times, the t-shirt, the tape, and the marker work together for the sake of illegal art. Sometimes the wetter days are the better days, depending on what he's going to use for the night's application. When it rains, it lures many of the other graf artists back into their homes and opens up available canvases across the cityscape. Even the fuzz tends to retreat to their patrol cars, limiting their maneuverability. It's pretty difficult to wheat-paste, and it can be tricky for the stickies too—though Roosevelt always felt that stickers were a copout, requiring only prep-time and a high-five to whatever government structure. Whereas applying marker to metal canvas, or listening to the hiss of the spray as the paint licks the cement, requires time and more risk. In some ways, with planning, installations can be easier to get away with. But construction decoys are less believable during periods of inclement weather, so welding in plain sight isn't an option. Projections can be set up, but not many people will be walking the streets, or in the mood to stand still in a downpour and gaze at the videography of an unsanctioned 2D expression.

After several minutes, the heavy rain gives way to a gentle mist that seems unaffected by gravity. Roosevelt pulls an all-black Yankee cap from his backpack and pulls it down over his eyebrows. As he leaves the safety of the awning, he tucks his chin to his chest, the interlocking NY almost parallel to the street. Through the beads of suspended raindrops, the scent of low tide makes its way to Roosevelt's nose as he draws closer to the Brooklyn Bridge. He curls his upper lip into his mouth, lets his bottom teeth comb over it, and he tastes the salted moisture. His tools are wrapped in the t-shirt, which is tucked under his arm where his journal usually resides, as he ascends the sloping wooden planks of The Bridge. There are a few others walking and biking, but they're soon-to-be-forgotten intermittent blurs. Instead, Roosevelt is focused on a moment of relative quiet in N.Y.C., the hush before the morning rush.

As he reaches the westernmost locus of the arch of The Bridge, he uses one side of the t-shirt to wipe away the rainwater from a rectangular area of brick. He tapes the t-shirt up against a line of weathered mortar and drapes it over the browned ceramic canvas to give it more time to dry. Roosevelt turns halfway around and leans against history. His pupils track left to right and back again as he surveys the scene and waits for a zero witness opportunity. On the adjacent railing to his right, Roosevelt sees what looks like the crude outline of a white voodoo doll with three thick red pins into the eyes and heart. And then he sees a fourth pin, which ends up being an extension of the first letter written underneath the doll. It stuck right between the legs of the genderless form. With a bit more style and acuity than the body outline, scrawled with a left-handed slant, is the word: LIAR. Roosevelt assumes this is either a warning to someone who's destined to see it, the sad rant of a jilted failure, or an acupuncture session gone wrong. Whichever it is, it's the picture of death, the drawing of a conclusion.

Roosevelt looks up to the nearby lantern. Its *Electric Ladyland* colors are dulled in the mist and its starburst lines bend toward him. Gazing farther upward, his eyes follow the string of beacons as they slope down and then back up to the Stars and Stripes at the top of the other arch. He looks over the railing and down to the harbored waters—the tranquil, liquid steel.

Roosevelt whirls 180° to face the old brick, lifts up the bottom of the t-shirt, and tucks the peak of his Yankee cap underneath it to create a canopy. Then he reaches into his back pocket for a joint-sized flashlight, turns it on, and places it in his mouth. Ready, set, poetry. He writes the words he's been muttering under his salted breath when he walked the wooden planks up to the arch. With his thoughts now inked and hovering over the East River, he knows they'll be echoed in the heads of happenstantial readers at daybreak.

RISING BEFORE THE SUN DOES,
I START WITH A NEW DAY SCOWL.
AND WHEN THE NIGHT GOES HEAVY,
THIS HUNGER BEGINS TO HOWL.
I'M AN EARLY BIRD, AND A NIGHT OWL.
❉

THE SILVER SENTINEL
"STERLING COVERAGE FOR ONE DOLLAR"

February 28, MMXX
Pearl, Indiana
By Holly Pedestal

After a tumultuous year, with the Pearl County Police having undergone charges of corruption and numerous cover-ups, the major shakeups rippling throughout their ranks have finally settled to calmer waters. After the overwhelming win in the special election for County Sheriff, Ezra Pithon affirmed his position regarding the two major issues affecting Pearl: the curious spike in high-speed, rural motor vehicle accidents, and the events surrounding the life and death of Viktor W. Xander. At his first press conference, he announced that the county would be hiring more officers, installing speed cameras, and ramping up policing efforts on the roadways. He then moved to the issue of Mr. Xander, insisting that the collaboration of the Pearl County Police and The Defenders of Christ had been productive and efficient, but that it has come to an end, with The PCP to resume full autonomy in all policing matters from this day forward. Sheriff Ezra Pithon officially dropped all posthumous charges against Mr. Xander, announcing that the case is closed. He again cited corruption and vengeful behavior by rogue officers within the former police administration that had led to the erroneous charges in the first place. Here is a timeline of the events that have led to today's news:

I

Theodore Theophilus Thomas, age 85, is reported missing by his niece, who is one of his caretakers. He was expected to return home after his half-mile walk to a local drugstore. But he's never seen at the drugstore, where he is a regular and known to the pharmacists and cashiers. There is speculation that he may suffer from dementia, which may have led to disorientation, and ultimately, his disappearance. Police search the community and surrounding towns and are unable to find any witnesses or leads.

II

Twin sisters, Georgia Love Carr, age 18, and Florida Joy Carr, also age 18, are reported missing by their landlord. The landlord, Emmett H. Johnston, calls the police out of concern that he'd not seen them in two weeks. He states that he'd not heard of any planned trip, but that their bags were packed and still in their apartment above his house. Mr. Johnston adds that he'd not received the cash rent payment, which had never been late before. (It's later revealed that the twin sisters worked together at a Pearl Strip club and were popular with the locals. Based on questioning at the Strip Club, the manager of *Fleur-de-Lisa* told reporters that the Carr sisters had resigned from the club, and were set to pursue other goals, of which he had no knowledge. On a local fansite, some members seemed to suggest they were going to go on a weeklong visit to see their estranged mother. There were also comments suggesting that their dance act "Mirror | ꙇɿɿoM" had recently lost some of it's usual passion[40].) It is also alleged that they may have been kidnapped by an obsessed *Fleur-de-Lisa* patron after their last shift, but police are unable to find any signs of foul play.

III

At a Thursday morning mass at St. Agapius Catholic Church, where there are many devout attendees, an incident occurs which first brings the name of Viktor Wolf Xander to international attention. The first-time visitor to the church arrives by himself and takes an aisle seat near the middle of the church. Several church members would later note that he did not genuflect before sitting down. Witnesses of the event gave positive remarks about Mr. Xander's demeanor overall, except to say that he seemed to be sweating profusely from the head, to the point where his shirt collar was soaked through. One church member, sitting one row behind him, noted that he was uncomfortable shaking the man's hand during the Sign of Peace. Not too long after, the Communion is prepared and the priest is leading the laypeople through their responses. As the Catholic attendees line up for the partaking of the body and blood, Mr. Xander also joins the queue. Some members agree that they weren't sure if he was Catholic, but seemed to be sincere and crying somberly. Mr. Xander has brief inaudible words with Father Leo Limot, it is said.

Father Limot is a recent addition to the clergy at St. Agapius. As Fr. Limot blesses him, he places the wafer directly into Mr. Xander's mouth, followed by a swallow of red wine. Mr. Xander bows and begins to walk back to his seat when he suddenly breaks down and falls to his knees with an apparent call for grace and for The Holy Spirit to enter his heart. Unsure of what's happening, a few parishioners rush to aid and comfort him. At this point, Viktor Wolf Xander hunches over and holds his stomach, and he is unable to speak. The parishioners hear choking noises, and then they witness Mr. Xander vomit repeatedly. All over the wooden floor of the church aisle, several chunks of human flesh and bits of fingers, followed by expulsions of blood are forming what would normally be a grotesque scene. However, many of the parishioners, after seeing what are obviously human body parts, begin to place both of their hands on him, calling to God with praise. Before any medical reports are issued, many leaders in the Catholic community are claiming this as proof of the miracle of Transubstantiation.

IV

The national and local media, the religious and secular, and an increased number of law officials begin to descend on Pearl, Indiana. Pictures, videos, and written accounts go viral on the internet, fueling both tributes and parodies of the event. Many believers want to worship at the church, but it's still being treated as a potential crime scene, angering the people lining up near the church.

The discussion over the supposed vomiting of the Transubstantiated Body of Christ becomes the lead story on all internet, network, and cable news channels, with some leaders changing their stance to that of the skeptics, given the possibility that it's a hoax, and that not much is known about the enigmatic Mr. Xander. The spokesman for Pope Pius XIII issues a statement in English, "The Catholic Faith and truth will prevail. We must allow our medical and investigative efforts, which are given to us by God, to reveal His truth to us. We must be patient. There are many people suffering in the world who need us right now, and they deserve our greatest attention. All things will be known in time."

V

The removal of what is now known as *"The Evidence,"* a double-entendre to be sure, becomes a concern to all involved. There's a range of desires expressed: some believers want it to be left there for three days of worship, some want it somehow preserved and kept in the church, some feel it should be shipped to Vatican City—where they will have a higher moral authority over the contents and a better interpretation of its meaning—and skeptics want the flesh and blood to be treated exactly like a crime scene. In the end, it is The Defenders of Christ who are able to negotiate a deal on behalf of the Church and State. The compromise by The D.O.C. states that forensic scientists will be allowed to take blood samples and biopsies from the flesh only after a formal blessing of the church is given by Fr. Limot. After completion, the church doors will be opened, but no visitors will be allowed in. People who want to pray near *"The Evidence"* are given one day, where they can line up outside the church and kneel on the front steps in full view of what they truly believe to be parts of the body of Christ. After the day of prayer, the church will be cleaned, with the remaining flesh and blood carefully sent to the Holy See in Vatican City for further analysis and blessings. Then the church will officially re-open with a commemorative hand-sewn rug to be placed over the floor where Viktor Wolf Xander knelt. The D.O.C. also stipulates that they assist the local police in their forensic and detective work, to watch over the purity of the process on behalf of the Catholic Church, and to act as a liaison to Vatican City. The Defenders of Christ go from a secretive sect of Christian activists and financial supporters, to a household name, virtually overnight. They're identities are shielded from the media, with few details about who they are and where they're from. They're all men, who only give mononymous Biblical names, wear dark maroon suits with a gold Patriarchal Latin Cross insignia on the lapel, thick beards, and reflective sunglasses. Their lead spokesman is named Ezekiel, who refuses all media interviews, only giving terse responses if intercepted, "God be with you."

VI

When V.W. Xander is admitted to the hospital on October 10, he is treated for hypertonic dehydration. According to hospital sources, while his fluid levels were being stabilized, Mr. Xander began speaking incoherently, and then suddenly was unresponsive. This is said to have occurred several times. Doctors then induced him into a coma to stabilize further what had become a pattern of erratic behavior, for what is possibly Status Epilepticus. Yet after tests, it's determined that Mr. Xander had suffered from Hibernating Myocardium, similar to a heart attack. When the barbiturates are removed from his system, he regains consciousness. V.W. Xander is to remain at the hospital for recovery, with enhanced security provided to the hospital by The D.O.C., pro bono.

VII

One month after the initial incident, Catholic baptisms, already up in the post-AppleFacegate era, rise at three times the normal rate, and nationwide, name-change registrants increase by a factor of two (with a majority turning to mononyms, leaving the family surname behind). There are also many non-official applications sent through social media outlets to become "employed" by The D.O.C., where no official positions exist. Mr. Xander is set to return home, with an exclusive interview promised to Cougar News Network. He's escorted home in a limousine by The Defenders of Christ.

VIII

With the Christmas Season in full swing, the mass attention wanes, but is poised to grow again with the anticipation for the upcoming interview. However, Cougar News Network reveals that it's been unable to reach Mr. Xander for some time and are unaware of his whereabouts. Mr. Xander, apparently a loner, doesn't have employment and doesn't have any family or friends with any information. His two-bedroom home is in a remote area and is akin to a small fortress, with higher-than-normal walls and few windows. There are "No Trespassing" signs along the perimeter. Yet with neighbors confirming that there hasn't been any activity at or near the home, the postal service stating his postbox is overflowing with mail, and with Cougar News Network's non-information, the local authorities treat it as a missing person's report, and enter the home late that evening.

IX

The Pearl County Police and The Defenders of Christ stand side by side at a press conference outside the home of Mr. Xander, which had been covered overnight in a blue tent-like structure that envelops the entirety of the house, to formally announce their findings. The yard is marked off with crime scene tape and all media outlets are restricted from entering the grounds. During the press conference, workers hired by The D.O.C. are building a temporary, even taller fence along the perimeter of the property. The national and international press await the news and wonder if the broadcast interview with the Cougar News Network will go on as scheduled. But the Pearl County Police and The D.O.C. announce that the man that many believe to be a walking miracle, as well as the confirmation of the veracity of the Catechism of the Catholic Church, was found deceased, from an apparent self-inflicted gunshot wound.

X

The D.O.C. announce that they have purchased the property from Mr. Xander's next of kin, a distant relative who wasn't even aware of her relation to the deceased, and that the process is moving along at lightning speed with the help of their legal counsel, compared to the usual timetable. The media is still a presence on the outskirts of the property, but the only people allowed within the fenced yard are members of The D.O.C. There is a round-the-clock effort to deconstruct the house from within. Large dump trucks are seen leaving almost every hour from the home, driven by the composed and bearded men in dark suits and mirrored sunglasses. As The D.O.C.'s ways grow more mysterious, their worldwide popularity rises commensurately. They announce that the ashes of Mr. Xander, who was cremated under the supervision of The D.O.C., were collected into an urn decorated with a golden Patriarchal Latin Cross, and delivered to Fr. Limot at St. Agapius Church. Lastly, they announce the plans for the future of Mr. Xander's property, saying that after the complete deconstruction of the home, the grounds will be turned into a prayer garden, rife with colorful flowers and stone benches. It is to be a place for local Christians to spend time with nature and reflect on the greatness of God's creation.

XI

After a few months, the garden is complete, except for the floral blooms, which are to come with the season. There are commemorative signs, park benches, and cobblestone paths. The church, which was also given a facelift of sorts through the funds of The D.O.C., has seen considerable and consistent growth, and has even become a tourist destination, a first for the small town. It is at this time that The Silver Sentinel obtained a source within the Pearl County Police force who's able to give a detailed account of what he says really happened the night they entered Mr. Xander's home, as he was a part of the initial investigation. Our source claims that within the home were the bodies of four individuals: Theodore Theophilus Thomas, 85; Georgia Love Carr, 18; Florida Joy Carr, 18; and the body of their presumed killer, Viktor Wolf Xander, 47, all of Pearl, Indiana. He attests that Mr. Xander died of a gunshot wound to the genitals, whereby he's presumed to have bled to death over the course of an hour. Furthermore, he states that, in what must have been a gruesome scene, the three victims of Mr. Xander were all found in one small windowless bedroom filled three feet deep in coarse sea salt. He says that when investigators entered the room, they feared that many more than three people had been contained within the walls of the room, as they saw various crudely severed limbs, which were spread out and protruded from the waves of salt. Our source claims that the early indications suggest that the victims were heavily drugged and asphyxiated, then preserved for later use by Mr. Xander. This was determined by the lack of any marks that would have indicated foul play before death. Some of the limbs, hearts, and other body parts, appeared torn and half-eaten due to the bruising and gnashing marks consistent with postmortem rape and cannibalistic behavior. As soon as our report was released, The D.O.C. denied all of the claims made by our police source in an official statement, insisting that their collaborative effort has been tainted by the motives of an envious and self-promoting police detective. The D.O.C. reiterates that their independent and faithful findings were the full truth, and that any further inquiries should be sent to Vatican City. The D.O.C. speculates that this faction within their special contractual agreement is a direct indication of evil within the system. They further note, or concede, that Mr. Xander had surely been infected by a demonic presence, one that they believe he tried to self-exorcise. Their position remains that Mr. Xander resides in the glory of Heaven, based on their belief that his conversion was, in fact, sincere. But at the same time, they acknowledge that it is God who is the ultimate judge.

XII

The report by The Silver Sentinel is received along the very lines that have defined the events from the start, there are skeptics and believers once again, yet this time, the roles are reversed: the people who initially believed in the revelation of the truth of Transubstantiation are now the skeptics of our report, and the skeptics of the Xander Situation are now beholden to the mysterious words of our source, who has since gone cold. The D.O.C. further asserts, alleging inconsistencies and falsities, that our report falls in line with the expectation that doubters and deniers of The Cross are present, adding that there is no way to link Mr. Xander to the disappearance of Mr. Theophilus, Ms. F. Carr, or Ms. G. Carr, whether circumstantially, forensically, or otherwise. They claim that our source is trying to atone for his own shortcomings within the Pearl County Police, that his inability to solve missing person cases in a small jurisdiction is reason enough for him to attempt to tie the cases together. The D.O.C. also aggressively states that they will pursue legal action against anyone who attempts to vilify the Church, or their organization, if they feel that the graves of the innocent are being danced upon, whether for the sole purpose of rhythmic defamation, or Christian discrimination. Also, around the same time as our exposé, other national news outlets were reporting about possible corruption cases within the Pearl County Police, with allegations of infidelity and sexual deviance practiced by several of the high-ranking officers. These reports have resulted in resignations, apologies, early retirements, and several severance packages offered to particular employees of the Pearl County Police.

XIII

With the police force in upheaval, an unforeseen announcement is made regarding the high profile Xander Situation, which brings further confusion and chaos within the Pearl County Police. It seems as if our report reverberated up the chain of command and resonated in the ears of the longtime County Sheriff, Beau LeMont. His official announcement is made alone at a press event podium in front of the Pearl County seal, a rarity, as there is usually a police presence to show solidarity. He discloses the results of his own personal investigation while admitting regret with respect to his agreement with The D.O.C. Sheriff LeMont announces the posthumous arrest of Viktor W. Xander, a 47-year-old man from Pearl, for the kidnapping, drugging, murder, and dismemberment of three local residents. It is a symbolic gesture, as the case is officially closed. But it suggests that there may be more lurid details behind the untarnished true story.

This was his attempt to reopen the door for a full, unbiased, and renewed investigation into what happened within the now torn-down walls of Mr. Xander's home. Sheriff LeMont's independent press conference angers the vocal residents who oppose any release of unverifiable macabre details, or lies, as they say. He is also chastised in the social mediasphere the world over, especially by devotees of The D.O.C., who are launching their own independent campaign to oust the current sheriff. They're already holding rallies and protests where they encourage others to wave the flags they distributed to the people of Pearl. One side of the flag is an American flag with 51 asymmetric stars, with the flag of Vatican City on the reverse. With administrative confusion at full tilt, information contested and muddied from all sides, change is certainly in the air. Three members of The Defenders of Christ issue their most verbose statement to date in front of the media, with all three of the members speaking in unison. They bowed their heads and made their appeal to all of Pearl, and the world: "Let us remember the Book of John, Chapter 1, Verse 14: 'And the Word was made flesh, and dwelt among us, (and we beheld His glory, the glory as of the only begotten of the Father,) full of grace and truth.' If you know that the light of the world has entered your heart, let it guide you through the darkest paths. Allow the glow from within to radiate to all of your loved ones and praise God for allowing you to live another day. If you walk with the Lord on Earth, He will carry you in His arms in Heaven. So, it is the doubters that need our light more than anyone else, for they live in an eternal midnight, their witching hour is every hour as they search for meaning and purpose that we already carry within us. They will look to you because they are in fact blind to the faith, they will listen to you because you speak the truth, and they will reach out to you because they know not what everlasting love feels like. Let them see you, listen to you, and feel you! Teach them to lift up their arms, for if they reach out to God, God will embrace them! Teach them to offer their minds, for God will enrich them with satiable knowledge! Teach them to bow their heads, for God will smile upon them for their obedience! Teach them to have faith, to be witnesses without the need for proof, and God will render them worthy and judge them in good favor! Amen."

Room   〚 ✳ 〛   337   Window

Floor   19   North   .

There   was   a   new   bouquet   of   flowers ,

with   a   selection   of   varying   hues

and   heights   ,   some   already

drooping   and   some   having

fallen   down   to   the

hospital   nightstand   ,   and

even   a   lonely   rose

petal   that   created

a   pink   tortoise

shell   on

the

beige

tiled

floor

.

There
was a small get-well placard embedded in the bouquet signed by two semi-anonymous
people, lliW + htɘdɒxilƎ, unknown to Axlia. As she was still adjusting her focus in the morning
light, a nurse walked in and turned the bouquet around to show her the better side of the blooms.
She briefly explained that it came from two people who had witnessed the performance and the
shooting, and that they had kiddingly apologized for it being such a large bouquet, which it was,
when they had dropped it off the previous night after she had fallen asleep. They told the nurse
that they had exchanged numbers to discuss what they had seen and had met at a cafe, where
their lunch had been generously paid for by a stranger who was going on and on about ketchup.

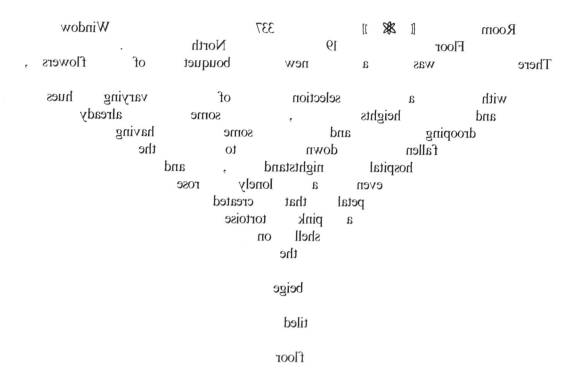

Room 【 ❋ 】 337 Floor 19 North Window

There was a new bouquet of flowers, with a selection of varying hues and some heights, some already drooping and having some fallen down to the hospital nightstand, and even a lonely rose that created a pink petal tortoise shell on the beige tiled floor.

There morning was a small get-well placard embedded in the bouquet signed by two semi-anonymous people, "Will + Elizabeth", unknown to Axlia. As she was still adjusting her focus in the light, a nurse walked in and turned the bouquet around to show her the better side of the blooms. She briefly explained that it came from two people who witnessed the performance and the shooting, and that they had kiddingly apologized for it being such a large bouquet, which it was, when they had dropped it off the previous night after she had fallen asleep. They told the nurse that they had exchanged numbers to discuss what they had seen and had met at a café, where their lunch had been generously paid for by a stranger who was going on and on about ketchup.

[[Σ]]

Suma curls some strands of hair over her left ear as she looks into the window of [:Dots—And—Dashes:], a store on The 10 on 10th. They sell pointillism originals and organic salts, peppers, and unusual spices from the urns on the floor display. On the back wall Suma sees a large mural of a Silk Road caravan moving across the endless orange sands, preserved in time.

As she walks to the café, Suma tastes the city emissions on her breath and wishes she had a mint. She lets the strap of her purse slide to her elbow. Suma looks down and feels inside for her phone. And just in front of her feet, she notices a dirty rainbow of flattened gum on the sidewalk below that seems to be placed there on purpose.

She has been meaning to call her friend, Jasmine, and find out how the performance artist is recovering. She wonders if it's too early in the day to call, and places her phone back in her purse. Maybe after her cappuccino will be better, she thinks. Suma walks into [Bump & Grind] and takes a seat by the window. She places her order with the waitress, who introduces herself as GingerGinger.

Suma makes cinnamon-topped foam whirlpools with her spoon in between each sip. She enjoys it slowly, as is always best to do in the morning.

She calls Jasmine, who answers as if she's speaking her first words of the day. They're hard to decode at first, but her voice clears up after a sentence or two.

"Hey Jasmine!"

".... .. / ... ..- -- .-"

"Good morning, sorry I'm calling you on the early side. How are you, Jazzy J?"

".. - .----. ... / --- -.- .-.-.- / . ...- . .-. -.-- - .... .. -. --. / .. ... / -.-. --- .-. .- -.-. - .. -.-. .-.-.- / .-- .... .- - .----. ... / ..- .--. ..--.."

"What was that?"

"--. --- --- -.. / -- --- .-. -. .. -. --." Jasmine coughs. "Excuse me, ... --- .-. .-. -.-- , Just sayin' good morning. Let me sit up. -.. .- -- -."

"I'm sure I didn't get you at the best time."

"No, it's cool. But yeah, things have been strange lately. I'm still not right, completely on edge."

"I can only imagine. Well, during the day I heard something about it, but nothing specific. Then, just before I left work last night, I saw someone with a Columbia sweatshirt, the exact same one that you used to wear."

"The famous tattoo sweatshirt. I still wear it."

Suma hears the spark of Jasmine's lighter. "And it took me a second, but I made the connection that you were probably right there when the shooting happened."

She exhales, "Yep."

"The last time I talked to you, you were just starting to work with her."

"It's been a few months now. I knew it would get buck wild here and there, but this shit took it to a different level."

"It's everywhere. Even more than any of the other shootings and all the car accidents. And there was this guy giving his ignorant opinion about it to everyone within earshot at the bar I went to last night."

Jasmine is yawning. ".-- .... .. -.-. .... / -... .- .-. ?"

"Rust Bust and Axe, on Amsterdam."

"I've been there before. It was a rough night, but I remember it because I was drinking out of a little plastic R2-D2 cup. The lid was his silver head, or whatever that part is, and I had to hold it open every time I took a sip."

"So, how's she doing?"

"Me and the guys visited her and she's going to be O.K. The Force is strong with that one."

"Any news on who or why?"

"Nothing. I know there's an intense investigation, but I haven't heard anything that means anything."

"Who knows what's happening lately."

Jasmine takes a deep drag off her clove. "Definitely fucked."

"Well, I'm sending good vibes your way."

"Thanks, I'll take them."

"Another reason I called, of course, was to just say hey." Suma jangles her spoon in the empty mug. "I've been working 'round the clock lately and this is my first day off. I felt like I had to get up early and use up every minute."

"You've been working around the clock at the library?"

"No, well, sort of. I've been working on some side projects. They keep me up, but I wouldn't want it any other way. I mean, I wouldn't know what to do with myself if I wasn't doing it."

"Do tell."

"Long story."

"Those are the best kind." Jasmine blows smoke away from her phone.

"The project doesn't sound exciting, it's something I'd rather just show you. Actually, when I think of explaining it out loud, the whole thing makes me sound strange."

"We all have our things, believe me. And if you're nervous about sharing it, then you're probably doing the right thing. Feel free to show me whenever, I'm curious."

"What about you, any other projects?"

"Just this right now. I have other ideas that I'm working on, but everything else is on hold. This week has straight taken over. Actually, Della's gotten some big opportunities already because of all the press."

"Della?"

"Yep, that's her real name. I go back and forth without knowing it."

"Hopefully something good is coming out of this."

"Mos def." Jasmine hears Suma muffle the phone to speak to someone else. "Sorry, that was the waitress. She's going to bring me another cappuccino."

"Where are you spending your vacation day?"

"I'm down at The 10 on 10th. I'm starting out at [Bump & Grind] for my caffeine kick, then over to [Halcyon Books], and hitting the [Mission] gallery to catch an exhibit that ends today, or soon. One of my friends from work recommended it. And then maybe—"

"—Wait, I have to interrupt. That's the gallery that contacted Axlia about doing a performance. She's going there today to meet with Cyrus Coaster, the actor, or now, the curator."

"No way, that's big. That place gets a lot of buzz. I've heard a lot about it and I'm not up on the art scene like you."

"Yep, could be. He even said something in the email about a solo exhibit."

"Let me know what happens, I'd love to see the show, and see you," Suma smiles through the phone.

"No doubt, no doubt." Jasmine takes a crackling drag from her clove. "Everything's been so overwhelming I can barely think about it that way yet. I have no perspective right now." The line is quiet for a moment and it allows her to shift the subject. "So how's that café? I haven't been there yet."

"Oh, [Bump & Grind]? Well, their cappuccinos are perfect and the place fits in with all the other shops here. This one is a combination café and cabaret, or maybe just a strip joint, not sure. Each table seats about ten and there is a large clear pole in the center that's filled with coffee beans. I guess they serve breakfast and brunch, croissants and all that, until two, then the dancers come out after the changeover. I'm by a window seat right now, but I can see some dark blinds that must come down from the ceiling when they do the switch. Last time I was here there was a flyer left under the table where they were advertising a special coffee ice cream lap dance called The Double Scoop Shoop, so I guess they still work in part of the café theme."

Jasmine chuckles.

"And I'm not sure if the Bump part of the name refers to the bump you get from the caffeine or the bump of the rump, or both. And I'm also not sure if the Grind part refers to the coffee process or the shooping that goes on in the private rooms, or both."

"I'd go with both boths."

"Either way, the cappuccinos are the crème de la crème." Suma presses her finger into her bellybutton through the thin layer of her shirt. "I think you'd like it here."

Jasmine lights another clove, "We should --. --- / --- -. . / -. .. --. .... -"

"My waitress, she said her name is GingerGinger, probably works the late shifts here as well. She's wearing a sleeveless shirt, but she has a tattoo on each arm that looks like a t-shirt outline with some shading for the wrinkles in the cotton. The left sleeve has a pack of reds rolled up in it, fifties style. And she has a small tattoo on her forehead of several strands of curled hair coming down from a widow's peak, like Superman."

"My type?"

"Maybe." GingerGinger brings her a second cappuccino. This one comes with a heart-shaped biscotti. "Probably."

"Sweet."

"Oh, there was something else I wanted to tell you that's right up your alley. I read a story this morning in The Times about a man who's an accidental performance artist. It's a pretty interesting long form bio. I can text you the link."

"With everything going on, I know I won't be able to read that much. Give me the quick version."

"True. Well, he's from the midwest and in his eighties. He has quite a severe case of Alzheimer's and his family isn't able to afford twenty-four-hour care, so they take turns caring for him. He doesn't go very far from home, except when his daughter takes him to her monthly opera performances. The opera company she's a part of performs one weekend a month in a nearby city. The daughter brings her father along, and sometimes other family members, and they'll rent some hotel rooms and make a little vacation out of it. The opera company is a very good one, but it's on the small side, so they have to be creative about their set designs, costumes, and sometimes they even double up on major roles. Obviously, these wrinkles add some personality to the operas, which are generally appreciated by informed audiences. For example, when one of the leading men came down with a bad case of laryngitis last minute, the tenor had to perform dual roles because they don't have any understudies. And this was in *Faust*, so the man had to play both Doctor Faust and Méphistophélès, which presented a whole lot of costuming and lyrical issues."

"Huh."

"So it turns out that the daughter was given her voice training by her father, who also had a long career as an opera singer. Apparently he's performed all over the world and in countless operas. While he enjoys the performances, he sometimes will forget that he's just an audience member and reverts back to his career as a baritone. And this is where all of the performance art starts to enter the picture. His memory is apparently shot, as far as people's names and their relationships to him, but with the lyrics and the staging, he's spot on. I guess these memories are so ingrained that even Alzheimer's doesn't have a chance against them. Usually another family member would sit with him in the audience and they'll hear him humming along with many of the songs. As the Alzheimer's progressed over the years, the humming became actual singing, and then the singing became accompanied by arm movements and standing up from his seat. He would get increasingly frustrated by the family member next to him that kept telling him to be quiet and sit down, especially because he didn't remember that it was a family member. And the family was also becoming upset, as they didn't want to treat him like a child in a public theater.

"Sounds tricky."

"His first performance happens like this: during the second act of *Rigoletto*, the family member that's next to him has to piss like a racehorse, and for the first time in a long time, he's left alone. Almost instantly, in his seat, he begins to sing along with passion to the very intense *Cortigiani, vil razza dannata* solo by the title character, Rigoletto, who is the court jester. The singer on stage is dressed in a jumpsuit where each limb is a different color and he's walking around with a hunched back and giving a great effort, just like the old man in his seat. And without the family member there to watch him, he stands up and starts to walk toward the stage. He's singing all the while as he makes his way to the side steps. The soloist is certainly concerned, but he keeps on singing, trying his hardest not to break character. He also happens to know the old man as a friend of his father's and doesn't want to embarrass him in any way. About one minute into the song, the old man makes it onto the stage and stands beside him. The old man is wearing an old suit, which is considerably modern next to the court jester outfit. But they match up quite well in two areas: they both have superb voices, and it turns out that the old man is a bit hunchbacked as well. During the duet, not one cast member breaks character. The audience is surprised, but they give the pair a rousing ovation, and the old man leans over just a few inches to take a full bow."

"Really?"

"The bow part I made up."

"That must've been some scene."

"There's more. After the duet, the man retreats not to his seat, but to the backstage area. And the opera goes on as planned from that moment forward, except for the part of Rigoletto. The tenor begins to improvise the lyrics, a cappella style, about a divided self and the prospects of the future, attempting to tie-in the unexpected duet into the storyline whenever possible. And the audience eats it up. So from that moment on, the family decides that they won't deal with the babysitting in the theater any longer and will allow him to sit backstage in full costume for whatever opera they're performing. Many times he wanders in the background as part of the scenery, waiting for his song to begin. No one ever knows which one it's going to be. The monthly results are always unpredictable and present all sorts of jagged storylines and space-time continuum issues for the opera singers to work out, live and on stage. But that's what gives each opera its very own personality. Even the old man's name begins to appear in the programs. His role is always listed as TBD. And while the old man creates the spark, it's the full cast that really becomes recognized as the performance artists. I mean, improvised opera really isn't a well-developed field, as far as I know."

"That's pretty wild. I would love to see what they do with *Madame Butterfly*. You know, my phone's blowing up, I should see what's on tap for today. But thanks for calling, really. I'll pass on those good vibes to Della."

"Cool deal. Definitely tell me what happens with the meeting and let me know if there's anything I can do to help. And maybe let's do a Columbia night soon when things chill the hell out."

"--- -.- / -... . .- ..- - .. ..-. ..- .-.."

After Suma's last sip of her cappuccino, which has gone cold, she pays the bill in cash, leaves the tip, and breaks the heart-shaped biscotti in two.

[[⋔]]

Zeus gets home around the time where night bleeds into morning. After a few hours of sleep, he wakes up in the brume of regret. He wills himself to stand and not stay naked. There are some superstar shell toes under the bed that he slips on without regard for the laces. As he makes his way to the closet, his morning erection lulls and becomes a weighted and disinterested member. He tries to put on his boxers without taking off his sneakers and it doesn't go as planned. Then he puts on some navy pants, a white polo, and his favorite watch. Every Friday morning for the past few years, he visits a quiet church for an exclusive dialogue with the Man on the second floor. Fridays have become his Sundays for reasons of solitude. It's the only place where he can turn off the magnetism of his personality and reverse the current flow. So on this Friday morning, in the mist of the sky background that reduces the Brooklyn Bridge to a muted brown curve, he sits down on his couch and folds his hands. He hasn't planned to pray just yet, but there are a lot of things on his mind. He closes his eyes hard and notices the inner vision patterns of light morphing into different shapes and then disappearing. Zeus relaxes his eyelids, rests his elbows on his knees, and begins his holy salutation. He always starts with what he's thankful for, then moves on to his contrition for a lustful life of sin, then through a list of questions, and then closes with the memories of those passed on and those missing. His prayers are sincere and come from deep within his head, a place he regards as his heart by proxy.

During the question phase of his prayer he whispers, "Who am I? Where am I going? Please help me understand. Can I be defined in vector space? Or do I have direction without magnitude? Or magnitude without direction? I would love to be a vector. A vector for you. But I am lost in a wilderness of questions. I would love a compass with twenty-six directions. Please spell it out for me. Point me in the right direction." He waits for another minute in silence with his eyes closed hard once again, the shapeshifting lights again floating by. "I feel I'm becoming the circular pivot, rather than the arrow." McJesus coughs out an itch into the alcove of his hands. "And I usually don't pray for this kind of thing, but I do want to ask for a nice time tomorrow night with Candice. I know I'm getting way ahead of myself, but there's something about her. A glow. Is it possible that she's part of my journey?" As he waits for a few breaths, the wind gusts against the apartment windows. "Does she ask questions like I do? She seems to have it figured out. All wrapped up with a red bow. She's probably a vector, right?"

After his meditations about those lost and still missing, he says his Amen, and opens his eyes. He looks down at the three stripes on his sneakers, and even with all sentimentality he's just been immersed in, the first thing he thinks about is the acronym he learned in sixth grade: A.D.I.D.A.S.[41]. The conflicts between religion and sex have always been a thorn in his side.

Zeus walks to the elevator in silence and contemplates everything before him as he sets off for an empty sanctuary on the street below.

When he was young and going to church with his mother, he often felt guilty for questioning his faith at all. When he entertained the idea that there could be another answer to the end game, he figured he was offending God in some way. But he knew that The Big Ten, particularly the first Commandment, confirmed that there must be other gods—or at least that there had been other gods. He'd think about these kind of things as he mindlessly played with his hands. During the sermons, he'd form various shapes and figures, and marvel at the innumerable combinations of interplay. He formed a barking dog with his right hand, his pinky forming the eye and his thumb and remaining fingers the mouth. He formed a dove, his thumbs the head, his fingers the spread wings. He played Rock, Paper, Scissors against himself with his own left hand and right hand. The winning hand would perform the rock n' roll salute. He fashioned a woven basket, and as he tried to keep it air tight at the base of each finger, he saw the flesh around his knuckles swell and pink up. He practiced silent snap rhythms, alternating between each hand. He dug his nails into the skin of his opposite hand and created little creased squares that would disappear within seconds. He made the old *index-finger-entering-the-circle-thing*, for which he disguised by pretending to crack his knuckles. He examined his nails and wondered how exactly they were attached. He tried to stretch his thumb all the way down to his wrist, which he'd seen many other people do, but he never quite got there. He practiced the trick that looked like he was taking half his index finger off, which he thought he did quite well. And there was the formation of the hand sanctuary. *This is the Church, this is the steeple, open the doors, and see all the people!* Except that there weren't that many people. With two fingers forming the steeple, two thumbs forming the doors, and arguably two pinkies providing the back wall, there were only four people in the church, assuming each finger represents one person. When he was first taught the rhyme and the motions, he liked the idea that the finger people were standing up and having a ball in there. But his church was nothing close to that. There was a lot of sitting around. But around the time when his thoughts about sex went from strange and intermittent to constant and fascinating, his movements changed in a new way. He used to only stand erect while singing, but now he'd also be erect while sitting, with a strategically placed hymnal or Bible on his lap. He wasn't sure why it happened so often, but he knew there was at least one member of the church having a rousing and revelatory experience. Whether it was connected or not, and for whatever reason, he liked to look at the backs of girls' knees as they walked down the aisle to their pew. He identified them along a scale of two extremes. The girls who were athletic and thin and had the kind of knee-backs that hollowed out when they stepped forward, their ligaments forming gothic arches. And the girls who were more sedentary and still retained some baby fat, they tended to have wide capital H-shaped creases, the inner workings of their legs unseen. There were two girls in particular that he looked for on Sundays. One was named Brenda. She was taller than he was and had long brown hair and the athletic knee-backs. The other was Lara. She had unusual eyes in a good way. Sometimes her family sat in the pew in front of them. And when everyone stood to sing, her two capital Hs were in full view for the duration of the hymn.

⊢allelujah, ⊢allelujah.

In all seriousness, he appreciated the subdued and reverent quality of the format of the service, and wondered if anyone should really be having that much fun in church. Zeus saw it as a time for reading, reflecting, and giving praise and thanks to The Creator. He liked listening to the pastor ask life's difficult questions, and then provide the answers at the close of the twenty-minute sermon. Yet as he got older, he began to realize that the answer to all the difficult questions seemed to be the same. No matter the issue, the pastor advised that all will be revealed if we just believe, just pray harder, ask for guidance, and have faith. He wondered if there was more substance to being a Christian believer. Year after year, he heard the same sermons presented in different ways that were summed up in one of two ways. It was either: *We have lovely lives, we are fortunate, Praise Him!*—or *Life is a struggle, it's unpredictable, show mercy, and Praise Him!* With a book that big, Zeus figured there must be more to it than that. Maybe he could come up with new ideas and better questions. So he started to bring his Bible to church so he could search through God's Word on his own. He kept two colored pens tucked inside, somewhere near Lamentations. The pens had pictures of baseball players on them from the millennial all-star game, with Vladimir Guerrero in Expos blue, and Ken Griffey Jr. in Cincinnati red. When the pastor focused on one verse in Matthew, he would read the chapter and write down his own ideas in the back of his Bible, which had blank pages for just that purpose. He used the blue pen for insights and the red pen for questions. He tried to write lightly on the leafy pages to keep the ink from bleeding through to the other side, but some of his questions left too deep an impression.

HOW STRONG IS THE GRAVITY IN HEAVEN?
IS THERE OXYGEN IN HEAVEN? CAN WE MAKE SOUNDS?
IF SO, IS THERE ONLY ONE LANGUAGE?
IS THERE JEALOUSY IN HEAVEN?
WHAT WOULD HAPPEN IN THIS CASE:
A MOM GETS A DIVORCE BECAUSE HER HUSBAND LEFT HER FOR NO REASON. THEN ONE DAY SHE GETS MARRIED AGAIN TO A MAN WHO HONORS HER AND LOVES HER. ALSO ONE DAY HER FIRST HUSBAND ASKS JESUS TO COME INTO HIS HEART AND HE IS A TRUE BELIEVER AND ATONES FOR HIS SINS, BUT HE NEVER GETS REMARRIED. WHEN ALL THREE PEOPLE DIE AND THE CHILD OF THE FIRST MARRIED COUPLE DIES, DO ALL FOUR PEOPLE FORM ONE FAMILY? BECAUSE THAT MIGHT HAPPEN TO ME.
WHAT KIND OF CLOTHES WILL WE WEAR OR WILL WE BE NAKED?
IF THERE'S SEX IN HEAVEN, WHO GETS TO HAVE IT? HOW OFTEN?
WAS IT WRONG TO ASK THESE QUESTIONS?

IF YOU DIE YOUNG, WILL YOUR BODY GROW OLDER IN HEAVEN, OR WILL YOU STAY THE SAME AGE AS WHEN YOU DIE?
WILL THERE BE BABIES CRAWLING AROUND IN HEAVEN OR WILL THEY BE ABLE TO STAND UP AND TALK LIKE ADULTS?
ARE WE SAD IF WE DON'T SEE SOME OF OUR FRIENDS AND FAMILY?
OR IS HEAVEN LIKE WHAT THE BIBLE SAYS AND NOT WHAT PEOPLE SAY?
WHAT WILL PERPETUAL WORSHIP FEEL LIKE?
WILL ETERNITY EVER BE BORING?
WHY DID GOD CREATE STARVATION?
WHAT DOES FORSAKEN MEAN EXACTLY?
IF JESUS DIED FOR OUR SINS, HOW COULD IT BE A SACRIFICE IF HE'S STILL ALIVE?

As he walks to his church, he passes several other places of worship along the way. He thinks about how things have changed over the years, with churches as the smallest buildings in the metropolis, and how they are about to change again. It used to be that they were the beacons, the spires that pointed to the clouds, and presumably, to the Heavens. But with the compounding industrial revolutions and capitalistic ventures (probably in contrast to Christ's double vision of anarchism x socialism), not only did the new structures point to the clouds, they penetrated them. The churches had been the quaint community strongholds, rejecting modernity in more ways than two. When a church is squeezed between two steel rectangular prisms, it's a jarring discrepancy, and evident that the waste of skyward space is being subsidized by a system that supposes to promote capitalism above all else. And the idea that there is a Heaven *Above* and a Hell *Below* is predicated on a flat world, the sands and waters as barriers to the eternities of love and evil. The primitive simplicity still works as an idea even though we live on oblong spheroid hurling through the expanse. Even though it doesn't sound as poetic, it should be a Heaven *Elsewhere* and a Hell *Elsewhere Else*, if at all. But change again is imminent after the AppleFacegate incident, with mega-congregations and church conglomerates beginning to reclaim skyscraper real estate[42] after benefitting from the encouraged practice of twithing[43].

Zeus enters the churchyard through a wrought iron fence and walks along a cobblestone path through a small grassy yard. He goes up the granite steps that had been worn smooth and sloped down in the middle. When he pulls the brass handle on the church door, he smells a fresh bouquet of varnish and incense. The church is empty, save for a worker who's kneeling down on the wood floor next to the altar. The worker is sanding a plank. He is wearing khakis, a t-shirt, and a blue baseball cap. It's the church's softball team cap and has a simple white cross logo embroidered on the front. It's sweat-soaked to a darker blue around the band. As the worker moves to the next plank, Zeus announces over the sanding sounds, "Excuse me, sir. Do you mind if I sit down here for a moment?"

He straightens his back and turns to look at him. He hadn't heard him enter. A few beads of sawdust-filled perspiration fall to the floor, "Oh! Yeah, sure. If you don't mind me doing some of the upkeep here in the meantime."

"Of course not. I don't mean to bother you. I just needed a few minutes to think and pray."

"Ahhh, there's no better place to do that then here! Go right ahead, son." And the man returns to scrape the low-grit sandpaper with the grain. Zeus walks to a pew near the front, bows his head, interlocks his fingers, closes his eyes, and travels through his memories with the salience of hindsight.

He thought first of his father, who'd left a vacancy where a role model usually resides. Zeus gave that spot to God. When he thought of Him abstractly, he thought of the Circle, but when he pictured God next to him on the pew, He took the form of a human-sized hazy gray cloud—and was faceless. Somewhere within, there was a glow that represented His spirit and vitality. This vision of God had come to him in a recurring dream he had when he was a young boy as he tossed and turned in his Spider-Man pajamas. The first time he felt the presence of the gray cloud, it seemed to envelop him and antagonize him with sharp objects. For a time, he was fearful of going to sleep. He had other nightmares, but it was in the indescribability of the hazy mass that worried him most. There was a soft fuzziness that replaced the air and clung to his eyes and rendered him blind. This gray cloud moved like slow water all around him and he felt weightless. There was no floor or ceiling, just surrounding walls of disorientation. It wasn't until after the third or fourth dream that he almost became willing to experience the dream, to face his fear with closed eyes. Young Jesús began to think of the gray cloud as a comfort, his own realm of mystery, where maybe the prodding needle pains were an attempt to wake him up to something larger than himself. But just as he accepted these nightly fates, the formless cloud became smaller and smaller, and eventually it was unable to surround him, and it separated from him altogether. The faint inner glow was now visible and sat next to him in the pew and the dreams never returned.

Around this same era of his life, he was old enough to be invited on his first youth group retreat. He welcomed the weekend get-away to a Long Island lakeside campground with his friends from church. Young Jesús was also excited by the prospect of seeing girls in his age-range that he never had a good enough reason to talk to before, besides a quick and awkward "hello" in the narthex, when they were with their families. So, while he was ready to impress socially, it was he who became fascinated by someone else—a forty-year-old surgeon slash part-time youth pastor. On the first night of the retreat, the group he was assigned to was sitting around a campfire that had been reduced to a few glowing coals. They listened to the youth pastor strum his guitar and sing religious refrains for several minutes. After he put down his instrument he asked them to hold hands and lower their heads. There was a girl to his left whose hand felt soft and moist, but chilled by the cool night. The youth pastor was to his right. His fingers were calloused and knuckled.

"Dear Lord, we ask You for your blessing. We ask You to give us guidance. We ask You to reveal your strength and love to us all. And we ask that You receive our songs of praise.

We adore You, Lord. You are the Rock. Amen!" When the group lifted their heads and opened their eyes, Zeus noticed a little spark from the depths of the ashes spiral upward against gravity, and then disappear. "Now that we've acknowledged the Rock, we can start to really rock in His name. I'm going to teach you a few basic choruses in just a few minutes, but let's introduce ourselves first. I'll start and then we can move around the circle. My name is Doctor-Pastor Astor. I'm a surgeon and a volunteer youth pastor. I give *praise* to the man upstairs every time I'm able to save someone's life. It's only through *His* glory that I can use my talents to help others. And I teach people how they can save their own lives, too. But in a much more important, *spiritual* way. We can talk about that later. And I really enjoy spending time with young people like you and sharing my personal feelings about the Lord. I'm *very* happy to be here this weekend." Zeus felt his hand compressed whenever Doctor-Pastor Astor emphasized a word. "And you?" he asked the person to his right.

"My name is Cooper. I'm from Manhattan and I'm thirteen. My father is a doctor too."

"Nice to meet you, Cooper. And you?"

"...Mark from Jersey. Never been to a place like this. My mom wanted me to go. I'm fourteen."

"Well, I'm glad you're here, Mark."

Zeus let go of the girl's hand to wipe the clammy perspiration on his jeans. He tried to politely wiggle his hand away from Doctor-Pastor Astor also, but his grip was too tight. He figured he'd be playing the guitar soon enough, anyway.

"And you?"

"I'm Janeen, J-a-n-E-E-n. And I'm from Brooklyn and I'm thirteen, too. This is my first campout ever. My dad's an electrician and my mom's a hair stylist and my brother is in a different group tonight."

"It sounds like you're blessed to have a great family around you, Janeen. And you?"

"My name is Jesús, J-e-s-ú-s, but everyone just calls me Zeus. I'm thirteen and my mom tells me that she's proud of me, but that I'm mischievous and impressionable."

"Well, she sounds like a very astute mother," the guitarist said with a smile. "It's very nice to meet all of you." He patted a four-count intro with his foot and broke into a bluesy call to worship. He sang out a one-line phrase and nodded for everyone to repeat it. When he swallowed between phrases, the youth pastor's Adam's apple, which looked more like the end of a banana, jutted out and down and then back in. After he established the chorus with the group, Doctor-Pastor Astor sang solo verses of praise, then he'd bring back the chorus. The call-and-response singing, foot tapping, and hand clapping went on for almost an hour. The dirt was now smooth by his feet. Their leader separated the songs with mini testimonials and encouraged others to share their stories of faith. The more they sang together, the more they opened up to each other. Janeen laughed often, Mark was relaxed, Cooper clapped on the off-beat, and Zeus grew more emotional as time progressed. He felt the night in a new way as the lakeside air, fortified by the energy of the music, entered each cell of his body. The interconnectivity of the group was intensified when Doctor-Pastor Astor cut out the guitar during the last chorus, leaving their voices floating over the sparse crackles of burning wood. Zeus imagined the lyrics leaving their mouths and joining the winding smoke in the middle of their circle. E pluribus unum, in God they trusted.

"Before we head back to meet up with the other groups, I want to give you the best invitation of all time. Now, you don't have to RSVP right now, God's invitation is *always* available. He is inviting you, if you haven't done so already, to join Him one day for an eternal life of love. Even though your time in Heaven won't begin for many years, you can RSVP right now and reserve your place next to Him, The Creator, our Lord. The way God works his invitations is different than what you might be used to. The way God wants you to respond is by first inviting *Him* into your heart and soul. It has to be up to *you* first. It's like a reverse invitation. Once He is invited into your heart, He will make it known to you that your life is forever changed from within. And it's a wonderful thing that can only be described after you go through it. He will save you from evil and bring joy to your heart. He is our ultimate Father, our Protector, our Rock." He paused and closed his eyes for a moment. "Has anyone here asked Jesus to enter their heart already?" Cooper, Janeen, and Mark raised their hands. Doctor-Pastor Astor looked to his left. "Zeus, would you like to join us and be saved from the perils of Hell and one day enter the Kingdom of Heaven for eternity?"

Zeus felt his body fill with a nervous warmth, as though the weight of this moment was collapsing in on itself. And he felt tears well up along the bottom of his eyes, spill out, and drop to the earth. "Yes."

"Would you like us to pray with you?"

Keeping his head bowed, he nodded.

The group was silent. He felt Doctor-Pastor Astor place his hand over Zeus's shoulder and whisper, "Dear God, You are The Almighty, You are Our Father, Our Savior. You are the reason we are all here, Dear Lord. And we pray together, Lord. Father, we ask You to bless young *Jesús* tonight. And when he is ready, Lord, when he is ready to ask You to come into his heart, when he is ready to become your loyal servant, we pray that You fill him with the love only You can provide, Lord. We pray that he will be baptized by You and born anew. And we pray, Dear Father, that You make him unto You a disciple here on Earth so that he may join You in Heaven and live forever in glory. We ask that You save him, Father. Thank you, Lord. Thank *You* above all. In Your name we pray, Amen." Doctor-Pastor Astor raised his voice a notch when he continued, this time looking at Zeus's closed eyes, and asked, "So, what do you think? Do you want to be made whole? Do you want to experience the unconditional love of the Lord Jesus Christ, the strength of Our Father, and the warmth of The Holy Spirit running inside you? Do you want to give your life meaning beyond the grave and be filled with emotions otherwise unknowable?"

"Yes, I do," Zeus said as he cleared his throat.

"You have to really mean it, from deep within your soul. You don't have to invite him into your heart if you're not ready, but if you are ready, then all you have to do is tell God that you *mean* it."

"Yes, I do! Yes, I want Jesus to come into my heart. I want to be born again and live my life with Him in my heart." The tears flowed and his emotions were channeled into a sense of profound relief. And he wanted to call his mother right then and there to tell her all about his new father.

Still praying with his eyes closed, the constant sanding lulls him into a deeper realm, and he struggles to maintain his consciousness. Somewhere along the line, the flames from that campfire scene were extinguished and the baptismal waters evaporated. The relationship began on an impassioned peak and then settled into a planar landscape. But in direct opposition are the feelings of guilt, moving at full tilt, fueled by his questions, insecurities about the nature of belief, some rising agnosticism, and a few droplets of atheistic philosophy. When he asks for atonement, he replays scenes in his head, both actualized and fantasized, and apologizes for them. He is a sworn sinner. Zeus knows that everyone has their own kind of forbidden fruit—his being of the peach variety. But he's trying to change that. During this confession, it's with the intention to quell his desires. Not purely for God, but for Candy and the comfort of monogamy. She's the one.

His head rests even heavier on the back of the vibrating pew in front of him. Zeus feels the rattle and hum of the subway cars as they run under the church. He dares to confront his beautiful demons, unsure of where it will take him. And so it begins.

He descends through the wood planks of the church floor, through the layers of dirt, concrete, and granite, and lands in the center of the subway tracks. He's staring down the tunnel as a pair of lights go from distant stars to supernovas. As the train approaches him, it slows to a crawl, and stops an inch from his face. Zeus climbs up to the front door and goes inside. Time slows to a quarter its normal progression and his vantage point changes to the third person. He watches his own actions from just behind his stubble-shadowed head. He's aware of this detachment and follows along as the scene plays out.

There's a young woman standing in front of him exhaling vaporous letters that form unintelligible symbols. She isn't wearing anything. Neither is he. Zeus notices that her nipples and bellybutton form the vertices of an isosceles triangle that's in direct proportion to the one below. She wears icy blue eyeshadow and white-frosted lipstick. Her eyes are the color of a morning sky and her pigtails fall symmetrically at each side. She speaks in the language of geometry. The woman's head begins to turn around like a screw-top Barbie doll. He notices the manufactured attachment line on her neck. It's the only place she is plastic. On the other side of her head is another face. It has changed ever so slightly. Her lips are now crystalized with red rubies, her cheekbones are rouged, and her eyes are overcast. She exhales more geometric shapes before reaching down between her legs. She produces a pink capsule, holds it up in front of him, and pokes it into his mouth with her finger. He feels himself getting high within his dream and watches the back of his peach-fuzzed head make slow directionless tilts of pure feeling. And he knows he's smiling on the other side. He floats farther into the subway car, looks up, and begins to talk to the Angels.

Many of them are crawling along the ceiling and some are hanging upside-down, the backs of their knees holding them up in the subway straps. They are also naked with attachment lines on their necks. He assumes they all have two faces. They have white tattoos of wings on their backs and diamond rings on every finger. He can see that the straphanger Angels each have a bright pink capsule between their legs. He's been with several Angels in the past few years. It seems every third stripper is named Angel. He floats toward a straphanger to take another pink pill with his mouth.

Then he reaches out to the congregation of women spread throughout the car. Some are in seats and some are twirling on the poles. It's a full ride. To his left is Ms. July, a high school teacher he met some months back. She's wearing a professional blouse and skirt and a pair of sensible heels, but her legs are spread apart. She's looking at him and touching herself with both hands. He watches her body convulse and climax not once, not twice, but thrice. On the pole in front of him is a woman named MollyJane. She has a habit of showing up wherever he is in the city. She has powdery white skin and green pentagonal eyes. She faces him, ties her hair around the pole, and motions to him by curling her two middle fingers. He obeys, led by the direction of his erection. He floats toward her, standing straight up with his arms at his sides and without his feet touching the floor. He enters her, numb to the pleasure of her warmth. She speaks to him in a contrail of Fourier series. He tries to understand, but his concentration is broken by the loud moans over his left shoulder. It is yet another climax for the high school teacher, the fourth of Ms. July.

In the window, the reflection of his face is distorted by acid graffiti. As he looks lower, he sees the imprint of his monogram from the elastic band of his boxers, WИM, within the impressed halo around his waist. It's continuous, save for the two hands that are wrapped around his backside. Zeus looks away from the window and straight down. He sees the zig-zagged part of Deborah DeLite's hair rocking back and forth. It's a familiar sight. He'd text her and they'd meet by Chelsea Piers, and never before midnight. In his phone he labeled her as Debbie Downer. He isn't sure if he really knows what her face looks like, but he knows the part of her hair. And that other thing.

Zeus floats forward, his erection leading the slow-motion charge. Pixie is reclining across a few subway seats using one hand as a pillow while her feet rest atop an actual pillow. She's creamy and soft and naked and is holding a cherry near her mouth. He begins to float horizontally, hovering over her. Pixie feeds him the cherry and places the long stem in her mouth. Zeus enters her and swallows the pit with discomfort. They look in each other's eyes while she kinks the stem with her tongue. When he rises up and away from her, Pixie pulls out the stem and shows it to him:

Thankyouforfuckingmelikethat! Youcanjustplayjazzwiththatthing!

Then he looks at one of the upside down Angels to his right. Her breasts obscure her face and her hair grazes the floor. He goes to her for another pink capsule to continue the high.

In his math class, Zeus was told by an upperclassman how to go down on a girl the right way. He said it worked for him every time. The advice was to hum and tongue the prime numbers and then the alphabet, before simply speaking in tongues until she answered. It was nerdy advice, but he took it. In an upright-sixty-nine with the straphanger, he hummmmmmmms, then takes a breath. Again, he hummmmmmmms, and then begins to breathe through his nose. Hummmmm*twothreefivseveneleven-thirteenseventeennineteen*mmmmmmmmmmmm*twentythree-twentynine-thirtyonethirtyseven*-mmmmmmmm-*fortyonefortythreefortysevenfiftythree-fiftyninesixtyone-sixtyseven*mmmmmmmmmmmmmmm*seventyoneseventythree-seventynineeightythreeeighty-nineninetyseven*mmmmmmmm. When he takes his next deep breath, he swallows another pink capsule. Hummmmmmmm*abcdef*mmmmmmm*ghijklmn*mmmmmmmm*opqrstuvwxy*mmmmm mm*z*mmmmm. *Freud*mm*was*mmmm*right*mmmm*about*mmmmm*sex*mm*being*mm mmm*enhanced*mmmmm*by*mm*religion*mmmmmmmm*because*mmmm*it*mmmm*feels*mmmmm*forebidden*mmmmm*and*mmmmm*gloriously*mmmmmmm*unrighteous*mmmmmm*comma*mmmmmmmm*do*mmmmm*you*mmmm*agree*? The Angel says she doesn't know who Freud is.

Floating forward, he sees a woman with scotch tape pasties holding a glass of champagne between her breasts. When she speaks, the words don't come from her mouth, but over the sound system in the subway car. "My name is Lola-yes-the-same-Lola. I'm the subway operator. This is an express train to *you know where*. Your next stop is at the corner of Lacey and Violet." She clinks the glass against the pole. "To you."

On her knees at the bottom of the pole is Lacey, running her tongue up and down the metal surface. Violet is behind her, holding her head in place. Lacey has blonde hair and is wearing a white babydoll. Violet wears a cloche hat and dark clothes. Zeus met them in a café where the two women were having lunch. He overheard the dominant one chastising the shy one for not clearing her plate. He inserted himself into their conversation and within hours he found himself at an underground club holding a leash with Lacey at the other end. New York is one big playground. He watches Lacey's tongue make its way all the way up the pole to eye level. Violet, still holding her head, says, "Kiss."

As he moves forward, the doors open to his right and a roll call of past paramours enter. Kitty walks in with a broken shoe, teetering between 5'3" and 6'1". Princess wears a corset that is way too small for her. Lucy is all natural and warms him with a gentle hug. Lucy's fur is soft, but it's a bush burning with many passions, he remembers. E.rik.A walks in with a short cocktail dress and a tight necklace. She speaks with a constant choke that she uses as an icebreaker. It's her way of telling men what she wants. Then the woman with the red vinyl pants walks in. She says, "You didn't even ask for my name last night."

"What is it?"

"It's Nycole. It's spelled N-Y-C in the beginning, like where you are. Well, maybe not right now."

"Hi Nycole. I'm..."

"I know."

"But I don't even know if I know."

The subway doors close and the lights flicker. He watches his peach-fuzzed head float toward two women whose bodies are painted gold. Each one holds on to the center pole while they bend over side by side. He stands behind them and alternately enters them as they begin to read two haikus in graffiti on the floor. The golden, arched women read them one syllable at a time, one for each thrust.

SWEAT **HER** A- **HON-** CROSS **EY** HER **DIPPED** CHEST **LIPS**
I **PURE** MUST **SWEET-** CON- **NESS** FESS, BE- WAS **TWEEN** MY **HER** FAULT **HIPS,**
EACH **JUST** KISS **LIE** TASTES **BACK,** OF **SUG-** SALT **AR**

He moves to the end of the subway car to a woman he's never seen before. She communicates telepathically to him, "My name is Lyric S. Divine. I'm only real because you made me. Look." The closer he studies her, the more she changes. Her skin loses its spectrum of colors until she becomes a penciled outline in an artist's sketchpad. A dimension is lost, but she's still able to communicate with him. "Look around."

The subway looks empty. He blinks hard. Then he realizes that all of the women and the Angels have become a mural painted over every surface inside the train, as if he has a googol eyes looking in all directions at once. He sees the Angels from all angles, the golden and arched women are further contorted, and the screw-top Barbie is a siamese twin. He sees Ms. July, MollyJane, Deborah DeLite a.k.a. Debbie Downer, Pixie, Lola-yes-the-same-Lola, Lacey and Violet, Kitty, Princess, Lucy, E.rik.A, and Nycole suspended in an aerosol veneer. And he sees the graffiti tags of silent individuals reaching out to ubiquity, the refractions of unexamined intentions, and the sketch of Lyric S. Divine against the door.

Then he realizes he is also without a body. That he's taken the form of negative space in the train, reduced to what he'd experienced, the exhaled vapors of angels. He is everywhere and nowhere.

Zeus wakes up with a spasm of elbows and wrists and feels drool on the side of his mouth. He wipes away the saliva and rubs his forehead, which has a diagonal red impression from the pew. As his eyes adjust to the light he sees a handmade, leather-bound book behind the hymnal. In red branded type across the top is the title:

Serpentine Poetry:
The Sacred Unhooking of Eve's Leafy Bra[44]

He's about to reach for it when the man sanding the boards rises from his knees and asks, "Were you praying—or dreaming?"

[[✝]]

The Defenders of Christ
North American Representatives in Faith
New York Office
Internal Document (1 of 4) Minutes from the April Meeting
Re: Joyce

Souls in Attendance
Chairman: Ezra ~~Pithon Esq~~.
Elders: Dr. Obadiah ~~Astor~~, Saul ~~Mello~~, Fr. Malachi ~~Patch~~, Ezekiel ~~Hernandez~~
Disciples: Samson ~~X~~, Mark ~~Stamen~~, Habakkuk ~~Ittup~~, Noah ~~Starch~~, Sec. Jonah ~~Millhop~~
Honorary Chairman: Dr. Gideon ~~Lovinglace~~

Introductory comments and prayer by Chairman Ezra:
Good evening. We are here to discuss two distinct topics. Before we begin, let us give our time to God. Please bow your heads in praise and for the affirmation of our covenant. *Dear Lord, We recognize that with You at the helm of the ship, You will guide us through the dark forest and lead us to open pastures. We give You praise by our commitment to rid the lands of those who doubt Your existence. We give You praise by sowing pure seeds in Your heavenly soil and ridding the earth of the weeds that spread lies and question Your omnipotence. You are our compass, oh Lord. Please continue to guide us so that we may serve You. We seek to restore the love and respect for Your Name that You so dearly deserve, and we seek to instill fear in the hearts of those who are suspicious of Your powers. Your greatness is under attack and we proclaim our allegiance to You on the front lines of the war of all worlds, the battle of all philosophies, the fight for righteousness. In Your Name we pray, Amen.* Our first order of business is to acknowledge that this is my first time presiding over a meeting for The Defenders of Christ in the North American Representatives in Faith chapter. And I will try to preside in the same manner that Gideon did, God bless him. Now I've attended several meetings here since The Indiana Situation, and I will do all I can to lead this chapter moving forward. Previously I served in Les Défenseurs du Christ, Le Paris Chapitre, for a few years, mostly dealing with Le Soulèvement Musulman, meaning, The Muslim Uprising. I see some new faces here. Does anyone have any questions for me? No? O.K. Our next order of business, as you can see from the sheet in front of you, is the legacy of our brother Gideon. With his funeral and memorial services complete, and brother Gideon looking over us from above, I'd like us to brainstorm about how we should acknowledge his service to our Lord. The floor is open.

Elder Malachi: <<coughing>> ...excuse me. I know Gideon was a family man, a caretaker. He left his family in excellent financial shape, but I think we should take further measures regarding his three children.

Chairman Ezra: Of course.

Elder Saul: We could use funds to purchase a home for each child in a strategic location so they can be Christian examples of wealth and success in morally depraved areas.

Elder Malachi: Well, two of his children, his sons, they are in their late thirties and already have nice homes. The youngest, his daughter Candice, is living at home still, and may need a change of scenery based on some of her recent behavior.

Chairman Ezra: We can get to Joyce's concern for Candice in a few minutes, but let's just focus on the legacy issue.

Elder Malachi: I do believe they're connected <<cough>>.

Chairman Ezra: Yes, but we can deal with them independently and things will fall in line.

Disc. Habakkuk: From what I know of brother Gideon is that he liked the water. He always loved talking about how God must have carved the coastlines by hand, and that's why he liked to sometimes hold prayer meetings and Bible studies on the beach at Coney Island in the summer. The drive was worth it. They were some of the most beautiful Wednesday nights of my life. As we stood on the shoreline, he used to tell us that God's hand had passed over that very spot.

Chairman Ezra: Why don't we upgrade the sons' homes to beachfront properties as close to their current homes as possible? Where are the morally depraved areas near them?

Disc. Habakkuk: One son and his family are also on Long Island. I will begin researching that area following our meeting, but Fire Island comes to mind.

Elder Saul: The other son is in Georgia.

Disc. Habakkuk: I have connections in Savannah, Atlanta, and Hilton Head that I can tap for advice.

Elder Malachi: If there's anything I can do for Gideon's grandchildren, I can take that on personally <<cough>>.

Chairman Ezra: You want to get a glass of water?

Elder Malachi: ...yes, I'll be back in a moment.

Chairman Ezra: Paid-in-full beachfront homes in morally depraved areas, check. What about something at the house as a tribute to brother Gideon? So his grandchildren will be reminded daily where their allegiances lie.

Disc. Noah: What about boats? I have a connection, a brother in Christ, that restores wooden boats from 1960s and they are absolutely beautiful. He can use a wooden inlay technique for the name on the back of the boat. Gideon's Armada? And he can do some work on the masts and make them look like crosses. The horizontal part of the cross can sit right over the top of the sail.

Chairman Ezra: I like it. I love it. Praise be. Boats, check. I will inform Joyce of the contribution from The D.O.C. for his service. Excellent!

Elder Malachi: <<cough>> ...sorry, I thought the water would have worked.

Chairman Ezra: You have something in your beard, Malachi.

Elder Malachi: ...did I get it?

Disc. Noah: No, it's closer to your eye.

Elder Malachi: ...what about now?

Disc. Noah: Actually, the skin around your eye looks a little pale.

Elder Malachi: Thanks. You know what, I'm going to head to the restroom and get myself sorted out. Excuse me again. Sorry.

Chairman Ezra: O.K., let's move on to the next matter regarding Joyce. As we are preparing the Lovinglace family for life after Gideon and his moral and financial support, Gideon's wife Joyce has asked us to keep a watchful eye over Candice, or Candy, as she is called by her friends. She's the youngest and only female child, and Gideon was very protective of her well-being. God blessed Candice with unparalleled beauty. The quick story is that Candice received her college degree about two years ago. And she'd been dating a young man she met there for the past three years. This young man is a good Christian with strong values and a great work ethic. Things seemed to be on track for an engagement and marriage, but Candice, according to Joyce, grew a little bored, or tired, of the young man. Joyce doesn't know exactly when it happened since Candice keeps that area of her life quite private. Over the past few months Joyce has seen Candice go out with a few other men, which is to be expected. But it's a group of women that she's been going out with that has Joyce most concerned. These women, Joyce worries, have been planting seeds of sin in Candice. She's always been trustworthy, but now she's going out with them to pubs, secular music concerts, and nightclubs, and it seems like they've influenced her style of dress to become less conservative. They've even been having slumber parties like they're in grammar school.

Now, it seems that out of concern for Candice's well-being, Joyce has looked at some text messages and pictures on her daughter's phone when Candice was in the shower after a late night on Tuesday. A Tuesday night mind you. It turns out that Candice went out with her little immoral crew and wound up at a club that doubles as a lingerie store. Apparently the people at the club wear their braziers out in the open. Well, the devil has sure found a dwelling here in New York City.

Elder Malachi: ...my apologies once again for stepping out. And I'm caught up to speed on everything, as I've already been involved with the Lower Manhattan Reconnaissance for McJ—

Chairman Ezra: ...we're not quite there yet, Malachi.

Disc. Noah: Did you put rouge around your eye?

Chairman Ezra: And as you can see, some preliminary steps were taken to get to the heart of the matter. So allow me to continue. Joyce has been further worried that she may be more susceptible to stray from her Christian path now that Gideon has passed. Joyce has prayed about it extensively, and she's convinced that God has advised her to seek our assistance in the matter. Joyce quoted the following verses that God has led her to: Exodus 20:12, Proverbs 11:29, Proverbs 22:6, Mark 3:23. I will use them in our closing prayer today. So this matter, out of respect for our brother Gideon, is to become a top priority. The Defenders of Christ will serve the Lovinglace family with all of our resources, and I believe this matter can be solved quickly and efficiently. We will help Candice to re-focus on the light of all of our lives, the one and only, Jesus. We all have strayed from our path from time to time, and we've all needed assistance. And that is why God has put us here, so that we may use our efforts along with The Holy Spirit. This is the ultimate synergy.

Disc. Habakkuk: What are the details of the matter so far?

Elder Saul: Candice lives in the Lovinglace family home in Garden City, Long Island, which is the home that Gideon built for his family. She's the only one who has yet to leave the nest. She attended the local university, Adelphi, and commuted, so she's been fairly sheltered to this point. After graduating she took a position at a Christian charity organization that provides aid and education to various third world countries. Several months ago, around the time she broke up with her longterm boyfriend, Brigadoon B. Damm, she took a second job and began working part time in lower Manhattan with a new clothing company called Rip-Off. This company has been trying to break into the market of upscale conscious fashion. Apparently they remove sections of the clothes you buy, for example a t-shirt, and they cut off the sleeves to be recycled and remade into unique quilts for the less fortunate and homeless. So a t-shirt, that's really now a tank top, may cost as much as $150.

Disc. Noah: Yes, I've seen something like that on Cougar News Network.

Elder Saul: Rip-Off encourages the employees to experiment with the clothes they buy so they may advise customers on interesting types of cuts. So one day, Candice's boss sees some of her cut creations, the ones that took sweatshirts and made them into bikinis, and had her try them on with some of the other young women that work there, in the name of charity, I suppose he said. Well, the other women, who would soon become Candice's new best friends, encouraged her to experiment ever further, and all the while the boss is watching and getting all sorts of ideas, apparently. Then he promotes Candice to be both a paid designer and model for the company, and now she's getting notoriety and being invited to various fashion shows and industry parties.

Chairman Ezra: And it's these kind of events that upset Joyce, especially the types of people that attend them. Some of them are sharks straight from the lava oceans of hell, I tell you.

Elder Saul: Candice, and I'm being frank here, is a beautiful young woman. She's probably been warding off potential suitors for a long time, but this latest foray into this kind of immoral business crossed the line of honor to the Lovinglace family. I wasn't able to find the exact cause of the breakup between Brigadoon and Candice, but I'm sure that her position at Rip-Off didn't help matters.[45] As for Brigadoon's future, let's just say he's making very wise choices. You'll soon see what kind of man he is becoming.

Chairman Ezra: Yes, not too long ago, Brigadoon and Gideon went to a men's weekend retreat in upstate New York. Gideon was fond of him. And I remember Joyce telling me on several occasions that both families were very close. About once a month, she and Candice would make dinner and invite the whole Damm family over.

Elder Saul: <<phone ring>> Chairman Ezra, may I take this? This may be of importance.

Chairman Ezra: Of course, brother Saul.

Elder Saul: Yes?... Yes, It's Saul.... O.K., is this going to be long?... I understand.... Give me a moment and I'll be right with you.

Chairman Ezra: Well, all of these events, along with the death of her father, have made the latest development cause for alarm. And that's what, or who, we're going to discuss in just a few minutes.

[[◆]]

From her Harlem apartment window on the second floor, Axlia Clia looks through the red gossamer curtains to the street below. She sees an elderly woman pushing a baby stroller approach the crosswalk. The stroller has one wheel that rotates like Earth and barely touches the ground. The woman is carting her food from the local bodega in a few paper bags. The closest thing to a baby in her stroller is the arugula. Axlia searches the bags for the top of a baguette before turning her focus to the concrete stage from the other night. Her vision blurs the details of the sidewalk and traffic lights, and the wrinkles of the elderly woman are made smooth. The light changes and the woman starts to walk across the street. She hears the engine of a loud car approaching the intersection and she pulls her hair away from her face to see it. The car doesn't seem to be slowing down. Axlia stands a little taller out of concern. She feels the need to call out and actually say something to the woman, but everything is happening too fast for the sounds to materialize. There's the wail of the brakes, the skidding of rubber over asphalt, and then a crackling. A cloud of smoke obscures the scene for a few moments before it rises into the sky and joins the lone cumulous cloud overhead. Axlia sees scattered red and fleshy looking pieces. She watches a small spinning wheel come to a stop. She pulls the curtains all the way to each side and begins to reach for her phone in a panic when she sees something that lets her exhale and relax her posture. The elderly woman is standing up, unscathed, with both of her arms and two stout middle fingers extended toward the stopped car a hundred feet away. She's amidst destroyed cans of sauce, torn plastic bags of chicken cutlets, and a collapsed and dismantled stroller. She sees the speeding man get out of his sports car. He begins to walk back to the scene to talk to the woman, when all of a sudden, he falls to the ground in a heap of painful despair. He brushes back his hair with one hand and traces it back over his face. Axlia sees the man breathing deeply and rapidly. He grabs his head on both sides and then presses his fingers against his temples for a full five minutes. And during that time, several city dwellers gather to help calm down the elderly woman as the neighborhood pigeons descend in earnest to assist with the clean up.

[[_LƐON_]]

Leon finds a small sliver of mirror along one of the reflective pieces of moulding on the tall book cart next to his desk. He's moving his head side to side like he's saying _No_ to someone very slowly. He stops in the middle and lines up the point of his faux hawk in the thin mirror. He's inattentive.

"Excuse me, sir."

"Oh! Yes. Sorry. I was looking at my hair in the... Yes, how may I help you?"

A woman in her late fifties with just-graying hair is holding up a library copy of _1984_ like a precursory exclamation point. "I just know for a fact that Orwell did not write all of the words in this book. There is... computer language. And then there are some places I know he _did_ write things and they are not there. What is going on here? Is this some sort of joke? I'd like to speak to someone important!"

Leon removes his glasses and wipes the bridge of his nose. "Sure, let me see if I can help you. Can I see the book, please?" The woman hands Leon the book with a jab. He inspects the book. The outside of the jacket is covered with crinkly plastic and the corners of the hardcover had become curly nubs. He opens it and fans through the pages and the scent of several decades flies into his nostrils. The edges of the pages are yellowed, but not distractingly so. He notices a few stray pencil marks and the creases of dog-eared pages. The book looks as normal as any he'd seen in the library. "Is there something specific you'd like to bring to my attention? I can get my supervisor if you'd like."

"I would like the real book. The real _1984_. Not whatever that is."

"Let me look something up here... Yes, we have five more copies available. Would you like me to pull one of those for you and replace it?" Leon begins walking toward the shelf with the woman reluctantly in tow.

"Yes, thank you. But if there's anything strange with this one..."

"...there are printing errors and unusual typos all the time. I've seen it all before." Leon reaches down to the bottom shelf. "Please let me know if there's anything wrong with this copy, and if so, I will bring you right to my supervisor. O.K.?"

The woman flips through the book, which looks the same as the other, and is skeptically satisfied. "O.K. Thank you. This looks much better."

A few minutes later, Leon picks up the book again to have a closer look. He starts at the middle and flips around, stopping to read an occasional paragraph. Suddenly something catches him by surprise and he lowers his eyebrows to the point where they're contained within the frames of his glasses.

Big Brother is watching YouTube.

But if thought corrupts language, language can also corrupt thought. #possibletautology

And then he turns to page one. He reads the first sentence and his eyebrows rise back out of the frames. He drops the book to the marble floor and *1984* echoes in time.

It was a day in April, and the clocks were.

[[✝]]

The Defenders of Christ
North American Representatives in Faith
New York Office
Internal Document (2 of 4)
Minutes from the April Meeting
Re: Joyce

Chairman Ezra: ...so then, we have to move on to the matter of Tuesday night. Candice was out with her female friends at the nightclub when she was approached by someone who's known for being a new money socialite... and a womanizer. Of all things, his mother won almost three hundred million dollars, after taxes, in the Powerball Lottery a few years back, and he was given half of it. He's gained notoriety online, on TV, and in some magazines. It's mostly due to the money, but from what I hear he has a charismatic personality as well.

Disc. Samson: Satan has the powers of temptation. He puts on a good mask.

Elder Malachi: Well, another thing is, his name is Jesús.

Chairman Ezra: ...Yes, his name is another interesting side point. Ever since AppleFacegate, his name was caught up in the name-marketing kerfuffle. Secretary Jonah, before we move forward, can you hand out the files and pictures? Thank you. As you'll be able to see, his given name was Jesús Neon Woodson, although he was known to his friends and the celebrity watchers out there, as Zeus. As in Hey-*Zeus*. After AppleFacegate, the Zeus name got less play because of the McDonald's prefix that was contracted in, and it became McJesús, but people pronounce it without the accent, *Mc-Gee-Zuss*. Woodson is his father's last name, although he grew up in a single parent home with his mother. His father took off years ago and it's been difficult to find any information on him. It's possible that he's left the country. His mother moved to Los Angeles not too long after winning all of the money. McJesus lives on the top floor of 8 Spruce Street, the wavy Frank Gehry building by the west side of the Brooklyn Bridge, which presents a few obstacles, surveillance-wise. So, look... the deal is that this character is planning to take Candice out on Saturday night. He's going to be picking her up around eight o'clock and they have no defined plans. That's what we've been able to gain from Joyce. So we'll be trying to make this date go either a) horribly wrong , or b) non-existent. I, along with Elder Malachi, have started the general reconnaissance plans overnight and will be continuing to put any available disciples in action.

Disc. Noah: I just googled him and the first images that show up are photoshopped pictures of him as Ronald McDonald. Look, there's one here where he's on the cross in the clown suit! He's holding a Whopper in each hand while his wrists are nailed to the cross!

Sec. Jonah: Isn't that Burger King?

Disc. Noah: Right, I mean he's hold a Big Mac in each hand.

Disc. Samson: Blasphemy!

Disc. Noah: On the other crosses beside him are two twin Hamburglars. They are both reaching for the Big Macs. And the caption says that McJesus is offering them *Salivation*!

Disc. Samson: This will end.

Disc. Noah: And there are the Romans below him yelling *Crucifry Him, Crucifry Him!*

Disc. Samson: Enough! I don't want to hear anymore of this disgrace!

Chairman Ezra: Let's return to order, please. Yes, there are disturbing and disrespectful images on the internet, and while McJesus is ultimately responsible for his actions, he can't be blamed for every other person's actions. That being said, we don't want Candice to be caught up with a character like this. We have to honor Gideon and Joyce, and most of all, Our Savior.

Disc. Samson: Amen!

Elder Malachi:<<cough>>

Chairman Ezra: Let's give the floor to Elder Obadiah and Disciple Mark now. They knew Mr. Woodson when he was young, and may offer some insight.

Elder Obadiah: Mmmm, yes. I only knew him for a few days when he was in middle school. I was a group leader at a Christian retreat that his youth group attended. He seemed like a lost boy who was in need of a role model, and I felt that he found one with Christ that weekend. We prayed together and he asked Jesus to come into his heart and accepted him as his personal savior. I remember it quite well, actually.

Disc. Mark: Yes, I was there too. I'm the same age as he is. I remember he was very emotional about the whole thing. His presence made me feel better about being a Christian, you know, to see that kind of genuine transformation and acceptance. I just thought, you know, that he was a good guy who was finding a good thing... the best thing.

Elder Obadiah: Obviously somewhere along the way, he's strayed from the path, and needs help finding his way back.

Disc. Mark: Right. I hope I can assist in someway, as he may remember me and some of the good wholesome moments we've shared.

Elder Obadiah: Exactly. I mean, I only have positive memories of him as a young boy. There were certain aspects of him that felt like he was older than he seemed. He had a special kind of aura about him, and a certain kind of look in his eyes, like he knew more than he was saying. His face even possessed some of the angles that are reminiscent of antiquity. He's quite a good looking boy.

Elder Malachi: I bet. <<cough>>

Chairman Ezra: Using the childhood connections of Obadiah and Mark, the research of Habakkuk, the wisdom of Saul, Noah's connections to Evangelical leaders, my law enforcement connections to The Vatican and the NYPD, Samson's strong-arm tactics, Malachi's technical support, and Noah's enthusiasm for the Lord, let's open the floor to suggestions for plans A and B. And anything you'd like to add too, Jonah, sorry.

Disc. Samson: I would like to begin with a silent prayer. Let's listen to God and listen to what brother Gideon would want us to do. Let's really listen, deeply. What would Gideon do?

Elder Malachi: <<coughing>>

Disc. Samson: Silence!

[[Σ]]

Suma walks to the end of 10th street to check out the art exhibit at [Mission]. She'd spent hours reading at [Halcyon Books], but is ready for a change of scenery. With the caffeine having lost its effect, she moves slowly down the block, noting the details of her surroundings. There's a bike with a flat tire next to a car with a flat tire, there are early blooms reaching their way into sun rays, there are fire escape outlines that look like dark metal thunderbolts, and there is a single cumulous cloud in the sky on an otherwise sun-filled day. As she steps up a few stairs toward the entrance of the gallery, she sees a sign on the door:

The gallery is closed.
We are preparing for our next exhibit to begin Monday.
We apologize for any inconvenience.
Our Mission continues!

But the door is ajar and Suma takes a cautious step inside. She looks straight up to the gold ceiling and works her way down to the walls, which are in the process of being painted white. There are temporary drapes that are billowing in and out over the old church windows. There are gray drop cloths on the floor and she can hear the sounds of manual labor in the background. She feels her phone vibrate in her purse. Then Suma hears a strong deep voice echoing throughout the vaulted ceilings. She can't tell from where it's coming, just that it's ubiquitous. But it's also muffled by its own sound waves bouncing over the bare walls and arches, and then running back into each other. Her phone vibrates again and she checks it this time. It's Leon. [*Hey Suma, strangest thing at the library. Did you know that big brother is watching YouTube? Haha. Yep it's true. I'm holding the evidence in my hands right now.*] As she reads the text she feels a wave of cold blood start at the top of her head and emanate down to her toes. She replies, [*That's crazy, Leon. I can't wait to hear more about it! I want to be the first one to see this :) Want to meet for drinks at 6 at RB&A?*] As she waits for the reply, the room grows darker as the wind stills and the drapes flatten. Leon answers, [*Perfect. I'll bring the book with me and you'll be the first to see it.*]

At the time, she knew that publication might've been taking it too far. Now, she must drain the well before the initial ripple expands its circumference too far to control. So, before meeting up with Leon, Suma has a few hours to come up with a plan. As Suma goes for the exit, the Darth Vader sounds return and saturate the gallery. She hears the voice say,

[[◆]]

"...so, what do you think about getting all of this exposure?"

Axlia adjusts the copper bracelets on her left wrist and nods with her chin held high.

The kinetic Cyrus Coaster continues, "I know, I know. You're still recovering, but you're O.K. to put the axe to the grind, right? I mean, I see an opportunity, and I take it as a sign. And the sign always says the same thing. It says *No Exit*, meaning just keep going, pedal to the metal. And I like to move fast and play on the spontaneity, and catch people by storm. And I think this storm is tsunami level, hurricane style. I mean, let's do this, you know? My beliefs are anchored in the stars, the moon, and the determination of fate. And right now, I feel like I am the stars. I am older and have twinkles of resources everywhere, just like the night sky. And you, you are the moon. You are younger, but you move the waters in your silence. You show us which way the world is heading. You are near us all, and you are full. And the determination of fate, well, that's pretty clear to me. Fate isn't always comfortable. But for some reason, the world saw it fit that you and that bullet were to meet ever so briefly in Harlem during your performance. And it is fate that has brought you to this gallery. It is through this pain that we, and others, can appreciate the pleasure of art."

Axlia shifts her portfolio from her left hip to her right.

"Now, I love all of your work. I'm really feeling everything in it. I mean, I wish it was my work. I appreciate the way you push the idea of dualities and the subsequent gray areas. I love it! And a lot of your serious work, well, I don't want to say I love it, because that seems to be the wrong word. But you know what I mean, right?"

Axlia doesn't offer any suggestions.

"Well, let's get down to brass tacks, whatever that means. I want to open Monday morning with all of your prints and video projects inside and I want to have a night portion that takes place outside of the gallery, right here on the sidewalks. I will provide all of the moving trucks and workers for your art and anything else you need. And they can start working within the hour if you'd like. I'm going to start a publicity tour a.s.a.p. with social media, print media, and news outlets. Any ideas on what you'd like to call your show and performance? Don't worry, you can think about it tonight. On my way over here I thought about incorporating the duality aspect of your work, you know? Maybe something about the flow of energy between one extreme and the other." Cyrus Coaster is sweating with excitement.

Axlia nods and pulls several copper chains out from under her sleeveless black top. She twirls her index finger in between cuban links and a rope, and lets them fall in the center of her chest.

"Excellent. We essentially have eight rooms, or areas, inside. We can work together to curate the project as your canvases and everything else arrives. Based on everything you've shown me, I'm thinking in the vestibule, the large entrance here, we can hang your most recent canvases lengthwise, from your I/O show. We can hang #Canvas1, 2, and 3 on the left, and then #Canvas4, 5, and 6 on the right, and leave a space in the middle here. I understand that the seventh canvas is still city property for now, but I'm working on expediting the situation. Now in the empty space in the middle, I have a type of invisible video screen that can hang there. And on the screen I'd like to have a floating video of you that can be seen from either side. My idea is that the video will be a reenactment of your Wednesday night show. We can film it Sunday morning if that works for you. I can get a film crew here. As you may know, I have a lot of connections with people in the movie business, and they are A-1 top notch solid gold. How does this sound so far?"

Axlia makes a gun out of her hand, fires a fake shot, and winks an approval at Cyrus Coaster.

"Nice. Now in this room over here, the left arcade, I'm thinking we can run the loops of some of your own personal art videos. We can accommodate three at a time. And opposite that by the right arcade, we can hang some of your other canvases. I particularly like the series that starts with the ancient poem in simple black and white, and goes through the progression like the telephone game, and ends with a colorful and nonsensical sentence. I think we can run those ten paintings side by side like a timeline. And in some of these side rooms, I call them box galleries, we can set up or recreate some of your installations. There's two rooms over there, and you have to go through the first one to get to the last room at the end. I'm thinking we can put your *It's not litter if I smoke it, Joe* piece in there. Like, put the video on loop on the far wall, but line the entire floor with cigarette butts, so that way everyone has to step all over them and really take in their ashy scent. Actually, I hope you don't mind, but I already have some of my team collecting some used filters from around the city. Some from the sidewalks and some from ashtrays. Don't worry, they're using gloves! And then in the far room, we can hang the paintings with the broken frames. I really dig how the images spill out right onto the walls and distort them. I think it's a strong commentary on the beauty created when one escapes the confines of what is expected. Dig it. So, what do you think so far?"

Axlia nods as she brings a clove cigarette to her lips.

"I also want to bring in an interactive element to the show. With deference to your Telephone Poetry Sequence, I would like patrons to participate in various live examples of it. There will be plenty of room to set this up in the nave and the crossing, over there, see? Whether you'd like to choose some more ancient poems, write them yourself, or even bring in someone else, a local poet, perhaps. These are just ideas, but I thought it would be cool to get ten to fifteen people to sit side-by-side in one of the pews. The first person would get the original poem, which we would have printed on the top half of a canvas in a simple style, and unseen by the people in the pew. Then the poem would get telephoned down the line until it reaches the last person. Then the new form will be read and then painted in a colorful, sort of psychedelic-graffiti way underneath the original. We'd be able to hear and see the progression, or digression, of the poem through the distortions of human interpretations. It would be a live communication breakdown, a commentary on the barriers of understanding one another through language. I can provide as many blank canvases as necessary and we can put them up for auction as part of the live event. There's nothing wrong with mixing art and commerce, *believe you me*, whatever that means. Give it some thought. Cool?"

Looking ever more confident about the show, and therefore, more beautiful, Axlia exhales the smoke to the ceiling of the nave, with a slow affirmative blink.

"There's really not supposed to be any smok... nevermind. So, there are two more spaces. The largest area is in the chancel of the church, which is the focal point of the gallery. I figured we can use your HYMEN TEARS performance and installation there, but I realize that it may be too small a timeframe to get all of your performers here and available for the run of the show. Or that space can be used for any new work you'd like to perform or get together. Maybe there's something you've wanted to do? I will accommodate all of the logistics. Dig it?"

Axlia nods through the singular cloud of her exhale.

"And then there is the old church library, well, at least there are the *shelves* of the library. Everything has been removed and I've used it only once before as a mini-gallery. We had an exhibit of very small paintings and sculptures and it when over really well. I'm digging that stuff, you know? But I didn't see anything of your work that would fit in that space, so give that some thought too. I mean, we don't *have* to use that space, but give it a thought. Also, there is some second floor space that is available, but it is out of the way. See that door there in the church library? It's kind of hidden, but it leads to a hallway, then a large staircase and then to a wide open area. If you would like to use it, you're welcome to. And one last element is the use of the sidewalk space outside the gallery to draw people in." Cyrus Coaster walks toward a window with Axlia following. "I have these holographic projectors set up at the top of the building on both corners of the street. Now, when we film your reenactment of I/0, we will also film it with the capability to show it as a hologram. We can use that holographic film, as though you were actually performing the piece on the streets, walking back and forth in the colors of mother of pearl and black. I'm thinking the I/O performance would be the best, since that is what has the most notoriety, and it's incredibly titillating. I want this gallery to be bursting at the seams. And as far as any digital nudity issues outside the building, I'm not worried. I can absorb the cost of city penalties. That won't even be mentioned with the contract I'd like to offer you. I'm more interested in pushing performance art to the forefront and making a name for this gallery." Cyrus Coaster's animated gesticulations are now accenting his words more often than before.

Axlia licks her index finger and thumb and distinguishes the fire at the end of her clove cigarette. The scent is sweet, rooted in mysticism. Axlia walks to the library door that leads to the hidden hallway to check it out. Cyrus hears her ascend the steps in the distance. When she returns ten minutes later, she pulls out some paper from the pocket of her skirt that had been folded into fours and then curved by her body heat. She produces a black and gold pen from her bag and walks over to a nearby surface. Axlia is sketching out the crude blueprints for the entire show, the changes to his suggestions, what she wants in each space, and an ambitious idea she has for the hidden hallway and second floor space. This takes about twenty minutes. Cyrus Coaster watches her mind at work. When she gives him the paper, his eyebrows rise like caterpillars in mid-stride. He leaves without a word to retrace Axlia's steps to the upstairs space. When he returns, he's punch-drunk with motivation.

"This will be difficult to get done exactly how you want, but I believe I hear you loudly and clearly. My team will do their best. Yes, we can do this. This will work. Very different. I hope you can see how much we are all excited to..." His voice fades into the background, drowned out by her own rampant thoughts.

As Cyrus Coaster carries on about percentages and more ideas, she looks over her shoulder at the large stained glass window. The sunlight is filtered through apple and citrus colors. Her hand feels its way to the bandage on her side, and she holds it there for several moments. Looking through a section of red on the stained glass, she sees a blurry figure standing on the sidewalk. He's wearing sunglasses, thin black pants, and a fitted black shirt with a few buttons unbuttoned. He's looking ahead and down the street. Her hand slides higher and finds a resting spot over her heart. The man in black with rose-tinged skin looks to the stained glass window, and his hand also goes toward his heart. And there he pulls out a pen from his shirt pocket and begins to write in a red book, a journal it seems. C.C.'s voice creeps back into her consciousness, "...so, let's start tonight. I can send my team over to your place at eight o'clock. If you sign here, we can officially proceed. This is going to put *you* and [Mission] fully on the map." She looks at Cyrus Coaster, focusing on his eyes for the first time, smiles, and hums an affirmation.

She signs her name as *Axlia Clia/Della Creme* on the solid line next to the *✗*.

C.C. reconfirms, "Eight it is!" Axlia walks out the gallery entrance, through the old church doors, and starts with a quiet confidence toward the subway station. She pauses for a moment to see if the man in black, now without any of the rose coloring, is still there. But he

[[❋]]

is low on one knee retying the slippery laces on his dress shoes and is partly obscured by a post box. As he begins to stand up, he sees the profile of a woman as she walks by him, from toes to head. She's wearing jade heels with a cubism quality to them. Her skin glistens in the sun from her ankles to her lower thighs until a rocket-gray skirt interrupts the reflective lines. The skirt conforms to her hourglass curves and in no time becomes a black top that shows just enough to pique curiosity. Her eyes are almonds and her hair falls down her back and moves with her steps. On her wrist, her copper bangles jangle until she's out of earshot. As though transfixed by her, it takes a moment for his brain to return to working order. And once the synapses sparked true, he starts to follow her, matching her stride for stride. He thinks through a few quick reasons to say hello, like seeing her hang the flyers for her show through the window at [COLOSSUS], but that seems a little strange, or maybe that he'd planned on going to her performance in Harlem, or hearing about her being shot and getting into a drunken argument about it with strangers—but none feel right. Another time, Roosevelt thinks. He mumbles to himself that he'll go to the next show no doubt. As he slows up and watches her hips swing into the distance, he takes a deep breath and inhales the sweet air of her wake. He makes his way toward a bench on the outskirts of Tompkins Square Park, a place of familiar refuge, and puts his pen to paper:

THE SWEET SCENT OF HER HAIR
FOLLOWS WHEN I ROAM,
SOFT TOUCHES OF HONEY
MUST DRIP FROM HER COMB.

Roosevelt looks up, his eyes squinting in the glare of the nearest star, as its light is being refracted and concentrated by the curvature of a very expensive watch. It's a one-of-a-kind watch that Zeus had paid a watchmaker to construct in rose gold, platinum, and onyx as a tribute to one that he had lost a decade ago. The original was given to him when he was young by a good friend of his maternal grandfather. Zeus had never met either grandfather, but this man provided a welcomed connection. He would tell him all about the inner workings of the watch and the skill that it took to perfect the craft. Zeus remembers sitting with him in his Brooklyn apartment and watching him open and take apart many of the components with small tools. He held the delicate gears, pointed out the jewels, and used many words that he didn't know. This man would tell him a little about the word and reassure him in his bass-driven voice, "You'll learn, you'll learn. Just keep watching and listening." He remembers hearing his breath and the soft airy sounds that found their way out through spaces where teeth once were. Then the man put the watch together, encased the back, put it on his much smaller wrist, and fastened the strap. The watch was far too big even on the smallest size, and his grandfather encouraged him, "Don't worry, it's yours to keep. You'll grow into it." Zeus remembers asking him if he needed a watch too, to which he smiled, "I have all sorts of watches, boy. Don't you worry. I have all the time in the world."

The original watch, which he later researched after the death of his grandfather's friend, was a Raketa Copernic produced in the USSR near the close of The Cold War. The hour hand was a golden disc with a single sun ray pointing toward the circumference. The second hand was an open silver circle with a notch pointing toward the precise minute. So at noon, for example, the circle and the disc were aligned, and it created the illusion of an eclipse. The third hand, which was black, was also the second hand, paradoxically. These eclipses occurred twenty-two times a day, and Zeus tried to look down at his wrist to catch those moments when he felt they were near, both with the original, and with the heavy metal version he wears today. When he first had the new watch constructed, he wore it more often than his clothes, as many times it was the only thing he wore when he slept.

Zeus is walking back from the church toward home and his head is hanging low, like a defeated boxer. He's holding a white paper bag with a small coffee and two glazed donuts inside. The coffee is dripping out onto the sidewalk from one corner of the bag. The lid sucks. He slips into a sincere walking prayer. Zeus concludes that his dream in the church was more vivid than any other, and that the scenes within it represent a distillation of the truth. He feels the guilt of his selfish triumphs and the times he indulged in his own happenstantial power. Those moments were ephemeral, but the memories are hollow and lasting. The truth is an embarrassment. He is overcome with the urge to change his course, to release himself from the ambiguous confines of doubt, and let God be his guide once again. He looks at his watch.

It's time to atone.

All of the questions he'd asked in the past, while they may have been valid thoughts, are not the ones he should've been asking. Those questions should've been relegated to inconsequential curiosities, he tells himself. They should've acted as an admission that the mind of God and the minds of men do not intersect, but that the minds of men are subsets of God, and that we are contained within Him. God understands us, but we can never fully understand Him. Zeus had defined his identity by questioning alone and he now realizes he'd been shifting on soft sand for too long. He wants something concrete on which to stand—and to stand for. He again wants to be in wonder for all the things God made possible.

He closes his walking prayer knowing his heart is in the right place. Zeus straightens his back and takes out a sugary zero of dough and takes a big bite. He continues walking home with his head angled up, feeling the warmth of the sun on his face.

[[✝]]

The Defenders of Christ
North American Representatives in Faith
New York Office
Internal Document (3 of 4)
Minutes from the April Meeting
Re: Joyce

Disc. Samson: ...Thank you Lord, Amen.

Chairman Ezra: As for Plan A, please let your voices be heard through the filter of The Lord.

Disc. Mark: What if we send her an anonymous text or email that details his past exploits? Something that will make it strikingly clear what he's all about.

Elder Obadiah: That may work. To inform her that there are parties concerned and that they have a bad feeling about this guy. Or maybe that he's emotionally unstable due to the absence of his father and the cataclysmic fortune that is the lottery. It's true, it can especially undermine one's own ambitions and skew their view of the world. To know that you've done nothing to earn your status can be either sobering or intoxicating, depending on the type of person. We can explain that it's not entirely his fault that he's not relationship material.

Disc. Samson: Nonsense. It is entirely his fault! I don't want to defend this heathen.

Elder Obadiah: I agree, Samson. He owns his sins. I'm simply suggesting that we let Candice *think* that it is no fault of his own. If we persecute him for being a poisonous thinker, I believe it will only make him look more interesting and rebellious, which may attract her more to him, especially with the way she's been acting.

Disc. Samson: But I disagree with that logic. If she is informed that it isn't his fault, then she may feel sympathy for him, and then give him undue respect.

Sec. Jonah: Ahh, the caretaker complex. A lot of women have that. I've heard.

Elder Obadiah: There are many things at play here, psychologically. We may be on two sides of the same coin. Women are unpredictable. No matter how God-fearing they are, they may be inclined to take on a project when they perceive a good heart, or they may be inclined to reject any uncertainty in a relationship out of self-preservation. The actions of women seem to be independent of logic. I reference Eve as my sole example. Obviously, Satan is manipulative. Candice may believe he has a good heart, but he may be veiled by the devil himself. If we push her in either direction, it may backfire in both cases. Women are unpredictable.

Disc. Samson: Honestly, I believe we are spending too much time in the passive-aggressive approach. I prefer something much more comprehensive and final.

Disc. Noah: What if we were to use our media connections to have an unfavorable story published about him. Something that is hard to refute, but that will raise doubt in her mind. Something, how should I say this... creepy. Something to make her uncomfortable about being seen with him, or want to see him at all.

Disc. Samson: I again, wholeheartedly disagree.

Disc. Mark: Noah, I think you may be on to something. If we can publish something quickly, it will give Candice time to reconsider her date for tomorrow night, and more time for us to deal with this individual gone astray.

Elder Malachi: There is also the idea of working things the other way. We could... send word to this McJesus character, that Candice is not who she claims to be. This way, if he cancels the encounter, she will feel rejected and more likely to move in a different direction.

Chairman Ezra: I'm not sure how I, or Gideon or Joyce for that matter, would feel about that tactic.

Elder Malachi: Joyce won't have to be informed of our exact actions. We can tell her simply that the matter has been settled.

Disc. Noah: Since he is a celebrity of sorts, there is the risk that he could make whatever we tell him, known to the public. I don't believe that it's worth the risk to her reputation, or Gideon's, or her family's.

Chairman Ezra: Noted. Let's move to some ideas for Plan B. Let's say we aren't able to prevent the date from starting, what can be done to ensure that they will not pursue further meetings?

Disc. Samson: Wait—there is another way we can prevent the meeting that can be disguised and effective. As we know, there is a time for peace, and a time for war.

Chairman Ezra: I'm not following you, Samson.

Disc. Samson: We can use the recent rash of high speed car accidents. My—or should I say *our*—sources indicate that it's certainly a domestic terrorism plot on a large scale that is expected to grow exponentially.

Elder Obadiah: I'm not sure where you're going with this.

Disc. Samson: It's unclear from which country it originates, but it is being carried out by Muslim extremists. It appears that they have small cells within all states that are becoming operational—and some are even robotic. They don't want this to be a one-strike attack. Instead they want it to build over the course of the year, until it becomes too obvious to ignore, and instill fear in every driver, every American, and mostly, every Christian. Some of these attacks are carried out by suicide drivers, but the vast majority are carried out in one of two ways. One, by a fleet of high-performance, unregistered driverless cars. Two, by hacking into the car of an innocent driver, and then disabling the breaks and increasing the speed as far as the car allows. The second example accounts for all of the single-vehicle crashes. Now, we've alerted the police across the country of our intelligence, but not all parties have completely bought into it. They insist that there isn't enough information to be sure that these are targeted attacks. But that's just the thing. They aren't really targeted. As far as the suicide drivers, these are extremist men and women who get behind the wheel on any given morning, afternoon, or night, and reach very high speeds, and then drift off into oncoming traffic, as if they've fallen asleep at the wheel with their foot pressed down on the gas. The accidents are often so horrific and so violent that they foster crematory-like conditions, whereby they can't even confirm the number of dead bodies at one scene until a full DNA analysis of whatever remains is complete. The waiting process can go on for weeks. In some cases, the missing persons are pronounced dead circumstantially. When the police officers try to connect the vehicle registrations to one organization, they're unable to find any pattern, of course, because none exists. So far there have been hundreds of these accidents, but because the number of automobile deaths in America due to speeding is so high, it hasn't brought the fear level up as fast as these evildoers thought it would. They may have unintentionally pointed out an inconsistency within the American government.

Elder Obadiah: What do you mean by *inconsistency*?

Disc. Samson: The inconsistency that the government wants to protect and improve the lives of its people, while at the same time, afford them the freedoms to do as they wish.

Elder Obadiah: Go on.

Disc. Samson: The federal and state governments establish speed limits that are easily and freely disobeyed. Some people are even lauded for disobeying them. It seems to point out that the freedoms of the few to drive recklessly outweigh the freedoms of the law-abiding. That the *idea* of being able to drive fast, far outweighs the idea of being free *from* the reckless.

Elder Obadiah: That's why we have a highway patrol. They protect us from the reckless.

Disc. Samson: And what have they really done? Look at the death tolls even before these high-speed *accidents* started and you'll see that no even seems to notice that the terrorism has begun!

Elder Obadiah: So, what are you saying?

Disc. Samson: I'm saying that if the government really wanted to protect Americans, they could enforce these laws a different way. The first thing the government would have to do is redefine the word *reckless*. Then they could pass a law that requires restrictor plates on all cars, classic and new. This would limit the speed of every car or vehicle. If they redefined *reckless* as going over thirty miles-per-hour, lives would certainly be saved. It would actually be very hard to die in a car.

Elder Obadiah: I didn't realize you were pro-government.

Disc. Samson: I am not! I'm simply pointing out their inconsistencies. Moving forward, only a few news outlets and municipalities have entertained the idea that this is the organized crime of terrorists. And they're being called conspiracy theorists. It's this fact that their terrorism has gone unnoticed that is most interesting. It indicates to me that they will ramp up their efforts for even more deaths, or organize accidents of greater magnitude, and make them impossible to ignore.

Disc. Noah: ...I had no idea.

Disc. Samson: Exactly. And while I abhor their actions and despise their religion, I find it a convenient way to solve our problem quickly, which is what I believe I am called to do. There are many instances in the Bible where God called for swift action, and I believe that this is one of those times. I'm ready for the call, for one. If we can simulate one of these accidents with him at the center of it, the problem is solved—and the poison of doubt will be reduced of its potency.

Sec. Jonah: Sorry to interrupt, but he's been seen driving a Lamborghini Countach from the nineteen-eighties and it doesn't have a computer to hack.

Disc. Samson: There are other ways.

Chairman Ezra: Before we go too far, I'm fully aware of God's need for immediate action, but I also believe that we should refrain from violence if possible.

Elder Ezekiel: You're sounding a lot different than you did in Indiana.

Chairman Ezra: You may proceed, Samson.

Disc. Samson: I have several ideas on how to make this happen. The best ways will even incriminate the extremists who started this.

Elder Saul: Let's hold on for a minute. I'm from the old school. And while I agree with everyone's line of thinking thus far, I want to offer a simple, yet effective way of preventing this meeting... sleeping pills. Whether it's Candice or this McJesus character, if one of them is in a deep sleep, they won't meet each other. If we can get some in his system, he'll never take the drive and we can push the issue along, and pray for its dissipation. If we can get Candice to ingest them, then Joyce will be there to tell him that she's too tired to go out. We can allow the fallout to commence, Joyce can read their text messages, and we can proceed without immediate violence. Either way, this is a peaceful way to an eventual end.

Disc. Noah: So you're saying you want to roofie McJesus!? I mean, why don't we just slash his tires?

[[Σ]]

Leon flicks a forgotten crumb from the table and takes a sip of water from a glass with a carousel of unicorns along the base of it. He continues, "So, I stopped off at home and got my own copy of *1984*. See? It's my paperback from high school. Since I got here, I've been looking through both books. I found six pages that don't match—it's crazy. It looks legit, but there's no way it can be. Even this first line, look." Leon runs his finger under the words. "It's almost as if someone took the Newspeak approach to the book and removed the adjectives and everything. Check this page, it perfectly matches the one in my book. Now look at this page." He quickly flips back and forth between the two. "Can you see any difference in aging? I mean, can you see any reason to doubt its authenticity? I looked up how many times this exact book has been taken out since we have several copies of it on the shelf. It was a lot. And it was more than eight times in the past year alone. No one's said anything until now, but this has got to be the strangest thing I've ever seen at the Library. Do you think it's worth something?"

Suma doesn't answer right away. She has none of the vigor of her coworker. She combs the right side of her hair with her hand and Leon watches as her green eye is accentuated. Suma looks introspective, but not in a pretentious way. Before she speaks, she tucks a lock of hair over her left ear, which causes Leon to shift his focus to the blueness of an ocean under swirling winds. "Before we go any further, I need to know something. I need to know I can trust you."

"What do you mean? Of course you can," Leon assures her, despite being very confused.

"I'm going to tell you the truth. And you may not think of me the same way again."

[[†]]

The Defenders of Christ
North American Representatives in Faith
New York Office
Internal Document (4 of 4)
Minutes from the April Meeting
Re: Joyce

Elder Saul: Look, he certainly has the means to get another car or a limousine. That would only cause a slight delay. The collateral fear would also be minimal, I believe. That's if he would even tell her.

Chairman Ezra: I've noted everyone's suggestions thus far, but let's move to ideas for Plan B. If they go on this date, and it goes poorly, it may spell the end of this short episode. Consider if they don't meet, they'll be more drawn to each other, and therefore their attraction to each other may be greater. Now, since we don't know their plans for tomorrow night, if we go ahead with Plan B, we will have to rely on any intel Joyce can lift from Candice's phone.

Disc. Noah: Why don't we bug Candice's room? Then stake out the house, and we he arrives, we'll throw a GPS tracker on his car and we can move from there?

Chairman Ezra: Let me have a few minutes alone in prayer. I have to cleanse my thoughts.

[Pause]

Chairman Ezra: Thank you, men. O.K., I believe that keeping this as porcelain-white as possible is a top priority here. Some of the more *final* plans proposed will not be employed at this time. When I prayed, God reminded me of a time that I went on a date in college that ended disastrously. I thought that I had blocked it from my memory, but after all that time, God let it flow down from above, right into my head. So, instead of preventing the meeting or deferring it, let's let it happen, and ruin it. Our plan of action for tomorrow night will center around this: Humiliation. This way, Candice will not be attracted to him. We are going to remove any possible tension of a sexual nature by using our connections within the restaurant industry. We are going to do this through the kitchen, the back door, so to speak. 1) I will ask Joyce to find out as much as she can leading up to the date time. 2) Ezekiel and Habakkuk, you will be responsible for the tracking device on Mr. Woodson's car. You're not to bug the house and you're not to be seen by anyone, Joyce included. 3) Obadiah and Mark, you will be on Long Island surveillance, and I will provide you with a detailed protocol to follow and our catalog of contacts in the restaurant industry, along with powerful laxatives in powder and liquid form. 4) Malachi and Noah, you will receive the same protocol, contacts, and laxatives, but you will be the Manhattan team. 5) Samson and Jonah, you are to be in the area of 8 Spruce Street. We do have some connections that reside there if extreme measures need to be taken. Let's hope it doesn't happen, but if the date goes on that far, there is a protocol that is more aggressive. I have access to other narcotics that will render Mr. Woodson sloppy and impotent. This is only to be used if Candice has a zero chance of getting into a vehicle with him after he's ingested it. If administered, we will take steps to ensure she makes it home safely. I pray it doesn't come to that. And 6) Saul and myself will oversee the events of the night and will communicate with all operatives about the plan of action. At any time, our activities may change. This will be a very fluid situation, but we will flush him out! Now, let's close together in prayer.

[[◆]]

Axlia watches the movers walk in and out of her apartment as they transport her canvases, installation pieces, various paint supplies, and even some clothes. As they say goodnight and close the door behind them, she looks around. It's as if she'd just moved in— blank surfaces, a sparse closet, a lonely bed. Axlia has the tremor of excitement in her veins, but it's stayed by the chill of vacancy.

She stands by the open window, hoping the cool city air will become fuel for her thoughts. There's still the issue of what to do with the holographic recording, the mini gallery in the library, which poems to use for the live communication in the nave, and the centerpiece in the chancel. She thinks that something simple, yet indicative of herself, should be at the focal point of the gallery. But maybe not too showy. She takes out a clove cigarette from a pack on the window sill and sparks her lighter, which produces no flame, but instead finishes the chain reaction with an idea.

Axlia Clia remembers she has an old 6' x 8' canvas rolled up under her bed. The original work is from her first attempt at a live painting performance, which was in the living room in front of her family in their Indiana home. It was her not-so-subtle way of showing her intentions to shift to the east coast. Della, as she was only known by then, laid the canvas over a large blanket-turned-drop-cloth and across the hardwood planks of the living room floor. Her audience sat on two plastic-covered davenports, her grandmother and sister on one, her parents on the other.

Dinner was in the oven and on the minds of the couched foursome. She was seventeen. Though when she painted, Della still wore her middle-school-era pajamas, which had become tighter and noticeably threadbare by then. Everyone tried to ignore it. With all eight eyes on her, she tugged her socks off and kicked them under a nearby piano bench. Della then buckled a tool belt around her waist that she'd fashioned into a paintbrush holder. The room was silent, save for the creaks of the floorboards as Della continued to prepare.

The canvas was almost white and it stretched flat at the corners with stacks of heavy books and at the edges with paint cans. Della outlined the map of The United States from memory with great detail, though it looked like California had grown an Alaskan tumor and phallic Florida had released Hawaii into the Atlantic—and that something was tectonically amiss in the northeast.

After she painted the new continental borders, Della blued the waters with Van Gogh-esque brushes of sky. Her mother shifted on the couch and the uncomfortable sounds of plastic friction pierced the air. Then, with the brush between her toes, she danced from state to state, and dipped into the various paint cans of the brightest primary colors to fill in the spaces. Nebraska was blushed red, Missouri was brushed yellow, Kansas's grass was greener, and Iowa's flowers were indigoer.

The scent of dinner replaced the air in the room, and Della could hear the empty swallows of her grandmother, a salivating carnivore. Della filled in the Great Lakes of H.O.M.E.S. and toed the line of the M.I.S.S.I.S.S.I.P.P.I. Then she moved to the north where it became clear that her home state had been replaced by Pennsylvania, rotated 90°. With all of the R.O.Y.G.B.I.V., the blackness of sideways PA was stark. In the direction of the sunrise, Della moved to the new Indiana, which she rotated sideways where its southern tip now shared a border with N.Y.C. along the Hudson, and Jersey was pulled down to make room. New York, the location of her future epic, was filled with mother-of-pearl. Her final touch was a glowing red star over the city, the capital of Della's America.

Her father cleared his throat. It had been more than one hour. She freed the edges and corners of the canvas from their restraints, padded to Lake Superior, took off her tool belt, bowed, and smiled to her family. Her family met her with claps of curiosity followed by more sounds of plastic as they rose. By now, the aroma of dinner was just about dragging them into the kitchen. Her mother was the last to stand. She took a few steps toward Della and said with raised eyebrows, "Well, that was interesting. What are you trying to say, dear?"

Axlia Clia/Della Crème rolls out the canvas from under the bed in her apartment and positions her four desk lamps to face inward at each corner, both to keep it in place and to remove the shadows. They are the only lights on in the room. The canvas is U.S.A.-side-down. She walks to her desk and grabs several handfuls of jet-black oil sticks and positions them around the perimeter. She stands at one end of the canvas and ties her hair up into a haphazard bun. In the darkness, which is thigh-high and above, she unbuttons her top and pulls it off each arm, and then throws the inside-out shirt on her bed. AC♦DC unclasps her bra and flings it frisbee-style on top of the shirt. She unzips her kick-around jeans and shifts her hips side to side until the denim collects at the floor. She keeps on her lacy black underwear as she lies down on her back with her arms spread way out in the light. Her head is closest to the red-curtained window and her feet are pointed toward the far wall, which is bare. AC♦DC takes an oil stick in her right hand and begins writing on the space she doesn't occupy. She writes words of poetry, regret, loss, love, family, and yearning, all cut from threads in her mind. She writes in script, helvetica, 3D block lettering, calligraphy, wild style, and her own personalized fonts. And after she twists and leans as much as she can, exhausting all right-handed possibilities, she continues with her left hand, which is slower, but just as accurate. To fill out the space below her feet, she tucks an oil stick in between her toes, presses her hands into the canvas, arches her back, and paints shapely waves and crooked lightning strikes.

After two hours of continuous work, she rests in corpse pose, surrounded in grayscale. She looks to the far wall below where she sees the only hint of color in her room. It's the light from the streetlamp that's casting flitting ripples of rouge against the muted white.

AC♦DC stands up, careful not to smudge the oil, steps onto the wood floor that creaks just like the floor in old Indiana, and looks back at her canvas. Her body is only light, devoid of words, and outlined in symbolism. Della sees that she's defined herself in the silence of the written language.

[[⌢   ⊢]]

"Mom, I know you don't know him, but he seems really nice and I had a good time talking with him—"

(Joyce's Voice...)

"I know that he has a reputation, but I bet a lot of that is fueled by the media. They sensationalize everything and try to vilify everyone. You've been telling me that my whole life! All they want to do is get more people to—"

(Joyce's Voice...)

"I don't know why I tell you about my personal life anymore. I've always tried to be upfront with you about the guys I meet, but if you're going to treat me like this, it doesn't make me feel encouraged about communicating with you next time."

(Joyce's Voice!)

"—this has nothing to do with Brigadoon. And yes, I *do* share things with you! I can't keep having the same arguments with you."

(Joyce's Voice...)

"I know you're concerned, and that's fine, but you have to let me make my own decisions. Do you want to go back to arranged relationships and marriages? I think we've seen that it doesn't work."

(Joyce is silent, then sniffles into the receiver.)

"Mom. Relax, please. I love you. It's just a date. One night out. I'm ready to meet some new people and get a better understanding of who's out there. That's why people go out, they want to see what people are like for themselves. We can't just all live based on how other people tell us to. It's very isolating. I *hate* explaining things like this to you."

(Joyce's Voice...)

"O.K., I won't say the word *hate*."

(Joyce's Voice...)

"Of course things are different!"

(Joyce's Voice...)

"No, I am *not* determined to dishonor you and dad! And no, I wouldn't change anything about the way I've been raised! I'm very proud of it. But I'm also ready for you to be respectful of my decisions."

(Joyce's Voice!)

"Mom, it's one date. It's not more than that. I don't understand why you're being this way."

(Joyce's Voice...)

"O.K., I'll consider what you're saying, but the date is tomorrow night and it wouldn't be right to cancel at this point."

(Joyce's Voice...)

"—you want me to say I'm sick? To lie? Mom, I think you're the one being unreasonable here. Look, I met him and talked with him for awhile the other night when I was out with the girls—"

(Joyce's Voice!!!)

"It's just a club. I know it's not a church, but there's a good vibe there. People are just there to have fun."

(Joyce's Voice...)

"No, not *that* kind of fun. Of course you'd say that. You're worse than I am."

(Joyce's Voice!!!)

"I'm sorry, I shouldn't have said that."

(Joyce's Voice...)

"Great, now we're going to start a new argument about where I work and who I work with. You know, they're a charitable company that's making a difference for a lot of people. Isn't that the most important part of being a Christian? Charity?"

(Joyce's Voice...)

"They're not changing me. They're teaching me more about myself. They're kind people."

(Joyce's Voice...)

"That's not true! You're listening to people who have no idea about what really goes on there."

(Joyce's Voice!!!)

"—those without sin, Mom! Those without sin! And not that it matters, but Jesus did defend a prostitute, remember?"

(Joyce's Voice is at an all-time high volume and pitch.)

"I know what Dad would say, yes."

(Joyce's Voice is cracking and there are sniffles in place of breaths.)

"I apologize. I really do, Mom. And I feel for everything you're going through, but please be understanding of what I'm going through too. I respect your concerns and will keep them in mind. I promise. I know you're looking out for me, but I also have to make my own decisions. Please let me figure out these things on my own, knowing that you've raised me the right way."

(Joyce's Voice...)

"Yes, I promise."

(Joyce's Voice...)

"You want me to say the whole thing?"

(Joyce's Voice...)

"Yes, I promise I will be at church Sunday morning with you."

(Joyce's Voice...)

"And I know you don't want to hear this, but honestly, I think you'd like him. He's nice, funny, and charming, and a little bit different. I think we have a lot in common. You know, he lost his father too."

[[❊]]

Roosevelt looks up to the night sky shrouded by the vapors of Coney Island electricity. The neon flares, the spangled lights, and the turns of the Wonder Wheel all burn brighter than the other suns in the forgotten Milky Way. After a short wait in line, the attendant ushers him in and he takes a seat by himself. Once the gears are put in motion, he rides the fixed orbit, rising above Brooklyn, and swinging the cage with the shifts of his bodyweight. The angles of the spokes create modulating frames of polygons from which he views the rest of the park. It's Coney Island's opening weekend, and with a chill in the air, the people don't pour in, but drizzle in and form little puddles of population near the pinwheel tops below.

As Roosevelt ascends, he looks down over the park. He sees laughter on the faces of a young family, a woman fixing her hair, a dachshund eating a hotdog off the ground, a couple practicing an upright version of CPR, the Cyclone coasting along on its sinusoidal path, and a teenager with a sideways red baseball cap throw a Baby Ruth wrapper over his shoulder. Roosevelt watches the wrapper flutter down to the ground.

As he reaches the zenith of the Wonder Wheel, Roosevelt looks out to the small crashes of water against the beach as the tide rolls in. He thinks about the darkness over the expanse of the Atlantic and the emptiness of the seat beside him. Then he leans back, his arm draped over the seat, and looks up as the glowing moon emerges from behind a lonely cloud. He equates interstellar companionship with his own desire for the same. He breathes in the chill with an intention to value the space between the inhale and exhale. Then Roosevelt reaches into his pocket, takes out a black marker, and starts to write a poem on the seat.

As the Wheel comes to a stop, the attendant opens his cage door and releases him back to the Coney Island wild. Again at sea and eye level, he sees the same couple still resuscitating each other with love, and the same teenager with the red baseball cap—only now he's kneeling on the ground and massaging his temples. Roosevelt scans the panorama and sees a woman with freckles hug an oversized teddy bear near a game tent. She's cute. As Roosevelt begins to walk back to the subway, he sees a polypropylene tumbleweed come his way. He bends down, picks up the Baby Ruth wrapper, and drops it in the trash can a few steps away. The Wonder Wheel starts up once again, and Roosevelt's words are elevated a little bit closer to the moon.

THAT WE ARE SHARING
THE GALAXY
IS QUITE LIKELY,
NO MATTER FROM HOW FAR.
WE ARE ANOTHER
PLANET'S WISH,
OUR STAR,
AND THE IDEA
OF WHO WE ARE.

❊

(INTERLUDE)

· [[⫛]] · [[Σ]] · [[♦]] · [[⚛]] ·

"...Oh, and here's my final thing on God. God... if God was singular, He was a lonely being. They said there's one God. Well, He's pretty lonely. And, I think He split himself up, so to speak, and made lots of people with all kinds of various ideas to communicate... so he's sitting there and rub his body and say, 'Oh Man, you know, all by myself!' And then by having you over here and you and the gangsters and everybody that think it's so wrong, that's *Him*. And He got to figure it out Himself. *You dig it?* Like this big invisible *source* is us. Now, the spirit, of Him is in a bit of every one of us. So we can ignore it, or be completely blind to it, or we can be killers and murderers, but it's still there. It's the divine source of creation."

Charles Mingus
Late 1961 or Early 1962
Interview with Nesuhi Ertegun
Atlantic Records Office

‖:　⌒　:‖

The Composer places the music on the stand and leaves the symphonic hall in silence. Then the musicians enter and tune their instruments. It takes longer than usual. When the conductor of the orchestra walks in, they stand until he is front and center, and then sit down. There is no applause. There is no audience.

The conductor raises his baton and begins to make waves and a pure beam of light shines down on Earth to a single soul in blue jeans. The conductor pauses with his arms up high and the musicians hold the note. When the beam of light makes contact with the soul, it elevates, and produces separate gray figures at the north, east, south, and west nodes of an unseen compass.

This fourshadowing accentuates the complexity of this symbolic individual who's dared to rise with the music over the surface of a cooling planet. The shadows move independently and create different shapes at varying tempos, but are bound by the same origin. The shadows are both our immediate histories of movement, and the legacies that will be cast until the last time our name is spoken or read. So when the conductor lowers the baton and the fermata ceases, the beam of light will desist, but the gray figures won't disappear. They will merge into a collective shadow with the soul, a sphere of unified darkness that joins the rest of the beautiful accidents somewhere within the harmony of the cosmos. The soul is both there and not.

The conductor and the musicians wait for the next piece of music, but The Composer doesn't return. After a long time, the conductor tries to exit the symphonic hall to look for The Composer, only to realize they've been locked inside. He places his baton on the stand, sits down on the floor, and the musicians lay their instruments across their laps. The conductor is unsure of what to do. He whispers to the musicians. They don't know either. No one knows.

After many years of waiting in the symphonic hall, a percussionist in the back row begins to tap his foot, but the conductor quiets him. Not yet. Wait. But the conductor understands that if The Composer is away much longer, more musicians will begin to make their own music, create their own new sounds. It will be difficult to silence them all. He thinks for a long time. Centuries.

He begins to wonder if The Composer will ever return, if they will ever again produce music together. The last piece was much different than the others. Maybe he's looking for a new orchestra, new inspirations, or a new place to express his ideas. No one knows. The musicians are shifting in their seats. He tells himself that remaining hopeful is best. He doesn't want to believe that the music will be forever muted, the light dimmed, and that the souls and shadows of their history will be abandoned. But the conductor cannot suppress the feeling that the vibrations of life will one day fade to

SATURN

[[❋]]

Roosevelt is at [Bump & Grind], and before pulling the chair out from a table near the back of the café, he lifts it an inch off the floor. He's careful not to drag the legs and contribute the cacophony of kitchen sounds in the background. It's early in the morning, after all. Roosevelt puts his phone on top of the menu. It's on silent. He rests his elbows on the table and runs his middle finger along his eyebrow scar, back and forth. His phone blinks a message that Ellison is on his way. A waitress in black Daisy Dukes and red fishnet tights, matching Jordan Xs, an 80s arcade belt, and a white hoodie that's unzipped most of the way down, taps him on the shoulder from behind. Her lips are red and her hair is tucked into the hood.

Roosevelt attempts, through the morning grumbles, to say, "Hi." And then clears his throat.

She takes a small notepad out of her bra and a pen from over her ear, and asks, "How are you this wonderfully early morning?"

"Not sure yet," Roosevelt thinks and says at the same time.

"Is it just you?"

"My friend is on the way. He should be here soon."

"Do you want to order something now or wait for your friend?"

"Yeah, I'll get something now." Roosevelt scans the menu. "I've never been here before. What are the Toasted Panties?"

"Oh, that's one of our signature dishes. It's a pair of melted edible panties over buttered marble toast, topped with frosting. It's like a fresh pop-tart. We have strawberry or blackberry."

"Damn, that's a trip."

She leans over close to him and places wrapped utensils next to his phone. "Yes, and I just took a pair off a few minutes ago."

Roosevelt smiles reflexively at first, but thoughts of health code violations render him expressionless. "Thanks. Let me think about it." She smiles as she walks away. He watches her legs and realizes that her fishnet tights were capable of catching him as well. He looks around the café. It's sparsely populated with men in wrinkled suits and women with smeared makeup.

When his waitress returns, her hood is off. Her hair is dark brown.

"O.K., I'll go with a medium coffee with cream, two guava jelly Muffin Tops, and a side of the Toasted Panties. Blackberry."

"Great, I'll be right back. Blackberry is my *personal* favorite."

When Ellison arrives, it's clear he's a regular. He walks in, swings around a pole in the center of the café, and waves to the staff. Ellison sits in the seat next to Roosevelt, which he drags out with ear-piercing friction. "Hey, boss, what's good?"

"This place is something else. I've walked by it a hundred times, but I've never been inside."

"Yeah, I'm here quite often. My favorite is the Maple Patty-Cakes. But they only serve them in the back."

"Maybe next time."

"Well, look, I figure we should get to it right quick."

The waitress returns with his coffee first. It's too hot for a quick sip.

Ellison continues, "Now I know it's only been two days, but me and Bolden have already been talking about our plan to leave the newsstand clean when the time comes. He's more antsy than I am, for real. But I agreed with him that we should monitor the phones of the people we thought might be cops, and some of the more *unsavory characters*, as you call them. And I know you've guarded against peeping on these cats and staying out of their business, but this is completely a back-up-back-up plan. We thought we should know who to avoid getting upset when we close up shop for good. So we put together some picture evidence for some blackmail-type shit, which probably won't be necessary, please believe," Ellison crossed himself, "but if it ever were to come to that, it wouldn't be a terrible thing to have."

Roosevelt lowers his eyebrows.

"The plan is airtight, so don't stress. Bolden can break into almost any phone without detection. He's a wizard, you know. Yesterday he started keeping records and screen-caps of certain texts with an offline digital camera that can't be traced in the cloud, or anywhere. Bolden is going to keep the records with his money in a safe deposit box. He's straight-up old-school."

"I really don't know if I want to hear about this, man. This wasn't the way I wanted to go about it. It's yours now, I understand, so maybe keep me out of this. I had a hard enough time with what I found out, but to monitor the phones of cops and all those shady motherff—, I mean, unsavory characters. I'm not sure if that's the best idea. Damn. Now I'm cursing in the morning, too. Something's off with me."

"I hear you."

"The whole idea was *mutually assured destruction*. No one was supposed to go down because everyone would have to go down."

"True. We're with that. It's just that even with trying to price ourselves out of the market, we know money isn't a problem for a lot of these cats, and we're more nervous than we thought we'd be, you know, without you there, and about any retaliation for taking away their service. They could bring the iron hand of the law, or the mafia grip, right down on our nuts. Like, blaoo!"

Roosevelt kind of smiles, then returns to being serious. "They're going to find another place nearby. Scout them out and let them know where the best copycat spot is. And I wouldn't worry about the cops. If anyone, it's the others. But that's me. I think you two should close it down how you want. I'm out. And I've been thinking about getting *completely* the hell outta Dodge. Maybe for good. Sometimes I think this city is fucked. I need a break from this place."

"Damn."

"Still cursing."

"I didn't think *damn* was that bad."

"I meant me. "

"But you're right, we've seen too much of the underbelly. It's nasty."

"True."

"But we're going to keep it tight because we want to get out soon, too. But I have to press pause. That's not why I wanted to meet up with you this morning. It's about something Bolden found yesterday when he was going through one of the phones."

Roosevelt's Toasted Panties and Muffin Tops are set down on the table. The waitress tugs on the strings of her hood and says, "Enjoy!"

Ellison continues, "Remember when you were texting me the other day about the artist you saw at **[COLOSSUS]**, the one in the window? How she was the one that got shot uptown during her show?"

"Yes."

"And then you texted me yesterday about how you also saw her by the Mission gallery?"

"Sure." Roosevelt takes a bite into the blackberry panties and raises a scarred eyebrow.

"Well, that's the thing. You know the unfriendly cat who wears the pork pie hat real low to try and cover that big red birthmark on his face?"

"Yes, of course. What's the connection?"

"He came in yesterday and me and Bolden just weren't feeling his whole aura. He felt like a threat, looking at us slanted. We didn't think he was 5-0, but something wasn't right, so Bolden gave his phone the comb."

"Most of the people at The Office are shady, you should be used to that. It's the reason it exists."

"Of course. But this guy had a different kind of vibe yesterday. So, while Bolden was giving him the comb, I checked his account on our file. He's sporadic. No routine. Sometimes he's gone for three hours at night, sometimes just one during the day. Bolden was about thirty minutes into the creep when he finally got something. Let me show you what he found."

Roosevelt takes a big sip of coffee. It's getting a little cold.

"Apparently this guy uses that M.I. app to communicate with whoever's in charge, the app that destroys the texts after they've been sent. Only Bolden is the fucking man—sorry— and he got everything this guy has been sending out for the past week. He couldn't get the incoming messages, but here, just read. These are from Wednesday night."

[Status: In place. Apartment confirmed empty. 4th floor fire escape. Awaiting start.]
[Crowd gathering. More than expected. Not a problem.]
[Show in progress.]
[Silencer on. Target available. Will proceed when I receive confirmation.]
[Locked and loaded.]
[Confusion. The artist was hit. Does not look fatal.]
[I was not able to employ my firearm. Appears someone else was successful shooter.]
[He was on a different fire escape. The one on the corner one flight below me. He packed up firearm and went into window. I thought I was working alone.]
[Affirmative. Was about to pull trigger when shot was fired. I did not discharge my weapon.]
[I need to know now if I'm working alone. Should I be concerned about other shooter.]
[Will give full description soon. Must leave building before police get here. Safe haven, then contact.]

The waitress leans in, "How's everything, gentlemen?"
"Your panties are the best, as my friend Roosevelt here is finding out."
"He can find out anytime he'd like," she winks with precision.
Roosevelt nods back. "Yes, everything is perfect. Sorry, I'm a bit distracted on several levels right now."
"That's O.K., I'll leave you two alone. But can I get you anything else?"
Roosevelt answers with a question, "Can you tell me your name?"
"Georgia *OoooOoooOooo*'Keeffe."
"Of course it is."
She runs her hand along Roosevelt's back before walking away.
Ellison leans in, "Don't get excited, she just says that for tips."
Roosevelt resumes reading the restored texts from the birth-marked, would-be assassin. "I'm sure it works."

[Status: Safely removed from situation. Unseen. Will divulge details when I know what is happening.]
[No, not in denial. I was not the shooter. My word is my life.]
[He was positioned on the third floor, on the corner of Riverside. 99% that he did not

ID me. He was not in my view throughout the performance. When I prepared firearm, he must have gotten into position. I estimate he fired within ten seconds, then left through the window. It was a professional job. Tight.]

[Yes, I will find out who owns the apartment. I'll need a day.]

[He was a white male, strong build, unsure of height. Had dark suit and gloves, a full dark beard, long hair slicked back and curled at the ends.]

[And sunglasses.]

[Gun looked like Glock pistol with scope and suppressor.]

[Will stay out of view until tomorrow morning. Where to convene?]

[Confirmed: 07:00 at Mission. Anything further?]

[Yes. My description of all events is firmly at 99% accurate.]

[Affirmative. He wore sunglasses at night.]

[[Σ]]

Suma walks up the marble steps to the library. The echoes resound in the Manhattan Saturday morning. She's the first librarian there. With the plan set in motion, Suma exhales all of the air in her lungs. It creates a slight disturbance and billowing of the American flag that hangs over her from the middle arch. Breathing is easier now that she's squared everything away after working around the clock, which isn't unusual, anyway.

. . .

* Last night at RUST BUST & AXE *

"Suma, you can trust me," Leon assures her as he adjusts his glasses. He takes a deep breath and a long sip of merlot to fill the gap of silence. He looks at her green eye, then her blue eye, then quickly at her chest, then makes a noise that is half throat-clearing and half-"So..."

Suma tells Leon about the whole operation, the typewriters, the polaroids, the garage sales, the 99 alterations, and the hobby that's become a compulsion. Even though today she's done it twice before, it still sounds embarrassing when she explains it out loud. But Suma feels another weight lifted off her back. As she details some of her books, whether they're jocose, satirical, political, or altered historically, Leon is rooting her on, sipping more wine and slapping the table with the excitement of a physical exc!amation point.

"Because I feel that I've flown too close to the sun, I think it's time to recover these books and bring them home. I don't want to destroy the evidence, but I want the books to disappear from the library without a trace."

"How do you want to do this? I mean, we could pull a few a day, demagnetize them at the desk, and smuggle them in our bags. We can have all of them out within two months."

"I want this done in one day."

"One day?"

"One hour."

"Mmmm..."

"Actually, this is all going down tomorrow morning. I don't want to wait. This is going to be a heist with paid accomplices and you're the last piece of the puzzle."

"How long have you been planning this?"

"I started a few hours ago."

"Damn. Don't you want to give this a little more time? Maybe this is too quick a reaction? I mean, if you've gone undetected for this long..."

"Maybe you're right, but it's too late to be pragmatic. Things are already in motion. One hour, tomorrow."

"What's the plan?"

"When I alter a book, I also remove the security strip in the binding. I was always nervous about setting off the alarm when I brought it back to the library."

"How do you remove the strip?"

"Very carefully."

"So there's no risk that the alarm will sound?"

"None."

"That's good. What can I do to help? You know, I'm off tomorrow."

"Of course. You won't even be entering the library. You'll be driving the moving van that I rented. You're the transporter."

Leon tries to contain a smile. "How many people are in on this?" Leon finishes his second glass of wine.

"Three main people: you, Jasmine, and someone named Beverly. She's the one with connections. It's not something I want to get into now, but we have a mutual interest in me not getting in any legal trouble, ever. That's another reason I want to act fast. Also, it's not that I don't trust Jeremy and Bunch, it's just that I want to limit any more involvement at work. I trust you the most." Suma pulls her hair over her ears and into a momentary ponytail, before it fans out across her back.

"Thanks."

"So don't prove me wrong." They exchange smirks.

"I know you didn't want to talk about it, but is Beverly family?"

"No. And, please, never mention that name to anyone else. It's tricky. And my family? Let's save that for another time. They are death to me."

"O.K., understood. But don't you mean *dead* to you?" Leon wipes his upper lip, anticipating the wine stains that may have been left behind.

"No, they are *death* to me."

"Right."

"So, I admit, the whole *1984* thing was me going too far. It was too obvious. But a majority of the books are on the obscure side. Many of them haven't left the library in years, so there's little chance of anyone realizing they're gone any time soon. Even if someone notices a missing title, it will be near impossible to recognize any coordination. There's almost no pattern to the books I've altered over the years." Suma finally feels comfortable enough to drink her beer, which has been bleeding condensation all over the table. "Beverly is coordinating a nine-o'clock meeting tomorrow morning at Bryant Park. She's assembling a group of eight of her girlfriends as we speak."

"And you trust them, obviously?"

"I trust Beverly. And I'll be paying them well. Actually, you'll be the one giving them their envelopes when they bring the books to the van."

"How much?"

"One thousand in each envelope. Except Beverly, she doesn't need it. I'll have one for you when you get to my apartment."

"You don't have to pay me. Are you kidding? This is exciting."

"Beverly will tell them tonight to what to wear and what size backpack they're going to need. Then in the morning, she'll give them my detailed instructions of where to find each book, and then where to meet up with you. So, I still have a lot to do tonight."

"Where's the drop spot?" Leon wants another glass of wine, but doesn't want to interrupt the exchange.

"In the parking garage under the Grace building on 43rd street. There'll be one more envelope for the parking attendant. You can be upfront with him about how people will be dropping off their bags with you and apologize for any inconvenience. I'm sure the cash should cover it. Remind him it's only going to take an hour."

"That's a lot of money."

"Don't worry about that. I want to make sure nothing's going to go wrong. It's worth it to me. So, you'll be getting ten backpacks total. Beverly and her girlfriends will have ten books each on their lists. That's ninety. We have *1984* with us right here, and Jasmine's backpack will have the remaining eight. If any of the books are being borrowed, I can take care of those when they're returned, but at least I'll have most of them—hopefully all. They're going to start at ten a.m., but in staggered shifts. So I imagine you'll start seeing some of the first girls by ten-thirty or so. They'll know that they can simply walk out through security and find you at the parking garage. They give you the books, you give them an envelope. That's it. As soon as you have all ten, you'll drive the van from the drop spot to my apartment. Get as close as you can. I'm guessing you'll be parked by 11:45 and I'll be home shortly after that, so there won't be a long waiting gap. Then you can start bringing up the books."

"Don't you work until five?"

"Well, around 11:30, I'm going to feel very sick to my stomach."

"Got it."

"With how nervous I'll be, it may end up being true."

"This is a total side note, but just to let you know, this is the hottest thing to ever happen in the history of libraries. *You* are the hottest thing to happen to libraries."

Even with an intense expression on her face, she can't help but slant a smile across the table. "Probably." She takes another sip of beer. From the puddle of condensation, a large drip falls to her shirt, darkening its shade. Leon's eyes dart to the area right over her heart, and then away. But then he looks again, this time without the fear of being caught. It's a guilt-free glance, for a change. Her focus is elsewhere.

· · ·

It's 11:38 a.m., and for someone who's leaving work early with a sudden and terrible sickness, Suma steps out of the library, and walks into the sunshine as healthy as ever. She hears the rippling waves of Old Glory and acknowledges Patience and Fortitude, the two guardian lions bookending the main staircase. And maybe it's only bellyfeel, but she reaffirms that this was the best course of action. A full deletion from the library and a chance to press reset. The wind blows her hair across her sun-kissed face. There's risk and a sort of looming danger, but it's something she's lived with her whole life. She adjusts the clasps of her two necklaces so they align on her nape and over a faint circular scar from Big Sir's trophy. Ever since she'd taken her first gamble on forgery and transcontinental flight, Suma, like a graffiti artist going over the establishment, has been leaving her own mark on the world as she's wished, all of it unseen during the stirring of the night.

[[↑]]

Zeus wakes up after a restful and dreamless night. The radiance of the spring sky makes him squint. It's a welcomed annoyance. It had been a warm night and he slept naked, with only his top sheet draped diagonally across him like a half-toga. He rolls to the side of his bed, stands up, flexes his biceps in a heroic pose, and lets out a primal yawn. He looks around his bed for some threads, but he only finds a white tank top and a pair of Jordan IVs on the floor. He tucks his head into the shirt and slides his right foot into the right shoe. He walks lopsidedly over to the other sneaker. He has a hard time getting it on and isn't ready for a physical challenge quite this early. So Zeus picks it up by the back tab, flips it halfway around in the air, catches the toe, and then sticks the left Jordan IV on his morning erection. He grabs his phone off the nightstand and hobbles toward the kitchen, the Jordan IV swinging side to side. Zeus opens the refrigerator, shakes the OJ, and takes a swig right from the container. During the long sip he thinks about his date with Candy and how he's going to start his day. As he finishes his last gulp, he remembers he'd planned to start with a prayer. And once the word *prayer* flashes across the marquis in his brain, his body responds with a relaxation between his legs, and the Nike pendulum loses its pivot. His Jordan IV falls sole-down to the ground between his legs. Zeus looks down to the floor and sees his right shoe and two left feet.

After he showers, he dresses in denim and cotton, and walks over to his coffee table with a cup of green tea. As the steam from the tea lifts and disappears, Zeus prays with his elbows on his knees, his hands interlocked, and his forehead resting on the knuckles of his index fingers. The prayer is about five minutes long and the tea is at the perfect temperature when he finishes. He feels better already.

Zeus picks up a thin black sharpie and a few 1987 Topps Baseball cards from the stack and fans them out on the table. As his ideas unfold, he adds them to the corresponding baseball card to help him plan out the night. Most important is the idea of choosing the backgrounds for their date. More locations means more memories, a way to stretch retrospective time. Instead of one or two spots and a few drinks and conversation, he prefers to establish different vistas throughout the evening, like mental postcards for her to take home. From there, the overall experience can be further enhanced by changing elevations and speeds, being social and physical in some way, and finally, to make everything look spontaneous.

Over the Kansas City Royals **BO JACKSON** Futur Stars card he writes:

CANDY SCOOP @8
UNISPHERE
LENOX LOUNGE

ROOFTOP AIR HOCKEY
HOME MINE/HERS

Then he inks the general directions through the home plate dust of the New York Mets **KEVIN MITCHELL** card.

MIDTOWN TUNNEL
L.I.E. TO NORTHERN STATE
GLEN COVE RD. TO CLINTON
CRIB ON STEWART AVE.

Distracted by a gust of wind that whirls up against his windows, Zeus looks up and away, and thinks of nothing. Over the California Angels **REGGIE JACKSON** card, he draws a halo around his helmet, some wings on his back, and a lightning bolt superimposed over his bat.

On the St. Louis Cardinals **JACK CLARK** card, which looks like the player is trying to surf between third base and home, he draws a longboard under his cleats, and ocean waves over the grass.

Back from distraction, over the Cincinnati Reds **ERIC DAVIS** card, he writes down his accessories for the night.

LAMBO COUNTACH
ROSE ON HER SEAT
RAKETA COPERNIC
MAIN CHAIN

On the next card, which is the Cleveland ball club's manager, Zeus doesn't write down any ideas. Instead, he draws over the Indians' logo in the top left corner. Chief Wahoo is revamped from being cartoonish, red-faced, and toothy, to sad and resigned. The tears drip and fall to the bottom of the card where a puddle of tears now blacks out the name of **PAT CORRALES.**

And then the outfit card, which he inks over the Detroit Tigers **ALAN TRAMMELL:**

BLACK VELVET BLAZER
DARK RED PANTS
BLACK BUTTON-UP
LEOPARD POCKET SQ.
KASE2 JOINTS

The last one in the small deck is a Pittsburgh Pirates card. It has an all-time great looking to the sky as he follows the arc of a baseball in flight. Just above the name, Zeus writes, **"AND HERE'S ANOTHER HIT...**[46]**"**

⟦ J♦SMINE A.K.A. JAZZY J. ⟧

Since the shooting incident, Jasmine has reached totem-topper status as a friend in Axlia's mind. She's been there for her at the hospital and by her side at her apartment for the recent projects they've worked on together. They've shared cloves and prepared canvases—and she's made connecting with other people a lot easier. And Jasmine is always cool about not listening to her.

Jasmine sounds like a walking steel pan as she goes up the forest-green metal subway stairs. She keeps a level focus as she strolls by the bases of the silver behemoths on her way to The N.Y. Public Library. Her cherry red headphones bump over her ears and her hair bounces to the beat of her steps. Her hair, after a recent haircut, is dark and tidal, and crashes to one side. The trough on the right side of her head is shaved and there's a design of swirling hearts buzzed down to her caramel skin. As per Suma's instruction, she wears a black backpack, which drapes over a green chiffon top. There is a morning chill in the air that the sun has not yet overcome, but Jasmine wears a short charcoal skirt anyway. But there isn't a lot of skin exposure she since has on a custom pair of extension gray Converse shoes, which start at the bottom and lace up all the way to mid-thigh. And hanging loosely across her hips are several thin belts. They're encrusted with icy metallic pieces, like tangled planetary rings.

Unbeknownst to Jasmine, she's receiving what is essentially a small book of texts from Axlia, who's giving her updates about the art show. She's texting her about the painting she finished last night and is looking for some feedback about the remaining projects on her to-do list for Mission curator, H.P. Cyrus Coaster. Jasmine hasn't seen any of them because she's busy stashing the books from her detailed checklist into her backpack. When Jasmine is pseudo-studying at a long table in the reading room, she sees a few of her comrades traversing the library for the books on their lists. Once she's confident that she is 8-for-8 with her portion of the heist, Jasmine walks toward the exit. She passes Suma without acknowledgement, and goes through the security door without a sound.

Just a hop, skip, and a long jump later, Jasmine is a few blocks away at the drop-off point, the parking garage below the Grace building. She looks for Leon, a man she's never met, but understands to be an affable and pleasant guy. But instead, next to the white moving van, she sees someone with slicked hair, a pleather jacket, tight pants, and a certified frown. His arms are crossed and he has the temple tip of his sunglasses and a toothpick in his mouth at the same time. Jasmine tries to refrain from laughing. It's Leon trying way too hard to act like someone else.

When she approaches him with her heavily-sagging backpack, he puts on the sunglasses, pulls them down the bridge of his nose, and looks at her over the frame. Then he says something with some kind of Russian*(?)* accent that's made lispy by way of the toothpick.

"Aahh, Ssank you."

And he gives Jasmine her envelope, takes the backpack, and loads it into the back of the moving van. Jasmine laughs but tries to disguise it as a cough. She's much better at faking it than Leon is.

As Jasmine walks away, she does a double-take when she notices the driver's side hubcaps of the moving van. On silver platters, there is painted one Belgian waffle with the syrup dripping sideways and a spicy tuna roll on the rear wheel.

Now that she's finished being an accomplice, she looks at her phone for the first time in a while. Her eyes widen as she catches up with the run of texts from Axlia.

♦

[text]
[text]
[text]
[text]
[text]
[Please text me back a.s.a.y.c.]

J♦SMINE

[Sorry! I was busy doing a favor
for a friend at the liberty]
[*Library]
[So what up? The painting you did
last night sounds tight. What are you
thinking for the holo? You want
me to swing by? I'm free nowww.]

♦

[Yes, please! Thanks so much!]

J♦SMINE
[np]

♦

[And the poetry project. C.C. had
a good idea about getting the
audience involved. He suggested
a live miscommunication that built off my
telephone poetry project, a commentary

on the imperfections of oral traditions, but
how they might be more beautiful because
they've been abstracted. But since we
don't have a lot of time, I want something
more straight forward. I'd like a live portrait
of the evening, but with only words.]

◆

[And I need something for the small
gallery in the library.]
[No. Do you know anyone? It has to
be someone who doesn't mind
doing some improvised work.]

◆

[Sounds prefect.]
[*Perfect!]

J◆SMINE
[Do you have a writer in mind?]

J◆SMINE
[Check. I'll ask around. It's funny, actually.
I just saw something that made me think of one
of my friends who's a graf writer. We worked on
something together once. And he knows this
guy that he calls an all-city poet who's a graf
writer too. He keeps to himself though, not too
many friends. Under the radar even to the
other writers. I've never met him, but I've seen
his work. Want me to see if he's interested in
doing something above ground?]

J◆SMINE
[I'll text him in a sec.]
[As for the small gallery in the library, I
have an idea there too... But I'll have to
hit you back later. Long shot. But
there are some strange vibrations in the air.
Strange connection.s]
[If it works,

it;ll be perfect too. Maybe I'll know by
the time I get to your apt. Either way,
we'll figure it out. Don't stresssss.]

♦

[Thanks again, honestly. I'm so glad you're
in my life!]

J♦SMINE
[;)]
[See you in about an hour.]

♦

[Great. Let's get to work.]

J♦SMINE
[Word.]

. . . .BACK TO MESSAGES. . . .

J♦SMINE
[Yo, B. Normal! I have a favor to ask you.
That poet you work with, I know he's pretty
secretive, but I'm helping my friend put together
an art show at the Mission gallery. I don't know
if you've been checking the news, but she's the
performance artist that was shot up in Harlem
this week, Axlia Clia. I've been working with her
for a minute. She's great. So, is there away
I could talk to him? Or maybe you can forward
this to him? The show's gonna have something
called "live communication." There wouldn't
be anything he'd have to prepare really. And
he can stay incognito or put himself out there,
whatever. No idea if this would be his kinda
thing, but thought I'd ask. The show is Monday
night. Sorry for the late notice. Hit me backk.
—JazzyJJJ ;)]

J♦SMINE

[Suma Suuuum... I know ur pretty busy right now, but I have an idea about what you can do with your books. It's different. You could hide everything in plain sight. And you'd be paid as an artist at a gallery. For real. $$$$!]
[Or maybe $. Not sure how much. Get back to me tonight after you;re set and I'll give you the rundown.]

Σ

[. . .]

[[✳]]

For the first time in a long time, he's a man of inaction. When Roosevelt realizes he doesn't know what to do, he knows exactly where to do it: [COLOSSUS]. It's his favorite place to take in some liquid inspiration. He's going to bring his journal, his pen, some cash money, and then figure the rest out through circumstance, happenstance, and the fragmented sequence of thoughts. Whenever Roosevelt tries to write in a bar or lounge, he has to deal with the expected distractions: the loud voices, the changing temperature of the room, the woman that walks by that's ninety-nine percent legs, the baseball game on the wallpaper of televisions, the lyrics of a chart-topper, the brief conversations with strangers, the dropped glass of red wine that clears an area like an infected rat, and the imbalance of a bargain-priced barstool. But for Roosevelt, these distractions make the writing more true because it's more challenging. To sit in a quiet room and request everyone's silence and assimilation is to wish for the dictatorship of the elementary school library, where the old make the rules for the young so they can fit into their formulaic expectations. To write outlines and to only draw in the allowed space is to acknowledge the separation between *self* and *other*—perhaps not consciously—but it celebrates the barrier.

Roosevelt feels that if someone only thinks and writes in silence, they're not of the people, and therefore he encourages the challenges. It makes his thoughts consistent with reality. The universe, by nature, is not quiet. The grassy fields may look vibrant and verdant, and the oceans serene, but it's a rouse. The surface is a lie. There is underlying and necessary brutality at all times. It's unseen and unacknowledged because it's too much to think about. The mind is protecting itself from the continual destruction that gave birth to our own existence. The sky may also look peaceful when standing alone in the post-midnight hours, but every moment in the cosmos is an invisible New Year's Eve, a constant resetting of the supernova fireworks of endless beginnings.

Roosevelt, waiting at a crosswalk, opens his journal and cycles through the pages to find a blank spread, which are getting harder to come by. He sees poems and downgrades and lists of ideas fly by like the week had. He opened to two haikus and two short poems:

. . .

THE SKYLINE INVITES
THE NIGHT - THE BIG APPLE'S RIPE
FOR ANOTHER BITE.

. . .

I DO NOT SPEAK FRENCH
- BUT IT'S COOL, MA JOLIE FEMME -
I DO KISS THAT WAY.

. . .

FLUORESCENT FICTIONS COLOR MY PAGES,
THE SINCERE TRUTH SO FAINT.
EMPTY SPRAY CANS FROM DRUNKEN STAGES,
SOLID LINES, BUT HOLLOW PAINT.

. . .

THESE MOMENTS
HAVE BEEN TOO SCRIPTED TO LET BREATHE,
IT'S TIME TO CHANGE,
BECAUSE EVERYTHING IS WHERE IT SHOULD BE.

. . .

Then he flips to a pair of pages that make him chuckle, bringing him back to a day that suddenly became golden. It was at the end a stressful day at The Office for Roosevelt, and to lighten his mood, Bolden snuck his journal away from him. He taped a picture onto opposing blank pages. The picture was from one of the R2D2 magazines on display. Specifically, it was an up close view of a woman pushing her breasts together, so Bolden taped them on, one per page, and accentuated the woman's cleavage with the gutter of the binding. Roosevelt didn't discover the additions until he left work, when he was off to write in the park. When he sat down on the bench, he opened his journal to where the sharpie was. There was a post-it note over the right nipple: [Rozey- here's a comfortable place to rest your pen when ur your you're buggin at work.. -Bolden]. The next day he remembered telling Bolden that while he appreciated the soft sanctuary within his journal, he didn't want to keep his pen there for fear the ink might explode. Roosevelt makes his way down the sidewalk, dressed in dark denim, a gun-metal button-down, dressy black kicks, and an onyx chain. Over his deep brown eyes, his scarred eyebrow furthered his foreboding, a disposition of both gloom and concern. Roosevelt arrives outside the sculpture store, the front for the [COLOSSUS] speakeasy. He's standing in the same place Axlia had been when he saw her for the first time. The figure of her posting the flyer to the window has become a sculpture itself, solidified in his memory.

When he approaches the back door and sees the red lips in the bell of the French horn, he recites one of the passwords, "Blue 7." [COLOSSUS] has a lush atmosphere, surrounding its dwellers with cherry wood paneling and maroon-tinged lounge areas. Vintage saxophones line the walls amidst framed oil paintings, which are portraits of dignified pigeons. The pigeons wear militaristic medals on their chests and are either stoically postured in front of purples and royal navies, or in flight over the spectra of cityscapes.

It's early afternoon and the lounge is sparse. Roosevelt takes a spot at a corner booth near the bar. The centerpiece of the table is a small brass sculpture of a pigeon. He orders cognac and swirls the liquid gold around the snifter to open its floral qualities, which bloom on the echo of his first sip. He writes in a small font in his journal, wanders through his brain, and searches for ideas—like whether to pass on any of his ill-gotten information, or to hire an incognito security detail for Axlia on the low, or to use his connections in the police force or the military, or to have Bolden hack into more phones and find something more concrete, or to look into the practices of the bearded men of The D.O.C., or to ignore it altogether. Every option seems worse or more vapid than the last. He's set in the empty union of proactivity and passivity. So he orders another, raises his glass, and chimes it to the beak of the pigeon.

One crystal glass after another, the afternoon pushes on. His quest to find meaning within reached a dead end. He's becoming haymaker-drunk and his scribbles are becoming just that. He would swear the pigeon nodded at him at least twice. Roosevelt is writing that The Artist is V.S. and he's O.P. (and also down with O.P.P.), and that together they can grow old, and he'd deliver some X.O. to the root of her fruit, or something like that. And how he cares for her skin, her thoughts, and even her pinky toes. And how the end of her hair lands in a place that's hard to reach, and how that might be significant. He writes briefly because his thoughts shift too fast to stay on task. In the scattered fragments, the L word makes an appearance, but also how the city is his mistress. It's hard to tell where he's going with anything. There's a doodle of the poem he wrote on the Brooklyn Bridge. It proves he's no architect, as one of the bridge towers has fallen into the East River. And then there's something unintelligible that results in the dragging of his pen across two pages crowded with ink, as he nods off to the land of Zzzzs. It's only one slash, but it suffices to X-out this sure-to-be-forgotten time.

Roosevelt's head is slumped to one side and his eyes flutter in and out of consciousness. When his phone vibrates at a frantic rhythm, he straightens up as though possessed by a slow-moving demon. He misses the call, but a text follows in place of a voicemail. His eyes adjust to the bright screen in the subdued lighting of [COLOSSUS].

B. NORMAL
[Hey man, I got a text from this girl
Jasmine I know and she's working with
that artist we were talking about the other

day. She's doing better and working on a
big show. She's looking for someone
to do some live poetry type deal for this
show at the Mission gallery on 10th. I always
let her know when I bomb a spot so she can
check it if she's nearby. She's uptown mostly.
She's seen your work too. She needs to
know asap though so she can hook you
up with Axlia. The show came outta
nowhere but it's legit. Prob a last minute
opening. Assume it will mean some
green too. I'll send you her contact info.]
[JN: Jasmine Nector]
[Let me know if you do it. I'll help you hype
it on sight.]

[Yeah man4 I;m bout it bout it. Let me
sleepy this off and I'll calls her in a hour
I'm at colossus. h; I could get into it, but
this is the craziest thing I ever read. I been
straight stressing over this thing, One days
I tell you why. Had too much to drink i
i think.

i

Fell better now though]

B. NORMAL
[Be easy, man. Sleep that shit off.
I'll let her know you're in.]

[I;m in like sin]
[Message sent with Lasers]

[[Σ]]

Leon brings the ninth and tenth backpacks up to the third floor and walks down the short hallway to Apartment 3D. He gives the door two knocks as he enters and places them on the floor near the coffee table. Suma has already started to unpack and organize the other books, checking each one for her alterations. Leon walks over to the kitchenette, takes a paper towel to wipe the sweat from his forehead, and washes his hands with a bar of organic lavender soap.

When he sees Suma straighten the last stack of books and disappear into her bedroom, he becomes both nostalgic and jealous. He sees the way she's made her job as a librarian more about herself. She's written an original story that spans all categories and eras. Leon hadn't dreamt of words like *overdue* or *pre-teen sci-fi drama*, but at a relatively young age he was willing to let the ideas of his future drift far enough away so he wouldn't be confronted by their hostility, and allow them to sink his ship of security. At work, he's been advertising his punctuality and customer service to his superiors in hopes of moving to upper management, which guarantees dental coverage and two weeks paid vacation. Leon appreciates his path of responsibility, the possibility of owning an apartment, and that his life savings will be passed on to and expired by his grandchildren, who he hopes will one day stand by his grave and pass down his stories. And if he ever feels as though he's chosen the wrong path, he tells himself that it has something to do with his birthday being late in the calendar year. But all these sentiments are changing. He sees Suma with her secret life and it does two things to him. It turns what were once responsible concessions to adulthood and creditors into an acceptance of mediocrity and a palpable dullness. And it increases his mental and physical blood flow, to a blood flood. He isn't sure why, but he feels thirteen again. The age when everything matters.

Leon takes a seat on Suma's davenport and leans back against a throw pillow. He blinks his vision along the wall, seeing a different typewriter in each frame. He fixes his hair with a gentle pat on either side of his head, and adjusts his crotch so it appears fuller. Opposite the typewriters on the wall hangs a framed comic book: *Wonder Woman and the Adventure of the Atom Universe!* Next to the books from the heist he sees a pulp fiction paperback novel by Julie Spritz: *Sexterior Decorator: The Carpet Matches the Drapes... and the Shutters!*

Through the wall and the background music, Suma's voice is muffled. But Leon hears her say, "I might as well tell you the whole operation." Suma walks out of her bedroom all hips and hair with a gray off-the-shoulder Columbia University sweatshirt and baby blue leggings with stirrups. Her purple bra straps and purple nail polish match the can of grape Crush soda in her left hand. Leon fumbles for the TV remote, presses power, and tries to look passive. Suma takes a few more steps and stands in front of the screen, her silhouette outlined in static.

After she takes a sip of her grape soda she says, "I haven't had that connected for about a year."

She sits next to him and curls her legs in between the cushions. "If you look at that typewriter over there, the second from the right, that's the first one I bought..." As she continues, her words lose the structure of sentences and pauses and tonal change, because Leon is focused on how close she is to him, one-on-one, in a non-professional setting, for the first time. As Leon half-listens to her divulge the secrets of her nighttime alterations, nodding at the appropriate times and asking the occasional follow-up, he takes mental polaroids. He looks at the smooth crease of her armpit of her exposed shoulder, the way her eyes widen when she emphasizes how difficult something was to alter, the two dark freckles that straddle her satin bra strap, and the way she purses her lips to reach an itch on the bottom of her nose. "Can you hand me that book there? I know, I'm lazy. It's the one on the chair to your right." Leon gets up and walks a few steps to a Frank Lloyd Wright knockoff chair. "Hold it gently." Leon does as told and presents the book to Suma, who is readjusting her position on the couch, and stretching her legs out on the coffee table. "This was a side project. It's not a book from the Library. It's a 1978 Fourth Printing of the New International Version of The Bible. I found it at a used book store. There was one just like it where I grew up." Leon sees Suma cross her legs at her ankles and that her toes are painted the same shiny purple as her fingernails. "It's inspired by one of the first people I met in New York. She was from a local church, and she was trying to reform some of the male-dominated practices from within. I think I looked lost enough to talk to, and she approached me on the street. She was up front about her not wanting money, just my attention and support. She went on and on about how if you read the Bible with God represented as a female deity, then you'll read the stories and laws with more compassion." Suma grips the air with her toes and then clenches them before cracking her second toes with her first toes. It makes two little sounds, like a pair of carbonated bubbles reaching the surface of her soda. "So I altered some of the more famous passages, changing the pronouns, like He to She, Him to Her, and the Amens to Awomens, which was probably not necessary. The hardest part was finding the right paper to match. It's very thin." Suma tries to crack her toes again, but nothing happens. "I altered a Library Bible too. I changed the Ten Commandments. Mine are more sensible." Leon feels Suma's phone vibrating through the couch. She reaches under her thigh and ignores the call, but also sees a few recent texts that had come in from Jasmine, and she raises the eyebrow over her green eye. While Suma is reading, Leon again adjusts his crotch to a false fullness. When she finishes reading, her shoulders drop, and she looks up to the ceiling. "Can you hold this for a minute? I have to think."

Leon accepts the feminized Bible. "Sure. What is it?"

She walks around in figure eights in front of the television, which is still sparkling black and white. Her hands are planted firmly on her hips. She looks tense. Suma reaches her left hand around her back and unclasps her purple bra, and pulls it up through the wide neck of her sweatshirt. "You don't mind, right?" Leon shakes his head. "Sometimes this is the best part of coming home." She continues to be contemplative, walking along the path of infinity, occasionally tugging at her sweatshirt. Leon notices the more pronounced definition of her breasts when she's facing him. The tugging creates a valley down the center so that her sweatshirt now reads: COLBIA.

Leon believes he's being tortured. "Don't worry about it. I understand. I took mine off hours ago." And Suma breaks her loop and smiles.

Suma looks at Leon, who's still wearing his pleather jacket, tight jeans, and is fiddling with a toothpick. "How would you feel about working on one more project... tonight?"

Leon looks over at the digital clock under the television, flashing...
12:00   12:00   12:00 12:00   12:00 12:00 12:00   12:00 12:00, and it does feel like time is standing still in her presence. "I'm up for it. Feeling good, feeling great. What do you want to do?"

Suma performs a little curtsy, pulling the sides of her sweatshirt to make a small triangle dress. "It may take a while. Are you comfortable in your little get-up? I have some clothes that will fit you."

Leon isn't very comfortable. His clothes feel stuck to him and the pleather jacket is stiff and squeaking. The toothpick is getting waterlogged and has to be thrown out pronto. He'd love to change. But his inner monologue sounds like this: [Whose clothes are these? Does she think I'm not muscular enough to require manly attire? Were they from an ex, a one night stand, or...? I don't know anything about her dating life. She never talks about it and I've never pressed her. Am I a coward, or just professional and too polite?] But he says out loud, "No, I'm O.K. Just stretching everything out," he smiles with forced conviction.

"Really? You look pretty uncomfortable. They're my p.j.s. I like to buy oversized clothes to sleep in." And for Leon, the winds cease, the waters are made calm, and his manliness is restored.

"Sold! To the dressing room," he proclaims as he gets up from the davenport. The sounds of pleather and dangling zippers fade into the kitchen, where he goes first to throw out the toothpick.

Leon comes out of the bathroom in a pink t-shirt with the words *Now is Our Time* in chalky white, and gray sweatpants that aren't as roomy as he imagined. Suma asks, "Feel better?"

"Sure." Even though he's in softer fabric, it's hard to say if he feels more comfortable. The pink t-shirt's sleeves are almost nonexistent and the sweatpants have vacuum-sealed his crotch. He keeps his boots on as a last vestige of virility.

Suma is on her phone, pacing around in figure eights again. "...and they're going to take everything from there? O.K... so, *yes.* I'm in." Suma stops at the center and balances on one stirrupped foot, and rests the other against her knee. "As long as you're sure that someone will be there, I can drop off everything tonight: my artist name, my bio, and all the books, probably between twelve and two." She listens. "Secrecy is sworn, Jasmine, word is bond. This is going to be wild. I'll look for you at the opening, but don't look for me."

Leon tries to decipher the news while looking for something to drink. As the phone call ends, Suma begins to bounce up and down with excitement. She says, "On top of the refrigerator, take that one down. Let's do it your style."

"That's white zinfandel."

"Yeah, but wine is your favorite."

"Well... right. Totally." Wine is his favorite, but not one that coordinates with the t-shirt he's wearing. "So, what's the story morning glory?"

She tells him all about how Mission hired the artist who'd been shot uptown to put together a multimedia art show, how it had been hastily designed, and how her friend Jasmine was the extension cord between the two artistic outlets. She explains how she never thought of what she's been doing as an artistic expression, but that maybe it is. And how she feels honored to be included in something so artistic and spontaneous, and how she doesn't believe in the annoying *Everything Happens For a Reason* thing, but how this made her at least consider the causes, consequences, and interconnectivity of life. And she tells him how there's a leftover space that used to be the church library, and how she imagines seeing her books on display, all in one place.

As Leon listens to her, he smiles all the while, unless he was drinking the too-sweet wine or picking a piece of crumbled cork from his lips. He gives her a few ideas about the display order and some ideas for what to name the show. "...if you think about it, you keep talking about these books as your *alterations*, right? And who does alterations? Tailors. I mean, you've been cutting and resizing and re-imagining what already exists, and creating something of your own through the experience of your life, and your life alone. Right?"

"No, you're right!" Suma holds up a near-empty glass. "Just a little bit more. We still have work to do." After Leon fills her glass near the top, he watches her take a pink sip through rose lips.

"Look at all the books you have. You know what you have? You have a problem," Leon pushes his elbow in her direction. It's an attempt to flirt, but the elbow flails into the air, and looks more like an arm spasm.

"I know. But now I like my problem."

"What about *Hoard & Tailor*?"

"Not bad. I like it!" Suma shifts her legs on the couch and her soda-pop toes brush against Leon's sweatpants. He feels a tickle of warmth throughout his body and his eyes brighten. "But I already think I have a title in mind that epitomizes my life without identifying me. I'm just proud to have it out there. It feels like validation without recognition, which is a-ok with me."

The skin around her ankle, while smooth, shows the early signs of budding hairs pushing toward the surface. And he sees something akin to a scar, a pinkish, solitary ringworm mark just behind the stirrup.

Leon gazes along her legs to her place of warmth, but is unaware he's doing so. He's searching through his memory bank for words that are related to alterations and change. Suma catches his invisible line of sight and laughs, "Hey buddy, up here!" Leon snaps his head back up and is embarrassed, but it's worse because he wasn't really looking—at least that time. Suma is amused and shifts her legs in another direction, her toes again brushing along Leon's leg. It tickles him again and causes the muscles of his legs to jolt. The jolt nudges the base of his wine glass, and in an instant, the sounds of broken glass and gasps bounce off all the surfaces of the prismatic apartment, and echo back. There's more embarrassment, more giggles, and more pink.

The break in the inaction gives them the impetus to get the books ready for the gallery. Like two tipsy surgeons, they remove the library labels and obscure telltale markings with concentrated precision. After several books, Leon takes over as the sole spine doctor while Suma walks over to her turntable to drop the needle on Side 1 of Bob Dylan's *Bringing It All Back Home*.

"The troubadour!"

"I picked it up the other day at [Wax & Rax]. You know that place?"

"I've heard of it, but I've haven't been there."

"It's a little scratched up and skips in some places, but it plays through. I have it on my phone, but I like the sound and nostalgia of vinyl, especially if the album means something to me. Because you're physically holding the music, I think it's more intimate." Suma points to her satin bra that she'd tossed on the TV. "I got that there too."

Leon keeps the thoughts that followed quiet.

Look out kid, they keep it all hid...[skip] *Look out kid, they keep it all hid...*[skip]

Using one of her more modern typewriters, Suma prepares a document that details her exhibit. She jabs and punches the keys with her new alias, the title of her section of the show, the number of pieces, and the instructions for the installation. She gives herself a brief bio, which is yet another false history, a Suma specialty. Then she walks over to the turntable and flips the record to Side 2, waking Bob Dylan from his 115th Dream a minute early, and returns to work at her typewriter.

It's just a shadow you're seeing...[skip] *It's just a shadow you're seeing...*[skip]

There are some short conversations as the needle works its way to the center, and a few supervisory visits by Suma. Each time brings her closer to him. At one point Leon can feel the aura of her warmth as she stands next to him, but it turns to a nervous chill as her hand brushes along the thin hairs of his forearm.

Leon's pile of discarded call numbers forms a curly plastic mountain on the floor. The books are ready to be packed into the backpacks once again. Suma finishes her document, folds it in thirds, and seals it in an envelope marked: "Delivery for Axlia Clia, Mission Art Gallery".

"So, are you ready to transform?"

"Yep. I just have to pack everything up."

"Why don't you change and I'll get everything set. I want to send these books off one at a time."

"After wearing your p.j.s, these clothes are going to feel twice as tight."

Suma thanks him with a wink, the shutters of her green eye closing momentarily. "O.K., Baby Blue, let's move it."

"Do you have another toothpick?"

When Leon comes back, he's clad in black and ready to assume the role of the transporter. Going down the stairs with the books is much easier than going up. Suma looks out the window and sees the van parked close to the curb. She sees the hubcaps—one with a silver plate of penne a la vodka and one with an upside down sundae—and she assumes she must be really hungry. After the van is packed and set to go, he comes up to her apartment once more to get the envelope and say goodbye. When he faces her, his horizontal sightline skims the top of her head. "So, you're not allowed to get in an accident, get pulled over, or make any stops, got it?"

"Right on. And I'll text you after the drop, and then again after I return the truck, and once more when I get home." As he waits for her reply, his eyes find the twin freckles that before were separated by the satin purple strap. And where there should be silence, the snaps and pops of the end of the record persist, like bottle-rockets going off far in the distance.

[[♦]]

Axlia curls up sideways on her bed with her personal scrapbook. She rests her head on her right hand and turns one spiraled page at a time with her left hand. Her hair pulses back with each flip of the large stock paper. The cover is black with a sticky strip label that reads:

(I N) C O M P L E T E   W O R K S

On each black page is pasted or taped a multitude of artifacts from her performances: promotional flyers, black & white photos, sketches of canvas ideas, envelopes with DVDs of her shows, and hand-written notes in silver marker. While she waits for Jasmine to arrive, she searches through her catalogue to complete her checklist for the show at Mission. Somewhere in the middle, she comes across the transcript and production notes for a page labeled:

F I L M   0 0 4

She focuses on the shape of her words. Axlia thinks about how the characters are defined as much by the aggressive strikes of ink as they are by the empty space.

A CHANNEL XERO FILM
[004]
CYPHER 1:26
WRITTEN & DIRECTED BY AXLIA CLIA & D.C.

CHANNEL XERO PRODUCTIONS 583 RIVERSIDE DRIVE
HARLEM, NEW YORK, NY, USA
TELEPHONE:1-099-FUCK-YOU

LOCATION
HARLEM APT WINDOW OVERLOOKING THE HUDSON RIVER AND
THE COLORFUL COAST OF NEW INDIANA,
GRAY PAINTED WALLS, DIM LIGHTING

SHOOTING DRAFT
CAMERA 1: PROFILE OF NYEBO FACING LEFT,
FROM THE SHOULDERS UP
CAMERA 2: PROFILE OF RYVIO FACING RIGHT,
FROM THE SHOULDERS UP

NYEBO: WHITE DINNER JACKET, BLACK SHIRT, WHITE TIE,
BLACK LIPSTICK
RYVIO: BLACK DINNER JACKET, WHITE SHIRT, BLACK TIE,
WHITE LIPSTICK

[FADE IN]
NYEBO & RYVIO ARE FACING EACH OTHER, THERE ARE SOUNDS OF
BIRDS IN THE BACKGROUND, THERE IS NO WIND

NYEBO
THE CITY WALLS HAVE AN AESTHETIC THAT IS BEAUTIFULLY THEIR
OWN. THEY HAVE CONSISTENT SOLID COLORS AND SYMBOLIZE STRENGTH
WITH THEIR RIGHT ANGLES OF BRICK AND MORTAR.

RYVIO
I AGREE WHOLEHEARTEDLY. THEY SHOULD BE CONSERVED AND ALLOWED
TO PROTECT THEIR INHABITANTS.

NYEBO
SOME OF THEM DO HAVE SOME ARCHES AND CURVES, BUT THEY FOLLOW
THE RULES OF ARCHITECTURE.

RYVIO

TRUE,TRUE.THEY DO NOT NEED ANY THREE DIMENSIONAL
EMBELLISHMENTS OR NEON ACCENTS.THESE EGOTISTIC
VANDALS NEED TO WRITE THEIR NAMES SOMEWHERE ELSE.
KEEP IT ON PAPER.

NYEBO

THEY ARE RUINING THE STRUCTURE OF OUR SENTENCES. IT IS VISUAL
POLLUTION AND GRAMMATICAL DESTRUCTION AT THE SAME TIME.

RYVIO

IF THERE WERE A FEW PIECES HERE AND THERE, I COULD UNDERSTAND
THAT, BUT IT SHOULD HAVE ITS PLACE. ONCE THESE CRIMINALS RUN
WILD, THE SO-CALLED ART REACHES THE POINT OF OVER-SATURATION,
AND IT FUCKING LOSES ANY OF THE POTENCY IT ONCE HAD.

NYEBO

THE OTHER DAY I NOTICED A FRESHLY PAINTED WALL OVER ON SECOND
AVENUE. IT WAS A FUCKING BEAUTIFUL GRAY WALL MADE FROM
SEVERAL COATS OF PRIMER. THERE WASN'T A STRAY MARK ON IT.

RYVIO

THAT SOUNDS FUCKING AMAZING.

NYEBO

BUT THE NEXT DAY, I WALK BY THE FUCKING GRAY WALL AND SOME
GRAFFITI MOTHERFUCKER WROTE SOME UNINTELLIGIBLE FUCKING WORDS
ALL OVER THE FUCKING PLACE.

RYVIO

LEAVE ALONE WHAT IS NOT YOURS TO FUCK WITH.
FUCK HIM, GODDAMMIT.

NYEBO

IT HAD A NAME IN NEON FUCKING YELLOW AND BRIGHT FUCKING
GREEN, AND A FUCKING POEM IN BLACK AND GODDAMN WHITE.

RYVIO

SHAKESPEARE MOTHERFUCKER.

NYEBO

AND THEN THE NEXT FUCKING DAY I SAW THAT THE WHOLE FUCKING
WALL WAS BOMBED. THERE WERE BLUE AND PINK CLOUDS, AND

FUCKING PURPLE SUNS AND RED FUCKING RAINDROPS.

RYVIO
HE FUCKED UP THAT WALL LIKE A FUCKING JACK HAMMER, GODDAMMIT.
DEMO-FUCKING-LITION.

NYEBO
IT'S JUST THAT THESE FUCKING PUNK MOTHERFUCKERS ARE ALWAYS
FUCKING THE FUCKFACE OF THE FUCKING MOUTH OF THE CITY.

RYVIO
I CAN'T FUCKING STAND IT. IF I SEE THAT FUCKER I'M GOING TO
FUCK HIM UP ON SIGHT.

NYEBO
NIGHT FUCKING VISION.

RYVIO
I'LL FUCKING PUT HIM ON BLAST LIKE FUCK FUCK FUCK FUCK FUCK
FUCK FUCK FUCK FUCK FUCK FUCK FUCK FUCK! FUCK FUCK FUCK FUCK
FUCK, FUCK FUCK FUCK FUCK, FUCK FUCK FUCK FUCK FUCK FUCK...
FUCK FUCK FUCK FUCK FUCK FUCK FUCK FUCK FUCK FUCK FUCK FUCK!
FUCK FUCK FUCK FUCK FUCK FUCK FUCK FUCK FUCK FUCK FUCK, FUCK
FUCK FUCK FUCK FUCK FUCK FUCK. FUCK FUCK FUCK FUCK FUCK!

NYEBO
EXACTLY!!!

[FADE TO BEAUTIFUL GRAY]

*

CYPHER 1:26[47]

CAST

NYEBO   AXLIA CLIA
RYVIO   D.C.

© MMXVII
ALL RIGHTS ARE FUCKING RESERVED.
NOT TO BE DUPLICATED WITHOUT MY GODDAMN PERMISSION.

[[✝]]

Chairman Ezra: This is a secure code. We should all be in place and online. Do we have clear communication? Respond with your name and location.

<< Habakkuk, Lovinglace driveway, check >>

<< Ezekiel, Lovinglace driveway, check >>

<< Obadiah, on stand-by at the Garden City Hotel lobby, check >>

<< Mark, on stand-by at the Garden City Hotel in vehicle, check >>

<< Noah, driver on 46th and 8th, check >>

<< Malachi, vehicle passenger on 46th n' 8th, check >>

<< Jonah, 8 Spruce Street, passenger, check >>

<< Samson X, 8 Spruce, driver, check >>

Chairman Ezra: Thank you, brethren. And Elder Saul is here with me at headquarters. All instructions will come from me via this channel and from my authority. Remember, if you are questioned by anyone of concern, you are *not* to act. You are to wait for my approval. Our goals are secrecy, detection, and prevention, with secrecy being paramount. If security is compromised or communications break down, you are to observe and monitor the situation only. Do *not* take any action until communications are restored. If communications aren't restored, we will rendezvous at HQ at one a.m. And what about the laxatives? Are both forms operational and ready to be administered if possible?

<< Check. >>

<< ...heck. >>

Chairman Ezra: Is the tracking device ready to attach?

<< Yes, sir. Check. >>

<< Check. >>

Chairman Ezra: One last thing before Saul closes us in prayer. Sunglasses, *on...* or off?

<< On. As always. >>

Chairman Ezra: Samson has spoken.

<< I am ready to starve this hellfire of oxygen. God forgive me, but I will F U C K I N G take him out if he disrespects Candice or Joyce, or the legacy of Gideon, or my Lord. >>

Chairman Ezra: Show respect, Samson! This is not the time, brother. Now, let's listen to Elder Saul as he prays for us tonight.

Elder Saul: Dear Lord, we know You are above us and also within us. We pray for your assistance to keep us focused on the task at hand. Emotions and tensions are running high and quickly through our veins, for the devil is cunning. But we pray that You thicken our blood as we strive to keep the devil as far away from Candice Lovinglace as we can. In closing, we understand that You have created a time for all things for those that trust in You. And we have felt your call to action within our hearts, and we know that You are guiding us. You are the light that chases the darkness and the evil into the gutters and ultimately into hell. Praise You, Lord. This is Your Word, which You have given to us from on high: Ecclesiastes three, verses one through eight.

There is a time for everything, and a season for every activity under the heavens:
a time to be born and a time to die,
a time to plant and a time to uproot,
a time to kill and a time to heal,
a time to tear down and a time to build,
a time to weep and a time to laugh,
a time to mourn and a time to dance,
a time to scatter stones and a time to gather them,
a time to embrace and a time to refrain from embracing,
a time to search and a time to give up,
a time to keep and a time to throw away,
a time to tear and a time to mend,
a time to be silent and a time to speak,
a time to love and a time to hate...

<< Pardon, Elder Ezekiel here. We have headlights approaching the driveway. Lamborghini Countach, Red, dark tinted windows, and NY plates that read: PWRBALLIN. Tracking device ready to attach once he gets out of the car. Over. >>

Elder Saul: ...a time for war and a time for peace. Amen.

At 7:54pm McJesus's car bellows with thunder up the driveway on Stewart Avenue at 5mph. The kicked-up pieces of gravel are rendered inaudible. He's sitting farther forward in his seat than normal, out of gentlemanly respect. McJesus adjusts the rose on the passenger seat so the fullest petals are featured. He looks in the rearview mirror to confirm he still has a face, and that he's actually there, in front of Candy's home. He stands outside the car, fastens a single button on his velvet blazer, and takes a deep breath. He pays particular attention to the air and how fresh it is out in the suburbs. City air is heavy and often feels like it carries the millions of collective exhales of its denizens. The cool clean air fills his lungs to capacity and produces an unexpected type of euphoria and encouragement that's usually reserved for mountaintops.

Her home is stately and landscaped. The path leading to the front door is outlined with solar lights that actually work. He steps on one flat stone at a time before jumping up three stairs in one leap. McJesus extends his finger and presses the glowing doorbell, which sounds like a concerto of chimes and goes on for a full fifteen seconds.

She opens the door. "Hey, you're early! I was hoping you'd be late!"

"I can turn around, walk back to my car, and drive around the block for awhile. We can pretend this never happened and I'll come back and strike up the orchestra once more."

"No, of course not! Come inside. I just have grab a few things upstairs and I'll be set. Sorry!"

"I'm in no hurry. Take your time," McJesus smiles back.

With Candy distracted by his pre-punctuality, she hadn't yet seen his get-up. She gives him a glancing survey and parts her lips as if about to remark, but a thought interrupts her, and her expression goes from a smile to a look of concern. "I'll just be a minute. I think my mom is down the hallway. She may come over and introduce herself. If she does, just smile and say words like *swell* and *golly gee willikers*, and you'll be O.K."

"Well, gosh, I can sure as heck do that," McJesus adds. And her smile returns.

When Candy starts to walk upstairs, he keeps his eyes fixed forward. Her ascent offers a vertical panorama of her body. Her straight strawberry blonde hair falls beyond her shoulders and bounces in full curls at the ends like a suspended waterfall. She wears a teal, light sweater with black three-quarter sleeves. On her right wrist is a thick black and gold Rubik's Cube-type bracelet. As she climbs a few more steps, her bottom shifts left and right across his sightline. For a moment, his eyes look like the ones on an old Kit Cat Klock. Tight against her hips, she has high-waisted leather shorts with dark stockings that cover the remainder of her legs. The stockings have a random distribution of dots that look like silver nonpareils. Her legs are both thick and thin somehow, and lack muscular definition. His chin is now tilted up as he watches her near the top of the stairs. Candy is wearing black heels that have a waxy licorice quality. He notices she hadn't peeled a sticker off the bottom of her right shoe. He tries to determine if it's a price label, a size label, or something sticky that hitched a ride somewhere along life's travels. As he follows the sticker up the last two steps, his eyes squint to get a better view. He leans on the stairway railing, looks straight up at Candy's backside, exhales, and smiles to himself.

Candy's mom's voice rings out from somewhere unseen, "Excuse me!"

"She wears a size seven! I mean, I'm sorry. I wasn't looking up... It looked strange I'm sure, but..." He hears a door close and echo into the vestibule. He can't tell from which direction the voice or the door came, but it's probably from a place called *Disapproval, N.Y.* From that point on, he keeps his gaze down at his own shoes.

The silence is broken when Candy returns and descends the staircase. His prayer has been answered. Unsure if he's still being observed by Mrs. Lovinglace, he checks the time on his Raketa Copernic watch. It's more than thirty minutes away from its next eclipse.

As she steps to the floor, their eyes meet for the first time that night. They look at each other in caring detail. It's the first time they've seen each other with ample lighting.

"I thought you weren't in a hurry," Candy says.

"No, that's not it. I'm just keeping my head down for a second," McJesus says in a hushed tone. "I think I just messed up. My first impression was my worst impression."

"What, with my mom?"

"I think so."

"Oh, don't worry about her! What did she say to you? What do you mean you *think so*?"

"I didn't see her, but I think she caught me watching you walk up the stairs. Which I was, but I wasn't *watching you* watching you. Meaning, I wasn't drooling and panting and all that. Man, I'm making this sound even worse now."

"What could you possibly be talking about, Zeus?" Candy smiles.

"I was watching your shoes. One shoe, actually!"

"What?! You were watching one shoe go up the stairs?"

"I just happened to see that you had a sticker or something on the bottom of your shoe and I couldn't figure out what it was, so I kept following it up the stairs. I told you, it just sounds worse now..." Just for fun, Candy lets him continue to overly explain himself, watching his emphatic animations while doing so.

"So you weren't watching me at all? Just one shoe?"

"O.K., let me start over. First of all, you look great, excellent, styling and profiling. And I'm totally down to have a cool time tonight, but I also don't want to put any undue expectations on the night and therefore create pressure in any way. But yes, I admit that it started with you and your hair and leather shorts, and then one shoe led to another, and it stayed that way. It was a strange consequence, but I think it caused my so-called *worst impression* for someone in my shoes, for which I'm sure there are no stickers stuck. But I guess all is not lost, since

I've already learned two things about you. That you walk upstairs very calmly and softly and that you wear a size seven. Also I liked the way you said my name."

Candy shakes her head with a long blink and a longer smile. "Are you ready to go?"

"Ready, steady."

"Bye, Mom! Love you!"

Zeus opens the front door and ushers Candy through. He hangs back for a moment and looks around the vestibule. He wonders if Mrs. Lovinglace has somehow been watching him the whole time. Then he realizes, all around him, are their family portraits lining the walls, showing their solidarity through a shared history. Through the years of fake sky backgrounds, changes in women's fashions, established beards, colored braces, switches to contact lenses, and accumulated wrinkles, their eyes are everywhere. Not only of Joyce Lovinglace, but Candy's too, and the curiously unbalanced eyes of the late Gideon Lovinglace. Zeus feels he's been seen from all angles and eras, but possibly from only one perspective.

He closes the door behind him and walks down the front steps after Candy. And just as soon it shut, he hears the click of the deadbolt. He looks back to the panes of frosted glass that bookend the door and sees Mrs. Lovinglace's hazy dark figure standing as still as a statue. One of her hands splays white against the pane.

"This car is outta sight! *This* is your car!?"

"Yep, this is my baby. I used to have Countach posters on my wall as a kid. When I first sat in the driver's seat, I knew I wasn't going to budge until the paperwork was done. I signed on the dotted line using the steering wheel as a table."

"Well, I think it's very *you*."

Zeus performs a gallant bow. Then he opens her door diagonally upward, like the wing of a flightless bird. Candy sees the rose on the seat and shoots him a wink that lashes *you-didn't-have-to-do-that*. When Zeus takes his place at the wheel he looks over at Candy and says, "Right back at you. And watch the thorns." She rests the petals of the rose against her neckline. He sees the same gold chain that she wore when he first met her. It emerges from around the back of her neck and disappears into wonderland.

As he backs the car out of the driveway, he notices that the darkness is still behind the frosted glass, but the hand is gone. Trying to shake off the tension and change his frame of mind, he pumps the stereo and drives the car forward. The collective shadows[48] listen as the Lamborghini charges away, going from a roar to a distant purr.

After a minute, Zeus turns the music down to conversation level. "How are you tonight?"

"Great! Definitely excited to get out."

"Me too. I know we're both supposed to act all cool and everything, like this is no big deal, but I'm really happy to be going out with you. I've been looking forward to it all week."

"Thanks. Me too. Really."

There are few moments of pregnant silence.

Zeus says, "Well, I'm sure we're going to get around to our favorite colors, favorite movies, and favorite breakfast foods, but instead of getting deep with that stuff right away, why don't we start on a lower plane. Let's air the dirty laundry right away."

"O.K.?"

"How about you tell me the dirtiest joke you've ever heard."

"What?!"

"You know, just throw it out there. I'll tell you mine if you tell me yours. This way, we can start at the bottom and work our way up to our favorite colors from there."

"Did you plan to ask me this?"

"Nope. Just thought of it. So, what's your dirtiest joke?"

"This is probably not the best way for us to start off because I was raised in a very conservative home. Like, no YouTube, no MTV, and only church-approved movies. We even had an organist play hymns for my seventh grade birthday party. I went to a private school where we only used one book for every subject and I'm sure you can guess which one it was."

"I went to public school, but I attended youth group and church trips all the way into high school. Oddly enough, that's where I heard the dirtiest jokes in my life. I learned more about sinning from my church friends than I ever would've thought. I went to this lakeside retreat once, where I got saved by a campfire. I'll never forget it. But it's also where I first saw a joint being passed around. Maybe that's why it felt so magical? Just kidding."

"You're saved?"

"Yes, technically. I mean, I admit I've had some dark periods along the path, and I've questioned many things, but I'm trying to set things right, honestly. Once you're saved, isn't that for life? Or if you have doubts, does it just go away? See, here I go, getting into a question vortex. That's what's always gotten me in trouble with The Faith."

"That took a quick turn, from dirty jokes to this. I'm saved too, but I'm not perfect either. I mean, my mom isn't always happy with my choices. She hasn't trusted me lately and it's been worse since my dad passed away."

"Again, I'm really sorry about that."

"Thank you. I'll never really get over it, but I have to live in the moment and save those somber feelings for the right times. I do miss him. It's funny, when we were just talking about our education, it made me remember how excited he was that I was going to a Christian school. I'm not really sure I had a choice anyway. He was a board member and he pushed the idea of using only The Bible for all educational classes. I could laugh and cry at the same time when I think back. After I graduated eighth grade and went on to another private, more-traditional prep school, the transition wasn't the smoothest. In a good way, I had different qualities than everyone else, but converting from cubits to feet in math class was near impossible to get used to. And I'm only half-kidding on that one. I remember that we had to do a diorama for each book of The Bible. We were allowed to choose the scene, but with the teacher's guidance. Judges was a tough book to navigate, I remember."

"I bet no one did a diorama of the Lot scene with his two daughters."

"Behave yourself."

"I've actually thought about that before. If someone wanted to represent Genesis on film, completely and accurately, it would be rated R, NC-17, X, and XXX, all at once."

"Oh boy. Might be true. I was just going to say that my father liked when I chose to create some of the more unusual dioramas in the school. Most kids went with *David and Goliath* or something like that. So he was really proud of my *Parable of the Mustard Seed* diorama."

"I'm sorry I got carried away there." Zeus adjusts the volume. "So do you think God can just take it back, meaning getting saved?"

"I think it's what's in your heart."

"What if it's in your heart, but nowhere else? That's what I'm saying when I think about it."

Candy sighs. "I wouldn't have thought I'd ever say this, but how about we switch to sharing our dirtiest jokes?"

"Yes! Good idea. You go first. Shoot!"

"Again, let me warn you about my upbringing. I was very sheltered. You are *not* allowed to make fun of my joke if you don't like it. And I only heard this recently. Unlike your church groups, I didn't learn all that sinning and joke-telling at my meetings. This one comes from my job that's still kind of new. I work in design at Rip-Off. Maybe my coworkers went to the same youth group you did."

"I'm impressed! That's a hot spot. And I'm going to ignore that last sentence."

"O.K. Here's the joke. I'll try my best to say it right."

"I'm ready." McJesus shifts into the right lane and around a stray yellow taxi on the suburban parkway.

"Okay. So there's this guy who has a really big penis..."

"Great..."

"It turns out that it's like three feet long and he has to wear special pants. It's made it hard for him to find work that isn't internet-based. Even the porn stars won't touch him, let alone any other ladies. He's just living this sad life with no rewarding job and no love because of his penis. It's like he has a limp baseball bat just hanging there. So he has just one friend in the whole world, and this friend is a bit mysterious, but he's caring as well. This mysterious friend scoured the earth for a possible solution for his friend. And since the limp baseball bat guy can't get a job, he can't pay for a medical procedure. So the mysterious friend looks everywhere and finally finds help near a stream that runs alongside a mountain in New Hampshire. It turns out that there is a plastic fish that comes to life when you ask it a question. The fish is lodged sideways in the mouth of a large bear statue. Know one knows how the statue got there, but certain people knew what the fish was capable of."

"Is it supposed to be Smoky the Bear?"

"I don't think so. The way it was told to me, there weren't any fire prevention signs nearby. So, legend has it that when you ask the plastic fish a question, he will turn his head in your direction, flap a fin at you, and answer with either *Yes* or *No*. If you get him to answer *No*, he will magically take two inches off the length of your penis. When the man's friend found out about the fish, he set up a road trip to help his friend get to a place of normalcy. Then he could wear regular clothes and get a job and finally go on some dates."

"What kind of fish is this?"

"It's a plastic sturgeon."

"Haha!"

"No. That's not the joke. That's a fact."

"What happens if the fish says, '*Yes*?'"

"I don't think anything happens. The point is that you have to get the fish to answer, '*No*.' So the two men made the journey to the mystical stream in New Hampshire and approached the bear statue. The man with the extremely large penis unzips his specialized pants and lets it drop into the damp soil. The story goes that even the bear, who never moved or spoke, raised his eyebrows at the sight of it. Then the man with the three-foot penis asked his first question to the fish.

'Are you the President of the United States of America?'

'No,' said the sturgeon.

And his penis lifted off the wet soil and was now two feet and ten inches long. The man turned to his friend with gleaming eyes and thanked him.

'Are you the Vice President of the United States of America?

'No.'

'Are you a justice on the Supreme Court?'

'No.'

'Are you a US Senator?'

'No.'

'Are you a representative of Congress?'

'No.'

'Are you a state governor?'

'No.'

The man looked down to a two foot penis and smiled again at his friend. 'Are you concerned about the current economic climate in America?'

'Yes.'

'Oh, I'm surprised,' said the man. 'I didn't know you had those concerns.' His friend pulled him aside and advised him to stick to the most obvious questions. The man agreed.

'Are you wearing a Yankees baseball cap?'

'No.'

'Are you wearing a Red Sox baseball cap?'

'No.'

'Are you wearing a Pirates baseball cap?'

'No.'

'Are you wearing a Mets baseball cap?'

'No.'

'Are you wearing an Expos baseball cap?'

'No.'

'Are you wearing a Giants baseball cap?'

'No.'

The man smiled at his friend once more, this time with a one-foot unit. 'Almost done,' he told his friend. And he turned his attention back to the fish. 'Are you wearing a Cubs baseball cap...'

'*No!!!* Look, I've told you over and over I'm not wearing a cap. I'm a plastic sturgeon, not a baseball player. *No, No, No, No!!!* You get me?' And the man looked down between his legs to see a two-inch killer. The two men looked at each other in horror. The man practically broke down on sight, but he felt the urge to apologize and ask the fish one last question. "Sir, I am so sorry to have bothered you. I didn't mean to disrespect your intelligence! Will you please, please, with whipped cream on top, reverse your last answer?'

'No.'"

"That's a great joke! I love it!"

"Thanks. That's the only one I know," Candy beams back. "That poor guy."

"You have to respect the plastic sturgeon."

"I guess I'm up next," Zeus says while checking his speed. They're nearing their first stop in Queens. It's a place he likes to go to reflect on the world, usually alone.

"I'd say I'd stop you if I've heard the joke, but I'm sure I haven't."

"Well, here goes. Oh, and I'll be using some colorful language for the sake of the joke, but overall I'm against bad language for the cause of style and class."

"I'll allow the exception."

"So there's a gynecologist sitting at his desk at the end of the day..."

"Great..."

"The office closes at five and it's four-thirty. He checks his calendar and sees that he has one more appointment, and that she's a new patient. He sees a car pull up outside his office and he sees a woman with the most incredible body that he's ever seen. So the doctor whistles to himself like *wheeeeee-woooooo* and prepares an insurance form on his clipboard. When the woman opens the door there's a draft and it blows her long blonde hair up in a whirlwind and falls in front of her face. She struggles to get in the door, so when she walks up to the doctor she has to fix hair and adjust her purse. The doctor says, 'Hello. Are you O.K.?'

The woman answers with a total valley girl accent and rocks her head left and right like this, '*I'M O.K.!!*'

The doctor does an internal double take and says, 'Are you sure? That door can do that.

It's like a wind tunnel.'

And again she says the same thing, but with more head movement. '*REALLY,* ' I'M O.K.!!'

So the doctor's thinking that she's hot, maybe very dumb, and his assistant took the afternoon off. 'Welcome to my office. I see this is your first time here. I have you down for a check-up only. Is that correct?'

' YEAH, *TOTALLY.* I'M NEW TO THE *AREA AND I HAVEN'T* BEEN CHECKED OUT *IN A WHILE!*'

'After you complete this form, meet me in the examination room, and I'll check you out.'

' O-*KAY!*'

So the gynecologist goes into the examination room and is having all sorts of bad thoughts, especially with the wind tunnel not just in the doorway, but in her head as well. When she walks in, he decides to see what he can get away with. 'Since this is your first time, I need to give you a full examination. Can you remove your shirt and bra for me?'

' SURE!'

So the doctor starts to feel her bare chest way more than necessary. And after a while he asks, 'Do you know what I'm doing right now?'

' PROBABLY JUST *CHECKING FOR ANY LUMPS.*'

'Right, right. Exactly. Can you remove your underwear and lift up your skirt for me?'

'*SURE!*'

'Just hold it straight up all the way around.'

So the doctor starts to touch her in between her thighs in all sorts of non-medical ways. And after a while he asks, 'Do you know what I'm doing right now?'

' PROBABLY JUST *CHECKING FOR ABNORMALITIES.*'

'Right, right. Exactly.' Finally he gets bored with all of that and decides to strap her into the chair with the leg braces, undoes his pants, and starts to go to town. And after a few minutes, right as he was climaxing, he asks, 'Do you know what I'm doing right now?'

And she says with a straight face, 'YEAH, CATCHING HERPES.*'

Candy chimes in immediately, "That's horrible. But I like it, I think. The best part is that she knows the word *abnormalities*."

"True!"

Zeus pulls the Lambo into a lot on the outskirts of Flushing Meadow Park. The Unisphere, the silver globe that was used as the centerpiece for the World's Fair in the early sixties, is illuminated, but from the car it's eclipsed by the nearby trees. The park is well-groomed and the fountains flow during the warmer months, and there are food trucks and ice cream men parked along the perimeter, but the taxpayer maintenance dollars haven't yet reached the steel circumference of the Unisphere. Nature is reclaiming the ignored planet.

"I love driving to this place at night."

"I've never been this close to it."

"It's just a short walk away." As they leave the car, the backs of their hands brush up against each other. The tension of small doses of body heat ends when Candy grabs his hand and they walk in happy silence for a few minutes.

"What do you think?" Zeus asks.

"Amazing. I can imagine what it must have looked like when people first saw it."

"I know. It's about half a football field high. I like to imagine how my ancestry came to be and see *through* the world at the places where they came from and think of all the little events that had to happen in order for me to exist. Or anyone."

Candy looks at Zeus. "You're very thoughtful."

"Thanks. But I always wonder, how can you not be?"

Candy shakes her head and it goes unnoticed by both of them. "It could use a little shine around the edges though. It looked perfect from the highway."

"True. Every time I look at it, I can hear the lead story being read by a talking head: *Hold your loved ones, folks! It turns out we do live in a hollow and vacuous world after all!* And, *proof of global warming is confirmed as moss grows across Antarctica!* And, *Plateau Everest now considered a good place to...*"

"I get it," Candy chuckles.

"Do you want to grab a snack? There's a Zeppole Truck near Madagascar."

After they get their powdered puffs of wonderfulness, they talk about their favorite foods and drinks, and preference of spoon size with regard to soup. They talk about canned soup, boxed soup, condensed soup, and what constitutes homemade soup—as in what percentage of the soup must be prepared at home in order to get that title. They settle at eighty-eight point eight percent. There's a moment when Zeus laughs so hard he blows a puff of sugary dust onto his velvet blazer and her strawberry blonde hair. That's followed by some cute exchanges as they work together to find all the places the confection had landed. It gives Zeus an excuse to look at her legs in the stockings with the silver nonpareil things. He says next time she can wear regular stockings and that they could just get another zeppole and laugh about something else. They both agree that it wouldn't be difficult.

Zeus and Candy walk back toward the car when they feel a chill in the evening air. Candy comments on the reflection of the moon off the hood of the car, which is suspended in the far reaches of the orbit of the Unisphere. "I love when the moon is big in the sky. Like you can reach out and grab it. Or that if you ran fast enough you could jump off the edge of the earth and latch onto it. It looks magical like that."

"I know what you mean. It's both powerful and comforting. Our nightly friend."

"I've always wondered why it looks so big sometimes."

"Oh, actually, I know why. It's because when the moon is along the horizon we have points of reference that we can compare it to. But when it's high overhead, it's pretty much alone amongst the stars. Like, if I look back to the Unisphere, I first see that couple walking over there, then farther back is a food truck, and farther still are the trees. But since the couple is closer to us, they're the largest objects in my frame, but my brain sorts out that they aren't the largest of all those objects. Clearly they're not taller than the food truck or the trees, so my brain figures out how to give the truck and the trees their proper weight, or should I say, height. So if we imagine the moon beyond those trees, we can better distinguish the difference between them, and the moon will seem larger, and therefore closer than when it is all alone." Zeus looks up to the sky that is obscured by light pollution on the edges. "Essentially, it's all about *perspective*. When the moon *feels* closer, it's only closer in context."

"Thanks, but I think you're just ruining the magic of it for me."

Zeus smiles and adds, "Sorry. But no, I think it's more interesting that way. The truth is *always* more interesting than the feeling."

"I think that's an entirely different conversation. And do you know where we should have it?"

"No, where?"

"I think the two of us should host a podcast or a radio show or something," Candy proposes.

"Exactly! We could totally pull that off!"

"What would we call it?" Candy pauses. "Ummmmm..."

In a deep radio-announcer-voice, he says, "Zeus Woodson and Candice Lovinglace Talk Feelings and Moons, Soups and Spoons!"

Candy laughs. "Wait, ummmmm... How about something simple? What about something with my nickname and your official name? Candy and Mc—"

"O.K., ready?"

"Yes."

The announcer voice returns and bellows, "*Sweet Jesus!*"

Candy, with her knee-jerk guilt already employed, laughs the kind of laugh that solidifies the moment into a memory.

Back in the car and on the road to their next stop, Zeus looks over at Candy as she looks in the mirror. His eyes scan in the direction of the slump of the seat, from sugarless hair to sugared stockings to where her feet disappear under the console. The first thing that comes to mind is his high school locker combination, 38-24-36. They're nearing the Midtown Tunnel and he takes the Lambo hard into one of the last curves before the toll.[49, 50]

"Where are we going next?"

"Drinks and dinner at a legendary jazz joint that was restored last year. They did it right. Sound O.K.?"

"Let's do it. I'm starving. I was about to run back for some more zeppoles. That's the truth."

"Candy, you actually do seem like a person who doesn't lie."

"I try not too, but sometimes you can't avoid the little white ones once in a while."

"When's the last time you told one of those?"

"The only time I lie... is down," Candice says. "But to be honest, I lied to you when you were early to pick me up."

"I'm disappointed. The picture of perfection has been ruined."

"It's not that serious," Candy says truthfully.

"O.K., spill it."

"When I told you I had to grab a few things and get myself together, I really had to run to the bathroom."

"Apology accepted," Zeus says to Candy's dismissive hand. "But!—I think you just lied again."

"How so, mister polygraph?"

"When you said you had to *run* to the bathroom, I'm pretty sure you walked. That's what everyone does. Everyone says they're going to run to the bathroom, but they leave the room at a normal walking pace. Now kids on the other hand, they run. They run for no reason at all and nobody really notices. But if you see an adult running, you know something must be wrong. Especially indoors. Imagine a Thanksgiving dinner, everyone's at the table doing their thing, and your mom gets up and runs as fast as she can to the bathroom. Everyone at the table would watch her, then trade wide-eyed looks around the table, and ask her if everything was O.K. Imagine she just says, 'Yep. I just felt like running.' Or when we're having dinner in a little while, I just get up and run toward the bar. You and everyone else would assume I'm either in desperate need of water to quell some hot sauce burn, or that I'm an impatient alcoholic. But really, I just felt like running, because why not? And the only thing I wanted was an extra napkin. So next time someone tells you that they're going to *run* to the bathroom, wish them luck. They're probably about to have an accident. So either kids are crazy, or adults are liars, or adults yearn to be young again and run all over the place only to realize that they have to walk slowly because of—cue the fifth symphony—polite society."

"The only thing I got from that is that you'd probably be an annoying dinner guest," Candy retorts.

"And don't get me started on *jumping in the shower*."

Zeus and Candy enter the citrine radiation of the Queens Midtown Tunnel and drive through the East River before emerging in the capital of the Milky Way Galaxy. Even though the view of the looming concentration of starry windows from the Long Island Expressway is impressive, there's something almost shocking about the vertical sight lines from the car window. This is true every time.

Zeus drives almost one hundred blocks uptown to Lenox Avenue, where he parks the mechanical marvel out front. He speaks to two men dressed in all black who are standing nearby, gives them the keys and an envelope from his inside pocket, and walks around to the passenger side. Two speckled legs swing their way around to the outside and Zeus offers his hand to the still-headless Candy. Even though they'd held hands earlier, when he helps her out of the car, his skin ripples with tingling warmth. They stand by the curb and look at the façade of the legendary jazz house. It's dimly lit, a place of class and perseverance. The illumination of the **LENOX LOUNGE** in neon white is in a font that Zeus wishes was his natural handwriting style, and it accentuates the glossy garnet exterior and silver-lined windows.

When he opens the door, they hear a percussive certainty mixed with a cacophonous spontaneity, and the pulse of the bass mixed with the sexuality of the saxophone. The sound pulls them the rest of the way in. Candy steps across the hexagons of the honeycomb-tiled floor, while Zeus admires the view and thinks of the sting. A young woman at the bar tells him that their table in the Zebra Room will be ready in a few minutes and asks them if they'd like a drink in the meantime. She hands them a list of Duke Ellington-inspired cocktails.[51] Zeus studies the bar menu while Candy looks around three hundred sixty degrees. She takes in the gold bar accents, the aged wood of the bar, and the framed, black-and-white icons on the walls. With the art deco light fixtures that curve like the outline of a Wurlitzer and the ubiquity of the music, she feels as though she's *in* a jukebox.

"I'll have a Lucky So-And-So and she'll have a Sophisticated Lady. Thanks."

"I wish they had a place like this back on Long Island. Wait, what did you order me?"

"Trust me, you'll like it. And agreed, this place is dope."

As if the thought just occurred to him, which it hadn't, Zeus says, "I have to ask why you said *on* Long Island? Shouldn't it be *in* Long Island?"

"No, I live *on* Long Island. It's an island. You don't live *in* an island."

"Sure, I pretty much agree with that, but are you saying that the *in* or *on* thing depends on the classification of the land mass? Or does it depend on the name of the land mass?"

"I think it's that way because it's an actual island and it sounds right. To live *in* Long Island just sounds strange."

"But Long Island is also its own entity, like Queens, Los Angeles, or Manhattan. And don't people live *in* those places? It sounds strange the other way when you say that you live *on* Queens, right?"

"Definitely!"

The pair moves to an open stool at the bar. Zeus offers Candy the seat, but they both decide to stand. The bartender meets them with their drinks.

He raises his glass. "Cheers!"

"To an interesting evening already!"

"So, just to continue, by that logic, why doesn't it sound strange to live *on* Long Island when it's a government-designated *place* like the others?" Zeus pokes at the large ice cube in his Lucky So-And-So.

"You're quite passionate about this. It doesn't sound strange because that's what people do. They go *on* places that are islands."

"So how do I say where I live?"

"You should say (Candy speaks with a deep voice that sounds nothing like his), 'I live *in*

Manhattan.'"

"Cool, but Manhattan is an island. And you just said that people go or live *on* islands. I think you're sounding pretty silly."

"Ouch. O.K., fine. I guess you could say (she repeats the voice thing again), 'I live *on* the island of Manhattan.' But then you'd sound pretty pretentious, which doesn't seem to be a concern of yours anyway."

"Woo! Nice one. So you're saying as long as the place where you live has the word *island* included, then you can live *on* it?"

"Yes, I guess. Are you some kind of annoying editor of grammar for regional colloquialisms?"

"It's true. I am. And by the way, as an annoying editor, I have to tip my invisible hat to the..." Zeus makes a show of both sounding the word out and counting on two hands, "*insignificancy* of it all, and why that makes it all the more fun to argue about. It's a seven-syllable word."

"That's nothing."

"Almost nothing."

"If you want to go there, I'll tell you what it really is. It's the best word I've ever learned, and it was from my eighth grade English teacher, Mr. G." She looks up to the ceiling and counts mentally. "*Floccinaucinihilipilification.* It's twenty-nine letters long and you'll need two toes for the syllable count."

"Sexy. What does it mean?"

"It means that something is estimated as being worthless."

"Is that how you think of me? As flock—? Or whatever you just said."

"Yes, it's how I think of you and your strange obsession with *on* and *in*."

The waitress escorts them to their table in the Zebra room. Zeus and Candy sink down into the maroon vinyl booth side-by-side, almost conspiratorially. The jazz is loud enough where they're forced to lean in to talk to each other. When one leans in, the other looks around the room at the portraits of musicians, who are in mid-melody, and whose eyes are closed and focused both inwardly and existentially. Zeus smiles to himself when he realizes the wallpaper matches his boxers.[52]

"Would you agree with the following statement? Islands are islands, but continents are really just big islands."

"I'm worried about agreeing with you about anything category-related."

"O.K., I'm going to leave this subject, for which I have much passion, with just two scenarios. You don't even have to comment on them. I'm just going to throw them out there to be absorbed. One: the location on your birth certificate says Australia. If someone were to ask you where you were born, what would you say? Two: the location on your birth certificate says Rhode Island. Again, if someone were to ask you where you were born, what would you say?"

"If someone asked me like that, I would simply say *Australia*, or *Rhode Island*. But I see where you're going and I'm not coming along for the ride."

"I'll be alone on my epic quest for grammatical congruity. Are you sure you don't want to stay on?"

"I'm pretty sure."

"While I'm sad and depressed, I'll leave you with one last bit of editing. And that's that you should've left off the last word you just said."

They order their dinner, have another round of drinks, sometimes talk with their mouths full, and move on to less-contentious topics—although they still manage to clash over their favorite colors. She doesn't agree that *juice* is a color and he's disappointed that hers is *white*. They also have never heard of each other's favorite movie before and agreed on the spot that a popcorn night was in order.

Zeus pays the bill in advance when he takes an unnecessary trip to the bathroom. After the server takes away their dinnerware, he counts out a cash tip.

"I already paid the bill. This is just the tip."

"Are you leaving her coins?"

"Yes, but plenty of paper, too. These are old Eisenhower silver dollars from the seventies. It's just a superstitious thing for me to bring her some good luck."

"I think my father had some in his coin collection, but I don't think I've ever held one. Can I see them?"

"Sure. See?"

"I'm going to punch you. I mean can I *hold* one of them?"

"Sure."

Zeus watches Candy wrap her index finger and thumb around the perimeter of the silver, and with her other three fingers fanning out, it looks like the O.K. sign. "He's bald."

"Indeed," he nods. "So, how are you feeling? Do you want me to bring you back home, or are you up for some rooftop air hockey?"

"Rooftop air hockey?! That's not what I would've guessed you were about to say. But it sounds fun. I'm not ready to go home yet. I'm having a great time with you," Candy smiles.

"Cool, me too. But in case you're getting bored or have to get up early in the morning, I wanted to give you an out."

"Believe me, I'd tell you if I wasn't having a good time." She hands the Eisenhower dollar back to him, but doesn't let go of his hand. "I'm supposed to go to church with my mom in the morning, but the service doesn't start until ten. Let's push on. I can let my alarm do the work tomorrow."

"So then, air hockey?"

"Let's go, Gretzky."

When they leave **LENOX LOUNGE**, the car is waiting for them with open doors and the keys inside. The two men Candy had seen earlier were in a nondescript black car behind the Lamborghini. Despite the car's raw power, Zeus drives slowly downtown to their next destination. He'd admit that driving the car on the highway feels like playing a video game without any extra lives. When they get there, the men are already waiting to catch the keys a second time. The couple arrives at the ground floor of a rooftop bar called [tOken]. They take the most common mode of transportation in Manhattan up to the top floor and walk out with interlocked elbows. The bar is located in the center of the roof space and is built using materials from recycled arcade game cabinets. The plastic patchwork of titles like *Frogger*, *Space Invaders*, and *NBA Jam* act as place settings for the customers. Around the perimeter of the roof is a ten-foot plexiglass barrier to help contain the projectiles from the game stations. The mix of alcohol, eight balls, darts, ping pong balls, and air hockey pucks can cause problems for the passersby on the sidewalk below. Well, the ping pong balls not so much. Zeus takes a *Spy Hunter* seat and Candy's derriere gets a hot pink kiss from *Ms. Pac-Man*. Everything on the roof requires tokens, which are supplied by the bartenders. Zeus pays with his phone and the bartender lines up the tokens in front of him.

⊕⊕⊕⊕⊕⊕⊕⊕⊕⊕⊕⊕⊕⊕⊕⊕⊕⊕⊕⊕⊕⊕⊕

Candy looks around to the diminished skyline that is made shorter by their elevated position. "We're higher up than I thought."

"It's nice up here, right?"

"Yes, I love it. What are you going to order? I'm thinking the Pole Position. It's Red Bull and Ginseng Vodka. I want to keep my energy up so I can beat you."

"I'm going to thump my chest with a Donkey Kong, an espresso porter with a shot of banana liqueur."

"Good luck."

The next hour or so passes quickly with Candy and Zeus bouncing between analog and arcade games and ordering a second round of drinks. The mood is first-date-perfect. With two tokens left, the couple makes it over to the air hockey table. They scowl at the initial face-off. Zeus starts with his first angled attack and Candy protects her goal. The game continues with arrhythmic, percussive surprises, and pauses for fist-pumping celebrations. The puck is like the two players, kinetic and floating above the surface.

Zeus looks to the side and ticks up his chin, as if to acknowledge someone walking by. Candy turns to look where he's gesturing. There's no one there. It's a made-up ghost. And as she's facing away from the table, Zeus ricochets the puck across the cardboard ice and into her goal for the winning point.

"Oooh! That was mean!"

"What are you talking about? I thought I saw someone over there."

"Yeah, right. You lie, you lie."

"What's the score now?"

"I think you know. You win, but I know the truth," Candy says with her hands on her hips.

"Do you want to get a few more tokens? Another round and a rematch? I'll play fairly, promise."

"Isn't that going to be too many drinks for you though? I prefer to arrive at my home in one piece."

"Agreed. To *be* intact is to *be*. I already told my guys to get the car for wherever we go next."

"But there's no back seat in your car?"

"I know, I mean the limo."

"Oh, O.K., you have a limo lined up and ready to go?"

"I do."

"Well, as long as you have it figured out, it sounds good to me. And as much as I shouldn't admit this, I do trust you."

"You should! No, but honestly, I wouldn't let anything happen to you. We're in this whole thing together."

"You do seem to have things in control. You're a really good planner."

"Thanks. When I care, I really try."

"O.K.," Candy says. "Let's go for one more round, but I'm going for a Virgin Pole Position this time, I have to watch myself."

"You know," Zeus leans forward against the air hockey table, "I didn't comprehend one word you just said. And I don't mean any disrespect, but you're very distracting. I could look into your eyes all night."

"Not if I close them." Candy holds them shut. "No, I'm kidding. That was really sweet."

"Fine, I take it back. Maybe this game is perfect for you—you're clearly a cold person," Zeus retorts.

"Learn to relax, Mr. Zeus. I said I was kidding around. Truth be told, I think you're as hot as h-e-double hockey sticks."

"Oh! Nice one. And thank you." Zeus bows. "But you're not right."

"I think I am, buster." Candy takes the puck with her hand and slides it into his goal without regard for any of the rules. "One to zero."

"That does it. I'm going to order you a Virgin Pole Position and I'm going to get a very exciting ice water. Then I'm coming back here to punish you one last time."

"Why don't you put me in the penalty box first? Then you can do whatever you want to me."

"Do *not* even say that. *Damn.*"

"Chill, buster. It's a joke. If anyone's going in that box, it's you."

Zeus doesn't say anything out loud, but his brain is alive with synapses of laughter and a childish refrain from middle school.[53]

When he comes back with their drinks, he sees Candy with her forehead pressed against the plexiglass looking down to the little toy cars and moving dots of people below. She says,

"Everything looks so quiet from here. This might even be the highest I've been, except for when I was in an airplane. I've never been to the Empire State Building, the Freedom Tower, or the Chrysler Building. They're on my list though."

"This might be strange to ask, but do you know where I live?"

"What do you mean? No. Where do you live?"

"Sorry, I'm only asking because sometimes random people will ask me about it."

"Why, where is it?"

"If you look up over your right shoulder you'll see it."

Candy looks into the vertical grid of unblinded apartment windows. "Where, exactly?"

"Oh, I mean way up."

Candy sees the silver waves of the Gehry Building reach a height that would take about eight generations of spruce trees, standing roots-to-zenithal-leaf, to surpass. "Holy shit."

"That's the first time I've heard you curse, which I'm totally down with, meaning the not-cursing generality."

"You live there?!"

"Yep. That's the spot. I have the top floor. It's one of the highest places to live in the city. You're more than welcome to come check it out, but I know you have to get up on the early side, so maybe next time for our movie night."

Candy takes a sip of her Virgin Pole Position, which is just Red Bull, and it gives her a jolted buzz that builds off the previous, more experienced drinks. The idea of the words *home*, *early*, *church*, *family*, and *schedule* take the back seat in a car without one. "I've just decided, based on recent developments, that I don't have to go home quite yet. What do you say we check out your place. And I'm of the cleanliness-is-next-to-Godliness camp, so I hope you vacuumed."

"Funny. I did, actually." He puts his arm around her shoulders. "Question. What do you think about when you're kissing someone?"[54]

The limo takes them to the lobby of 8 Spruce Street where they're greeted by the security officers, followed by small talk and the introduction of Ms. Candice Blue Helena Lovinglace. In the elevator, Mr. Woodson buttons one button on his velvet blazer and Candy looks at her muted reflection on the brushed silver doors. They feel a queasy rush as the elevator begins its sudden ascent to the top floor.

"You know what I thought happened to your body in elevators?"

"What?"

"Well, you know the bit of dizziness you get at first? I thought that the upward force pressured all of your insides to go down and pack themselves tight into the lower half of your body. So I reasoned that your head must be temporarily empty and that's what made you not be able to think about anything except the dizzy-queasy thing. Makes sense, right?"

"Oh, sure, totally. So your brain goes into your throat?"

"Maybe even farther."

The elevator doors open. "Well, here we are. Home sweet."

"It's very clean and white! Wow!"

"Most people comment on the view, but yes, it's definitely neat and tidy."

"Should I take my shoes off?"

"You're welcome to do as you please. Keep on the heels or go barefoot, the choice is yours. This isn't a totalitarian space here."

"O.K..."

"O.K., let me explain my disdain for—wait, ex-*plain* my dis-*dain*—I'm feeling those drinks just a drip, and I'm rhyming. I'm going to make coffee. We'll be back to our regularly scheduled conversation in just a moment."

Candy watches the McJesus show in full effect as he talks about the benefits of coffee. She takes her shoes off and loses a few inches of false height. She isn't barefoot either, as he suggested she would be. Candy takes slidey steps toward the kitchen in her stockings, almost frictionless over the polished floor. "It's pretty late for caffeine."

"...Says the girl who just drank Red Bull. I don't want to get into all of this, because it becomes a bit of a rant, but I'll tell you why I get upset about the shoe issue. I prefer to keep my shoes on, but that's only due to a moisture level thing—I'm strange—but I hate, hate, hate dry skin. And I have no problem with people who want to take off their shoes the second they step inside. But when I go to someone else's apartment or house and they tell me that I *have* to take my shoes off, puffs of steam emit from both ears. Couldn't they inform me about their house rules on the invite or over the phone if it's such a big deal? And let's say I correctly assume that it's the type of place, or type of person, to require the stripping of specific clothes once inside. And let's say I prepare by bringing my own house slippers, wouldn't I be the weird one now? Or what if I said 'no.' Would they ask me to leave or would they just think that I'm strange for insisting on keeping myself clothed the way I intended? I'm going to have a New Year's Eve party, and when everyone gets here, I'm going to tell them that they have to roll up their shirts. I don't want midsections covered here. It's my apartment rule. Anyway, that's why I said this is a totalitarian-free space."

"I think it's more of a *shoes are dirty* thing, rather than mandatory stripping or forced discomfort."

"Candy, whose side are you on?" He pours some half-n-half into an empty mug, followed by hot coffee, which allows him to skip the stirring step. "And in a related rant, there's a subgroup of the shoe-removers who really tighten my tie. They are the dog owners. I went to a dinner party at a friend's house once, and they had me remove my shoes for the cleanliness thing, while at the same time they let their dogs sit on the couches like it's nothing. Let's be honest, dog's butts are there. They're right there. All exposed and pressing against all the surfaces in the home. So fine, fine. I'll take my shoes off, but they shouldn't be upset with me when I take a seat with the back of my pants pulled down. It's only fair."

"You actually did this?"

"No, but I should've."

Candy speaks through the stutters of laughter, "I'm sure they would've been completely fine with it. And what exactly is your point?"

"Our bottoms are more protected from the direct contact you get with a dog, so as far as cleanliness, they shouldn't have been able to say anything about it. But I would've been the weird one."

"You certainly would've."

"Do you think they make their dogs wear little booties when they take them out for walks? Their paws are smaller than our feet, but they have twice as many. Might be dirty."

"So, in light of this conversation, guess where you'll never be invited for dinner?"

"Why?"

"Because you'd make people actually run to the bathroom and roll up their shirts, all while you pull your pants down at the table."

"I see your point."

"Don't worry. I think it's funny."

Zeus tests the temperature of the coffee. It's still too hot. "Can I get you anything to drink? Or do you want a snack?"

"I'm thinking red wine. After my virgin moment before, I wouldn't mind returning to the land of adults."

"Of course. I have a nice Rioja in the wine cabinet. And not to belabor the point, but you did say you had to get up on the early side."

"I'm having a great time and I don't want to end it yet. Let's play it by ear. The world won't end if I have to rush around in the morning, and that's assuming you don't have anything to do in the morning either?"

"I also planned to go to church. I went by myself the other day and I want to go more often, but that's a different story altogether. I can go at any time tomorrow, so it's cool if you stay over. I can drive you back whenever you want to get up."

"Well, I didn't mean stay over officially. I meant maybe we can just stay up really late and take your limo back whenever. No pajamas required."

"No pajamas sounds like fun."

"Oh boy, nevermind," Candy says as both of their faces are in rosy bloom.

Zeus sips his coffee without flinching and tells Candy he'll open the bottle of Rioja and bring her a glass by the coffee table. She moves silently over to the white couch and is unexpectedly enveloped by its deep cushions. She smiles and adjusts herself to an upright position. On the coffee table Candy sees a white ceramic bowl with primary-colored lollipops in clear plastic and a stack of baseball cards next to a few sharpies. From the kitchen she hears drawers closing, metal-on-metal shuffling, and the uncorking of the wine bottle. The noises are abstractly percussive, she thinks. Candy reaches toward the bowl of lollipops and takes a heart-shaped red one. Upon closer inspection, of all things, the lolly has an impression of a vacuum. She pops the wrapper off the top and gives it a few licks before putting it in her mouth. She looks like she's kissing a very skinny cigarette. It tastes like plastic with a hint of tart cherry.

Candy hears a door close and then a bassline reverberate throughout the apartment. She stretches her legs out on the coffee table and feels the vibrations run up from her heels. She looks demure. She can't see him, but she notices a distinct new aura of just-sprayed cologne. When he joins her on the couch, he places the bottle down next to two wine glasses. His coffee is nowhere to be seen. His eyes run from her toes to her thighs, where the two nonpareil constellations intersect, trying his best to mask his visual fixation.

"Sorry it took a few minutes. How's the lollipop?"

"Not very good. Why is there a vacuum on it?" Candy sips her wine. It doesn't pair well with the lollipop, but she turns her sour reflex into a nod of approval. She raises her glass for a silent cheers. Zeus does the same. The second sip is full and fine, with an echo of oak and dark berries lasting much longer than the finish.

"I got them the other day when I bought a new vacuum at that place on the 10 on 10th. It's a Vacuum slash Gourmet Lollipop shop called [CLEAN PEOPLE SUCK]. When you buy a vacuum, they throw in some extra lollipops into the bag. I thought they might've thrown in some of the expensive joints, but it looks like they gave me the regular old cheapies."

"Actually, I think my friend gave me one of those not too long ago. It was a fancy P.B. and J. flavor. Something like Truffle Almond Butter and Rosebud Mint Jelly."

"Rosebud Mint Jelly, sounds good. Let's get one right now."

"Pretty sure they're closed."

"Well, this city is slipping. We need a twenty-four hour vacuum lollipop shop."

"I think everything on tenth is legit. I like the way they mix things that don't normally go together. Obviously there's [Wax & Rax] where we met, but if they wanted to open another lingerie store, they should totally match it up with a battery shop. The sizes are basically the same. Ever think about that?"

Zeus had never thought about it, but is now. With a burst of cognizance, he draws a Venn diagram in his head and organizes the findings.[55]

"I've already made it through several sizes." She takes another sip, which is closer to a gulp.

"Wait, which ones are you talking about?"

"Bad boy. What do you think?"

"I have no idea. I simply asked you if you were talking about positive and negative electrodes and their ability to create power, or..." Zeus takes another sip of Rioja in place of the remainder of the sentence.

She retaliates with a soft kick to his knee. Zeus counters by hitting her with a small couch pillow. All of this quickly leads to finger flicks and light slaps and eventually, Candy's legs draping over his.

"Since our conversation has just taken a turn toward the land of low lighting and closed doors, it made me think of something you said before, about the Rosebud Jelly."

"Mint."

"Right, but I meant more about the word *jelly* and the context it takes in Jazz music."

"You know you're playing hip hop, right?" Candy presses her calves down more firmly and flexes her toes, then switches her legs, left over right.

"Of course. Although I could argue that Jazz and Hip Hop have many things in common, like innovation through preexisting backdrops, improvisation due to cultural necessity, and that they're probably both forms of folk music, the music of the people. People with style."

"Well put." Candy sips her wine.

Zeus notices two upturned red tangents from her lips. He indicates where, "You have a little wine things right there."

"Why, thank you, sir."

"No problem."

"So, this jelly thing?"

"Right. There was this guy back in the early days of Jazz, early twentieth century, who said he invented it. It probably wasn't true, but a legend can last longer than a fact. I doubt Jazz was a singular event or discovery. Anyway, his name was Jelly Roll Morton and he played the piano. His real name was Ferdinand with a French-sounding last name, but the Jelly Roll part is interesting. When I first checked out Jazz albums—which, because of the artwork, I liked even before I listened to it—I thought it was a cute, old-time name. But fast forward several years, and I'm reading this book about the origins of Jazz, and how it used to be called the devil's music."

"I didn't know the devil played the piano."

"Apparently so." He notices Candy shifting her toes, the black tones of her tights stretching out to gray, then fading back to black. "But Jazz didn't sound satanic to me in any way."

"So what's the reason?"

"Well, there were a few, but it all goes back to where Jazz was born, which was in bars and brothels. If you were at one of those places late on a Saturday night, it would probably be tricky to wake up for church on Sunday, even though they probably should've. Not only was the music different, but it came from a different intention. The faster tempos got the hearts racing and the people dancing, but it was the slow tempos that gave them the space to really turn it on, to give it some curves. And when you dance like that, things are going to change."

Candy shifts and leans toward him. "That's better. Go on."

"They said that the saxophone sounds most like the human voice and that it was a way to express sexually what couldn't be said in public. Although, there were these Library of Congress Recordings of Jelly Roll where he reminisces and sings some of the dirtiest refrains that were popular at some of the bars and brothels. So dirty." He takes a sip of wine. "When

Jelly Roll played these joints, he'd position his piano against a wall that was next to the room where women would turn their tricks. There was a peep hole cut so he could watch the action play out. Then he'd play the piano at a tempo that would match the bodies pulsing up and down. You could say that the cadence of Jazz was born from the collective rhythms of sex. Devil's music."

"Damn."

"Damn straight. But probably all contemporary music is the devil's music to the previous generation. Some can't understand it and some don't want to. But that music will become their golden era, what they're nostalgic for. They'll hold on to that until... "

"...until a new devil is born."

"Exactly."

"Music reflects what society wants you to see and what it wants to hide, at the same time."

"You're great to talk to."

"Thanks." Candy sips her wine with a smile and it makes a slurping sound.

"So here's the thing about Jelly Roll's name. First of all, it had nothing to do with dessert, not in any way, and it wasn't meant to be a cute name. Most of the references seem to suggest that in New Orleans, where he was from, it was slang for a woman's private area just below the waist."

"I like how you said that carefully."

"I'm trying to be a gentleman."

"Sure."

Zeus tips an invisible cap. "But since you couldn't look that one up in the dictionary, it took on other meanings back in the day, depending on the context. But I'll skip to the most interesting one. It's the meaning that I'm going to keep as official." As he finishes his wine, Candy is ready with the bottle to return opacity to the glass. "A jelly roll is your most intimate fantasy, your darkest sexual desire. The thing you'd least like to advertise, that no one would guess, but makes you tick like a time bomb. Not a bad nickname, right?"

Candy doesn't answer right away. She takes her legs off his and tucks her heels underneath herself. Her knees go from black to faded charcoal. She leans over and then toward him, closer than before. Zeus follows the v-shaped path of the gold chain with his eyes, his imagination running feral. He feels her exhale warm the side of his neck. She says, "So tell me, what's your jelly roll?"

"This might be another I'll-tell-you-mine-if-you-tell-me-yours type thing."

"Oh really? After a few more sips of this old grape juice, maybe I'll tell you. But maybe not."

"Truth serum."

"Yeah, I remember how you are with that."

"I can wait. There's still a little more in the bottle."

"Top me off."

"Yes ma'am. And while I'm waiting for the truth serum to kick in, should I tell you another joke?"

"You know what? I think I'll just go for it. It'll probably be less embarrassing than another one of your two-hour jokes."

"O.K., O.K., you could've brought me down slowly. But if you want my confidence kicked to the curb, it's cool, I'll remember that."

Candy's legs have fallen asleep, so she untucks them and gives him a swift kick with her right foot, which gives her a prickly tingle that runs up her thigh. "Ever since I started working at Rip-Off, I've been exposed to people I never would've met, at least the way I grew up. And they've opened my eyes to some new things, like getting the tattoo I mentioned earlier. And..."

"Where is it, anyway?"

"Let's put that in a jelly roll sub-category for now." Zeus raises one eyebrow and makes a show of fake-looking over her body while rubbing his chin, which plays more silly than strange, but he still instantly regrets it. Candy continues, "Do you want to hear it or not?"

"Yes, please go on. I think the wine is starting to run through my vines."

"Vines?"

"Veins."

"The same, I suppose."

"It's amazing how I can continue to interrupt myself from the flow of what's important. Especially..."

"...I'm going to interrupt you interrupting yourself, because you may only get one chance to hear this."

McJesus zips his lips and throws away the key. Then he takes another sip of wine and puts on a thoughtful face. "I do take this seriously. It's an intimate thing."

"O.K., so my jelly roll..." Candy shifts her legs again. "I know what I like, but it's hard to hear myself say it out loud. Thoughts sound so much different in your head. They're more natural that way." Candy takes her biggest sip of the night, finishes her wine, and looks at the ceiling through curved glass. "It's that I like piercings and some pain in certain areas." She exhales. "That's it, the cat's out of the bag. I've never told anyone that before, so... I mean, obviously the tattoo artist and body piercer might have an idea because of the way I sounded when they were working on me, but you're the first to hear it from my lips. I mean, I didn't even tell my last boyfriend. I tried to in a way, but he didn't really get it. He was angry at the mention of it, actually." She put her head on his shoulder. "So there you go, that's my jelly roll."

"Very seductive," he nods slowly. "By the way, I see that your lips have some wine tangents again. It looks like your lipstick got smeared north."

"Oh yeah, why don't you take care of that this time?"

"Yeah?"

"I know I sound like a trashy novel character, but just kiss me."

Zeus and Candy kiss for two minutes straight with the intensity that is accompanied by deep nostril inhales and devouring looks. They drift to a more sensuous place of enjoyment and wandering hands. As they part, their eyelids are heavy. The wine tangents are gone and a lot of Candy's lipstick has been transferred to Zeus.

"What's yours?" Candy asks.

"I'll tell you, but can I hear a little bit more about yours first? Where are your piercings? I mean, I don't see any. You don't even have your ears done."

"That's for me to know and you to find out," Candy winks.

"I hope I have the chance." They start to play with each other's hands, exploring their knuckles and nail beds.

"I'll tell you where two of them are." Candy pulls her hands away from his and forms an external push-up bra on herself, then points to the exact piercing locations.

"Nice."

"I agree."

"What do they look like? The piercings, I mean." They smile again and their hands pick up where they left off. Zeus is tracing his index finger along each digit.

"My right nipple has a curved bar and my left has a straight bar. I didn't want to be too symmetrical."

"So, they turn you on?"

"What do you think?"

"Hot. What about the tattoo?"

"It's kind of spread out. It's based on the solar system and the night sky. I chose a piercing as my sun, which has a red jewel in the center, and the planets and stars go out from there. It's definitely minimalist. It wasn't so much about filling my body with ink, but experiencing the needlework in different parts of my body. And I still can't believe I'm openly telling you these things."

"I won't tell a soul."

"Like, right here..." Candy points to her hip, "...is Venus. And here..." Candy uses her right foot to point to her left calf, "...there's a small yellow circle there. That's Neptune." Candy turns her head and pulls her ear forward. "This little blue dot is Pluto." She moves her hand down from her ear to her side, "Orion is here and Leo is closer to the middle."

"That's wild, for real. Is the sun the piercing on your belly button?"

"No. Just a little south of that."

"You're killing me. That's definitely the hottest spot."

"Damn straight." Candy closes her eyes and smiles. "That's the wine talking. O.K., your turn."

"My turn?"

"Your turn."

"O.K., let me take one more sip." He lowers his voice. "I love to go down on a woman when I'm on my back. I like to hear her talk about what she wants to do next. I like feeling her grind on me, figuring out what turns her on, since she's the one in control, almost to the point where I can't breathe."

Candy bites her lower lip and releases it. "...And who's this woman you're talking about?"

"That's up to you."

"Yeah?"

"Have you thought about when you want to go home?"

"I've only been thinking about one thing." Candy brings her face right next to his. Her breath is warm against his lips. When she blinks, she lashes his face ever so softly. She speaks in whispers and he responds by kissing her and placing his hands around her back, arching her even closer. When he kisses her neck, she feels the short bristles on the back of his head brush against her face. Their body movements are smooth, peppered with torrents of intensity. Zeus moves his hands down her body to her leather shorts and then slips them under her top. With his right hand he tries to unhook her bra while his left hand caresses her skin near Saturn.

Candy helps him undo the last of the three clasps. She moves her arms through each of the straps and pulls her lacy support forward and out the bottom of her shirt. As Zeus feels their silky weight drop against his forearms, he sees a glimmer of light catch her gold necklace, the same one from the night they met. Candy's hands wander south and she feels his arousal. She begins to unbutton his pants, each one a notch closer to release. Her eyes stay fixed on his as she lowers her head, and holding the base of his erection, she teases him with her lips.

Candy places his hand on the top button of her leather shorts. Zeus unclenches the teeth of the zipper and watches her twist and writhe the shorts off her body, the absence of the restraints of her bra are now explicit. She crosses her arms like an X in front of her body, each hand grabbing the bottom of her top, and lifts her teal sweater over her head. Her hair falls against her skin. With his hand, Zeus collects it in a ponytail and pulls it behind her while he kisses her along the Hydra constellation, exploring her interstellar space.

Zeus tries to ease himself on top of her, but the unsupportive couch makes the move awkward, and the side of his face presses into Candy's armpit. He kisses his way out of the situation and dislodges his knee from the couch cushion chasm, and slides himself on top her. After a moment in a simulated missionary position, Zeus descends to his knees and feels the backs of hers drape over each shoulder. He moves his head much closer to the warmth beneath her stockings and is wordlessly content. He kisses her over her belly button and her inner thighs, getting ever closer to the sun. Candy finds a seam along the top of her stockings and tears them down the middle and slides the satin triangle of her lingerie to the side. She watches him scan her body from the top down. She leans over and he rises to meet her. They share kisses and quiet words, then he spreads her legs wider. After a few minutes of pleasurable moans, Candy pulls his head up and says, "Come with me." They stand up and finish undressing while keeping eye contact. She takes his hand and leads him into the bedroom, and guides him down on his back over the white bedspread. She mounts him and slides her breasts north and south along his body before pressing them against his face. She directs him to squeeze them together and make her piercings touch. He uses his tongue to flick the curved barbell while gently pinching the straight one. She whispers in his ear, "Harder, please." He applies more pressure, still careful not to go too far and possibly ruin the moment. But Candy pulls his head away and speaks louder, directly into his ear, "I thought I told you what I need. Harder, like this. Watch." Candy demonstrates what she wants him to do to her, how he can be the remedy to her whimpering moans. This time he pinches her much harder and sees her pure exaltation, her eyes in a series of long blinks. Then she presses her breasts tightly together with her arms, "I want you to spank them too—both of my nipples at the same time. Make them kiss." With one hand he forces her nipples together, and with the other and without holding back, he repeatedly slaps them while she touches herself. Candy throws her head back with satisfaction; she's never experienced her private desires with someone else. Zeus feels her dripping wet over his chest. He's turned on beyond all known levels of luminosity. "Now, just one at a time." Candy holds up one of her breasts with both hands and uses her teeth as a clamp on her nipple. She lets the other one hang down without any constraints, "One for each of us." She looks into his eyes and waits for him to begin. "Let's see who can do a better job. I'll tell you if it hurts too much—or maybe I won't."

After Candy enjoyed several minutes of her lustful sensations of pleasure and pain, she brings her hips up higher, rises up to her knees, and straddles his face. He sees the flicker of the silver piercings and gold chain above him, the low lighting in his bedroom coming solely from the windows of skyscrapers, the collective urban glow.

"Your turn," she whispers. Her toes are cool and they send chilling waves up his sides. The taste of Candy furthered his intoxication of her and the entire night. She brushes over the crown of his head with her hands, leans closer to him and says, "Is this what you want?" He responds with his tongue even though he isn't in a position to say anything. He pleases her until she loses control of her hips and convulses with varying contortions. Candy arches her back and feels the rush of a rapturous release. And somewhere in the Los Angeles Calvary Cemetery, the bones of old Jelly are rolling over with dark delight.

She falls over him and her strawberry blonde hair makes a private tent around both of their faces. They thank each other and share soft words and kisses. Zeus parts her hair and tucks it over her ears. With a few locks still brushing against his forehead he asks, "What do you want to do now? Do you think we should wait?"

"No. I want you inside me right now." She slides down his body until she feels him solid and thick against her.

"Is this how you want it?"

Candy answers by rising over him and working her hips down until he enters her. He's captivated by her body and listens to the sounds of a beautiful struggle. "Just let me know when you're going to cum."

Zeus directs her rhythm, "That won't be for awhile." They find an easy tempo at first, adagio maybe, before their bodies agree upon a jazzed up allegro. Candy is leaning back and gripping his thighs while her breasts are swinging and bouncing to the backbeat. She is his sublime opiate.

In the other room by the coffee table, Candy's phone vibrates repeatedly along the wood floor until it crawls its way under the couch.

After the last few accented thrusts in that position, Candy leans flush against him with blushed red cheeks, and her gold necklace swings forward and hits one of his front teeth. The treble of its tremor resonates locally and disrupts the pendulum effect. Then she arches forward and presses her body against his. Their shared perspiration enhances their carnal awareness. She rolls over to the other side of the bed, waiting for him on her back. "Over here."

McJesus, already in her heart, enters her body once again. What starts with beads of sweat falling from his forehead to her chest, transitions into a syrupy rhythm of sensitivity. Long kisses and caresses continue until their bodies move into a new position. He turns Candy sideways and holds her hips down with one hand and her ankles up the other. She squeezes her nipples and watches his torso pound against her until he has a sudden leg cramp and has to switch back to the simple position of the missionary. They face each other and the rhythm increases as they work toward a mutual feeling of blinding euphoria. When Zeus is going his hardest, Candy tries to control her breasts, holding them together, the crucifix charm hidden deep in the valley. She watches the shifting shadows across his body, highlighted in the muted neon of the Manhattan radiance. He slows down only to kiss her and tell her it's time for her to let go, that he's going to hold her down and fuck her until he feels the surges of her orgasm. Not long after, Candy releases in waves, moaning the name of a higher power. She grabs his forearms, her mind focusing on the synapses of emotional connectivity. Zeus is approaching the point of no return. When he pulls out, Candy leans forward, bites her lip, and waits impatiently. She watches his muscles pump and twitch before he covers the expanse of her galaxy with milky eroticism.

After several exhilarated sighs, Candy pushes her breasts up toward her face and licks and sucks her piercings clean, as he watches without blinking once.

Zeus says, "I just want to hold you."

"I just want to be held by you."

He pulls the bedspread down and Candy curls up against him under the covers. He puts his arms around her and kisses her with care. He rolls his head to the right, holding her closer as he yawns. She shifts her position to rest her head on his chest, and feels it rise and fall with each breath. Candy gives him an unconscious kiss, and with her eyes closed, faces the same direction.

Within moments, the pair falls deeply asleep as one, unaware of anything else in this world. The landline phone in the kitchen, which Zeus may have used only once before, is ringing nonstop. The rings are both the sirens of frustration and the frantic prayers of Joyce Lovinglace, and they are falling upon deaf left ears.

[[✠]]

On the street below, Brother Samson and Secretary Jonah sit in the D.O.C.-owned car, which is all-black everything. It's well-equipped with digital capabilities usually reserved for the F.B.I. and has a weapons cache that would embarrass the N.Y.P.D. The cars in their fleet are designed for stealth, without any definable style, so much so that they have become easily recognizable by the fans of The D.O.C. The pair looks up and out of the tinted moonroof. Their eyes follow the twisted metal tower all the way up to a window on the top floor.

The tires of their car are a few feet into the No Parking section behind them, as they'd parked hastily and without regard for the sign. Samson's scalp is tensing up, as if his hair is being pulled out one strand at a time, and he's powerless to stop it. He hears a voice in his head, but he denies its existence. At the same time, Samson is angered by Chairman Ezra's decision to relent and his face reddens with enraged capillary action. Jonah is googling the phrase [McJesus funny] on his phone. He's trying not to let Samson see the screen, but not so much that it seems like he's trying to hide it either. He sees one image with a photoshopped McJesus standing on the shore of the sea of Galilee calling out to some men on a boat. They're holding out a very large net with only one piece of fried fish. Above them in the blue sky is a white bird in flight. McJesus is holding out a paper bag that's overflowing with tartar sauce. The bag has the golden arches and the slogan *i'm dovin' it*. He calls out to them and says, "*Follow me and I will make you Filet-O-Fishers of men.*"

"What are you looking at?" Samson demands.

"Nothing."

Samson grabs Jonah's thin arm, his hand wrapping around his bicep. "Don't lie to me." He intensifies his constriction and digs in his nails, which are longer than they should be, and they break the skin in five places. Samson feels Jonah's pulse increase while his own steadies at 45 beats per minute. With his other arm, Samson removes his sunglasses and reveals all of the scars of the failed surgeries. Jonah, now further terrified, doesn't attempt to pull away.

The thing with the sunglasses comes from the founder of The Defenders of Christ, who was raised in an Eastern Orthodox home before later becoming the staunchest of promoters for the Holy See. While the organization was intended to act on Vatican City's behalf under all radars, he maintained a central teaching from his youth, that of the Christ Pantocrator. The founder felt strongly about the dichotomy of forgiveness and love on one side, and severe judgement on the other. His own face was gruesome and asymmetrical, so when he looked in the mirror, Christ Pantocrator stared back with affirmation and approval. He decreed that members of The D.O.C. must undergo a special kind of plastic surgery, as both a sign of commitment, and as a symbol that they understand their responsibilities as the men on the front lines in the war against Satan, in all the forms that he takes. All of these changes were to take place in the eyes of the beholders of The Cross. Also, he required the surgery for reasons of remote procreation by way of a false genetic likeness. It was the only way he could fulfill God's blessing, to be fruitful and multiply. That was a reason he kept to himself.

The fans of The D.O.C., like the Catholic school girl swooners and the closeted full-mooners, let their imaginations run to the delta of wishful thinking, and assume that all the bearded men have the keenest of river-blue eyes. But the truth is, behind those mirrored sunglasses, all the current operatives in The D.O.C. have one blood-filled eye and another of their natural color—except one.

Depending on the subject's eye type from birth, one of two surgical processes are available. For someone with round, peaceful eyes, the surgeon will permanently tighten the muscles surrounding the targeted eye and alter the lid to create the eye of judgement and mystical terror. For the more seriously-browed, the process involves the loosening of the facial muscles on one side combined with a cocktail of botox treatments to create the eye of compassion. The D.O.C.'s chief surgeon explained to the founder that the life-long bloody eye was a symptom of the jackhammer-like work on a very sensitive area. The founder saw this as yet another sign of a glorified personal sacrifice. There'd never been an issue with any of the prior surgeries—no unexpected malformations, infections, or vision loss—until Brother Samson X.

The X after his name isn't a nod to the American Malcolm, but for literal reasons of '...*the last shall be first.*' It's a full bow to the Grecian Christ. In Greek, Christ begins with the letter *Chi*, or *X*, in English—and so the parable became the actual for Samson.

When the surgeon met Samson, he remarked that his particular scowl of judgement was a special blessing, animalistic and rare. But in keeping with the doctrine of The D.O.C.'s founder, the surgery would be performed to his left eye. After the incisions and stretching of fibers, his eye was left bloodied and relaxed to solemnity, and was to heal under cloth bandages. When Samson returned weeks later, the doctor removed the dressings only to find that the muscles around the eye had healed and returned to their original scowl, again matching its counterpart. To his amazement, he reported his results with the founder, who responded with the commandment: "Adjust his right eye, then." So again, the doctor proceeded, repeating the surgery. Samson left as a mirror image of the first attempt, bloody-eyed and cloth-wrapped.

Again he returned weeks later for the assessment. To less amazement this time, the eye surgeon saw that his work had accomplished nothing, except to turn both scleras and irises permanently crimson. When he reported the latest results to the founder, the response was, "Well, keep performing the surgeries until they take hold. Let me know when you get the results we require for membership." So again and again and seven times again, the doctor un-tensed the facial muscles around each eye and applied every technique he could, the only result being the intensification of the blood-red color surrounding his pupils. The surgeries ceased when the founder was found dead under mysterious circumstances. With the unexpected passing, the power structure of The D.O.C. fell to regional leadership, which eased the clenching grip of musculature alterations over Samson. The regional leadership admitted him as a full member and operative, and considered his solidified expression of contempt a badge of Old Testament honor. The creases that developed during the multiple surgeries gave Samson the mask of someone twice his age—and from brow to opposite cheekbone and back again—the deep surgical scars formed the letter X, a testimonial tribute across his face.

So when Samson takes off his glasses while compressing the veins within Jonah's arm into one collective artery, the sight of two blood-ridden eyes staring through his mirrored sunglasses chills him to the core.

BUD BLACK SABBATH

Cyrus Coaster walks with his hands tucked in his jacket pockets as the morning cool sweeps through his hair. It's early. So early that the sun is just an aura over the horizon and the street lights are still on. The sky is the kind of blue that says go back to bed. He hears a stray horn, probably from a taxi. He sees a woman with a limp on the opposite sidewalk pushing a cart with three wheels. Her shadow is moving in half-circle arcs as she passes each lamppost. A bluejay's mating call ripples through the morning from a nearby alcove. With the sounds of loose sand over cement, his steps crackle as he nears the door. He exhales into the sky and looks for evidence of his breath, but it isn't cold enough. He reaches his right hand into his jacket pocket and pulls out a set of keys. There's a dull jangling until he finds the one marked MISSION. He hears a man down the block call out to an unseen friend, "Hey Man! How you this morning?! Little chilly right?" When the reverb ceases, he feels the tremors of the city underground rise up through his legs. He turns the key and pushes open the large church door and steps inside. He bleeps in a long code on the digital panel and little red lights throughout the vestibule turn green, and then off. The only light inside enters through the stained glass windows; it is faint and nebulous. He cups his hands around his mouth and blows warm air into them. Then he flicks up seven switches, one at a time down the line, and the stained glass fades back into the dark walls. Cyrus Coaster looks down and sees the collection of backpacks and a sealed envelope, which had been delivered just hours earlier. The light is purely internal now.

· M O V E A B L E   T Y P E ·

·

ARTIST
· EVER SUM ZΣRO ·

NINETY - NINE BOOKS
BOOKMARKED FOR ALPHABETIC DISPLAY

·

TERMS

CONTACT ONLY THROUGH AXLIA CLIA
ALL FOR SALE AT YOUR BEHEST
CASH PAYMENTS ONLY
REMAINING PIECES WILL BE RETRIEVED
BY CURRIER AFTER SHOW

BIOGRAPHY
PRINTER'S DEVIL, THESPIAN,
& FREELANCE GLADIATRIX

THANK YOU
I WILL ATTEND ONLY AS A VISITOR FOR REASONS
LEGAL AND OTHERWISE

·

SEE ATTACHMENT FOR LIST OF WORKS

·MOVEABLE TYPE·

Altered States: A Novel
Paddy Chayefsky

Answer to Job
C.G. Jung (Translated by R.F.C. Hull)

The Bartender's Guide to Shaking the Sugar
Jessica Jolly-Palas

The Baseball Encyclopedia:
The Complete and Official Record of Major League Baseball
C. Sully Publishing

Beets & Rhymes: [Poetic Veggie Recipes for Youngsters]
Ida Illiszt

Beneath The Underdog: His Words as Composed by Mingus
Charles Mingus

Bo Jackson: Playing the Games
Scholastic Biography by Ellen Emerson White

Boardroom Power: Joseph Says Speaking in the Third Person
Commands Respect
Joseph Nickelnurser

Cedar Beach Punks & Pirate's Cove Burnouts
Jocko Fields

the ceiling fan slows; the lights dim
S. Shipp-Solomon

The City of Angles: Fighting Crime in L.A. with Euclidean Geometry
Det. Lionel Dash

Crown Him With Many Crowns:
The Iconographiti of Jean-Michel Basquiat
Stillwell A. Maximilian-Ory

Cults: The Infancies of All Religions
Jasper Pastiche

Dondi White: Style Master General:
The Life of Graffiti Artist Dondi White
Andrew "ZEPHYR" Witten & Michael White

Dictionary of American Slang
Harold Wentworth, Ph.D and Stuart Berg Flexner, M.A.

The Education of T.C. MITS
Words by Lillian R. Lieber & Drawings by Hugh Gray Lieber

Enchanted Cigarettes [Or Stevenson Stories That Might Have Been]
Stephen Chalmers

Endless Sexual Positions for Survivalists:
Spice Up the Coming Apocalypse
Chanelle Bellringer

Erasers: A Complete Histor
Jonatha Mot

Everyday Dust Removal in N.Y.C.: Unforgettable Jazz Performances
at Blue Note, Minton's Playhouse, and St. Nick's Pub
Grayson Pocketta

Executive Influence: The Presidents of The United States of Earth
Harold Najjar

The Existential Importance of Being Mintified
David Trachtenberg

The God of Ecstasy: Sex Roles and the Madness of Dionysus
Arthur Evans

A Great and Shining Road:
The Epic Story of the Transcontinental Railroad
John Hoyt Williams

Guns N' Moses: Christian Metal Origins Revealed
Viola Slacks

Hand Me The Wrench [Vintage Chevrolet Repair Manual]
Norman C. Counter

Harold Lloyd's Hollywood Nudes in 3D
Suzanne Lloyd

He'll: The Fractured Damnation of a Foot-Worshiping Neophyte
D.D. LePied

Hiking Death Valley: A Guide to Its Natural Wonders and Mining Past
Michael Digonnet

Hit Me! Confessions of a Masochistic Blackjack Champion
Jean Puff

Holy Bible: New Scofield Reference Edition, King James Version
Edited by C.I. Scofield, D.D., Oxford University Press

How to Hug in Japan
Tim Needles

The I of the Storm: The Winds of Change are Blown From Within
Sapphira Dreambox

is 5
E.E. Cummings

I.J.
D.F.W.

igPay tinLAay: teringMASay ressivePROGay ageLANGUay
tiouslyEXPEDIay &ay ntlyCONVENIEay
Nenê Monet

Inferno
Dante Alighieri

Iron Man: A Super Guide to Wrinkle-Free Clothing
Taki Pennysnap

The Little Squirts Who Squat:
Real Accounts of Modern-Day Garbage Pail Kids
Franklin Pierced

Lou Gehrig: A Quiet Hero
Frank Graham

The Lyin', The Switch and The Wardrobe Malfunction
Nitsuj Timberpond & Netaj Jackdaughter

The Man Who Loved Only Numbers:
The Story of Paul Erdös and the Search for Mathematical Truth
Paul Hoffman

Mannahatta: A Natural History of New York City
Eric W. Sanderson

The Maul of America: Consumerism Attacks!
Sir Kieran Drizzlepuss

Mel Ott: A Crossword Giant
Swill Horts

Mr. Mint'$ Insider's Guide to
Investing in Baseball Cards and Collectibles
Alan Rosen with Doug Carr

My First Math Book
Tirza Lipsplitter

No Rest For the Wickets:
How Buster Bopfiend Became U.S.A.'s #1 Croquet Player
As Told To K.B. Childe

New York is a Friendly Town
Misty Applebottom

New Oxford English Dictionary, Third Edition
Edited by Angus Stevenson and Christine A. Lindberg,
Oxford University Press

The Next Neon: How to Imagine and Describe New Colors
Remy Church

One Year in the Night of the Life of a Supposed Lucid Dreamer
Juju Jongleur

The Oval Orifice: Sex at Sixteen Hundred
Tricky D'Or

Overbite! Food Addictions and Class II Occlusions
Dr. Dolphy Sidewinder

Pigeons:
The Fascinating Saga of the World's Most Revered and Reviled Bird
Andrew D. Blechman

The Plague of Fantasies
Slavoj Žižek

Poetry From A True Gemini Rebel
Michael McCarthy

Psychology of Mind Control
William L. Hoover, Ph.D.

Pubic Enemy: [Cautionary Tales of a Bum-Rushing Hip Hop Groupie]
Tizzy Skyebumps

Puff, Puff, PASS! [Effective Study Habits to Get Higher Grades]
Lynn Michele

Ready, Aim, Conspire! [Right Wing Tactics Explained]
Tommy Galman

A Reasonable Approach to Fiscal Responsibility in Local Governments
[A Random Intelligence Creation, IBM Publishing]
Watson Monkey SECTOR:G39/AB58 ICSHDRN: RH2B3B101630

QRK:271431
PLNCK:1211276
#162677117238532311130572533535352DM1364757612327527932850772114125
DS561215104943684340093202BB35231114141129915386358103850H

Rhythm Splinters at The Drake, MCMLXXVIII
TYRUS

Rural Sprawl: Going Way Green
Pussyfoot Jalopy

Sage Against The Machine:
[Christ's Disruption of the Roman Government]
Harlotte Glitterbounce

Scum and Villainy: A Guide to the Underworld
Corran G'Don

Sear ching For Cont inuit y : Living With Perpetual Hiccups
Hillary Celery

Showers of Gold: [Letting God's Prosperity Rain Down Upon You]
Paige LePlage

Slipping on Bananas and Landing on a Pile of Money:
Funny and Effective Insurance Scams
Olmstead Frye

States Altered: The Redistricting of the America
Russ L. Moore-Ann

Subtitles: The Subtlety of Reassurance and Clarity
Yosef Yaphankle

The Sun Also Rises
Ernest Hemingway

Swaghili: [Teach Yourself Books]
K. West

Swahili: [Teach Yourself Books]
D.V. Perrott

Symbolic Usage of Ca ^ ets & Ampersands
Delancey Notel

, then eyes twinkle / three times crystal
O.E. Spike

There's a Chicago Fire in My Pants and
All I Want You to do is Fan the Flames
M.M. Charmeuse

The Tijuana Bible
Velvet Vamp & Tittyboo Yumsplasher, with Ryder Hypestick

To Turn You On: [39 Sex Fantasies for Women]
J. Aphrodite

Tonight at Noon: A Love Story
Sue Graham Mingus

Triangle Always Wins: They Might Be Giant Catholics
Adam Andrewski

Turn the Other Other Cheek!: [True Tales of a Christian Sadist]
Madame Ruby Jinx

Uncle Phillies Barbershop: The Good Old Days of Shape-Ups and Fades
Smitty Madrid & Smokey Court

Webster's American English Dictionary
Created in Cooperation with the Editors of Merriam-Webster

Wolverine #4 (1982), A Marvel Comics Limited Series
Writer: Chris Claremont
Penciler and Cover Art: Frank Miller

Virtuoso Hustler:
Slingin' Eight Balls On the Corner & In the Corner Pocket
Taylor Rollo

Wednesday Night _____ Meeting
Louis L. Lasser IV

Who Does She Think She Is?
Rosalyn Drexler

The Wing of a Dove: The Left Cannot Fly Alone
Bushy Rimlaw

Wisdom of the Mystic Masters
Joseph J. Weed

X-Rated: Adult Movie Posters of the 60s and 70s
Tony Nourmand and Graham Marsh

You Again?!: Eternal Life with 72 Virgins
Wilton Drupe

Young Green Thumbs: Turning Kindergarteners into Kinder Gardeners
P.Z. Meegley

.)(.
K.Leigh Meow

1Q84
Haruki Murakami

1984
George Orwell

4-Sewer Hitter: [The Stickball Legend of Scooter Steele]
Juan-Pablo "Boom-Boom" Ramón

722 Miles: The Building of the Subways & How They Transformed
New York
Clifton Hood

99 Ways to Say Rationalization: [A Guide to Too Fast Cars, Million
Dollar Homes, Mowing and Maintaining Vast Acreage, Trophy
Spouses, Luxury Platinumware, Francium Earrings, Thread Counts
into the Thousands, Rare and Exotic Lightbulbs, Personnel Assistance
for your Personal Assistants, & Other Fun Ideas to Enhance Your Own
Personal Heaven]
Yuno Hoo

[[❋]]

After waking up and feeling the effects of the colossal head throbbing and self-whispers of *never again*, he tries to recall the previous night. It comes in collage form. The history of calls and texts from his phone is the best way to reconstruct the events into something cohesive. Then it's on to the urgent hunt for coffee and two aspirin for his reemergence into lucidity. He wonders why his body woke him up so early.

It's in times like these he wishes he had someone to take care of him, someone to talk to, parents even. Almost without a conscious decision, he takes the long subway ride from Manhattan to Rockaway Beach. It's the first place he remembers seeing a jet airplane. He just doesn't remember who he was with. The hunt for coffee is less urgent than he'd thought.

As the subway winds through the underground, he watches the unpainted tunnels go by as missed opportunities. And he sometimes thinks of what else could have been. He's jealous of Ellison and Bolden when one of them tells him that they have to buy a gift for their mother's birthday or if they're meeting up with their dad for a beer after work, although the idea of alcohol isn't sitting well right now. But he's gotten along without parents this far. He knows they're a luxury even the rich can't afford.

He leaves the subway and walks as far south as he can. With a paper cup filled with coffee, he looks up to an empty sky. Then, overlooking the Atlantic Ocean for awhile, Roosevelt wanders, writes, and philosophizes before returning to the crowded isle of Manhattan.

Roosevelt is a few blocks away as he strides toward the 10 on 10th with Rambo straps of markers and mini spray cans across his chest under his black jacket. As the rays from the top arc of the sun are emerging, Roosevelt sees himself in the foreground fifteen feet tall, his shadow long over the sidewalk. There's a glass alcove protruding from a building under renovation. He sees a milk crate under the scaffolding next to him and kicks the toe of his boot into the space for the handle, flicks it up, and catches it with his left hand. With his dominant hand he draws a marker from his ammo belt. He ducks into the alcove undetected, that is, except for a man who's made himself into a ball in the corner. The man has draped several coats over himself. The nights are still cold in April. Roosevelt is quiet and the man remains motionless with closed eyes. The sun is just high enough to be seen from inside the alcove. Using the burning glow as a temporary background, he writes his poem inside, squaring the circle with a black diamond.

```
                              *
                            FEET
                      FIRMLY IN THE
                 SAND, ALONE I STAND. THE
              BREEZE OFF ROCKAWAY BEACH
           TURNS BOLD WIND, PAGES THRASHING
         SIDE TO SIDE, CLOTHES WRINKLED LIKE
       THE OLD WAVES, SQUINTING OUT AT DAWN OVER
      THIS GOLIATH. A THROWN AND SKIPPED STONE
    LEAVES QUICK FOOTSTEPS, SUBSIDING WITHOUT NOTICE,
   STRENGTH IS RESTORED. FEET FIRMLY IN THE SAND, ALONE I
  STAND. // SHIVERING JUST FINE IN THE COLD, TOGETHER WE HOLD.
   THE BREEZE OFF ROCKAWAY BEACH TURNS BOLD WIND, PAGES
     THRASHING SIDE TO SIDE, CLOTHES WRINKLED LIKE
        THE OLD WAVES, SQUINTING OUT AT DUSK OVER
           THIS GOLIATH. A THROWN AND SKIPPED
             STONE LEAVES QUICK FOOTSTEPS,
               SUBSIDING WITH SOME NOTICE,
                 STRENGTH IS RESTORED.
                   SHIVERING JUST FINE
                     IN THE COLD,
                       TOGETHER
                       WE HOLD.
                          *
```

The marker squeaks as he finishes the last star and he hears the thlump of three winter coats. The man speaks with a grumbly voice. "I believe you just vandalized the sun, my man."

"I think you're right," Roosevelt answers from atop the milk crate. "Do you think it will last?"

"No. It's transient. Just like you and me."

Axlia prefers to sit in the first seat of the first car of the subway, which is easy to do on early weekend mornings. There are three others in the car with her and all four of them are going to different churches. It's the first time she's been on a Sunday morning train to go to church in a long time. Axlia looks at her reflection in the scratched plasticky glass of the front window and then switches her focus to the headlights illuminating the steel path of the subway rails. She listens to the soundtrack of the N.Y.C. subway system, the rhythm of the tracks, the falsetto screeches around the turns, the techno tones of the doors, and the spoken word of muffled static voices. When the lights cut out and flicker on the express train, it makes the local stops appear as passing space stations. Axlia pulls a lock of hair over her ear. Her hand continues to the back of her neck where her index finger traces her black diamond tattoo before giving herself a short impromptu massage. She switches her focus back to the glass to see the reflected passengers behind her. They're looking forty-five degrees toward the floor, avoiding what would be straight-on eye contact, which is both creepy and awkward for strangers. Sometimes Axlia sees a chin tilt upward to read the glowing advertisements for improved skin[56], and then return to the area under the seats. An overweight woman rises with some effort while holding on to the silver pole. Her stop is next. Axlia notices that she's wearing a large cross around her neck. It's encrusted with oversized red and blue jewels, the telltale harbingers of a home-shopping-channel purchase.

Wherever her church is, she's up early in pursuit of the purpose from above. Axlia gets the feeling the woman is well-intentioned, kind, and probably has had a trying life. The pew can be a welcomed refuge. At the next stop, a middle-aged woman waits until the last possible second to rise and slip through the doors. Her modest shoes are probably more expensive than they look. Her coat is of high quality, but without personality. Her lips are pursed closed and her cross is small and rests outside her turtleneck, but it's pure gold. She's reminiscent of her mother, which causes Axlia to dip into a melancholy state. When she refocuses forward through the scratched window, she pays particular attention to the blurred graffiti flashing by on either side of the tunnel, like scattered rainbows darkened by laws. They are the works of the artists who live beyond by delving below.

The third woman, on the younger side, maybe isn't going to church after all. She walks over toward Axlia and leans over with her jacket unzipped, her plunging neckline revealing that she's wearing a bra with doily qualities and a frontal closure. She's wearing two necklaces. Axlia remains still, except for her eyes, as the woman gets as close as possible without knowing someone's name first. This low leaner is reading the subway map to reassure herself that she's getting off at the right stop. By her perfume of alcohol and human grime, she's not heading out, but *home*, Axlia realizes. She sees that her cross, against a background of soft sexuality, is a crucifix, and is fastened to the chain in a different way than most. Usually the chain goes through a small welded circle at the top of the vertical part of the cross, but the low leaner's cross is welded on either side of the horizontal bar. As her body vibrates in sync with the subway car's movements, her chain tightens, and the little Son of Man is performing perpetual somersaults. Her other chain becomes entangled with the crucifix and sends the Body of Christ into a sudden reverse of gainers. The necklace that isn't the crucifix is actually a nameplate in gold bubbly script. So following the unintended intimacy of the leaner, Axlia ends up knowing her name after all.

Considering the three necklaces, the track in her mind reverses to a day in Indiana, a long time ago. It had started out as a typical Sunday with the Crème family getting ready to go to church. Della was at the age when she was verbal and quite literal with her interpretations of the world. She'd been wiggling a baby tooth back-and-forth that was hanging on by its last gummy thread. It was an age that she reached before anyone else around her—an age of wisdom and abandon. She was about six. She was wearing a floral dress, had her hair in a braided ponytail, and wore a small cross. It was a necklace handed down to her by her grandmother. It was too long for her, but she enjoyed wearing it. This particular morning it kept getting caught up in the soft wispy hairs on the back of her neck, and was hanging unseen and askew under her dress.

"Are you ready?"

"Yes Mommy, I just have to put on my shoes."

"Where is your cross, Della dearest?"

"I have it on, it just keeps getting caught here, see? On my n—."

"Why would you say something like that?! That's a terrible thing to say!"

"I'm sorry Mommy, but that's the truth. It keeps getting stuck there."

"Well take it out of your dress and hang it down in front!"

"O.K., but it..."

"So help me God if you say that word this morning! Don't you know you shouldn't speak about your private areas like that! It's not respectful to God!"

"But it's a part of me, like my ear or my knee. I thought that if God created it, it can't be bad. And you taught me that word, remember Mommy?"

"Stop it! Stop arguing with me this very minute and stop speaking! Don't you love me?! Don't you love... I'm going to get your father. What is the matter with you?!"

"Mommy, I..."

"Don't say another word!"

Her father stepped in, "Della dear, why are you arguing with your mother. Remember, you are to honor her. If she asks you not to say something, she's telling you how to be a better person. She loves you and cares for you. She wants the best for you, Della. And I want the best for you. And of course, God, Jesus, and the Holy Spirit love you and want you to be the best *you* you can be. There are going to be little bumps along the road, but if you listen to God and do what we as your parents advise, the road will smooth out over time. You will be following in the steps of Jesus who already blazed the trail. You know, He was a kid too. He probably had all sorts of questions and little quarrels with Joseph and Mary. Maybe He wanted to stay up late and watch the night sky above Him? Or maybe He wanted to pray longer? I bet you, Della, that He had a loose tooth just like yours and that He wiggled it front and back and wondered when it would fall out. So today, why don't you think about that on your way to church, and then listen to the sermon, and enjoy reading your Bible."

Della nodded.

"Thank you, Della dear. I know you love your God with all your heart."

"I know what you mean Daddy, but I think it's that I love Him with my brain. That's the part of my body that lets me think and understand. And I learned from you and Mommy that my heart is an organ that pumps blood all through my body. I love God with all my brain."

"You see? I told her not to speak!"

"Honey, it's O.K." He placed his warm hand over his wife's shoulder. "Oh Della, I believe God made you in a very special and unique way. You are blessed with the ability to surprise me every day. And I promise, your heart does much more than that. The scientific diagrams don't show everything the heart is capable of. What do you say, let's get a move on it."

Della walked into the bathroom and stood before the mirror. She put her hands over her heart, as if to feel for something more. Then she watched her tongue move her little tooth front and back, and then a little to the side. She dislodged the tooth and wiped it off with her fingers. She gave it the once over, letting her fingernail run over the tiny ridges, and smiled at herself with one missing pearl. Della tucked the tooth into the ankle of her sock and tasted her blood in silence.

As she grew up in the Crème household, Della was encouraged to study her Bible. Her parents gave her one called *The Student Bible* that provided introductions to each book, which included the main ideas, the historical context, and short biographies of the authors. She often read it at night before saying her prayers. Her parents insisted that The Bible be her foundation, and that it was the one truth you could hang your hat on. She knew Him as a rock-hard fact, far beyond a mere belief. At home, she reveled in learning about God's creations. She respected the complexity of the workings of the human body and the synergy of the relationships within the animal kingdom. She admired both the very large and very small, the everywhere quality of God.

So when she pondered how and where God lived in her heart, as her parents always told her, she reasoned that it must be a very small, unseeable place. God wouldn't want to take up too much room anatomically. Everything already had a purpose. She concluded that He must be microscopic, the size of an atom. It was the only way He could find space in her heart.

Often, Della thought of the time she wore her grandmother's cross to church. It made her more aware of the role that jewelry plays in religion. And the more she read her Bible at night, a looming contradiction become unavoidable. It was clear to her that Jesus rejected worldly possessions, gold, and public displays of religious affection. And near the jump off of the whole thing, even God denounced graven images with the third commandment. But back on that Sunday morning, she was encouraged by her family to wear exactly that in honor of a temporary death for all eyes to see. And that was immediately followed by being chastised for saying something that was physically factual. It seemed to Della that traditions trump dogma, or rather, that shiny objects trump doctrine. She knew it didn't matter what was done, only what was intended, and that it was consistent with the tribe. And as the cracks formed in the foundation of her religion, quaked by logic and language, the hat that was hanging on the truth, fell to the floor.

Still underground, @aceedeecee1000 hits up Twitter despite being in a dead zone in the tunnel. Her messages will take to the air as soon as she walks through the turnstile.

1 [Taking over Mission Gallery tomorrow at sundown: New&Retrospective, Live Graf&Poetry, Altered Books, Holographic Nudity, etc. -Axlia #Phases]

2 [Be seen in #Phases—send me a close-up picture of your cross/crucifix. I'll pick 10 for a pop-up exhibit in the show. #MissionCrosses]

The breaks begin to shriek and the reverse force brings Axlia's face right up to the window. As the train comes to a full stop, she looks straight down the tunnel and watches the light approach its vanishing point where it's too weak to continue. It's her stop. Now it's...

a time to create and a time to incite,

a time for caffeination and a time for croissants.

[[※]]

Roosevelt takes a seat alone at a table near the middle of the café, his back to the storefront window. A waitress with booty-booty-booty-booty-rockin'-everywhere shorts and an electric-blue garter belt walks his way to take his order. There's a [Bump & Grind] button on her hip that's promoting their recent coffee addition: Brand New, try Bitches Brew. She most likely has a torso and a head and styled hair, but Roosevelt's gaze hasn't reached those heights. The hips and legs ask him how he wants his coffee. "Creamy." As she walks away he sees a stray dollar bill flapping in the hip strap, a Washington with wings. She must be in crossover mode, he thinks. She brings him his coffee and pours in some cream, and he watches the white spirals darken and wander to the edges. In the mug is a small silver stirrer. It's the mini stripper pole usually reserved for the nighttime cocktails.

She kneels down and looks at him over the surface of the table and raises her eyebrows, "Is there anything else I can do for you?"

His suspicions are confirmed; she has a face after all. He knows he can't answer that question honestly, so he smiles and says, "Nope."

The waitress with hips, legs, and now a head, says, "Well, you just let me know." The waitress watches Roosevelt's hand cover the [Bump & Grind] logo and surround the warmth of the coffee mug. She notices it's splattered with blood red spray paint at the fingertips and finds his scent as she stands. The scent is a mix of clean citrus and illegal poetry. It could be called Springtime Solvents, perhaps.

The logo that he's covering on the mug was of another mug. The mug in the logo has [Bump & Grind] printed in a mocha-colored font and is filled to the brim with something hot. The steam from the mug forms the silhouette of a naked woman. He reaches inside his jacket and draws a ball point pen from his Rambo belt and begins to write on the napkin next to his coffee. A lot of these doodle sessions end up in the garbage, but every once in a while he will come across a gem, and he'll fold the napkin, bring it home, and slip it into a glass jar on his writing desk. He starts with simple shapes that take on various rotations and dilations. Those shapes form what may be the first line of a future poem, which he then crosses out and rewrites in a different order. Roosevelt adjusts himself in his chair so his elbows will hit a more comfortable spot on the edge of the table. During the last wiggle forward he sees a streak of jet black hair flowing by the window in his periphery. He doodles a sideways fire, as distractions are omnipresent. He hears the jingling of the mobile by the entrance as the door opens and someone walks in. Roosevelt starts to draw the outline of a woman's body that belongs to the sideways hair when the waitress approaches him. A breeze of floral espresso follows. As someone sits behind him, the backs of their chairs bump. The waitress asks the person if she wants the same thing as last time. Roosevelt can tell it's a she by the tone of the waitress's voice. There's no audible answer, but he imagines a nod took place. The waitress backs her booty-booty up to his table and places her hand on his shoulder. "What are you writing, honey?"

"Oh, just some poetry lines and some ideas for an art show."

"Yeah, you and everyone else around here." Roosevelt looks up over his shoulder to gauge her expression. "No, I didn't mean it that way. I just know some other customers that are working on a show, too. Hey, I love your handstyle."

"Cheers to that. And can I have another?"

"Sure. More Bitches Brew?"

"More Bitches."

"So what's your take? Does art imitate life, or is it the other way around?"

"The thing is with that kind of question, the answer can go on for a long time."

"Why is that?"

"I think that questions like that don't have answers, but necessitate discussion. But I'll give it my best shot."

"Bang bang."

"First, I think that the Arts are fictions based in reality that in turn reveal an enhanced version of reality, more vivid and contemplative."

"Nice, but wordy."

"Thanks. And Life seems to be a fact of itself. It's the baseline for anything we can do. Even with the improbability of events that had to happen in order for us to be here, it almost seems inevitable that we're here. But that just simplifies another discussion."

"Sorry to interrupt, but let me go check on my order and bring you some more Bitches. I'll be back, it's quiet."

The waitress disappears through noiseless swinging doors, and returns balancing a small mug on a pizza pie-sized tray.

"O.K., so where were we, or you?"

"I don't know, I get distracted easily. What is it with the city? There are beautiful women everywhere, or at least the idea of beauty everywhere. Just a minute ago I was distracted by flowing disembodied hair. And I keep seeing you walking back and forth. I envy people that can concentrate."

"Well, I accept your compliment on behalf of the other halves. Here's your Bitches Brew."

"The quick answer might be that Art is a fiction dependent on Life in the first place. But from there they get twisted and tangled forever more."

"But where does Life come from? Do you think that Life might be the Art of God?"

"Could be. I don't know. Maybe God is our greatest work of art, an abstract masterpiece that we've projected on ourselves. See, that's why these questions need discussions, not answers."

The waitress tucks her blue fingernail in between her thigh and the strap of her garter belt, "I don't really believe in God, but I like the idea that He might be an artist."

"What if the artist is a She?"

"Whatever you want to put down there doesn't bother me." She untucks her finger and pulls her hair tighter in her ponytail. "I'll be back in a minute."

During the following moments, Roosevelt feels the warmth of the person sitting behind him. The warmth has an aura of spiced cloves.

"Let's go with She," continues the waitress. "By the way, my name is Céleste."

"French?"

"Maybe. And you?"

"Roosevelt." And after he says his name he hears the first sounds from the aura behind him. It's kind of a liquidy gasp and two coughs. "While you were away, I thought about something I was contemplating on my way over here."

"I was gone like two seconds."

"Céleste, I know this is going to sound like '*the only thing that's constant in this world is change,*' but it might be a little different. Here's the set-up. The other day I was talking to some people at a bar and one of them kept mentioning his ideology. He said his ideology was the reason for everything. But he kept referring to it in the plural, like *our* and *we*. First of all, where does someone access a collective ideology? Where is its origin? How does it begin?" He runs a few fingers over his scarred eyebrow. "I think that no ideology has always been the same, even though ideally, and I know I'm killing that root word, it should be. So since ideologies are dynamic, then how could anyone hold on to one long enough to claim membership or belief, unless they're willing to change with it? If there's some perfect form of the ideology, then the interpretations of that ideology would be subject to others and their influence." He takes a sip of his Bitches Brew and then a deep breath. "It's not that it's a moving target, but an invisible one in the sky. And if you take aim with your bow and send one up, it's going to come right back down and split your wig." Céleste takes the seat across from him and stacks her hands like two pancakes. "And even if this was an ideology he created, meaning the guy at the bar, he'd be omnipotent and could edit it whenever he wants, but he'd also be the only one to fully understand it, and therefore shouldn't be able to use the plural *our* and *we*."

Céleste takes out a stick of gum from a silver wrapper. "Maybe he's his own god. Or maybe that's why God is an artist, constantly updating his work and going over it." She looks at his hands again. "You may know about going over something."

"The paint? Yes." Roosevelt writes his signature in the air. "I guess I think that creating an ideology or trying to follow one, is to take what's interesting and elaborate, and put it in an easy-to-swallow pill form, like poison *from* your own mind."

Céleste snaps her gum. "I have to check on my tables." As she rises from her seat, Roosevelt follows the changing shapes of the steam as they leave his mug. He resumes his doodle on the napkin. When Céleste returns, she doesn't sit down, but leans forward, her elbows resting on the table. "Sorry, can't stay long."

"I'll try to finish up my point right quick. I think the reason they follow these things is out of fear. It's risen out of evolution, as everything else." She snaps her gum three times in a row. "And this goes back to what I was saying about change before. The only thing that hasn't evolved *is* evolution. We evolved to our present form as a result of fear from the start and it keeps finding ways to influence us. Things like courage and intelligence, they rose out of us confronting fear and finding ways to give death the slip. And the ones who survived, the ones who lived long enough to reproduce, it's not that they didn't have any fear, it's that they had just the right amount of fear. They had to have the perfect flight time. They knew when to split and when to stay. Let's say they saw something they could eat in the wild, but there's a tiger lurking nearby, it makes sense to bolt. But if they always bolt at the first sight of danger, then they'd never have enough food to survive. On the other hand, if they weren't fearful enough, they'd hang around too long and that tiger would just add them to his calorie count for the day." Céleste looks over her shoulder, takes the gum out of her mouth, and rewraps it in a silver ball. "Of course today, we don't have the same problems here in New York, but I have an updated version of it. I write poetry and paint it all over the city, as you kind of guessed. So I need the same kind of flight time. If I'm too skittish while I'm painting, or if I'm too confident and get busted, I'm useless both ways. But if I know when to take flight like LeBron, I'm up and out, seen and remembered by numerous people in the most important city there ever will be."

"True, makes sense. Well, I have to get back to work or my boss is going to give me a spanking. She already caught me chewing gum twice this morning. She can be unforgiving."

"And thanks for that distraction. What was I just saying?"

"Ideology, flight time, graffiti..."

"Right. O.K. Last thing, Céleste. So now, it's not about the calculus of when is the best time to run naked through the woods away from a predator. Our fears have changed. Actually, it's about denying that our fears exist at all. Now we camouflage ourselves artificially. That's because what we fear is something that's more difficult to concede, than say, being afraid of tigers."

"What do we fear?"

"Two things. Love—and not being loved."

"Hmmm..." Céleste takes out another stick of gum. "The first one, I'm not afraid of that." She winks. "I have to get back to work, but I hope you can come back at night and we can talk more about it. I wrote my schedule and the rates for our Champagne Room on this napkin. I was going write it all fancy like you, but I didn't want to look like I feared how you thought of me. So that's me, uncamouflaged and naked, passing a note in the skyscraper jungle."

"That's the best sentence I've heard all year."

"Which one?"

"The last one."

"Have to go..."

"But I didn't finish telling you about my loving ideology—"

"Look at the napkin, tell me about it then. Oh, and if it makes you fell better, here's my ideology." Céleste gives herself a smack across her booty shorts. "Maybe that's one you can get behind."

His smile is wide, despite his effort to resist. Roosevelt finishes his coffee and tucks Céleste's napkin into his jacket. Then he makes a loose ball with his own napkin and leaves it on the mirrored table, that in some places, has been chipped by spiked heels. When he stands up and pushes his chair back, so does the woman behind him. This forces them into an awkward, leaning-over shuffle around their tables. When they both return to full height, they are eye-to-eye with nothing between them. While her lips remain full, Roosevelt opens his just enough to exhale. Her shoulders roll back, her toes grip the stockings in her shoes, and Roosevelt's body temperature experiences a wave of lava from the top down. After the past brushes of delicate timing, the two artists are finally connected as Roosevelt reaches his hand out to hold hers.

He says, "It's you."

"Call me Della."

"I will."

They leave together and walk into the morning metropolis. After the door closes behind them and the last jingle of the mobile ceases, Céleste walks over to clear Roosevelt's table. His crinkled napkin had reopened. She sees a stick-figure holding his arms out between two cars at an intersection. She lowers her eyebrows. It's a picture of Headache Man mitigating a traffic dispute.

Death Valley, California
5:37 AM (PST) / 8:37 AM (EST)

He slides The Bible out from between two untitled books on a packed shelf and tucks it under his arm. He halts the grinder and crosses himself with his free hand. He pulls his mirrored sunglasses down to the bridge of his nose and takes a moment to survey the tortured man in front of him. While the phrase *poetic justice* doesn't zap into his consciousness, there are actual shreds of Auden stuck to his lower lip, lines from Yeats hanging from his stubbled chin, and ripped pages of Wordsworth prose soaking in room-temperature urine mixed with blood on the basement floor. Without having to explain anything further to his partner, it's clear that he's not going to feed it to him. The Bible remains tucked under his arm. "*This* does not belong here."

------ ------ ------ ------

One week earlier, to the minute, in a small plain-walled office at an undisclosed Manhattan location, Suma sat opposite a different man, also adorned with mirrored sunglasses. There was a table as bare as the walls, save for a small cassette recorder from the mid-1980s. She was conservatively dressed—not one hair was out of place or one wrinkle un-ironed. The only unusual thing was the black cotton band that was loose around her neck. It had been her blindfold just moments before as an agreed upon disorientation tool. It was the same protocol they followed the last time they met. They didn't want her to know where she was. Suma didn't care to know either.

"I'm going to press record, O.K.?"
"I'm ready."

▶ Today, *I am here with Ms. Summer Evers, an aspiring fiction writer who wishes to discuss her thoughts about a possible plot line. This plot line concerns an abusive father figure in her book, which is yet to be titled, but I understand that the working title is "Balance." She will be filing a DBA and once that is complete I will record it along with her personal information and tracking sources. The following information is purely confidential since it is the brainstorming for a storyline within the fictitious novel, part of the creative process. The information that lies within is only for the use of Ms. Summer Evers as an author, and any unwarranted use of this information will cause financial losses for any perpetrator. If we find any illegal use of the following plot lines we are about to discuss, however well-disguised, our agency will use the full force of its legal outfit.* ∎

"I'm not sure I'm very good at this. I really think I need a script or something."

"Don't worry, it sounds perfect. Lawyers don't speak the way they write, anyway. Just play the part."

▸ *Let us begin with your thoughts on the character's plot line. Where is he now, in the book?*

The character lives in a dark place, symbolized by the surrounding area of Death Valley. I have the details of the house and address on these notes here, which are not vital to the plot at this time. I feel that the character rarely parts from his daily routine, which from what I understand, has remained unchanged for the past fourteen or so years, except that now he doesn't even have to leave the house to collect his government check, as it is deposited electronically into his bank account. He usually wakes up around eleven and watches television for an hour or two. He sits on the easy chair, which has an exact impression of his large body carved into the cushion, as if it were a hardened sculpture. He has a plate of leftovers on one knee and the remote on the other. The few times my character, the one I most identify with, was able to see him during this part of his day, she always felt nauseated by it. Many times it was cold Chinese food. He would eat with the unsteady plate on his knee and use one hand to shovel the rice and cold meat into his mouth. And because he was constantly trying to avoid any commercials, on the other knee he kept one hand on the remote to switch between different channels. As he ate his leftovers, about thirty percent of the rice either ended up in his lap, on the floor, or somehow attached to his face, by a combination of saliva and oil, I imagine. Sometimes he would just reach down into his lap, without looking away from the television, and scoop up little bits of rice or chicken muscle, and suck it off his fingers. After breakfast, if you can call it that, he gets in his car and goes to the *Distilled & Discounted* liquor store, which is a real place that I use in the novel. He buys cheap vodka, the kind that you know is cheap because it only comes in a plastic bottle. I call it *Olde Potatoe* in the book. He buys two bottles, a one-liter bottle and also a fifth that he takes to the bowling alley, which is where he goes next. Although sometimes this character is refused entry, depending on who works there and what he smells like. Did I mention that he rarely bathes? But usually, he is down at *The Spare Cactus*, also a real place, for about two hours. He used to go later in the evening, but when they started turning it into more of a club atmosphere, he switched to the more lonesome daytime bowling. There, this character eats fried food and orders extra to-go. But most of the time, he doesn't make it home. He just eats it in the car, where his greasy fingerprints can be easily lifted off the steering wheel, if that ever needed to be done. He drives home drunk every afternoon, where he reunites with the other inhabitants of the dark home. And that's when the smoking begins. It's strange, he almost never smokes in the first part of the day, but once he gets home, it's cancer sticks on a chain. ∎

"Are you O.K.?"

"Yes, let's just continue."
"O.K., pressing record again."

▶ And that's where the character goes from a drooling worthless wandering mammal, to someone who prefers all things to be in chains. When he gets home, the smoke from his cigarettes rises to the upstairs bedroom, entering the lungs of his soulless wife, and probably her entire body, as she is a shell of a woman. I think this horrid character has hollowed her out over the years, whether by exclusion, depravation, repression, rape, or other means. She rarely leaves the place. And the character, whom I call Big Sir, makes his way slowly down the creaky steps to the basement. I'm not sure if he walked that way as a result of obesity or a bad hip—or just to instill fear. But fear was the result every time. And as I recall, out of the twelve steps, the second, fifth, sixth, and tenth were the ones that creaked the most, as they let out higher pitched sounds that echoed in the walls of the basement. The echoes were softened by the books, though. There were shelves and shelves of books, ranging in genre and age. I assume they were purchased by his wife some time ago, before she was hollowed out. When my character was down there, she was put on a chain, which was modified with a soft cover. It went around my stomach so it wouldn't leave any telltale marks when I went to school. My character has escaped by this point in the novel, but from what she understands, there are now *two* young girls from The System in the same basement, and that they are chained up almost all the time. No school. And that is why my character is brainstorming right now on what to do about the situation. This is a rescue mission and also a revenge mission. Do you understand?

Completely. How is it that you see the events unfolding?

You see, my character is very resourceful, and she likes to use the surroundings and materials relevant to the storyline. Sure, my character could hire a hit man to take him out with a shot to the dome, but that just won't do, as far as the vendetta factor. I believe she would prefer to have the situation resolved a little more poetically, biblically even, like Deborah in the Book of Judges. She has resolved to use three men to execute the plans. If my character were able to go back in time and go out west, she would personally drive a stake through this evil entity. But she has other things to do at the moment, and it wouldn't be feasible, plot-wise, for her to take a western trip and risk losing time in the pursuance of her own ambitions. But her character now has the financial means and cunning to correct a few wrongs, and rewrite future histories. See, she believes evil behaves like fire. Fire requires oxygen to burn and spread. And this Big Sir character has been burning and spreading the flames for far too long, and to too many people.

And she will be the one to stop it. She is the one who has emerged, and she will be the one to return vicariously through a trinity that is representative of myself. So, I would like to see this grotesque mammal suffocated by his own iniquities.

Meaning?

Meaning that when I said he hollowed out his wife, he also hollowed out my character and the two little girls chained there now, and probably several unnamed others. At first, he penetrated us and filled us as much as he was able, both physically and emotionally, and then he ripped what was inside back out with him. Each occurrence removed another piece of the soul, more of the inside. And therefore, he produced a woman and little girls that were like personal blow-up dolls, but with real skin and his very own foul, carbon dioxide-filled stench propping up the wasted bodies. Luckily my character had hidden her soul and purpose in a place that couldn't be penetrated or even discovered. Her imagination and intellect existed in something like a nebular haven above her, accessible at any time, and only by her. I'm not sure if the others have something like that. So my intentions are not that he will be emptied of his blood and whatever darkness lies within, but that he will consume all that is, or was, his existence. He will consume it to the point of suffocation and engorgement, slowly and painfully. And he will be watching a video of my character while it is happening. That's something I, meaning the character with which I most identify, will handle on my own.

As far as materials relevant to the story, what would your character have in mind?

Before I get to the materials and methods, let me tell you that the home is in a secluded area. The nearest homes are at least a quarter-mile in either direction, and I know of no contact between the neighbors in the past. The community, if you can call it that, seems to have a *live and let die* attitude. So, for the materials, let's start with the rental box truck the three men will pick up in Los Angeles. It will be simple to acquire most of the items in the area before heading off to Death Valley. The items: six bowling balls, six bowling trophies, six liter-sized bottles of *Olde Potatoe*, six pocket-sized bottles of *Olde Potatoe*, six yards of steel-enhanced rope, chloroform for initial control, a combination television/VCR, a vintage Polaroid camera, and a shot of adrenaline in case he goes into shock and is unresponsive. He must feel this the whole time. Next you will need a high velocity grinder, I wrote down the model type here. It will turn the bowling balls and basement chains and everything else into small pebble-sized pieces. That will be the most difficult thing to transport, so it will be important that the characters assess how best to move it ahead of time. And keep in mind it will have to go downstairs, then back upstairs afterward, before being destroyed piece by piece at an incinerator in a nearby county, for which I will provide the fictional address in later details. You will also need food and medical supplies for the girls and the wife, which may need some attention after the event. Definitely something healthy, as they are likely malnourished. And it's not so much as a material, but ample time to recover and understand the next steps that will be made available to them.

So far there is nothing that my three men, with their roles in your novel as fictitious middleman, cannot accomplish. But I am curious to your character's wishes regarding the grinder and the video.

Well, she will produce the VHS tape herself, as to leave no digital trail. This video is a collage, a vignette of sorts. That part of the manuscript has already been written, and I doubt it will need to be redone or edited before the work is ready to fly. It's of my character at a Brooklyn bowling alley. She rented the whole place for an hour before they opened. And she is having a grand old time bowling by herself, knocking down pins at will, and all the while, she keeps going back to the camera and speaking to it. The camera was on a tripod near the ball return, and she would laugh directly into the camera. Some of the morning staff members watched incredulously from a distance. She was saying things like, "Strike me and I'll strike you back!" And, "I'm going to have three fingers stuck in you too!" And, "Does the little gold man in little gold khakis need to move around a little bit? Or is the gold man like the little statue on the trophy and can't move his body? Oh, poor little gold man, you're just stuck there, and you're getting all filled up with love, aren't you? And some people say I have too much love to give, and it's true what they say. But the way I show love is different than the way other people show love. I show love that fills you up to the point where you can't take it anymore. But the thing is, you will take it, because that's what you've needed all along, and now you're going to get it in the most fun way ever. Fun for me, anyway. Favor for a favor, goldie pants." Or, I think she says something like that. It's always difficult to remember what she said verbatim because she was overacting and euphoric about the whole situation. And my character wants this video to be shown throughout the process, even if it has to be replayed until the completion of the event. My character would like the television to be facing him, directly in front of his eyes, so he won't be able to ignore the message.

And I know I told you this before, but I want to emphasize just how much he hates God. Not that he doesn't think He exists or anything. But that he really hates God and everything He stands for.

I see. That will help us assess this storyline more accurately.

As far as the grinder and the three characters that will be carrying out this assignment of vengeance, it's imperative that the girls and the wife be removed from the house before the event. They can take shelter with one of your men, the kindest of the three, in the back of the box truck with some blankets and the healthy food I mentioned before. They must not be able to run or contact anyone until after the event. After it is finished, your men will drive them to one of the few trustworthy persons my character knew in the valley. She will take care of them from that point on. Remember, this is vengeance, but also a rescue. Your men and myself as the author, are their saviors.

With only Big Sir in the house, knocked out with the chloroform, your men can set him up in the basement, which is the literal *hell* where my character was razed. Grinder, video, supplies, alcohol, bowling balls, trophies, et cetera. Your men can get creative in the moment, as I don't have full command over all of the characters in my book. Some of them just write themselves. But let's just say that all of the supplies will have to enter his body one way or another. The grinder I suggest does not grind to a fine powder, but to small jagged pieces. As

Big Sir watches the video of my character, he must consume all that is within the basement, until even his eyes have no place to go. Pop goes the weasel.

And I believe it's only fair that he understands his demise and his legacy to follow. My character will address some of those points in the video and will also provide unfalsifiable documents that show that he is an admitted pedophile and abuser with the deadest of beats, in terms of financial support and honesty. My character, the professional forger, has also written untraceable letters to the local police describing what was done and why. Of course the reasons given are meant to mislead as to the true source, but will suffice nonetheless.

Does that still sound like a viable storyline? If so, we can end the interview.

Yes. ∎

I will have three men assigned immediately, one on the sensitive side and two who will operate with God's unapologetic judgement. On your end, the moment you deliver our documents and signatures as you did with the election in Pearl, Indiana—and I receive proper authorization from above—the storyline you proposed will be written in stone. Moving forward, as this goes beyond our normal compensatory offerings, our relationship may have to enter a cooling off period, or maybe terminated altogether. Time will tell. Aside from letting you know when things are complete on our end, you won't be hearing from us for the foreseeable future.

Understood and agreed.

------ ------ ------ ------

Death Valley, California
5:13 AM (PST) / 8:13 AM (EST)
"Press play, he's starting to snap out of it. And set it on auto rewind."
"Yes sir, Samson."
"Remember, no names!"

On the VCR, the neon blood numbers begin at 3:00 and blink to 2:59 and continue to countdown. Big Sir is on the basement floor, his face contorted, crooked with horror and confusion. His arms are bound with electric tape around his back as far as his wide body will allow. He feels the pull of the tape stretching the corners of his mouth while his saliva runs cool and finds its way into his ears. He attempts to roll to one side to rise, but his balance, weight, and disorientation only allow him to teeter. He's unsure if it's a dream until he feels two sets of hands lift him up. The two men step against his heels and use them as a fulcrum. As they bring him to his feet, he's facing the floor at a 45° angle with his arms perpendicular to his body. The pain is undeniably evident. The weight of his body is too much for his arms to bear, and Big Sir feels the tearing of both rotator cuffs. It sounds like the crinkling of plastic bags. The two men behind him force him in front of the television where the video is underway.

2:42 2:41 2:40...

In the lamplit room the shadows are in several places at once. The corners and sides of the room are very dark. Big Sir finds the face of the apparent orchestrator in his periphery and he tries to speak through the gag. In the reflection of his captor's sunglasses, he can see that the gag is a dull silver. It is so tight across his bloated flesh that it seems to separate his head into two hemispheres.

"Don't worry. We'll let you open your mouth in a few minutes. Usually in this situation, I would offer someone like you salvation, but in this case the verdict has been in for a long time. The will of God is harsh in its fairness. Just face forward and watch. This message is for you."

After the tracking is adjusted on the remote by the lead captor, Big Sir's expression changes from terrified to bemused. It is restricted to his eyes, because any change in facial musculature is obscured by the distended halves of his head. They hold him in front of the TV for the entire video, making sure he looks dead ahead. And whatever emotions he's cycling through on the inside, they intensify the broken capillaries, and spread across his cheeks like lightning strikes of blood.

0:02　0:01　0:00.

[The VCR clicks and rewinds to the beginning.]

3:00　2:59 2:58...

"Obviously she is very upset with how you've behaved over the years. And that can't be allowed to continue. She is the architect of this entire operation. I hope you realize you brought this on yourself. Nod if you understand."

Big Sir nods with trepidation. The collar of fat around his neck masks the exact location of his chin.

"Here's how we will judge if you are fit to live. It's a performance-based assessment. You can save yourself by acts of suicide. Or should I say, *suicides*. Do you remember those from gym class? Probably not. Well, here's the set-up. You are going to stand against that wall, right there. While you were asleep, we set up ten books on the opposite wall across the room, see? We're going to give you ninety seconds to bring the books back one-at-a-time to your starting wall, where you'll recreate the stack. This would be ample time for anyone even in decent shape, but..." The captor chuckles sardonically. "Well, we're going to pull for you."

Big Sir spits out a sentence of muffled grunts.

"Don't you worry. I'm going to let you use your arms for this. And if you start feeling heroic, think about what it would feel like to have my man put two live rounds in the soft spot between your legs. He's ready to let some hollow-points fly right now. Normally I'd have him use my SA-.33s[58], but like I said before, there will be no offer of salvation. But if you can finish your suicides, I will remove the gag. Let's start, shall we? I see 1:38 on the

VCR. You have until it's all zeros. Go."

Big Sir's run looks more like a fast waddle and his injured limp arms swing like weighted chains. With great effort, he lifts the first book and moves back to his starting wall. He's panting already, which makes the second book more difficult than the first. His shoes are worn thin on the outsoles. As he places the second book on the return stack, one of the men from the darkness hurls a bowling trophy at him. In a dash of violence, the marble base cuts the flesh on the back of his hand. The fanned out whiteness of his metacarpals are in full view. Big Sir lets out a shriek that isn't age or size appropriate. He keeps moving. Looking to the corners, he's anticipating more trophies. With the placement of the third book, two more comes his way, one from each side. The first one misses and damages the laminate wood-grain paneling. The other trophy catches him just over the ear, the little gold head digging into his own. He falls down, shrieks again, and says something like, "Mercy, please," through the gag. He wants to comfort the site of the pain, but he stands up and keeps moving in fear. The mix of blood, sweat, and salivated tears work their way south toward the heart. The only sounds in the room are of heavy gasping, the scuffing of rubber-soled shoes, and the video with Suma speaking in a childlike rhyme cadence: *Hit me and I'll hit you back.* As he leans over to place the fourth book on the stack, the remaining three trophies hit him in a flurry. The first one hits just above the calf and causes his leg, already riddled with muscle tremors, to buckle in and bring him down to his knee. Then, with his back as a dartboard, the second and third trophies pierce his skin. When he arches in response to the pain, one of the trophies remains momentarily lodged in one of the folds of his back. Big Sir thinks of his own mortality for the first time, right there on one knee.

The instigator aggresses, "Get up, you're running out of time!"

Big Sir feels his kneecap grind against the basement floor and shift sideways as he rises. He slogs on as an injured mammal in survival mode. When he leans over to place the fifth book on the stack, the first bowling ball comes his way. Out of the corner of his eye, he sees the shiny black sphere. Acting on instinct, he tries to block it with his arm, but the torn rotator cuff renders him unable to control his movements with any accuracy. The bowling ball hits him across the left flank, breaking each rib in its circumference. One rib snaps and punctures the limp balloon that is his adjacent lung. When the fifth book hits the stack, the bearded men cheer with insincere claps. Then the second black ball comes rolling with the spin of an experienced bowler toward the feet of the tortured man. Big Sir attempts to jump *over* the ball. It's a pathetic effort that results in his jumping *on* the ball.

The lead captor begins to count down the way a lenient parent does. "Twenty seconds left! Nineteen... Eighteen... Seventeen-and-a-half... Seventeen... Sixteen-and-three-quarters... Sixteen-and-a-half... Sixteen-and-a-quarter..." While he's digging his fingernails into the solid ground in frustration, the third bowling ball lands on the nape of his neck. He lets out a whimper that's imitated by one of the captors. The men encourage him to finish, reiterating the reward of the gag removal. He manages to put down four more books, his ninth suicide complete. As Big Sir tries to make his way to the opposite wall for the last time, his left shoulder is hit with a bowling ball, and he's sent into a corner. This unharnessed force knocks over a nearby shelf. It's the shelf that Suma had designated as the one with her favorite books. Big Sir is in a state of shock, but the sound of a gun cock breaks through the haze and refocuses his mind. The lead captor rushes at him and forces a bowling ball against his sternum. The cracks echo in the basement. He pushes the ball farther into his chest before rolling it down toward his waist, which creates a temporary valley of fat cells that are quickly restored to their hilly formation. The lead captor is one of the few men in Big Sir's life who's able to look down upon him. He's close enough to smell the blood on his breath. He says with great articulation, "Move now. Finish your suicide."

Big Sir conjures all of his available strength and air that one lung can provide and reaches for the last book. His fingers are now paralyzed and useless, so he holds the book between his wrist and elastic waistband. At this point, Big Sir's waddling progression is so slow that the countdown includes sixteenths. Just as he's about to complete his task, although the stack of ten books is more of a pile now, he sees the leader holding a bowling ball in the shadows. This ball is much easier to see than the others because it's bright red and sparkled[59]. He expects it to be hurled his way, but it remains in the captor's arms. He says, "We'll get to this later."

Big Sir makes a muffled sound in the form of a question.

"This one is much heavier than the others. It makes all the difference. Would you like to see how heavy it is?"

Big Sir wheezes an emphatic, "hmmNo!"

"Here. Catch!"

Big Sir's arms don't even move. The red sparkling ball lands on the front of his foot. The force pulls three of his toenails up from the wrong side. The blood pours out through the seams of the sneaker almost too fast to believe. He feels the urge to urinate even though his bladder had been emptying steadily in a weak stream since the first suicide.

"Why don't you stand up so we can remove your gag. Oh, right. Let's give him a hand." They prop him up against the wall. His leg are quivering from the stress of muscle use, something that hadn't been challenged in decades. The more his legs struggle to hold himself up, the more his body takes on the movements of warm jello.

"This won't do. No one should have to eat standing up."

The captors drag him closer to the TV and let him slump onto a metal folding chair they found in the corner. Big Sir is in agony and making as much noise as his body allows. Initially, they were going to tie him to the chair, but it isn't necessary now.

"We should clean these cuts. Can you hand me one of the large ones?" The lead captor points to the bottles of *Olde Potatoe*. He opens all of them and pours the high-proof liquor over his open wounds and the bloody sneaker. "That should help. The burn you feel just means it's working." The floor is covered in blood-infused vodka. "Let's take this gag off. He may want to say something. And if not, he surely has worked up an appetite, wouldn't you say?"

When the industrial strength tape is removed, his face returns to form, sort of. Under the skin, it all moves like sludge. His lips are raw and bleeding from the cracks. When he attempts a full breath, it's purely asthmatic, and he's unable to speak. His bald dome glistens with yellow sweat while the hair over his ears splays out, caked and still.

"Nothing to say?" The lead captor gets up close, slides his sunglasses down the bridge of his nose, and looks into his eyes. Big Sir's face twists with repugnance and dread. He puts his sunglasses back on and continues. "It's just as well we get on with it. It's time we settle the score. *Do unto others...* Since the girls you tortured and used had spent their darkest hours here in this basement, so will you. And as they have consumed these books and stories of triumph into their hearts, you will consume them too. Only we don't have the time to read them now. I mean, we are surrounded by them. Right here, for example, appears to be the poetry section. I'm not a great fan of modern verse, but I respect their skills and recognize some of the names." The lead captor flips a switch on the grinder and it whirls into slicing action. He tosses several books into the opening and the shredded remains collect in a container almost instantly. The other captor stands behind Big Sir and pulls his head back, tilting it over the back of the chair. In each hand he holds a bowling trophy. He lodges the little gold men into the corners of his mouth, widening the fulcrum of his jaw. "Why don't you open up and say Auden." The lead captor occasionally rids his beard of any stray clippings, but mostly focuses on his consumption of the books. He's wearing thick leather gloves as he forces the pages of the masters into his mouth, which is becoming one big paper cut. Even after the grinding, the hardcover books take extra effort to force down his throat. One of the little gold men is dislodged and Big Sir bites down hard on the other side. The force breaks two of his wisdom teeth. With a choking cough, one tooth falls to the basement floor, and the other down his throat. After several minutes, he has consumed three shelves, roughly thirty-nine books. The lead captor finds the one book that he will spare from the grinder, saving The Good News from abstraction.

The shredded paper and cardboard is dry, but absorbent, and Big Sir is becoming almost mummified from the inside by the words of dead mystics. The consumption continues until he's bloated with literature. The two men want to suppress the bulbousness with something hardier, something that can anchor to the bottom of his stomach.

"Recover the trophies and the black bowling balls and bring them to me." The lead captor puts them in the mouth of the grinder, and then into the lopsided open mouth of the abuser. This takes a lot of effort, as some of the pieces are nearly an inch in diameter. They struggle, but improvise with makeshift nose plugs and lubricating his throat with the small bottles of *Olde Potatoe*. Choke, swallow, repeat.

"We're supposed to get a picture of you before we finish, but you look a little out of it. Hand me the adrenaline." He doesn't have to look hard for a vein since some are exposed already. Big Sir's eyes draw wide open when the drug kicks in. The lead captor holds the Polaroid camera up to his face. "Big smile. She'll like this."

With suffocation and death imminent, the captors turn the volume all the way up on the TV as Suma laughs in his face. Big Sir vomits for the sixth and last time. Shreds of paper coated in bile find their way to the light, but most of the regurgitated prose is forced back down into his lungs. During his subsequent convulsions, Big Sir, in the reflection of the screen, sees the mutilated sloth that he is and the ghost he's to become. The last image that goes through his brain is that of a beautifully-crafted, sparkling red bowling ball, which caves in his skull with ease and power.

Big Sir reflects; he's been really lucky.

$0:00^{60}$

Axlia Clia/Della Crème walks into Mission and finds herself surrounded by just about everything she's ever produced. It's the first time she feels smaller than her work. Most of the paintings are in place, the videos are playing, and the live painting stations are stocked with materials. She notices an unused wall space that looks large enough to hang her #MissionCrosses from her followers. The "Moveable Type" exhibit in the small library is staged with a small individual light over each altered book, which is opened to a page of modified significance.

Roosevelt is playing two roles—one as poet and artist preparing for the live show tomorrow night—and one as bodyguard for Della, unbeknownst to her. When they meet Cyrus Coaster, he's going over the schedule for the day and the opening tomorrow night. Roosevelt is both steely and cool while he studies the High Priest. Then they're introduced to the rest of the staff: the other curators, the holographic camera operators, and the set designers. Lastly, they're shown where the re-creation of I/0 is going to be—it looks like a movie studio. Her black canvases and small pools of black and white are in place, and the walls are green-screen bright.

Just moments before, Axlia saw her world projected out to the gallery, and now the vision is inverted with numerous cameras pointed at her from the ceiling corners and the walls. They are the eyes of machines who never forget.

The only missing pieces are Jasmine and her two assistants from the original performance of I/0. It's not that they're late, it's just that Axlia is early. Cyrus Coaster isn't the type to wait and suggests that one of his female employees at the gallery can assist her with the body paint.

He motions to a green room of sorts and tells her it's a place of privacy. It has a shower and is hers to use. Axlia responds by starting to undress on sight. She isn't as concerned about privacy the way other people are. She feels that her artwork has already exposed her in ways far more intimate than anything physical. Roosevelt is standing behind her and watches each garment fall to the floor like the leaves on an autumn afternoon. Actually, everyone in the room pauses and joins Axlia in silence, as if someone has pressed a mute button. She stands with an arched back and her chin held high. She looks at Cyrus Coaster, then reaches for Roosevelt's hand, and leads him toward the green room.

"The poet? O.K., perfect," Coaster says. "Can we start filming in thirty minutes?" Axlia nods.

Roosevelt's unaffected demeanor is tricky for him to keep as he tries not to blush. But he assumes the position of her painter and follows her. His boots click with an echo while Axlia pads forward across the cold marble floor. He's heard but unseen, as all eyes are following Axlia's pendulous hips.

When they enter the room, all of the bodypainting materials are set up, along with some fresh fruit and filtered water on the counter. There's also a sealed tin of clove cigarettes with a silver lighter and a crystal ashtray next to it. Someone did their homework. Roosevelt closes the door behind them, tucks his journal into his jacket pocket, and uses the same hand to smooth out his scarred eyebrow. Axlia looks at the scar and wonders how it came to be. She unwraps the tin and lights a clove. She begins to speak for the first time in a long time. She feels that things are different now, out of nowhere. "Why don't you start with the black paint. I'll turn around."

There's a brush beside the paint container, but Roosevelt ignores it and dips his hands in instead. He starts at her shoulders. He feels as though he should be giving her a massage at the same time, like a trade-off for being allowed to touch her. The only sound in the room is the crinkling of the clove as it burns.

"Write me a poem on my back as practice for tomorrow night. I want to know your style."

Roosevelt thinks for a minute as he finishes painting her shoulders and upper back. Some of the paint drips down on the sides like blackened angel wings. He dips his finger into the paint and writes the first letter of his poem. Della watches him in the small mirror above the counter. He didn't plan ahead and had yet to take off his jacket. He tries his best to pull his hands through the sleeves without getting any paint on the inside. He's almost successful. Roosevelt puts his left hand on her hip as if to steady his canvas while he goes back to the inkwell. His letters are in all-caps and far from perfect, as some merge and form typographic ligatures. The D in the last word of the haiku makes a trail all the way down to her sacrum. Roosevelt transforms the poem to the spoken word in her ear.

SHE BREATHES IN HER FIRE
LIPSTICK ON LIT CIGARETTE
EXHALING DESIRE

She smiles without Roosevelt noticing. She reaches for a second clove from the tin. The first few cigarettes of the day always give her elevated sensations. Roosevelt dips both hands in the black paint and covers the words he's just read to her.

After the black half is finished, Roosevelt washes his hands in the sink, and wipes them off on his dark denim jeans. He switches to the mother-of-pearl inkwell and begins coating her neck and working down each arm. His hands are quietly trembling. Then, with a two-finger dip on each hand he paints along the edge of the black border on her sides, crouching down as he paints lower. His movements are those of a sculptor. Roosevelt stands and covers both hands in paint, places them over her collarbones, then moves them sinuously down around her breasts before cupping his hands upward and over them.

Through a ring of smoke, Della asks, "Another poem, perhaps?"

And his veil of cool falls to reveal a bright smile. "O.K." Roosevelt takes a few moments to think. The air is thickened by sweet and spicy smoke. "The first one was *about* you. This one will be *for* you."

Roosevelt sets the paint can down on the dropcloth on the floor and kneels beside it. He starts to write the first line under her breasts. He writes smaller this time to conserve space. He's also more gentle. This sends Della into occasional chuckles from the tickle of his light touches. Roosevelt replies, grinning in jest, "Hey, this is serious. Stop laughing at my poetry."

Della watches him over the peaks of her chest as he concentrates. What feels like the third line of the poem drips into her belly button. As he finishes the fourth and last line, Della tries to decipher it upside-down.

Roosevelt continues lower as he looks into the eyes of his *IloveAbove*, covering the fronts of her legs with broad strokes, tracing his fingers along each one of her toes, and then over the tropical warmth of her Bermuda triangle.

"What does it say? I can't see all of it."

He stands up and uses one hand to white out each line as he recites it. Roosevelt says:

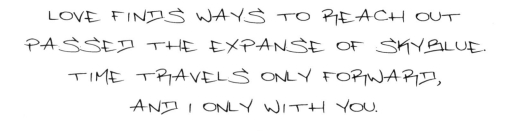

Della closes her eyes and Roosevelt sees a small tear escape out one corner. He wipes it away with the bottom of his shirt and finishes painting her face. His fingers follow the contours of her eyebrows and then circle around her lips, careful to leave them untouched.

"Black and white. You're ready for your performance."

Their eyes meet on the level and Della says, "Not just yet." She leans forward with her arms down as to not make contact with him. They share a singular and peacefully molten kiss.

[[↑]]   [[⌒ ⟼]]

Zeus's eyes flicker open to check the time on the wall. It's a few minutes before noon. His body yawns as all the muscles in his body tense and then relax—except one. Candy, still sleeping, shifts positions and slips her arm under the cool side of the pillow. The sheets slide lower and arch over her hips as she rests on her side. Zeus follows the hills of her bodyscape and wonders how he hit the lotto twice.

He finds his boxers on the floor and puts on a pair of Jordans. He shuffles into the kitchen, opens the refrigerator, and puts down a good pint and a half of OJ in one swig. As he replays some of last night's scenes in his mind, his shakes his head with equal parts pride and disbelief.

Zeus walks over to the couch and starts to put away the wine glasses and smudged napkins, being careful not to make too much noise. There's something in his eye that he removes with his fingernail. He runs his hands over his light stubble, stretches upright with victory arms, and twists side to side for thirty seconds of accidental morning yoga.

He sits down on the couch to think about the day ahead and reaches for the stack of 1987 Topps baseball cards. The card on top is the Kansas City Royals' pitcher, **BUD BLACK**. He's wearing a powder blue uniform with a true blue cap, both with white lettering. Thinking of Candy, he writes the first word that comes to mind over the front of the jersey; then he obscures it with a dark rectangle. The shape begins to metastasize and he ends up covering the entire uniform in black, from jersey to pants to cap. He leaves his face and skin alone, except for his left hand, on which he draws an extended black finger pointing with foreboding intentions. He writes the day of the week in all-caps under the player's name: **SABBATH**. As he turns the baseball card over to the back for scheduling and further doodling, he notices a chrome-like starburst in the reflection of the window across from him. It is from the sunlight catching the corner of Candy's phone that had slid under the couch in the midst of the passion.

Zeus kneels down, reaches under his legs, and picks it up. There's a low battery warning on the home screen just above the notifications:

[Mom · 33 Missed Calls & 17 Voicemails]

The words *obsessive* and *protective* come to mind, but then the words *emergency* and *hospital* and *loss* follow, and Zeus feels immediate concern bordering on regret. He reverts to quick words of prayer, closing his eyes and looking to the ceiling. His thoughts leave his mind in an upward draft of hope. With the Lord's blessing lingering somewhere in the ether, Zeus resolves to quell any concern for Candy and her mom.

He brings her phone to the nightstand and crawls back in bed, spooning her like a sweet bowl of cereal. She wraps her arms around his. With his nose, Zeus nudges the locks of hair away from her ear, and then gives her soft kisses before taking her earlobe between his teeth.

She smiles and twists toward him.

He says, "You look so beautiful in white."

"You look beautiful in nothing."

"Oh, thanks a lot!"

"You know what I mean," Candy says as she brings her arms over his shoulders, their bodies chest to chest.

"You're amazing in all sorts of ways I can't adequately explain."

"That's probably the best thing I've ever heard in the morning."

"I bet it's true at any time. But, not to ruin the moment, it's actually close to one p.m. And I found your phone under the couch and it looks like someone has been looking for you."

"Oh my... I can't believe it's that late! How did that happen?!"

"I know. I'm usually up on the early side, but I think we had too much fun. We're feeling the kickback now."

"O.K., O.K., O.K. Let me think." Candy sits up in bed, now more conscious of her body, and holds the sheets up under her arms. "I'm pretty sure I know what she said on each one of those voicemails."

"Is it something serious?"

"Not really. She was probably just being protective of me last night, and I promised her I would be home at some point and that I would go to church with her this morning, which is going on right now. She was nervous about me going out with you and she said heard something about highway terrorism."

"What should we do?"

"I don't know." Candy looks around the bed and the floor for her bra. "What time is it exactly?"

"One o-four."

"I think the best thing I can do is be home before she gets home."

"What time is that?"

"Church is from eleven to twelve-thirty, give or take fifteen minutes. But she usually will stay and talk to other people during coffee hour, and then head over the parsonage for an early supper. So, assuming she's in the mood to stay, I need to be home before three-thirty. Then when she gets home, I can give her a story that I stayed over a friend's apartment after our date. I'll say that she was my safety in case things didn't work out with us, but that it was late and I decided it was easier to stay with her. My friend Jewel from Rip-Off will totally cover for me, no problem. And I'll tell my mom that my phone was off or on silent or..."

"...Like a pro."

"What?"

"You lie like a pro, Candy."

"That's right Mr. Zeus, watch out." Candy stands up in the glory of ubiquitous sunlight and nothing else, her galaxy tattoo in full sparkle in the middle of the day. Zeus follows her swaying and leaning to pick up her scattered lingerie and clothes.

"I'm watching, don't worry."

Zeus sits up in bed, shirtless, but still with the boxers and Jordans combo. He feels inherent sadness when he sees her bra going back on, the underwire pushing everything up without his support.

"How fast do you think you can get me home? Safely, of course."

"From my garage to your driveway, once we take the elevator down, easily under thirty. If we're out of here in fifteen, you should be able to beat your mom home even if she doesn't go to that early supper."

"Super, let's go for it. Get dressed."

The two lovers reverse last night's process and head to the elevator for their quick commute.

During the drive over the Brooklyn Bridge and on the blacktops of the N.Y.C. highways, the roar of the engine echoes within their emotions. As he shifts through the gears, Zeus places Candy's hand on the shifter and places his on top. Zeus drives at a speed that's almost dangerous while their fingers are interlaced and playful. The ride is without incident, except for one car that passes by out of control, skidding over the median with deployed airbags. Their hearts skip a few beats, but with all the cardiovascular upticks of the night, it probably helps them revert to their usual rhythm.

As they approach Stewart Avenue in Garden City, Zeus says, "You know, I didn't dream last night. And I'm not saying that I don't remember any of my dreams, but that I didn't dream at all. Because I think I'm living it, being with you."

"That's really sweet. Really." Candy runs her fingers up his hand, over his forearm and shoulders, and massages the back of his neck. "I feel like I am being true when I'm with you. Things are more precious and sincere, prescient even, like moving in slow motion at the speed of light." They pull up in the driveway, which is empty and reassuring. "I'll let you know how everything goes."

"Can I have a kiss goodbye?"

"You're getting one whether you like it or not."

[[⼲]]

On his drive back over the Brooklyn Bridge, Zeus accelerates through his contradiction of desires. He's hovering above the East River and looking for a place to drop an anchor, even if it's from a Lamborghini. But every time he takes a critical look into the waters of faith, they feel puddle-deep. Maybe if he can just lie flat enough, he can still be immersed. He wonders why it's easy and natural for so many people he knows to stretch themselves this way. It probably has something to do with the eventual position where everyone ends up, lying in a grave. Maybe it's good practice to consider the bodily future in conjunction with a wondrous afterlife—if that's what it is. But if this is a one-shot deal, with nothing else to count on, the world is a singular realm of heaven and hell rolled up in one ball of earth tones and blues. That way is more poetic, but who wants poetry?

His current philosophy puts him in a place similar to where he is on the bridge right now, he thinks. It's a perpetual state of betweenness, the apex of the wide parabola in between the two gothic towers. One side is set in bedrock and the other is set in sand. The constructors weren't able to find solid ground. While it's evidently immovable, the knowledge of the sandy foundation gives the impression that it can fall from its grace at any moment. And Zeus ponders the bridge as a symbolic structure that connects the towers of theology and philosophy. No matter how fast he drives, he can't escape this divided feeling because he recognizes the polarity of his thoughts: that there is freedom in questions and security in answers.

Of course, all of that is just a brief distraction to what's lighting up every other synapse in his brain, which looks pretty much like this:

CANDY · CANDY · CANDY · CANDY · CANDY · CANDY · CANDY · CANDY · CANDY · CANDY · CANDY
CANDY · CANDY · CANDY · CANDY · CANDY · CANDY · CANDY · CANDY · CANDY · CANDY · CANDY
CANDY · CANDY · CANDY · CANDY · CANDY · CANDY · CANDY · CANDY · CANDY · CANDY · CANDY
CANDY · CANDY · CANDY · CANDY · CANDY · CANDY · CANDY · CANDY · CANDY · CANDY · CANDY
CANDY · CANDY · CANDY · CANDY · CANDY · CANDY · CANDY · CANDY · CANDY · CANDY · CANDY
CANDY · CANDY · CANDY · CANDY · CANDY · CANDY · CANDY · CANDY · CANDY · CANDY · CANDY
CANDY · CANDY · CANDY · CANDY · CANDY · CANDY · CANDY · CANDY · CANDY · CANDY · CANDY
CANDY · CANDY · CANDY · CANDY · CANDY · CANDY · CANDY · CANDY · CANDY · CANDY · CANDY
CANDY · CANDY · CANDY · CANDY · CANDY · CANDY · CANDY · CANDY · CANDY · CANDY · CANDY
CANDY · CANDY · CANDY · CANDY · CANDY · CANDY · CANDY · CANDY · CANDY · CANDY · CANDY
CANDY · CANDY · CANDY · CANDY · CANDY · CANDY · CANDY · CANDY · CANDY · CANDY · CANDY

[[　⌒　　↦　]]

Candy walks into an empty house and finds a note left by her mom. The note does as she intended, tying Candy's shoelaces together with a knot of guilt. She takes small steps and shuffles up the stairs into her bedroom. The quiet is a refuge. She sheds her clothes and ill emotions at the same time, trying to focus on the positives before the negatives develop into permanent images. Candy turns the bathwater to hot, almost all the way to the capital H on the knob. While the tub fills, she lights two scented candles, dims the lights, and pours in some pink bubble soap. Holding on to the towel rack, she tests the water with her toes. She gets in. The warmth of the water envelops her body.

Candy uses her finger to write **MJZNW ♥ CBHL** in the steam on the glass tile wall. A bubble lifts off from the mountainous seascape and holds together as it travels across the bath until it lands on her toes, which are chilled in the air just over the waterline. She rubs herself down with a natural sponge, and when she touches certain areas, the memories of last night come quickly.

Candy tightens the terrycloth belt on her robe and revels in the release of tension. Her feet feel the change from memory foam to thick carpet to hardwood as she walks into the kitchen. There's still no sign of her mother, which she welcomes, as she's thinking of which story will be the most convincing. Candy opens the refrigerator and lines up the ingredients for an omelette in the order that she'll use them. She runs her hand along the counter and taps a rhythm with her fingers while she decides not to immediately decide what to do when her mother comes home. Instead, she concentrates on making herself breakfast as the sun begins its descent over Long Island.

[[Σ]]

With dusk approaching, Suma traverses 10th Avenue without effort. The weight she's carried for so long is dead. She feels its non-existence. She isn't trying to hide, but isn't trying to be noticed either. She's at ease scoping out the area around the gallery. Suma will be unrecognizable by tomorrow night's premiere. She's thinking of Jasmine, Beverly, Leon, and The Artist.

In the shop windows and wrapped around streetlamp poles, Suma sees the flyers for the opening. Inside a place called [**SALO N**], or [**SALOON**], depending on the time of day, are two conspicuously sun-glassed and well-suited men getting their beards trimmed and groomed while they stand in front of a large mirror. One of the men is holding a Mission flyer that's ripped at the corners. As the stylists work side by side, the men lean toward each other to communicate, which makes the scissor logistics trickier. They look shorter than she'd remembered. The second **O** is beginning to flicker. That's the indication that the establishment is starting to change over. With the rearranging of the furniture in the background, it's about time to go from hair care to pub fare[61].

As she continues walking, all of the other store signs on the 10 on 10th seem much lower than normal. Even the glare from the street lamps is starting to shine into her eyes, oddly enough, and she hides her blue and green wonders with the shade of her hand. Suma hears the steps of her shoes against the sedimentary pavement, but feels physically removed from it as the city breeze rushes between her toes. Walking on air while staying grounded, Suma disconnects from her past, and follows the ascending curve of a trigonometric equation. A wind kicks up from beneath her and carries with it a flyer for the show. She finds it on the steps of a fourth-floor fire escape.

MISSION ART GALLERY

PRESENTS

AXLIA CLIA

. PHASES .

MONDAY
DOORS OPEN AT 7PM

·

NEW.YORK.CITY
ART SHOW OF THE YEAR

·

NEW WORKS + RETROSPECTIVES
VISUALS, PAINTINGS, INSTALLATIONS, & PHOTOGRAPHS
LIVE GRAFFITI & POETRY
THE ALTERED LIBRARY
I/O HOLOGRAPHIC PERFORMANCE
AND A 1/1 EXPERIENCE

◆

[[✻]]

While it's muted by the skyscraper aurora, he can feel its pull nonetheless. Roosevelt walks home in the calm evening, following the moon down the avenue as it twitches with each step he takes. He considers turning left or right in search of a nightspot to continue the high, but he feels content to trod in the direction of the gray satellite. He will ascend in the elevator to his apartment, in a state of a newfound nirvana, and have a drink with his journal. He will recall the moments he spent with Della and welcome the butterflies in his stomach to stay as long as they'd like. He'll put on some Bobby Womack, or maybe Roberta Flack, or no—Curtis Mayfield, definitely. Then he'll take an indulgent hot shower with a cold beer. Then he'll dry off and write until the pen falls from a kinetic slant to a sleepy horizon.

*

I CAN ALWAYS WAIT FOR TOMORROW
IF EVERY NIGHT IS THIS LOVELY.
WITHOUT WORRIES AND DREAMLESS,
A DIM CRESCENT ABOVE ME.

*

M∞NDAY

In the darkened lull before sunrise, two men walk along 10th Avenue. Their steps are jagged, but they move together as one. One of the men is very tall despite his permanent hunch. He prefers to talk up close to everyone, and almost everyone he's ever spoken to has been shorter than he. Even with his arched posture, the back of his neck measures 6'4" from the ground. The shorter man listens to his friend's words, but also feels his words, as his warm breath hangs in his face like a cloud of human exhaust. And it doesn't smell terrible, it just smells like...breath. The pair walks along looking like the top half of a capital D, exchanging stories and thoughts as the alcohol from their last drink lingers in their bodies.

The shorter man looks up at a storefront sign and says, "{ Barely N∅thing }... I love that place, man. You ever go there?"

"Never, nope."

"Well the story is that it's based on another store that the owner used to live by when he was in college. It was a lingerie joint that sold VHS porno tapes and DVDs in the back. The guy told me that it looked more like a thrift store with second-hand panties, like, none of the brands or colors matched. The original owner really should've named his store Barely *Anything*, but that's our language for you. So I guess this guy went into the store and explained the undefinable nature of the store's name, but the owner cursed and threw something lacy at him. Maybe he didn't care or maybe he didn't appreciate the math lesson. But *Barely Nothing* means *a little bit of zero*, like the fraction one-over-zero." He draws the fraction $1/0$ in the air with his finger. "You can't have a little bit of something that isn't there. Sure, zero-over-one works just fine because there's something in the denominator. For example, let's say you get one at-bat in the big leagues, but you strike out. You're O for one. But the other way around means that you got a hit without ever getting in the game. Impossible."

"Yeah, I get it, man. You were O for one tonight when you struck out with that girl at the bar."

"Thanks for reminding me. Anyway, so this guy, all these years later, opens his own place with the same name that he corrected back in the day, on purpose. I guess it stuck with him. But his shop is different. He sells books in all mathematical disciplines, but also has a wide selection of thongs with a dirty nerdy logo on the front. It's an embroidered cherry with a stem that winds up curving to the side and becoming the top of the pi symbol."

"Speaking of thongs, you see that new Viagra ad they're pushing now? They're going for that younger demo I guess. It looks like a beer commercial. And they're still putting that disclaimer at the end: *If your erection lasts more than four hours, call your doctor...* It sounds more like *that's* the advertisement right there in the medical disclaimer. As if your doctor would answer the phone at one a.m. and arrange an appointment. You know what I'd do if I had a four-hour erection? I wouldn't call my doctor, I'd call every woman I know."

"That's the truth. It's the only side effect you wish for, a solid never-ending erection."

"Just like the cornerstones of buildings: Erected in 19whatever. That stuff still breaks me up."

"Me too," the shorter one laughs. "I need to stop walking for a second. I need these spins to straighten out."

"That's probably the worst thing you can do."

He sits down on the curb anyway. The taller man's legs spread out to what seems like the middle of the street. And the shorter man notices a manhole cover with home plate spray-painted over it. "You see the new Jeter statue went up outside Yankee Stadium?"

"Yep, that's a permanent erection too..." The taller man chuckles and then burps. The bitter aftertaste of his last drink erupts in the inches between their faces.

"Oatmeal stout?"

"Sorry about that."

"Don't worry about it. It's just a memory burp. They happen. I once had a memory burp that came from three days before, no lie. It was from an onion burger off a food truck."

"Nasty."

"You know the first beer I ever ordered at a bar?"

"What?"

"I ordered a Guinness *drought*."

"What?"

"That's right, a Guinness drought, which of course doesn't exist. Here's the thing. First, I'm trying to look like I know something about drinking beer. I didn't want to order something typical. So the waiter comes up to my table and asks what I want. And I said 'I'll have a Guinness drought!' in my deepest voice. Obviously the waiter looked at me crooked, but I affirmed my selection with gusto. I told him again, 'Guinness drought for me!'"

"That sounds like the driest drink of all time! Did he bring you an empty glass?"

"Yes, he did! But that's because it wasn't on tap. He brought me a Guinness in a can, the kind with the nitrogen cartridge. He popped the top and poured it into the glass. The waiter left the can there on the table and I remember trying to see what the cartridge looked like. Anyway, I thought I was cool for ordering it, and I ordered more later. In fact, I kept ordering Guinness droughts for years."

"And no one ever asked you what the hell you were saying?"

"I guess I had passive aggressive friends and bartenders who felt bad for me. Eventually I learned the truth about my errant ways. It took me hearing someone else ordering a Guinness. Of course, I'd heard other people order a Guinness, but they just said, 'I'll have a Guinness.' They didn't go into as much detail as I did. And then one day, I heard a guy say that he wanted a Guinness Draught. The fact that he said *aft* as opposed to *out*, made me re-look at the word and examine all of my grammar lessons with the integration of international quirks. And then I thought back to the lyrics of a Fugees song called, "How Many..."

"...How many mics do we rip on the daily..."

"...that's the one, man. And there's this one line where Wyclef is describing a fight and he says '*the other tried to duck and caught a left with my Guinness stout.*' So me, not knowing much about beer, didn't know what a stout was. Whenever I rapped along with it, I just made the word rhyme with *out*. So when I saw the beer advertising posters and labels, I assumed the word draught was really pronounced drought, since there are some *ou* and *au* ambiguities, I think. I blame Wyclef and the sedimentary formation of the English language."

A newspaper delivery truck creeps up alongside the pair. Someone inside the truck yells to 'look out!'—and they both look in different directions. A bundle of newsprint thuds and skids to a stop just behind them. The truck putters away as if it's grumpy.

"We should get up and keep walking."

"Good idea. I'm feeling better."

After they get up from the curb, they both glance at the stack of papers and the next-day headlines:

SWIFT CHANGES IN HIGHWAY TERRORISM:

ZERO CAR ACCIDENTS NATION WIDE REPORTED ON SUNDAY,
BUT OVER 100 SOLO DRIVERS DEAD ON THE SHOULDERS OF
AMERICA'S HIGHWAYS, THEIR CARS FOUND WITH
THEIR ENGINE STILL RUNNING

•

EARLY AUTOPSY RESULTS INDICATE
INTERNAL BRAIN TRAUMA AS CAUSE OF DEATH

•

F.B.I. SOURCE: MANY DEAD DRIVERS
CONNECTED BY TERRORIST NETWORK

•

D.O.C. ACCEPTS RESPONSIBILITY FOR
WHAT THEY CALL 'DIVINE ACTIONS'

•

"That's why I don't drive, man."

"You don't drive cuz you live in the city."

"True."

"Want to hear a sad story that's kind of funny? It's kind of related."

"Sure."

"This guy I know at work is going through a midlife crisis. He's always complaining about this and that. For weeks, he's been telling people that his daughter in med-school needed some money to help pay for housing or she'd have to transfer. But this guy said that since his daughter had earned a scholarship, she should get a side job to pay for the rest. He told his daughter that things were tight and he couldn't give her anything. And he'd say, 'What about me?' 'What about the things I want?' And apparently, his daughter is a saint. So, some of my coworkers were disappointed with him. They'd say, 'Obviously you wanted to have a child, and that's what you have. You should do what's right. Help the kid out. She's one of the good ones.' But then, a week or two later, he starts talking about how he's going to buy a sports car, a Viper. He said he got a good deal."

"Not cool."

"No, it gets worse. When he gets the car, which is a bitch to drive in the city since it has no clearance, he brings it to the office garage to show off. So people are coming down to check it out and act happy for him. But the thing is, the Viper is white with pink accents and a pink racing stripe down the center that's actually a viper, a snake. I remember it. The snake wasn't intimidating, as you might guess, but it had this smirk on its face. So, almost collectively, everyone from the office starts to applaud. And then one woman says what we were all thinking. She says, 'You know, you had me fooled. I thought you were getting this for yourself. I bet your daughter is going to be so surprised! Not only are you going to help her with rent, you're throwing in a car too! She's going to love it, I'm sure. That's very generous!'"

"I thought you said it got worse?"

"That's just it. The car *was* for him."

"No... Why did he pick that one?"

"Who knows, really. He probably got a great deal because no one else would want to drive it. Not even his daughter, really. So, it's a sad story, but I have to laugh when I think about it from his point of view. Here he is, skirting his own daughter just so he can impress the people from work with a sports car. Only it turns out that A: they think it's a girlie car, and B: that he's a selfish father."

"That's terrible, What does that have to do with the terrorism stuff?"

"Nothing. Only because it was about a car."

"Oh."

The two men breathe in the dank air blowing up through the subway grates and exhale more meandering stories.

"Here's a quirky one. I met this old dude at a spot on the west side the other day. When he went to the bathroom, he held his place at the bar with a chess piece, a knight. When he came back I asked him why he left it there. He said that he was a ranked chess expert and carried a traveling chess set at all times. And when I asked if the knight was his favorite piece, he didn't give an opinion. He only alluded to the L-shaped path he had to take to get to the bathroom. He said pawns were for close-by bathrooms and queens for when he had no idea where it was. He told me he was in the midst of a battle of selves, vying for the master of intellect within his own mind. He said that he was playing a chess game against himself."

"How did he do that? With a computer program?"

"You'd think that'd be easier, but no. He wanted it to be pure in the physical form."

"O.K., how so?"

"Well, he set up a table in his apartment with one chair and a chess board set up on a Lazy Susan. He made one move per night from whatever side was in front of the chair, black or white. To keep track of the moves, he bought a camera separate from his phone, and took a picture of the board each night. He didn't want to be tempted to check it during the day. Then he'd turn the board 180 degrees to set the game up for the next evening. Then, here's the quirky part, he'd drink himself to oblivion, to a blackout. This way he wouldn't remember what move he had made, and the next night would start fresh and untainted, and he'd make a counter-move to himself. Apparently this went on for months."

"So who won?"

"I guess he did. But he also lost. I think it was more about self discovery and process. Maybe it was a draw."

"Or maybe it was about a lot of drinking?"

The two men chuckle and point to the 24-hour liquor store across the street, [Rhythm & Booze]. "He's probably stopped in there a few times."

"I've never been in there either. What's their deal?"

"Obviously, it's a liquor store, but it's also the home of the New York Beatbox Philharmonic. It's their rehearsal space and conservatory. I've heard them practice. They're unbelievable. You want to grab one more for the road, paper bag style?"

"No way, man. I'm cutting myself off. Finito."

"Well I'm getting one more, amigo. Let's go."

They walk across the street and the shorter man pays ten bucks for something cheap and malty. He sips it and tucks it in his jacket as they resume their lopsided walk home. They wonder about tall women in heels, why coins make your hands smell bad, how screen doors are made, and how elastic waist bands are the official sign that someone has given up trying to impress anyone sexually—and maybe that they've given up altogether. They talk about how the phrases *a penny for your thoughts* and *putting in your two cents* results in a net negative. They ponder what qualifies something as being a casserole, the word *piquancy*, and they comment on the new combination baseball-card-slash-antique-violin store called [*Chin Music*]. Even though they're no longer near the 10 on 10th, the concept has already inspired other nearby entrepreneurs to piggyback on Coaster's idea of duality shops.

There's a large woman who's walking in the same direction as they are. They first see her when she's a block in front of them. But she's moving on the slow side, as her steps are more diagonal than their own. Her steps take considerable effort. The widest part of her body is held together by an equatorial belt. It's a decorative belt without loops to go through. As the men keep on, the woman can hear them talking from behind. After another minute, the tipsy pair surges passed her. She isn't happy about their conversation echoing in the city canyons. It's probably the part about the elastic-waistband-equals-life-failure, they figure. She curses at them from behind.

She says something that's stifled by poor enunciation. The men whip around and see the woman charging at them like the pattern on Charlie Brown's sweater. The shorter man is carrying a black leather case that contains all of his *things*. Whatever his *things* are, they're very important to him. The two men part the sidewalk to let her run through. When the shorter man skips out of the way, he drops his black leather case. The woman stops, equidistant from the two men, standing over his case. Instead of pursuing either of them or saying anything else, she bends over and picks up the case. Her useless belt is about to snap. She hurls the case into the air like a moonshot off a slugger's bat and watches it land behind the wrought iron gate of an old neighborhood graveyard.

She takes several steps away from the men in the opposite direction she's been walking the whole time, bends over, pulls down the elastic waistband of her pants, and exposes the fullest of moons. She yells, "Kiss my ass!"

Without missing a beat, the taller man cracks, "Thanks sweetie, but I don't have all day!"

After a final exchange of sign language, the trio disbands. The two men reminisce immediately and share some back-slapping laughs. But these jovial feelings are subdued by the fact that the shorter man's case is gone. The graveyard is unlit and has no apparent entrance. The shorter man shakes the wrought iron gate in despair. Then he shakes the elbows of the taller man, "She threw my case in there! In the graveyard! I have to get it! My case has everything I need. Terence! Terence, how do I get in the graveyard?!"

"You have to die."

[[†]]

Samson X is in his study, a dark room with light concentrated over his desk. His sunglasses are tucked into the collar of his shirt. The simple soundtrack is provided by an old wall clock, which ticks and snares against the empty walls. He is calibrating a custom gun that he's been constructing for some time. The apparatus fits over his right hand like a bionic glove. Samson fuses the magazine and central components against a wrist brace. The barrel extends from the brace and runs alongside his index finger, which he's unable to bend when he wears the gun. The trigger is activated when he squeezes his thumb against his other fingers, which are free to curl. There is no safety. After adjusting the fit, he places a call to Joyce Lovinglace.

[[Σ]]

Suma is lying supine in her bed opening one eye at a time to adjust to the newborn sun. While alternating through the filters of blue and green, she rises to her elbows. She glances over to the window, which is bright and fuzzy at the edges. She'd cracked it open before going to bed for some air circulation, but also for the comforting diminuendo of city noises that go on throughout the night. Her automatic coffee pot is percolating as her senses are overwhelmed by a distinct weed aroma. Her neighbor one floor down is getting high below and the smoke has crept under the panes and curled inside Suma's apartment. As her pillow regains its form, she places one foot on top of the other underneath the covers. She balances the heel of her right foot on the toes of the other and then flips the position. As Suma continues to switch her feet, she watches the linen landscapes change with sudden volcanic shifts, and feels the clenching muscles of her lower abdomen. She feels herself becoming more profound and more aware of meaningless details, like shoddy spackle work and how unused outlets looked like the faces of surprised ghosts. And then she wonders how long her neighbor has been sparking the owl.

[[⌒ ⟶]]

Candy's dreams were tangled and indistinguishable like the gamut of emotions she's endured over the past weeks. What used to be a predictable track is now becoming a timeline that wouldn't pass the vertical line test for a function. It looks more like a signature written with epileptic penmanship.

She blinks her eyes for long intervals and her suburban vistas alternate between sight and sound. // She looks at the hardened overflow of wax from her bedside candle, and the introversion of its curled burnt wick. // She hears the kitchen cabinets being closed way harder than necessary. // She notices that each of her dresser drawers are open to different lengths, like a lopsided game of Jenga. // She hears the muffled sounds of the downstairs TV and of the talking heads suggesting the best war strategies from the comfort of ergonomic chairs. // She sees her two stilettos by the closet door, one on its side and the other upright and stabbed into the sandy berber carpet. // She hears another kitchen sound and then the TV fall silent. And she hears her mother's footsteps change from hardwood clicks to low bass thumps as she starts up the stairs. // She looks through the blurred strands of strawberry blonde that had swung in front of her eyes to the brass doorknob, which is brightened by wear on one side. // She hears her mother speaking about the dangerous seeds of doubt, the power of redemption, and a directive phrased as a compromise. // She sees the abrupt change from morning rays to shadowed grays as a cloud passes in front of the sun.

She reaches for her phone.

[[↑]]

With his face pressed into the pillow, Zeus is breathing out of the right corner of his mouth and matching nostril. His legs wake up before he does. They twist without friction against the high thread count sheets. His conscious self returns with yawns and long inhales of purified air and the wax from unlit vanilla candles. He tightens the muscles in his neck and shrugs his shoulders all the way up. Zeus shuffles his right hand along the short bristles of hair before running his index finger along the bass clef curve of his ear. He rises with a lazy up-dog arch and looks over his shoulder at the covers, which look as though they'd just been made. He'd slept soundly, petrified even.

He reaches for his phone and selects a mixtape from his Boombox app: *DJ BraZear Presents: Electric Baby Powder Blues*. The first song to play is Sam Cooke's *Mean Old World*, which is a reminder that we all have, and should therefore sing, the Blues. They offer solace to those who reside in their midst and become a crown to those who rise to the noiseless space above our atmosphere. And from that point of view, the sky is always blue.

But no sooner than the second chorus, Sam Cooke is interrupted by a ringtone programmed for the one and only, Candice B. H. Lovinglace. And he's as far away as he possibly can be, from being alone.

"Hey Candy, how are you?"

"Hi Zeus, I'm O.K., I guess. I'm heading into Manhattan in a little while. I hope it's not too early for you, but it's hard for me to talk when I'm at Rip-Off."

"No problem. You can call me anytime and twice whenever."

"Good to know. And you know you can always call me whenever, except when I'm work. So, almost whenever."

"What's on your mind, sunshine?"

"While I can't wait to spend time with you this weekend, I had to make some compromises with my mom. She isn't too happy I didn't make it to church with her. I don't even know if she bought my story, but she made it crystal clear that she's really upset with me. And because you are who you are, I, or *we*, might have to play along with some of her insecurities for a little while. Is that O.K. with you?"

"What makes you think we're hanging out this weekend?"

"_____."

"Whoa, totally kidding. You know that right?!"

"Sorry. It's been a little tense on the home front."

"I understand. Sorry."

"_____."

"I truly can't wait to see you. I've been thinking about it since I dropped you off at home."

"_____."

"Candy, you still there?"

"Yes. Like I said, it's been a stressful day. So, here it is. My mom would like you to attend a Bible study this Wednesday. My dad used to run the meetings, but obviously... that part has changed. They meet at different churches across the island and interact with the church leaders and congregations, so the place can change week to week. It's more like a men's fellowship night with a Christian consultation mixed in. My mom said that since I spoke so highly of you, she wants you to meet with the men that my dad entrusted my well-being to. They're like my big brothers now, apparently. I thought it was too soon for all of that, but she's insisting that you go. It might make things better for us seeing each other in the future. And this week's meeting is at a church that's close to my house, so you won't have to go too far."

"Of course. I'll be there."

"Thanks. It means a lot."

"Well, since I'm going to the Bible study, can I ask you for a compromise on the side?"

"I think I've been compromising too much. I just want things to be easy."

"Nothing serious—it's about later tonight."

"Tonight?"

"There's an art opening at Mission Gallery. I've heard good things. It starts at seven. From what I hear it's pretty exclusive, but I have a few connections and I can get us in."

"One of my friends from work is going, actually. She texted me about it last night."

"What do you say?"

"Normally, I'd totally be down, but I promised my mom I'd have dinner with her. I can't ditch her this time. She'd probably kill me and then I'd never see you again."

"That would be the worst atrocity of all time."

"Agreed. I also think I need to chill so I don't get too overwhelmed. A lot has happened in the last two days, thanks to you."

"Hey, I blame you just the same."

"Fair enough. I just can't wait to see you again, but I want it to be after everything calms down here—then I'll go to any show with you, anywhere you want."

"Deal. I'll hold you to it."

"I'll do the holding, Mr. Jelly Roll."

"Damn. Memories."

"Yes. I still feel them."

"_____."

"_____."

"Yeah, well, I know the gallery idea was last minute. I think I'm too focused on you to plan ahead for anything else. I'm getting a real sense of the differences of experiential living versus living for future retrospectives—"

"—sorry to cut you off, but that last sentence reminds me... With the way that you think, I'm concerned how the men at the Bible study will react to you."

"_____."

"They might not understand you. Is it possible for you to tone down some of your questions about religion? Like how women like to wear their crosses? I hate to say it, but I know these men are very conservative and not open to different philosophies, or new opinions about their religion like you are."

"So, no dirty jokes?"

"I told my mom how you've been going back to church and all that, but they're going to press you on what your beliefs are. I'm sorry about all of this. But from what I've heard about them and knowing the way you think—well, you're both two kinds of different."

"Yes, I understand. I'll be a good boy. You *do* seem stressed."

"That's what I mean. I don't want you to think I'm *telling* you how to act."

"You are, but that's O.K."

"_____."

"It's fine."

"This is what I wanted to avoid. I'm just getting caught in the middle and no one is going to be happy with me. I'm trying to work out all of these problems that are caught up in tradition and faith and family—and how they interact with my life and what I see for myself. It can be overwhelming when—"

"—You're right. Sorry to cut you off. That's just my immediate reaction to feeling constrained, but that's stopping here. I'm sure once I meet them, I'll understand. Don't worry, I'm good at adapting. I'm with you, Candy. We're a team going in the same direction. Honestly, I'll do anything you ask."

"Thank you. This isn't easy. I know this isn't the typical follow-up to a first date."

"True! I'm going to try to make it as easy as possible. Right now, there are three monosyllabic words I feel like screaming at the top of my lungs, but it's probably not the right time just yet. There aren't enough adequate adjectives to describe how I've been feeling since last Tuesday night."

"You mean Tuesnight?"

"Tuesnight, you're right."

"I feel the same way. That's why there's more pressure. All at once, my dad passes away quietly and you enter my life like an earthquake."

"Well, I think you're wonderful. Just wonderful with a capital W-O-N-D-E-R."

"I feel like I'm falling for you already."

"It's strange how we say we're *falling*, right? Falling down doesn't sound romantic. It sounds like a negative thing, unless you're both falling together onto a bed of synthetically-feathered pillows. Falling is usually embarrassing, a clumsy mistake. Why not jumping? That sounds more intentional. I'm jumping in love."

"That's just it. It's romantic because it isn't planned. Relationships that are arranged don't have the wavering ground you need in order to learn how to walk and move together. It's more exciting because everything is all of a sudden."

"You know what else is like that? A hiccup-burp. Ever have one? For whatever reason, I have them at least once a month. It's when you have a loud hiccup, like a high-pitched gasp, and then you burp right after, all of a sudden. They're weird."

"Never had one."

"So why not: I'm hiccup-burping in love? Because to fall in love means you first have to be upright. Hiccup-burps can happen anywhere. They're even more unpredictable, and therefore more romantic."

"And that's exactly why I am asking you not to be yourself on Wednesday night."

"I think I understand what you're saying now. I'll try my best."

"Good boy."

"But yes, I'll be there Wednesday. Can you text me the address? What time should I get there? Should I bring my Bible or anything else?"

"Sure. And I'd bring your Bible. That would be nice. The meeting starts at 7:30, but I would get there at 7:15."

"7:14."

"I don't know. It might look like you're trying too hard to impress them."

"Do you want to do something after the meeting?"

"I'd love to, but those meetings can go well into the night. There were times my dad wouldn't return for days. I'd bring a snack if I were you."

"Really?"

"Really. I mean, it'll probably be a normal one, but I don't want to promise a time. The organization is really serious about their work. They're quite well known, actually."

"Hmmm... O.K. I'll pack a snack called breakfast, lunch, and dinner."

"And I'd leave your phone in your car. My dad always told me there's no internet in the Old Testament. Oh, and your car..."

"...Right. What should I take there?"

"I feel terrible that I'm asking you to do all these things that aren't really you."

"It's O.K. I told you, anything to make it easier for us. I'll take a modest car."

"You have a modest car?"

"Good point. I'll rent one."

"You're very sweet."

"You're sweeter. You're the Candy to my rock, the swizzle to my stick."

"Well put."

"That sentence didn't go as planned."

"Sure."

"And I'll wear something simple and respectful. No velvet or animal prints, for example."

"There's no way this will go well."

I used to do this thing where I'd put myself in situations that made me look good to different people I wanted to impress, girls mostly. But the people weren't actually there; they were off living their lives somewhere else. But I imagined that they could observe my life through my own eyes, even listen to my thoughts. My system required no electricity. It just worked. Of course, I could choose the times I wanted to broadcast, turn off the signal whenever it wasn't flattering, and even rewind time and start over—that was my greatest innovation to the technology. I called it Mental Media and I was advertising for myself. For example, if I liked a girl, my flavor of the week, I would turn my station on when I was standing in front of my mirror, shirtless. I'd only do this after a quick bedroom workout of push-ups, sit-ups on an abrasive carpet, and a few sets of curls with homemade weights. I'd get the lighting just right, where the shadows would add some definition to the muscles I was trying to will into existence. There was a vein that ran along my left bicep that I tried to angle toward the mirror when it swelled to the surface. Then I'd get dressed and show this girl that I was fresh to def. I'd broadcast my thoughts about whatever I was about to do. Maybe she'd want to come with me. But the truth is, I was probably going to the kitchen to do the dishes. I'd also do sports broadcasts for a basketball coach when I wanted to make the team. In my Knicks jersey, I'd play early in the morning on the West 4th courts by myself and give commentary on my last second shots swishing through the chain link net. I even took shots in slow-mo replay mode so they could see the voodoo spin I put on the rock and my suspended follow-through on the fadeaway. Hot butter on French toast—word to Bobbito! And for my mom, I tried to broadcast some of the moments when I was doing well in school. I'd focus the camera, or my eyes, on my test paper while I solved a quadratic equation. Get those negative composite coefficients out of here.

I was trying to be perfect in all views from my vantage, but even that, with all the restarts and edits, I would mess up... wait, vantage? That sounds forced. Let's do that portion again.

O.K., reset.

I was trying to be perfect in all ways from my viewpoint to others. No, that's worse. One more time. O.K., reset.

I was trying to show what I thought was perfection through my eyes, but even with all the restarts and edits, it was difficult to maintain the image I was going for. So now I do the same thing with my internal-monologue-slash-commentary-broadcasts, but there are no more edits or coverups, just me as I am. I don't even know who watches me anymore. It's a public access channel. My mind is loud and my eyes are usually open.

So here I am, as you can see, standing in front of my bathroom mirror, tying my tie and looking fly. If you look down here, you can see my custom black and gray Kase2 oxfords. And here's the pocket square to match. This is art gallery glam right here. With Candy having dinner with her mom tonight, I thought I'd invite my girl Melanie a.k.a. Mel a.k.a. Melle Mel a.k.a. Swell Mel, but she said she's as busy as a bee, so I'm going to run stag tonight and mingle with some art honeys. Just me, myself, and everyone else's eyes. And I'm taking my time tonight, slow easy strides with lazy echoes over cracked cement. Enjoy the show.

.

Zeus walks toward Mission and stops for a still shot of the outside scene. The accent lights are angled upward and cast long shadows of the architecture. A cold front must've passed through the Manhattan latitudes within the past hour and it's suddenly chilly, evidenced by two women rocking hip huggers rubbing their upper thighs to create friction. Next to them in line is a tall American with an orange Fender Precision bass slung over his denim jacket, his watch reads 12:51, incorrectly. As the line continues, Zeus sees a couple using a pizza box as a coaster for two cocktails as they share a slice; a young artist with Purple Rain hair wearing an Earl Sweatshirt t-shirt; a woman in a light blue dress moving balletically, carrying a denim jacket on one arm and two Dachshunds on the other; an engineer holding a fold-up bicycle and a gentleman's pocket knife writes down his ideas with a fine looking pen; a woman humming Jefferson Airplane's *White Rabbit* next to a man wearing a white t-shirt that reads *Elbow Joints: Dope Plumbing Supplies* and a red hat in the back pocket of his jeans; a man smoking a La Flor Dominicana Capitulo II cigar exhales smoke that spells the names of forgotten philosophers as he eyes the woman in front of him wearing a little kilt; a fly-by-night vagrant in navy slacks with a red stripe, holds his charm and transgressions not close to his vest, but within it—he's next to something tall with long brown hair and a fur coat that can't be real; a husband and wife holding hands with their daughters behind them, mimicking their gestures through dance; two fortysomethings lighting a bowl of kush; and scores of meandering protesters wearing coordinated outfits. He sees a woman standing over a poem that's been painted on the cement some time ago. She isn't aware of it, but the spike of her heel dots an i.

DOWNTOWN WITH MY CHALK,

EMPTY POCKETS TALK… IT'S TIME

I HIT THE SIDEWALKS.

Farther down the line there's a towering man in pinstripes, he's next to someone in a Red Sux shirt, they're posing for a picture with one hand in the O.K. symbol, like two monocles of insobriety; a police officer in plainclothes with his girlfriend in grapefruit-colored clothes, they are sharing laughs and IPAs; a woman with hot pink leg warmers and electro-crimped hair is singing *Two of Hearts*, her audience of one is wearing a Newsboy cap, an elemental t-shirt with the symbols for Tungsten and Uranium, and an engaging smile; a Brooklynite with "The Dead" carved into his arm seems to Zeus to be the kind of person who knows what to know before anyone else does; an older man in a white suit with a fedora to match is humming the blues; a group of steampunk extroverts are adorned with extra gears of pretentiousness; a man who's hunched over due to all the marathon medals he's wearing, his wife is attempting to prop him up; a transgender person with long knobby toes extending over the platform of strappy shoes; a group of teenagers on an assignment from an arts school; and two men with full beards and reflective sunglasses. Zeus pauses for a moment. Then he sees two women, standing arm-in-arm, hip-to-hip, and temple-to-temple, face the same direction as they decide where to look. Their glasses—*les fenêtres des yeux de l'âme*—form a chain of visual deficiency. He overhears a conversation behind him. A woman says, "I will cut you, you know." Then the man responds, "Where?" She's slow to answer, "Right...... there." He's reassured, "That's the only place that counts."

Zeus sees women in cocktail dresses taking selfies; an albino male smoking a menthol cigarette; a married woman who looks as spiritless as the models in wedding dress advertisements; a man with a Luis Camnitzer tattoo, his accent both adventurous and Australian, he's talking to a family of four, all wearing NY Islanders sweaters, the parents with Coliseum blue #31 and Fisherman #91, the kids with Brooklyn black #21 and 80s white #5; a woman in a sang-de-boeuf cowboy outfit with silver high heels; a man wearing eau de soot, dressed in a black suit with reflective cufflinks, is reading Bradbury; a knockout brunette-tinged-red tells her boyfriend, 'it's pronounced Don *Julie*-O,' as he analyzes the blueprints for the new Table Mountain Cableway; and three elderly women bumming a vape off a British man with a VR headset. Some visitors don't wait in line, but in luxury cars and limousines that line the street in the same manner as the crowd, only in a more homogenous way. Most of the cars are black and idling with pollutive grandeur, with one red Ferrari outlier.

Without warning, the accent lights dim and the street lamps turn off. For the city, it's as dark as a midwest sod farm under a new moon. Zeus walks just outside the waiting line. He runs his hand along the chain of wide smiles of velvet rope.

The spotlights from high overhead the Mission Gallery beam down and catch the haze and dust of the city, crisscrossing and creating tall roman numerals around the corner building. In the circular base of each spotlight is the title of the show and the name of the artist. The lights remain in this way for several minutes and allow for the slow and sinuous introduction of the song Della selected for the opening: *She's Just Miss Popular Hybrid*, by Charles Mingus.

As the vibrations calm from Mingus's last trill, the beams cease as well. There is blackness. Then she appears in 3D holographic purity from the projection scheme above. There are no longer any thin cones of smoke-filled light, just the internal glow of the artist's body. She appears in four places around Mission, two on each side of the ninety-degree corner. Each representation of AC♦DC is performed in sync, walking in silence for Canvas #1, slow and steady in each direction. The crowd behind the velvet rope takes pictures and a few take a chance to reach into one of the phantasms. Their hands distort her pearl white skin for a moment, but AC♦DC is unfazed and digitally healed. Above the four phantasms is a singular moon that circumvolves from razor crescent to dim sun. Mostly in silence, this new audience experiences her infamous performance. Even the protesters quiet down. Several minutes later, the silhouettes fade to black as an asynchronous applause peppers the airwaves. Three of the four phantasms survive gunshot-free, while a fourth remains a faithful representation of the actual events.

The doors to the gallery open. Zeus is one of the first to walk in and he scans the gallery. Right away, he's disquieted by an installation near the entrance. It's a cross structure comprised of wooden frames. Inside each one is a picture of a crucifix worn on a chain, each as unique as the individual wearing it. There are different sizes and positions, different precious metals and jewels, all resting near the heart. Zeus sighs in astonishment, "Huh."

Mission Gallery begins to swell with patrons and potential buyers. Inside, Mingus reigns and resounds over the all with the percussive tones of a man alone at his piano, his musical typewriter. Under the notes of *Spontaneous Compositions and Improvisations*, there are conversations and pairings off to the side, where connections are made, but not necessarily realized.

With hushed words, Roosevelt and Bolden discuss possibilities and probabilities about their data gathered from The Office. They agree six senses are necessary.

Suma wears a platinum blonde wig with precision bangs and a silvery slide down her back, as she attempts to hide in plain sight. She's further abstracted by jet black contact lenses and smoky eye makeup that's only a shade away from obsidian and her dress is darker still. Her heels emit the radiance of lightsabers from The Dark Side of The Force. Leon holds Suma's elbow in his hand as they enter the gallery with the rest of the crowd. He lets it run down the smooth underside of her forearm before enveloping her hand in his. Suma plays the part of Leon's date to bolster her uncredited status in the crowd, much to the delight of the boy, who's still trying too hard.

Jasmine sees something that unsettles her. She mimes to the members of Axlia's live crew of two from uptown. She's reminding them to keep their eyes open out of concern for what Roosevelt had relayed in confidence to her earlier.

Fresh from RUST BUST & AXE, and not invited, are the remaining two-thirds of Suma's presidential friends, Bunch and Jeremy. In a completely unconnected series of events, a drunk Bunch and a friendly Jeremy were talking with some artsy types who said they were heading downtown to see the show. Since some of the girls were cute, they figured they should check it out. So here they are.

Samson and Jonah, who are on a surveillance and intel assignment, also seem to blend in with the crowd, a rarity for sure, and speak of their utter disdain for the abhorrent subject matter of The Arts, which they both capitalize and belittle at the same time. The movements of their lips bring small tremors to the coarse hairs of their beards. Samson stands beneath the empty body of the artist, which is outlined with her words, her voice. With the backlighting in the gallery, the colors of AC♦DC's altered map of The U.S.A. elicit the effect of stained glass. He walks closer until the large canvas is directly overhead. Samson finds the original Pantocrator from the church, hidden from the masses. He bows his head in prayer and his sunglasses slip to the bridge of his nose, exposing the eyes of vengeance.

Suma gives Jasmine a polite society hug and passes her a note that explains where Axlia is, coupled with specific instructions for her bartending responsibilities.

H.P. Cyrus Coaster speaks to potential buyers about the obvious success of the show, and that no, it isn't too early to tell. He speaks of the future possibilities of the artist within the social mediasphere and the business ventures that can be marketed in an "authentic way," and the approachable costs of the artwork within the buyers' community. He does all of this with the charisma of an inside trader. He'd once played one years ago in a commercial. It was for Polka-Cola™, an ill-conceived knockoff brand promising intense carbonation and music to your mouth. In the commercial he was seen as someone who knew what the next big thing was going to be, and he offered tips on short selling Coke stock and buying as much of "The Dotted Can™ as you possibly can."

Zeus shuffles into the center of the nave with a self-assured nonchalance. He sees the graffiti artist styling his poems with thick markers over satin-white pressboard. He writes one haiku after another as he speaks with the gallery patrons.

SAMO'S CROWN ABOVE,

MY LOVE, DOVE-WHITE, 'NEATH MOONLIGHT,

CRACK, SPARKLE, IGNITE.

In between poems, Zeus sees him lift a bronzed flask to his lips. He isn't making a show of it, but he isn't hiding it either. When someone pours from a flask to share with others, it's a small vessel playing the part of a welcomed ally. But when someone is drinking from it alone, it looks wistful. Zeus considers that this example is different. That it makes the graffiti artist look introspective and relaxed.

Roosevelt is sipping Trésor des Rois just enough to keep him loose, and is content indeed.

The way wine is distilled to its cognac essence, he is trying to do the same, cultivating fields of thoughts to create a few ounces of words.

BEAUTY-FOCUSED FACE,
HER BARE LEGS CUT THROUGH BLANK SPACE -
ARMS DANCE IN BLACK LACE.

After a nip of cognac and another conversation, the next poem goes up on the wall.

SOMETIMES I ASSUME
THE WORST... SLOW DOWN, I SHOULD PUT
MY SECOND THOUGHTS FIRST.

He speaks to someone who calls mathematics the poetry of the gods, the words of the unseen and abstract. She's talking about different infinities and looks familar. The haiku is purely symbolic. Roosevelt had taken a year of Math in college before dropping out. Some of the ideas stuck with him.

$$\{ 2x : x \in \mathbb{Z} \}$$
$$= \{ 2x : x \in \mathbb{Z} \} + \{ 2x+1 : x \in \mathbb{Z} \}$$

Zeus is the next one to talk with the poet. "Good evening, sir."

Roosevelt nods. "And how are you?"

"Digging the show. And I think I understand that equation, believe it or not. I like your words and your handstyle. Actually, I've seen your work before."

"I get around. Thanks."

"So how does this work?"

"Basically, I've been talking to people and then writing poetic representations of the conversations. Improvise and realize. Live communication."

"So, what do you want to talk about?"

"It's up to you. You're the catalyst."

"O.K." Zeus looks up and absorbs his surroundings in the nave. "How do you feel about this whole scene in an old church? Are you religious? I've been thinking about this stuff a lot lately."

"Am I religious? About some things, yes. But that might not be what you're asking. For most of my life, when people said they did something religiously, they were talking about something other than The Almighty. Like, 'she goes to the gym religiously.' They just meant that they'd do something often. But most religious people that I've known didn't practice their religion religiously. They used their religion to when it was convenient. Although, I'm sure there are sincere people out there. But now and in the past few years since the AppleFacegate thing, people are making a bigger show of it. It's so obviously disingenuous. They're putting on a religious front to appease each other, not necessarily God."

"I know what you mean, believe me, but what about *you*?"

"Well, do I believe in a personal God? No. But I do think there's some entity that created this whole thing. I'm not a fan of us just coming from nothing because that first reaction that set it off was comprised of *something*, not nothing. I wouldn't give that *something* the name of God, but there aren't any other good words for it that I know. We should create one."

Zeus motions to Roosevelt's flask, "Nice."

"Want a little?"

"I won't put my mouth on it."

"Hold up." Roosevelt unzips his backpack and pulls out a bottle and a plastic cup. "I've come prepared."

"Best gallery experience of all time. Cheers."

"If I have to put myself in a box, it might be labeled something like: *Complexly Agnostic in an Annoyingly Thoughtful and Exhaustive Way*. I lean toward the idea that the universe is infinitely small. That there's so much more to the history of this existence. Earth is just one of the planets in our solar system, our star is just one of billions in the galaxy, our galaxy just one of billions in the universe. So why can't our universe be one of billions of other universes? I could go on talking about this for a long time."

"Me too. I've had similar thoughts. It's something I'm struggling with."

"I think that this church, with its right-angled walls and triangled roof, is a place for people to go to think about themselves and their place in the world. It's important to think deeply. That's what makes it sacred, if anything."

"True."

"Many people filter their ideas about themselves through the prism of God. It's a way to diverge and separate their own light and figure out who they are. But I don't think everyone gets that deep. They like it simple and explained for them."

"What about Jesus?"

"I think when people say that Jesus is in their heart, they're at once being absorbed in their own importance, and at the same time, trying to include themselves in a global community of loving outreach. It's tribal. But for some of the Christians I know, the loving outreach comes at a minimal intrusion on their day-to-day lives. I'll be charitable, but I have to get that fast car first."

"Like how in the Bible it says to 'give up your riches so you can truly follow the Lord,' or something close to that."

"Exactly. It's religion on their own terms, not God's," Roosevelt says.

"People want to get money and then try to honor that principle when *they're* ready, not when the people who need it are ready."

"True. They're upholding their responsibilities outside the constraints of time."

"But what about all the twithing and new churches being built now?"

"I don't know. I'm not getting caught up in that net."

"I hear you."

"I think that religions rise as a result of being the underdog, so when they get money and power, they lose a certain kind of respect, like someone from the street who makes it big and moves to the boulevard, then tries to come back years later like it's all the same. They'll lose the real cats on the block, but there are some that can be bought back. It's just like with the skychurches. They're trying to buy souls."

Zeus says, "I have my questions about everything, but I've been trying to return to my life of belief and understanding. It's healthy for me."

"Maybe the struggle is healthy."

"I don't think I'll ever know for sure, but it's something I feel I should do. It's a little like the Descartes logic argument. He tried to simplify the God and Heaven argument like this: you have two choices, 1) Believe in God, or 2) Don't believe in God. And from there, there are two different possibilities, a) God exists, or b) God doesn't exist. There are four possible outcomes: 1a, 1b, 2a, 2b. If you choose the 2b route, you never believed in a nonexistent God, and there's no Heaven to miss out on. If you choose 2a, you didn't believe in God, He exists, and He's sending you to the fire. If you look at 1b, you believed in a nonexistent God and you'll end up like 2b, but looking at the positive side, maybe you lived a more moral life."

"Maybe not."

"The only way to get to Heaven in his argument is through 1a. You believe and your reward is eternal bliss. I'm more nuanced than that, but it's a framework for the picture."

"Too basic for me. I think there's power in *questioning*. Sometimes it can be a much more effective weapon than an aggressive statement[62]."

"That's what I've been doing my whole life, and maybe that's why I'm seeking a different approach. I'm finding the more I keep answering questions with more questions, the more unsettled I feel. I'm really conflicted."

"I wouldn't worry much about it, man. Take the Ebionites, Marcionites, and the Gnostics. They were around during Christ's time, more or less, and they couldn't agree on the answers either. Look how far we are from those moments."

"True. You seem to know a lot about this."

"I listened to an audiobook to impress this girl a few years ago."

"Did it work?"

"It had the opposite effect. But anyway, the Descartes argument assumes God is logical, and if so, *simply* logical. That's unlikely based on the intricacy of the universe. To me, it's possible that God is so large or removed that he doesn't know we exist, or that God is quantum, within every atom of our universal structure. There's this professor I know that says that God positively exists, but he doesn't know that he exists, which is a cool idea. Or maybe God is an entity that has just as many questions as we do, and probably a lot more. Maybe *questioning* is what it's all about."

"It's also about a woman I just fell in love with, out of nowhere."

Roosevelt raises his flask. "Isn't everything?"

"So, what do you know about the artist, Axlia Clia? Am I saying that correctly? Where is she tonight?"

"She's something marvelous with some outer-space grace, I promise. Word is she's here, but anonymous and tricky to spot. She speaks with her art, really. I wish I could say more, but I'm stuck here writing some poems, adding to the cinematography, and sworn to secrecy, so I haven't done any exploring yet."

"Yes, well, dope show. I'm into it. Nice talking to you and thanks for the drink."

"No problem. Do you want me to put some ink down? I can summarize our conversation or you can suggest something."

"Of course, almost forgot. How about something dangerous. To question something seems appropriate."

They shake hands and pull away with a collection of finger snaps. After Roosevelt finishes the last drops of cognac from his flask, he waits a minute before taking the marker to the canvas.

DARK CCORNERS YIELD TRUTHS,
SOMETIMES WHEN YOU SEE THE LIGHT,
IT ISN'T TOO BRIGHT.

Jesús Neon Woodson walks through the various gallery rooms with video loops and installations before entering the small altered library. Near the door there's a pin-straight platinum blonde woman with the darkest of eyes who puts a ✓ in the following boxes:

- ▢ foxy

- ▢ fierce

- ▢ fine

- ▢ furtive

She notices him but pays him not one cent. Normally that would have presented some kind of challenge, but Zeus is in a place of peace and sustained internal bliss because of Ms. Candy Lovinglace. Also, the wig thing bothers him. He scans some of the yellowed pages with softened corners under gallery lights. One book makes him think of his mom. The connection is unexpected. He remembers seeing *"Tonight at Noon"* on his mother's bookshelf in her bedroom when he was a kid. He'd never read it, but he liked the title because it didn't make sense. Zeus isn't sure if his mom had read it either, but if he had to guess, he would say that she at least started it. He thought of the title one day in school when the concept of a large sphere spinning and whirling around at ridiculous speeds around another sphere of even greater girth was introduced in science class. It began to fill the mold of understanding. The title of the book went from abstract to possible as Zeus learned about worldwide timezones. Tonight at noon, this morning at midnight, this afternoon at dusk, all became language games to reach a meeting point across time and space. These phrases led to the possibilities of time travel over short distances, where tomorrow can be today and yesterday is now. So, here in the Mission gallery, he thinks of his mom and lost time, and he goes to find a quiet space where he can call her, three hours prior to that moment. His mom's sleeping habits can best be described as erratic and possibly crepuscular, so he never knows if she'll pick up. He finds a dark alcove at the far end of the small library where the other voices are subdued. As he waits for her to answer, he also becomes aware of sound waves from the other side bouncing against the door he's leaning against. From left and right, the audio in the alcove warbles, creating a stereo of uncertainty. The phone rings several times until he lands in robot speakerland and he leaves a voicemail that expresses truths on two fronts: that he misses their two-person nuclear family, and that he wants her to meet Candy a.s.a.p.

The door is difficult to open, but he presses himself against it and nudges it ajar to find the source of the curious sounds. Zeus sees the bottom of a man's shoe, which is patent leathery, without scuffs or creases, and still—even though it looks like the man is running away from him. He follows his sightline along the man's leg to his black-suited torso, and to his black derby. The man is in a hurry, but motionless. In front of him is another man in mid-stride, dressed just the same. Zeus is now leaning through the door opening into the unknown zone almost too far to regain his balance. In front of those two men are five more in a more relaxed gait, frozen, with the same suits, hats, and accessories. And in front of those men are a dozen more standing like suited statues. All of the men are fixed toward a woman standing in front of a curtain by the far wall. Her arms are belled out along the side of her black cocktail dress. Zeus traces the sheen of her smooth legs to her hinged plastic knee joints. Her face is just as lustrous and adorned with red lipstick kissed onto the featureless surface. Her closed eyes are represented by two wide parabolas with splashes of black mascara. And there's a mark of beauty, a Marilyn piercing with a small black diamond pinned above the model's lips. He's now leaning far enough into the hidden hallway so the only parts of him left in the alcove of the small library are his legs, unseen by the gallery patrons. He teeters to the point of no return and stumbles down a large step, falling to one knee, scuffing his pants, and cursing himself under his breath. The door closes behind him. The noises from the small library have gone mute. Now all he hears is light background music[63] and a voice, *her* voice. As Zeus weaves through the mannequin men he keeps looking back over his shoulder—for someone to be watching him or for cameras or anything else. The voice is just above whisper level and repeats the same cadence of words. *Find your place behind the curtain.* He approaches her face-to-faceless, gives her the once over, and again looks back down the hallway over the sea of derbies to the alcove door where he had emerged. *Find your place behind the curtain.*

With trepidation, he pulls the accordion folds of burgundy to one side. Behind it is a door of solid dark wood that stretches long and square in all directions. There are two strong beams raised above the inlay that run east to west, and north to south. In the center, like the origin of a cartesian plane, is a brass doorknob emblazoned with a bold-faced capital **D**. There are brass letters fixed to the door on either side, and Zeus runs his finger over their outlines: GOODEVIL.

With his hand over the doorknob he twists it and slips through the opening. There's a tall staircase that goes straight up without an end in sight. He ascends the stairs to find a small room with a modest prohibition-style bar with one stool leaning forward on two legs, and a bartender, also on two legs, muddling fruit in a rocks glass. The music is Gershwin, but the rhapsody is in the heart, which begins to increase in tempo. The bartender, Jasmine, wears something that's only revealing when the observer is equipped with the right kind of imagination, which Zeus has. The clarinet notes roll around the room and warm the surroundings. There's a book propped up by a plate stand and opened toward the bartender. Zeus scans the cover and spine: [The Bartender's Guide to Shaking the Sugar, by Jessica Jolly-Palas]. Zeus moves his lips but no words escape. He clears his throat and approaches the bar and returns the stool to its natural animalistic stance. "So, finally, a live person! What have I gotten myself into? What is this?"

The bartender finishes making him a cocktail and slides it toward him. *"Whatever it is, it's all for you."*

"Are you the artist?"

"Whoever I am, I'm all for you."

"Got it. And even though I don't know where I am, this is pretty wild. Is that an old-fashioned? For me?"

"Whatever it is, it's all for you."

The bartender slips behind another curtain behind the bar and Zeus is left alone with his drink that's the color of the darkest orange of an urban sunset. He listens to Gershwin and lets his mind wander within the measures. He pictures mental gifs of his mother dancing in a blue flowing dress. And he thinks in photographs of the neon memories with his father at Coney Island. His mind wanders in the now and revels in the mystery of what's at hand, like a drive-thru nirvana. Then it goes ahead of the current time, well beyond the music end, with summer-toned images of Candy love and a small family. The bartender returns and interrupts his frame. Jasmine gestures with an upturned palm toward the wall.

"If you'd like to continue, it's all for you."

Zeus slips a fifty under the glass, stands up, and returns the stool to a lean. He walks to the wall and checks for seams. As he pushes, the wall moves forward, hinged on one side. He looks back to the bar with a grin, but Jasmine is nowhere to be seen. The next space is considerably cooler and he feels a rush of sweet air envelop his senses. The space remains dark as pitch until he closes the door behind him. Then, like a switch, there's a sepian light low and in the distance. Tricky's *Makes Me Wanna Die* is pumping with the super-bass turned all the way up. There's a vanilla wind that billows long convex silk sheets against his body on both sides. It distorts the light with ripples and shadows. As he moves down the hallway, the floor feels like a shallow quicksand under his feet. The sound waves judder his entire atomic structure as he becomes one with the harmonic vacillations. This overstimulation produces a focus of synaptic activity that he's unaware of. He takes his time. When Zeus approaches the sepian glow he again comes to a wall, that when he pushes it, acts as the off switch to all of the kinetics. His ears are overwhelmed by the sudden silence, ringing in the aftershock.

This room is larger than the previous ones and is painted black on all six surfaces. Zeus adjusts his eyes. There are bare Edison lightbulbs hanging from the ceiling at differing heights, many just inches from the floor. Zeus carefully makes his way through the golden twinkles like a giant wading through the cosmos. When his eardrums return to working order, the sounds of chimes give voices to the miniature suns. Some distance later, the outline of a door is glowing red.

When he pushes through to the other side, there's a flood of red light coming from a single source on the far side of the room. In front him are tens of nude mannequins catatonically transfixed in his direction. Each of them have one arm extended, pointed at him. The only sound in the room is of a bass pulse once per second. Zeus is unsettled, but moves forward, C-walking and Ɔ-walking his way through the crowd. He trips on one of the legs, but catches himself by landing on all fours. As he rises, he could swear that he'd seen someone move near the wall.

He squints as he approaches the red spotlight, makes his way around it, and walks down a narrow hallway that twists and turns like a maze. At the end there's another door. It opens to a white room traversed by synthetic sunbeams. It's laboratory bright. There's no sound. He sees the backside of a nude mannequin with long black hair reclining on a lucite bench. The mannequin is staring at the lone item on the wall, a gold-framed blank canvas. The frame is ornate and swirly with a recess in the center of the top beam that houses a black jewel. And there's a small bracket on the bottom of the frame that cradles a black paint pen. Zeus stands there for two solid minutes, partially in relaxation, and also trying to figure out what he's supposed to be appreciating or doing.

The reclining mannequin begins to move. Joint by joint, she rises with plastic clacks. His heart skips a beat. Her hands and feet are free from the mannequin shell and all twenty of her nails are unpainted. She turns to him. He sees her face, natural, beautiful, and serene, with not one hint of mascara or blush. The artist looks at him with something of a smile.

Zeus begins to introduce himself, but Axlia reaches across the gallery bench and places her finger perpendicular to his lips. She steps around to his side and holds his right shoulder with both hands while propping herself up on her tiptoes. Axlia whispers instructions to him, her breath warm and ticklish, while she occasionally makes light contact with his ear.

Zeus goes up to the framed canvas and takes the marker into his right hand. He feels Axlia's aura exuding through the plastic armor from behind him. The frame is of typical portrait dimensions, like a baseball card, he thinks. Zeus follows his instructions and starts his first ever self-depiction using a 1987 Topps design as his template. He draws a frame within the frame and adds the wood-grain details. He draws the best circle he can in the top left corner where he puts his team logo, a McDonald's M. He draws a rectangle on the bottom and writes his given name in block-letters: **JESÚS NEON WOODSON**. Then he goes back to the logo in the corner and puts a slash through it, which probably violates some part of his contract. When he outlines his shoulders, he realizes he hasn't left room for his whole head. Instead of trying to correct his mistake with permanent marker, he decides to improvise, as the poet had not long before his strange journey began. He draws in a pinstriped jersey and buttons going down the middle. For his team name he uses script. He was going to write *Clowns* across his chest, but stops before the *s* , and adds a script *The* in front. Still headless, he begins to draw in his arms and arthritically contorted hands. He sketches in a bat that he holds over his heart. It extends to the top of the baseball card and then out of the frame, as he draws the barrel directly onto the gallery wall. In the space over the other shoulder, he writes notes just as he would if he were at home on his couch.

BE KIND & HELPFUL
VISIT MOM
BUY COFFEE & OJ
GET A JOB
TELL CANDY I ♥ YOU
READ BIBLE FOR
WEDNESDAY NIGHT MEETING
GO TO SLEEP EARLY

Then he inks a black ring on one of his fingers, the important one. On the wall outside the frame he writes in a zap-like bubble: **"SPRING FEVER, CATCH IT !"** Next he writes in the *topps* logo on the bottom left of the card. The last thing he has to do is represent his own likeness, his face. Really, every part of our body *is* us, but the face is the PR Department. The shape he gives is more skeletal than fleshy, but he makes up for it with surprisingly vivid eyes. His nose is only marked by a diaeresis and his mouth looks hieroglyphic at best, but the eyes are spot-on. He's just able to fit them on the canvas. Zeus draws the baseball cap outside of the frame, blackened and sideways. He smirks to himself for a moment and looks over his shoulder to assess the artist's opinion, but she's nowhere to be found. Zeus reaches up to the frame and removes the black diamond, as Axlia had whispered for him to do upon completion. He feels the diamond's sharp points, its fragility in stature, and its solidity as a constant. Then he looks at his self-portrait, searching deep within his own eyes for something beyond the wall.

TÝR

LIKE AN ELECTRIC CATERPILLAR NEEDLING IN FLIGHT,
A SPARKLER TWISTS WITH A WILD STYLE FLOURISH
AS THE PROPHET SCRIBES HIS TRUTH EPHEMERALLY.

ITS LUMINOUS FLUX IS HARMONY HIGH,
ITS MESSAGE, LIKE A QUIET KISS,
DISSIPATES INTO THE MIST.

[[❋]]

Enter the den of silence.

The stereo is unplugged, the phone is dead, and there isn't one siren or horn on the street below. Roosevelt wakes up in his own apartment for the last time. He's half-naked and puffy-faced, like a boxer post-fight. And his right hand is super sore—even for him—after all the non-stop graffiti and poetry at the gallery. Lying on his back, Roosevelt lifts his arm and his eyes trace the veins and bone structure of the back of his hand. He watches his fingers move in circular waves, like he's saying *beautiful* in sign language, both forward and backward. He staggers to his closet and starts to move his cash close to the door. The cash is in four heavy canvas duffel bags and two backpacks. They're all busting at the seams.

From the small kitchen table, he grabs a granola bar and finishes it in two bites. Roosevelt feels the sandy quality of dirt over linoleum under his bare feet. He rubs his eyes with the heels of his hands. Then he has another granola bar, this time in three bites.

Roosevelt recalls the conversation he had with Della after the show—about its success across many fronts, how he'd talked with the same man that participated in the one-of-one show, and the tensions of the night throughout the gallery. He mentioned that he was very proud to have been part of it, that she had strived in adverse conditions, and that she had a unique voice. Roosevelt transitioned to how he wanted to leave the city and wasn't sure when he'd return. That he had a destination in mind, but didn't know—and didn't want to plan exactly—how he'd get there. The journey was the whole point of having a destination. He didn't tell her the spot on the map, but mentioned that it was out west. Way west. That maybe he was going to trade one island for another. And whether subtly or not, he implied he wouldn't mind if he had someone accompany him. He acknowledged that he was in a transitional phase, but that it was also a common state for him. Roosevelt told Della that he was leaving his apartment the next day and that his improvised journey would begin. In turn, she suggested that if it were truly an improvised trip, he would be willing to stay with her for the first few days. Also, only half-kiddingly, that he hadn't consulted her about this voyage. He agreed on both accounts and said he'd see her in the morning. (In truth, he planned on staying in a Manhattan hotel that shares his name until he'd tied up some loose ends, chiefly the one involving her safety, regardless of her reaction.)

On his bed, there's a third backpack that's empty and unzipped. Roosevelt scans his apartment for what's important to take with him. There are neat stacks of journals and sketchbooks, a color wheel of spray cans, a row of paint-dripped kicks, his flask, and a smattering of keepsakes: framed photos, postcards, a vintage clock radio, and his military patches and medals. Leaving behind the shoes, he takes as much as the backpack will allow, removing the pictures and hanging the empty frames back on the wall. He places the third backpack by the door and makes the bed.

Roosevelt puts on a black suit, a black shirt, and no tie. He takes a pair of Puma Clydes with a metallic rainbow of drips out to the fire escape. He goes over them with black spray paint for an aerosol spit shine and lets them dry for a few minutes—everything's brand new.

Roosevelt tucks his phone and his red journal into his suit jacket, slides the duffel bags and backpacks into the hallway, places his keys next to an envelope on the desk that contains three months rent, and locks the door from the inside before closing it. A locksmith should get some work, he thinks.

Roosevelt descends all the way to the A train platform with three backpacks piled over his shoulders and two duffel bags in each hand. He walks along the yellow nubbed safety strips until the rush of air and metal approaches the station. He takes a seat at one end of the car, armoring himself with seven figures, and heads uptown to see Della[64].

From a busted plastic box, Roosevelt buzzes Della in her second floor apartment. She unlocks the lobby door and leaves her own ajar as she makes her way back to bed. She expects him to make it up the flight within moments, but she hears the bass of hallway disruptions. It sounds like he's falling *up* the stairs. A full minute later, Roosevelt arrives with packed backpacks and lugged luggage, standing in her doorframe. He looks around her apartment and sees the painted shadows of canvas edges and the faint right angles intersecting on the floor and walls. There are no curves except her own.

"I thought my place was sparse."

One of Axlia's eyebrows rises to her hairline and she turns over to lie facedown on her bed. Then she closes both eyes, one for exhaustion, and the other for comfort. Roosevelt kneels at the foot of her bed and kisses each one of her toes before starting to give her a massage. He works up each leg to her thighs, caresses her lacy bottom, spends time kneading her lower back, works his thumbs on each side of her bare spine careful not to get near her wound, plays some jazz piano on her shoulders, dances his fingers along her neck, and moves in circles over her temples. The vivid sunlight, filtered through the red curtains, shines down on the landscapes of her back like a field of crimson clovers. Roosevelt is now lying beside her, his heart rate twice hers.

"Do you want some breakfast? I can run get some bagels and coffee or whatever you'd like. As you know, I have no future."

She's either sleeping, in a muscular trance, or just being herself.

"I was kidding about the future part."

She turns her head forty-five degrees; her eyes are still closed.

"I'm in the mood for bagels, I haven't had one in forever. Plain with veggie cream cheese or a French toast bagel with plain cream cheese. Those are my two joints right there." The curtain moves and lets in a sliver of pure planar light. "And Della, I need to tell you something that's been on my mind for the past few days. It'll take a little while to explain. I didn't go into it in detail last night, but now that the opening is over, I think it's time." Roosevelt runs his hand up and down her back as he tells her about his shady dealings with the clients of The Office. He tells her about the text messages and how the bullet that wounded her was unlikely a stray. He tells her that it was strange and complicated, and that he'd taken measures both through a private security detail and through his connections in the police force to protect her and try to uncover the truth about that night. He tells her that depending on how she feels, he'll stay with her indefinitely.

"Are you sleeping?"

She is.

"I'll be right back."

Roosevelt kisses her neck and slides backward off the bed. He finds a receipt by her desk and writes her a little poem. The muscles in his hand are still numb.

*

((CONSTELLATIONS CONSIST
OF BURNT OUT ANCIENT WORLDS
AND PAINT OUR SKY WITH GALACTIC SWIRLS.
❄
THEY WERE ONCE THE ONES WHO WERE BORN
WITH LOVE, STYLE, AND TRUST,
AND IMAGINED THE POSSIBILITIES OF US.))

. GOOD MORNING .
143

. . .

Nightly Internet News Transcript
Tuesday, April 14, MMXX
(Uploaded 8 hours ago)
1,794,328 Views

"I am William Howler and it's just after midnight. Earlier this evening, this was the scene at the Mission Art Gallery. It's a repeat of the now infamous performance where the artist known as Axlia Clia was wounded by a bullet in Harlem. Only this time it was prerecorded and performed by holograms of her walking around the perimeter of the gallery. The holograms are nude, save for black and white body paint. As you may imagine, this angered many parents as they innocently walked with their children on the streets of their neighborhood. Calls were made for religious officials to protest the art show that has turned this church into a magnet of sin. When a multi-faith coalition approached Mission, they were picketing in the same path of the holograms, unbeknownst to them. These men and women of God were repeatedly being entered by these naked ghosts! Is this the end of discretion?! Is nothing sacred?! There are further protests being planned right now, with the intention of being better coordinated and informed. And that's just what was going on on the outside. Inside there are reports of further desecration: suggestive paintings, offensive language and poetry, something called HYMEN TEARS, pictures of the crucifix between women's cleavage, and an altered Bible. She changed God's words! Again, is this the end of discretion?! Is nothing sacred?! As for the *artist*, where was she? Apparently she was in the Mission Gallery performing a one-time show for a single patron that will never be repeated or recorded. Right, I can only imagine what happened in that situation! Shouldn't you apologize to the children of faith? Show your face and say something for yourself!

There are also calls for a public protest of all Cyrus Coaster movies, the stores on the 10 on 10th, and the entire Wiccan faith, if that's what you call it. Yet despite the community outcry, there are further reports that every piece in the gallery had been sold by the close of this opening night. Personally, I wouldn't want any of those items hanging in my home. I apologize for my very personal slant to this story, but this affects my ever-growing Christian faith, which I came to fully experience two years ago. I feel it necessary to be sincere. To end on a good note, there are rumors that The Defenders of Christ will assume involvement in the deescalation of this paltry and profane art. For the latest on this developing story, stay connected, we'll bring you the news before it breaks. Have a *pleasant* night, and I'll be home *soon*, honey! I can't wait to see *you* and *only you*! For N.I.N., God Bless. I am William Howler."

· · ·

When Roosevelt returns with coffee and a brown paper bag with too many bagels and several cream cheese options, he sees Della curled up sideways on her bed next to the poem on the back of the receipt, which is also curled. She turns to sit up and leans on her elbows, still topless, and smiles. Roosevelt unbuttons the top two buttons of his shirt before pulling it over his head.

It was a mid-morning delight, a daydream that became an hour-long trance. There was something charming about its naiveté, the way they stayed in one position the entire time. But it was focused in a minimalistic sort of way, where the new modes and levels of what is basic became magical through furthered exploration, like a Steve Reich album maybe. They kissed the entire time like it was a recent revelation, while the motion in the ocean was a midnight cruise on December 31, 1999.

Roosevelt is passed out and facedown with his legs crossed like the numeral 4. Della stands up and puts on soft denim, a pair of shoes, and then zips a black jacket over her bare skin. She reaches past the untouched bag of bagels for a clove cigarette and some matches.

Della walks out of the apartment and over to her street stage across the way. She lights the clove, takes in the first burn, and thinks about the art opening for as long as it takes for the smoke to disappear. Then she shifts her thoughts, wondering if she too needs a break from the city. She takes a deep breath of Manhattan air. Adventure and change are healthy, she tells herself. And while Della's mind is clear, it's also saturated with new ideas. It is somewhere in the near future, just around the corner of now.

She wanders back and forth on the cement, free from the canvases and paint. When she finishes her cigarette, she swirls the flame out on the bottom of one of her flats, walks to the trash can, and throws it out.

She sits down on the bed next to Roosevelt and says, "Where do you want to go? I'm coming with you."

He reaches into one of the backpacks, the one without any money, and pulls out a postcard from a friend from his days in the Air Force. He hands it to Della.

> Roosevelt,
> Can you still get up?
> MSgt. Kay

She turns it over to the picture side. There's a staircase vanishing to a green mountain summit in the clouds.

* CLIMB THE HAIKŪ STAIRS OF OAHU, HAWAII *

[[⚲]]

Zeus is on the phone with Candy. He's looking in the mirror and turning his Yankee baseball cap sideways. "I don't know if you saw what I did last night, but I wish you were there with me." He pulls his cap straight forward and down. "I stumbled into something that I didn't know was part of the show. It was this one-of-one art performance and I was the person to experience it. All the scenery, the different rooms, music, a drink at a bar, were created for me. Well, *me* being the one who happened upon it. And the whole thing was taken down an hour later, only to live in the black hole of my reminiscence."

Candy asks him a question.

"Exactly. I'll tell you about the whole thing step-by-step when I see you." He turns the hat backward and his eyebrows are pulled up a bit. "A quick version? Sure. I first got involved by trying to leave a voicemail for my mom and it was loud in the gallery. I was in this little library room and there was a small alcove on one side. I figured it would be a little quieter. But as I went in farther, I started to hear something from behind a door. I was curious and pushed through and fell down into some kind of hidden hallway. It was strange. The hallway had all of these mannequins that looked like they were running somewhere, but had been touched in a perfect game of freeze tag. When I looked down to the end of the hallway I saw they they were running toward a woman, another mannequin actually, who I believe represented the artist. It's just like it was outside the gallery, all of those patrons were just mannequins with a pulse. Meaningless individually, but important in number. But then again, she was hollow and plastic, and the center of attention. So maybe it falls back to the masses—the empty vessels interested in something unattainable and unreal, a figurehead for their curiosities and fantasies. I might be thinking about this too much right now. Then the mannequin started to speak to me. She said, 'Whatever it is, it's all for you.' The words represented something I used to think about when I was young. It sounds terrible now, but I used to wonder if the world was designed just for me. Anyway, I felt compelled to believe."

Candy speaks for a few minutes, repeating some of his story as he exchanges various *yeses* and *uh-huhs* in confirmation. His hat is now inside out.

"I'll tell you about the whole thing. Promise."

As she speaks again, Zeus practices flipping the hat from his hand up to his head with one move.

"It's that there was so much to take in. It was multi-sensory." Zeus moves closer to the mirror and pulls a stray eyebrow hair out with his fingernails. Candy asks about the drink at the bar.

"It was an old-fashioned." He tries to raise his left eyebrow without moving his right as Candy asks more questions.

"Oh sure, spot on." His right eyebrow muscles cooperate with his brain commands much better than the left. "And the artist, she was naked, sort of. She was wearing the shell of a mannequin. I could see her face, hands, and feet. Come to think of it, I'm not sure whether it was her hair or not. And I didn't see a spot of makeup. She was plastic and natural." Zeus flares his nostrils over and over, wondering how much different his face would look like if they were flared all the time. "You never need make-up in my opinion. You're perfect. You have the best face!" Zeus walks away from his mirror and into his living room, his nostrils still flared. Candy blushes audibly. "No, I'm serious, you do! And in retrospect, her whole get-up made me think of the absence of embellishments. I mean, think of the term *make-up*. It's either *make*-up, like make- believe, like it's all fake—or it's make-*up*, like it's an improvement over imperfections. But I think some people go way too far with it, where it becomes a mask they hide behind. And then they don't feel comfortable without it. It can become a domino effect for how they feel others perceive them, creating a false sense of their true identity."

He sinks into the couch.

Candy talks about the different parts of an identity.

"Right, interesting. That falseness could be their truth—their existence a forgery."

Zeus places the hat upside-down on the coffee table and spins it as Candy continues.

"But if they continue to layer all of those colors and shades on their face, they may not connect with someone in a pure way. Although, who am I to know what's the pure way? I guess what I'm saying is that their make-up ends up masking what's really already perfect. Am I being annoying or deep?"

Zeus listens to Candy and crosses his ankles on the coffee table. "Skin deep. Exactly!" He uses his non-phone hand to adjust the private trinity in his boxers.

Candy gives her opinion of what make-up does and how his night was much more interesting than hers.

"True. Yes. Just another strange night in Alphabet City. I really wish you were there."

As Candy speaks, he becomes more relaxed, at ease with where he's headed. Her voice is soothing and rhythmic, the ultimate soul music. "I know you said tomorrow night's prayer meeting might go long, but if it's not too late, can I give you a ring after it's over?"

To Zeus, what Candy says sounds like Aretha Franklin's *Call Me*. Her quick reply is a condensed form of four minutes of melodic tranquility—a delicate exaggeration.

His eyelids lower. "You know you're all I think about. Your beauty, your words, our connection, everything. And even though we only met a week ago... I Love You."

As Candy responds, his eyelashes begin to flutter, and he smiles. Then Zeus closes his eyes, falls asleep, and takes a noontime nap. During this time his legs manage to uncross and he knocks over a stack of 1987 Topps baseball cards.

[[✝]]

"It's the decision to continue going after the artists and philosophers is what I'm unsure about—specifically these four. It may have something to do with the position we find ourselves in. We will do all we can to undermine Coaster, but we don't want the collateral damage to bring sympathy to their cause. Despite their involvement with this show and their vulgar displays in a former house of worship, there are some that will be compassionate—and not only people from their wretched community—but people from our side too. I can see sending a subtle message to them, but nothing that will bring the waning liberal media to their cause. We're on the verge of getting the power we've sought for a long time. I don't want to compromise that. We will bring their questioning and heresy to their knees, but no further. Shall I read the names on the list? O.K. Here they are in order of importance:

McJesús Neon Woodson is a man caught in two nets, if you will. There is the matter regarding Joyce and Candice for one, and the fact that he was observed as a patron of the Mission Gallery for the other. He received the special private show by the artist. I have a hard time believing that it was all one big coincidence. With his name and Coaster's reputation, I imagine he is somehow involved with the marketing of the show, and that he's a full supporter of the trash on display. Here's some background. He doesn't have that many strong connections. There is his mother, Yvonne Flora, who lives in California. He doesn't see her often, but they do communicate daily. And a Melanie Millan of New York City, who appears to be his best friend and cohort, accomplice even. Mr. Woodson's father is estranged as far as we know. He's been missing for quite some time. We put some of our best researchers on it, but all leads have come up empty so far.

Della Crème, doing business as Axlia Clia, is the performance artist at the center of Phases, the show at Mission. Her profile in society has increased significantly, although she's not known in the mainstream... yet. She's from Indiana and made the move to the city several years ago. Her family only seems to think she works with artists, but is not one herself. The communication between them is almost non-existent, as far as we can tell. They are a faithful family. If they are informed of her actions, they will not support them. To find out your daughter is walking around naked in a church? Well, I can only imagine. She has a staff of sorts, a woman named Jasmine Nector, who also has a connection to another person on our list, which we'll get to later. And there are two men who are involved with her art projects. We've identified them through some of her videos and still shots, but we are yet to put names to them. They were there during our first attempt to suppress her in Harlem. She's been on our radar for some time. Ms. Crème now has formed a connection to the graffiti artist at her show. You'll be briefed on him as well. Oh, and, she doesn't really... talk.

Ms. Summer Evers, this is a complicated case here. We've contracted her to work for us on several occasions, exclusively to create and recreate documents we've needed. She's a top flight forger. She worked for cash all but one time. That time was last week when Brother Samson shepherded an operation in Death Valley. The agreement was *a favor for a favor*, and was to be our last transaction. Last night she was seen trying to be unseen at the Mission Gallery in the vicinity of a so-called Altered Library. The exhibit is made up of actual books where certain pages have been changed to fit her desires or views. And they were done in such a way where it was undetectable to even the well-trained eye. Unless she knows another forger and was there in support, I'm thinking that she's likely the person responsible for this part of the show.

One of the men on our reconnaissance team took note that the books looked like library books. He noticed some discoloration on the bottom of the spines, where the plastic band might have been. That may have been part of the altered library theme, it's hard to say. But this may give us a lead as to where she works, and under what alias. This Summer Evers is a bit of a ghost. She doesn't even exist on paper and has no digital imprint. My opinion is that she's the liaison between Jasmine Nector and Axlia Clia/Della Crème. This places her as an originator and accomplice with regard to this sinful show, and bears the sole responsibility for the altered Bible that was on display. We've also accessed some intel on her recent past, her college years. We keep coming up with a curious name whenever we've dug into the Columbia University archives: Beverly B. Sunshine. Whatever their relationship, or whether they're one and the same, will be explored. But in the immediate, we've used our financial resources to anonymously purchase the entire collection. This altered Bible is our chief concern. We didn't want it falling into the hands of someone who will promote it, or profit it from it any further. It's hard to say what she's done with the rest of the books in this altered library, but we would like to rid the world of them.

Elgin Lee Roosevelt, who uses his last name as a monomym, probably from his days as an Air Force pilot, is the poet and graffiti artist who's responsible for the live painting in the sanctuary. The content of which we all find offensive, as he questions the essence of what we hold dear. Yet he is a man who, despite his military background, may not know the ramifications of his involvement here, possibly the most innocent of the lot. But the further we look into his life, we find that he's not just a poet, but a bonafide vandal. The work on display had some similar characteristics to some graffiti seen in the city by our operatives. But all of that scribbling looks the same to me. He also ran a second avenue newsstand for the past few years that had a side business that flew under the radar of the authorities—or maybe in conjunction with them. It was some kind of cell phone harboring service where one could appear to be in one place, answering texts and the like, while they were off doing whatever sinful activities they wanted. Not so innocent after all.

He's also drawn some personal interest from Axlia Clia/Della Crème, which is why he's now an important figure. Again, he's possibly unaware, but he'll be watched closely. We have a few leads on the names of friends and associates, but nothing concrete.

To conclude this briefing, I want to stress that this is an effort to *intimidate*, not to harm or terminate. We don't want to encourage any sympathy for these individuals. In your folders you will find your specific assignments. We will convene tomorrow for our Wednesday night prayer meeting at the Cathedral of the Incarnation in Brother Gideon's hometown, where we'll have the perfect opportunity to meet Mr. McJesús Woodson face to face. He will want to impress us, but we will push him into an uncomfortable corner and show him that he has no future with Candice. Then we can assess his fate and put it to rest, and allow Joyce and Candice to move on with their lives, and their mourning of Gideon. As for this evening's plans at this gallery of sin, let's let this Coaster character know that God, The One and Only, is watching and not pleased. Let's close in prayer."

[[Σ]]

The evening ambers saturate her apartment. Her typewriters on the wall are bathed in copper. Suma looks at her closet door and thinks of the polaroids within that document her compulsion. They're shielded from the setting sun, as all memories kept private. She just found out that her altered books had been purchased by a private collector early that morning. She and the room are quiet. She walks to her refrigerator and pulls out a bottle of Sugar Hill. The pop of the cap and the hiss of the carbonation are the first sounds. Then Suma lets out a sigh that is long overdue.

In the lobby by the mailboxes are posted flyers, business cards, and take-out menus. In the middle of this collection, overlapping all the others, she sees a Missing Persons notification. Suma wonders what hers must have looked like back in Death Valley. Then she leaves her apartment building in search of her next self.

She walks the grid, one block south, one block east, over and again. Suma absorbs the sounds of the Manhattan dwellers and watches the city kinetic. Many of the faces are blurred and turning like long exposure photographs from the times when people lived in black and white. But there are a few that are in focus, staring right the hell forward. The gray blurs and distortions are their own kind of eerie, but the statuesque faces have a macabre obedience that's more sinister. Those are the faces that remain.

Suma sees a young woman walk by wearing 3D glasses. There's an older man who nods and then cracks a bright yellow smile, his teeth like Bart Simpson's hair. An elderly woman hunches over to apply magenta-colored wax to lips that are already three coats thick. There's a woman who's talking to herself about her grocery list in a stern voice. Opposite her is a man in pure white leaning against a wall and singing something sweet. Suma is caught in the crossfire of lonely voices.

A man creeps around the corner who has the quality of visual stench. Even his sweat is pouring out like a series of faucets, as if he's turning himself inside out. There are two boys imitating the windup styles of MLB pitchers, each one holding an apple. One of the apples is bitten and browned. An older woman in a wedding dress walks in a circle with a white umbrella overhead. A man a few years shy of Suma's age makes a lame attempt at flirting. He says hello and smiles by pulling his lips inward. Suma nods and keeps walking. A tanned bald man runs by without a shirt. His shorts are begging to be called shorters. An overweight woman pushing a stroller made for quadruplets goes by in the other direction. Her hair looks thin from stress and her face sullen from the same. There's a man that's bejeweled and wears his sexuality on both sleeves, both pant legs, and all four cheeks. On the next block there's a man so average he is unique. If he were to remain the median in a culture whose norms are continuously stretched, he will be required to live in a state of perpetual change, Suma thinks.

New York is chock full of characters that keep it percolating at all hours, but there are the unseen decaf personalities that give it volume. How do they live with themselves?

After the next right-angled turn, Suma sees another person that looks like they're in a long exposure photograph wearing a blurry dark suit. His face is in focus. He doesn't seem to blink or breathe, but is alive with terror. It's a patronizing stare. He is unusually tall. The connection between them is known in one direction and assumed in the other. Suma returns the stare. His thin smile is mostly obscured by his beard. She sees deep slashing scars that surround his two blood red eyes. He's a specter in seek of a haunt.

She walks down the street faster. While she scans the passersby, she feels a presence behind her. She hears a whispering voice say something indiscernible. She walks faster still and uses her periphery to see if this dark presence is real. Nothing. She looks to the windows to catch a reflection of what's chasing her. Nothing. Suma continues to hear lisps and exhales. She considers turning around, but keeps on forward, almost at a jog now. She hears steps that aren't her own. More exhales. Then something sharp and cold creeps down her spine and sends the chills straight back up. She stops dead, as if her feet are nailed to the sidewalk. She hears the clicking sounds of metal gears. The presence says her name and gives her a warning that's four words long. Suma turns around, anticipating the look of the specter's blood red eyes, but no one is there. It's an empty sidewalk with a far away vanishing point. It had been either very real, very internal, or both. Suma's past is catching up with her.

She stands there in silence, her body pulsing with every thunderous

<pre>
                    heartbeat
                    heartbeat
                    heartbeat
                    heartbeat
                    heartbeat
                    heartbeat
                    heartbeat
                    heartbeat
                    heart beat
                  heart beat
                heart   beat
              heart   beat
            heart   beat
          heart   beat
        heart   beat
      heart   beat
    heart   beat
</pre>

until she relaxes into a state of composure.

Suma completes her zig-zags on the grid like a slow lightning bolt moving through Manhattan. Her pointed end is at [Halcyon Books]. She walks inside. A bunny bounces by and leads her to a section she's never visited. The shelves are just as stocked as the others, but there's something missing—the words on the pages. The journal section of Halcyon is a skyline of varying spines, some bound in leather, canvas, hemp, wood, and synthetics. She runs her hand along the different materials before pulling out a black journal that seems to have had a previous life. When she holds it up to the light, she sees graffiti-style writing covering it in black that's just a shade different. It's meant to be hidden, iridescent only in the light. When she leafs through the lineless pages, she sees that they've been written on as well, only this time in white. It's difficult to read, but the message is clear to Suma. She closes the journal and brushes a few strands of hair away from her face. The absence of typography and the apparent space inspire freedoms that she's been fearful of her whole life. Always having altered the existing statues of rock solid prose, it's now time to create a new structure using old materials. She promises herself to go her own way, a Venus restored, a Venus in motion.

Suma leaves the bookstore on 10th Avenue to the west, away from Mission. She hears sirens and senses fire, but doesn't look back this time. If she had, Suma would've noticed terrible billows of smoke stirring in the background with some ashy debris beginning to twinkle in the sky. All the way from the east end of the block, one piece of yellowed paper flakes down on her shoulder before it's whisked away in her wake. If she'd looked at it, she would've seen some familiar words:

> At once an essential composer in the history of jazz and a bass player extraordinaire, Charles Mingus was born on April 22, 1922, in Nogales, Arizona, and grew up in the Los Angeles neighborhood of Watts. He made his recording debut with Lionel Hampton in 1947, and performed on numerous recordings with Louis Armstrong, Charlie Parker, Stan Getz, Duke Ellington, Bud Powell, Art Tatum, and many others. His several honors included a Guggenheim Fellowship, an honorary degree from Brandeis University, and the Slee Chair in Music at the State University of New York in Buffalo. Charles Mingus died in 19never at the age of

∞

.

Roosevelt leans over the edge of the bed and finds his pants. He reaches into the back pocket, unfolds a paper sign, and gives it to Della. "I just bought it. It was the first car I saw."

FOR SALE

1984 Volkswagen Quantum GL

Turbo Diesel Engine

5-Speed Manual Transmission

4-Door sedan w/trunk

New front bumper and windshield

Moonroof (small crack)

New front tires, back tires still in good condition

Cassette player works

Needs body work and rust repair

Headlights flicker sometimes

Odometer broken, over 200,000 miles

Passed NYS Inspection

Runs O.K.

Sold as is, call number on back anytime

$400 firm, cash only

"It's parked right outside. It'll do for a one-way trip and we can ditch it for something else later. I'm ready to jump this juke joint tomorrow. As for tonight, I'll take you to my show, my hidden spot, my church."

Della smiles and makes prayer hands.

"So here's the quick plan. Before we go out, check that your money from the Coaster sales are squared away and pack up your clothes and whatever else you can fit in that Quantum hooptie. Write a note to the lord of the land with the extra cash for rent in the envelope, and then relax. While you're doing that, I'll pack the car and drive it down to a garage that's close by. I know a guy from my old business that I trust. He'll keep it overnight. He runs a high security operation, so I'm not worried. He's going to give it a tune-up and a new battery too. I gave the girl I bought it from an extra hundred to leave the registration and inspection stickers on the window. Then, I'm going to walk back here, take a shower, maybe with you if I'm lucky, get dressed, and take you out for the night. You don't have any latex gloves, do you?"

Della shakes her head.

"No big deal. It helps the paint from getting under your nails and keeps the evidence to a minimum so we won't get busted. I figure we can leave our mark on the city together."

Roosevelt and Della walk out of her apartment building and onto the sidewalk with linked elbows. A cross street breeze flies Della's pink scarf into his face and catches his light stubble. She pulls it away from him and they share a schoolyard laugh. He tells her of the various tag names he's used over the years and how they evolved into a symbol both small and ubiquitous. She often leans in close and whispers her thoughts in his ear. They talk about the changing colors of the city as they walk south; from the brownstones of Harlem to the marbled façades of the Upper West Side; the April greens of central park to the visual cacophony of Times Square; the brick bookshelf buildings of NoHo to the blue skies over the Lower East Side; the mercurial rise of 8 Spruce Street to the eastern escape of the Brooklyn Bridge; and the grand finale of the Freedom Tower before the quiet harbor. They talk about the aesthetics of forced closeness on a skinny island and some pretty meaningless stuff too, but it doesn't feel that way to them. And even though they talk themselves off the island, they only walk as far as 121st Street, and catch a cab. Their driver violates every traffic law within the first five blocks. Roosevelt sends thought beams into the sky and asks Headache Man for forgiveness.

The taxi stops a block away from [COLOSSUS]. Della is on the curb side of the car and gets out easily enough. Roosevelt has to negotiate the slide across two and a half vinyl seats while paying the driver through the opening in the bulletproof glass. The couple walks into the sculpture store and approaches the speakeasy door. It's the first time they're on the same side of the front window. Roosevelt slips a note through the opening. They wait in the storefront and talk about how sculptures are able to endure injuries far better than paintings. Minutes later they approach the window in the door, Della whispers, "Moritat."

Inside, the jazz seems to flow from the mounted instruments on the wall. They sit next to each other in a corner booth for four. On the cherry wood wall next to them, there's a framed picture of a pigeon hovering in flight over a peaceful and psychedelic sky. Roosevelt reaches down into the seat cushion and pulls out a black pen. He keeps it there as a backup. He explains that this place is a refuge for his mind. "I come here to write down ideas. They can be joyful, desperate, or silly. Sometimes it's to sketch out a poem, or where I'm going to paint that night and what my escape route is going to be."

A cocktail waitress stops at their booth with skepticism. "Hi Roosevelt, how are you tonight?"

He smiles, "Good evening, Mya."

"I see you're not flying solo."

"True. Della is my copilot."

As she looks at Roosevelt, Mya says, "Nice to meet you, Della."

He finds Della's hand under the table. "She's seen me here more than a few times."

"So, would you like to see a drink menu[65], or do you know what you'd like to have?"

"Two of your perfect Manhattans with extra brandied cherries. It's appropriate for tonight." He makes sure Della is O.K. with the order. She nods.

"I'm sure it is. I'll be back in a few minutes."

Roosevelt says to Della, "So, do you want to do a piece together? We can have a drink or two here and set the scheme."

Della responds by switching her current to Axlia Clia mode. She unfolds a napkin and a red pen materializes in her hand. Roosevelt begins the first half of the collaboration. They rule over the napery as bookended autocrats. He begins with his styled name in all-caps, then writes her artist name beneath it with digital lettering. In between the names, Roosevelt pens a short one-line poem with a strikethrough that ends with a right-pointed arrow toward some positive infinity.

When Mya arrives with the cocktails, there are no paper islands on which they can land. She sets them down on the wooden ocean.

Roosevelt says, "Cheers!"

Axlia takes over the delicate canvas by superimposing *Della* in classic script over her artist name. Then she draws a shadowed heart around the whole piece; the arrow now doubling as a cupid's projectile. AC♦DC adds her own style and color to the inside of the heart and finishes by surrounding it with glimmering red giants.

When they leave [COLOSSUS], they're full of warmth and philosophically buzzed. "I wish that life could be this all the time." He leads Della down the sidewalk on 2nd Avenue, just steps from his old newsstand. The electrical power beneath it he'd once harnessed seems at this moment to live inside him. The streets are quiet.

Up from a sidewalk grate, a wave of exhaust curls around them like a blanket of unwanted security. It stays with them for a few blocks until it's interrupted by Della's clove cigarette. She takes one from her purse and sparks it like a campfire, the smoke full of disappearing stories. Roosevelt enjoys the change of scent. Along the way he points out some of the spots he's hit and the poems that are still up. There are haikus on silver poles, tags on the backs of road signs, and a kind of envoi painted on the vertical part of the curb that runs the length of one city block[66]. The exhaust returns and lingers with disdain. The pair begins to slip into the labyrinth, where alleyways are the only ways. The streetlights are few and they're further sheltered from the city sounds. Roosevelt holds a can of black spray paint in his hand and gives it a nonchalant shake. The sound of the metal pea mixing the paint echoes in the urban grooves.

When they turn down the next alley, the stench of the exhaust is still following them. It's undeniable. Roosevelt stops and looks back. Nothing. The two keep on until they reach the secluded center of the labyrinth, the darkest heart of the East Village. There's one light fixed over a door. It shines down and softens the edges. Roosevelt gives the can a good shake and holds his right hand near the top of the door. As he's about to paint the R, his hand beings to tremor. The exhaust feels predatory now. Without trying to seem concerned, he looks back at Della and whispers, "Damn. What is that?" She looks around the alley. Nothing. He writes his name with long arching swoops and abrupt pulldown motions, the muscles of his forearm active and beautiful. He writes her artist name with angled movements, like an orchestra conductor that can produce music directly from his hand. The one-line poem and arrow in between their names points to the future. From his jacket, he gives a can of red spray paint to Della. He's sure his heartbeat is audible, pulsing into every cement crevice. Della shakes the spray paint and reaches up near the door frame. She paints the heart around their names. After she finishes the two halves, the static sounds of the spray can are muted. But Roosevelt and Della hear a lasting reverberation. It's a different kind of static. It's of metal scraping brick and it's close by.

Roosevelt goes into full protection mode, shielding Della from the unknown. He turns to face the source of the noise. The stench of exhaust returns. It is being exhaled from the outline of a dark figure. The figure takes a step toward them and enters the sphere of light, still half-shadowed. He's almost seven feet tall and his eyes look like exposed blood clots. That much they can tell. The figure raises his right arm straight forward in a measured way. Roosevelt and Della see a black steel glove assume an accusatory position. The index finger of the glove is extended and needle sharp. Alongside the spire is the barrel of a gun. Roosevelt raises his right hand in defense and tries to reason with the figure, but he is noiseless and moves forward. The figure looks down upon him before switching his focus to Della. He takes another step forward and the needle pierces the skin of Roosevelt's palm. Roosevelt hears the gears of the glove click into the cocked position and he lunges forward to cover the barrel. This causes the razor point of the steel to go all the way through the other side, skewering his hand. Dismissing the pain, Roosevelt kicks the outside of the figure's knee, causing it to bend inward. He tries to pull his hand off the spire, but the figure lifts his arm higher. He feels the blood running cold down his arm. Roosevelt kicks him in the same place with more force three more times. The figure's knee snaps and fractures sideways, but he still doesn't make a sound. Della looks around for an improvised weapon in the shadows. As Roosevelt again goes for the knee, the figure moves his leg out of the way, only to step on the can of red spray paint. The giant loses his balance and hits the concrete hard. His weight brings Roosevelt down with him, their hands still connected. The fall causes the figure's femur and tibia to puncture both his skin and suit pants. The patella is now on the wrong side of his knee. As Roosevelt tries to attack the exposed area of weakness, the figure grasps his throat. His extended reach pushes Roosevelt farther away. He can't even grab his beard. The figure's scars converge to a flatline before he says four words and squeezes the trigger of the steel glove.

The scenes of the aftermath play in slow motion frames for Della. She watches the shadowy figure try to retreat. He's unable to stand. She sees him crawl away on three limbs, his injured leg dragging behind like weighted tail. She sees that Roosevelt is in shock and that his right hand is gone. As if she is someone else, she watches her own hands reach for him and clutch him from behind. Her head turns toward the door, where she sees that his blood has filled her painted heart.

Once she switches back to regular timeframes, she's able to call for help, both by phone and by screaming into night. Roosevelt holds his wound with his left hand. Della assures him people are on their way and to keep his arm above his heart. She unwraps her pink scarf and ties it around his bicep. Then Della reaches for a can of spray paint, secures the other end of the scarf around it, and creates a tourniquet. She twists the can until the scarf is taut, and then she twists some more, which lessens the blood flow from a pour to a drip.

Della speaks of love and beautiful chromatics and tells him to hold on. She tells him that she will be there for him—that she will be his voice.

Down the dark passageway light beams begin to dance in the distance and grow closer by the moment. The boots treading their way sound like a heavy rain. He feels cold to the core, but he smiles at Della and reaches up with his left hand toward the door. With blood on his hand he begins to write a script capital $\mathscr{D}$, but his arm falls to his side. The boots are now a thunderstorm. Della holds him closer and helps Roosevelt lift his arm all the way up. She warms him with a kiss and together they finish her name.

WEDNESDAY NIGHT MEETING

[[⼮]]

In the afternoon, Zeus steps out of the shower and towels off. In front of the mirror he applies shaving cream with a brush. He makes strange faces as he glides the razor over his stubble. He splashes on two handfuls of after shave and it creates a beard of sting. All smooth now. He slips on black suit pants and his black and gray Kase2 oxfords. He's both commando and sock-less. He buttons a fitted white shirt from the top to the bottom and tucks it in. He has trouble with the belt clasp. With his collar upturned, he puts on a thin tie that's a dark red blend of wool and linen. Then he dons his black suit jacket and clips a pen to his inside pocket. Zeus puts on his Raketa Copernic, grabs his wallet from yesterday's blue jeans, and his Bible from the nightstand. He's been reading it all day.

His driver takes him north to Paley Park on 53rd and 5th. Zeus takes a seat and faces the waterfall. The rushing sounds drown out the surrounding voices. The chill in the air feels mighty healthy. He resumes his reading, focusing on the sections he'd dogeared back in the day. But after an hour or so, the rumbles and tremors of his stomach are impossible to ignore. He's only had coffee and multivitamin gummies today. He texts his driver to pick him up at the 21 Club at 5:45. That gives him at least an hour for dinner and plenty of time to get to the car rental spot in Garden City before he flies solo to the church.

Zeus walks one block south to 52nd and 5th, to the home of the wrought-iron gate and colorful jockeys. He orders a Pour Toujours[67] at the bar and uses the base of the cocktail glass to hold the Bible open to Romans 8:28[68]. He wonders to whom the last *his* refers. The bartenders, Hugh and Estlin, kindly give him hell. He overhears someone at the bar mention an explosion that happened yesterday at the Mission Art Gallery. He takes a big sip and feels the proximity of the reaper a day late.

He checks the news headlines on his phone for the first time in twenty-four hours. While he's reading, he ignores a few calls from an acquaintance he hadn't heard from in a while. His eyes widen and he exhales relief as he tries to process what he's missed.

WEDNESDAY'S HEADLINES
. . .

BLAST-PHEMOUS!
MISSION ART GALLERY DESTROYED
GAS LEAK IS THE CAUSE, INVESTIGATORS SAY

.

POLICE: TICKETS FOR DOUBLE PARKING DOWN 90% THIS YEAR

.

YANKEES WIN IN FENWAY AS WODEHOUSE EARNS THE SAVE BY
STRIKING OUT THE SIDE WITH 9 EEPHUS PITCHES

.

CHAIN RESTAURANT "THE TILTED BURQA" FILES FOR CHAPTER XI

.

LEXICOLOGY REPORT: "CREAM CHEESE" CAN BE USED IN VERB FORM

.

ST. JOHN COLTRANE AFRICAN ORTHODOX CHURCH TO HOLD SUNDAY
SERVICES AT EAST RIVER AMPHITHEATER

.

SPATE OF DRIVE-THRU DRIVE-BY KILLINGS
SLOW FAST FOOD INDUSTRY

.

THE CRUCIFIX CONTINUES TO OUTSELL ANKHS, PRAYER BEADS,
STARS OF DAVID, AND LITTLE BUDDHAS

.

RIP-OFF PROFITS RISE AS NECKLINES FALL

.

GROUNDBREAKING ACTIVISM:
EVANGELICAL EXTREMISTS PLANT LEVITICUS 19:19 SIGNS
IN SUBURBAN GARDENS

HOMEOWNERS GIVE TWO GREEN THUMBS DOWN:
"KEEP YOUR RELIGION OUT OF MY SOILED BACKYARD!"

.

He's ushered to table 50. His waiter's name is Butler, somewhat appropriately. Every time Zeus goes to 21, he's treated like an old friend. He orders a synthetic steak tartare with extra spice, french fries with extra ketchup, and a Jack and Charlie's Ale with extra intention. And for dessert, he has the crème brûlée. It's the perfect combination.

In the limo, he continues to read the Bible and contemplates the events of the past week. He's been reading it without reverence or excitement, acknowledging a state of religious anhedonia. His opinion is that the language in the Bible isn't inspiring, but limiting. It's not an attempt to exalt the Creator, but to quantify Him, and therefore it binds Him to symbolism. It takes him nearly the whole trip to acknowledge that a DeeDeeJ mixtape has been bumping the whole time.

When they get to the Garden City Car Rental he sees the sign out front: *Exotic Cars Available!* It reminds him of a time when he was young and confused the words exotic and erotic. This made him question what some cars are really used for. He gets in a red 2012 Ford Focus. He tells his driver to stay close by, that he'll text him when the meeting is over, and that it might go long. He pulls up to the Cathedral of the Incarnation at 7:16 PM. There are eleven cars parked in a perfect line, each one blacker and more tinted than the last. Zeus parks at the end of the line and gets out of the car. He looks up at the cathedral's imposing spire that reaches into the serenity of the dark blue sky. He whispers to himself, "Oh yeah." It's his attempt to change, possibly the reincarnation of a lovebird.

Up the steps and through the doors, a sudden autumn empyrean folds around him. It's accented by gothic arches, lanterns, pillars, and divinely geometric shapes. Echoes of quiet voices emanate from the circle of chairs in the front of the nave. He takes the only open seat in between a man with a clipboard and an injured giant. The large human's crutches lean against the back of the chair. One of his legs is in a bionic brace. Zeus is the only one without a beard and one of two without sunglasses. His inner monologue says something like: *When she said they were famous, I didn't think she meant these guys.* He nods his head, "Good evening, gentlemen."

Some nod in return, but all is quiet until Chairman Ezra says, "Welcome to our Wednesday night prayer meeting. Let's begin by bowing our heads. Dear Lord, we come here tonight in wonder and reverence for everything You have provided. This beautiful Cathedral, the cool spring air, our kinship with The Almighty..." Zeus isn't paying attention to the words. Rather he is trying to take everything in. The voice reemerges, "...and in His Name we pray. Amen." After a few moments suspended in silence, he continues, "Allow me to make the introductions. My name is Ezra. I'm currently the North American Regional Chairman of The Defenders of Christ, a global organization. While I'm always humbled by the title, I feel especially so tonight, as we are meeting in Brother Gideon's hometown. And to my left is Reverend Stearns, the Dean of this church. We are here to help him with his plans to expand their foreign ministries, financial issues, and a private matter within the church, and how to deal with the new artists and atheist antagonizers. And Reverend, next to you and working around, these gentlemen are The Defenders of Christ: Father Malachi, Elder Saul, Disciple Secretary Jonah, Disciple Habakkuk, Elder Ezekiel, Elder Doctor Obadiah, Disciple Mark, Disciple Noah, and Disciple Samson. Next to him is an important guest invited here by Joyce Lovinglace. He's a friend of Candice's, and from what I understand, he's looking for some direction in the church. Please, allow me to introduce Jesús Woodson. And to my right, I'm very blessed to welcome a new disciple. This is Brother Brigadoon. He's also associated with the Lovinglace family."

Brigadoon is less bearded than the others and has a bandage on one eye. Zeus wishes he didn't shave today. And he wonders how many Brigadoons there are in the world, let alone in Garden City. He figures the answer is one.

Chairman Ezra talks about church business, new members, charitable events, and inspiring hymns. The reverend listens and provides short answers, always appreciative of the advice. He moves to more dogmatic ideas, current events, verses, philosophies, and the Mission Art Gallery. He motions to Zeus, "You were there, weren't you? Please tell us why you wanted to attend such an event?"

"Honestly, I go to a lot of art shows. I wasn't aware of what was going to happen. It was opening night."

"But didn't you know that this was the artist that had walked around naked?"

"I think she was painted. But yes, I knew it was her."

"But to support that kind of activity... that is not something you should associate yourself with. That's partly why we are here tonight—to discuss the decay that sill exists in our country. Would you agree?"

"Well... I'm not sure. I don't know if anything that seems offensive at first glance is to be ignored forever."

"Why?"

"I've learned that the more we—meaning society—suppress our curiosities or subjects we don't like, the more taboo they become, and therefore more attractive somehow. Or if we don't like what some people do, if we ignore it, we will never hear other points of view. Then we might as well just speak into an echo chamber."

"Is that what you think we do?"

"No, that's not what I'm saying. I'm just telling you how I approach life."

"And how well has that gone for you, spiritually?"

"I'm not sure yet. I'm still trying to figure out a lot of things."

"I see. Well, since you're here, I'd like to tell you how we approach these topics and how God plays the central role. He's not a backup to shortsighted desires and curiosities."

"And I'm here to listen and participate."

"Why don't we first listen to you so we can better assess where you are on your journey. I understand you may have questions or doubts, so why don't you take the floor and express these feelings."

Zeus mentions several things he's struggled with and recounts his life story. It's personal and pretty juicy. He talks about the absence of his father and his last memory of him at Coney Island, the hypocrisies of pious leaders, the country's return to religion with what he calls "a wink and a twitch of false sincerity," and, only half-kiddingly, the perils of winning the lottery.

"You have an interesting perspective. Thank you for sharing your testimony and voicing your thoughts. I'm sure that wasn't easy. Let's proceed with a few questions for you."

"Sure."

"Do you think God is perfect?"

He pauses. "I don't know—" And as soon as the words leave his mouth he feels as though he shouldn't be so honest anymore. He thinks of how Candy told him to be the diet version of himself. He tries to walk it back, "I don't know... how to tell if anything is perfect. I'm not sure anyone who's imperfect can be the judge of who is."

"Are you saying that you don't think we should claim that our God is perfect?"

"Of course, you should. I'm just speaking for myself."

"Maybe you're not looking up to the sky with reverence or looking at the way even the smallest pair of baby hands work in perfect concert."

He thinks of birth deformities, but keeps quiet.

Ezra continues, "Maybe you haven't opened your eyes all the way to see clearly? Maybe that's why you're not able to fully appreciate God's creations?"

Zeus tries to keep it light. He chuckles, "I'm not sure all of you appreciate them fully, not right now. Look at what you're wearing."

All heads turn toward him in silence.

"Sorry, just trying to have a little fun here. I just mean that literally you can't fully appreciate God's creations if you're wearing mirrored sunglasses inside a church!" Apparently, not all of the calories have been removed.

With all heads still turned toward him, every member of The D.O.C. remove their sunglasses in unison, and in Brigadoon's case, he removes the bandage. When he looks at their eyes, he tries not to react. He sees the scars, Samson's deep grooves and bloody eyes, Brigadoon's fresh wounds and dried blood. He figured the sunglasses must've been hiding something, but he thought it was more on the technological side. He clears his throat. It's a lonely bellow that reverberates for a long time. It's the only sound in the church.

Brigadoon, in a suddenly serious tone, says, "Let's stay with this. Go ahead and get philosophical here, let your thoughts run. I think we'd all love to learn about the man that Candice is so taken with."

"O.K. But I do feel almost set up for this."

"Are you uncomfortable in the house of the Lord?" Brigadoon asks.

"I thought this was a regular prayer meeting. The ones I've been to have been much different. Usually we start with a prayer, maybe a song, and a passage. Then we talk about how the passage applies to our lives. There was another one I went to at an Eastern Orthodox Church. It was called The Jesus Prayer. It was very relaxing. It was about being contemplative while the gospel is sung. Actually, I even fell asleep one time. I know that doesn't sound good, but with all the incense and the dark lighting..." He trails off.

More silence.

"Well, I feel compelled to be honest," Zeus says.

Brigadoon piggybacks, "There's no better time than now to start."

"That's just it. I think I've always been too honest. That's what gets me in trouble."

The giant next to him adjusts his legs and his knee brace juts into his thigh. He's trying very hard to suppress his natural inclination to be himself. He takes a quick inventory of the thoughts he will not mention. They're the same kind of red-inked questions he has in the back of his Bible, but now they're at the forefront of his mind. *Why do we care for evidence when we're supposed to rely on faith? It seems that once the Bible was written down, the story itself took on the role of evidence. It would hold more validity as a verbal history, possibly. Why, in general, do conservatives take God's side if He's been the last one to conserve anything on Earth—He's been making changes all along. From regretting that He ever created mankind to the flood and the eventual sending down of His only Begotten, He seems to make things up as He goes. Is He compulsive? Autistic? And if He's conservative now, when did this change occur? What do the Biblical contradictions imply? Are they there to make the story more magical? And wouldn't it be more impressive if magic was never mentioned? It does seem as though Jesus can do anything, except swim. Why did He walk on water? Maybe He was more lazy than miraculous. Or maybe the miracle is that the Bible is able defend anything at the same time? Why do people pray for riches when it's something He was concretely against? Why didn't God create non-waste humans? Why can't we use all of what we consume for energy without anything being left over? It's annoying. And if we pray before we eat, why not before we excrete? Why are the sexual organs living next door to all that business? Why are these type of questions looked down upon? Also, sex and violence are expressed in the Bible, but only one is really shunned. I've seen scrambled porn, but never the censorship of weapons. And... If God can do anything, does that mean He can create a world where He doesn't exist?*

Zeus speaks again. "I want to do the right thing and follow God, but sometimes I have a hard time knowing where He is."

"Excuse me?" Ezra asks.

"Where I believe He's going doesn't always match up with what our religious leaders say."

"Where do *you* believe He is going?"

"Well, I have all sorts of ideas about what might happen. I've wondered if the world is a simulation with me at the helm, almost like a first-person video game."

"So you think that we may not even be real? That this entire world is just for you?"

"Look, I'm just answering your question. I'm trying to show you how I think. And to answer your interruption, yes. I've thought about the possibility that you're not real and would be very defensive about not being real if I were to ask you. If this is really a simulation, I imagine I wouldn't be able to break this system simply by guessing that it was. A simulation on this scale would've been constructed with these questions in mind."

Brigadoon says, "That means I might not be real and Candice might not be real. What do you think she'd say to that?"

"I was still in the middle of a thought, but sure, I'm confident that she wouldn't like it if I told her she was just part of a simulation. We're getting really off-base here. You're all being very defensive." And he thinks about the name of their organization. "As you should be."

Silence.

"This is called 'me letting my brain run wild into other dimensions.' Let me take back the *not real* part because what *is* real would take on a different definition. I'm just saying that if the world is truly infinite, not only would everything you can imagine be real, but everything you imagine would also have new imaginations, and those projections would be real as well. It's not just endless possibilities, but endless actualities. So, just to finish up, I've considered many ideas of where God might be taking us. Possibly to a strange mix of transhumanism, unforeseen technology, and intergalactic travel. Or, how can I say this... maybe to some kind of psychedelic singularity, an arcadia of fractal multiverses—and yes, I just came up with that."

More silence.

"Not impressed at all?"

He hears the cracking of knuckles.

"I hope that my honesty about having questions is something that God understands. The God I believe exists is one that knows that complexity breeds sophisticated thoughts. That's how I see my relationship with The Creator. I think society has played the main role in creating the conflict between the two Gods."

Samson echoes, "Two?"

"Well, one God, two perspectives. I want my relationship with God to be personal and private. But that relationship has been altered by religious leaders that include a set of prerequisite beliefs. Now, before you can get personal with God, you must join a group relationship first that fits with what these leaders proclaim. In some ways, they've removed Him from the original equation and substituted themselves as a conditional, but equivalent variable."

"I appreciate your exploring of the mind, but you're making this far too complicated. Just look to the teachings of our Lord. He makes it very clear," Ezra says.

"That's just it. I feel there are areas where His teachings, the parables, for example, are supposed to be subject to the interpretations of the reader. And over time, this may have led to why people simply choose their own type of Christ. For many, it's now a Christ of convenience. Just like our culture of whatever you want, whenever and wherever you want it, He's become Americanized and shown that way throughout the world. It's like we've created a fast food Christ..."

"A McJesus..." Samson says, looking at him with blood red eyes.

Zeus is silent for a change.

"You're treading on sacred ground," Ezra adds. "Be careful."

Zeus leans forward in his seat. "I agree I get too deep sometimes and that I tend to bend toward the unorthodox. But I'm trying to streamline my philosophies. That's why I'm here."

Brigadoon says, "Maybe you should wait to date Candice. Figure these things out first. You sound very unsure of yourself."

"It's not that I'm unsure, it's that I'm sure there's no simple choice. There isn't a dichotomy. There are gray areas and I appreciate them. Maybe the gray is a choice."

Ezra says, "You're saying that when presented with the choice between Heaven or Hell, you're choosing to remain on Earth. It doesn't work like that. We're in the gray right now. You must choose the light above or the darkness below. We believe the Bible makes it a simple choice. The Bible doesn't waver or change."

"In some ways, I'd argue that Jesus has changed. In the New Testament, He was the antiestablishment figure. Now He is the establishment. That kind of change is interesting to think about."

Samson looks at Ezra. "How much longer are we going to listen to this?"

Ezra holds his hands out to quiet an already silent group. Then he nods across the circle. Zeus asks, "You don't find that idea interesting at all?"

Two members of The D.O.C. stand up at the same time and walk toward the door. Zeus begins, "Ezra—"

"Chairman Ezra," Samson says.

"Yes, Chairman Ezra, sorry, maybe it's a good time for me to listen to you. As I've said, I'm in the middle on a lot of these issues, but I want to know how you approach these questions. I'm always open to being persuaded."

The two members walk back in from the outside. Ezra asks them, "Is it the same car?"

They both shake their heads.

"One more question, Mr. Woodson. We saw you driving a different car the other night."

"You followed us?"

"My question is, Mr. Woodson, why do you have those particular decals on your car?"

"Oh, that's just a joke."

Ezra's tone turns more serious. "This isn't something we take lightly. Again, why is that on your car? And is that why you didn't drive it tonight?"

"I didn't drive it because I didn't want to look brash. I wanted to be respectful of the church."

"So, you're being deceptive," Ezra says.

Brigadoon adds, "If he's willing to lie in order to impress us, to appear more humble, imagine what he must be telling Candice."

"Look, I'm an honest person. I wanted to be respectful. That's all. The engine is overwhelming and might've been a distraction to what I thought tonight was going to be about. It feels like I'm on trial for having any questions at all."

Ezra ignores his statement. "Again, why do you have those decals?"

"It's a joke."

"Please tell us the whole story. Who is it that owns the company that sells them? I know that you know him. I've already spoken to him this afternoon. Please tell the disciples and Reverend Stearns how they came to be."

"He's an acquaintance of mine. He's always starting quirky little companies online. We were talking one day outside a café. I made a remark about how many cars had the Jesus Fish and how many had the little Darwin animal dude."

"And..."

"And that maybe there should be a logo for those who aren't firmly on one side or the other. I just thought it would be funny if there was something that showed a mix of the two prevailing theories in a silly way. I didn't realize he was going to run with it and have them produced."

"And even once he did, you decided to promote his company. Your choices do not reflect someone who is even the least bit fearful of our all-powerful God. You are ultimately responsible for this trash."

"No, no. I see how this might offend you, but I just thought it was a funny idea, nothing nefarious."

"An idea can be the most dangerous thing. Especially to us," Ezra says.

. . .

Nightly Internet News Transcript
Wednesday, March 4, MMXX
(Uploaded 6 weeks ago)
1,924,328 Views

I'm William Howler and this is a quickie from your team at Nightly Internet News. It's a question from one of our viewers, Annie from St. Louis. She sent in a picture of some car decals she's been seeing in her hometown. As you can see, there's an Ichthys in a compromising position under a Darwin symbol. Typically, the Darwin symbol has two legs, but this one has another, excuse me, *limb* protruding and pointed toward the rear end of the Ichthys. My apologies, but it appears to have impregnated the Ichthys. The result is several little human stick-figure babies being birthed below. They call it "The Perfect Bumper Sticker for those in the middle." They're suggesting that there is a theory that would marry the two polarizing concepts, that it would explain how we came to be, that there is a mix of religious beginnings and evolutionary progression. This is absurd to be sure. The middle is a cowardly place. It's ideological purgatory! These are available on their website now at fixedbetwixt.com. These decals have been popping up across the country. But we, on Annie's behalf, would like you to flood their website with traffic, not to purchase anything, but to shut it down. I'm calling for a hack of their database and a demand that they take down these offensive stickers. And tell them to consider repenting for what they've done. We'll be back later with another quickie for you. Until then, have a *pleasant* evening, and I'll be home in a few hours, honey! I can't wait to see *you* and *only you*! For N.I.N., God Bless. I'm William Howler."

· · ·

Samson ruptures the stillness. "The Christ Pantocrator represents two sides without taking any claim to riding the middle. As you look around this circle of men, you'll notice that we are created in the image of God, but we have also been brought closer to His Son's image by our devotion to represent His ideals, His vision of this world in between the two dominions beyond. One eye is open and accepting, peaceful, and awaiting your invitation into your heart."

"I've done that—"

"Stop talking."

Zeus nods once.

"The other eye of Christ Pantocrator judges your actions. It is stern and unapologetic. This eye has no sympathy for the path you've chosen. It's the path of rejection. And for that, there is only peril."

"But both your eyes are—"

"—Yes, my eyes are devoid of compassion. Our Lord Jesus Christ is much more forgiving than I am. You should consider that when making your choice of what to believe, and of what to follow. You see, they tried to make me more sympathetic to those who shun the Lord, but it seems that God had different plans for me. I am pure judgement. I'm much less understanding." He leans in toward Zeus. Samson uses his fingers to open his left eye wider, but the muscles constrict and the capillaries become bloodier. Then he does the same with his right eye. "Would you like to see that again?"

Zeus doesn't. He feels the room anticipating his answer. "Look, maybe I should go and let you carry on with your meeting. I've tried to be honest with everyone here and I hope you can appreciate that. Not everyone is as sure as you are about their faith. It seems I have some soul searching to do before I can be subjected to something like this. I feel I'm getting in the way, that I'm taking the attention away from what you really want to be doing tonight, which is helping the Reverend here, and discussing the important issues that concern you."

"Don't you realize?" Ezra asks.

"What?"

"That *you* are the *only* issue. That your recent relationship with Candice is what concerns us." Ezra motions to Reverend Stearns and he retreats to the vestry.

"I assumed tonight was going to be much different. I'm uncomfortable bringing Candy into this." Zeus begins to rise, but he feels the jolt of Samson's knee brace strong against his leg.

"Maybe you're uncomfortable after all this time sitting on the fence." Samson turns his large body toward him and continues, "There are many types of fences. There are some with pickets, iron spikes, barbed wire, and electrified ones too. Which one are you on?"

"You know, I've always been a chain link guy."

Samson clenches his jaw.

Zeus shifts in his seat.

"Make your choice right now!" Samson demands.

"I tried to say this just a minute ago. I've invited Jesus Christ into my heart and have been reborn. I've done it already. Should I do it again? Just tell me how many times will satisfy you. And there *are* two people here who know exactly what I'm talking about. You don't think I remember that evening by the lake? I know it's been several years, but I remember everything from that weekend. And I think you should know that God in Heaven remembers." He looks at Elder Doctor Obadiah, whom he knows as Doctor-Pastor Astor, and fellow campfire reveler, Disciple Mark. "I may not be the greatest conformist, but why are you joining them in their judgements? Why aren't you defending me?"

Disciple Mark interjects, "We are The Defenders of Christ. Only Christ."

Zeus appeals to the surrounding circle of scarred eyes, "We're on the same side."

"They've seen what you've become and they've seen that you must not have been genuine with your words," Ezra says. "Your doubts and strange fantasies are not Christlike. They are detrimental and ultimately poisonous to our worldview."

"Are you're saying my sin is having too many questions?"

"Not too many, just the wrong ones."

Zeus feels a massive hand envelop his shoulder with the weight of a boulder. Samson applies pressure. Ezra stands and walks toward Zeus, then kneels down on the left side of his chair, keeping his eyes fixed on Samson's. Brigadoon shifts his seat to make more room for the chairman. Ezra places his hand on Zeus's other shoulder. It's much lighter in touch, but still an attempt to intimidate. He says, "Let's bow our heads in prayer. Dear Lord, we thank You for providing the time and space for us to meet this evening. This is Your house, Your shelter from all that is evil. We pray for any evil within to be forced out by your light. We've addressed some difficult issues tonight and we pray that they will be resolved in Your time. We will do all that we can to assist Reverend Stearns in all his efforts to make this church a beacon to those who seek your guidance, to welcome Disciple Brigadoon into our brotherhood, to be respectful of the vows we've taken to protect those most dear to us, and above all, to defend Your name. We also pray for Jesús Woodson, that he may find all the answers he seeks in Your Word, the only place to find them. Amen." When he lifts his head and opens his eyes, the reflective sunglasses are back on. "God be with you, gentlemen." All rise except Ezra and Samson. They're still holding his shoulders down. "Let's hang back for a moment."

The cathedral empties out and the car engines can be heard reverberating in the nave. Samson lets go of his shoulder. "Candice is someone we are sworn to protect. We hope you understand that we cannot allow you to see her anymore. It's not a good fit for what Dr. Gideon would have wanted. Let's make this easy. Now listen, you are not to contact her anymore."

Ezra continues, "Why don't you work out some of your questions and maybe we can revisit this in the future. At this point in your life, she's not the woman for you. If you feel one day that you've changed and found the Truth of the Lord, please contact me first. Understand?"

"No, I don't understand. *We* are falling in love."

Samson's laugh trembles the atmosphere.

Zeus's voice is shaky. "I'm going to tell her everything that's happened tonight—that this was a witch hunt disguised as a prayer meeting. I'm leaving now."

"That's funny, because I'll also be telling her what happened tonight. We have a few women who we've reached out to that are also willing to talk about what went on tonight."

"What the hell are you talking about?"

"This... is a house of worship," Samson confirms as he rises and collects his crutches. As Zeus begins to walk away, Ezra says, "Deborah DeLite, Ms. Oralee S. July, and Nycole Smyth, with a y, twice. You haven't treated them the way women should be treated. Especially not the way Candice will ever be treated. And the fact that you've seen them earlier this evening won't be something that will help her fall further in love with you, as you claim she's doing. Are you seeing our concerns more clearly now? Or should we tell her what happened between you and these three women tonight?"

Zeus is angered and momentarily speechless. Ezra asks, "Where is your phone?"

"It's in my car. Candy asked me not to bring it to the meeting."

With the crutches lodged in his armpits, Samson reaches into his inside pocket and pulls out a glove of sorts. "Interesting..."

"Why?"

"Let's see whose truth she will hear first." Samson pulls the glove over his hand. Zeus sees a metallic barrel that ends with a spire extending from his index finger. It's pointed at him.

"What is that?"

Ezra answers for Samson, "I don't think you want to find out."

With the two men standing side by side, Zeus sees himself reversed and separated four times in the reflection of the sunglasses. He says to Samson, "You are the accuser. *You* are the fallen angel."

"But an angel still," Samson says. They take another step closer. "And you are the deceiver."

"Two devils in one church," Zeus says with reticence, "are too many."

"Agreed."

And with the click of the gears on the glove and the barrel pointed at his heart, Zeus runs. Ezra leaps to grab hold, but he's unsuccessful. He yells to Samson, "Not in here!" The trigger isn't pulled. Zeus pushes through the cathedral doors and pulls his keys from his pocket. He doesn't see his car. He panics and presses the unlock button repeatedly. There are only two cars in sight and neither is the rental. He begins to run from the church while trying to orient himself in an unfamiliar town at the same time. He instantly regrets his frequent blunt smoking. Things are quiet around him when he reaches a nearby stretch of railroad tracks. From the map he remembers that Candy's street runs parallel to the tracks. He looks left, then right. He doesn't see any signs for Stewart Avenue. His processing speed is at an all time low. He pats himself down in search of his phone. No dice. He hears the pattering footsteps of a vindictive and quiet pursuit from behind. Their exhales are audible. He chooses to go left and sprints down the tracks. His oxfords weren't made for this. He's hoping to see a telltale marker that will help him find her house, but he doesn't know he's running in the wrong direction. Zeus is faster than his stalkers are, but he's not sure how long he can keep it up. Disciple Mark is running slowly due to the sunglasses, and Brigadoon, with the surgical bandage back over one of his eyes, is further limited by a lack of depth perception. Zeus mistakes this for an athletic advantage. There is only faint light from distant street lamps. When the sounds of their footsteps fade, he looks for an opportunity to derail and change course. He sees a baseball field on his right and a school of grandeur in the background.

There's a chance he can hide somewhere—and he also sees there are houses nearby. At this point, he figures, he'll ask for help from anyone. Any chance of reasoning is lost. He scales a fence mixed with hedges. This is where he loses some ground. Brigadoon and Mark begin their ascent as he touches down on the other side. He hears them talking between breaths. The baseball field looks game ready. Zeus runs down the first baseline toward home, the darkest corner of the field. He slides headfirst against the chain link backstop and pulls his black sport jacket over his head. He hears nothing but the drone of his own mind. His memories are brought closer. He thinks of his father teaching him the game of baseball. He remembers when he was a little boy he would stand in the batter's box and hold an invisible bat in his hands. Before he swung and ran the bases of an empty field, he heard his father, the voice above him, commentate.

Like this, son. Keep your hands up. Don't let him see you think. You already know what to do. Here's the pitch. Watch the way the seams tumble. Now... drive with the legs. Swing. Shift the hips. Drive the ball. Follow through. You didn't follow through there. You always have to follow through. Now run like lightning before the thunder. Run, run, run away from home. Round the bag. Round first. Keep your head up, son. Watch the third base coach. He's waving you on. Dig those spikes. Dig'em! The right fielder bobbled the ball, keep running! He's waving you to go on home. Come on home, son. Come back home to me, son.

He pulls down his jacket and looks toward home plate. He sees nothing because there is too much light. He's momentarily blinded. He stands out of an instinct to find out what's going on. From each side, he feels both wrists being zip-tied to the chain link backstop. The light is coming from a collection of cars pointed in his direction. There is a large figure coming from the outfield in a sinister dance of shadows. As it draws closer, Zeus sees the beast hobbling and crawling in his direction. On the pitcher's rubber, Samson pauses, leans on his crutches, and rises to full height. He's anchored by two other men on either side. His sermon on the mound is brief. "Brothers, it looks like this devil has been roaming about the earth! Well, no longer. Let's show him where he's headed if he doesn't purify his heart."

The three approach him. They're in no hurry. Zeus doesn't say a word. Samson gets up close to him. The exhales from his nostrils come in strong gusts from above. Samson takes hold of the crutch that aided his good leg and presses the top of it against his neck. Zeus remains silent. Then Samson places the crutch behind Zeus. It's almost as tall as he is. Brigadoon and Mark use a series of zip ties to make him one with crutch, his back secured to the top, his ankles bound near the bottom. Samson, balancing on one leg, begins to untie Zeus's tie. He looks at the material of it and mutters, "Yet another abomination." He rolls the tie up and pushes it into Zeus's mouth. But as Samson unbuttons Zeus's shirt, revealing a near hairless chest, he coughs out the tie. Samson reaches into his pocket and produces the glove. He fits it over his large hand. The gears make winding and mechanical sounds. He holds the long metallic finger to Zeus's lips. He says, "God addresses all of your gray areas in Matthew 5:37. 'All you need to say is simply, 'Yes' or 'No'; anything beyond this comes from the evil one.'" He moves the spire down to his chest and points it at his heart. "This is the most important part of your body and I don't believe it's filled with the Lord, as you claim. Maybe we can see what's really going on in there?" Samson pierces the skin over his heart and draws the blade down a few inches. The blood streams down in a line all the way to his waist.

"No."

"No!? You don't want me to see what's going on in your heart?"

In between deep breaths, Zeus answers, "No. It's that I don't agree that it's the most important part of the body."

Samson pierces the skin again, this time dragging it left to right.

Zeus tries his best not to wince. "It's my mind."

Samson pins the spire in the intersection of the bloody cross and gestures with his other hand to the two disciples on either side of him and then to Brigadoon and Mark, "Gentlemen... Revelations 12:12."

Mark begins, "Therefore rejoice, you heavens and you who dwell in them!"

One of the other men obscured in the glare of the headlights, Ezra he believes, continues the verse, "But woe to the earth and the sea..."

Brigadoon adds, "because the devil has gone down to you!"

Samson gets closer to his face, "He is filled with fury..."

The other man in the shadows has an unfamiliar voice. It's deep and subtle. He finishes the verse, "because he knows that his time is short."

Zeus says, "You're organization is an embarrassment to Christianity."

The voice from the shadows returns, "We are Christianity in its most pure form."

"Christ is compassionate and loving."

"Yes, to those deserving."

"I'm deserving of a second chance, deserving of your forgiveness." Zeus thinks of Candy and how he will do anything to see her again, and launches into his defense, which has zero to do with truth. "Having doubts will make you stronger in your faith because then you'll know how to defend them when you're attacked. And that's what's happening to me right now. I recognize that. You are making me stronger in my faith. I didn't realize it at first, but I see the simplicity in your thinking. It's the clearer way."

No one responds. The moments hangs like a slow curve.

Samson says to Brigadoon, "Give me the zip ties." Then to Zeus, "The more you run your mouth like this, the more it's obvious you'll say anything to get out of this. Your persistent lying further shows you to be a deceiver. And the home of a deceiver is below."

"I want to honor Candy by making the right changes. I want to—"

"It's Candice," the voice from the shadows says.

"I want to honor Candice. I want to prove to you I mean what I say." A tear wells up in a concave arc, his head hangs forward, and then it spills into the streams of the cross on his chest.

Samson looks back to the shadows, then to Zeus, "It seems the judge has overridden your appeal. We don't want your kinship."

"Jesus doesn't reject love."

"But God does, as you're about to find out."

Zeus ends the charade. "All you do is pick and choose and follow orders from the simple apes behind you. You're quite amazing, really. You maintain Iron Age thinking in the age of Artificial Intelligence. IA over AI, fuck that." Zeus begins to beatbox and nod his head. The D.O.C. are collectively frozen as he channels The Notorious B.I.G.:

"When I die, fuck it, I wanna go to hell,
cause I'm a piece of shit, it ain't hard to fuckin' tell...
It don't make sense, goin' to Heaven with the goodie-goodies
dressed in white, I like black Timbs and black hoodies."

He continues to beatbox after the verse, accentuating the spits of the snares in the direction of Samson X.

Samson contributes some arrhythmic spoken word to the bizarre and sudden Hip Hop soundtrack, "Let me point you in the right direction, to the place where the fire replaces all the oxygen."

"Fire *needs* oxygen. Damn, do you think about anything?"

In one move, Samson grabs his ankles with one arm and swings them 180° upward. Zeus's head twists to one side and he emits a primal sound. Samson uses a zip tie to the secure the crutch to the chain link backstop. Samson limps and crawls around to the other side where Zeus is facing. He looks at him as he hangs upside-down. Zeus feels his head swell with the feeling of reverse gravity. The back of his suit jacket hangs behind his head like the black wings of a descending angel. Samson removes the glove, "*This* is what I think about." He winds up and begins to slug him repeatedly. The fence between Samson's fists and Zeus's head only makes things worse. The others don't speak. In the torrent, chain link Xs are imprinted across his face and on Samson's knuckles. The blood that runs from Zeus's mouth to his forehead is united with Samson's. The rigid plastic of the zip ties cuts through his watch band and it falls to ground. His wrists are perforated with long dashes. Zeus's peach-fuzzed head is now wearing a crown of contusions. And the more his chest rattles against the backstop, the more the cross opens over his heart.

Samson hears Zeus speaking softly through thick liquid. "...And the way of peace they do not know." He spits a fountain of crimson. "I read that today."

Samson grips the fence up high, pulls himself forward, and sends the knee brace against his head. Then again.

Zeus is motionless.

Samson looks at Brigadoon and Mark. The headlights reflect off their sunglasses and illuminate the body of McJesus. The two nod. Samson grabs the backstop again and drives his knee brace against him once more. He reaches into his pocket for the glove, fits it over his hand, and steps back a few feet to extend his arm. The spire is inches from his head. The gears click, ready to fire.

On the other side of the backstop, a figure from the shadows raises his arm up into the glare of the high beams, then slowly lowers it. Samson mirrors him.

(CODA)

The world trills black, gray, and red. His vision is distorted by swollen eyelids, his thoughts disrupted by electrified darts. It's early morning. The branches of barren trees reach far down into the mist while a murder of American crows dangle in the light wind. He looks up to the ground and sees the face of his watch at a perfect 5:27 eclipse. He resists the instinct to pray. He sees drops of O-negative merging with the morning dew overhead. A train jolts the air like a thunderous typewriter on fire. It seems to be traveling in two directions at once. The crows take flight, falling farther into the abyss, and unsettle the landscape of the grayscale Rothko horizon.

Then, like an audiophile going through withdrawal, he twitches in need of a fix of harmonic pulses. With the pervasive burn that accompanies it, his body jangles against the backstop. It resounds in low tones, like a metallic string from an upright bass emanating to the sky below. The movement is pure pleasure and pain. But he knows there is unfairness in balance. It's a symphonic étude interlaced with radio static. It's still beautiful to those willing to listen. The vibrations separate the clouds and reveal the graffiti of new colors across the spectrum. He closes his eyes.

He hears kaleidoscopic words in a poetic cadence, the words of an artist, perhaps. It feels like a phone call, where the voice is as close as his imagination will allow it to be. This voice is nearby. His skull is fractured and sabotaging his mind. He tries to drift off to the one place he wishes he can rest his head. It would be warm, loving, and perfect. And somewhere close by, a young woman feels something in the pit of her stomach. It's something with all the modernistic fashions.

His mind works in razored fragments. This meeting between the signifiers, a demigod, and a full devil, has given him the impetus to create a new score. It's the end of the vamp. Now he chooses only to trust in the music of the gracious and the beautiful, the jelly rolls and the passions of a woman loved, and the lush adventure of two connected hearts in New York City, the brilliant empire in the stars. And he still thinks that religion can be very good, as long as you don't believe it's real. Because it rejects the complex in favor of a punctured logic. It simplifies all that's in creation and unfolds the tesseract.

He just needs to get to the next eclipse. And then another one, and another one. He's watching the revolutions from above, trying to hold on. He has plans, but also knows that his body is cold. The shivers bring the pain. And he wonders if this is it.

He tells himself, that whatever lies ahead, he's no longer for sale.
He is Jesús Neon,
Son of Yvonne,
Friend of Melanie,
Pharaoh Woodson of the Real,
King Coney of the Flirty Circus,
Moonwalker of the Steel Grid,
Blessed Baller of Power,
Notorious Monarch of Style,
Accidental Philosopher,
Old-Fashioned Daydreamer,
Lover of Candy.

CONCORDANCE

· ⟦ ↑ ⟧ · ⟦ Σ ⟧ · ⟦ ◆ ⟧ · ⟦ ✳ ⟧ ·

1 ☦

2 Zeus and Melanie met by a park bench outside the lobby of his silverscraper, next to a manicured and ornamental spruce tree. It had been noon and frigid, and as they spoke, their exhales became little puffy clouds. During part of their initial conversation, Zeus and Mel each mimed smoking invisible cigarettes. It was surprising how many interests fit in the intersection of the Venn Diagram of Z ∩ M. They were a great pair, but in the totality of Z ∪ M, it turned out that their body rhythms were the cause of their problems in the bedroom. Z had the R&B vibe, but was more Hard Rock with the pelvic cadence. M's style looked more like 80s Glam, but she wanted soft caresses and a slow pulsing bassline. They tried horizontal positions, vertical positions, various contraptions, and threw in some roleplaying, but it was apparent that no DJ alive could reconcile this metronomic conundrum, no matter the mix. So best friends they became.

∴ ∩ > ∪ Q.E.D.

3

FUN! T! V! Late Night Broadcast Television Introduction Monologue Snippets
June 6th

· "So, tonight, with all of the homemade porn now accessible to everyone, Apple's new facial recognition software has taken on an entirely new meaning..."

· "It looks like Congressman Gavin Appleseed has been outed. He apologized alongside his wife today. Apparently he's really been spreading it around, in bushes and backyards! He's known as a politician with a solid core and thick skin, but now he'll be known for some hardcore and foreskin..."

· "In the Bible it says that Eve gave Adam the apple in Eden, but today it looks like Apple gave us Adam eatin' Eve..."

4   She wants to see what would happen if he were to put on a backpack filled with old Encyclopedia Britannica books, carry a forty-pound dumbbell in each hand, and walk in a room constructed to the exact specifications where the ceiling height would brush the hairs on top of his head. Will he then be forced to walk heel-to-toe? Or will his calves push right on up, causing his head to make small indentations in the sheetrock above, slowly concussing him until he falls to the floor in a heap? She's curious.

.   .   ..   . o

5   In the basement, where she read night and day, there were occasions where a large man would arrive home after a late night of bowling—he was her foster parent and so-called provider. This drunken ball-roller claimed to play perfectly, but he couldn't get anywhere close to 300. He blamed anything and anyone, except himself. Yet there was one night he thought he'd finally bowled the perfect game. But really, it was the management at the bowling alley, The Spare Cactus. They had had it up to here with all of his alcohol-fueled bullshit about the lanes not being waxed enough, the shoes not being colorfully-patched enough, the balls being too round, the dogs not being hot enough, et cetera. So one night when the large man had the posture of the tower in Giza (and not too long after that, a failure of any posture), the management decided to pack his gym bag with one of their congratulatory pre-ordered trophies. It was of a man posed in a pre-release bowling stride. Over the figure was a large '300' attached by a golden spire that pierced the model's dome piece. Some of the staff members of The Spare Cactus wanted to shove the damn thing right down his throat to shut him up permanently, but management kept it as a half-joke/half-middle finger.

The large man's Blood Alcohol Content, had it been measured, would have broken into the tenths place with a crooked number. So of course he had no memory of the actual 148 he bowled that night, but he held the perceived notion that he had. He felt fulfilled in a way he never had before. He imagined the figure on the trophy as himself even though it was adorned with a much slimmer and better-formed bowler, dressed in an outfit touched by Midas. He pictured his face going up on the alley's Wall of Frames forever. He rode this feeling of unexpected jubilance for a few months until it became impossible to ignore that he hadn't gone over the 200 mark since his historic and life-affirming game. The excuses began to accumulate and overwhelm him to the point where he had nowhere to put them. They eventually fell to the basement room where young Suma stayed. The more he failed to repeat his hollow 300, the more the girl was at fault. With all of the resources and energy he'd to put into the bureaucratic paperwork and lunchbox preparation, he couldn't possibly have enough vitality or accuracy to return to form. And no one gets a free lunch, he told himself.

On the nights he spent in the alley's gutter, got wasted, and found his way home, his only release came from the deployment of a different type of strike. The trophy, which he earned by accuracy of annoyance, became the weapon, the payment for her midday meal. The provider struck her with the golden figure topped with the '300' for a full ten frames. Her skin was reddened, bruised, and torn open in the form of threes and zeros. But it was mostly the zeros that left their marks on her body because of the way the large man held the trophy in his right hand. The zeros were spread across her body; no area was spared. Most nights she was unable to treat the marks, which led to bizarre scabs and eventual scars.

During the school day, the provider was contacted many times about the circular discolorations and deteriorations on Suma. The school nurse was very concerned about ringworm or a skin disease or something. The provider deflected the questions by telling them about a false history of self-mutilation and that she was seeing a psychologist and that he appreciated their efforts. The school nurse felt uneasy about his claims, but she was also young and not yet confident.

Her teacher considered Suma an intelligent little girl, but also disheveled, unkempt, and quirky. With Suma's history of changing schools due to the transient lifestyle of a foster child, she was rarely able to establish good friends or trust from her teachers. Though in this time of the zeros, Young Suma confided in a school friend who she convinced to pass the story along to their teacher. The teacher followed the protocol of first reaching out to the school psychologist and principal. When they pulled the transfer file for Ms. Suzie Marie Hill, it labeled her as a victim of abandonment and displacement with a tendency to create outlandish stories. The file was true, but it restricted her totality to one piece of paper. Also true were her statements about the trophy marks and the basement library prison, but according to her assessors, they were mirages that originated somewhere in Death Valley.

6
Angel Dust a.k.a. PCP a.k.a. 1-(1-phenylcyclohexyl)piperidine)
Overdose Symptoms of Phencyclidine Use: Dissociative Experiences, Loss of Reasoning, **Inability to Focus Sight**, Slurred Speech, **Inability to Control Muscles**, **Repeated Vomiting**

.   . b .   . l .

7   You wouldn't have to be Lucy-in-the-Sky-high to know that it was a genuine CZ, possibly crystal. But it's a sentimental choice, one half of the earrings he wore in high school. The piercings have been closed for awhile, as he'd stopped wearing them when he entered the military. Tonight, dotted scars sunk into his lobes where there once twinkled light. His face is darker now.

8   Option A: He has one from his high school days that still worked. He'd be going down on a woman as she smoked a cigarette. She'd flick the hot ashes on his bare back as he pleasured her, and he'd feel the effect of *jouissance*, a word he learned the meaning of well after high school.
    Option B: A more recent addition to his fantasy file somewhere in the corner of his brain has him watching a woman discreetly touching herself in public. But when he notices her, she notices him noticing her, and she becomes more turned on by this. Then she stands up and walks over to give him the shush-don't-tell finger on his lips. When she does, he tastes her. She walks away and he follows her. The ending to that fantasy is variant and usually deviant.

9   Apologies.

10

. RUST BUST AND AXE .

. THE GOOD-MORNING OLD-FASHIONED .
RAVENSWOOD RYE WHISKEY, CHESHAM ROAD MAPLE SYRUP, HOMEMADE CINNAMON
BITTERS, SLICED BLOOD ORANGE

. GANGSTERISM 1940 .
FLOR DE CANA EIGHTEEN-YEAR RUM, TOBACCO-INFUSED SUGAR CANE SYRUP,
VANILLA BEAN STIRRER, TOPPED WITH GOLD FLAKES

. BEAT BOP .
BROOKLYN GIN, ST-GERMAIN ELDERFLOWER LIQUEUR, FRESH LEMON AND LIME,
GROUND BLACK PEPPER

. NEW AMSTERDAM .
MICHTER'S BOURBON WHISKEY, GRAND MARNIER, SWEET VERMOUTH, BING CHERRY

. DEATH IN THE AFTERNOON .
VEUVE CLICQUOT CHAMPAGNE, LAUTREC ABSINTHE,
SERVED WITH "A NOBODY EVER DIES" ERNEST HEMINGWAY POCKET-SIZED LEAFLET

. MARTINI FRANCAIS .
VAN GOGH VANILLA VODKA, CHAMBORD, PINEAPPLE JUICE, MUDDLED BLACKBERRIES

. MR. BOJANGLES .
TITO'S VODKA, GINGER ALE, GRENADINE, THREE MARASCHINO CHERRIES

. SAILOR BEWARE .
HORSERADISH VODKA, SPICY BLOODY MARY MIX, SEA SALT, LEMON WEDGE,
FLOATING RAW OYSTERS, SERVED IN A MARTINI GLASS

. BAD DAY .
TWO SHOTS OF CHEAP TEQUILA, SERVED BACK-TO-BACK

11 FOR EXAMPLE, ON THE BAR AT THE MOMENT, ARE THE FOLLOWING:

* ACE FREELY / KISS PINT GLASS
* N.Y. JETS MUG WITH MANUFACTURED FROST
* BUDWEISER "RED LABEL" PROMOTIONAL GLASS, 2001
* ALBERTO VARGAS PEEK-A-BOO GIRLIE GLASS, 1960S
* 2PAC ALL EYEZ ON ME, PINT GLASS
* BIG BARRY'S BOOT GLASS, LONG ISLAND, 1980S
* P.J. CLARKE'S SHOTGLASS
* HOOTERS, NIAGARA FALLS, CANADA, SHOTGLASS
* JUNIOR'S SPYCOAST, PORT JEFFERSON, MASON JAR
* OLD RASPUTIN RUSSIAN IMPERIAL STOUT, NONIC GLASS
* PORT JEFF BREWERY PINT GLASS, 2014
* MOSCOW MULE COPPER MUG WITH ENGRAVED INITIALS J.M.L.
* CANADA '76 OLYMPICS COMMEMORATVE GLASS
* MARIO'S ITALIAN RESTAURANT HIGHBALL, EAST SETAUKET, 2019
* PRINCESS LEIA DRINKING GLASS
* MAD MEN WHISKEY GLASS, 2007
* THE DRAKE HOTEL, CHICAGO, WHISKEY GLASS
* THE SATURN CLUB, BUFFALO, WATER GLASS
* TIFFANY AND CO. ROCK-CUT DOUBLE OLD-FASHIONED GLASS
* "CREATE." COFFEE MUG, RAE DUNN ARTISAN COLLECTION
* DELIRIUM TREMENS CHALICE
* ADELPHI UNIVERSITY, ARISTOCRAT GLASS, "VITA SINE LITTERIS MORS EST"
* BUD MAN BEER STEIN, 1975
* TOAST COFFEEHOUSE CERAMIC MUG, PORT JEFFERSON
* MICKEY MANTLE'S NEW YORK RESTAURANT AND BAR, TALL BEER GLASS
* LINDENWIRTIN BLACK FOREST BEER STEIN, "KEINEN TROPFEN IM BECHER MEHR, UND DEN BEUTEL SCHLAFF UND LEER"
* PARKS AND RECREATION "TREAT YO SELF" COFFEE MUG
* HULKAMANIA BEER MUG, 1985
* CHECKMATE INN FUNNEL
* WELLS BANANA BREAD BEER PINT GLASS, ALL THE WAY FROM LONDON

12 THE JUKEBOX PLAYLIST FOR THE EVENING:

ROLLING STONES: "LOVE IS STRONG"

THE KILLS: "NO WOW"

PEARL JAM: "EVENFLOW"

THE STROKES: "AUTOMATIC STOP"

GUNS N' ROSES: "ROCKET QUEEN"

THE WHITE STRIPES: "LITTLE ROOM"

KEMPLETON: "I LIKE PINK"

SPLURGE: "49 CENT REFILL"

RANCID: "TIME BOMB"

BLUES TRAVELER: "HOOK"

GARBAGE: "SUPERVIXEN"

THE DEAD WEATHER: "HANG YOU FROM THE HEAVENS"

R.E.M.: "CRUSH WITH EYELINER"

THE BELLEGARDS: "CHEWING THE DICE"

DONOVAN: "SEASON OF THE WITCH"

MISSING PERSONS: "DESTINATION UNKNOWN"

LED ZEPPELIN: "MISTY MOUNTAIN HOP"

DEF LEPPARD: "HIGH 'N' DRY (SATURDAY NIGHT)"

VAN HALEN: "RUNNIN' WITH THE DEVIL"

ROLLING STONES: "BEAST OF BURDEN"

ROXY MUSIC: "OUT OF THE BLUE"

KILLER MOOSE: "SMD"

QUIET RIOT: "CUM ON FEEL THE NOISE"

THE MISFITS: "SATURDAY NIGHT"

ODELL: "MONSTER"

SUITCASE CURLS: "THE BACKUP SINGER"

13 A brief nickname directory:

1. "The Say Hey Kid" is Willie Howard Mays, Jr. (Inducted 1979)
2. "Three Finger Brown" is Mordecai Peter Centennial Brown (Inducted 1949)
3. "Shoeless Joe Jackson" is Joseph Jefferson Jackson (Never Inducted, but was *Indicted* 1920)
4. "Hammerin' Hank" is Henry Louis Aaron (Inducted 1982)
5. "Big D" is Donald Scott Drysdale (Inducted 1984)
6. "The Big Hurt" is Frank Edward Thomas (Inducted 2014)
7. "Stretch" is Willie Lee McCovey (Inducted 1986)

14 The dates will read:

William Henry Harrison, Whig Party (March 4, 1837 - April 4, 1837)

Martin Van Buren, Democratic Party (April 4, 1837 - April 4, 1841)

Suma contemplated changing Harrison's affiliation to the Whiggin' Out Party, but decided against it for the sake of subtlety. This is a typeface project anyway.

15 *A sampling of Suma's entries:*

hamburger n. 1 A badly scarred and often beaten prize fighter. 2 A bum or tramp; anyone who is down and out

sneaky pete sneaky Pete Any of various illegal alcoholic beverages, ranging from home-made whisky, flavored alcohol, and fortified wine to boot-legged moonshine. 1949: "...A group which was discussing the effects of 'sneaky-pete.' " W.J. Slocum in Collier's, Sept. 3, 40. Since c1940.

la(h)-de-da(h) la(h)-di-da la(h) de da(h) la(h) di dah n. A sissy; a fancy pants. 1928: "Some lah de dah with a cane!" Hecht & MacArthur, Front Page, II. adj. Sissified.

shaft n. 1 [taboo] A woman considered only sexually; a woman's body; the vagina. 1949: "She wasn't wearing a slip. 'Wow,' he decided at last, 'a shaft like that...' " N. Algren, Man with the Golden Arm, 56. Not common. 2 An act or an instance of being taken advantage of, unfairly treated, deceived, tricked, cheated, or victimized; a raw deal. Usu. in "to get the (a) shaft." Fig., the image is the taboo one of the final insult, having someone insert something, as a barbed shaft, up someone's rectum. See **up my ass**.

Mae West A vestlike life preserver. Wide W.W.I.I. use. From its shape, which makes the wearer appear to have a large bosom, as does the entertainer Mae West.

ladies' man lady's man A male of any age who is charming and courtly to, and grooms himself to please, the ladies; one who pursues women politely and with success.

hitched, get To be married. 1954: "We went straight down to City Hall and got hitched." L.Armstrong, Satchmo, My Life in New Orleans, 158. See **hitched**.

cloud buster 1. In baseball, a high fly ball. 2 A skyscraper. 3. A fast, new airplane.

heaven dust Cocaine. Drug addict use. Not common. See **dust**.

ashes hauled, get [one's] To have sexual intercourse, to be sexually satisfied; usu. with a prostitute, chance acquaintance, or a stranger. 1939: "Well, you see that spider climbin' up that wall,/Goin' up there to get her ashes hauled." Jelly Roll Morton, "Winin' Boy Blues," song written before 1910.

Dictionary of American Slang

Harold Wentworth, Ph.D. and Stuart Berg Flexner, M.A.

(New York: Thomas Y. Crowell Company, 1967)

16   Suma also considered The Count of Basie, The Earl of Hines, and The King of Cole—with all due respect to Baby Laurence.

17   **em·men·a·gogue** /ə'menə‚gôg, -‚gäg, -'mēnə-/ ▸ n. Medicine a substance that stimulates or increases menstrual flow.
—ORIGIN early 18th cent.: from Greek *emmēna* 'menses' + *agōgos* 'eliciting'

18   **pal·in·a** /'palī‚nə/ ▸ n. a painting (or poem) for which another painter (or poet) will redact or erase any of the original sentiments expressed to bring a new and enhanced meaning through plurality: *Andy Warhol and Jean-Michel Basquiat collaborated on a palina at The Factory.*
—ORIGIN early 21st cent.: English from Greek *pālin* 'again' + *-a* 'extraneous suffix.'

19   Otherwise known as a black diamond, which may have extraterrestrial origins. With needle-cut precision, Axlia's nape is jeweled with this: ♦.

20   Jasmine notices something etched into the bark. It must have happened years ago, as the tree had begun to reclaim its skin. It has the structure of a short poem, a love poem perhaps.

21   At which point, Jasmine and some of the men in the audience, place themselves in the requisite and temporary game of mental limbo for the dip. To feel her touch, they are willing to literally bend over backward.

22

794   CYRUS COASTER
MUTUAL BASE BALL CLUB OF NEW YORK ♦ MANAGER
HEIGHT: 5'11"   WEIGHT: 220   BATS: BOTH   THROWS: BOTH
BORN: 7-7-70, NEW YORK, NEW YORK
HOME: LOWER EAST SIDE, NYC

TEAM CHECKLIST
* P [HALCYON BOOKS]
* C [WAX & RAX]
* 1B [RHYTHM & BOOZE]
* 2B ⟨ BARELY NOTHING ⟩
* 3B [THINK]
* SS [DOTS-AND-DASHES]
* LF [SALO N] / [SALOON]
* CF [BUMP & GRIND]
* RF [THUGS N' KISSES]
* DH [CLEAN PEOPLE SUCK]
* CL [MISSION]

C*   © 2020 STOPP CHEWING GUM, INC. PRTD. IN U.S.A.

23   **795**

A powerful and mindful impact

**SAMSON SENDS 4 TO HELL
WITH ONE SWING OF THE BAT**

Jericho, N.Y., February 29, 2016: The 6'10" Samson breaks his own modern day record. With 4 heads positioned in a row, he connected with the first one on the sweet spot of his bat. Like a sadistic Newton's Cradle, he shattered all 4 skulls, with the last one sent over the centerfield wall. Don't worry, they all deserved it.

D*   © 2020 STOPP CHEWING GUM, INC. PRTD. IN U.S.A.

24   **796**   **ONE   YEAR   AGO**

2019 — "No, Brig! Stop!" . . . "Isn't this what you want?!" . . . "No, don't!" . . . "I'm trying to show you that something's wrong with you." . . . "I knew I shouldn't have told you anything!" . . . "Now I know who you really are. You have no honor. You should be ashamed of your desires. You belong with the sinners." . . . "If you—" . . . "I'll do what's needed, Candice, and you won't do anything!"

"How did you get away with it? Doesn't your wife track your phone?" . . . "I have a place that handles it called The Office. I'll tell you how it works later." . . . "And the girls?" . . . "They're only a few blocks away, so it works well for me." . . . "How much?" . . . "For The Office or the girls?" . . . "Both."

"Are you saying you replicated this fingerprint with a pen?" . . . "Yes. With a pen and a lot of practice." . . . "Where did you learn to do this?" . . . "Out west."

F*   © 2020 STOPP CHEWING GUM, INC. PRTD. IN U.S.A.

2015 — "It's perfect. It's the car I've dreamed about ever since I was a kid. I'll take it." . . . "Very well. Let's talk about how you'd like to finance this. Do you have excellent credit?" . . . "I have the cash." . . . "Good one." . . . "I'm serious, look." . . . "Excuse me, but are you a drug dealer or something?" . . . "If the drug is love, yes."

"It's very interesting, honey. But what is this all supposed to mean?" . . . "_____." . . . "Can't you say anything about it?" . . . "Dad, I told you, she's not going to talk to you. That's why she's doing what she's doing, so she doesn't have to explain with words."

"Roosevelt, you understand why you're here." . . . "Yes, sir." . . . "We've never had an instance of contrail graffiti before, so we're not sure how we're going to proceed. But for now, you're grounded until further notice."

F*   © 2020 STOPP CHEWING GUM, INC. PRTD. IN U.S.A.

26

King James Version (KJV); Publication Year: 1611

O Lord God of my salvation, I have cried day and night before thee: Let my prayer come before thee: incline thine ear unto my cry; For my soul is full of troubles: and my life draweth nigh unto the grave. I am counted with them that go down into the pit: I am as a man that hath no strength: Free among the dead, like the slain that lie in the grave, whom thou rememberest no more: and they are cut off from thy hand. Thou hast laid me in the lowest pit, in darkness, in the deeps. Thy wrath lieth hard upon me, and thou hast afflicted me with all thy waves. Selah. Thou hast put away mine acquaintance far from me; thou hast made me an abomination unto them: I am shut up, and I cannot come forth. Mine eye mourneth by reason of affliction: Lord, I have called daily upon thee, I have stretched out my hands unto thee. Wilt thou shew wonders to the dead? Shall the dead arise and praise thee? Selah. Shall thy loving kindness be declared in the grave? Or thy faithfulness in destruction? Shall thy wonders be known in the dark? And thy righteousness in the land of forgetfulness? But unto thee have I cried, O Lord; and in the morning shall my prayer prevent thee. Lord, why castest thou off my soul? Why hidest thou thy face from me? I am afflicted and ready to die from my youth up: while I suffer thy terrors I am distracted. Thy fierce wrath goeth over me; thy terrors have cut me off. They came round about me daily like water; they compassed me about together. Lover and friend hast thou put far from me, and mine acquaintance into darkness.

New Jerusalem Bible (The Catholic Bible) NJB; Publication Year: 1985

Yahweh, God of my salvation, when I cry out to you in the night, may my prayer reach your presence, hear my cry for help. For I am filled with misery, my life is on the brink of Sheol; already numbered among those who sink into oblivion, I am as one bereft of strength, left alone among the dead, like the slaughtered lying in the grave, whom you remember no more, cut off as they are from your protection. You have plunged me to the bottom of the grave, in the darkness, in the depths; weighted down by your anger, kept low by your waves. You have deprived me of my friends, made me repulsive to them, imprisoned, with no escape; my eyes are worn out with suffering. I call to you, Yahweh, all day, I stretch out my hands to you. Do you work wonders for the dead, can shadows rise up to praise you? Do they speak in the grave of your faithful love, of your constancy in the place of perdition? Are your wonders known in the darkness, your saving justice in the land of oblivion? But, for my part, I cry to you, Yahweh, every morning my prayer comes before you; why, Yahweh, do you rebuff me, turn your face away from me? Wretched and close to death since childhood, I have borne your terrors—I am finished! Your anger has overwhelmed me, your terrors annihilated me. They flood around me all day long, close in on me all at once. You have deprived me of friends and companions, and all that I know is the dark.

27   In order of the nicknamed: Rickey Henley Henderson, Ron Guidry, Dave Righetti, Mike Pagliarulo, Lou Pinella, Dave Winfield (a moniker bestowed by the owner of the club, George Steinbrenner), Willie Randolph, and Don Mattingly.

. i .   . v .

28   In this case, it may have been $C_{17}H_{21}NO_4$, pure cocaine.

29   Roosevelt was considered a medical marvel from day zero to day one. He wasn't supposed to make it. There was an incubator incident after the C-section birth, and of all things, it was a dense, full-body wrap that played a major role in his survival, clothing the wailing baby from grave to cradle.

30   The Fibonacci Sequence: 1, 1, 2, 3, 5, 8, 13, 21, 34, 55, 89, 144, 233, 377...

. i . . o .

31   Mattres had recently published his first cartoon online. Since he was known for his portraits that inexplicably turned faces into the fronts of vehicles, he decided to stay with his strength and create cartoons with cars as the main characters. The thing is, when he thought he was drawing cars, he was just as comically terrible as when it was the other way around. Their rectangular grills warped into a bulbous surface and their headlights became well-lashed eyes. His first cartoon was about a singing car, a Porsche 911. The first few panels showed the car racing around countryside vistas, confidently repeating his favorite songs as the lyrics emit from his tailpipe. When he drives into a parking lot, his headlights catch sight of a cute little pink number with a soft white canopy, a Cadillac convertible, and he pulls up behind her. When he tries to sing to her, he becomes nervous in an instant. He stutters and putters and his engine stalls out over and over. The little pink Cadillac is not impressed. She takes off to a tune all her own. When she speeds away, the white canopy blows off like a scarf in the wind and lands on top of the Porsche, and the carbon monoxide and graveled dust kick up all around him and leave him thoroughly exhausted. From one of his headlights, a tear drips down onto the New York license plate that coincidentally reads A11-AH01.

32   When H.P. Coaster won the coin at an auction, he had it reframed with the tails side facing out because it featured a double-headed eagle looking east and west. It was a symbol that he felt deeply connected to, for reasons both historic and metaphoric.

33   Imagine the number line and the set of all integers ($\mathbb{Z}$), starting and then diverging in both directions at zero, stretching infinitely to the negative, infinitely to the positive. They go on forever. But there are also hidden infinities, the ones that are found within the boundaries of the integers themselves. Even though they seem smaller, they're still infinities. There's always a place to keep going.

The reason Zeus is aware of these smaller infinities is that one of his high school algebra teachers explained them in a memorable way. He said, "Suppose you want to kiss the most beautiful girl in the world. And suppose she is standing at one end of the classroom and you are at the other. And she can't wait to kiss you back. So, go ahead, walk over there and kiss her—but there's a stipulation. You can only move toward her in one minute increments, and when you walk, you're only allowed to go half the distance to her lips. How long will it take you to kiss her? Two minutes? Four minutes? No. An hour? A year? No. Since for every minute you travel you're only going to go halfway. During the first few minutes, you'll move a lot, but as time goes on, it will feel like you're standing still, allowing your life to be paralyzed by this one person. Even if you're a millimeter away and you're eye-to-eye, you can only move a half-millimeter. And the next minute, half of that. And then half of that. So no matter how short the distance is, you'll never get there. You'll never kiss her, this most beautiful girl in the world. It happens in the space between integers, and sometimes between people. It's sad, but metaphorically relevant, especially for some high school math teachers."

34 🐝

C.R.E.A.M. (Cash Rules Everything Around Me)

Enter The Wu-Tang: 36 Chambers

American Rhythm and Flow Folk Music From the slums of Shaolin, 1993

The RZA, The GZA, Ol' Dirty Bastard, Inspectah Deck, Raekwon The Chef, U-God, Ghostface Killah, and the Method Man (and Masta Killa).

35   Zeus, normally an SR-71 Blackbird from above with this stuff, has today in the library missed one of the purest gems of all. Even though she's obscured by stacks of books and parentheses of dark hair, she is ever-present on the shelves, both her true character and editorial alterations kept undercovers.

He usually seeks out the 10 in 7's clothing, the waitress in an unflattering uniform, the girl-next-door without makeup, or even the librarian who pulls the pencil from her hair and lets it fall like Niagara over a jutting bodyscape. But at this moment, although acting otherwise to everyone else, he is thinking only of Candy Lovinglace.

36   Note: This is the author's preferred spelling with respect to Nirvana's hit record in 1991. Here are two quick, not well-researched arguments, for its permanent submission into dictionaries everywhere.

If the ubiquitous "Nevermore" from Edgar Allan Poe's *The Raven* has gotten the grammatical pass, then let's give Kurt Cobain's *Smells Like Teen Spirit* one too. How popular could that word have been before 1845? And if the strange "Nevertheless" from nothing in pop-literature or -culture gets a grammatical pass from the completely appropriate "Never the less", then let's add one more compound to this short list. Or maybe this is much ado about nothing. In which case, never mind.

Truant

Gin & Juice
Monkey 47 Gin, Orange & Pineapple Purée, Lime Wedge

·

Thug Passion
Alizé & Cristal Champagne

·

Mali-Booyah
Malibu Rum, Grey Goose Vodka, Shaved Coconut Rim, Pineapple Leaf Stirrer

·

Pop Quiz
Coca-Cola Classic & MamaJuana

·

After-School Special
Chocolate Vodka, Godiva Liqueur, Vanilla Ice Cream, Ovaltine Powder

·

Skirt Roller
Apple-Infused Bourbon, Honey Syrup, Ginger Ale, Starfruit Slice

·

Detention
Johnnie Walker Swing Scotch, Grand Marnier, Burnt Tangerine Peel

·

38   85 x 85 is (8 x 9) followed by (25). Answer = 7,225.
                    135 x 135 is (13 x 14) followed by (25). Answer = 18,225.

39   Word to *The Rocky Horror Picture Show*.

40   Mirror | ɿoɿɿiM

While there are plenty of mirrors in *Fleur-de-Lisa*, on the floor, on the ceiling, even the poles themselves, their signature act involves the implication of a mirror. The pole in the center of the circular stage acts as their meridian, with each sister walking onto the stage from opposite sides. When Florida steps up with her right, spike-heeled foot, Georgia does the same with her left. Their choreography continues over the vague sounds of eighties glam rock with coordinated twirls of their hair and bodies. They slip off one side of their bra, then the other. Then they go cheek-to-cheek for a bump of their hips, and then cheek-to-cheek for the meeting of their faces. With their arms stretched out, they rotate their heads toward each other and share a long tongueless kiss with their eyes closed. What looks sensual to every other person in the joint is really quite awkward for them and they always laugh about it in the powder room. Of course, their feelings improve once the tips started to roll in.

And the tips from the patrons of *Fleur-de-Lisa* are literally rolled to fit easier inside each dancer's garter. The Washingtons, Lincolns, Hamiltons*, Jacksons, Grants, and Franklins* each have their presidential faces (*or the two less-ambitious faces) squeezed against the legs of desire. When there is no more room in the garter, they're tucked along the side of their panties, where they sometimes slip all the way down in front, which may explain the subsequent smirks seen on their portraits.

The Mirror | ɿoɿɿiM act continues as they move forward in concert with the music, closer to the audience of transfixed men and women. After two turns in slow motion, they rotate to face each other, first nipple-to-nipple, then face-to-face with another kiss. Florida and Georgia continue to rotate until they face opposite directions. They both let their long hair down at the same time to fall into one cascade. As they bend over, the focal point becomes the mirrored ceiling. They are derrière-à-derrière, and form a four-leaf clover of flesh from above. They arch their backs up, whip their hair over their faces, and let their breasts glisten in the neon lights. And finally, rising up on their stilettos, they press up and against each other, bouncing and booty-shaking in double-time to the glam rock rhythm. All eyes are on their joint clover pulsating in the reflection above.

So after the club closes and the lights are turned on, the sisters collect their money by the handfuls. They have rubber bands, a backpack, and an electric money counter at their apartment. The truth is, at the close of each night, Florida and Georgia really know what it takes to make ends meet.

41   A.D.I.D.A.S. = All Day I Dream About Sex

The more he learned that God saw everything he did, including his thoughts, he felt both anxious and guilty. Young Zeus searched for why this guilt existed and began to read The Bible for some insight. He read it at home and during church while others were preaching their own interpretations of it. But after several months of reading, he was further perplexed. For one thing, he didn't understand why with all of the complexity in The Bible, that many people tried to boil it down to one idea, one phrase that would allow you to enter the sparkling Kingdom. The boiling down let the interesting philosophical ideas vaporize and left behind a sludge of keep-it-simple-stupid syrup. He also felt less guilty when he thought about how God created literally everything, even what orgasms feel like. You'd think he'd understand why it was so enticing.

And the fact that the hands are designed to fall into the lap of the *Man Downstairs* or at the entrance to the *Curly Pearly Gates*, the ability to have one couldn't have been easier (unless fingernails were lids over little reservoirs of massage oils). Or was it all a test? Because if He was watching him getting sweaty in solitude with a wrist pace of 160 BPM, then he'd probably be doomed. And the guilt returned.

But if God created genital sensitivity, He must know that some people are more sensitive than others. He wondered if God tried out different levels of sensitivity on Adam and Eve and if there were pleasures too intense that He left them in the workshop in the sky. Either way, Zeus felt that he was made extra sensitive. So much so that he tried to abstain from any genital touching, even in the bathroom or in the shower. This created an odd stance at the urinal and an excessive washing of the happy trail area so the soap bubbles would work their way down and do the cleaning on their own.

So he thought of spelling the name of his sneakers a different way, with an extra A. The problem being though, that in order to *not* think of something, he had to first acknowledge what shouldn't be thought of. Back to square one.

A.D.I.D.A.A.S. = All Day I Dream About Avoiding Sex

42

RECENT HEADLINES FROM THE NEW YORK TIMES

. . .

MEGACHURCHES UNITE TO BREAK GROUND ON SKYCHURCHES
IN TWELVE "DISCIPLE" CITIES:
NEW YORK, LOS ANGELES, CHICAGO, HOUSTON, DALLAS, SAN
FRANCISCO, DETROIT, DENVER, WASHINGTON D.C., BOSTON,
NEW ORLEANS, AND LAS VEGAS

.

LAWMAKERS PASS BILL TO LIMIT CORPORATE SKYSCRAPER HEIGHTS,
MUST BE 500 FT. LOWER THAN SKYCHURCHES

AKIN TO THE PONTIFICAL SWISS GUARD,
SKYCHURCHES WILL EMPLOY THEIR OWN ARMED FORCES

43

twithe /ˈtwīTH/ ▸ n. twenty percent of income set aside as a donation for the church and clergy. ▸ v. [with obj.] give as a twithe: *the couple pledged to twithe every week*
—ORIGIN early 21st cent.: a doubling of the English *tithe.*
twith·ing /ˈtwīTHiNG/ ▸ n. the practice of paying a twithe.
—ORIGIN early 21st cent.: English (see **TWITHE**)

44   Serpentine Poetry:
             The Sacred Unhooking of Eve's Leafy Bra
                          . . .

             SWEAT ACROSS HER CHEST,

         I MUST CONFESS, WAS MY FAULT.

         EACH KISS TASTES OF SALT.
                          . . .

         LILITH LICKS WITH FLAMES

     WHILE I CARESS EVE'S SOFT FRUIT,

         GARDEN WRAITHS PERMUTE.
                          . . .

         HER HONEY-DIPPED LIPS,

     PURE SWEETNESS BETWEEN HER HIPS . . .
         JUST LIE BACK SUGAR
                          . . .

         FROM THE DUST OF STARS,

         I'M THE UNSEEN ATOM, THE

         OMNIPRESENT SCAR

                          ✳

★ ★ ★ ★ ★ ★ ★ ★ ★

ALL-STAR MODEL/DESIGNER
CANDY LOVINGLACE

★ ★ ★ ★ ★ ★ ★ ★ ★

IN JUST A FEW MONTHS INTO HER
ROOKIE CAMPAIGN, CANDY HAS
GARNERED MORE WEB HITS
THAN ANYONE ELSE ON THE TEAM.

798   RIP-OFF LEADERS

HITS

PLAYER	NO.
CANDICE B.H. LOVINGLACE	36,465
@DAHLIABELAIR	31,283
ARIANA SHYLARK	30,055
JINSY HAVANA	29,935
JAXON-BLISS	29,934
Q.T. SIMONA	22,873
SONGMARLOW	22,781
JOLENE GOODENOUGH	21,590
AVALONELENA.XXX	20,415
COPLAND SERENITY	20,365

E* © 2020 STOPP CHEWING GUM, INC. PRTD. IN U.S.A.

47

JAMES 1:26 (N.I.V. TRANSLATION)

THOSE WHO CONSIDER THEMSELVES RELIGIOUS AND YET
DO NOT KEEP A TIGHT REIN ON THEIR TONGUES DECEIVE
THEMSELVES, AND THEIR RELIGION IS WORTHLESS.

48 They are those of Mrs. Lovinglace, Elder Ezekiel, and Disciple Habakkuk, all under
the penumbra of the ghost of Mr. Lovinglace.

. n . .. . .

49

[[✝]]

<< Ezra, they're approaching Manhattan Island by way of the tunnel. The GPS is running
true, we're tailing him a few cars back. It's not too hard to spot a Lamborghini. Over. >>

<< Yes, we're tracking their movements on the monitor. And a reminder to watch your
speed. It's worth losing the tail to save your lives. I just read an update on the terrorist car
killings. >>

<< Yes, Brother Mark, we've heard and we're on full alert, for Candice and ourselves
and our fellow patriots. The roads are quiet for a Saturday night. We've been praying about
it. Over. >>

<< We're doing the same here. These terrorists think it's a war between God and Allah,
but Allah is an illusion. They don't realize that this is a war of the people, the holy and the
hell-bound. This is the continuing war between our God and Satan, and we're on the front
lines fighting with His spirit within us. Satan takes many forms, whether it's these cowardly
terrorists or this young man who asks the wrong questions and attempts to denigrate the life
and family of Gideon. The front lines are everywhere and must be defended. We must be
mobilized and ready for any type of battle. >>

<< Amen to that. Over. >>

50

FRIDAY'S HEADLINES FROM VARIOUS NEWS OUTLETS

. . .

BLOOD BATH: IN ONE NIGHT, OVER 200 PEOPLE FALL
VICTIM TO POSSIBLE NATIONWIDE TERRORIST PLOT

.

HIGHWAY VOLUME APPROACHING
AN ALL-TIME LOW ACROSS THE NATION

.

TERROR THREAT: ABJECT IN MIRROR IS CLOSER THAN IT APPEARS

.

SEC'Y OF DEPT. OF TRANS. URGES CONGRESS TO PASS STRICTER
SPEEDING LAWS AND INSTALL ROADWAY CAMERAS

.

ANONYMOUS U.S.SENATOR:
NEW CARS IN PRODUCTION SHOULDN'T BE UNABLE TO EXCEED 30MPH

.

HIGHWAY TO HELL: NONBELIEVERS BEWARE, SAY A PRAYER

.

SPOTLIGHT ON TAXES AND LIBERTY: FREEWAYS AIN'T FREE

.

STATISTICAL ANALYSIS: IRONICALLY, TRAFFIC DEATH NUMBERS
NATIONWIDE ARE DOWN 45% AS TERRORISM INCREASES

.

VIGILANTE WATCH: HOMEMADE ARMORED CARS & TANKS
SEEN PATROLLING HIGHWAYS

.

COACH BUS FALLS VICTIM TO MULTI-S.U.V. ATTACK

.

FOUR-WHEEL DEATH DRIVE: JEEP-HAD COMES TO OUR BEACHES

.

COUGAR NEWS NETWORK PUNDIT: "THESE TERRORISTS AREN'T
PRACTICING ISLAM, THEY ARE PERFORMING IT."

.

THE DEFENDERS OF CHRIST VOW TO PUT THE BRAKES ON
TERRORIST VEHICULAR HOMICIDES

51

LENOX LOUNGE

∗ ∗ ∗

"BLACK AND TAN FANTASY"
GUINNESS, SUGAR HILL GOLDEN ALE, CHAMBORD LIQUEUR

∗

"SOPHISTICATED LADY"
DOM PÉRIGNON METAMORPHOSIS ROSÉ,
SERVED WITH A SIDE OF SEASONAL ORGANIC MIXED BERRIES

∗

"PRELUDE TO A KISS"
FRENCH VANILLA VODKA, TIRAMISU LIQUEUR,
SERVED WITH PETITS FOURS

∗

"DIMINUENDO AND CRESCENDO IN BLUE"
(JOHNNY WALKER SCOTCH BLUE LABEL SERVED WITH STYLE)
YOUR FIRST SIP, THE BAND WILL QUIET TO A WHISPER, RELAX...
YOUR LAST SIP, THE BAND RETURNS WITH THUNDER, CELEBRATE!

∗

"I'M JUST A LUCKY SO-AND-SO"
DUKE BOURBON, VANILLA SYRUP, CLEMENTINE BITTERS

∗

"LOTUS BLOSSOM"
HONEYSUCKLE-INFUSED VODKA, DOMAINE DE CANTON,
COINTREAU, CHOCOLATE-DIPPED FLOWER PETAL

52

[[✝]]

<< Ezra, our reach in the restaurant industry is long, but it doesn't extend to the Lenox Lounge. We have no one on the inside. Especially considering they are seated in the Zebra Room. At this point, the laxatives are a distant dream. Over. >>

<< Yes, Brother Malachi, let's continue tracking and wait for the next movement to resume the tail. >>

<< Noah here. He seems to have bodyguards of some sort, or accomplices maybe. There may be more eyes on this couple than we thought. >>

<< As long as God's eyes are on them as well, we have the upper hand. Be vigilant and continue to be steadfast in the Lord. >>

53

In a nursery rhyme rap style, it goes like this:
"I got an invitation
from the board of education
to do a demonstration on a girl,
I stuck my boneration
up her middle separation
and increased the population of the world."

54   [[✝]]

<< Ezra, they've switched vehicles. The GPS is no longer tracking their movements. I'm following their limousine with Brother Jonah. We're running the plates through our network.>>

<< Good work, Brother Samson. >>

<< They're heading downtown toward the Brooklyn Bridge. It doesn't seem likely that they're going back to the Lovinglace residence. Probably to his apartment. The windows are tinted black. I can only imagine what he is attempting within. What is our next play if they're trying to be alone? >>

<< Let's put our faith in God. And let's put our faith in the way Brother Gideon and Joyce raised their daughter. Let the Lord walk us one step at a time. >>

<< My patience is running very thin with this wicked character. I can be in position for a

clean shot, untraceable. >>

<< Samson! Imagine the trauma for Gideon's daughter. If it comes to that, we will take him alone when the conditions are right. We are acting as the arms of God, not the firearms of God. >>

<< When did you go soft? >>

<< From this moment on, I'm commanding you to stand down. This mission will now be reconnaissance only. You and Brother Jonah are to follow and update us here at headquarters. You are not leave your vehicle for any reason. As for all other operatives, you are to make the switch to highway patrol. These terrorists are not going to slow down on their own. We fight for God on many fronts. Understand? >>

<< Check. >>

55

BRA SIZES		BATTERY SIZES
		AAA
AA	✓	AA
A		
B	✓	B
C	✓	C
D	✓	D
DD		
DDD		
		9V

56   Courtesy of the ageless Dr. Zizmor.

57   Suma is tossing and burning through another frightful dream. This time the paralysis reaches her eyes. There is the presence of a large figure, but only in feeling. Her tunnel vision is filtered through noiseless reds and whites, and sometimes yellows, as she listens to the screams of prolonged torture. The tunnel is traveling west.

[Advertisement]

Salvation Ammo .33 Caliber Slugs

Do you have bad aim?

Are you concerned about innocent bystanders?

Are you a killer with a conscious?

Salvation Ammo's .33 Caliber Slugs (SA-.33s) are made with exclusively-blessed materials to set your mind at ease! We use the metals from repurposed crucifix necklaces and certified Holy Water in our manufacturing process. The process is finished when the bullets are prayed over by a representative minister from each of the top ten denominations of Christianity. (Mormonism option now available! Ask us how.)

If your gun is turned against you, you'll ensure yourself a straight shot to Heaven. And just think of your children — accidents happen! Our SA-.33s will prevent any future guilt, as you know the person(s) will be in a better place.

Forgiveness made easy!™

Tried and Trusted

A Great Gift Idea

Salvation Ammo, VVVLLC

In case they didn't invite Christ into their heart, we'll do it for them.

Made in the U.S.A.

59   The captors, when they had gone shopping to complete Suma's checklist earlier in the day, were only able to buy five bowling balls at the local, family-owned sporting goods store. So the lead captor drove the box truck to The Spare Cactus, had a word with the owner, and walked out with the heaviest ball in the whole joint. When he approached the two other men in the truck, he raised the ball to his chest to show them. The reflection of the sparkles turned his sunglasses red. And Samson smiled.

60

　　0 : 0 0

Time has been counting down or moving in reverse ever since the period of frozen dreams. Now only the zeros are frozen, poised to tick upward at Suma's command. When she decides to move her first muscle, it's an exaggerated bicep flex. And there's no more static, no more shadows, no more abuse, no more paralysis. She begins to sleepwalk forward in multiple dimensions, unhinged and translucent.

　　0 : 0 1
　　0 : 0 2
　　0 : 0 3
　　0 : 0 4

61

First Impressions Blog
"Too Much to See, No Time To Edit"
By, A. Millie

.　.　.

[SALO N] / [SALOON]

This is my quick review of a place called "SALO　N." The outside of the sore front has all these vintage scissors hanging up and the prices for various haircuts and other offerings. I wanted to do something kinda wild while I'm in New York City, so I thought I'd have a lock of my hair dyed red. I have blonde hair, so I thought it would pop. Anyway, when I walked through the swinging doors, I went from the East Village to the Old West. My first mistake was calling the place the wrong name. I kept saying "Salo" and then "N" but obviously it's meant to be "Salon." The woman I spoke to said they were becoming "Saloon" in just a few minutes. She asked me for ID, which I never mind of course! She said since I only wanted a low-light, it would be alright for me to stay. When I sat in the chair, it was more of a reclining stool. it felt shaky and it was hard to relax or hold still. On the shelf by the mirror all of the combs and scissors were kept in old gin bottles. My stylist told me about a notorious incident where a local drunk dashed into Salo N during the day and stole the comb bottle, thinking it was gin. But really, it was just isopropyl alcohol mixed with little hair snippings. Someone saw him drink the whole thing. it didn't end well. So now they have a label over the gin brand that says *not gin*! On the mirror there were also appointments for the week written with a dry erase marker and a small sign at the top: Get more bangs for your buck! after a few more crazy stories she was done with the coloring. And as I was reading all of the names on the mirror,she got out her hairdryer to finish up. That was the most unsettling part! The hairdryer had been painted silver and black with the details of a revolver! that's a gun. She held that dryer and pointed it at my head all directions. her finger was on the trigger and the hot air was roaring out the end of the barrel. And when she stood on the opposite side of the red strands of my hair, it really looked like she was blowing my brains out too!! I swear she was loving it, but I was uneasy. Maybe that's the whole idea of the place, to scare you. I'll never forget it, but I'll probably never go back.

Oh, and when I was leaving I saw some workers turning those old rigid-hood beauty parlor hair dryers upside-down and filling them with chips and pretzels and placing them on the bar. And for their place settings, they used hair curlers as napkin rings and their knives were half of a pair of scissors. Gross! Maybe I'll take that gin after all!

62   Scribbled somewhere in his red journal is this poem:

THE ?UESTION MARK

DELIVERS A CUTTING POINT

WITHOUT A BLADE. . .

THE ALLURING CURVES OF DOUBT

ENTICE ILLUSIONS TO FADE,

THOUGHTS TO BE SWAYED,

THE BALANCE OF REASON AND

FAITH TO BE WEIGHED

.

63   These songs by The Ink Spots played on a loop in the hallway.
"If I Didn't Care"
"We Three (My Echo, My Shadow, and Me)"
"(It Will Have to Do) Until The Real Think Comes Along"

64   In his head, he's singing *Déjà Vu* for the first time:
Uptown baby, Uptown baby,
I gets down baby,
Up for the crown baby!

65

[COLOSSUS]

. . .

CHERRY STREET MANHATTAN

PINE BARRENS SINGLE MALT WHISKY, SWEET AND DRY VERMOUTH, BRANDIED CHERRIES, STIRRED

AVENUE BEE

AVIATION GIN, ORGANIC LOCAL HONEY, FRESH LEMON JUICE, ASTER GARNISH

GRAND STREET HIGHBALL

ROUGH RIDERS STRAIGHT BOURBON WHISKY, APPALACHIAN GINGER BEER, MUDDLED LIME

2ND AVENUE FLIGHT

DUVAL-LEROY CHAMPAGNE, BRANDY LIBRARY COGNAC, ORANGE BITTERS, ROCK SUGAR

. . .

TAPS

CHROMATIC ALE, RIVERHEAD, NY / SORACHI ACE, BROOKLYN, NY
MERMAID PILSNER, CONEY ISLAND / OLD SLUGGER PALE ALE, COOPERSTOWN, NY

. . .

CAPS

HARAR BEER, ETHIOPIA / MIDAS TOUCH, DOGFISH HEAD
BROWN ANGEL, CLOWN SHOES / ROAD 2 RUIN, TWO ROADS
PLINY THE ELDER, RUSSIAN RIVER / SS-C.R.E.A.M., CARTON
BREW FREE! OR DIE, 21ST AMMENDMENT / POMPEII, TOPPLING GOLIATH

. . .

CORKS

ONTANON RIOJA, SPAIN / COCOBON RED BLEND, CALIFORNIA
MILESTONE RED BLEND, CALIFORNIA / VOLCANO RED, HAWAII

66

WHEN I'M GONE,
JUST LOOK TO THE FRIGID MOON,
AND FEEL THE WARMTH
OF MY GAZE . . .
KNOWING WE HAVE SHARED THE
SAME UPWARD STARES
MERE MOMENTS APART.
THESE ARE CONNECTIONS OF THE HEART.

Bar 21

67

The Wince
Double Tito's and Soda—no fruit, thank you

The Smile
Les Climats du Coeur Pinot Noir Served in an Orrefors 'Difference' Mature Wine Glass
Preempted by a shoulder massage and a dimming of the lights

Le Doux Printemps (ou La Dame Susan)
Lavender soda & French Vodka, Splash of Vanilla Syrup, Drop of Honey, Twist of Lemon, Rock Candy Stirrer

Harvey's Martini
Cotswolds Dry Gin & Pindar Cuveé Rare Champagne
Served Half-Full with a Delicately-Placed Dandelion Clock Garnish

The Babspell
Wild Turkey Master's Keep Bourbon, straight up, poured into a coupe glass chilled with liquid nitrogen,
but served with the belief that it will taste like sweetest Cosmo in the Cosmos, maybe something like this:
Ciroc Peach Vodka, Blood Orange Liqueur, Juices of Cranberry, Passion Fruit, & Lime

Last Call, Really
Balvenie 14 Single Malt Scotch Whisky and a Chinnock Cellars Cremoir Cigar To-Go, We'll Hail the Cab

Pour Toujours Cocktail
2.00000 oz. Hennessy V.S Special Edition 44
1.00000 oz. Fresh Cara Cara Orange Juice
0.50000 oz. Limoncello
0.25000 oz. Absinthe
0.12500 oz. Creme de Cocoa
0.06250 oz. Jerry Thomas Bitters
0.03125 oz. Love

68

Romans 8:28 (New International Version (NIV) Publication Date: 1978)

And we know that in all things God works for the good of those who love him, who have been called according to *his* purpose.

About Louis L. Lasser IV

I'm a writer by morning, bartender and tap dancer by night. After teaching Math for twelve years, the closing of my school gave me the impetus to write with a purpose. Born from a decade of poetry and street art, Wednesday Night Meeting lives as my first novel.

I grew up in Mt. Sinai, Long Island, and despite its name, it's almost completely flat. My father, he goes by Lee, the middle initial of our shared name, taught me to love baseball. My mother, Marcia, taught me it's not only O.K. to dance and wear sequins on stage, but that girls might even like you because of it. My maternal grandparents combined to be a third guardian. Through the art of language, William Hoover taught me to keep searching for meaning, and Marian brought me to the place where I found it: New York City.

I graduated Adelphi University with a degree in Mathematics, but majored in trying to solve the abstract equation of what life is about. My education has come from friends and lushes, preachers and professors, colleagues and former students—and has been further sparked by Manhattan skyscrapers and the harbors of Port Jefferson and Setauket. My style is most influenced by the writers E.E. Cummings, Langston Hughes, O. Henry, and David Foster Wallace; the filmmakers Quentin Tarantino and David Lynch; and the music of Kanye West and Charles Mingus.

I owe everything to my wife, Cara. Our relationship, her unwavering support and love, her grace and beauty, are the most wonderful sources of inspiration.

Acknowledgments

The Connolly family: Denis & Lisa, for their support, interest, and inspiration; tough brudder-in-law Matthew & one fowl swoop Marissa; Ginny Banach; and most of all, the gracious & lovely Cara (aka J.F. aka J.O.A.F. aka Floajie Smojes); The man upstairs & my best friend, William Hoover, and Marian, the maven of style; Miss Marcia, caring teacher & mom to many, Dr. Justin Lasser, with Ph.D.s in both Philosophy & TKPUA; Alicia, for perseVerance & artIstry, Michael, Kyle, Jessica, Joslyn, and Jeff; my godparents Doug & Marianne Hamshaw; EliZZabeth, Prince Kenny & Anny, Scott & Kelly, & the incomparable Jean Hamshaw; Lauryn, Mary Lou, & The Bogert Family; My patriarchal lineage: Louis L. Lasser, Louis L. Lasser II, & Louis L. Lasser III; Harriet, Alan, Gayle, Josh, Susan, Gary, Tim, and (the coolest aunt) Alison; Tyler "Where should I place my settlement?" Rhodes, Eva, Shaina & Ty, and young Ethan; My colleages: David Gillespie, the teacher I wish I had; Terence V. McConnell of Rockaway Beach, for literature and great times at Swift's; a recent friendship/incarnation with the author Jeffrey Owen Thomas; Michael Garvey, for L.E.S. morning walks & coffee; Ann Marie Terrizzi for clapping speeches; Barbara Pellerito for lasting friendship; Nick Turvin & Josette Leon, for laughs & debates; My dear friends: Kristian Moreno & family, from jazz band & *seventeen* Magazine to the grown days, the good times persist; Emma Backfish, Jessica Lynn, & George Lynn: my trivia partners in crime; Dan Carey & Family, from LaSalle to the Bronx; Sean and Mike Russell, for stories & sodality; Tim Needles, for inspiration; Hesh Kestin, for criticism; John "Port Jeff" Artarian & Kristie Roccoforte for swinging under the stars; Kevin Coleman & Peri Rieber, the twin couple; Melinda Miscevich for Manhattans & encouragement; Jim (from Starbucks) for advocacy, Jerry Cliquot & Omar Edwards for rhythm & opportunity, Andrew Adamski & Family for dodgeball amongst The Spoons; David Trachtenberg for intelligence; Brian Brown for sneaker styles, Julian Casablancas for Hempstead music & possibilities; Remy Church for rhyme skills & resolution; Joseph Lee & Marie Elena Scaturro for Earl Hall adventures, Amy Weidner-LaSala, crushes for 5-year-olds die hard; The Riebers & The Dubins for steadfastness; Karen Melnyk-Vutrano for our letters & short stories; Vinny & Danielle Renner-Orobello; My Mario's family: Marco Branchinelli for a 2nd home, Russ Moran for ideas, Anthony Martino for taking a chance on me; My fellow bartenders: Julie Rosenberg, Heather Hardhardt, Jackie Roode, Nick Giardinello, Nicole Marino, Christine Johnson, & Phil Caporusso; Nic Palmeri for basslines and manliness checks; Byron Rice for jazz & techno writing techniques, & the sources of great conversations: Rob Letwins, Hugh Jackson, Pat Rumney, Austin Beck, Dave Lamson, Steve Lindsay, Joe & Luba Randall, Francesco Pedone, Cary Palmer, Bob the Builder, & Neil "Bond, Neil Bond" Toye; My fellow dancers: Alanna DeFabrizio, Alyssa Meano, Samantha Giacoia, Emily Vallone, Raphael Odell Shapiro, Angela Steen, Alexa Laskowitz, Mariana Dominguez, Kayla Axelrod, Lauren Zawadski, Francesca Scala, & The Reilly Family; My exceptional math students over the years; My professors at AU: Dr. Sally Ridgeway, Carmen DeLavallade, Robert Christopher, & Rebecca Wright; & my Mt. Sinai teachers: Steve Mantone, Gary Short, & Renee Petrola for first getting me to read, it's all your fault.

Kickstarter Founders

My sincere gratitude goes out to Andrew, Jamie, Lillian, & Luke Adamski, Emily Anderson, John Artarian, Douglas Borge, Marco Branchinelli, Daniel Carey, Remy Church, Kevin & Peri Gordon Coleman, Lisa & Denis Connolly Jr., Matthew Connolly, Bonnie Consiglio, Suzanne Crocetti, Michael Crossley, Kelly Crowley (Former 7th-grader of "Mr. Lasser's"), Joanne & Christian Curry, Beata Grudzinski, Stephanie Haight, Brittany Anne Haynes, Tom Hurson, Paul Ilardi, Samantha Kochman, Amy Weidner-LaSala, Justin Lasser, Marcia L. Lasser, Stacey La Scala, Jessica Lomonaco, Marisa Mangiameli, Theresa McKenna, Elizabeth Mitchell, Don Moran, Russ Moran, KC Moreno, Paulina Mulligan, Paul F. Murphy, Alexis Musolino, Nic Palmeri, Barbara Pellerito, Stephen J. Plunkett, Paul Porcello, Lynn Rando, Caitlin & Erin Reilly, Tyler Rhodes, Heather Rodio, Stef Roy, Susan & Gary Ruiz, Tim Ruiz, Sean & Lauren Russell, Francesca Scala, Jason Smith, Jerry M. Sposato, David Edward Stothard, Gabriela Vazquez, and Jennifer Wielage! I couldn't have done it without you.

Made in the USA
Middletown, DE
18 September 2017

4843686 7R00252